Juliet E. McKenna has been interested in fantasy stories since childhood, from *Winnie the Pooh* to the *Iliad*. An abiding fascination with other worlds and their peoples played its part in her subsequently reading Classics at St Hilda's College, Oxford. While working in recruitment and personnel, she continued to read across all genres, and started to write herself. After combining book-selling and motherhood for a couple of years, she now fits in her writing around her family and vice versa. She lives with her husband and children in West Oxfordshire.

Find out more about Juliet E. McKenna and other Oribit authors by registering for the free monthly newsletter at www.orbitbooks.co.uk

By Juliet E. McKenna

The Tales of Einarinn
THE THIEF'S GAMBLE
THE SWORDSMAN'S OATH
THE GAMBLER'S FORTUNE
THE WARRIOR'S BOND

THE SWORDSMAN'S OATH

The Second Tale of Einarinn

JULIET E. McKENNA

www.orbitbooks.co.uk

An *Orbit* Book

First published in Great Britain by Orbit 1999

Reprinted 2000, 2002

Copyright © Juliet E. McKenna 1999

The moral right of the author has been asserted.

A CIP catalogue record for this book
is available from the British Library.

ISBN 1 85723 740 4

Typeset in Erhardt by Palimpsest Book Production Limited,
Polmont, Stirlingshire
Printed and bound in Great Britain by
Mackays of Chatham plc, Chatham, Kent

Orbit
An imprint of
Time Warner Books UK
Brettenham House
Lancaster Place
London WC2E 7EN

For Steve,
sternest critic and staunchest support.

Acknowledgements

I continue to rely on the invaluable assistance of Steve, Mike and Sue, for their dedicated scrutiny of each line, while Liz and Andy valiantly take on the big picture and Helen comes up with those key questions. Everyone reading these books has reason to be as grateful to them as I am. I am also indebted to Jenny and to Sharon for friendly, flexible childcare and thereby peace of mind as well as peace and quiet.

As my most immediate contacts within Orbit, I am most fortunate in having Tim and Lisa for good-humoured editorial expertise, while Cassie and Adrian spread the word. Of the many booksellers whose enthusiasm is doing so much, my local Ottakar's team are closest to me in every sense. My thanks go to all, as well as to their colleagues.

I would also like to thank the ever expanding circle of friends, family, friends of family, family of friends and members of IPROW who continue to support me with curious facts, plausible names and ongoing interest.

This circle has, however, been sadly diminished by the untimely deaths of Zoey Ducker, through tragic accident, and Graham Skinner, after long illness. They are not forgotten.

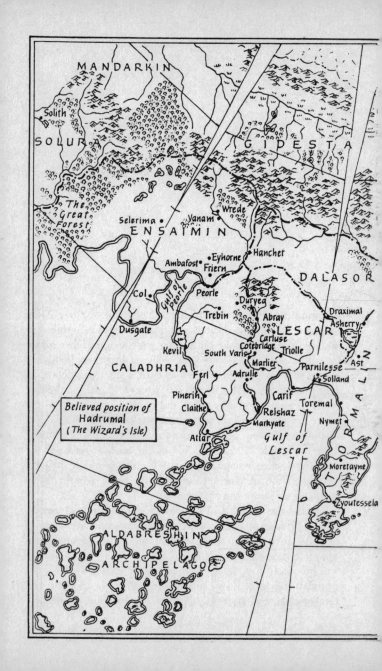

ISLANDS OF THE
ELIETIMM
(The Ice Islands)

Sholvin Cove

Inglis

Blacklith

Bremilayne

Kalaven

KEL AR'AYEN

CHAPTER ONE

From Planir, Archmage of Hadrumal, to Messire Guliel
D'Olbriot, Sieur of that House and Keeper of the Honour of
the Name, Adjurist of the Convocation of Princes and Patron
of the Empire, Solstice salutations and most heartfelt wishes
for prosperity and health in the year to come.

My dear Sieur,

   I am most grateful to you for intelligence of the Elietimm
ships wrecked on your coasts over the For-Winter season.
I have not forgotten the narrow escape of both your man
and mine in their recent encounter with that race and may I
assure you I remain sensible of the threat to your domains and
the wider peace of the Empire. Beyond such important but
necessarily impersonal concerns, I would venture to remind
you that just as you lost a sworn man in Aiten, I lost a
scholar in Geris, a man of much learning who might have
aided us both against this threat, though of course, nothing
outweighs the loss of both their lives. I do not forget such
debits in the scales, as I am sure you do not.

   Your letter encourages me to think that you realise, as do
I, that our interests lie along the same road in this matter.
Just as you face the very real danger of hostile forces landing
on your coasts, or worse, to lie concealed in the unpopulated
reaches of Dalasor or Gidesta, so I am faced with the threat
of a complex magic whose mysteries we in Hadrumal are still
unravelling. On that subject may I assure you that there can
be no shame or blame attached to your man Aiten for his
attack on my mage Shivvalan. There can be no doubt that
had his mind not been invaded by the foul enchantments of

the Elietimm, he would have fought to the end in defence of his honour and your Name.

Thank you for your enquiries after Shivvalan; he is quite recovered and eager to do his part in foiling the schemes of the Elietimm. You also mentioned the pleasure with which you received the sword that I discovered so unfortunately concealed by an elderly and somewhat eccentric wizard, but your thanks are unnecessary. It is sufficient recompense that you approved my suggestion to present the blade to your sworn man Ryshad Tathel. I was most impressed by his resourcefulness and courage in the face of dire trials and it seemed only fitting that such an heirloom should be used once more to defend the Empire, in service of so great a House.

On that subject, I have a favour to request of you. I continue my researches into the mysteries of this ancient magic. As you will know from your own nephew's fate, this seems to attract the unwelcome attentions of those Elietimm at large in our lands. While my wizards have many talents, swordsmen they are not. Should you be willing to grant me the use of your man Ryshad, I can certainly put his undoubted talents to a use worthy of your House. The more we learn of these Elietimm and the quicker we do it, the better it will go for both of us.

*The High Road towards Cotebridge, in the Lescari
Dukedom of Marlier, 8th of Aft-Spring in the
Second Year of Tadriol the Provident*

How do you apologise to a grieving mother for not being the man who killed her son? Another might have Aiten's blood on her hands but I was still more deeply stained with shame that I had been unable to raise my sword against my friend of so many years to free him from the foul enchantment that had claimed his mind and his will, even at that ultimate cost. I'd tried to explain away my failure but my halting words had hung in the air, twisting awkwardly like crows on a gibbet. Had that visit to his family all been a dreadful mistake? No; my honour demanded it, if I were to be able to look myself in the eye as I shaved of a morning and see a man true to his oath.

Things had improved a little when Aiten's father and brothers had decided getting soaked in home-made applejack was the best way of honouring his memory. Everyone had told a story about Aiten and some of them even stayed funny when I recalled them sober. A sour morning-after with a head as thick as winter fog and my mouth tasting like a pissed-in boot had been a small price to pay.

My smile faded as I recalled Tirsa, Aiten's sister. A middling brown-haired girl with soft brown eyes and a pleasant smile; the sort of lass you see by the handful at markets clean across the Old Empire. Only I'd be able to pick her out from a festival crowd at a hundred paces, and it would still cut me like a whetted knife in ten years' time, she was so like Aiten to look at.

Remembering the grief in Aiten's mother's face as she

clutched the bundle of his possessions to her breast, trying to breathe in the last scent of her lost child, had me sufficiently distracted not to notice the bandits lurking in the hedgerow. Showers of rain on and off all morning had left the sky as grey as my mood, and despite it fairing up, I still had my hood raised. None of this excuses my lapse; I certainly should have remembered that the roads in Lescar are always more dangerous outside the fighting seasons, as perverse as anything else in that benighted land.

One of the vermin had my bridle before I could gather reins or wits. The startled horse reared backwards, and as I felt its hooves slip in the mire of the sodden road, I kicked my feet free of the irons, barely keeping my own footing as I leaped clear. Shaking and sweating, the horse snapped at the grabbing hands of the bandits and escaped up the road, leaving me facing the filthy gang of them.

'Pay your toll, pal, and we'll let you pass,' the foremost said, grinning widely, blackened stumps in his slimy gums.

I shook my head at the leader. These sorry discards from some defeated militia weren't going to be much of a challenge to me. They were all gaunt and hungry, matted and filthy, driven to scavenging like desperate dog-foxes after a long winter of lean pickings. Still, desperation makes for dangerous men, I reminded myself.

I backed down the rutted road a few paces, to draw them out far enough to be sure there were only four of them. Lescari, cowshit between their ears as well as between their toes since I could now be certain they had put no one behind me to cut off any retreat. I could certainly outpace them if I chose to turn tail and run, but I didn't fancy trying to make my way through the unknown muddy byways off the highroad. As my hand moved towards my sword hilt, parchment in my pocket crackled, reminding me of my duty to my patron's orders.

Besides, I didn't feel inclined to run; Dast's teeth, why should I? I wanted my horse back too. It was a good beast from Messire's own stable and I'd been riding it no more than seven or eight leagues a day to husband its strength. 'Sorry,

friend. You didn't say whose authority you had to levy a toll.'
I kept my voice neutral.

'This is all the authority I need!' He struck a challenging
pose with his notched sword, evidently aiming to impress in
his rusty breastplate fringed with inadequate chainmail.

His pack grinned, all bold in remnants of ill-fitting armour.
More fool them; the leather of my thick buff coat covered a
layer of metal plates without the vulnerabilities I was assessing
in my opponents as they smirked. I don't wear a hauberk; it
attracts notice and my usefulness to my prince depends on
going unremarked. I laid a hand to my own sword. It sparkled
silver on the pommel, the polished scabbard bright in a watery
gleam of fugitive sunlight now that the rain had stopped.

'What's your charge?' I asked, face calm, mind anticipating
the next moves. I spend long seasons trying to teach the militia
raised for the House of D'Olbriot that there's no virtue in
fighting if you can avoid it, but Lescaris learn the opposite in
their leading strings, from their warring dukes down, to the
endless grief of their torn and bleeding land.

The leader finally registered my unfamiliar accent. 'Tormalin
man, are you? Fancy words, fancy horse and blade. Let's see
what you've got in your purse, that'll be the rate for the
road!'

Evidently a man with no more sense than Dastennin gave a
flatfish. 'I'll give the price of a meal.' I smiled without humour.
'You can thank the Lord of the Sea for that.'

The other three looked tempted by the thought of food they
could pay for rather than a fight for their dinner, as I had
suspected. The leader scowled, unwilling to back down. 'We'll
spare a coin to Talagrin at the next shrine, when we've selled
your horse and your gear, thank the Hunter for sending us a
plump pigeon ripe for the plucking.'

'You want to try for my feathers?' I drew my sword. It slid
gleaming from the scabbard with a steely rasp and the rusty
weapons facing me wavered. 'Why? I'm carrying nothing but
letters from my patron.'

I wouldn't have been bandying words with outcasts before

I'd visited Aiten's family, I reflected. Not when I'd been carrying enough true-minted Tormalin gold to buy up half this sorry fiefdom. I wasn't the only one looking to defend my honour, the coin reflecting the value Messire D'Olbriot put on Aiten's oath now his death demanded its redemption. I forced myself to lay aside the burden of my own guilt while I dealt with these vermin.

'Sworn man, are you?' the foremost sneered, confident enough to let his sword point dip as he scratched at his lice-infested head. 'Lickspittle to some fat-arsed Prince who spends all his days with his head in a jug, playing with himself. That's how you pass your time, isn't it, wringing the goose's neck?'

His fellow footpads snickered at this, but I am long past the days when cheap insults enraged me. A true swordsman knows hot fury kills more men than cold steel. I backed away another pace, drawing him forward beyond the dubious protection of his fellows. Messire's militia are never so easily gulled, not after I've brought them to heel.

'So what have you got to say for yourself, curly? Come on, hand over your coin and that belt-pouch for a start! Well, answer me, curse you, unless you're too busy shitting yourself.'

My continued silence was unnerving Foul-Mouth's supporters by now, as I intended.

'All right, lads, let's have the bastard!' He took a bold step, rusty blade levelled.

I glared at the closest one to Foul-Mouth's off hand, who took an involuntary pace back. Idiocy was about to kill his mate, that and my sword, but if any of them chose to run I wasn't about to waste my time hunting them down.

Foul-Mouth lunged at me, off hand flailing. I stepped sideways to smack his blade up with the flat of my sword. He took his chance to swing his dirty blade round for a skull-splitting strike. I moved in and as his arm came up I rolled my wrist to drive the point of my keenly polished sword under and deep into his armpit. He collapsed like a ruptured wineskin, blood frothing from his mouth, drowning his shrieks of panic and pain. The others swore in guttural Lescari and one rushed me, stupidity apparently something they shared along with their lice. Sure of my footing, I brought my sword round at belly level, his instinctive parry sending him staggering back. He swung wildly, I evaded the blow with ease and swept low but he managed to leap sideways in time to save his kneecaps and I found I was facing two of them, his mate having found some semblance of courage.

If they'd had any more training than learning which end of a sword was the handle I might have had some trouble, but a few rapid strokes hacked through his guard and dropped the first to his knees, clutching the bloody ruin of splintered bone that had once been his sword arm. I punched the luckless mongrel with my off hand and he scrambled off into the bushes, howling through split lips, while the slowest to join battle took to his heels like a scalded hound, slipping in the mud in his haste to save his boil-scarred skin, without even the wit to try grabbing my horse.

That left me with a lad, tears carving pale streaks through the filth on his face, slime running from his crooked nose as he panted in terror through broken teeth. Life had been kicking this lad in the face since before he could walk.

I managed to rein in my anger; it had been a long and none too happy season for me thus far but that was no excuse for losing control. It had certainly felt good to give vent to the slow-burning rage at Aiten's untimely death that I kept locked in the back of my mind, but I could not afford to indulge such feelings.

I glanced quickly round, saw my horse now browsing on a patch of new grass and considered simply ignoring the boy. No, Dast curse him; he had done nothing to merit such consideration. I feinted to his off side, he swung his trembling weapon in a futile stroke but I had my blade at his throat before he had a hope of recovering. He dropped his stained sword and steam coiled damply around his feet as he pissed himself.

'Mercy, mercy,' he stammered. 'Please, your honour, I'll not do the like again, I swear it, any oath you like, mercy, for pity's sake, Saedrin save me—'

I leaned the edge of the blade into the soft skin of his neck to silence him. Could he be trusted? I doubted it; what would a lad like this know of honour, in a land where the so-called nobility change allegiance with every passing season, scrambling for advantage with rival dukes who have wasted ten generations in a futile struggle for a worthless throne?

'I swear,' he whimpered, desperately trying to swallow without cutting his own throat.

The issue here wasn't his honour, though, was it, but my integrity and self-respect. How could I kill some idiot boy who was begging to surrender, frantically offering me his paltry oath?

'Lie down,' I snarled at him and he dropped into the filth as if he'd been clubbed. Putting my boot heavy on his neck, I hurled his sword deep into a tangled thicket of thorns. I laid my own blade against his face, one red-rimmed, crusted eye blinking at the blood-clotted point as I stroked it slowly up his cheek. 'You lie here and you don't stir until you can't hear my horse's hoofbeats. If I see you again this side of the Otherworld, I'll gut you like a herring, do you hear me?'

He nodded frantically, eyes flickering between me and the crumpled heap of his erstwhile leader, the life drained out of him into the clotted mud. I backed away, ready to finish the lad if he was stupid enough to make a move. No, he had that much wit at least, more motionless than the still-quivering corpse next to him.

Checking there were no more surprises lurking among the unkempt hedgerows, I walked slowly towards the horse, not wanting to spook it with the smell of blood. However, it came readily enough; half a season on the road told it I meant fodder and water. This was definitely a relief; my chances of getting a remount in Lescar were about as slight as that boy's chances of dying in his bed.

I spared a glance back before the curve of the road took me

out of sight; the lad was looting the body of his late friend. I rode on, unconcerned. Even if he caught up with me, killing him would be no great task and no dishonour, since he'd have forfeited any claim to mercy along with his oath. The horse halted, raised its tail and dropped a heap of steaming gurry on the road, an entirely fitting comment, in my opinion.

The fire in the blood that comes from a fight, however trivial, warmed me for a while and in any case, this late in the season, the weather was increasingly mild. Still, a little anger at myself for getting caught like that seared me as the noon sun rode high above me, drawing wraiths of steam from the sodden ground, the spring air full of the green promise of renewal. I found myself gripped by sudden sadness and reined in to take a drink of water, trying to wash the tight dryness from my throat.

How long would it be before I could think of Aiten without that strangling ache? It was riding alone that was doing it, I realised, after so many years. I was missing his endless supply of dubious jokes, his blade matching mine as we protected each other in any fight we couldn't talk our way out of. One of the cornerstones of my life was gone, a certain loss of confidence leaving a hidden hole threatening to trip me, even if it was apparent to no one but me.

I unlaced the neck of my coat; a warm garment in the spring sunshine. My fingers caught in the thong of my medallion, the insignia I bore as a physical reminder of the oaths I had sworn to my Prince and he in turn to me. I had Aiten's as well, the bronze disc sewn inside my sword-belt, waiting for me to exact a double reckoning in blood from the bastard responsible for his death. Was I going to shove it down the enchanter's throat or ram it edgeways up his arse? I mused. Whichever, I'd sharpen the edges first, just to make a point. By rights that debt was our master's to claim or remit, but I had made a private vow of vengeance and hammered a nail deep into the door of Dastennin's shrine to affirm it. We make no formal vows as we do to our patron, but the loyalties between sworn men are no less strong.

No, it was time to move on, I told myself. After all but losing myself to the drowning sorrow of my sister's death from fever in my youth, I had found new purpose in taking service with Messire, hadn't I? My duty was to him, my sword his to command.

The usual rat-infested hovel that passes for an inn in Lescar came into view as I crested a rise in the road. I was still holding my sword at my side, sticky with bloody detritus, so I gave my horse his head at the water trough and took possession of a rickety bench where I spread out oil and rags to clean the solstice gift Messire D'Olbriot had given me in recognition of my trials in his service the previous year.

It says a lot about Lescar that it wasn't the sight of a man cleaning a bloody weapon that startled the pinch-faced little maid coming out to empty her ash bucket, but my accent; my Lescari has all been learned on Messire's business around the border with home. I couldn't fathom her concern; she only had about ten words of Tormalin, though I doubt she could have counted them. Eventually I gathered there was no fresh roast, so I took the gritty bread and sour cheese offered but declined the greyish stew, congealed in the pot from the night before. Evidently exceeding the reckoning with good Tormalin pennies, I won a startled smile when I declined the halved and quartered coin pieces she tried to offer me. I have no use for Lescari coin, even when it's whole.

As I ate I fished out the letter I carried, brought by the Imperial Despatch to rescue me from the taut emotions of Aiten's sorrowing family and sending me to ride the empty roads of Lescar over the Equinox festival. Well, that at least had been preferable to lining up with my brothers to entertain the nicely eligible daughters of Mother's sewing circle. I took up the letter and the description on the outside caught my eye again, still making me smile.

Ryshad Tathel. An armspan and four fingers tall, thinly built but muscular. Hair black and curly, eyes brown, dark complected, clean shaven. Softly spoken but with a determined manner.

My father would have phrased it rather differently: 'stubborn as a mule and twice as hard to shift when he digs his heels in' is what he had said of me to Messire's Sergeant-at-Arms. That last sentence was written in a different hand. So, Carmarl was rising rapidly in Messire's counsels if he was being allowed to add personal notes to the Sieur's letters. Saedrin grant it will be many years before the men of the family have to gather to elect a new head for the House of D'Olbriot, but it was starting to look as if I could win a tidy sum with a wager on Camarl. Perhaps I should lay some coin soon, while the odds were still long on a sister's younger son succeeding.

From Messire D'Olbriot, given at his Toremal residence, the 26th day of For-Spring, to Ryshad Tathel, sworn man.

I send my greetings and my wishes that your trip provides consolation both to yourself and the family bereaved by Aiten's loss. I take this opportunity to repeat my own sorrow at his fate as well as the esteem in which I held him. I ask you to communicate this to his parents once more.

You are no longer required to attend me in Toremal when your visit is concluded. I have received a request from the Archmage of Hadrumal, Planir the Black, that you travel to Caladhria and join with one Shivvalan Ralsere, mage. You will find him with a recluse called Viltred Sern who dwells in the forests to the north of Cote, seat of one Lord Adrin, on the highroad to Abray.

This mage requests your assistance in continuing the pursuit you shared in at the end of For-Winter past. At such time as the wizard Ralsere no longer has need of you, return to Toremal with all best speed. In the interim, keep me apprised of your movements with letters by Imperial Despatch or such other discreet means as you judge secure.

I am confident that you will perform this commission with your usual capability.

It was smoothly written in the fluent hand of Messire's personal scrivener. I could just picture the Sieur, sat with a pile of documents, disposing of each with terse commands. My spirits rose; I've worked for Messire long enough to read what wasn't written into the letter. I was to be his eyes and ears, his link to the Archmage's plans for foiling the Ice Islanders. This offered better prospects of vengeance for Aiten than chasing garbled reports of foreigners in the backwoods of the ocean coast, which is what I'd spent the latter half of winter doing.

I'd had no real dealing with wizards before getting caught up with Shiv the year before and we generally prefer to keep them at arm's length in Tormalin. I wondered what Shiv was up to; he and I owed each other a measure of our lives after that cursed trip to the Ice Islands. Still, his loyalties to his Archmage meant a different lodestone from mine governed his course, I reminded myself.

I ate and headed for the river. The false hope of the noonday sun faded, fine rain mizzling down like exhausted tears. I passed the remnants of a sacked village, reeking with the smell of burned wood rotting after the long winter and weeping black stains into the scorched earth. So much for the Dukedom of Marlier, where life was supposed to be safer than most. I found myself longing for the clean scent of salt on the wind from the ocean at home.

I looked across the valley with its coppices of hazel and ash, past the sprawl of a turf-roofed village amidst a striped patchwork of open fields and over the rough common grazing to the stark crag where the local Baron had his reddish stone castle. Tormalin villages cluster close to the protections of their patron and have done since the Chaos when lordless and landless men ransacked the ruins of the Old Empire. Lescari peasants grub a living from the land as best they can and hope the battles pass them by. I noted the battlements were being raised, straw and clay that had protected the half-built fortifications from frosts stripped away; that could be useful intelligence for Messire. What threat did Marlier see waiting now the Equinox had opened the fighting season? I knew the

Duke of Triolle had fouled his own nest comprehensively after heavy losses in the previous year's fighting with Parnilesse. Did he have ambitions here?

Arriving at the river in the mid-afternoon, I found a silent line of grim-faced peasants waiting by the bridge, salvaged possessions in bundles and handcarts, little children all unknowing smiles, older ones wide-eyed and glancing at parents for reassurance seldom forthcoming. I'd been passing pitiful groups like this all through Lescar, trudging along, heads down, locals stopping in their work to watch as the strangers passed, hoes and plough-staves in hand, ready to keep anyone moving who might be thinking about trying to stop. My own purse had lightened by a good measure on the road, common coin gone to those who would take it or else spent on as much bread as I could reasonably carry, so I had something I could casually offer those still clinging to the shreds of their dignity.

I rode to the head of the queue, not about to risk hanging about and getting drawn into the quarrels erupting here and there along the line.

'Rein it in.' A burly man-at-arms levelled his pike to bar my way and the rest of his troop stopped lounging on the parapet of the bridge.

'Good day to you.' I dismounted and nodded a precisely calculated half-salute. 'Is there a fee for crossing the bridge?'

He eyed me a little uncertainly. 'That depends on who you are.'

I bet it did; on whether one was a desperate peasant willing to give up a share of any hoarded coin worth having, or a fleeing mercenary who could end up costing a lax border guard a flogging if he slipped past and was caught looting or worse. Caladhrian lords know full well the bloody chaos of Lescar would soon spill over to choke their lands if it were not for the depth and swirling current of the Rel, and they take guarding the few bridges suitably seriously.

'I am a Tormalin prince's sworn man.' I pulled my amulet from the neck of my shirt and held it out.

'What's your business in Caladhria?' the man asked, open-mouthed.

'My patron's,' I replied crisply but politely.

He didn't know what to say to that but he didn't lower his pike either.

'Here.' I held out my hand and he closed his stained fingers on a couple of good Tormalin Marks, not the flimsy leaded coin of Lescar. 'Give some woman on her own with children a free passage, why don't you?'

He cracked a gap-toothed smile at that. 'I reckon I could.'

He planted his pike on its butt and my horse's hooves rang on the planks of the broad bridge. Tormalin-built Old Empire foundations were still solidly defying the murky flow of the mighty Rel, as you would expect, and the intermittently renewed woodwork above was dark from a fresh coat of pitch. More men with pikes lined the sides, ready for any threat of trouble. I stopped by one who looked barely old enough to use a blade for shaving, let alone for defending his Lord's domains.

I noted the colours and badge on his overlarge livery. 'Are you Lord Adrin's men?'

He nodded cautious agreement. 'That's right.'

'I'm heading for a place called Cote. Which road do I take?'

He frowned at me. 'Which Cote would that be, then, mester?'

I frowned in turn, perplexed. 'How do you mean?'

'Well, for Upper Cote, Spring Cote, Cote in the Clay and Small Cote, you go upstream, Cotinwood and Hill Cote are downstream, and you'd want the west high road for Nether Cote and Cote Fane.' This being Caladhria, the lad was genuinely trying to be helpful, not just tweaking my nose.

'Where's Lord Adrin's main residence?'

'He'm visiting Duryea, his wife's people, been there since the Equinox.'

'And where does he live when he's not visiting?'

'All over.'

The lad's painstaking Tormalin, doubtless learned from some local scholar, was oddly accented and I wasn't at all sure he was understanding me fully. The Caladhrian I know best is the coastal dialect and this far up country could well confuse things further.

'Thank you,' I said, belatedly recalling why Caladhrian was a byword for lackwit back home. This lad couldn't poke a dead dog with a sharp stick.

Once off the bridge, I spurred the horse clear of the peasants milling about. A knot of lime-washed, timber-framed houses with wood-shingled roofs clustered around the meeting of the roads; it could have been any small hamlet between the ocean coast and western Ensaimin, the most distant province, where the Empire's grip had never really taken hold and slipped loose first. I looked vainly for way-stones that might give me some heading and finally drew my lucky rune-stick from my pocket. I rolled it between my palms, the Drum came out upright and I headed north on that result.

The house of Viltred Sern,
west of Cote in the Clay, Caladhria,
9th of Aft-Spring

A sturdily built hut of logs and wooden shingles stood under a shallow crag in a forest clearing, a knot of figures gathered on the smooth turf before it. Their prisoner was an old man, withered with age, hair and beard frosted with white. Bound on his back to a freshly felled log, twigs and splinters pierced him not by deliberate design but through simple carelessness. Manacles were tight around wrists blackened with old blood, drawn by repeated writhing against the cruel restraints. His captors stood in a loose half-circle, black-clad in leather and metal, faces flat with disinterest, men with unvarying blond hair and stocky builds. Their leader stood at the head of the hapless victim, calm as his irons reheated in the small wood fire. The smoke rose and coiled away into the clear blue sky, the first leaves of the new season green and fresh on the trees. Blood dripped slowly from ruined hands, fingers broken, jagged edges of bone jutting through skin, nails ripped out with calculated brutality. The victim's ribs heaved in sudden spasm, skin stark white through the smears of blood as his chest fluttered like a half-killed bird and abruptly stilled. Gory pits where eyes should have been wept tears of anguished blood.

'That's a grim prospect, I grant you, Viltred.' The speaker swallowed hard as he stared at this stark picture. It hovered within a gleaming diamond hanging from the upper point of a crescent of hammered copper set before him on the table, a tongue of flame licking upwards from a candle at the bottom of the arc.

'When did you first see this fate in your augury spell?' He cleared his throat and looked around the homely clutter of the small cabin as if to reassure himself the vision of anguish and malice was no more than foul illusion.

'Four days past,' the old wizard grunted, face dour as he looked at the image of his agonised death, scant paces from his own threshold. 'So what do you make of it, Shivvalan? What has this to do with you turning up after the mighty wizards of Hadrumal have ignored me for close on a generation, believing me to be either liar or fool? When I was Azazir's apprentice and we made our voyage, no one believed us when we said we had found islands in the far Ocean.' He gestured towards the gem with one gnarled hand. 'Islands where a race of fair-haired men lived, as like to these as hounds bred from the same pack. Now you come to tell me that the wise and noble wizards of Hadrumal have discovered these islands for themselves and deign to believe me at last. Is it coincidence that I now see these curs hunting me? What trouble is Planir stirring up for us all now?' He huddled back into the worn and faded cushions that lined his heavy oak chair.

Shiv rubbed a hand over his sallow chin, dark eyes thoughtful. 'Well, certainly the Archmage must be told at once. Believe me, Viltred, I told you the truth. Planir sent me to find out what you could recall of your own voyage to the Ice Islands with Azazir. I'm sorry, I should have explained; it seems these unknown islanders, Elietimm they call themselves, have some means of enchantment that we know nothing of in Hadrumal. Worse, they had some role to play in the fall of the Tormalin Empire, most likely by means of magic, but you know how much lore was lost in the Chaos. Planir is hoping to recover some of that knowledge. We had no idea that these men would be seeking you out as well, I swear, but that must be what this means.' He paused for a moment before continuing briskly. 'Still, now that we have this warning we can make sure none of this comes to pass. How often is an augury fulfilled in all its particulars? Not above one time in a handful, less maybe.'

'I'd prefer longer odds of seeing the Solstice than four

chances in five.' Viltred drew a shuddering breath, and as he did so the vision in the crystal shook and dissolved. With evident effort to regain his composure, the old wizard leaned forward to rest his hands on the table once more and slowly turned the stone with the shimmering fingers of azure light that revealed the mage's elemental link with the air that surrounded him. The answering amber glow rising within the heart of the gem spoke of magic born of the earth as slowly a shimmering haze cleared and new pictures focused on the bright surface.

The image sharpened: a knot of figures standing in a large airy room. Framed in an open window behind them, masts and rigging moved gently with the motion of unseen waves, sails square-set on stubby spars.

'There you are, Viltred, and showing no signs of ill treatment.' Shiv sighed with relief.

'I'll allow being caked to my eyebrows in the filth of the road and looking nigh on exhausted is preferable to dying spitted like a festival hog,' muttered Viltred.

'Those galleys, they're the kind that ply the Caladhrian Gulf,' continued Shiv thoughtfully.

'What I want to know is who are all these other people,' the old man snapped.

Shiv frowned as he studied the tiny figures in the spell's vision. 'The woman with red hair is called Livak. She travels Ensaimin, a woman of many talents, a gambler for the most part.'

'That sounds dishonest as well as disreputable,' snorted Viltred.

Shiv stifled a sudden smile before continuing. 'The tall man at the back is the sworn man to Messire D'Olbriot – Ryshad, the one who should be here any day now. You recall me telling you about him?'

'I am not yet in my dotage. I can generally remember things I have been told the same day,' the old wizard replied acidly. 'Who's the plain-faced piece with shoulders like a farm hand?'

'That's Halice,' said Shiv slowly. 'She's a friend of Livak's who's been laid up over the last few seasons with a broken leg.'

'And what possible reason could I have for being with such an ill-assorted crew, down in Relshaz?' demanded Viltred, his sunken eyes flashing with annoyance. 'And before you ask, I recognise that beacon tower. I knew the city well enough in my youth.'

'That other man's face is weathered like sailcloth and with those rope scars on his hand, I think it's safe to assume he's a sailor,' Shiv murmured, more to himself than to the old man. 'Those parchments that Livak's weighting with tankards would probably be charts, don't you think? Are we taking ship somewhere? Relshaz is certainly the biggest port on the western side of the Gulf, but in a city that size a lot of other things could be going on. We could be looking to meet a ship?'

Viltred shrugged wordlessly, his lined face grim under his straggly grey brows. Shiv sat motionless at the dark oaken table, deep in thought, before suddenly slapping his hands down on the scarred wood. 'There's no point trying to second-guess these things, is there? Still, contrasting visions like these generally mean achieving one outcome precludes the other, doesn't it? We can make a good start down that route by getting everyone we're seeing together, and Ryshad's already on his way.'

'I wish you would curb your enthusiasm for telling me things I learned as a first-season apprentice before you were even thought of, Shivvalan. How do you propose we go about this, anyway?' Faint hope warred with the suspicion in the old man's faded eyes.

'I think I can find Halice, at very least, and I imagine she'll know where Livak may be.' Shiv rose from his stool and fetched a ewer from the old-fashioned dresser behind him, taking a little silver vial from his breeches pocket. Viltred watched in silence as the younger mage sprinkled black drops of ink on the surface of the water. A greenish glow began to gather in the water, rising above the rim of the jug to trickle over the sides and sink into the stained table top. 'A friend of mine was helping tend her leg,' Shiv explained in increasingly animated tones. 'He found he had a boot buckle of hers and passed it on to me. As he said, you never know when you might want the means of scrying for someone.' He dropped the trinket into the water, caught his lower lip between his teeth and bent closer to his magic, expression intense.

'Just get on with it,' muttered Viltred.

A sudden sound of rushing air and water filled the room and Shiv stood abruptly upright, his eyes meeting Viltred's where he saw his own consternation mirrored.

'You set wards of warning on your way here?' asked the old man, a quake of fear in his voice. 'Could that be this swordsman arriving?'

'No, I'm afraid my spells are woven only for the Elietimm,' Shiv replied breathlessly. 'After travelling to those accursed islands, I've no desire to find myself in those bastards' hands again, believe me. One of our number suffered much the fate we have to protect you from.'

'Let's remove ourselves to the safety of the village,' said Viltred more robustly. 'You have sufficient mastery of air to achieve that?'

Shiv scowled in frustration. 'We daren't take the time to gather all your valuables and if we just translocate ourselves away, we'll have no idea what the Elietimm do or where they go.' He swiftly crossed the dusty floor to open the varnished shutters just enough to see out. 'We'll be trapped like rats in a barrel if we stay here, though. No, we'll find a vantage point in the woods where we can hide ourselves,' he said decisively. 'With the greater moon still new and the lesser at last crescent, this is the blackest night of the season and that can help us as much as them.'

'If I see them coming for us I'll be away, clear to Hadrumal, if I can,' warned Viltred, grim-faced. As the old mage rose stiffly from his chair, Shiv drew back the bolts on the sturdy wooden door. He caught the shorter man under one arm and, throwing open the door, half hurried, half carried Viltred into the concealing gloom gathering beneath the trees as the sun sank slowly in the clouded western sky.

'Wait,' commanded Viltred a touch breathlessly.

Shiv bent his head close to the old mage's. 'What is it?'

'I've a few spells of my own woven hereabouts,' Viltred murmured grimly. 'I can set them for two-footed beasts as well as those with four.'

He rubbed knuckles swollen with joint evil and a faint blue glow gathered into a ball between his hands. Viltred released it with a gesture and it floated away like a wisp of marsh gas, alighting here and there on the fringes of the forest to leave a small, fast-fading imprint on the grass.

'We have to conceal ourselves,' whispered Shiv urgently. 'I've some means of confusing their enchantments but we have to stay absolutely motionless.'

Viltred nodded and the two wizards drew further into the shadows. A flicker of multi-hued light at the edge of seeing gathered round them, evaporating to leave the mages no more visible than the patterns of darkness merging with the twilight.

The final golden shimmers of the sun were scattered by a waterfall tumbling into a brook but everything else was muted to myriad shades of grey. Black as the night deepening under the surrounding trees, the shape of a man suddenly ran across the open ground to the hut, crouching low and moving swiftly. His yell ripped through the silence as a shock of lightning erupted from the ground beneath his feet, throwing him backwards to scramble in confusion for the shelter of the trees. Smoke drifted away on the night's chilly breath.

After a long still moment, two more figures slowly paced across the turf to vanish in the dark lee of the hut. A sudden flare of blue light outlined the frame of a window and startled curses were hastily hushed. After a tense pause a hooded individual strode boldly from the cover of the woods and stood in the middle of the grass, a handful of others respectful in his wake.

The stout wooden door exploded inwards in a soundless

shower of splinters and the black-clad men rushed inside,
only the faintest gleams of starlight catching on their swords
and one pale, uncovered head. Faint sounds filtered through
the ruins of the door, the scrape of nailed boots on the
floorboards, the heavy drag of furniture being hauled aside,
crashes spoke of shattering crockery while a series of dull
thuds suggested treasured books being tossed angrily to the
floor. One liveried figure emerged from the door, head down
and stooped shoulders betraying failure and fear. The hooded
man crossed the grass with impatient strides and struck him
with a gesture of disgust. The others emerged, one proffering
something that stayed his leader's punishing hand. With a
sweep of his cloak, the hooded man led his troop away to
melt into the forest night.

The pallid, wasted arc of the lesser moon rose over the
sheltering crag. Slowly tendrils of smoke began to ooze from
the windows and door of the cabin. Greedy flickers of flame
began to lick round the timbers, startlingly orange against
the deepening night. In an impossibly short time the roof
collapsed in on itself and the red glare of the inferno defied
the soft light of Halcarion's crown of stars, now riding high
and uncaring above the smoke. Feathery drifts of ash swirled
across the glade as grass withered and the bare earth began
to steam. Suddenly the fires melted away, leaving only a ruin
of blackened wood.

A motley-coloured cat made a tentative foray from the edge
of the woods but something startled it and it dashed up a
tree. On its second attempt, it reached the forbidding heap
of charred timbers and paced cautiously round, sniffing and
occasionally prodding with an inquiring paw. After a while, a
second cat appeared, ears down and tail clamped close to its
grey-striped side. The two animals explored the edges of the
ruin for a while, the air around them shimmering oddly, the size
and colours of the creatures shifting and altering until the spell
faded away to reveal the wizards in their own forms. Neither
man paid any heed to the magic unravelling around them and
continued to search intently, pulling wreckage aside.

'Let me.' Shiv hauled a blackened beam aside to reveal the smashed and burned remnants of a trap door. Viltred pulled at a twisted tangle of wood and metal with an effort, struggling with a racking cough as the ash and cinders were puffed up around them both. Shiv helped him clear the choking debris then made to go down the rock-cut stair now revealed.

'No,' snapped Viltred. 'This is still my home, what is left of it.'

Gathering his faded jerkin around himself, Viltred descended the steep steps awkwardly while Shiv waited, arms folded and one impatient boot raising little flurries in the soot as it tapped.

Viltred's cough echoed harshly as he emerged from the cellar some while later. 'Well, the Archmage is going to learn nothing new about these mysterious islands, their vicious people or their arcane arts from the few treasures I won from Azazir.' He spat into the dust and clinker. 'They've taken every last piece, so where does that leave Planir's hopes now, Shivvalan, tell me that!'

The High Road between Upper Cote and Spring Cote, Caladhria, 10th of Aft-Spring

'Ryshad!'

I was so startled to be hailed by name on the deserted early morning road that I jerked my reins like a novice. The indignant horse skipped a pace forward, shaking its head with a rattle of harness rings and bits.

'Ryshad, over here!'

'Shiv?' I looked round to see the wizard waving at me, lanky and raw-boned as I remembered him, leaves stuck to his breeches as he emerged from a spinney I would have sworn was empty of anything larger than a squirrel. 'What in the name of all that's holy are you doing?'

A second, hunched figure appeared and Shiv turned to offer his arm. 'May I present my companion, Viltred Sern. Viltred, this is Ryshad, the sworn man I told you about.'

A Prince's man soon learns not to betray surprise so I bowed, expressionless, as I looked to see what manner of man had been apprentice to one of the most notorious and dangerous wizards that the hidden city of Hadrumal had ever produced. It was something of a surprise to see a tired old man with a ragged grey beard and sunken eyes, soiled and crumpled after what must have been a cold night out in the open. Still, it had been a generation or so since Azazir had been given the choice of banishment to the distant wilds of Gidesta or death at the hands of the Council of Wizards for his irresponsible sorceries.

'Shivvalan, I need warmth and food before my joints seize

completely in this damp!' The old man scowled out from the
moulting fur of his hood.

'What's the story, Shiv?' I asked, concerned. 'Why are you
walking the road without so much as a bundle between you?'

Shiv shook his head. 'I could only tell you half a tale at
the moment. Let's find somewhere with a fire and some
decent ale.'

I let it go for the moment and dismounted to help shove the
old wizard into the saddle, where he rode like a sour-faced sack
of grain. 'There was a decent-looking tavern not far back,' I
suggested.

'Fine.' Shiv nodded. 'We'll be going south as it is. Take
us there.'

I wondered if I would have to find a tactful moment to
remind Shiv that, patron's instructions or not, he had better
not have any ideas of ordering me about. Messire gives me his
commissions, but I'm used to plotting my own course.

We soon turned into the well-swept foreyard of the whitewashed tavern and Viltred struggled to get off the horse.
Realising he was older than I had first thought as I saw
the greyness of his skin under his sparse beard, I offered him
my arm. Accepting my help after a sharp, suspicious glance
the mage stalked stiffly inside where Shiv was charming a
pink-faced tapmaid into letting us have the private parlour
off the common hall.

Once we were seated in the snug room which even boasted
some well-polished wainscoting, I poured three tankards of
the rich dark ale as Shiv drew the heavy oak shutters across
the clouded glass of the small window. At a snap of Viltred's
fingers the candles sparked to life, outshining a faint glimmer
of blue light spreading from Shiv's outstretched hands.

'Now I can tell you what's going on. We don't want to be
overheard,' he explained as the enchantment faded into the
wood and plaster of the walls.

A sensible enough precaution, given that putting up the
shutters would have aroused the curiosity of anyone who'd
seen him do it.

'If you could manage it, Viltred, the augury would be the clearest way to explain everything,' continued Shiv.

The old man sighed but nodded. 'Do you have a candle-end?' He took an oilskin bundle out of an inside pocket and unwrapped a crescent of hammered copper set on a little stand.

I watched, determined to keep my countenance. We don't have much use or experience of wizardry in Tormalin but I had seen it wielded to startling effect the previous autumn, when Shiv, Livak and I had been fleeing for our lives across the desolate wastes of the Ice Islands. I recalled Shiv was a wizard whose powers linked him principally to the element of water, an accident of magebirth which had played a crucial role in saving us from the merciless Ocean, thanks be to Dastennin.

Viltred's colour improved as he drank his ale and I took a long swallow of my own. Full flavoured with the bitter bite of good hops, it was more than good enough for me if I couldn't get a decent Tormalin wine. It was certainly a vast improvement on the sour dregs I'd been drinking in Lescar.

Shiv fixed a stub of tallow to the lower point of the crescent, and in his unguarded expression I saw he was weary as a brothel watchdog, woken ten times a night. Viltred carefully hung a gem from a tiny hook at the top and Shiv lit the candle with a snap of scarlet magic. I saw from the flashes of fire that this was a diamond, larger than any in the Imperial crown, and bit back an exclamation.

Viltred cleared his throat before speaking. 'Nowadays I live a quiet life with little magic, but one thing I do for the locals, in return for food and so forth, is take auguries for the coming seasons.'

I wondered how good the old man was; I've never seen a festival fortune teller I'd wager a Lescari penny on, netting the witless with their lies. A sudden flash of amber light set images dancing inside the diamond, seizing my eye and seeming to fill my gaze, everything else of no more significance than a mirror's frame.

The face of the stone was dark now, clouded with what

looked like smoke. It drifted apart leaving only the sooty
breath of torches steaming around a ruined hall. Greedy fires
devoured heaps of fine stains, lovingly embroidered hangings,
furs and gowns looted from Dastennin only knows where. Dark
oaken furniture, dutifully polished for generations, was hacked
and splintered, gouges showing pale in the old wood like bone
exposed in a mortal wound. My heart started pounding in my
chest as I recognised this place; it was the audience chamber in
the Imperial Palace in Toremal. I gritted my teeth in impotent
fury as I saw black-liveried figures crossing the broken tiles
of the floor with armfuls of looted luxury to dump on the
insatiable flames. I realised with cold horror and hot rage
that these were Ice Islanders, fellows to the villains who had
maimed and robbed Messire's nephew the previous summer,
that outrage setting Aiten and myself on the trail which had
ultimately led to my friend's death.

Darker smoke was gathering in one corner and I saw that
a ravenous tongue of fire had taken hold of one of the great
wooden pillars of the doorway to the throne room. As I
watched, the heavy double doors, shorn of their gold fixings,
swung open and a tow-headed man in bloodstained leather
waved a triumphant and terrible trophy at his fellows.

It was a head on a pike. From the lumpen shape of the
jaw and face, they had beaten their victim before despatching
him, savagely enough to break the bones of his skull. For
all that, I knew this man, I had seen that youthful and once
handsome face warm with contentment, those eyes, now dull
and lifeless, bright with excitement. This was my Emperor,
Tadriol, third son of Tadriol the Prudent, fifth emperor of that
House, still new enough in this seat of power to be awaiting
the acclamation from the Princes of the Great Houses that
would seal their approval or otherwise in the epithet their
Convocation bestowed on him.

I could not stop myself glancing at Shiv and our eyes met
for a moment, his face set like ice and just as cold. Realising
my hands were clenched into fists, my nails marking my
palms, I reached for my tankard, trying to wet my dry throat

before realising the vessel was empty. Viltred's magic flickered as he turned the gem once more with trembling fingers of enchantment.

Soft grey haze cleared and revealed mellow stone walls, warm in the light of fine beeswax candles. I saw myself standing on a dais in what I instantly recognised as a Tormalin Prince's great hall, lavishly decorated for the celebrations of either Solstice or Equinox. We had evidently all prospered; I was spruced up like a whorehouse apothecary in maroon velvet and fine linen with a discreet collar of gold links as I stood behind Messire's nephew, Camarl, his plump face genial but his eyes keen, deep in conversation with someone I recognised from a cadet line of D'Azenac. Realising I was looking at myself as other people must see me was an eerie experience, unnerving, and I stifled a sudden shiver. My lips parted in unconscious surprise when I saw Livak, seductive in a midnight-blue gown of silk, pearls caught in the exquisite confection of her hair and gleaming around her neck. I allowed myself a moment to savour her unaccustomed elegance and realised she was enticing the knot of eager and noble youth around her to wager on the fall of a delicate set of applewood runes, tucking silver and gold coin discreetly into the little velvet bag on a ribbon at her waist.

Shiv was down in the main body of the hall, standing tall and courtly in green linen, closely shaven and with his long dark hair tied neatly back for a change, weight resting easily on his back foot, arms crossed and relaxed. He was laughing with one of Messire's nieces, who clearly had no idea that her evident interest in him was doomed to disappointment. Viltred was in animated discussion with two noblemen, dressed in formal robes incongruous in this setting but possessing an unexpected air of authority as he waved a black-clad arm, his gnarled hand gripping a staff which he thumped down to emphasise his point.

'What you are seeing are alternate possibilities for the future,' began Shiv.

'What does it all mean?' I demanded curtly. Any concerns of

the wizards were secondary to the peril threatening everything to which I was honour-bound.

'We don't know.' Viltred's frank admission silenced me.

'You've taken no action?' I heard impatience sharpening the edge to my tone and forced myself to blunt it. 'When you've seen such a threat to the Emperor?'

'Taking action based on auguries is a very risky business.' Unexpectedly, Viltred was not cross or defensive but merely sounded weary to the bone. 'Every event depends on such a chain of circumstance and causation that in acting you can forge the vital link that brings about the very catastrophe you are trying to avoid.'

'Seeing yourself and Livak like that suggests you both have some role to play in securing a positive outcome.' Shiv gestured at the now lifeless gem. 'I'd say our most important task is getting everyone in that vision together as soon as we can.'

'Do you know where she is?'

'She's with that friend of hers, Halice.' Shiv nodded and poured more ale. 'I've been scrying for her last night and today, as well as for you. That's how we knew what road you had taken.'

Of course; those tricks with magic spells and coloured inks gave Shiv the means to keep track of people without them even knowing it. How long had he been scrying on me? I discarded that thought in the face of more immediate concerns. So Shiv was trying to find Livak; the woman who'd killed Aiten, who'd saved my life, who owed me a good measure of hers, skilled gambler, dextrous thief, latterly my lover when a sudden storm of passion had hit us both on the voyage home. I'm not given to nailing anything in a skirt, I did enough of that in my youth, but Livak, she had been something different, the first woman to really get under my guard in more than ten years. Just thinking about her red-haired passion set the blood pulsing in my breeches. What was I going to say to her? What did I want from her? Come to that, was she going to want anything from me, beyond a good time between the sheets? Hopes and doubts that had nothing to do with my duties warred within me.

I rasped a hand over a day's growth of beard but banished that minor irritation from my mind. 'What else do I need to know?'

Shiv hesitated before answering. 'The Elietimm attacked Viltred's home the night before last. It may be coincidence, but then again, they may have followed me there.'

My hackles rose at the idea of my enemies and those of Messire prowling, unchallenged, on our side of the Ocean. 'What happened?'

'They looted the hut for a few keepsakes Viltred brought back from his journey with Azazir and then torched it. We managed to hide in the woods.'

'It's lucky you were there, Shiv.' Was it luck or were the Elietimm hoping to take two coneys in one snare?

'They've taken the Spice Road.' Shiv took a drink. 'We cut across country when I scryed you reaching the river.'

I raised a hand. 'Shiv, last year these bastards were about as easy to track as a ship in stormy water. How can you be sure?'

'We've been scrying for the things they've stolen, that's giving us some clue. Viltred's had them in his cellar for over a generation; ordinarily he should be able to find them clear across the Caladhrian Gulf.'

'Do you know where the Elietimm are at present?'

'The best I can tell you is that they're not close enough to us to present an imminent threat.' Shiv's grimace told me he found this as unsatisfactory as I did. 'We want to find Livak and Halice, then try to pick up the trail again, catch up with the Ice Islanders, see what they're up to. We can attempt to recover what they've stolen, too; Livak's skills will prove useful for that.'

I didn't share his conviction that Livak would be prepared to help him out. I'd gained the distinct impression that she'd been put off thieving for life after the trouble going pilfering for wizards had landed her in. Shiv had needed to blackmail her into it last year.

'We can't be sure these people won't want Viltred himself

for some reason.' I frowned. 'Taking him closer to them means taking him into more danger. Isn't there somewhere safer he could go?'

'You're here to protect him now.' Shiv wouldn't meet my eyes. 'The Archmage feels it's better that we all stay together; this all relates to a project Planir has very few people involved in.'

I glanced at Viltred to see unhappiness in the downturned corners of his mouth. Did he know something Shiv wasn't telling me or was he simply in pain from the joint evil I had noted twisting his hands? There were a lot of unanswered questions here. I stifled unaccustomed frustration as I drained the last of my ale. 'Let's find you two some food, some horses and get back on the road to make the best of the day.'

Shiv may have had no more than the shirt on his back but he had a well-filled purse inside it. Once the two wizards were mounted, on a thick-necked black and a murrey roan, we made good time through the Caladhrian countryside. Sturdy yeomen were out ploughing their fields with a springtime optimism that came as a welcome change after Lescar, slaked lime piled in orderly heaps, ready to enrich the soil. Fine-looking stock grazed secure in neatly hedged enclosures and new wheat was pricking up through the rich, dark earth. I might have been a little more impressed if I hadn't been attending Messire when he'd spent an afternoon explaining to Camarl how all the vaunted Caladhrian agricultural expertise stemmed directly from the needs of Lescari dukes to keep their fighting men fed. Little enough of this bounty would go to relieve the lot of the wretched souls I had passed on the Marlier high road.

Gangs of peasants were clearing woodland and I noticed the distinctive headscarves the women wore. 'Those are Lescari, aren't they?' I turned to Shiv.

Shiv nodded. 'Lord Adrin lets some across each spring to clear land and settle between the River Road and the Rel. If they prosper, he gets tenants and rents; if raiders get across, Lord Adrin's own people might get off a bit lighter.'

I hoped the determined optimism in the faces of those

labouring so hard would be rewarded. 'Has there been much trouble lately?'

'Not much, and Lord Adrin's on the alert.' Shiv stood in his stirrups and pointed to the broad sweeps of a distant mill. 'If you see a mill locked in an upright cross, that's a signal to the militia that scavengers have crossed the river. They stamp out most of the vermin.'

I nodded approvingly; I would have to mention Lord Adrin to Messire, a man with wits as well as control of a strategically placed bridge.

We rode until the failing light forced a halt at a wayside inn. With the lesser moon waning past its last crescent to dark and the greater barely waxing at half, there wasn't enough light to justify risking the horses further. Viltred travelled without complaint but grew more and more hunched over his reins; when we stopped, he was barely able to straighten. Shiv helped him to our bedchamber while I visited the tap-room to ask a few seemingly idle questions of the underemployed tap-man. I was reassured to learn of no unusual blond-haired travellers in the vicinity and learned that Coteshall, where Shiv expected to find Halice, was only a scant half day's ride away.

Eventually, yawning and hoping for a better night's sleep than Arimelin had seen fit to bless me with lately, I accepted a flannel-wrapped hot brick from the motherly goodwife. Welcoming the warmth on my chilled hands, I climbed the narrow stairs in stocking feet, my boots tucked under one arm. Shiv and Viltred were already asleep, as I picked my way quietly through stale aromas of well-worn boots and the fresh tang of warm liniment to the vacant bed. Sleep was long in coming; every time I closed my eyes, I saw Ice Islanders sacking the very heart of Tormalin power.

A great house of pale stone, full of empty echoes

It was a cold and clear morning. Frost gleamed in the corners of the courtyard where the early winter sun had not yet penetrated and the blackened stems of some late autumn flowers overlooked by the steward drooped forlornly in an antique urn. The doorkeeper hurried to answer the summons of the bell, rubbing his hands briskly against the cold of the deeply shadowed entrance. A young man entered, tense and pale, twisting a bright sapphire ring on one nervous hand but with habitual manners ingrained enough to greet the servant with a precise bow. His highly polished boots clattered on the flagstones as he strode into the house, evidently needing no guide.

Once inside, Temar took a deep breath and checked his appearance in a handy mirror in the anteroom. The face he saw was curiously at odds with the rich clothes he wore. Lean, with high cheekbones tapering into a long, pointed jaw, it was more suited to armour or working clothes in his opinion. He'd certainly feel more comfortable in either, rather than chafing under the seldom worn constraints of formal dress. Blue eyes, so pale as to be almost colourless, stared back at him from under thin black brows. The severity of their gaze was heightened by his long black hair, drawn back and clasped at the nape of his neck. That was the fashion required, whether or not it suited him.

Temar straightened the collar of his shirt and brushed with irritation at a speck on his crimson jerkin until he realised it was in fact a flaw in the silvering of the mirror. That would have been enough to get the glass sent straight to the servants' quarters less than a handful of years ago, he thought. The realisation stiffened his resolve as he waited for a summons to his grandfather's presence.

Not Grandfather, he reminded himself; the old man was sitting as head of the House D'Alsennin this morning. Not that that meant what it once had; there were no clients waiting eagerly on the polished bench, hoping to present requests or offer services to their patron.

'Esquire.' The chamberlain opened the double doors with a flourish and managed to convey the impression that his presence there was to confer an honour on Temar rather than because the household had been forced to dispense with the services of the hall-lackey.

Temar bowed politely and walked stiffly into the salon. It was some time since he'd been in here and his step faltered as he registered the statues missing from their niches and the sun-faded silken drapes. An inadequate fire flickered valiantly in the massive fireplace, unable to do more than draw unwelcome attention to the chilly atmosphere.

'Temar, it's good to see you.' His grandfather looked imposing in his formal mantle of maroon velvet, seated in the ancient black-oak chair that dominated the dais at the end of the long room. Despite his scant white hair and deeply graven wrinkles, his faded eyes were clear and alert.

'Sieur.' Temar made a formal reverence and sank to one knee, head bowed.

'This is an official visit?' There was a hint of amusement in the old man's voice.

'It is.' Temar's voice was firm. With his head bowed, he did not see the dismay that fleetingly doubled the weight of years on his grandfather's face.

'Then make your petition.' The Sieur's voice was firm and even a little grim.

'I request permission to take ship with Messire Den Fellaemion.' Temar spoke more loudly than he had intended in his determination not to stumble over his words. The request rang through the room more like a demand and Temar forced himself to remain still, staring at the subtle curves of the ochre and cream tiles on the floor.

'Go on.' The old man's voice was quelling.

Temar looked up despite himself; momentarily at a loss.

'Make your case, Esquire.' The Sieur looked down at him, unsmiling. 'Tell me why I should allow the last of my line to risk himself in some unknown land the far side of the ocean.'

Temar took another deep breath while trying to conceal it. He'd expected confrontation, argument; he'd been counting on it to spur him into defying his grandfather.

'I know that I am the last in the male line of the House D'Alsennin and I respect the obligations of my blood. Therefore it falls upon me to restore the fortunes of our name, both materially and among our peers. As the Empire has withdrawn from the provinces in latter years, we have successively lost lands, wealth and position. I do not see any realistic prospect that these will be recovered and so I have sought another means to raise our House to its former glory.' He paused to collect his thoughts.

'The Emperor has announced that a military levy will be raised to retake Lescar from these self-proclaimed Dukes.' The old man's face was unreadable.

Temar looked directly at him. 'No Great House has sent troops to any of the levies announced since the turn of the year, my lord, and this will be no different. I have no more confidence in the commanders of the Imperial Cohorts than I do in a pack of middenyard dogs and every Esquire who served his turn in the last year will be saying the same to his elders. You know as well as I do that Nemith the Reckless will be the last Emperor of his line and likely dead and burned before the end of the season, given his tastes in wine and whores.'

The Sieur inclined his head slowly. 'That is very true and when the Convocation of Princes meets to elect a new Emperor, there will be all manner of opportunity for the Esquires of even the minor Houses to secure his patronage. I am too old to dance that measure and you cannot do it from half the world away.'

The cold of the floor was starting to strike up into Temar's knees and he was getting cramp in his calves. He cursed himself for a fool for adopting the formal posture and tried to ignore the discomfort, but it forced itself out in his increasingly terse words.

'We are not the only House suffering as the Empire retreats, Grandfather. Why should I stand in line with a pail for another man to grant me a turn at a shrinking well? Messire Den Fellaemion tells of vast lands overseas, fertile and free for the taking, endless, untrapped forests, wealth to be had in iron and gold, even gems.'

'That sounds more like your friend young Den Rannion talking.' The old man's tone was sour. 'Tell me, just what do the good Esquire's gambling debts stand at now? I'm sure his father is only too keen to send him to any shore empty of gaming dens and brothels, if only to save his purse!'

Was the old man deliberately misunderstanding him? Be that as it may, Temar was not about to be reined aside into an argument about Vahil's latest foolishness; he did not drop his gaze. 'Messire Den Fellaemion is offering passage to those dispossessed and fleeing the ruins of the Provinces. He is giving them the chance to build a new life for themselves if they join him in building a second Empire across the ocean.'

'So you wish to grub in the dirt with the scaff and raff of the homeless and landless? Must I point out that you are neither?'

The Sieur leaned forward, scowling down from the seat of his forefathers. Temar made an effort and schooled his face into something approaching an expression of calm reason.

'Messire Den Fellaemion is looking for men with experience of command to help him manage the colonists, to organise the work, to co-ordinate and direct their efforts. I'm sure I need not remind you that I managed our estates in Dalasor to your complete satisfaction for three years. When the Mountain Men struck south of the river, I served my time in the Cohorts and was given command of my own troop within a season. I can put the skills I learned to good use and be recognised for it and rewarded. Is that not a more fitting occupation for a son of D'Alsennin than hanging round the court and scrambling for favours like a dog begging scraps?'

'Not when you will be yoked to the likes of Messires Den Rannion and Den Fellaemion. Who do you think they are? I'll tell you; an aging visionary trading on the faded glories of his voyages with Nemith the Seafarer and a man looking to make his House sorry that they passed him over in the choice of their Sieur. You might as well try to restore our fortunes by melting down the plate and chancing your luck in the bordello games, like that pup of Den Rannion's!'

'Messire Den Rannion does indeed have an astute eye for commerce, Grandfather.' Temar's voice betrayed an edge of anger for the first time. 'He would not be supporting the idea of a colony if he did not think it would be viable and profitable. He intends to sail himself, to build a home and a future for his family, and he has been planning to do so since before the death of his father. His brother, the Sieur, supports him fully.'

'I'd say his debts must be pressing indeed if he's prepared to flee across an ocean to escape his creditors! No, I'll believe Den Rannion is setting down his arse along with his coin when I see it. You don't think he's simply turning a quick coin out of playing on the hopes of the gullible? From what I hear, he'll have to recoup a handsome sum to keep pace with your friend Vahil's spending.'

Why did the old man keep mentioning Vahil? With a shock, Temar realised his grandfather had no real argument to make and was simply trying to end the discussion by provoking a quarrel. He stared at the old man and blinked as what he saw changed, as if transmuted by some evil alchemy. This was no longer the impressive head of a once Great House, no lordly figure holding the reins of many lives, curbing some and slackening others to keep the whole equipage on an even course, not even the unquenchable source of reassurance and security that Temar had depended on as he grew, too early, to manhood and duty. His grandfather was simply an old, old man, weary and afraid, bereft of his sons and the future of his House, facing his dotage alone and uncertain.

Temar rose to his feet and grimaced as he rubbed his knees. He went to sit on the step of the dais as he had done so often as a child, when the hall was thronged with tenants and clients, his uncles circulating as the Sieur dealt with the suppliants. Temar made himself comfortable and looked up at his grandfather.

'I really want to do this, Grandpa. I'm never going to be any good capering at court, ferreting out gossip and trying to turn it into advantage and gold. You know me; I'm used to speaking my mind, as you taught me yourself. I'm tired of trying to salvage coin and dignity from every tide of disasters and knowing all the while that the next time the Emperor nails his own foot to the floor, I'll be back up to my neck in a flood of ripe gurry.'

The old man rubbed a hand over his face; his eyes dimmed with momentary despair. 'Better that than drowning in the deep of the ocean, surely? Do I have to remind you how many ships set sail with Nemith the Seafarer and never returned?'

'Messire Den Fellaemion returned, Grandpa, and he has made the crossing a handful of times since. I trust him.' Temar tried to keep any rebuke out of his voice. He failed.

'What is that supposed to mean?' The old fire flared in the Sieur's eyes. 'You trust him? You see a better future riding as his postilion, do you, rather than as master of your own team? You're planning to abandon your own name and take his, perhaps?'

Temar stood abruptly, shedding his efforts at unaccustomed humility. 'My concerns are for the future of my name, Messire. I intend that my sons and grandsons will revere my ashes and bless the inheritance I bequeath them.' He clenched his fists unconsciously and felt the band of his father's ring press into his flesh.

'So what will you be doing with my funeral urn, then? Using it as a doorstop? Ungrateful hound!' The Sieur raised one twisted hand and very nearly struck out at Temar. 'Am I to blame that first the Crusted Pox stole away the sons of my House and then a pox-rotted whoremonger has pissed away our lands through chasing his deluded ambitions?'

Temar opened his mouth to reply in kind in the usual fashion of D'Alsennin family discourse, but something in his grandfather's face halted him. Abiding grief underlay the wrath in the old man's eyes and prolonging the fight seemed suddenly pointless.

'I did not mean to insult you, Grandpa; I didn't mean it, not the way it sounded. I know full well our House would be ashes blown on the wind many years since, if it were not for you.'

Whatever the old man would have said was lost in a paroxysm of coughing and Temar looked around hastily for water or wine.

'Leave it.' The Sieur produced a handbell from the folds of his mantle and its silvery jingle brought the chamberlain scurrying in.

'I will consider your petition, Esquire.' The old man managed to control his coughing and looked up at Temar, high colour masquerading as a brief pretence of good health. 'I have other affairs to see to. You may attend me in my study before we dine.'

He got to his feet with some difficulty but waved away the hovering chamberlain with irritability and stalked out of the salon, head unbowed.

Temar watched him go and could not decide if he were more worried or annoyed by the old man's behaviour. What other business could he have to deal with? Most likely, he was just delaying a decision by going for a nap. Well, Temar wasn't going to kick his heels in this cinder-shrine all afternoon, he decided with characteristic speed. He strode rapidly from the room and slammed the ponderous doors with an energy that drew a startled plume of smoke from the little fire. The nails in his boot heels snapped angrily on the stone treads as he made his way down the back stairs and into the kitchen.

'Temar, my duckling, how lovely to see you.' A sparely framed woman in a clean if faded livery looked round a cupboard door, a half-full jar of spices in her hand.

'Jetta! Well, I must say I'm glad to find you still here.' Temar tried for a light touch but his words fell flat. He slumped into a chair and stared moodily at the grain in the white-scrubbed tabletop, picking at it with a ragged nail. 'I was starting to think everything and everyone had been sold off or sent packing.'

'You reckon it's all looking a bit bare above stairs, do you?' Jetta's sardonic voice made Temar look up, startled.

'If I didn't know better, I'd say we'd had loan-broker's men in!' he responded bitterly. 'What's the old fool been doing? Paying some alchemist for potions? Hoping to get him a doxy to bear him a better heir?'

'He's been keeping what's left of the tenantry in shelter and food, young man.' Jetta's eyes were bright and not only with passion. 'The Sieur is always mindful of the obligations of the House.'

'You think I'm not? Don't you start blaming me,' Temar snapped. 'I've been working from first light to last moon, both halves of summer, to keep what's left of the estates producing some sort of income. I'd have an easier time milking pigs for cheese and probably have more to show for it! Why do you think I've not been back here for so long?'

'Don't you start ripping into me, just because you're feeling guilty, young man. I put you over my knee when you wore soft shoes and I'll do it now if need be.' Jetta's smile belied her words and she put a plate of sweetcake in front of Temar.

'Thank you.' He took a piece and felt unaccountably comforted.

'Are you dining here?' Jetta closed the cupboard and moved to the hearth to swing a kettle over the fire.

'It would seem so. Grandfather has ordered me to attend him in his study beforehand.' Temar's sarcasm had somehow lost its edge.

Jetta sniffed. 'What have you been saying to upset him so badly, then?'

'How do you know he's upset?' Indignation coloured the guilt in Temar's face.

'Why else would Master Othneil be ringing down for a bridesbell tisane?' Jetta pointed to the open door of the lackey-lift in the corner of the room.

'Is he ill?' Temar tried to ignore the qualm in his belly at the thought.

'No more than any man of his age but his winter cough has started early and he's spending too much time in his study and not enough in his bed.'

So much for imagining his grandfather had nothing to do with himself. Temar dragged the newly polished silver clasp out of his hair with an irritable gesture and could not think what to say.

'So, how's your mother?' Jetta busied herself with cups and hot water.

'She's very well, thank you.' A fond smile lightened Temar's whole face. 'She's growing her hair for a wedding plait.'

'Is she now?' Jetta halted, smiling herself, herb canister in hand. 'So who's going to be cutting that to lay on Drianon's altar?'

'He's Rian Tor Alder; do you know the name?'

Jetta frowned momentarily. 'He deals in wool, doesn't he? The family run sheep in the mountains on the Bremilayne road?'

'That's him,' Temar nodded. 'They've been friends for a couple of years now and he's finally persuaded her to marry him. I'm so pleased, for him as well as her. He's a good man and I know he'll make her happy.'

'I'll tie a ribbon to Drianon's door to wish her well. She certainly deserves some happiness!' Jetta remembered what she was doing, and tied sharply fragrant herbs into a scrap of muslin. She dropped the bundle into a cup of hot water. 'Have you told the Sieur?'

'Not yet.' Temar poked at his tisane with a silver spoon. 'I think it would be best if she told him herself but she's always been so nervous of him. She thinks he'll feel she's betraying Father's memory and the D'Alsennin name.'

'Nonsense!' Jetta shook her head emphatically. 'He'll be delighted for her and I know your father would never have wanted her to spend so long as a widow, not once her year's-mind was spent in the Sieur's care.'

Temar fished the steeped herbs out of his cup and sipped the steaming drink carefully. 'That's what I told her.' He stared unseeing, into the fire. 'I wish I knew what advice he'd give me, Father I mean.'

'What about?' Jetta covered one of his hands with her own.

'I want to join Messire Den Fellaemion's colony.'

Jetta stared at him. 'Is that what you came to tell your grandfather?'

Temar nodded. 'I have to do something, Jetta, or I'll go mad from frustration. Things are going from bad to worse and I'll be cursed if I join the rest of the scavengers picking at the stinking carrion that's left of the Empire.'

'You sound more like your Uncle Arvil than your father.' Jetta blinked away an unbidden memory.

'What do you think my father would have done?' Temar held her with his pale gaze.

'He'd have done what he felt was best for the House.' Jetta gripped Temar's hand. 'But he'd have been honest enough to know that it had to be something he felt was right for himself as well.'

'I'm fairly sure that's what I'm doing,' sighed Temar. 'But I do sometimes wonder if I'm just looking for somewhere to run off to, some way of getting out from under all the duty and obligation.'

'It's hard being the only one left to carry the Name,' Jetta comforted him. 'You know, when your grandfather crosses to the Otherworld, it's not Saedrin who'll be asking the questions before he opens the doors. The Sieur is going to want some answers about just what that cursed plague was supposed to be for. They're going to have to be good ones!'

Temar smiled. 'Do you suppose the old man will demand free passage from Poldrion as well? On account of his ferry having so much trade from our House already?'

'I wouldn't put it past him!' laughed Jetta. 'Now, if you're staying for dinner, you can make yourself useful. Go and get some sea-coal in from the yard and then you can make a start on the vegetables.'

Temar made her a mocking bow. 'At once, Mistress.'

Doing something both useful and undemanding helped Temar to relax. He had very nearly managed to put aside all thoughts of the future, duty and conflict by the time he was concentrating on washing the earth out of the last greens of the autumn. The jangle of a bell high up in the house startled him and he looked ruefully at Jetta.

'I think that's my summons.'

She came round the table and wiped his hands on a cloth as if he were still a child. 'Try not to let him get you cross; you know what he's like. If you're sure of what you want, he's going to have to accept it eventually.'

That was easy enough for Jetta to say, Temar thought, without heat, as he climbed the narrow stairs back to the formal rooms of the house. How often did any man called D'Alsennin give in gracefully? About as often as a bitch whelped kittens, he'd say.

He remembered to pull the clasp from his pocket and clip back his hair before he reached his grandfather's study. He paused for a moment and looked at the gleaming silver, remembering how long it had taken to get the tarnish out of the deeply carved leaves. Temar sighed, remembering how the candlelight had used to catch at it when his father turned back to the door after coming to check on the children last thing at night. Well, he couldn't ask his father's advice, so all he could do was be true to himself and his Name.

He knocked on the black door and braced himself.

'Enter.' His grandfather's voice was firm and Temar saw that his face was determined but more at peace with himself.

Temar closed the door and took a seat across from the old man, keeping his face impassive as he wondered what part all the ledgers and rolls on the table were going to play in their discussion.

'I have been considering your petition,' the Sieur began

formally. 'While you are the sole heir of this House, safeguarding the future of the Name must be my first consideration. However, I realise I must also do justice to your own wishes and needs.'

He paused. Temar sat silent, trying to look attentive and deferential.

'I cannot see any benefit to you joining Den Fellaemion and crossing the ocean on your own.' There was a challenge in the old man's eyes as he took a sip of wine but Temar refused to take the bait, remaining still and quiet.

The Sieur snorted and replaced his glass in its silver holder. 'However, it is certainly possible that these lands overseas could offer us estates and position to replace what we have lost in recent years. I cannot ignore that. I have decided to allow you to join this endeavour on certain conditions. Provided you agree to my terms, you may go with my blessing.'

'What are your terms, Messire?' Temar asked politely, fighting to keep the relief and exultation out of his face.

'We have many dispossessed tenants and those that remain on our lands are suffering in the present tensions.' The old man began laying parchments before Temar. 'You need to see the figures to see the whole tapestry.'

Temar clamped his teeth on an impulse to remind his grandfather he was the one who'd provided most of the ledgers and records and looked where the old man was pointing.

'You see, here and here? Compare the figures with as recently as last year.' The Sieur sat back in his chair. 'These are good people, suffering through no fault of their own and if you are to go any way towards fulfilling your obligations to your tenantry, you should offer them the chance to join you in this quest.'

Temar stared at his grandfather, eyes wide; whatever he might have expected the old man to come up with, this was not it.

'We can raise the capital to purchase a couple of ships and, with a little ingenuity, we can fit them out with goods from our own properties.' The Sieur produced a freshly drawn-up list. 'I want you to look at this and see if you can see anything I've missed.'

Temar took the parchment dumbly and then grinned, as much at himself as anything.

An answering smile took a generation off the old man and there was a wicked glint in his eye.

'Nothing to say for yourself, my boy? That's unlike you, I must say.'

Temar looked up from the list. 'You are suggesting we take a major role in this project. How's that supposed to sit with Den Rannion and Den Fellaemion?'

'That's your problem, my boy. If you want to do this, you're going to do it in a way that benefits your House, or not at all.'

Temar tried to run a hand through his hair, forgetting the clasp and wincing as it tugged at his scalp.

'I accept your terms,' he said finally, wondering with a qualm just what he was committing himself to.

'Good lad. I knew you'd see sense.' The Sieur rose and poured them both some wine. Temar sipped absently, still trying to make sense of this new situation. He stopped and looked more carefully at his glass.

'This is the Califerian vintage, isn't it?'

'The last year before the Crusted Pox struck,' his grandfather nodded and savoured the glowing ruby liquid. 'It's the last carafe; it seemed appropriate.'

Temar could not think what to say, so he drank his wine instead.

'I have something else that I think it's time you received.' The old man put down his glass and walked swiftly to a long chest. He removed a ring of small keys from a chain around his neck and unlocked it. Carrying a long linen-wrapped bundle, he swept documents to the floor to make space for it on the table.

'This is the sword that I had made for your Uncle Arvil; I always thought he would be the next Sieur D'Alsennin, when it was time for me to step aside.' The old man untied the

linen bands with stiff fingers but waved away Temar's offer
of help. 'I can manage.'

He drew aside the cloths to reveal a dark green scabbard;
the sword's guard was intricately carved but the handle was
well fitted and workmanlike. This was no mere dress-sword.
When he drew the blade, it gleamed, bright and unspotted, a
tracery of leaves coiling down its length.

'Here.'

Temar took the sword and weighed its superb balance,
mouth open in delighted admiration. 'This is marvellous,
Grandfather,' he breathed as he made a few careful passes
with it.

'It should be, given the coin it cost me,' the old man snorted
gruffly. 'Just don't go using it to chop wood in these foreign
forests or some such.'

'Hardly!' Temar laughed. He stopped, his face suddenly
solemn. 'This is a prince's gift, Messire. I cannot thank you
enough.'

'Make a success of this expedition, give our tenants a new
life and our House a new future. That's the thanks I require.'
The old man fixed Temar with a burning eye. They stood for
a tense moment, the weight of obligation and the uncertainty
of the future hanging heavy in the air.

A silvery bell sounded in the hallway and the spell was
broken.

'You'd better start thinking about begetting the next generation as well. Isn't it about time you had your eye on some
girl? You can't afford your Uncle Sinel's tastes, you know.'

Temar laughed at his grandfather's jest and followed him
to the dining room.

Hill Cote, Lord Adrin's Fiefdom, Caladhria,
11th of Aft-Spring

Waking early from unsatisfying sleep tainted with vague dreams of people arguing, I found a sense of dissatisfaction spilling over into the grey light filtering through the shutters. I decided there was no point lying in bed, questions chasing themselves around in my head like the rats I could hear scurrying in the thatch overhead. There was also no point in trying to get back to sleep with Shiv snoring like a basket of piglets on the other side of the room.

The morning air was damp where it had sneaked around the window frame. I shivered at the cold touch of linen on skin and pulled on breeches and jerkin hastily. Wondering in passing just how I'd managed to avoid smacking my head on the beams the night before, I grabbed my boots and moved quietly past the heap of motionless blankets that was Viltred.

I was breakfasting in the tap-room, sitting in my stocking feet, when Shiv appeared and joined me.

'I wish I'd thought of that, I hate putting on wet boots,' he said with feeling, nodding at my footgear upturned on the fire irons.

'Any man at arms knows the importance of dry feet,' I shrugged as Shiv helped himself to bread and meat. 'The other thing he needs is information. There's a lot you're not telling me, Shiv.'

'I don't know much more than I've told you, I swear, not for certain.' Shiv sighed. 'This was supposed to be a quick trip to find out if Viltred knew anything useful and to pick up any bits and pieces that Planir could set his scholars to work on.'

I wondered what he meant by that but a jaw-cracking yawn distracted me.

'Tired?' Shiv looked concerned.

I nodded. 'I don't seem to have had a decent night's sleep since Solstice.'

'The goodwife's got a pretty well-stocked philtre-chest,' Shiv suggested a touch diffidently. 'Viltred's concocting something for himself.'

'No,' I said curtly. 'No, thank you.'

I'd taken to chewing thassin after my sister died, to get something between me and that suffocating pain. Being young, arrogant and sure I could dose myself safely had landed me with a habit that had taken two seasons of night sweats and persistent thirst to shake off. I'm not about to risk developing a taste for anything like that again. Seeing some affront in Shiv's eyes, I sought a more neutral topic.

'Why does Viltred insist in calling you Shivvalan anyway?'

He grimaced. 'Saedrin only knows. The last person to do that was my mother and it still makes me feel as if I'm waiting to shave my first whiskers for Misaen's altar. Which reminds me, my respected and venerable colleague was wanting hot water for his tisane.'

I don't know what Viltred put in his morning concoction but it must have been something pretty potent because the old wizard was in the saddle a cursed sight sooner than I would have expected. The roads were better after a dry night and we rode briskly through the clearing mists of a bright morning.

'This is where we should find Halice,' Shiv announced some while later as we rounded a wood-topped hillock. Stoutly built stone crofts, each with a patch of diligently tilled land, were loosely gathered around the market and the shrine. People were going about their business, barely sparing us a glance. Shiv led us down a side lane to a typical longhouse, thick walls four-square under mossy thatch. A sturdily built woman in a decent brown broadcloth dress over neat, unbleached linen was hauling water from a well and looked at us with a challenge in her eyes when we stopped. She rested well-muscled arms on her bucket and I noted the faint pattern of silvery scars around her knuckles and forearms. A farmwife would have the muscles, but I doubt many have swordwork scars. She was also the first woman I'd seen that day with an uncovered head, her dun-coloured hair cropped short.

'Can I help you?'

Shiv made a bow. 'Are you Halice?'

The woman looked at us, unsmiling, her dark eyes opaque in a coarse-boned face. 'Who wants to know?'

'Shiv Ralsere. I am looking for Livak.'

There was a flicker beneath the heavy brows at that but I couldn't tell what it meant.

'She's not going to want to see you, mage,' Halice said calmly, without malice.

'I'll take that chance.' Shiv smiled at her with warm charm but I could tell Halice was about as convinced as I was. I'd seen the type that Shiv fancies after a few drinks; generally tavern brawlers with arms as thick as my thigh and three days' growth of beard.

He reached behind him and brought a flagon out of his saddlebag. 'I recall Livak saying you were partial to Dalasorian vintages.'

A half-smile quirked at the corner of Halice's thin lips. 'You may as well stop to eat with us. I can spare a hen that's gone off lay. Put your horses in the byre. Livak's gone to the farm down yonder, she'll be back in a while.'

She reached for a crutch that had rested unseen on the far side of the well. As she moved, I could see that her skirts reached to just above the ankle of one leg but that her other foot barely showed, twisted sideways under her petticoats, the result of a badly broken leg that had mended seriously awry.

I dismounted and tossed my reins to Shiv. 'Let me take that.'

Halice paused, glanced at me and handed the water over. She looked at the fowls scratching their brainless way around the yard, reached down and unhurriedly picked one up.

'You wizards any good at plucking and drawing your meals?' She wrung the chicken's neck with casual expertise.

She turned her back on Viltred's startled indignation and limped heavily to the cottage, where a wide passage separated the byre end from the living half of the house

I handed the water to Shiv. 'I'll see to the horses.'

There was an old, stale smell of cattle but more recent scent and sign of horses: hay racked ready, a bin of grain and straw bedding. I wondered what schemes Livak and Halice had been working over the winter seasons. I was sorting harness when Shiv reappeared.

'Viltred all right?'

'Fine, now he's got a hearth to sit beside. That Halice's a hard one to read, isn't she?' He shook his head ruefully.

'Hard all round, as far as I can tell, and not wanting anyone's pity.' I slung my saddlebag over my shoulder. 'Didn't she used to be a mercenary in Lescar?'

'That's what Livak told me.' Shiv picked up his new satchel. 'She also said Halice's biggest advantage is that people take one look at her and treat her like the village idiot's foolish sister.'

I smiled. 'I can see that. How did she break her leg?'

'Took a bad fall with a horse on a rocky road.' Shiv grimaced in sympathy. 'She's lucky she kept the leg at all.'

I was about to speak when Halice appeared at the doorway and we jumped like slacking apprentices. She was certainly quiet on her feet for a cripple.

'There's wood needs chopping.'

'I'll do it.' Shiv tried for a friendly smile as he took the well-honed axe and I followed them out to the back of the house. As Shiv stripped to his shirt and made a competent start on a stack of wood, I caught an unguarded expression of surprise on Halice's face before she realised I was there and her countenance went blank once more. I piled split logs into the basket but turned when I heard evenly weighted footsteps behind me.

'Livak!' Shiv greeted her warmly, leaning on the axe.

She halted, opened her mouth, and closed it again. I allowed myself the luxury of admiring the way her closely cut jerkin clung lovingly to the curve of her bosom. Livak was a little thinner than when I'd last seen her and her red hair was longer, tied back in a rough braid that left her green eyes bright in her pale face, her wandering father's Forest blood showing through more clearly than I remembered. She was carrying a curd cheese, pale in its muslin wrappings.

'Hello, Shiv. Not got anyone else to bother?'

She stalked into the homely warmth of the flagstoned kitchen where Viltred was resting his beard on his chest, eyes drowsy. Starting at the sound of the door, his face brightened with curiosity about this bold female in her buff breeches. Livak ignored him.

'Drianon save me, Shiv, I really don't want your kind of aggravation,' she grumbled, but as she turned she flashed me a quick smile, which ran warmth through me like a shot of spirits.

As Halice turned from tending the broad hearth that dominated the far wall, I saw Livak raise an eyebrow in infinitesimal query, but she had no more than a minute tightening of Halice's lips in return. It meant nothing to me but I know that my mother and any of her sisters habitually tell each other more with half a glance than a hundred words. I wondered just how much attention Livak paid to Halice's opinion.

'So what have you been doing with yourself over the winter?' Shiv stacked firewood in neat rows.

'Whatever it is that you want, you've thrown a losing hand of runes, Shiv,' Livak warned him.

'I gather you've been over the border recently?' Shiv's tone was relaxed, but I wasn't fooled. I caught Livak shooting a questioning glance at Halice, who shook her head slowly to say she had not been talking out of turn. I held my peace; I'd plot my course when I knew if the wind was veering or backing.

'We've been working the recruiting camps along the Rel, me and Sorgrad and Sorgren, two brothers we know,' said

Livak slowly. 'All the mercenaries are just looking to drink and roll the runes until the better weather gets the fighting properly underway, and the corps-masters fix their contracts. We've been fleecing the little lambs trotting up to enlist, woolly heads all full of idiotic ballads.'

Livak challenged Shiv with a bold grin. She was rewarded with an ill-concealed snort of disgust as Viltred shifted on his fireside settle. Livak turned to him, a provocative spark in her eyes, deliberately coarsening her Ensaimin accent.

'Look at it this way, old man, if some young idiot off to fight in someone else's war loses his money and gear before he gets to enlist, at least he stays alive.'

Viltred fixed her with an unexpectedly steely gaze as she smirked at him. 'Young lady. Our business is far more—'

'All in good time,' Shiv interrupted him smoothly. 'What do you think of the prospects in Lescar this year?'

His pose was easy and careless, his angular face open and inviting. With his tone softened by the lilt of the fenlands around Kevil, he was every minstrel's idea of a typical Caladhrian, securely tied to land and family and probably none too bright. It was very convincing, or it would be if you'd never seen him throwing handfuls of power around and blasting Ice Islanders clean into the Otherworld, probably far enough and fast enough to save them negotiating Poldrion's ferry fee.

'The Duke of Parnilesse is dead in very murky circumstances, and his three sons all dispute the succession.' Livak managed a suitably thoughtful tone but I could see the wariness behind her eyes. 'Their territory will be ripe for the taking if they can't raise the coin for one of the better corps-masters.'

That was interesting information; surely the eldest son should have inherited without argument? After all, it's the obstinate Lescari insistence on line-of-blood succession that started their pointless wars in the first place.

'From what I've been hearing, the old Duke was almost certainly poisoned,' Halice observed as she briskly tended the chicken now split and skewered above the fire. She reached into the salt box hanging on the chimney breast and seasoned a pot seething in a trivet in the embers. 'Sorgrad reckons his sons'll start their own little war before Solstice.'

I wondered how best to get a letter to Messire from hereabouts, and if I could warn Aiten's family.

'Shivvalan!' snapped Viltred. 'Planir's business is far more important than Lescar's trivial quarrels.'

There was an awkward silence until Livak spoke up, sarcasm colouring her tone.

'Yes, go on, Shiv,' she invited. 'But let me give you one rune for free – there's no power this side of the Otherworld will get me mixed up with the Archmage again.'

There was no hint of compromise in her voice. I wondered just what throw of the bones Shiv thought he had in his hand that would get her working for wizards again.

'Viltred here has had some valuables stolen and we were wondering if you would help us trace the thieves and retrieve the goods.'

Unable to conceal her start of recognition at the old man's name, Livak characteristically went on the attack. 'Would you be the Viltred who used to work with that madman Azazir?'

The old man scowled at her. 'Azazir was one of the greatest minds magic has seen in ten generations, young lady—'

'Azazir was so far beyond reason he couldn't find it with a spy-glass and let me tell you—'

Shiv cut in hurriedly. 'Please, Livak, we really do need your help. The raiders were Ice Islanders.'

Livak paled. 'Have you got your hat over your ears? No!'

'We'll make it worth your while,' Shiv persisted.

'I don't need your coin, Shiv, or the Archmage's,' spat Livak.

'Think it through, Livak.' Shiv gestured with an eloquent hand. 'These people can't have been here long, not with the spring storms on the ocean only just over. We have an early scent of them – we can dig a bloody great pit for the bastards to fall into! We'll have them by the stones, ready to squeeze!' Shiv's face was as intense as I had ever seen it.

'And if Planir the Black decides this bear-pit of his needs

live bait in the bottom of it, he'll just grab the nearest warm body and I, for one, have no intention of being around to play the goat.' Livak crossed to the hearth, defiance in every line of her stance. She drew herself up next to Halice but I saw the other woman was staring at Shiv with an concentration that startled me.

The mage tried again. 'There are things you just can't ignore, auguries—'

'Festival fakery, Shiv,' Livak went on, eyes hard. 'I don't want to know. And you've got nothing on me this time to make me. I'd sooner take my chances walking naked through a wild wood.'

Shiv pursed his lips. 'You don't fancy the chance of getting a little revenge for Geris?'

'I shared his bed, Shiv. That lays no obligation on me to share his fate.' Her tone was scornful. 'Forget it, you can eat with us and then you can get on your way.'

With that declaration ringing in the air, she went out, slamming the door. Halice threw off a sudden abstraction and busied herself at the hearth. Raising a hand to still Shiv when he made to rise from his seat, I was glad to see he was looking faintly ashamed of himself. Trying to use Livak's guilt over Geris' death was a real horse-coper's trick. I frowned at the memory of Geris' lonely, agonised murder at Elietimm hands. I couldn't blame Livak for her refusal, but I reminded myself sternly that the auguries suggested we needed Livak to somehow help avert disaster for the Empire, so I had to do everything in my power to convince her to join us, didn't I? I only hoped I wasn't borrowing against an empty purse as I followed her.

The sound of a hayfork drew me into the byre. 'I wondered if you needed any help?'

Livak's face showed she thought that excuse was thinner than a beggar's blanket. 'Buckets,' she said crisply, pointing to a stack in the corner.

I followed her out to the well. 'It's good to see you,' I commented as I wound up the pail.

Livak gave a smile to lift my heart but I reminded myself that persuading this woman to share her life with me would probably be harder than convincing her to come and work for Shiv again.

'I did wonder if your duties might bring you this way some time,' she said lightly, but with an unmistakable edge to her tone.

'You should hear Shiv out. These auguries of his bear consideration.' I poured clear, cold water into the waiting buckets. 'Planir is warning that the Empire is in grave danger from the Elietimm.'

Livak's snort told me her opinion of that. 'All those gleaming cohorts and the Empire won't be able to fight off a few boatloads trying to steal sheep from Dalasor?'

'Gleaming cohorts won't be much use against those cursed enchantments of theirs, will they?' I replied honestly. 'And the Elietimm are hardly going to hack a settlement out of the wilds of Gidesta or take over a couple of Dalasorian fishing villages when they can find rich towns, decent anchorage and better weather merely by sailing south for a few weeks. Come on, Livak, you saw the place they live in, bare rock and barren grassland; they're not going to stay there, not now they have a way to reach the mainland.'

Livak grabbed a bucket, slopping water over the hard-packed earth of the yard. 'Well, it's not my problem,' she stated firmly over her shoulder.

'It's certainly mine.' I picked up the second bucket and followed. 'A lot of the older Princes don't want to admit it, but the days when Tormalin cohorts kept six provinces under their heel are long gone. When you add in the threat of this peculiar Elietimm magic, we'd be stupid not to look for help if the Archmage is offering it.'

'And your Emperor has the stones to admit that?' challenged Livak.

'Tadriol may be young but he knows when to take advice, Dastennin's blessings on him.' I moved closer to whisper dramatically into Livak's ear, savouring the lavender scent of her linen as I did so. 'The word is he'll get his acclamation at Summer Solstice. Messire favours "Tadriol the Provident" but he's keeping it to himself.'

Livak's eyes glinted. 'Place the right wagers on that title before the Convocation makes it official and Shiv'll be able to buy that Viltred all the trinkets he wants, forget recovering the ones he's had stolen.'

'Well, he has no chance of getting anything back if you won't help him.' I thought about putting an arm around her shoulders but Livak moved away, muttering something in an Ensaimin dialect that I don't know.

'The Archmage pays sound coin and in good measure,' I pointed out, trying a different weight to tilt the scales.

'Why does everyone think they can buy me?' scowled Livak. 'Anyway, Planir only offers the rates he does because he only has to pay out one time in ten. Everyone else ends up seeing the inside glaze on a funeral urn.'

'Have you got some of last year's coin put by?' I busied myself spreading straw.

'What, like the good little field mouse who hid every other grain for the winter? Your mother told you that tale as well did she?' The mockery in Livak's tone stung me. 'No, we used it to buy a Winter Solstice to remember, all four of us, new clothes all round, wine and good dining, ten days of the best that the Cavalcade at Col can offer.' Livak's expression challenged me. 'The Archmage's coin may be sound metal but it comes with too much blood on it to keep in my purse. Still, you're right, I should have found a better use for it; I should have spent it all on incense to burn to Trimon, to get Shiv dropped head first into a river gully if he ever tried to find me again!'

Making an offering to the god of travellers myself was starting to look like my best hope for getting this ill-matched handful on the road. 'The mercenary camps will soon break up,' I reminded her. 'What will you do for coin then? Halice won't be able to enlist with any decent corps with that leg of hers.'

'We'll manage and I'm certainly not about to go chasing

crickets with a hayfork for Shiv when Halice needs me with her.' Stabbing the hayfork into a bale, Livak went out into the yard, where she started slinging scraps of wood into a kindling basket with unnecessary force. I swallowed my irritation, and began to help.

'I don't know how you can do it,' she burst out after a few moments. 'How can you get yourself mixed up with wizards again?'

'I'm doing my patron's bidding,' I replied in as neutral a tone as I could.

'He sends you off like a fowling hound, does he?' Livak shook her head, her tone perilously close to a sneer. 'Coming and going at his whistle or risking the whip? Tell me, has he got some other poor bastard leashed in to replace Aiten yet? Doing his master's bidding didn't do him much good, did it?'

I closed my eyes on sudden flash of memory: Aiten's body in my arms in the midst of the pitiless chill of the ocean, his life blood warm on my skin where Livak had sliced open the great vessel in his leg and killed my friend to save the rest of us when Elietimm enchantments had stolen away his mind and turned him to attack us.

'I had to do it, you do know that, don't you?' she demanded abruptly, her face white. 'He'd have killed us all if I hadn't.'

'I know.' My eyes met hers as I fought to keep my voice level. 'I know and I don't blame you. Neither would he. The only shame to bear is my own, for leaving you to do what I couldn't.'

'I'll be answering to Saedrin for it, that much I know.' Livak's emerald eyes suddenly brimmed with tears that she dashed away with an angry hand. 'It's been that one killing the old mercenaries warn you about, the one that stays in your dreams, where you wake with the smell of blood in your nostrils.'

'You don't have to tell me that. I'm doing this for Aiten's sake as much as for anything,' I told her with a venom that startled even me. 'We swore the same oaths and we lived by them. I'm loyal to that trust.'

'I'm loyal to my friends, not some canting words and a tarnished kennel–tag,' snapped Livak, stabbing a finger at my medallion. 'I value my freedom too highly.'

Smarting, I clenched my fist on a handful of kindling and felt a splinter pierce my palm. 'Freedom to die penniless in a ditch? No sworn man with an injury like Halice's would be left hanging on the charity of their friends! The Sieur takes his responsibilities seriously.'

'He doesn't take any of the risks though, does he?' retorted Livak, turning her back to cross the yard again. 'That's not what I call responsibility.'

'And you'd know all about that, never staying more than half a season in any one place!' I set my jaw against my anger. I could only suppose it was the lack of sleep that I never seemed to quite make up on that was making me so uncharacteristically quick to anger. Pulling the sliver of wood from my hand, I sucked at the scratch for a moment. When I had myself in hand I found Livak collecting eggs from the long grass beneath a knot of fruit bushes. The pig trotted into his run, breath foetid as he snuffled up over the wall, ears flopping with palpable disappointment when he realised we were not bringing food.

'I should never have let Shiv talk me into going with him last year, Drianon rot his eyes,' Livak muttered to herself. 'I knew Halice was hurt; he said he had a friend who'd take care of her. I'd like to cut his stones for slingshot!'

'The Emperor's apothecary in Toremal couldn't have done much with a break like that,' I objected. 'You can't blame Shiv, or yourself, come to that.'

Livak looked up at me. 'I remember telling you the same about Aiten.'

'That's different!' I snapped before I could help myself.

'Is it?' Livak started pulling the first shoots of spring from a neat vegetable patch, an appetising prospect. The new growing season at home had given me a taste for early greens before Messire's commands had sent me north again, where the cold earth still waited for Larasion's smile. I shook off the distraction.

'Can you just stand still for a moment?' My words came out

as a furious demand rather than a request and Livak looked at me, eyes stormy as a winter sea. I got myself in hand with no little effort. 'We need you, Livak—'

'We need you?' she mimicked, mocking, 'I need you? You sound like a bad Soluran ballad, Ryshad, noble knight wooing lady fair!'

This unexpected shift wrongfooted me utterly.

'I had been hoping you might have come to find me on your own account,' snapped Livak, 'not just because Planir whistled you up. What's your next move? Try and coddle me into coming with you, like some trooper showing a housemaid a few tricks with his polearm? Forget it, that's how my mother got caught!'

'What are you talking about?'

'I thought you valued me on my own terms. Come and meet your family, that's what you were saying last year.'

'You're the one who said goodbye!' I objected. 'I only asked you to come to Zyoutessela with me for the Solstice, you're the one who refused!'

Livak shook her head. 'How long would it have been before your mother started embroidering hair ribbons, asking me to help darn the linens? If I wanted to be someone's maidservant, I'd have stayed at home!'

'Well, make up your mind!' I had had enough of this and it must have shown in my face.

'Never mind, forget it.' Livak blushed scarlet and pushed her way past me to go back to the house. Biting down on a few choice retorts, I followed, breathing heavily.

We entered to find Halice deep in conversation with the two wizards.

'There are a few things we'll need to sort out before we leave tomorrow.' Halice limped to the dresser to fetch a slate. 'We should be able to sell the pig easily enough but it might be better to kill the chickens and cook the meat.'

'What are you talking about?' Livak glared at Halice.

'I'm going with these wizards.' Halice had evidently served in those mercenary corps that specialise in storming defences.

'If they need a thief and you're not willing, there are people in Relshaz who will help for the right purse.'

The bowl of eggs fell to the clean-swept flagstones and shattered. Livak ignored it, railing furiously at Halice. 'Why on earth do you want to get mixed up with wizards? You know what happened, I ended up halfway across the ocean on islands no one's ever heard of with some evil bastard trying to push my mind out through my nose with a magic no one knows anything about. Ask Ryshad how he liked it. Does Shiv know how they did it? I'll bet Planir and all his useless mages still haven't worked it out. That lad Geris was tortured to death; have you forgotten what I told you? I only came out alive because Drianon spared me three seasons' luck! I've been making offerings at her shrines ever since on the strength of it and you know I'm not religious—'

Livak ran out of words or breath and there was a long pause before Halice spoke in a low tone of studied calm though she would not raise her gaze to meet Livak's eyes. 'What I remember is you telling me how Shiv got his arm broken. A sword blow that shattered the bone clean through, you said.' Her voice was hard beneath her level words. 'Most surgeons would have taken it off at the shoulder, wound-rot wouldn't be worth risking, not for an arm that couldn't be used even if it could be saved. Those wizards had a way to save it, didn't they? He was using an axe with it earlier, Livak, not just chopping morning-wood but splitting logs. I'll work with them to track down these thieves and they can pay me back by mending my thigh bone.'

The wizards and I sat motionless, knowing full well the dangers of getting between two women having a row.

'Two sound feet aren't worth that kind of risk, Halice! Believe me, I know. These Ice Islanders are killers, butchers—' There was savage anger in Livak's voice now and I heard wrath rising to meet it in Halice's tone.

'You have no idea what I'd risk to get two sound feet again, Livak, no idea at all! Have you any idea how I hate being stuck here? A goat would have more conversation than that slattern down the lane, and she's the brightest one for leagues around.

Try and talk to anyone in the village about anywhere more than a day's walk away and they look at you like you're a singing pig. You and the brothers go off and have a good time separating idiots from their purses while I do piss all and have to sit like some crippled old grandma and just take it when you three hand me a quarter-share. I was the one who got you into your first game in a hiring camp and now I have to sit and listen to you telling me all about the latest plans in the compounds, which corps-masters are taking contracts, who's putting together a raiding troop, and all the time I know I'll never be able to go back to it, not now my leg's more twisted than a claim to the Lescari throne! I'd almost rather green-rot had booked me passage with Poldrion.'

Livak turned on her heel to storm out of the room, face scarlet with fury and hurt. There didn't seem any point in following her this time so I stayed where I was and looked down at my amulet, the bronze gleaming against the linen of my shirt. Shiv pushed his chair back with a scrape on the flagstones and picked his way past the mess of broken eggs and greens to fetch the wine. I went with him and found some earthenware goblets on the dresser, thinking now about the undeniable justice of what Halice had said; that kind of crippling injury is something that we sworn men fear more than a clean death and quick passage to the Otherworld.

'You'll do that, mend her leg for her?' I demanded of Shiv in a low tone.

'Of course; Saedrin shut me between this world and the next if I don't.' Shiv spread his hands, all innocence.

He had just laid a weighty oath upon himself so I judged that should keep him honest.

'I hope you still have a decent weight of Planir's coin with you, Shiv, because we need to buy a light carriage,' Viltred spoke up suddenly.

'What for?' asked Shiv doubtfully.

'Because I can't sit a horse until you get my leg straightened,' Halice spoke with a commendable calmness, given the circumstances.

'I don't want to be tied to the high road with a vehicle.' Shiv shook his head. 'And what about changing horses? No, we need to move fast and—'

'If we need a carriage, we need a carriage,' I said firmly, catching Halice's set expression. 'The Elietimm'll be having to keep to the high roads themselves as well at this season. Apart from the local routes to the markets, every other track will be thigh deep in mud.'

Shiv's thin lips betrayed his annoyance. 'I don't see—'

'I can't ride all the way to Relshaz with my back the way it is.' Viltred waved his hand peremptorily at Shiv. 'Do as I tell you, Shivvalan.'

I handed round wine, managing to avoid catching Shiv's eye. As I did so, I considered how swollen Viltred's knuckles were with joint-evil and wondered how much pain his back generally gave him.

'Oh all right.' Shiv capitulated with ill grace. 'If you think you'll find anything suitable round here.'

'I know a few people to try, especially if we offer them the pig as part payment,' Halice assured him.

A flare of grease falling into the fire reminded us of the browning chicken and we ate in silence. At one point, Shiv looked as if he wanted to speak to me but Viltred's narrowed eyes and shake of the head silenced the younger man.

'Thank you for an excellent meal.' Viltred laid his spoon in his plate, wiped his knife clean and stood to make Halice a little formal bow. 'Now, if you will excuse us, Shivvalan and I will attempt to scry for our quarry outside.' Viltred's voice brooked no argument and Shiv shut his mouth on his objections.

Halice turned her attention to the mess on the floor, kneeling awkwardly.

I fetched a pail. 'What will Livak do if you come with us? Stay with these brothers you were talking about?'

Halice took the cloth out of my hand. 'I doubt it. They want to go off after the Draximal paychest. It was all they could talk about, last time they were here. Sorgrad has found out which corps will be collecting it and where to enlist.' Resentment darkened Halice's voice. 'He was saying what a shame it was we couldn't all go after it with them since no commander would take me on with my leg like this and the only way Livak would get taken on was as a featherbed, which he couldn't see her going for. She'll dress the whore to bluff her way into a camp but she knows it's too cursed dangerous to play the part for long without being willing to lie down for it.'

I only hoped Halice was right but reminded myself that I had other loyalties to bind me, especially if Livak was going to take such an uncompromising stand. Dast scourge the woman, why did she have to be so cursed contrary? No matter, advance information of this kind of plot would be valuable for Messire, wouldn't it? 'Which corps are collecting the paychest?'

'The Ironshod, on their way down to secure the border for the Duke of Triolle.' Halice shook her head. 'I don't want anything to do with it, I had their commander, Khys, serving under me a few years back; I owe him better than that.'

Halice's mercenary career hadn't been all foot-slogging in the mud then, not if she had friends like that. Most corps last a couple of seasons before they fall apart over rows about booty or because they've been stamped into the gurry once too often. There can't be more than a handful of troops as good as the Ironshod, who've been striking sound coin out of Lescari misery for more than seven years now. 'How do these brothers expect to take a paychest on their own?'

'I don't know.' Halice rinsed her cloth in the pail, eyes taking my measure. 'I can manage here, why don't you go and do something useful towards getting us on the road?'

I took the hint. 'Is there a scribe round here who might have a reasonably up-to-date set of itineraries he'd be willing to sell?'

'Innel, lives next to the Reeve.' I left Halice to prove her independence by cleaning up without assistance.

Finding Innel the scribe easily enough, after a little conversation I decided I could trust him with a letter for Messire, to be sent on to Lord Adrin with a request that he forward it through the Imperial Despatch. I double-sealed it but I wasn't too concerned about anyone reading it since I'd written all the sensitive sections in the southern Tormalin dialect of the ocean coast, the everyday tongue of our home city of Zyoutessela. If there was anyone within a hundred leagues who'd be able to understand it, I'd eat my sealing wax still hot. I wrote my favourable assessment of Lord Adrin in formal Tormalin however, just in case curiosity got the better of his sense of honour. Innel turned out to have several useful volumes to sell which I compared carefully until I was satisfied they agreed well enough. I'm always cautious about charts made outside Tormalin; you can get badly caught out if the mapmaker's information is out of date or just plain invented. These were almost good enough to be Toremal drawn.

While I was in the village, I made a quick survey of the inn, the shrine, the women selling their crafts and produce around the buttercross. Livak was nowhere to be seen, nor had she returned to the longhouse by the time I got back. Shiv went out to buy a horse and vehicle while Viltred showed Halice the auguries. She watched the horrors impassively, the stillness of her face unmoved but a catch of breath here and there betraying her shock. I did not need to watch again, needing no reminder of my duty, whatever attitude Livak might choose to take. Shiv came back some while later with a neat gig and a long-nosed harness horse with a winter-rough, light bay coat, which I helped him stable.

'Did you get a good deal?' I asked him with a faint grin as I spread straw in the byre. 'Planir's not too badly out of pocket?'

'It was a fair price, pigs seem to be a favoured currency around here,' Shiv assured me, his good humour apparently restored.

I looked at the horse, which seemed a little overdocile to me and wondered about that. Livak still hadn't returned by the time we went to bed and this time it was frustration keeping me awake long into the night. What could I do when the one woman we wanted was dead set against joining us, and the one who promised every chance of being dead weight in the water was determined to come?

CHAPTER TWO

Taken from the Library of the Caladhrian Parliament, being a true copy of the letter sent to the Lord of each fiefdom by Eglin, Baron Shalehall, later First Preceptor of the Parliament, generally dated to the 7th year of the Chaos.

I write this appeal in the hope that Caladhria may be saved from the calamities that beset our poor land on every side. Daily I hear the lamentations of the hungry, the despair of the beaten and the grief of the dispossessed; I can bear it no longer. Saedrin sees the woes of the common people and remembers, just as we take their fealty, so we take on an obligation to defend them against such misery; I have no doubt that he will ask some hard questions before some of us are allowed to enter the Otherworld. Yet all I hear from my peers are fruitless hand-wringing and divisive argument about which pattern of governance we should copy from those around us.

There are those who would step back a generation and set up an Emperor or King, but what would that achieve? How is such a man to be chosen? What qualities would we seek in a man to be entrusted with so much power? I for one, fear the shades of my forefathers would petition Arimelin to plague my dreams with demons, were I to deliberately submit to a tyranny that they struggled so long and hard to throw off. Are we perhaps to ape the self-proclaimed Dukes of Lescar and let the strongest seize what they may until no one dare challenge them? Their Graces' wealth and fine palaces may look very well now the grass has grown over the battlefields, but let us not forget they established themselves in a manner little different from bandits laying claim to a forest hideout. They work hand in bloody hand to carve up the bounty of Lescar like poachers portioning out a stricken doe. I hear you ask me; are we then left only with the prospect of the division and strife that plagues Ensaimin? Will our sons and daughters live only to see our beloved land disintegrate into a patchwork of petty kinglets and greedy cities, squabbling among themselves like a litter of starving mongrels? By Misaen's hammer, I will not have it so and I call on all honest men to help me.

Why are we looking beyond our borders for an answer? Let us look to ourselves, to the wisdom of our ancestors. Before Correl the so-called Peacemaker sent his cohorts to trample our land beneath the nailed tread of Tormalin rule, we were a peaceful and decently governed people. Our forefathers knew the dangers of placing too much power in the hands of one or even a few men and ruled themselves, fairly, through the Spearmote. All men of property could speak, all men of goodwill could work together for the common good. No tyrant, great or small, could hope to stifle the liberties that are all men's birthright, that our fathers won anew for us when they threw off the rusted iron hand of the House of Nemith. We have managed to restore much that was lost to us. Let us come together once more in the Spearmote and take charge of our own destiny.

On the River Road, heading south,
Lord Adrin's Fiefdom, Caladhria,
12th of Aft-Spring

Livak turned up in the morning as Shiv and I were discussing our route and Halice was harnessing the horse in the gig, ignoring Viltred's peremptory instructions. It was a bright morning, fine high cloud in a clear blue sky.

'What have you got there?' she demanded without preamble.

'Itineraries.' If she didn't want to discuss her decisions, neither did I. Finding the volume that showed the closest stages of the River Road, I unfolded the long sections of map.

'They're not Rationalist drawn, are they?' she challenged, 'You'll soon get lost if they are. All the distance and detail will be twisted to fit their notions of order and balance, you do know that?'

'No, they're fine.' I wasn't about to rise to this lure, pointing to an area marked with a stand of thick-branched trees. 'What do you know about this place, Prosain Heath?'

Livak looked over my arm. 'It's where Lord Adrin's lands meet the territories of these other Lords, Thevice and Dardier; they manage the forest between them as a hunting preserve.'

I tapped the river. 'This looks a bit too close for my liking.'

Shiv nodded. 'Cover for deer and boar will do fine for Lescari runaways as well, won't it? There probably won't be any trouble but we might as well join a larger group, if we can.'

'It's been a long, hard winter,' I agreed.

Livak pointed to a blue circle at the side of the road. 'That's a good place to stop and water the beasts; people tend to gather there before crossing the Heath.'

'I wonder if we might get some scent of the Elietimm there?' I wondered aloud.

'It's a thought,' Shiv nodded. 'They should be easy enough to trace; they'll stick out like the stones on a stag hound in Caladhria.'

Livak shifted next to me. 'Tell me, Shiv, do Caladhrians think it's just unlucky to go beyond the district where you're kin to at least half the population, or is it actually considered immoral?'

'Oh, both,' Shiv assured her cheerfully.

Livak sniffed but I saw a faint smile tease the corner of her lips. 'Wizards travel in style, do they? She stared disparagingly at the neat little vehicle. 'Where did you get this?'

'Short Merrick.' Halice slapped the harness horse on the rump and climbed awkwardly up on the seat.

'So what was he doing with it? It doesn't look as if he's been using it to haul turnips.'

'It seems his late wife was from Abray, where the roads are rather better and she'd learned ambitions beyond her husband's station in life,' Halice said drily. I was relieved to see her and Livak share a tentative grin.

'It's pretty gimcrack work,' Livak sniffed, picking at a piece of loose inlay.

'And who are you to say so?' Viltred looked down at Livak with patent irritation.

'A wagon is joinery, mage, only with wheels on it. I grew up polishing the most expensive furniture in Vanam and that makes me the best judge of woodwork you'll find around here.' Livak set her hands on her hips and cocked her head back to stare boldly up at him.

'You'll be riding Viltred's horse, then, Livak,' Shiv said hurriedly. 'Come on, the weather's holding and we should make the high road by noon if we set off now.'

Halice soon had her hands full with the harness horse, which had evidently recovered from whatever it had been fed to sweeten its mood. Viltred proved not to have much of a sense of humour about nearly getting tipped into the hedge and to start we rode largely in silence. As the morning wore on, Halice got the measure of the beast and, to my relief, some conversation started. I was not looking forward to riding three hundred leagues with four people who weren't talking to each other, and I was missing Aiten yet again.

'It'll be a relief to get on to a decent highway,' I commented to Livak as we negotiated a particularly soggy slough under a canopy of early leaves.

'I'll say,' she agreed, coaxing her mount round the puddles. 'Anyone who let his trees overgrow the road like this back home would be paying the Merchants' Conclave a hefty fine.'

With trade the life blood of Vanam and the other great city states of Ensaimin, that was hardly surprising. Still, she had a point; Messire D'Olbriot has a Highway Reeve who spends six seasons out of the eight criss-crossing his lands and making sure repairs are made to the roads, but Caladhrian Lords don't seem to see their responsibilities in the same way, flapping their lips in that Parliament of theirs like blackfishers drying their wings on the quay side. On the other hand they're quick enough to agree things like this new hearth tax of theirs, another way to plunder the peasantry and keep their ladies in satins.

'Shiv tells me it's considered quite respectable for Caladhrian ladies to pay social calls in an ox-cart, the local tracks can be so bad.' I shook my head, still not quite sure if he had been tugging my hood with that one.

Livak smiled fleetingly. 'Still, I do like to see trees left to grow tall, not always coppiced and confined.'

I nodded and wondered if that was a reflection of her Forest blood. It was always going to be an issue between us, one way or another, wasn't it? It may be an old joke but, from everything I've seen, it's undeniably true that the only way to get a Forest dweller stopped in one place is to nail his foot to the floor. The Great Forest may be clean across on the far side of the Old Empire, separating the western reaches of Ensaimin from the kingdom of Solura, but Forest minstrels have always been a common enough sight in Tormalin. Few other people would travel that distance simply out of curiosity and wanderlust.

I remembered what she had told me the previous year, before questions of loyalty and independence had divided us. Livak's father had been one of the Forest Folk, seducing her housemaid mother when the Western Road through Ensaimin brought him to the great city of Vanam. From what I had gathered he had stayed around while Livak was small, long enough to teach her more of her heritage than she seemed to realise through the songs of their race that would sing her to sleep. He had given up the struggle in her middle childhood, though, leaving her mother with only the child as a reminder of the bitter loss of her lover, facing the derision of her family alone. It was no wonder that Livak had a jaundiced view of family life.

On reflection, Livak's refusal to spend the Solstice with me had probably been for the best. Persuading my mother to calm down after hearing a highly edited version of our little excursion the previous year had been hard enough. I don't really think it would have been the ideal time to introduce her to a lover dressed in my spare jerkin and breeches, with a past that defied polite description. Mother still hopes that one of us will bring home a gently reared girl, with her own embroidery on her skirts and suitably long plaits for Drianon's altar. That's fine by me, as long as it's one of my brothers who does the honours. Hansey or Ridner can lay their mallets and chisels aside for long enough, if Mistal's too busy with his studies.

'I have business of my own in Relshaz, you know,' said Livak abruptly, some while later. 'If Shiv's managed to talk Halice into his schemes, I might as well travel that far with you all. As you say, the roads can be risky on your own.'

This was none too convincing coming from a woman who'd left home barely out of girlhood with no more than the clothes on her back.

'What business, exactly?' I enquired, tone mildly interested. I hoped it wasn't anything too dishonest. There were aspects of Livak's livelihood that sat ill with my conscience.

'There's a man called Arle Cordainer.' Livak's eyes were distant and cold.

'What's he to you?'

'He owes me,' replied Livak crisply. 'He's a deception man, one of the best because he makes sure he's set someone else up in line for the pillory or the gallows if things go wrong. The four of us nearly ended up swinging for him in Selerima a year or so ago; he couldn't have dropped us in more shit if he'd left us neck deep in a privy-pit.'

'You think you'll find him in Relshaz?'

'I saw him on the River Road just after Equinox.' Livak's face was intent. 'He was all dressed up like a Tormalin silk trader and wearing a full beard, but I never forget a pair of hands or ears.'

I nodded encouragingly and wondered if this Cordainer knew Raeponin was about to demand a reckoning from him to balance the ledgers of justice.

'I will come as far as Relshaz with you,' continued Livak briskly. 'I want to make sure Shiv does right by Halice, if nothing else. I still don't trust wizards, say what you like.'

Now we were getting to the truth of her change of heart, I decided.

'If we get a scent of these Ice Island thieves, I'll do what I can to get Viltred's treasures back, just as long as I'm sure it's worth the risk. If the wizards owe me for that, they can pay the debt by straightening Halice's leg.' Livak scowled at the pair of mages ahead of us but the anger in her eyes shaded to hurt when she gazed at Halice's back. 'That should settle any accounts between her and me. Shiv gets one draw of the runes and that's it, though. If there's any hint of the kind of trouble we were landed in last time, I'll be out of there faster than a cat caught at the cream pan.'

'I'll probably be two steps behind you.' I nodded again and ventured a warm smile, which Livak returned, albeit with a sardonic glint in her eye.

'Saedrin's stones!' Halice's inventive curses told us the gig had caught a wheel in a boggy rut.

'How's the horse?' Shiv asked Livak when we had the vehicle back on decent ground.

'Fine,' she dimpled a smile at him. 'But riding something suitable for Viltred was hardly going to be a challenge, was it?'

'I was a notable horseman in my youth, young lady—' Viltred began, stirring himself like an old mouser poked by an impudent kitling.

'We'll hit the high road about noon, won't we?' I spoke over the old mage, looking back at Shiv, who was taking a turn at the rear. Livak flashed Viltred a taunting smile and urged the horse to a canter.

'That's right.' He glanced from Livak's disappearing back to Viltred with an expression of faint exasperation. As we rode on, he kicked his horse up to a trot and drew alongside me.

'Can't you get Livak to stop baiting Viltred?' he asked in a low tone.

I shrugged. 'I'll mention it but as long as he keeps taking the worm she'll keep dangling it, until something more amusing comes along anyway. You could suggest he stops treating her like a maidservant turned out for flirting with the bootboy; that might help.'

Shiv muttered something under his breath that I decided to ignore. The gig slowed as the road wound up a long incline and we found ourselves walking, hearing Viltred's attempts to find out more about Halice. Since she answered most of his questions with one word, two at most, he grew increasingly irritated and his enquiries eventually moved from the impertinent to the downright offensive.

'I would have expected a woman of your age to have settled, with children.' Viltred slid a glance sideways to see Halice's reaction. 'In my day it was considered unlucky for a girl to pass her generation-festival unwed.'

'I'm going by Soluran generations,' Halice said unexpectedly. 'That's thirty-three years, not the Tormalin calendar's twenty-five. I've got another two before I need worry.'

That silenced Viltred and I shared a grin with Shiv. I wondered if I could persuade my mother to do the same; with her fiftieth year looming, she's desperate for a grandchild.

Viltred took a while to recover from that thrust but after a while began regaling anyone close enough with increasingly tedious stories of his youth, tossing around names that were evidently supposed to impress with all the subtlety of a plough-boy stoning crows.

'Who's Felmath of Broad Aile?' I muttered to Shiv.

'No idea,' he shook his head.

I frowned. 'I know that one, Lord Watrel, but his wife's called Milar; Abrine was his mother.'

I'd spoken loudly enough to attract Viltred's attention.

'You are a sworn man to Messire D'Olbriot, are you not?' The old mage was adopting an increasingly lordly manner himself. 'You must pass on my compliments to his lovely wife, Maitresse Corian. I had the pleasure of making her acquaintance some years ago.'

I didn't know quite how to answer that since the lady in question has been ashes in her urn some nineteen years. Luckily, Viltred seemed more interested in displaying his noble contacts than getting any response.

'Yes, we met when I was the guest of Sulielle, Duchess of Parnilesse. She's a very gracious lady, you know, elegant and a wonderful hostess.'

Halice reached out with her whip to get the carriage horse's attention. 'Dowager Duchess, you mean.'

'Pardon?' Viltred was visibly displeased to be interrupted.

'The Duchess is Lifinal, Duke Morlin's wife. Sulielle lives on her dower lands in Tharborne.'

'You seem very well informed,' Viltred began.

'I spent three years commanding the Duchess of Marlier's personal guard,' Halice said crisply and snapped the lash over the horse's neck. I couldn't say whether it was her remark or the sudden jolt of trotting that silenced Viltred but I, for one, was grateful that he gave up on his efforts to impress. I hoped the pace of this pursuit picked up soon; so far, it was about as inter-esting as escorting Messire's maiden aunts on their annual cir-cuit of the family estates to give them the opportunity of telling the minor ladies of the Name how best to rear their children.

Once we reached the high road we made better speed and reached the little lake I had marked in mid-afternoon. After seeing to my horse, I helped Viltred down from the gig before finding my sword and buckling it on; I hadn't bothered with it since leaving Lescar but if there was a chance of trouble on this Heath I would be ready. Looking round for the others in the various travellers thronging the banks, I saw Shiv was deep in conversation with a man I didn't recognise. I moved closer, though not near enough to break into their conversation in case Shiv was about to learn anything of use to us.

'Ryshad!' Shiv waved to me and I made a show of just noticing him. 'This is Nyle. He's a guard captain for that merchant train over there; they're heading south.'

The stranger nodded a brief greeting. 'We're carrying goods for Sershan and Sons, down from Duryea to Relshaz, finished woollens and ceramics.'

Misaen's supposed to have built the first men out of clay and this looked like one of the forge god's earlier attempts. He did have a neck, but at first sight Nyle's shoulders seemed to start just below his ears and he'd fill more than his fair share of any room. He was a few fingers taller even than me but so heavily muscled that you would think of him as stocky rather than tall if you saw him from a distance. His eyes had the hard alertness of a hunting dog, an impression strengthened by his square jaw and slablike jowls as well as his rough, brindled hair.

'How long will you take to cross the Heath?' Shiv continued.

'We'll reach the Spread Eagle at South Varis the day after tomorrow. We'll rest the animals there and then head on.' He cocked his head in Shiv's direction. 'Take it from me, you don't want to be crossing the Heath on your own.'

'Not at this time of year,' Shiv agreed.

'Pay the mule-master, a Mark a head.' Nyle turned to move towards the next group of travellers where I heard him repeat his offer of protection.

Wagon trains cost coin while they're travelling and they only make it when they arrive and sell their wares, so the mule-master was soon getting his charges into line after their water stop, forty or more beasts making their handlers work hard for their bread.

'Nyle said we should go between the mules and the wagons since the gig's got smaller wheels.' Shiv rode up on his black horse, which nearly unseated him as the mule train drew out in a clamour of reluctant braying and men cursing.

We moved off, with eight assorted vehicles joining the muletrain's handful of wagons. Viltred was soon giving us all the benefit of his age and wisdom again.

'Lord Adrin should put some of those mendicant Lescari to breaking rocks for road-mending instead of adding more plough-spans to his rent-rolls,' he grumbled as we left the farmland and entered the fringes of the Heath proper, where the road soon deteriorated again.

The scrubby bushes gradually gave way to bigger trees tinged with spring green above carpets of bright flowers. The mossy scent of springquills rose about us, their colour reflecting the blue sky up above the lace of twigs and new leaves while the creamy frills of Larasion's lace were starting to show among the wayside grasses. We travelled without incident but the road forced us to single file for the most part. I soon found my mind wandering with boredom.

'Ryshad?'

My horse shied and I snatched at the reins, startled.

'Dast's teeth, Livak! What are you doing?'

'I was trying to stop you cracking your head open by falling off your horse asleep,' she replied a touch acidly.

I scrubbed a glove over my face. 'Sorry?'

Odd fragments of what must have been half a dream hovered round my head, something about a pursuit over sweeping grasslands. Wasn't Arimelin satisfied enough with ruining my nights, that the goddess had to start me dreaming during the day? I must have dozed off for a breath or so, something I couldn't ever recall doing on a horse before, but then I couldn't remember being quite so weary, not recently anyway. I wondered uneasily if all this difficulty in sleeping meant I was sickening for something. A series of shouts was handed back along the mule train, scattering my confused thoughts. I realised we were stopping to make camp and saw that Nyle had fixed on a large grassy clearing, evidently well known to him. As Halice turned the gig off the main track, I could see the guards fanning out to hack down the early undergrowth all around. Muleteers were fixing picket lines for their beasts and fencing them in with thorn brush. As we headed for a comfortable spot, the wagons and carts drew in to form a defensive ring, canvases soon laced securely.

Nyle came over and spoke to Shiv while we were making our own little camp inside the circle.

'I want everyone to water their animals by that stand of withies.' He gestured towards a brook on the far side of the clearing. 'Use that gully over there for a latrine.'

I wondered why his eyes kept straying to me, even though he was talking to Shiv and I was curious enough to mention it to Livak as we circled the clearing later collecting firewood.

She shrugged. 'I don't think he wants your body; he hardly looks the type to drink out of both sides of the cup. I think you're seeing Eldritch-men in the shadows. You're just over-tired.'

I didn't pursue it but I still felt uneasy as I peered into the gathering gloom under the trees.

'Does anyone think there's much risk of trouble?' I asked the others as we sat down to eat.

'They'd have to attack in some strength to have a chance against a camp this size.' Halice scanned the area thoughtfully. 'It depends how hard the winter has been round here.'

'According to one of the muleteers, the local Lords usually send their foresters in to clear as many vagabonds out as they can before the does start dropping their fawns, but we're a bit early for that,' Shiv said, his words muffled by the chicken leg he was chewing. 'Nyle's not taking any chances, he's setting a full watch, look.'

We saw to the animals, decided who would sleep where and watched the guards earning their coin with patrols around the edge of the clearing as the night closed in around the circle of campfires.

'I do like seeing sentries being set, knowing I won't have to take a duty,' Halice smiled broadly as she rolled herself in her blankets.

Shiv was already snoring musically and Livak was yawning as she lingered over the last of her wine. I rolled my cloak for a pillow, tucked my blankets around myself, closed my eyes, half listening to the murmur of voices around the larger fires. A couple of verses of that Dalasorian song listing all the different boys trying to get under a virgin's blanket drifted over to us, occasionally lost in a burst of laughter from a friendly game of runes. The rich scent of wood smoke mingled with the moist breath of the awakening woodland and I drifted off to sleep, vaguely hoping Livak wouldn't be tempted to join in any of the gambling.

I was ripped from my slumbers by urgent shouts that my sleep-numbed brain could make no sense of. Halfway to my feet before my mind caught up with my body, I stared bemusedly at the black-haired stranger in front of me. His pale blue eyes were wide in his narrow-jawed face and he held out an urgent hand to haul me upright, a sapphire ring catching the firelight. I reached out but must have misjudged the distance, my fingers closing on empty air. He shouted at me again but I could barely make out what he was saying; it sounded like Tormalin but no dialect I had ever heard.

A yell behind me spun me round and I saw three ragged and filthy figures scrambling out from under the nearest wagon, notched harvest tools and rusty swords questing before them, eyes bright with greed and faces bitter with hardship. I could smell their stench mingled with raw spirits and chewing weeds. Well, I'd soon take the wind out of their sails. I'd met worse than them in the rougher parts of Gidesta.

As I drew my sword and moved to drive the scoundrels off, I spared a fleeting glance around me. Shiv was moving to the centre of the clearing, concentrating on weaving a dim tangle of light between his fingers, head turning this way and that as he looked for a chance to help. I couldn't see Viltred but assumed he was somewhere close to Shiv, probably with the small group of women and children huddling together by the main fire-pit. A sudden lattice of sapphire magelight sprang up around the vulnerable ones, startling the guards who'd hung back to defend them.

Halice had already moved to our far side where two startled guards were being pressed back by a larger group of bandits rising up from the cover of the stream bed. The black-haired stranger must have wakened her first, not knowing about her leg. Wet and desperate, the vagrants hacked blindly as they fought for the food and coin they coveted. They were a sorry-looking lot, gaunt and filthy, many with old injuries or disease, but there was no pity in their stained blades, only death in their eyes. I looked for the stranger, but he was nowhere to be seen.

A rat-faced man in muddy rags came at me, swinging a nail-studded club in a flurry of ill-judged blows until I dropped him with a scything stroke to his thighs. As he fell, he tripped the youth behind him who took the opportunity to cut and run. The third was made of sterner stuff, or was just more desperate; he came on with jabs of a once fine blade that looked as if he'd been using it to cut firewood. I feinted to his side, parried, feinted again; as he reached out, too far, I smashed the small bones of his hand with a hacking down stroke. If he'd kept the sense Misaen made him he'd have run but he had to try again, sweeping the sword round in his off hand, agony twisting the lines and filth of his face. I brought my own blade up and ended his problems with a cut to the side of the head that took off his ear and dropped him in his tracks. I jumped sideways as I thought I saw a shadow at my shoulder, but to my relief there was no one there, just a trick of the uncertain light, with the greater moon alone at its half and the lesser full dark. Still, it was an unwelcome reminder of how naked my flank felt, without Aiten's strong sword arm and burly frame to support me.

A sudden blow from behind sent me sprawling into a cart

and I scrambled away from the slashing hooves of a loose horse, snapped halter dangling as it dashed, panicked, from the sound of battle and the sickly smell of blood. Curses rose from the picket lines as the muleteers struggled to restrain their beasts as terror spread like sparks from wildfire. The high-pitched whinnying of the mules and the wails of a frightened child spiralled upwards to pierce the night sky.

'Aid here!' Halice's yell tore through the uproar of the fight and I looked out to see she was facing two men on her own. The other guards were unable to help as they held back attackers intent on a gap where they had dragged a wagon askew. Halice's crippled leg was tying her to the spot as surely as a man-trap; unable to move freely, her shirt was already torn over a bloody scrape on her off-side arm. Cursing freely, I began forcing my way through the mêlée.

Before I reached her, I saw a bright knife slice through the canvas cover of a wagon and caught a glimpse of auburn hair in the firelight. A stunted youth hanging back and jeering at Halice got a thrown dagger among the boils on his neck, fair payment I think. He dropped with a choking cry as foam filled his nose and mouth, his head jerking back in uncontrollable spasm, his cry lost in the din of the fight. Livak dropped from the cart to drive a second blade into the kidneys of a brutish heap of filth whose heavy hedging-blade was hacking at Halice's defences. He clapped a hand to his side, mouth open in soundless surprise as much as anguish before the venom forced his face into a frozen snarl. Halice left him to the poison, taking her chance to drive her sword up into the face of his startled partner, who went down in a splutter of blood and shattered teeth to gut himself on his own skinning knife.

A couple more hard-faced guards came up from behind me and charged into the suddenly hesitant attackers waiting on the edge of the firelight. I dodged past them and grabbed Halice round the waist, hauling her out of the fray. She cursed, startled.

'Stuff it, Halice, let him help.' Livak came with us, tense and alert, her face turned to the dark and the danger, a dagger glistening with oily smears held well clear of her body.

I dragged Halice bodily backwards; hopping to stay upright, she swore at me with all the fluency of a long-time soldier.

'I was wondering where you'd got to,' I said to Livak with some difficulty.

She shook her head in disgust. 'When did you last get into a fight in Caladhria? All my poisons were in the bottom of my belt pouch, double-sealed with wax and lead!'

'Are you hurt?' I looked round to find Shiv at my shoulder.

'What have you been doing? How about some useful magic for a change?' Livak spat at him.

'Just who do you suggest I immolate?' he snapped back and I saw a measure of my own frustration with the two women reflected in his eyes.

I paused to let Halice regain her balance and the four of us looked round to see the guards driving off three different attacks.

'I don't know who we're travelling with – how am I supposed to tell friends from foes?' Shiv turned on the spot with a sharp gesture; with the flickering half-light and dodging shadows thrown by the ring of fires, I had to agree with him.

'To me!' Nyle's bellow would have put a rutting bull to shame and I saw his square head leading the guards as a last desperate rush by the bandits threatened to break through the cordon at the final gap still under attack.

I sprinted across the grass, dodging loose animals and panicked merchants. A ragged wretch with raw sores running down his arms dashed out from under a cart and nearly tripped me with a rusty scythe but, before I could deal with him, a spear of blue fire dropped him to the ground, face blackened and hair smoking. I waved my gratitude to Shiv without looking back and stepped in to hold the line when a merchant stumbled back, clutching at a bloody gash in his guts.

I could see Nyle sweeping a massive blade around in a deadly arc, wrists rolling in a two-handed Dalasorian grip. Blood sprayed across him as the shining steel ripped up under an opponent's chin and carried off half his face, but Nyle didn't even blink. Eyes white-rimmed as he poured his fury into his sword strokes, he lunged into a gap and dropped another bandit into a howling welter of blood and entrails. The stupid bastard evidently had some training in swordplay, but it betrayed him now he had no militia armour to save his guts. Nyle pressed forward with each hint of advantage, nailed boots secure on the slippery ground, kicking aside anyone unable to regain their feet. Fighting shoulder to shoulder put heart into all of us and we formed a wedge behind Nyle's cutting edge. We began to mesh with the instinctive moves common to most militias and started to force the bandits back to the stream.

A long-faced man with a cattle thief's brand twisting down his cheek came at me. He parried one stroke, then another, but an old Tormalin move that I'd been practising all winter sent his notched sword twisting up out of his grip; I got him between the neck and the shoulder. That broke the nerve of the vagabond next to him and, as he ran, the courage born of drink and desperation deserted the rest. Their line collapsed like a child's game of sixpins, those too slow on the uptake paying for it as they were cut down trying to turn and flee. The faster ones made for the shelter of the stream bed, but as they reached it a flare of magelight drove the night out from under the trees. Yells of panic mingled with derisive laughter from the guards who had pursued them and odd, cracking noises snapped out along with the screams of dying men. I stood for a moment then turned back to my own companions. I wasn't going to risk myself unnecessarily; the men getting paid for it could do that. My responsibility ended with driving the bandits away, I judged.

'Come on, come on.' Halice was calming our horses with soft words and dried apple while Livak was rummaging in the gig for something to clean her daggers with.

'You know, Ryshad, I've heard of Arimelin sending people off walking in their sleep but I didn't know she could make them fight.' Her green eyes were wide in the firelight.

'What do you mean?'

'How did you know they were coming?' Halice looked over, now dealing efficiently with her own wound, her teeth holding one end of a bandage as she knotted it tight. She spat a fragment of lint from her mouth. 'What were you saying when you woke me, my Tormalin's not that good in the middle of the night?'

I blinked but Shiv arrived at my shoulder and interrupted before I could ask what the two of them were going on about.

'That should save the Lords' foresters a task.' He was looking extremely pleased with himself, brushing what looked like frost from his gloves though he had blood oozing from a long gash in his forearm.

Halice rolled back his sleeve and stripped the shirt from the wound with impersonal strokes of her belt knife. 'This needs stitches,' she warned briskly and turned to the gig.

'Saedrin's stones!'

I had my dagger out within half a breath as Halice started backwards, but it was only Viltred, unwrapping himself from his enveloping cloak like a tiggy-hog unrolling its spines.

'Have you been there all the time?' I asked incredulously.

'I am no warrior,' he said with threadbare dignity. 'I thought it best to stay out of the way so I made myself invisible.'

No one could find a reply to that, so I turned to Shiv as Halice held a curved needle in the flame of a brand from the fire.

'What did you do, exactly?'

'Most of them tried to leave along the stream bed, I'm not sure why. Anyway, I froze the water, which held them pretty much fast for Nyle and his men.'

Shiv's laugh caught on a gasp of sudden pain and Livak passed him a flask.

'What's that?' asked Halice.

'White brandy. I picked it up in the last camp, but we never got round to drinking it.' Livak looked under her lashes at me. 'I got a set of the latest engravings about the Duke of Triolle's love life, as well.'

Those promised to be ripely entertaining, if not downright obscene. I looked over towards the trees, the darkness hiding the carnage beneath them. I couldn't decide if I liked the idea of trapping men like that, to be killed like snared vermin. I shook it off. Dead is dead and Shiv had probably saved a few of the guards from injury or worse.

'Do you know these stars?' I asked Livak. 'What would you say the time is?'

She looked up. 'Halcarion's crown's just beyond zenith so it won't be long until dawn at this season.'

I wondered if Poldrion would charge the dead bandits more or less for their ferry fare on account of them striking on his side of midnight. Halice soon finished with Shiv's arm and made a neat job of it.

'I've seen worse stitching by Messire's surgeon,' I commented. 'Not many soldiers learn that kind of skill.'

'I grew up five days' walk from the arse end of nowhere,' she said in a matter-of-fact tone. 'I learned to turn my hand to most things before my tenth year.'

The beasts were still refusing to settle with the reek of fresh death all around and everyone turned to trying to restore some sort of order. I opted for helping drag the nearest corpses outside the ring of wagons. It wasn't a pleasant task, but a dead robber can't do you harm whereas a nervous horse stamping on your foot can ruin a fair few days, a lesson I learned good and early in Messire's service.

I looked the bodies over, just in case any of them had the flaxen hair of the Elietimm, but I saw none. I didn't bother looking any closer; these men had drawn their runes and would have to put up with the spread they threw the same as the rest of us. The only one to give me pause for thought was a scrawny boy I rolled over to get a better grip on his tattered jerkin. He had long lost half a hand and most of the meat of his arm, probably to a beast-trap, the sort farmers set along a wildwood margin for wolves and the like. If he'd had a livelihood, he would have lost it along with his fingers. Whatever his tale – thief or peasant, vicious or honest – someone's sword had sung the last verse when it ripped into his ribs, chips of bone gleaming white among the ruin of his gaping chest as I dragged him over the blood-soaked ground. Stupid bastard.

I looked over towards Halice, who was kneeling awkwardly with her twisted leg. She would never sink so far as this lad, not with Livak and her other friends to keep her afloat, but the life she'd known and relished was over and I saw the realisation plain in her face. In some ways she was as finished as the poor bastard with his guts trailing over the ground as I rolled him down a slope to lie in a tangle of dead limbs with the others. No wonder she was desperate enough to take up with a wizard's quest.

'Let's have some of that.' I came back to the fire and reached for the brandy. Taking a deep breath to get the smell of blood and voided bowels out of my nostrils, I coughed as the liquor caught at the back of my throat. We passed the flask around until barely a finger of spirit sloshed in the bottom.

'This wasn't a way I'd choose to drink four Crowns' worth of finest white brandy,' Livak observed as she took a swig.

'I'm glad you've got it.' Shiv was cradling his arm against his chest but the liquor seemed to be dulling the pain well enough.

'It's not as if I'd paid for it, anyway,' Livak said generously.

'We don't seem to be too popular,' Viltred remarked with some amusement, eyes bright in his lined face as he passed me the bottle.

I followed his gaze and saw the merchants who had been sleeping closest to us were now all on the far side of their fire, doing their best to edge a few arm spans further off still. Shiv in particular was receiving suspicious glances as the two burly men wrapped themselves in their cloaks and prepared to spend what was left of the night dozing on the seat of their cart.

I couldn't blame them; seeing that real magic works to kill and to help others to kill is a real shock, there's no denying it. We don't have much time for mages in Tormalin, but you'll find philtre-merchants and palmists in any sizeable village, and a fair few are genuine. I could remember a girl in the next street who left our little dame-school to study with the mage in the larger half of the city, on the gulf side of the isthmus. Pretty well everyone knows someone who had a friend or relation whose fishing instincts or touch with a garden turned out to be mage-born. It's just that you don't imagine you'll see them sending lightning shooting from their fingers to leave a bandit crisped like a baked fish. Still, that was Shiv's problem, not mine, for the moment anyway. I yawned, wrapped myself in my cloak and settled down to get my share of what little sleep was still on offer.

A spacious Tormalin steading, set among gardens on a grassy hillside

Temar watched with gathering irritation as yet another drove of rack-ribbed cattle were herded, lowing and snorting, into the holding pens. Shouts came from a group of men hastily lashing hurdles together to make yet more enclosures as some of the beasts threatened to stray and wreck their day's work.

'Where will I find Esquire Lachald?' a swarthy drover addressed Temar with scant courtesy.

'In the house,' Temar replied shortly. 'No, wait, I'll show you myself.'

It was time he had words with Lachald, he decided abruptly, time he made it quite clear what the Sieur had in mind when he wrote the instructions Temar had brought. He strode through the home gardens and shoved through the gate into the grassed courtyard, the shorter drover having to hurry to keep up with Temar's long-legged strides. Giving vent to his irritation, Temar flung open one of the doors in the long, single-storey building that enclosed the lawn on all sides.

'Can I help you?' Lachald looked up from his desk, all but hidden by parchments covered in figures, amendments, crossings-out and notes. His thick fingers were ink-stained and his sparse blond hair unkempt.

'Respects, your honour.' The drover gave Temar an uncertain glance but carried on. 'We've brought in the herds from the western grass, so that should make the last of the cattle. The sheep weren't far behind us; they should be here within the chime, two at most.'

'Thank you, Rhun.' Lachald dug among his parchments and forced a note into a cramped margin. 'Go and get yourselves a meal. Oh, tell the steward to open a cask of wine for you all; there's no point hauling it back to Tormalin if we can drink it here, is there?'

'Obliged, your honour.' Rhun ducked his head and then hurried out, glad to escape Temar's palpable irritation.

'Is this important, Esquire?' Lachald did not look up from mending the nib of his quill. 'I am rather busy.'

'Why are we delaying while the herders bring in yet another bunch of scrawny cows and some mangy sheep?' Temar did not bother to temper his exasperation. 'I told you that horses should be the priority; they're far more valuable to the Sieur. We should have left days ago.'

'The Sieur has ordered me to withdraw his chattels and tenants from this reach of Dalasor in the best order I may.' Lachald rested his hand on a parchment that Temar could see bore his grandfather's personal seal. 'I am not about to sacrifice the futures of those families who have loyally worked this holding, some for generations, just to satisfy your desire for quick coin.'

'Coin is what the Sieur has need of,' Temar snapped angrily.

Lachald consulted the parchment before answering. 'He has explained his wish to finance a part in a new colony venture and I have every confidence in his judgement. However, my task is to make sure everyone who leaves here does so with as much of their property as possible, and that every beast that can be found is taken.'

'What is the point of rounding up winter-starved cattle that will eat as tough as boot soles?'

'They can be fattened on the grazing around the Great West Road.' Lachald bent over his writing, as if the conversation were concluded.

'That means they won't be selling until Aft-Summer.' Temar slammed his hands down on the table and leaned forward, eyes hard and ominous. He stared down at Lachald who remained impassive. 'Den Fellaemion wants to sail no later than the turn of Aft-Spring and we'll need the full season to make ready if we're to join him.'

'Let Messire Den Fellaemion sail when he will.' The steel hidden in Lachald's bulk rang in his voice. 'The proceeds from the sale of those cattle will be used to help settle and support the tenants this side of the ocean. The Sieur's concern that none be left destitute is quite clear.'

'They won't be left destitute; they can come with me to the new colony! If we ever get a vessel bought and fitted, that is,' Temar said scornfully. 'Which is why we need to concentrate on recovering only those things of value that can be turned rapidly into coin: stud animals, horses for the Cohorts, wine and spirits mature enough to sell. We need to move fast and we won't be doing that if we're stopped every half-league by a milch cow dropping a calf!'

'And what of those whom the Sieur is forcing to leave, who don't wish to risk the open ocean in a quest for an untamed land, full of Talagrin only knows what dangers?' Lachald's voice betrayed an edge of weary irritation now. 'Are they to be discarded here along with the broken pots from the kitchens?'

'If they want to stay when every sensible House is drawing back from Dalasor, let them. There'll be no Tormalin presence this side of the Astmarsh within five years, anyway.'

'How is that relevant, exactly?'

Temar stared at Lachald for a long moment then turned on his heel, striding for the door.

'You know, Esquire D'Alsennin, if you are to make anything like a worthy Sieur of our House, you really are going to have to learn how to deal better with folk.' Lachald leaned back in his chair and folded his arms, a sardonic expression on his fat face.

Temar half turned, mouth open, surprise fleeting across his face a breath ahead of real wrath.

'I was sent here with a task to do and you are—' Temar was shouting now but Lachald remained unmoved, seated behind his desk.

'Oh, do shut up!' he countered with a full-throated bellow that easily drowned out Temar's intemperate accusations.

The younger man fumed, unable to decide between further argument or the satisfaction of slamming the door behind him.

'Have a glass of wine and we can discuss our options like sensible men,' Lachald commanded acidly. He rose and turned to a shelf, extracting a flask of wine and two glasses from behind a set of ledgers.

'Rielle thinks I'm drinking too much during the day,' he explained as he offered Temar one of the crude greenish beakers. 'She will insist on sending over small-beer when I ring for refreshment. Sit down, won't you?'

Temar hesitated for a breath then took the wine and found a stool under a pile of ledgers.

'That's better.' Lachald took a long drink and closed his eyes for a moment before continuing, smudges of tiredness grey beneath his lashes. 'I know it's the saddle horses, the bulls, the rams and so on that will make the Crowns to buy your ship and supply her. I wish you all the best and we'll burn some incense to Dastennin when you sail.' He raised his drink to Temar in a toast and the youth took a reluctant sip from his still full glass.

'So why aren't we—' Temar began, but Lachald spoke on over him, his tone commanding attention.

'In the meantime, I have to look at the whole game, see where all the runes are going to fall. I'm not expecting you to wait for the cattle droves and the ox-carts, not once we're past the Astmarsh. You can cream off the best and welcome, once we're under the protection of the cohorts again, but until then we'll need to keep together or one attack from the plainsmen could cut us to pieces. I'll also be cursed if I'm going to leave anything behind that those dog-lovers can use against any of the other settlements around here. If I didn't think it would be bad for morale, I'd fire the buildings as we leave tomorrow!'

'Why didn't you tell me this earlier?' Temar demanded, undaunted.

'Why didn't you ask?' Lachald shot back, dark eyes challenging. 'Why didn't you do me the courtesy of assuming I know my business after managing these ranges for the Sieur for close on a generation?'

'My apologies, Esquire,' Temar said stiffly.

'My pardon, Esquire,' Lachald responded with ironic formality.

Temar drained his glass and placed it carefully on the edge of the desk. 'I will see you at dinner,' he said crisply.

Lachald watched the young man leave, shook his head with a mixture of exasperation and amusement and then applied himself to the seemingly endless lists that this departure was generating.

Temar hesitated in the colonnade outside the office door. The sounds of disgruntled cattle and overworked men lifted over the stone tiles of the low roofs. He looked at the rope burn across one palm and the bruises on both arms and decided he'd done as much rough labouring to safeguard his House's prosperity as it was reasonable to expect in one day.

The sun was dipping below the main dwelling as Temar walked across the grass towards it; he looked up at the gilded clouds, dragged across the deepening blue of the evening sky by the ever present winds of Dalasor. Snapping a twig from a feverfeather growing in one of the urns along the colonnade, he paused to breathe in the sharp scent as he bruised the leaves. Temar closed his eyes and allowed himself a moment to think of his mother, who always favoured the herb in her tisanes. Her wedding at the Winter Solstice seemed to be the last time he could remember being free of apprehension and aggravation over Den Fellaemion's expedition.

He went into the entrance hall and his steps echoed against the bare walls. The intricate hangings that once displayed the quality of the wool raised here were already packed and stowed on one of the ox-carts. Sounds of activity could be heard all around and Temar hoped a little guiltily that he hadn't stopped work with the stock just to end up moving the last of the furniture. A maid appeared from one of the anterooms and bobbed a quick curtsey, almost as surprised to see Temar as he was to see her.

'Excuse me,' she mumbled as she passed with an armful of books and a travelling writing desk that Temar recognised as belonging to Rielle. They must be finally clearing the private apartments, he concluded. A thought struck him and he sniffed, turning his head towards the kitchen wing. There was no savour of dinner on the air, he realised gloomily; the clatter of pans and stoneware must be the last packing up of the kitchen. At this rate they were going to be leaving with more wagons than an Imperial Progress.

He returned to the colonnade and walked swiftly round to the shrine, closing the door behind him. The two statues stared at him with impassive marble patience, challenging him. Temar pulled up a chair and sat, looking thoughtfully at the half-size figures.

Talagrin was not a god he was used to worshipping; the favour of the lord of wild places seemed a little irrelevant when you lived in one of the biggest cities in Tormalin. Temar felt a sudden qualm; would the god have heard his half-meant irreverence? Talagrin's good will would be worth having once he was trying to carve a colony out of a wilderness, no argument there. Temar opened the drawer in the plinth beneath the figure, which was draped in the fluidly carved skin of a long-forgotten predator, and took out a stick of incense. It was stickily fresh and he saw recent ashes in the offertory bowl before the god; he was evidently not the only one looking for divine protection against the perils of journeys ahead. He snapped flint and steel against a twist of dry wool and lit the incense. Waiting for a moment he breathed in the fragrant smoke, feeling it loosen the tension behind his eyes that had been threatening to break into a headache for most of the day.

Larasion regarded him over her mingled armful of flowers, fruit and bare branches as Temar prepared a second offering. He had made enough of these in his time, he thought with a rueful smile, asking for fair weather when he reckoned he was in with a chance of spending a chime in the long grass with some pretty girl, beseeching cold winds and rain when one of those hopeful maidens wanted him to join some family celebration, to be presented for parental inspection. That was all very well but rain in due season and sun to bring a fruitful harvest was going to mean the success or failure of Den Fellaemion's colony, not just profit and loss in the D'Alsennin ledgers. Temar lit the incense with a sober expression and looked at the sternly beautiful face of the goddess, hoping she would understand his unspoken pleas.

The door opened and a small, pointed face framed in gold braids peeped round.

'Oh, Temar, don't let me interrupt your devotions.'

'No, Daria, it's all right, come in.' Temar rose and the girl entered, bringing with her a blend of scents that made a heady mixture with the incense. She seated herself with practised grace.

'Aunt Rielle has had me at work all day in the still-room.' Daria fanned herself with an elegantly manicured hand, now somewhat stained. 'Halcarion only knows how I'll get my fingers clean.'

She proffered some minor blemishes for Temar's inspection, resting her hand in his for a breath longer than was strictly necessary.

'I thought I would find some peace and quiet in here, maybe avoid being given another job for a little while,' she confessed with an mischievous glance from beneath her darkened lashes.

'You and me both,' Temar replied with accomplished charm. Daria had been sent to spend a couple of seasons up here after some escapade at Solstice, he recalled. There had been talk of a coppersmith or similar; certainly she'd overstepped the boundaries most good families expected of their daughters.

Daria yawned and stretched her arms above her head, the loose sleeves of her gown falling back to reveal tempting, milky skin. She reminded Temar of a pale-gold lapcat his mother had once had, all coquettish affection. He wondered how Daria would respond to a little stroking.

'I'm hungry,' she complained abruptly. 'No one seems to have done anything about dinner, did you know that?'

'Why don't I fetch us some bread and meat and we can find a quiet corner to eat in, just the two of us?' Temar leaned forward and was rewarded with a stirring glimpse of the downy swell of Daria's breasts.

She smiled pertly at him, her eyes knowing. 'I'll find some wine; no one's going to miss a flask or so in all this confusion. Meet me by the kitchen-garden gate.'

Temar spared the statues a glance as he followed Daria out. He smiled suddenly; whatever Talagrin or Larasion might be thinking, Halcarion was certainly smiling on him.

As a result Temar was feeling refreshed and even cheerful as he sat watching the wagons roll out in the early light of the following dawn. The herds had already moved on, plumes of dust rising in the cold air to mark the trail south.

'Is everyone accounted for?' Lachald was clutching a list awkwardly along with his reins, a charcoal smear on the side of his head showing he was stowing his marker behind his ear again.

'All done.' Rielle walked briskly to her carriage, having supervised the stowing of the effigies from the shrine. A tall, spare woman with an angular face, she took no nonsense from anyone, from the Emperor down, some said. It had come as no small surprise to Temar to hear her insist that the statues must be the very last thing to leave the villa, to avert ill luck. As a lackey opened the carriage door, Temar caught a glimpse of Daria looking distinctly disgruntled. To his relief her expression cleared when she saw him and she gave him a private, conspiratorial smile. He would hate to think their dealings the night before hadn't been satisfactory. It was a shame she wouldn't make a suitable wife, he mused. She certainly had the charm a Sieur needed in his lady but Temar didn't fancy being married to a girl with such a welcoming attitude.

A horn blew close by, startling his horse, and Temar was very nearly unseated. The wagons got slowly under way, the lowing of reluctant oxen mingling with the stubborn creaks of wood and leather, settling into a low rumble as the line of carts moved off down the track. Temar looked round for his scouts and nodded to Rhun, whom he'd marked down as a useful man, his lack of formality not withstanding. Rhun raised a pennant on a lance, settling it firmly in his stirrup. Temar kicked his horse on and cantered down the line, a contingent growing behind him as those previously nominated as guards left their families and goods behind. He led them to a little rise, where they paused to watch the carts winding on through the vastness of the grasslands.

'I don't expect we'll have any real trouble but it will pay to stay alert,' Temar began.

'What about the plainsmen?' one of the younger lads asked nervously. Temar saw concern darken the eyes of several others.

'The last true plainsmen were driven out by the Cohorts more than twenty generations ago,' Temar said firmly, frowning as a few sceptical murmurs came from the rear ranks. He raised his voice slightly. 'There are raiders, certainly, preying on decent, hard-working stockmen like yourselves, and they are taking every advantage of departures like ours, so you all need to keep a good watch. I don't suppose they'll have any more courage than four-legged carrion hounds, so if we make sure they see we're ready to defend our own, I imagine they'll scurry back to their dens, tails between their legs.'

That got something like a laugh, at least, and Temar briskly allocated each man a partner and a watch-roster. Luckily he'd woken for a trip to the privy in the night and remembered he still needed to draw this up, hurriedly finding a lamp and parchment and doing his best to recall the orders Lachald had posted, looking to put the men near their own kin and belongings to keep them that little bit more vigilant. He grinned to himself; the lamplight had roused Daria and she'd welcomed him back to the warmth of the bed with a rekindled fire of her own.

His good humour evaporated as he heard one of the lads behind him talking to his mate in an undertone.

'It's all very well saying the true plainsmen are dead and gone but I've heard tell that some of them can come back from the Otherworld; Eldritch-men, they're called, they step out of the shadows and shoot you full of them little copper arrows.'

Temar rounded on the pimply stripling. 'What nonsense are you peddling? I'll tell you what, why don't you go and tell your tales to the children round the fire tonight and see if you can't start a real panic for the women to cope with? Who's your mother? I'll wager she'd stripe your arse for you if she heard you talking such rubbish.'

The lad flushed scarlet as his mates laughed, perhaps a little forcedly but loudly enough to satisfy Temar that the boy wouldn't risk further ridicule with such tales.

'Get to it,' Temar ordered and he watched with satisfaction as the men dispersed, some a little awkward, unused to riding with a sword at their belt and all scanning the sweeping plains with intense eyes.

'Let's scout ahead,' he commanded, spurring his mount to a rapid canter. Rhun followed, managing the pennant and the reins with enviable ease. Temar led them away from the main track, to avoid the dust and dung the herds were creating. Rhun dipped the scarlet fluttering above them, an answering flash of red showing that the herd guards were staying alert.

Temar surveyed the horizon and frowned as an unnatural shape caught his eye in the featureless expanse of the plains. 'That plains ring's the only cover for leagues around here, let's make sure no one's using it.'

He didn't wait for Rhun to answer but dug in his heels, relishing the excuse for a gallop. His incautious impulse had faded somewhat by the time they reached the earthwork. He reined in some distance away, circling carefully, keeping a distance that would allow him escape if by some remote chance raiders were indeed lurking inside the grassy walls.

'No one here,' Rhun said confidently. 'Not recently, anyway.'

Temar frowned as a gust of wind brought him the odour of old fire, or something like it. 'Let's check inside.'

He moved his horse to the opening in the leeward side of the rampart and drew his sword before entering. As they expected, there were no waiting raiders, nor little men using the shadows to come back from the Otherworld, Temar smiled to himself. There was a dark scar on the close-cropped turf, though, and Temar dismounted to examine it, picking a shard of blackened bone out of the ashes.

'It's the old way of cooking a beast, the plainsman way,' Rhun said unexpectedly.

'Explain.' Temar looked up, curious.

'You strip the bones, empty the stomach and put the meat in it, make a fire out of the bones and cook the meat by hanging the stomach above it.'

Temar looked at the short and stocky herder, dark-skinned and black-haired. He also recalled the journal he'd once read; the recollections of a young D'Alsennin who'd served with the cohorts during the conquest of Dalasor and his descriptions of the area's original inhabitants.

'Plains blood in your family, is there, Rhun?' he asked with a half-smile.

'Hard to say.' The man's black eyes were unreadable. 'All I know is we're stockmen, always have been.'

'What did the plainsmen use places like this for, anyway?' Temar stood and turned slowly, staring up at the earthern walls.

'Marriages, parleys, death rites.' Rhun shrugged. 'Placating the spirits.'

He pointed to a line of bedraggled feathers stuck into the turf to the left of the entrance. 'That's giving thanks to the cloud eagles for taking the carrion.'

Temar stared at the barred pinions for a moment then returned to the matter at hand, determinedly shaking off a faint unease. 'How recent would you call this fire?'

'Three days, may be four.'

'Not really anything to worry about, then. Still, we can tell the others we've found recent trace of raiders; it'll give them something to stay alert for.' Temar mounted and led the way back to the wagons, now spread over the best part of half a league.

The long day and the next passed without incident, Temar's initial excitement at finally being on the move waning, especially as the length and frequency of the rest breaks needed by the oxen became apparent. Enthusiasm diminishing rapidly, he concluded sourly that his role as commander of the so-called guards was little more than a device by Lachald to keep him out of the way.

'At this rate Den Fellaemion will have sailed before we reach the Astmarsh,' he complained without preamble that evening, planting himself in front of Lachald, arms folded.

'Go and see if the herds have reached the ford, will you?' Lachald took a bowl of vegetable stew, thickened with grain, from Rielle. 'Thank you, my dear.'

Temar muttered an oath and strode off to his horse, Lachald shaking his head as he watched him go.

'Captain?' Rhun looked up from his own meal.

'Stay and eat,' Temar snapped as he yanked his horse's reluctant head round.

The smoke of numerous dung fires coiled upwards into the vast emptiness as he skirted the wagons and the hobbled oxen grazing with bovine contentment. Temar's lips narrowed as he saw the sun was barely on the horizon, yet they were already stopping for the night. Cresting a rolling ridge, he saw a silvery thread of water winding through the green. The herds were already crossing the ford, splashing through the muddied water.

'Why can't people just follow their cursed orders?' Temar fumed, using his heels to take out a little of his frustration on his hapless mount.

'What are you doing?' he yelled at a herder on the far bank. 'Lachald said we cross the river together, tomorrow!'

'You come and tell the cows, then.' The man evidently didn't recognise Temar. 'They started crossing—'

The man's voice was lost as urgent bellows rang through the lowing of grazing beasts.

'Gurrywit!' Temar swore and galloped through the water, looking for the men who were supposed to be guarding the cattle. He turned into a slight hollow and saw them, apprehensive, all seated round a fire with rough-cut steaks threaded on a hastily rigged spit.

'Get your arses up and your swords out!' Temar spat, threatening the nearest youth with the flat of his own blade. A confusion of hasty explanations drowned him out momentarily until he silenced the men with a trooper's obscenities.

'Come on!' Temar led the way out of the river gully and saw a group of ragged figures intent on cutting out a section of the agitated herd. Temar yelled a challenge but, able to see the guards from such a distance, the raiders melted away into the gathering dusk and the hollows of the grassland. Temar was just drawing breath to berate his ill-assorted troop when cries for help rang out from the far side of the throng of milling cattle.

'Bastards!' he swore in disbelief as he led the men in, forcing a way through the animals. They achieved little more than scattering the beasts still further; the raiders were nowhere to be seen, only a gang of startled herders clustered round one of their number who'd taken a club to the head. Real panic was threatening among the cattle now, and Temar's men began to move instinctively to use their horses to curb and control the herd.

'How many have we lost?' Temar demanded of a herder.

'Don't know what's stolen and what's strayed,' the man said helplessly.

Temar was about to pursue this when Rhun's horn rang up into the grey evening sky. Not waiting to check who was with him, Temar galloped back to the ford to hear screams and shouts from the straggling line of motionless wagons. A flare of orange blossomed in the gloaming as a burning brand sailed in from the darkness, scattering a bevy of shrieking women. A horseman was silhouetted against a cook-fire as he galloped in and snatched a waiting side of meat from the spit, his mount barely breaking stride. Frantic barking from the far side of a wagon was suddenly stilled and the wail of a terrified child rose to a shriek. Temar's hand hesitated over his throwing knives; in this confusion, he couldn't risk hitting friend rather than foe. A knot of grey shapes moved stealthily along the furthest edge of the firelight and Temar marked where they halted. He looked round wildly and saw Rhun cantering down the line, searching for the guards. Temar met him and caught his bridle, dragging him between two carts without apology.

'They're waiting out beyond the lead wagon. Get some men and circle round to drive them off.'

Rhun left without need of further instruction and Temar headed back towards Lachald's position. A cart stood abandoned, tailgate swinging and its sacks and casks scattered as its frightened driver had rushed his family instinctively to Lachald's protection. As Temar galloped past a small figure dashed out from beneath the axles and vanished into the night, some nameless loot clutched greedily to its chest.

'Are you all right?' Temar yelled, relieved to see Lachald's carriage in a circle with two other carts, the men staying close, swords drawn.

'Get whoever you can across the ford,' Lachald bellowed in a tone that brooked no argument. 'We're too spread out.'

Temar wheeled his horse round and pointed at one of the spotty youths.

'Get to the head of the line, tell them to yoke up and get moving. Wait!' he yelled in exasperation as the lad went to leave. 'Tell them to work and move in groups, not to get separated.'

Movement flickered in the corner of Temar's eye as he turned away from the lad and he caught a glimpse of shadowy shapes circling behind Lachald's carriage.

'Come on.' He dug his spurs into his horse's bleeding flanks and fury carried him into a ragged figure whose rough-coated steed had temporarily unseated him. Temar managed to lay a deep slash across the raider's back before he got his mount under control, but he could only watch, cursing, as the man was swallowed up by the concealing darkness. Every instinct screamed at Temar to go after the robber but he managed to restrain himself.

'Stay here, drive them off but don't go beyond the firelight,' he commanded the knot of armed men who had belatedly ridden up.

He began yet another circuit of the file of carts and was finally able to get his guards working in effective groups, each defending a section of the line against the harrying raiders. Gathering a smaller troop, Temar moved to concentrate on protecting the carts crossing the ford. Once the vehicles were formed into a defensive circle, the darting assaults soon tailed off, though Temar stayed on a knife-edge of apprehension until the first pale streaks of dawn showed above the eastern horizon. Exhaustion hit him like a mallet when sunrise at last revealed empty grassland all around. He went in search of Lachald.

'What are the losses?' Temar asked, shivering and looking hungrily at a kettle of porridge bubbling over Rielle's fire.

'None dead, some minor wounds,' Lachald responded curtly. 'Some food and supplies taken, and more scattered or spoiled.'

Temar sighed with relief. 'We've been lucky.'

'You mean you've been lucky. If those raiders had wanted to, they could have cut us into rags.' Lachald's harsh tone was uncompromising. 'You're in charge of the guards and they were a complete shambles.'

Faces turned as Lachald's voice rose and Temar stood, mouth open, unable to deny the accusation.

'I thought you were supposed to be sending out scouts? Exactly what instructions had you given, in case of attack? Why didn't you come and tell me at once that the cattle had crossed the river? Do you know where the horses and the sheep have got to? Go and find out!'

Temar turned without a word and found a fresh horse,

avoiding anyone else's eyes. He rode off, finally grateful to the ever present breeze as it cooled the humiliation burning his cheeks.

The River Road, Eastern Caladhria,
from Prosain Heath to South Varis,
13th of Aft-Spring

Getting the caravan moving once daybreak arrived was no simple task. After rides on wagons for the wounded were sorted out and the order was rearranged to take account of the reduced guard, the sun was well over the tree-tops before the beasts and carts were anything like ready. The mule-master, a thickset man with thinning hair, nearly came to blows with an arrogant type with expensive boots, now thoroughly muddy and scuffed. I gathered he was the negotiator and was getting agitated about delays that might cost them dear in Relshaz. Eventually Nyle stepped in to make peace, his scowl deterring the pair from any further argument. I watched, amused, but turned away when he saw me looking. He can't have liked that for some reason, because I soon caught him looking after me, checking my place every so often. By the end of the day, I was starting to get tired of it.

Either word had spread through the undergrowth or we'd finished off the only group of bandits, because we cleared the Heath with no further trouble. We reached the Spread Eagle just as the sun was sinking behind the western hills and the shadows of the trees were meeting over the road. It was a sprawling substantial building of local flint and brick, surrounded by a broad expanse of paddocks and barns of solid tarred wood. We could see South Varis spreading itself round the far side of a modest lake, a typical Caladhrian stretch of neat cruck-framed crofts and tidy workshops, all freshly limewashed in pale colours, lights already being snuffed as the inhabitants went to their beds along with the sun.

Metal-shod hooves clacked over the cobbles and the laden

carts rattled through the arch of the stableyard, Nyle and the mule-master loudly demanding service. The thin-faced negotiator dismounted with a sour expression and left his horse to an underling without a backward glance. I watched him stalk off through the front door and heard him calling peremptorily for his usual chamber and a hot bath. Stable hands appeared and helped the new arrivals sort themselves out, voices lifting above the racket of unco-operative pack animals.

'I'll help Halice with our gear and stowing the gig; Livak, you and Shiv find someone to take care of the horses. Viltred, you can find the innkeeper or whoever's in charge here – get some rooms before they're all taken.'

The old mage gave me a sharp look, clearly unused to taking orders, but he headed for the main door without argument. I was glad about that; I wasn't intending to spend any more of this trip nursing his self-importance along like a leaking row-boat.

I dismounted and yawned; this was getting ridiculous – a day's easy ride in clear weather shouldn't leave me this weary. Still, a good night's sleep in a decent bed should set me to rights.

'If there's an ostler or groom spare, see if they've seen any unusual travellers.' Shiv glanced round the stableyard.

'Help you, sirs?' A stooped old man followed by an over-powering smell of horses sidled out of a nearby barn. 'You'll need some help, ladies.'

It wasn't a question and he was staring at Halice's leg with ill-disguised curiosity.

'No we don't.' Halice's reply was understandably curt

'I think we can manage, if you're needed elsewhere.' I softened her words with a polite nod; it was important that our beasts were treated well, with the place so busy.

The groom leaned against the doorjamb and treated us to an ingratiating display of sparse yellow teeth.

'No call for me, just yet. You're on a trip to the south then?'

Livak turned to him with a bright smile, all charming innocence and wide, confiding eyes.

'We're on our way to Relshaz,' she said, with a nicely calculated touch of breathlessness. 'Grandfather has investments there and with both our uncles putting their coin in our cousins came along as well.'

I caught Shiv's eye to let him know to alert Viltred to this new chain of relationships and looked away fast so that we could both keep a straight face.

The old gossip's eyes brightened. 'What business are you in, then?'

I could see him imagining all the fascinating possibilities – spices, silks, gems, bronzes. Relshaz is the main port for eastern Caladhria and most of the Aldabreshin trade on top of that.

'Animal feeds.' The enthusiasm in Livak's voice nearly tripped me, despite myself. 'Barley, oats, that kind of thing. Fodder crops are too bulky, you see, and then there's the problems of transport, but grain is a different matter. If you time it right, you can get quite a premium, shipping to the Archipelago.'

'Oh,' The old ostler was noticeably less interested now.

'That's only if the Aldabreshi don't start importing for themselves,' Halice said sourly. 'I heard tell a group had been making enquiries around Trebin. You haven't seen them on the road, have you? A gang of about six, all dressed in black, keeping themselves to themselves?'

I mentally tallied up a Crown owed to Halice's quick wits but the little man shook his head with what I judged to be genuine ignorance. I couldn't decide whether I was relieved or disappointed.

I held out a silver Mark. 'Please make sure all the horses are settled and the harness is properly cleaned.'

'I'll get the boy to do it.' The groom took the coin and somewhat ungraciously slouched off, whistling sharply to summon two lads who were taking their time to get a bale of straw spread for some mules.

'Livak, next time, do you think we could agree on a ballad

before you start singing it?' Shiv's voice was muffled as he bent to loosen his horse's girths.

'What were you planning to do? Stand around and look shifty and get him imagining all sorts of possibilities?' Livak led the beasts away to the stables with a shake of her head.

'That's not the issue,' Shiv followed her, determined to pursue the point.

Unracking the gig's seat I reached into the body of the vehicle for our luggage. 'No harm done, as long as we make sure Viltred knows he's just become a grandfather.'

I tucked my sword under the flap of one of my saddle bags and passed it to Halice, while I leaned over for Viltred's bag.

Halice whistled with more than a trace of envy and I turned to see she was looking at the intricate leatherwork of my scabbard.

'Maybe I should try swearing to a Tormalin patron if that means I'd get to wear a Prince's heirloom at my belt.'

I wasn't about to pass up the first friendly remark she'd made to me that day so I handed the sword over.

She turned it this way and that and smiled as she felt the superb balance. Drawing the blade a little way, she peered at the bright steel.

'It's not a D'Olbriot heirloom, it's loot from the mad old wizard that Viltred used to know,' I explained.

'This is the sword that came from Azazir?' Her plain face lit with curiosity. 'No wonder Viltred wants to catch up with those thieves. What did he lose – do you know exactly? A couple of swords like this, we could be talking serious bullion weight.'

'Let's ask him,' I said obligingly before another yawn threatened to crack my face. 'Dast's teeth, I hope this place has clean beds; I don't seem to have had a solid night's sleep since Solstice.'

'You and me both,' Halice said curtly as we went to find the others.

We found Viltred in a pleasantly furnished tap-room, talking to a buxom lass with a snowy apron and glossy curls who was happy to take his patronising manner as long as it came with solid coin.

'Oh, there you all are, at last. Now, I've managed to get three bedchambers, one for the girls and you can share with Shiv, Ryshad. Supper will be ready in a few minutes so we've just got time to wash.'

No one was going to have trouble believing we were Viltred's grandchildren if he carried on treating us like this, I decided. Not until Livak tipped soup or something worse over him, anyway.

'It's the first three rooms overlooking the mere,' the maid-servant volunteered with a speculative smile at Shiv. 'I'll be up with a warming-pan later to take the chill off the linen.'

I'd been wondering if I might have the chance to heat up Livak's sheets for her but it didn't look likely. I sighed; it would have been one way of guaranteeing a sound night's sleep, if nothing else.

We trooped up the stairs after Viltred like the dutiful descendants we weren't and all followed him into his room.

'I think we should know just what these Ice Islanders took from you,' I began.

'Things get traded in places like this,' commented Livak. 'If someone offers me a two-Mark ring that should be worth ten, I'd like to know if it could be one of yours.'

'That's a good point,' Shiv agreed.

'So what did you and Azazir steal from the Elietimm?' asked Halice.

The old wizard bridled at the implication that he was a thief but shut his mouth on a retort, smoothing the front of his faded velvet jerkin for a moment instead. 'There were four swords, two rapiers for court wear and two broadswords; a couple of dress daggers; a chatelaine's key-ring; some plain gold signet rings, a necklet of pearls, several goblets and tankards with family insignia; a gentleman's note-tablet; an ink-well—'

I held up a hand. 'That's enough to be going on with, isn't it, Livak? Let's eat.'

We ate an excellent meal from a table of ten or more dishes

and lingered a little while over some fine porter. I bathed and shaved off the stubble of the last few days with considerable pleasure and still managed to be in bed before the chimes of midnight sounded faintly over the water from South Varis. Inevitably I slept poorly again, though I couldn't say if that was down to Shiv's interminable snores or frustration as I thought about Livak asleep on the other side of the lath and plaster wall.

The sound of more traffic in the yard woke me and I opened the shutters for a breath of fresh air as I dressed.

'I wouldn't mind giving that redhead a few turns on the spit.' A lone voice echoed up from a group of stable lads idly tossing runes, resonant in one of those unpredictable silences that open up especially for embarrassing remarks. I looked to my right to see Livak leaning on the sill of her window.

'Shall we find some breakfast?' I laughed. 'Or do you want to take him up on his offer?'

'You can stop smirking,' she growled, but I saw she was failing to keep her own face straight as she drew back from the open shutters.

'One of these days I'm going to take the Great West Road and search those unholy woods until I find someone who can tell me if Forest Folk really are as insatiable in bed as all the stories say,' she muttered as we went down the stairs. 'It's a cursed inconvenient reputation to live with, you know.'

'Oh, I'm not so sure. You might be able to acquire some useful information if that lot are more interested in watching your bodice buttons than what they're saying.'

'It wouldn't be the first time,' she admitted with an unabashed smile.

We watched the comings and goings in the tap-room over fresh bread better than any I'd had since leaving home and potted fruit my mother would have been ashamed to serve to her pigs. After a while we sauntered out to take the sun on a bench facing the stableyard and entertained ourselves trying to guess the origins and destinations of the various vehicles and pack animals. A varied collection of local merchants and independent traders came up from the south some while later and I saw a trader with Relshazri wheels to his wagon set down a dark-haired girl in a low-necked dress at the gate and drive through to the barns without stopping. After all, a ride for a ride is the usual deal, no more, no less, and that meant the girl was the type I was looking for. I watched as she headed for the rear of the inn without a backward glance.

'I think I might start asking a few questions.' If we were hunting, it was time we started trying to find a scent. I stood up and Livak nodded her understanding, casually unlacing the neck of her shirt a little and adopting an effectively deceptive guise of big eyes and little brain.

'I'll see what I can find out from the wagoneers who came in this morning.' She sauntered off, hips swaying just enough to catch the eye.

I walked round to the rear of the inn, treading carefully round a suspicious hound chained to a post and grimacing as I caught the scent of the midden. Voices at the door came round the corner of the building and I stopped, hoping the dog didn't decide to object as it watched me with pricked ears.

'I'll work for broken meat and bread, just until I get a ride out of here.' There was no pleading in the cart girl's voice, which I had to admire.

'We're not hiring.' The glossy-haired wench who'd served us was sharp with disdain.

'I'm not looking for a permanent place, just something to eat in return for giving you an easier few days.' The girl's instincts were good, I noted, making a reasonable offer rather than just begging. 'The house looks pretty full to me.'

'Oh, all right. You can help out tonight, but you sleep in the stables.' I heard quick steps on the kitchen flagstones then the scrape of a heel as the maid turned back with an afterthought. 'You do your business in the yard, I don't want you bothering customers in the tap-room. Any thieving, I'll send to Varis for the Watch and they can flog you in the market square.'

I leaned against a water butt until the dark girl came back around the corner.

'Are you heading north?' She looked me up and down and stayed out of arm's length.

I shook my head. 'South, and I'm looking for information about the road.' I tucked my thumbs into my belt and the coin in the purse hanging from it chinked softly as I nudged it.

'What sort of thing, exactly?' She looked cautious as well she might. Axle-greasers, harness brasses, call them what you will, these girls live a dangerous life; Dastennin only knows what the rewards are. She had the usual mongrel looks of the breed, thinner than she should have been, with a face older than her years should have given her.

'I'm Ryshad.' I held out a hand.

'Larrel.' She kept her arms folded defensively.

'I'm interested in finding a handful or so of men travelling together, black-liveried probably, all yellow-haired. We think they're on the road south of here.'

'What's it worth?' Her eyes told me she had seen them.

'That depends how much you can tell me?' I folded my own arms and smiled at her, not so pleasantly.

'There were six of them, all walking, one with a long cloak and no pack, the rest loaded like troopers who've lost their horses.' Her own smile told me she was no fool and more importantly, no liar, not about this at any rate.

I reached into my purse. 'A Mark for the name of the nearest village and a Mark for how many days since you saw them.'

'Tormalin Marks, not Caladhrian,' she countered, 'five pence to the Mark, not four, I'm not stupid, you know.'

'Fine,' I shrugged. The two extra coppers meant nothing to me but would buy someone like her a welcome hot meal.

'They were half a day's walk south of Armhangar, the day before yesterday.'

She held out her hand and I passed her the coin. 'My thanks.'

Surprise flared briefly in her eyes as she tucked the coin into a purse at her waist. I watched her go, found a bone in the midden to toss to the dog and went to see what I might find out from the kitchen staff in the lull between breakfast and the noon rush. It wasn't much of a surprise to find none of them had seen so much as a polished stud off an Elietimm livery; the Ice Islanders didn't strike me as the type of travellers to put up each evening at the nearest inn to share an idle ale and a joke. I frowned as I went in search of the others.

The stableyard was surprisingly quiet but a rising level of noise lead me to a crowd gathering on the far side of the barns. I found the rails of an empty paddock lined with a mixture of locals and travelling men. Shiv saw me and waved, so I headed over to him.

'So, have you heard tell of any black-liveried travellers?' Shiv leaned on the fence rail and ran a hand through his hair.

I told him what I had learned and then looked round for the others. 'Where's Viltred?' I asked.

'Resting in his room.'

Shiv and I watched as two men climbed over the fence, one carrying two polished staffs over his shoulder, the other with a bundle of inflated bladders dangling from one hand.

'He's not going to get much sleep with all this going on.' Fatigue betrayed me and I heard a slight sneer in my tone.

'He's an old man, tired, stiff and sore,' said Shiv mildly. 'Be fair, he's only a handful of years off his third generation festival.'

I looked at Shiv in some surprise and tried to think if I'd ever known anyone that old before. We would have to make some allowance for Viltred if he was carrying seventy years or more in his purse. I supposed Messire D'Olbriot's uncle, who had been Sieur before him, must be about that age and I had to allow he was hardly in any shape to go riding any distance, let alone day after day.

We watched as the men lashed together frames for hanging a bladder at each end of the field.

'This is spit-noggin, isn't it? Is it as hard a game as I've heard?'

'It can be,' Shiv chuckled. 'It depends if there's anyone playing who has a score to settle with someone else on the field.'

Two teams were sorting themselves out by the paddock

gate. After some toing and froing, the match resolved itself pretty much into local traders and a few farmers who'd been passing taking a line against the guards and wagoneers from the Duryea train; fourteen to each side was the figure finally agreed on.

'Is it only the man with the staff who can't cross the throwing line, or does everyone have to stay clear of it?' I watched as the men setting the field scored a deep line in the uneven turf at either end of the playing area.

'Only the staff-holder. Don't you play this in Tormalin?' Shiv looked surprised.

'In the north, on the western borders, but don't forget I'm from Zyoutessela. If you go any further south than that, you fall off the Cape of Winds,' I reminded him.

The first run of the game began. The wagon-train men were clearly used to playing together and soon had the staff passing smoothly between them as they ran through and round the local boys. A cheer went up as their man pitched the arm's length of polished wood at the suspended bladder, but he missed by barely a finger's breadth. Five men went down in the scramble for the staff but one of the grooms got it and the action came sweeping back down the field towards us.

'I'm going to see if I can find Livak.' Shiv stood up from the rail. 'Are you coming?'

'I'll hang on here.' I kept my eyes on the field. 'This is quite something, isn't it?'

Shiv laughed and slipped away through the crowd, and I concentrated on following the game. We don't go in for these gang sports so much in Tormalin; we tend to favour contests of individual skill instead. I started to wonder how my own spear-throwing talents would play in a game like this. The trick would be getting a chance to use them, I decided, wincing as a man poised to throw disappeared under a heap of dusty jerkins. One failed to get up as fast as the rest and limped off, clutching a hand to his chest. There was a short pause before another mule handler jumped the rails to take the injured man's place.

'Do you fancy a turn in a team?'

I turned to find Nyle at my shoulder. What was it the man wanted with me?

'What about your friends?' he went on. 'We could do with a decent runner?'

I shrugged. 'You'll have to ask them yourself.'

'You're Tormalin-born, aren't you? Do they play spit-noggin in the east?'

'Not where I live. Will you be playing later?' I can do idle conversation as well as anyone else but I wondered if there was going to be any point to this.

'Oh, yes.' Nyle moved a little closer and leant forward. 'The thing is, I wanted to talk to you first. I do a little trading on the side for myself as well, weapons mainly. I noticed your sword – it's Old Tormalin work isn't it? I wondered if you might be interested in selling?'

'Not really.' I shrugged again.

'I could do you a really good price, you know. I have a contact who is looking for just that kind of blade.'

A sudden yell from the field might have meant Nyle hadn't heard my answer, I supposed, but the keenness in his steely grey eyes made me doubt that. Was this just a random encounter, I wondered, or did we have some hounds who'd picked up our own scent while we were nose down for another quarry?

'Sorry, friend, but it's not mine to sell.'

I took care to colour my words with boredom rather than betray any suspicion and turned back to the game. Things were starting to heat up as a dispute broke out over whether or not a muleteer had stepped over the throwing line before the staff had left his hand.

'You could make your patron a coffer full of gold. Think about it; there'd be a decent purse in it for yourself, best part of a season's pay.'

'No thanks.'

There was a cry from the field as one of the locals threw a punch and a shout went up for Nyle. His broad nostrils flared briefly in ill-disguised irritation.

'I'll see you later.' He tried for an affable smile but his eyes were still hard; clearly a man not about to take a refusal as final.

He vaulted over the rail and was drawn into the game, leaving me to ponder this odd conversation. A great roar went up and I saw Nyle had the staff and was running with it. He was surprisingly agile for such a big man and when some luckless turnip-herder tried to grab the wood he threw the man off with a twist of the staff that sent him spinning into the gathering crowd.

'Nicely done! That's a Gidestan move; no wonder they haven't seen it round here before.' Halice pushed her way through the increasingly dense crowd and leaned heavily on the rail beside me.

I wondered what Nyle had been doing in Gidesta; he didn't look like a miner, a trapper or a logger, which is pretty much all there is to do in the northern mountains. His accent wasn't Gidestan either. I shook it off as irrelevant.

'Where's Livak?'

'Taking bets.' Halice pointed across the paddock and I saw Livak's coppery head in the middle of an eager cluster of people waving purses.

'What's she giving them?'

'Two wins five for the mule train, three wins seven for the locals,' said Halice, watching the game thoughtfully. 'Better if they win by more than five heads.'

'Heads?' I was puzzled.

Halice pointed to one of the bladders swaying a little in the breeze.

'The Mountain Men are supposed to have used heads taken in battle when they invented the game. Sorgren says it's the way they used to keep their fighting skills sharp. He swears his grandfather could remember seeing it played with the heads of some miners who'd pushed too far into the mountains, and I've seen pig's heads used in western Gidesta.'

There was a suspicion of relish in Halice's voice as she glanced sideways to see how I would react to this.

I laughed with a grimace. 'Messy!'

A group of the farmers seemed to have got themselves in step at last and managed to bring the game down to our end of the paddock. Five of them concentrated on flattening any muleteer who came within grabbing range and so their man managed to send the staff curling through the air to split the bladder clean in half.

'Have you found anyone who's come across the Elietimm on the road?'

Halice didn't hear me so I had to nudge her in the ribs and repeat myself, trying not to speak too loudly despite the cover offered by the noise of the crowd all around.

'What? Oh, yes. Well, a couple of them said they'd seen a small group of men camping out where the Linneyway goes off from the River Road. I think that must have been them – the wagoneer said they were all white-blond, that's why they caught his eye, all of them being so fair.'

I frowned. 'What were they wearing?'

Halice caught her breath and looked annoyed with herself. 'He didn't say and I didn't think to ask. Just ordinary clothes, I suppose; he'd have mentioned any livery, wouldn't he?'

'Can you try and find out?'

A shout went up and I saw someone waving a large sand-glass to indicate a break was due. It took a few moments to attract everyone's attention and then there was something of a lull, the noise muted by tankards of ale downed all round.

'By the way, that guard, Nyle, was asking me about your sword,' said Halice. 'He does a bit of weapons trading on the side, it seems.'

'He came to ask me himself. I'm still wondering what to make of it.'

The teams sorted themselves out and a few men evidently decided they'd had enough, limping off, cradling bruised hands or nursing bloodied noses and mouths.

'What's he offering?' Halice cocked an enquiring eyebrow at me.

'Doesn't matter.' I shook my head. 'Messire got it from

Planir and gave it to me as a Solstice gift by way of recompense for that little excursion to the Ice Islands with Livak and Shiv.'

I shivered abruptly and I heard a distant echo of my own screams at the hands of the Elietimm leader. That memory was going to fade about as fast as a pirate's tattoos.

'Caught the draught from Poldrion's cloak?' Halice joked, but her eyes were thoughtful none the less.

'Something like that,' I said shortly, looking back to the field where the fresh men were forcing the pace on as the game recommenced.

'Your Messire thinks well of you, then?' enquired Halice.

'I try to give him reason to.' That sounded a little more pompous than I had intended but Halice seemed unperturbed.

'So how did you come to swear to him? Is it a family thing? Are you following your father?'

'No,' I smiled at that. 'My father's a stonemason, and with my two oldest brothers picking up the chisels he let my next brother and myself choose our own paths.'

And in the year after the dappled fever had taken Kitria, the three of them had cut more stone and faced more buildings than any other masons in the city. My mother had spent half of each waking day either in tears or Halcarion's shrine and Mistal had fled the city entirely. I had sought every sensation I could in a vain effort to stop myself feeling her loss.

'How long since you gave your oath?'

'Twelve years, this summer.' I didn't have to think about that; twelve years since I'd spent an entire Solstice drunk on raw spirits and dazed with thassin in the arms of a succession of cheap whores. I'd woken up to bleeding gums, a splitting head, a dose of the itch. More immediately I'd realised that I had to do something different, and quickly, or Poldrion would soon be ferrying me back and forth in the Shades between the worlds until I could come up with some explanation to give Saedrin for the waste of that particular life.

'Livak's told me about what happened to you out there, on the Ice Islands.' Halice turned away from the game abruptly.

'Then you know all you need to.' Halice might be unbending a little towards me, but I wasn't about to start discussing those experiences with her.

'I know more than Livak thought she was telling me.'

That struck me as an odd remark and I turned away from the field myself.

'What do you mean?'

'She told me about the Ice-man and the way he got inside your minds.' Halice's eyes were dark and unfathomable. 'But she didn't say a lot about you and that makes me think you got inside her head, if nowhere else.'

I stared down at her with no little challenge but her gaze didn't waver.

'Livak's a smart girl and no one's fool, but every so often a man'll come along and she drops the runes completely,' Halice went on in a conversational tone. 'I try to make sure I'm there to help her gather the set, settle any scores, just so you know. I'm sure you don't want to make her sorry she met you, do you?'

A roar from the crowd drowned the rest of her words and everyone turned to see some unfortunate clutching his ribs being carried off the field. When I turned back to Halice she had slipped away.

I rubbed a hand over my face and wondered what to make of that particular conversation. I've been asked my intentions a couple of times by stilted fathers, several times by kindly aunts with speculative eyes and once, in that heedless period of my youth, I was warned off by three angry brothers with axe-helves in a back alley due to a miscalculation born of thassin-inspired overconfidence.

I decided this came somewhere between an enquiry and a threat and couldn't decide whether to be indignant or pleased that Livak had a friend who looked out for her interests. At least Halice hadn't waited for an answer; that was a relief. I didn't know where I might be going with Livak, not beyond the closest bed if I had the chance, that was. I wondered what Halice might have been saying to Livak. Dastennin curse the

woman for an interfering wharf bird, I muttered under my
breath; I didn't even know what Livak's own feelings were
and, until I did, I could do without Halice scratching up the
dust between us.

A shout came from the field. 'We need three more to make
up the numbers or we forfeit to Nyle's men!'

On an impulse I didn't stop to examine, I decided the game
looked like an excellent way to work off some of the building
frustrations of this journey. A handful of men climbed the
paddock rails with me and I was chosen for the locals over a
lad from South Varis who looked as if he was being fattened
up for slaughter. The sand-glass was turned and the next run
began. I found myself in the thick of the action, being tall
enough to stand out for anyone looking to throw the staff and
save himself a pounding. Luckily I have sure hands and I found
the footwork I've spent years learning for swordwork meant I
was agile enough to evade most of the tackles. I dodged and
weaved and found myself yelling with the exhilaration of it all
as I outstripped the pack and ran for the throwing line at the
far end of the field.

One burly muleteer managed to grasp one end of the wood,
but strangely no one had ever told him a staff is a two-ended
weapon. He drew his hands close into his body with a snarl
of triumph so I got my hip behind my end and just kept it
going forward. He went down like a sack of wheat when he
caught my full weight on the staff hammering into his short
ribs. I went straight over him, and when I saw him later I
could recognise the print of my boot on his chest. I thought
I was going to be flattened like a mudfish when a heavy-set
carter swung round towards me, fists clenched, but someone
appeared at my elbow out of nowhere and dropped the man
with a heavy shoulder straight in the stones that suggested a
personal interest.

A couple of local lads who must have built their muscles
wrestling bullocks proved that big men can put on a burst
of speed if they need to and drew level with me. I saw Nyle
and another wagoneer heading for me and I whipped my head

rapidly from side to side to check where the cow handlers were. One gave me a brilliant smile, nodded to his brother, and I dug my heels into the turf to let them surge past me. They hit Nyle and another wagoneer like a rock-slide and the field ahead was clear. I heard the thunder of hammering feet behind me and knew I only had a moment. Forgetting everything I've ever been taught about spear throwing, I sent the length of wood spiralling through the air and saw it smack the bladder high up over the frame before I caught what felt like half a cohort in the small of my back.

When I saw daylight again I spat out a mouthful of grass and some bits of a dried clod I didn't want to examine too closely, but my sense of elation was uncrushed.

'Good throw!' Livak's voice cut through the roars of the crowd and I saw her bright hair and lively face close at hand, by the rail.

I waved and blew an extravagant kiss in her direction before scrambling up to avoid getting trampled into the clay. As the game continued I managed another score and took out wagoneers with some vital tackles to help make three more. We finally gave it up after nine runs when everyone was just too tired and no more replacements came forward. I wasn't sorry; if we'd gone on, I reckoned there was a danger of it degenerating into a brawl, which is one reason it's a game frowned on in Tormalin. The final score was agreed as fifteen heads for the wagon train losing to my team's twenty-one and the mood suggested no one was disgraced by that. Once we'd scraped off the worst of the mud, everyone moved on to the tap-room where the serious drinking began. I looked round hopefully for Livak, keen to know how much she'd made on the betting.

'Over here!' Shiv stood up from a corner table and I pushed my way through the throng, trying to evade delays for congratulations from my erstwhile team-mates.

Halice poured me an ale and I downed it in one before taking a second a little slower; I didn't want to drink too much, too fast, not on top of all that exercise.

'I think dinner may be a little slower this evening.' Livak appeared from the direction of the kitchen and pulled up a stool next to me.

'Had a profitable afternoon?' I grinned at her.

'Very!' She flashed a smile at me and patted the billow of her shirt which clinked discreetly.

'Anyway, have either of you heard anything about our friends from the east?' Shiv was suddenly all business, voice low, although I don't know why he was bothering given the amount of noise all around us.

'I got a good lead on a group in black about a day and a half south of here, but Halice got just as clear a nod on some blond travellers away over near the Linneyway.' I reached for my drink and tried to drag my mind back to our chase.

'When I was taking bets I made out I was asking after a bad debt and was told both tales,' said Livak.

'Where's that map of yours? Could it be two sightings of the same group?' Halice sounded unconvinced and I didn't blame her.

'Could they have split up?' I asked.

Shiv shook his head. 'I doubt it; Viltred's been scrying and he's sure that everything that was taken is still together.'

'I checked and the group I heard about are definitely in local clothes, not any kind of livery,' added Halice. 'I'd say we have the thieves and another pack to worry about now.'

'But are they after us, after Viltred or after the other lot in black?' Livak frowned.

'Or going about some entirely unrelated business?' I took another drink. 'It's always possible.'

'I'll go and talk to Viltred. He might be able to scry for this other troop if he knows the area himself.' Shiv shot a regretful glance towards the cart-girl Larrel, who was doing the rounds with a tray of bread and cut meats to placate the hungry customers.

Livak caught his arm as he moved. 'Not so fast. That guard captain, Nyle, seems very keen to buy Ryshad's sword. Did you know about that?'

Shiv shrugged. 'That's hardly surprising, is it? It's an Old Empire sword; those blades are always in demand.'

'Don't come the festival virgin with me, Shiv, I know you too well.' She shook her head at him. 'There isn't anyone like Darni working the area, is there? Tempting people to sell off the family heirlooms so Planir can investigate them, letting idiots like me involve themselves in your daft schemes? You don't think I'm going to forget being caught like that, do you?' Her tone was distinctly waspish.

'I doubt it,' Shiv frowned. 'I can check, if you like, but I think Planir would have told me, don't you?'

'Nyle said he has contacts who are looking out for swords like that,' persisted Livak. 'The Elietimm were hunting for Old Empire artefacts last year, weren't they?'

And stealing them, I thought grimly. Messire's nephew had lost his wits in the beating he'd taken trying to protect the heirloom rings the bastards were after.

'Nyle might not know it himself, but whoever he's selling to could be tied in with them,' Halice chipped in. 'What if he tells them about this sword he couldn't get hold of? I'd say we should seriously think about selling it. I don't want to find I'm suddenly on the wrong side of this hunting trip.'

'I know it was a gift from your Messire, Rysh, but it could be putting us all in danger. Selling it might be best.' Livak turned an intense stare on me and I shrugged noncommittally. She and Halice were evidently up to something here.

'I really don't think we need to think about doing that,' Shiv replied just a little too firmly.

I gave him a curious look. The euphoria that I'd brought in from the paddock started to fade fast; it looked as if there was another game going on here and I started to suspect I was missing a few crucial pieces.

'You don't want him to sell, do you? Does Ryshad know just what it is that he's carrying?' Livak's emerald eyes challenged Shiv, but his gaze slid sideways.

'It's an Old Empire sword, he knows that.'

'What about the trouble he's having sleeping?' Halice chipped in.

'Are you hoping to hear all about some peculiar dreams, by any chance, Shiv?' persisted Livak.

'What exactly do you mean by that?' I gripped my goblet and cursed myself for forgetting that the Archmage could well have Shiv trawling for different fish to the rest of us.

'You tell him or I will,' Livak threatened.

'You remember I told you Planir was studying Tormalin antiquities, that was what he sent me to Viltred to collect?' Shiv scratched his ear as he struggled for words and I got a feeling I wasn't going to like what I was about to hear. 'I don't think I mentioned that some of these seem to give their owners strange dreams, detailed visions of the fall of the Empire. The Archmage wants to use them to find out more about the foundation of Hadrumal, which happened about a generation later, when the magic that governs the elements was first properly developed.'

'The mysterious city of wizards, hidden Trimon only knows where, to keep the arts of magic safe from the non-mage-born.' Halice's tone was distinctly sarcastic.

The corners of Shiv's mouth twitched downwards, betraying his irritation. 'It's where the Archmage and the most powerful wizards live and study. It's not really all that arcane.'

'Just as long as it keeps mages away from honest folk,' said Livak cuttingly.

'Most mages find it frees them from the distractions of life among the non-mage-born,' Shiv sniffed a touch pompously.

'What has this got to do with my sword?' I broke in impatiently.

'You remember when we tracked the Elietimm back to their islands last year, we found proof that the Tormalin colony lost around the fall of the Empire was not in Gidesta after all?' Shiv asked me, ignoring Livak. 'And that the Old Tormalins used this ancient magic, the aetheric enchantment that the Elietimm were using on us last year, whatever that may be exactly?'

'Yes, of course.' I looked at him suspiciously. 'It looks like the colony was somewhere on the far side of the ocean. Messire's been talking about trying to find it, Dastennin willing. Get to the point, Shiv.'

'It seems these colonists were attacked by the Elietimm but they somehow managed to disrupt the Ice Islanders' magic, not realising it would bring the roof in on the Empire at home, which also relied on using this old magic.'

I glanced at Livak in surprise. 'Did you know about this?'

She looked uncharacteristically defensive. 'Weren't you told? That old wizard, Otrick, he said they were going to tell D'Olbriot and the rest of the Tormalin Convocation.'

Shiv rubbed a hand over his mouth. 'Over the winter we've established that where we can trace the history of those artefacts that cause dreams they come from families involved in the colony. We think they may actually have belonged to colonists.'

'So?' How had they got back across the ocean then, I wondered.

'We're hoping the dreams might give us some clue as to just what the colonists did to disrupt the Elietimm magic,' said Shiv simply. 'We've been studying what little we know of aetheric spells, and so far we can't reliably detect or counter them.'

'So you want to know how to poleaxe their sorcery, in case the Elietimm decide to attack in force and with aetheric magic in support?' That made sense enough, I had to give him that, why be so secretive about it? Messire should have been informed, if no one else.

'It can't harm any of us now, other than baffle a few old priests whose miracles won't work any more.' Shiv shrugged. 'Aetheric magic was pretty well lost along with the Empire, as far as anyone this side of the ocean is concerned.'

'So I've been given this sword in the hopes that I'll start dreaming up some answers for Planir?' I could not keep an edge of outrage from my voice; how dare these wizards use Messire like a bird on a game board.

'We, that is Planir and the Council of Mages, they've been trying to match likely antiquities with people who should be similar to their original owners.' Shiv's tone grew more animated. 'You're a swordsman. Have you been having strange dreams? We might well learn something significant if you can try to remember what they are about.'

'As opposed to trying to put them out of my mind because I've been starting to wonder if my wits are turning to water and about to come trickling out of my ears, you mean?' I managed to keep my tone pretty well level; after all, an argument here would attract too much attention.

'I don't see why you should think that.' Shiv looked surprised.

That was easy for him to say; he'd not had an Elietimm enchanter turning his mind inside out. The idea of that kind of magic invading my sleeping mind made my skin crawl like the thought of wearing a pauper's shirt. I was tempted simply to hand Shiv the sword, but no – it had been Messire's Solstice gift to me and token of his admiration. I was not about to hand that over to any wizard. Arimelin willing, I'd ignore any dreams that might come.

'Whatever the colonists did, it would be worth their while for the Elietimm to know about it as well,' mused Halice. 'What if they could reverse it? Would that increase their powers? Just stopping us from finding out would mean they kept their tactical advantage. That could well be why they went after Viltred.'

I ran a hand through my hair, wincing as I snagged a tangle of curls that needed a trim. 'I'm going to get a bath before I stiffen.'

I stood abruptly and ignored Shiv's attempts to reassure me. The glossy-haired wench passed me and I caught her arm.

'I want a bath and plenty of hot water in my bedchamber, as soon as you can.' She shook off my hand, looking a little startled and I realised I had gripped her a little hard. 'Sorry.'

'I'll get it seen to, soon as I get a moment,' she said a little uncertainly, and I went upstairs to pace the room until it arrived.

I was starting to feel cold and sore and realised a little

belatedly that I must smell like a hard-ridden horse. A good
soak in nicely hot water loosened my muscles and helped soothe
away some of my indignation at what I had just learned, but
I can't say I was much happier as the water started to cool.
Hunting down Ice Islanders was one thing; I was quite content
with that task. Finding out that we might be the prey was
definitely unwelcome news and the suspicion that I'd been
somehow set up like a lamb staked out to draw wolves was
something I didn't even want to think about. Was that what
Shiv had in mind? Was it his idea or Planir's intention all
along? Just what had the Archmage told Messire anyway?
Had that devious charmer explained this peculiar business
with the dreams, or just suggested the sword would be a
suitable gift from a grateful patron? It had to be the latter,
no question; anything else wouldn't honour the oaths that
bound D'Olbriot and me together. That same oath meant I
was honour-bound to keep the blade, as well as committing
me to working with Shiv; I couldn't avoid it, but I could cursed
well make sure he wasn't keeping back anything else I needed
to know.

I propped my mirror on my knees and had a thoughtful
shave. We could play these runes reversed, couldn't we? Did
it matter if the Elietimm found us or we found them? Not
as long as the wizards could keep scrying on them, it didn't.
It certainly made no odds as far as my oath to Aiten was
concerned, I reminded myself. I just needed to make sure
that I kept alert, all my wits about me. My reflection in the
polished steel looked a little less grim and I recalled something
my father is always saying: 'Build for storms and hope for
sunshine.' It's a fair enough catchword for a stonemason and
I could do well to remember it. I shook my head at myself;
what would he think of me mixed up in a quest like this?
I imagined he would take it all with his usual calm; he'd
certainly understand once he met Livak. I hoped so; I was
relying on him to talk Mother round.

A knock on the door startled me and I turned to see the
latch lift.

'Need someone to wash your back?' Livak slid in and leaned against the door, her smile coloured by a little uncertainty in her eyes.

'If you're offering.' I held up a washcloth and shifted forward; drawing a deep breath of pure pleasure as she scoured my aching muscles with the rough towelling.

'I've borrowed some rubbing oil from Viltred too.' Livak bent down and brushed her lips against my hair. 'I thought it might help.'

'Good idea.' Stepping out of the water, I spread a towel on the bed. As I lay down I heard Livak bolt the door and smiled into the pillows; Shiv could have Livak's bed for all I cared, Halice's virtue would be safe enough.

'About what we were saying downstairs—' Livak sat beside me and rolled up her sleeves.

'I don't want to talk about it, not at the moment,' I said more sharply than I intended.

'Halice is going to see if she can get anything more out of Nyle.' Livak poured a little oil onto her hands and I smelled the sharp scent of dragonsbreath leaves. 'He seemed quite keen this afternoon, when they were discussing tactics for the game.'

'She's welcome to him.' I'd been wondering what kind of man would catch her eye.'

Livak laughed and began to lean deep into rubbing the muscles of my back. 'Halice likes men who make her feel small and feminine.'

'That must limit her choice unless there's a wrestling troupe passing through the neighbourhood,' I muttered.

'You'd be surprised; she doesn't do too badly for bedmates.'

Livak leaned over and I felt the weight of her breasts brush my back through the soft linen of her shirt. I wondered briefly if all we were going to be were bedmates, no ties binding us. As I started to speak, she kneaded a stubborn knot of muscle in my shoulder and the goose featherbed stifled my half-formed words.

'What did you say?'

'Nothing.' I stretched out under her skilful hands and

made appreciative noises as she carefully smoothed out the myriad aches.

'Still stiff?' she enquired after what seemed like half a season of pleasure.

'Only where I want to be.' Dragonsbreath has the same effect on me as most other men.

Livak giggled as I rolled over. 'I was wondering what Viltred was doing asking the ale-wife for this.'

'Forget Viltred.' I reached up for her and drew her into a fierce embrace.

She was as eager as me and shivered in delicious delight as I stripped her shirt over her head. The sight of her soft breasts tightening in the lamplight drove any thoughts of conversation clean out of my head. I reached for her with rising desire. Her answering touch was sure and firm and burned me anew with the fiery thrill of a new lover's hands and lips. She moved to my caresses eagerly, unhesitating pleasure given and received in the keen rapture of mutual exploration. For all the novelty of her body under my hands, we came together with the ease of a couple a generation wedded, moving with the fluid, instinctive rhythm that had come to us so naturally before. I drew on all the self-control I possessed until I felt the cadence of Livak's movement stumble into ecstasy and then gave myself up to the sweeping waves of delight that came crashing down to overwhelm me. We finally rested, her heartbeat pounding against mine, and I knew that my pulse would be echoing hers for a long time to come, no matter what her feelings for me might be or the prospects for our futures. Our breath mingling, we drifted into deep and refreshing sleep together.

CHAPTER THREE

Taken from the First Appendix to the Transactions of the Merchant Venturers of Col, Volume 8, 126th Year of the City's Freedom.

My esteemed brothers in commerce,

This leaves me well and in hopeful spirits, and I hope it may find you in health and prosperity. You will be surprised at this, I do not doubt, given my last missive from the chaos of Triolle.

So, to business. In the debit columns, I will not disguise from you that we face heavy losses. The port at Triolle Bay has been comprehensively sacked by the troops of the Duke of Draximal. The goods and profits of this year's trade between Triolle and Aldabreshi are now being gambled in the camps and sold to adorn the troopers' grubby trollops. Moreover, this war of theirs is no mere summer storm; if anyone tells you it will all be settled by Solstice, insist on recording odds at a gaming-house and take that fool for every Mark he has in his strongbox. It may have started with ambition for the throne but it is turning into a struggle for the most fertile land, access to the rivers and the sea, say what you will. I cannot see how Parnilesse will escape being dragged in, and with that the last decent anchorage this side of Tormalin will be no safer than a nest of pirates. Commerce in Lescar is as dead as a man with a sword through his neck.

How then can I be hopeful? Let me explain. This finds me in a village called Relshaz, no more than a collection of muddy huts on the delta of the Rel itself. Thus far the place has but one thing to recommend it: its position. Consider the advantages of a port so situated; the Rel is navigable for sizeable vessels as far as Abray and barges could penetrate even further, virtually to Dalasor. A settlement here could draw trade from most of eastern Caladhria, if the word were circulated discreetly, and should commerce in Lescar revive at all such a port would be ideally placed to garner the business and the ensuing profits.

We must be bold and move fast or we will lose this chance to control the future of trade in the Caladhrian Gulf. My sources tell me Lord Metril of Attar Bay wants to extend his anchorage and Lord Sethel of Pinerin plans to build a series of jetties along the Ferl Roads. Both proposals will be put to the Parliament at the Equinox Sessions and in this instance I do not think we will see the interminable talking in circles that those gentry commonly excel in. Both Lords have been working hard to make sure they get the backing to vote them permission; a cunning stroke has been to co-operate. I will do what I can to loose a fox in their hen-run, and in the meantime, you must find the means to start construction of a harbour before the winter storms set in. I know it will go hard with us, to find such coin in this leanest of years, but we must look beyond short-term losses to the long-term gains.

Your partner in trade,
Jeram Gilthand

The Relshaz ferry, Caladhria,
27th of Aft-Spring

No one could decide what to make of Nyle's interest in my sword, but I was soon confident we'd left that problem behind along with the mule train when we took the road west of Adrulle. This was partly to cut off a long curve of the river and partly to take in a stretch of the Linneyway, to see if we could get any scent of the second group of possible Elietimm. There was no word at any of the inns and we concluded they must have been heading for Ensaimin, if they had in fact been Ice Islanders. I didn't forget them but I certainly reckoned I could put them to the back of my mind.

Our route took us through a succession of those tedious Caladhrian market towns that become hard to tell apart after a while. Shiv's mood improved as the mages spent their evenings dabbling in their scrying bowl and determined the Elietimm that had robbed Viltred were still heading towards Relshaz. The weather grew steadily warmer as we moved south; we found ourselves riding through the heat of the days in shirt sleeves and Viltred's mood improved markedly as the sun soothed his aches and pains. The recent generation's trend for enclosure had started in southern Caladhria and the land was increasingly regulated and confined with hedges and walls, the stock sleeker and stronger as a result. We saw fewer cows and cornfields and more sheep and vineyards, the towns grew large enough to have slums and beggars and traffic on the road became more frequent. I could almost have convinced myself I was on the road running south down the lee of the mountains towards home.

My own mood improved as the weather and the countryside reminded me more and more of home. With Livak's assistance I was sleeping more soundly but had no more idea of her feelings, both of us preferring good sex to any potentially unsatisfactory conversation about what the future might hold for us. Finally the dank, murky breath of the great mouth of the Rel was carried over a rise on the morning breeze, a blend of mud, rotting wood, weed and fish. We crested the line of hills that dominated the shore to look down on the glistening city of Relshaz, a dense accumulation of whitewashed buildings clustered securely on a delta between the broad black arms of the river. The silt-laden waters from the hills of Caladhria and the plains of Lescar swept around the city and carried a great dark stain out into the shimmering sea. In the late spring sun the Gulf of Lescar was blue as a bankfisher's wing as the waves rolled in from the far horizon. I drew a deep breath and relished the tang of salt in the air; it didn't have the clean sharpness of my own rugged ocean coast, but at least it was the scent of the sea.

I soon lost even that suggestion of open waters as we followed the track winding down from the hills. The Spice Road and the River Road meet here in a broad trampled marketplace where some traders opt to do their buying and selling rather than spending time and coin taking one of the ferries to the city. We pressed through the throng of men, mules, oxen and carts with some difficulty, a handful of languages clamouring around us, dust rising to catch in our throats, taking knocks from all sides.

'Let me go first.' Shiv had his own evil-minded horse firmly in hand now Halice had taken the stitches out of his arm and I let him take the lead gladly. The thick-necked beast shouldered a brace of neat-footed mules aside and I slipped in behind, ignoring their owner's oaths. I was glad Viltred's horse did not have the brain to be unsettled by the chaos as I saw Livak having to take the harness horse by the bridle to help get it moving. Halice snapped the whip over its ears and it skipped forward reluctantly.

'How long will we have to wait for a ferry?' I shouted above the racket as we drew to a halt by the weed-draped wooden walkway, now beached on the noisome mud as the tide drew the river down into the central channel.

Livak shrugged. 'Anything up to a full chime, probably.'

As she spoke the sound of bells carried across the turbid waters.

'I do like to be somewhere with proper clocks and regular chimes,' she commented. I had to agree my own city-bred blood preferred it.

As it turned out, we crossed the river in less time than I had feared, for once I had the measure of the press of traffic I slipped ahead to greet the lading-master, giving him a warm handshake with a Caladhrian Mark in it. When a carrier's coach rattled down the walkway to the broad, flat deck of a ferry, leaving just enough room for us and our gig, he waved us on ahead of a very put-out wine merchant.

'That was lucky,' Shiv commented.

'No such thing,' I shook my head. 'The trick is knowing how things get done on a dockside.'

We stood at the rail and watched the gangs of shackled and sweating slaves lean into their oaken staves to drive the giant capstans that wound the great chains carrying the ferry across the dark and swirling waters of the river, the bustle of traffic waiting to leave the city seething behind them. Mud-covered children skipped and scavenged among the detritus on the exposed flats, hurrying to the ferry as it drew close to the shore, little hands upturned for any coppers.

'You'd think they'd build a real bridge nowadays,' Viltred remarked sourly. 'On the Caladhrian side at least.'

Halice joined us, her limp more in evidence than usual thanks to Shiv's horse treading on her sound foot.

'You can get fined for that kind of talk,' she warned. 'Relshazris take their independence very seriously and the river's saved them more than once. Anyone trying to build a bridge here gets executed.'

I nodded, 'I'd heard that—'

'When we get clear of the ferry, we will be heading for the Arril district,' Viltred interrupted with an air of importance.

'I'll drive,' he added, turning his back on Halice to climb into the gig.

'Where are we going?' I asked with some surprise.

'I have quite a few contacts here,' smiled Viltred with a somewhat irritating superiority.

'So do Livak and I,' said Halice mildly, yielding the reins without fuss.

'That's right.' Livak spurred her horse forward when it threatened to baulk at the planks of the walkway. 'It'll save time if we split up; we'll see what we can find out and meet you – where?'

'No, absolutely not,' Shiv spoke over her decisively. 'Let's stick together for the moment. There are some people I have to talk to before I decide what we do next. In the meantime, I don't want to alert anyone who might have a loose mouth to our presence here.'

Livak exchanged a glance with Halice that suggested they were going to take this about as readily as a purse of Lescari Marks. I'd have to keep an eye on the pair of them, I decided; Livak had a real problem with taking orders, I knew that, even from someone as easy-going as Shiv. I looked across as she stood staring down into the nameless debris that the water was bringing back to the end of the floating jetty. How were we ever going to reconcile my oaths and duty with her stubborn independence and love of life in the margins? The carrier's coach took its weary passengers off on the last leg of their journey and we soon cleared the ferry area. Halice and Livak exchanged a quiet word and rueful glance at Shiv's back as we passed an inn whose sign was a plume of feathers.

'Good ale there?' I enquired casually.

'Good ale,' confirmed Halice. 'Reasonably honest gambling, fairly safe beds and generally reliable information as well.'

'Wizards' fancy magic is all very well,' Livak edged her horse closer to mine. 'I'd like to back it up with some local knowledge bought and paid for.'

'You'll get no argument from me.' I looked around curiously. 'How well do you know Relshaz?'

'We've been here a couple of times over the last year or so.' Livak reined in her horse suddenly as a man stumbled in front of her. 'Festival gambling mostly, it depends how the runes are turning. The thing is, we know people here and they know us.'

'Make sure you tell Shiv,' I said firmly.

'Is he going to listen?' countered Livak sourly.

Viltred wove the gig through the busy streets, pausing frequently as traffic bunched around the narrow bridges crossing Relshaz's innumerable canals. I have to say, the more I saw, the less and less impressed I became. Close up, the famous White City of the Gulf is distinctly grubby and chipped, especially on the landward side. I saw green stains smudging the painted walls and garbage in the waters, the smell rising with the temperature as the sun climbed. Furtive beggars lurked in the shadows of narrow alleys and entries and I was glad we hadn't arrived at night. I sat straighter in my saddle and twitched my cloak back from my shoulder to clear my sword to deter anyone who might be thinking of trying his luck.

We entered an area of warehouses, manufactures, stores being winched to the tops of tall buildings by teams of horses sweating to draw ropes through lines of pulleys. Women moved handcarts of identical sections of furniture and metalwork, segments of tables, chair legs, all on their way to the next workshop for the following artisan to earn his pittance at piece work. Children ran messages, held horses, swept crossings. The press of traffic distanced Livak and me from the gig a little and I tugged at her sleeve to get her attention.

'What's the Arril district like?'

Livak shook her head. 'I don't know it, not as such; I'm usually in and around the inns and gambling houses and the Arril quarter is strictly solid houses for respectable merchants and the like. We manage the odd venture into the smart addresses along the Gulf front, but that's about it.'

'Where do you suppose some Ice Islanders would be making a den in this labyrinth?'

'Any one of a handful of places.' Livak turned to look at

me, her expression intense. 'Halice and I know people who could find out. Shiv's got to let us use our contacts.'

Viltred took a side street, the gig bouncing over the cobbles between tall houses that promised rather better things of the city. The white shining walls of the brick houses were freshly painted, their balconies already bright with pots of flowers and noisy with people enjoying the sunshine. Women dressed in fine silks passed us with clean and sometimes cheerful children in tow as they bargained with hucksters, gossiped with friends and ordered their servants around.

Viltred halted in front of a broad, high gate set in a wall of fine-dressed stone and climbed down stiffly from his seat. 'Wait here.'

His knock was answered almost immediately by a neatly uniformed porter.

'Please tell Madam that Viltred Sern is here,' said the old man in flawless Relshazri and with a courtly air that seemed to add five fingers to his meagre height. I realised with some surprise that this was his native tongue; given the fluency of his Caladhrian, I'd assumed that was his birthplace.

Livak raised a speculative eyebrow at me as the gates were opened. We were ushered into a spotless courtyard that gave in turn on to a broad swathe of lawn, ornamented with a sparkling fountain and blossoming fruit trees. Two grooms hurried out from the stables that separated the stone-built house from the street and took our horses while the porter led us towards a highly polished door. He opened it and ushered us onto a long sunlit salon with fine muslin curtains billowing around tall windows open to the spring breeze. My dusty boots rasped on the polished floor, and I noticed I was not the only one avoiding the silk rugs that splashed turquoise and leaf green across the dark wood. Watered silk hangings softened the walls with the same tones and framed an interesting collection of statuary and ceramics, nothing extraordinarily valuable but each piece chosen with an expert eye to the composition of the room. Elegance hung in the air with the scent of fresh flowers.

Viltred strode over to an elegant silk-upholstered day-bed and settled himself with enviable aplomb. 'Wine, thank you.' He waved a dismissive hand at the flunkey who took himself off at some speed.

I took a chair at a satiny fruitwood table and tried to match Viltred's air of ease, fighting a feeling that I should be standing at the alert as I would in formal attendance on my patron at home.

'Viltred, my dear!' A door opened and a superbly built woman swept in with a rustle of yellow silk and perfume. She embraced the old wizard with some passion and sat herself beside him, tucking her dainty feet under her before sweeping a queenly gaze round the rest of us.

'This is Mellitha.' Viltred kissed her hand with a courtly grace at odds with his travel-stained appearance and I had to curb an unexpected smile of admiration for the old mage.

'Who are your companions?' She arched a finely plucked eyebrow in a face as flawless as the porcelain vase behind her head. I wondered how old she was; her chestnut hair was finely brindled with white and I could see a tracery of fine lines around her keen grey eyes.

Viltred introduced us. The flunkey returned with the wine and was dismissed, our elegant hostess pouring for us herself.

'How are the children?' enquired Viltred with what sounded like genuine interest.

'Tref's travelling through Ensaimin, painting portraits of all the little lordlings with pretensions of grandeur.' Mellitha smoothed her expensive gown, bright with embroidered flowers, over her generous curves, and seated herself again.

'Tia's still in Hadrumal with her father; she's learning the book-binding trade and they've agreed she'll take over when he retires in a year or so. Sanan is getting married soon, a lovely girl from Col; her father owns a string of inns so they'll move there after the wedding. Patrin's soldiering in Lescar, which I'm less than happy about, as you can imagine, but I heard from her a few weeks since. She'll be back in Relshaz for Solstice and I'm going to try to persuade her to come into the business with me now.'

'I would certainly be happier if she did that,' nodded Viltred.

Mellitha laughed. 'There's no use you sounding so fatherly; I've told you often enough I've no idea if she's your daughter.'

I looked at Viltred; so the old bird had spread his wings in his younger days, it seemed, raising his crest to good effect, and he must have had some song to charm a woman like this. Mellitha was evidently a woman of substance and independence, no mere ornament in her silks and scents.

Shiv coughed. 'I'm afraid this isn't just a social call, madam.'

She dimpled a smile at him. 'I didn't think it was. How can I help you?' She smoothed a hand over her immaculate coiffure and was suddenly all business.

Shiv told her our tale with admirable conciseness, given the frequent interruptions by Viltred, not all of which I thought relevant. Mellitha surprised me a little by asking for my observations and I could see her eyes were alert, notwithstanding her demure self-possession. In a way it reminded me of conversations with my patron's current paramour, Lady Channis, one of those daunting women whose beauty is nevertheless a lesser asset than her wits. Halice and Livak sat silently sipping the cool white wine and occasionally exchanging a glance. I saw Mellitha looking at them as they shared one of those moments and realised this was a woman who was going to want to see both sides of this coin before she put it in her purse.

'Do you think you can help us?' Shiv said finally.

'I can certainly make some enquiries about foreigners in black livery for you.' Mellitha moved to seat herself at an elegant desk and took out smoothly expensive reed paper and ink. 'People like that should stand out, even in Relshaz.'

'Be careful about drawing attention to yourself,' warned Shiv. 'These are dangerous men, killers.'

'I'm a tax contractor,' said Mellitha confidently. 'I'm supposed to ask questions and I have plenty of people working for me who understand discretion.'

'You mean you don't get all your information through cunning spells and infallible sorcery?' Viltred laughed. 'That's what I heard last time I was here.'

'You're a mage?' I couldn't help the surprise in my question.

'I am, but that's not my main business. Still, I make sure I'm seen working enough magic to keep the rumour mill fed. It comes in useful,' Mellitha smiled sunnily. 'Most folk don't see any point in lying about their income when they're convinced you can see through desks and read their ledgers.'

Livak laughed and I saw she was looking more at ease, recognising Mellitha as a woman moulded from the same clay as herself. Should that worry me, I wondered wryly?

'I should scry for the thieves,' Viltred broke in. 'You might see something which you recognise.'

'It could help you direct your enquiry agents.' Shiv agreed and I murmured my own assent.

Mellitha rose and smoothed her gown over her ample hips. 'That's something we can do now. I'll need a few things, so please build me a picture of these people while I fetch them.'

She rang a silver bell and doors opened to admit a pair of maids who rapidly laid a selection of elegant lunch dishes on the sideboard.

These went initially ignored as Viltred sat forward and concentrated on creating an image of the Elietimm in the air above the table. Livak, Halice and I watched, absorbed as the old mage wove skeins of blue light into first wisps, then sketchy shapes, then solid figures with every colour and detail precise. Mellitha collected a bowl, a flagon of water and some small vials. Shiv was watching her preparations with interest.

'What are you using?'

'Perfumery oils.' Mellitha dripped precise amounts into the water. 'I've been working on a few new things lately and this has been producing very good results.'

Viltred came to sit beside her and the three mages peered
into the fragrant bowl. Mellitha looked at the image of the Ice
Islanders for a long moment then set the water spinning, the
oils on the surface gleaming in the green glow of her magic.
Dark, indistinct images half formed and then dissolved. Faces
loomed out of the depths and then floated away into nothing.
A stone floor suddenly appeared sharp and clear, and then
vanished just as quickly.

I looked over at Halice and Livak; we exchanged a shrug
and went to get something to eat.

'How very odd.' Mellitha sounded distinctly put out. 'I can't
keep the spell focused and I know I'm not doing anything out
of the ordinary. The best I can say is they're definitely in the
city but I can't even begin to guess where.'

Shiv sat back and ran a hand through his hair. 'I don't
think you've been doing anything wrong. There's something
interfering with the spell. I've seen it before, this is what has
been happening to us—'

'Are you quite sure it's an external problem?' asked Viltred,
doubt plain in his eyes.

Mellitha gave Viltred a level look. 'Who's the one with water
affinity here?'

'What do we do now?' Shiv's face was a study in frustration
and I couldn't blame him. We were finally in the same place
as our quarry and the wizards' magic chose now to desert us
again. I wondered how soon we could make contact with Livak
and Halice's associates.

'Wait a moment,' Mellitha held up a brightly ringed hand.
'You know, I came across something like this a few years ago.'
She rummaged through a pile of small journals in her desk
drawer. 'Here it is, a fine art dealer whose income didn't
add up. I tried to follow him on a journey to Tormalin and
something fouled up my magic for a couple of days.'

'What was it?' demanded Viltred.

Mellitha shrugged, leafing through her notes, a frown marring her forehead. 'I never was exactly sure. It was all rather
odd; he was trading in religious art, shrine statuary, the sort

of thing people used to keep in their houses. As close as I could tell the problem was caused by something in his possession. I wasn't even sure he knew about it. I mean, as soon as he'd sold on all the votive figures, the scrying came clear and I was able to see just how much coin he was making above his voting declaration and where he was banking it with a goldsmith in Toremal.'

She looked up at the stillness in the room and glanced at each of us in turn. 'I take it I've just said something significant?'

'It's complicated,' Shiv temporised.

Mellitha fixed him with a steely gaze. 'Young man, I am one of the leading tax contractors in this city. In order to purchase the rights to collect taxes, I have to calculate a tender that the Magistracy will accept while setting taxes that people will pay without too much objection. Expenses are the contractor's responsibility, so making my own profit adds a further complexity. I spend my life dealing with complicated matters.'

Shiv had the grace to blush and started to explain what the Archmage had discovered so far about the largely unknown, aetheric magic that the Elietimm could wield with such frightening ease.

The ocean dock at Zyoutessela,
before the watchtower was built on the heights
and while the old fishmarket still stood

The circle of the harbour was packed with vessels and not
the fishing boats that usually swung from the quay sides.
Tall-masted, high-sided ocean ships clustered awkwardly along
docks built for smaller craft, each busy with sailors and less
agile folk loading and stowing a wide variety of gear.

'Where do you want this, then, Esquire?' A docker halted,
red-faced as he balanced a weighty sack on one shoulder.

'That's beans, is it?' Temar checked the stamp on the leather
tag and then ran a careful finger down his list. 'Forehold, next
to the little casks.'

The man grunted and moved away, several others following him.

'Wait a moment.' Temar moved to check their loads. 'Fine,
go with him.'

He watched a second line of porters carrying caskets and
leather bags down to the accommodation deck, making sure
each had the charcoal mark that signified official permission.
As the last man disappeared down the ladder he heaved a sigh
and glanced up to check the sun; with all the noise, he hadn't
heard any chimes since dawn and had no idea how much of
the day had passed. At least it wasn't too hot this early in the
season, he mused, and the rain that had plagued their previous
days' labours was holding off.

Just as he thought this, a chance shift in the wind brought
a faint brazen ringing to Temar's ears. Dockers and porters
turned to look at him expectantly.

'Noon break!' confirmed Temar with a loud shout, the

workmen's faces mirroring his own relief at the prospect of a rest and something to eat.

He tucked his lists into the front of his dull-green jerkin and made his way through the crowds towards one of the fisher-inns, opening a waxed note-tablet pulled from one pocket and carefully scoring through the tasks he'd accomplished that morning. More were left than cancelled but at least it was all progress. Temar smiled a little ruefully to himself; what would Lachald think if he could see him now, ink-stained hands and charcoal smudging his plain cuffs?

'You're looking very cheerful, Esquire D'Alsennin.'

Temar looked up to see he had nearly walked into a thin man with a shock of grey hair swept back from a hatchet-thin face. Green eyes, pale as a cat's, stared at him, unblinking.

'Messire Den Fellaemion.' Temar made a quick reverence and wiped his palm on his breeches before offering it.

'How goes the loading?' Den Fellaemion acknowledged Temar's courtesy with a brief handshake.

'Very well, Messire, we should have all the dried goods aboard by the end of the day and almost all the accommodation problems have been resolved.'

'Good,' the lean man nodded approvingly. 'Do you have a current lading list for my clerks?'

'You'll have it by sunset,' Temar promised, hesitating a moment then taking out his note-tablet again to add it to his list of things to do. Better look like a child learning letters in a dame-school, he felt, than risk forgetting.

A faint smile flickered across the nobleman's pallid lips. 'Take some refreshment with me, D'Alsennin.'

'Gladly.' It may have sounded more like a command than an invitation but Temar was too thirsty to worry about that.

Den Fellaemion looked round the quayside and signalled to a lackey with a wicker basket slung over one shoulder. 'Let's find a quiet corner.'

That was an easier task than it would have been before the noon chime, but the dock was all but deserted now as the toiling throng pressed into the taverns and clamoured for a meal. Temar led the way to a ledge cut into a rocky outcrop where he'd seen women mending crab traps. He took the wineskin offered and quenched his considerable thirst gratefully.

'Ah, excellent.' Den Fellaemion opened the basket and took out fresh bread, spiced chicken, dry-cured ham and a yellow cheese wrapped in butter muslin. He passed Temar a dish with its lid tied and sealed. 'See what's in that, will you?'

It proved to be a medley of fruits in sweet wine, and Temar's eyes brightened.

'Den Rannion's lady still seems convinced I need feeding up,' observed Den Fellaemion in an amused tone. 'I think there's enough for two here; do help yourself.'

'Thank you.' Temar pulled his knife from his belt and cut himself a generous slice of the crumbly cheese.

'There's something I need to mention to you.' The older man leaned back and closed his eyes as he enjoyed a gleam of spring sunshine that picked out the subtle brocade in his severe grey clothing.

Temar hurriedly ran through his recent duties in his mind but was unable to find any immediate cause for concern. 'Yes?' Perhaps the Messire had some new responsibility for him.

'With your House providing four ships, provisioning several more besides and many of your tenants signing on for the colony, you are suddenly one of the major sponsors of our expedition, did you realise this?'

'My grandfather is the Head of our House; he deserves that honour.' Temar wondered what Den Fellaemion meant.

'Your grandfather is not here. You are.' The green eyes opened and fixed Temar with a piercing stare. 'Many people will be looking to you as their patron, both before we sail and once we settle across the ocean. You will have a significant client base, if you choose to exploit it. What are your intentions in that area?'

Temar spread his hands uncertainly. 'I hadn't really thought about it.'

'It is time that you did,' said Den Fellaemion crisply. 'If

you are intending to live off the backs of your tenants in the style of such Houses as Nemith, I think our venture can do without you, despite the resources you offer. If, however, you intend to take a full part in leading the colony, shouldering your obligations and responsibilities, then I can see you could even hope to become a valued deputy to Den Rannion and myself. There are precious few of the noble class involved in this expedition and since the commonalty will look to us, as they are used to doing, how we conduct ourselves will have a major impact on the success or otherwise of the colony.'

Temar abruptly snapped his mouth shut and swallowed hard before answering. 'D'Alsennin has always been a House most conscious of its duties to its tenants and the interests of the Empire,' he said stiffly.

Den Fellaemion regarded him, unsmiling. 'Then would you care to explain why you have been sampling the favours of nearly every willing maiden who has crossed your path since you arrived here? There are many outmoded traditions that I intend to leave behind on this dockside and the right of a Sieur or his designate to make free with the female tenantry is certainly one of them.'

Taken completely unawares, Temar said the first thing that came into his head. 'My grandfather wishes me to marry—'

'I do not recommend choosing a wife by trying her paces between the sheets; you test horses before purchase, not women, if you want peace at your hearth side anyway.' Den Fellaemion's sudden smile wiped away his stern expression. 'Keep your breeches laced, Temar. We are a small community and I don't want you raising expectations or outrage by mistaking a lass's meaning.'

Temar blushed and ran a hand through his hair. 'Of course, Messire, I hadn't been thinking—'

'No harm done.' Den Fellaemion stood suddenly and waved to someone on the far side of the harbour. 'Guinalle, come and join us!'

Temar looked round to see a young woman wrapped in a blue-grey cloak picking her way carefully across the cobbles slick with spray. She was of less than common height but neatly made with an open, heart-shaped face.

'Messire, Esquire,' she greeted them each in turn before seating herself composedly on a crab trap.

'Do have something to eat.' Den Fellaemion wiped his knife on a scrap of muslin and sheathed it with a decisive gesture. 'I have much to do, Guinalle; I'll see you at seventh chime, at the colony warehouse.'

'As you wish.' The girl took some bread and felt under her cloak for her own knife.

'Let me.' Temar cut her a slice. 'Cheese, ham or chicken?'

'Cheese, thank you.'

'The ham's very good.' Temar's knife hovered over it. 'Let me cut you some.'

'Not today, thank you.' Guinalle's tone was polite but firm. 'Perhaps another time.'

She looked up to see Temar's puzzled frown. 'At the dark of both moons, I make due observance to Ostrin.'

'You're a priestess?' Temar couldn't think of anyone less likely to be sworn to the god of blood-letting than this mild-faced female.

'An acolyte, of Larasion, but I observe the courtesies to all the gods.' Guinalle's self-possession did not waver and a glint of gold sparked in her warm brown eyes.

Since Temar could not think of any response to that, they ate in silence for a little while, Temar looking past Guinalle to the harbour wall and the open seas beyond. It made sense to have some priests and acolytes along, he supposed; seeking divine favour could certainly do no harm. He looked at Guinalle's modest cloak and her long nut-brown hair, unadorned with any clasp or jewel. The girl was probably one of the foundlings or orphans taken in by a large shrine and educated by them; without kin, she'd have no ties to this side of the ocean. He smiled at her. She was a tempting armful, no question.

'If you need any help, any advice, any introductions, don't hesitate to ask.' He moved a little closer. 'Do you have a lodging organised?'

'Thank you, but I'm sure my uncle will see to everything.'

Temar's gaze followed her gesture and saw Den Fellaemion's narrow back, an arm pointing emphatically to something in a sack.

'The Messire is your uncle?'

'His late wife was my father's sister.' Guinalle untied her cloak to replace her knife, its plain sheath on a girdle of gold chain, complete with jewelled pomander, silver mesh purse, several keys and a chased silver note case. Her dove-grey dress, though plainly styled, was of unimpeachable cloth.

'I didn't realise.' Temar hurriedly tried to remember what he knew of Den Fellaemion's family. His wife had been a daughter of Tor Priminale, hadn't she? Even from a cadet line of the House, this demure girl could claim precedence over half the nobles at a Convocation, if she was so minded.

Temar stood and made a formal reverence. 'I must be about my business, but I am at your service, should you require me.'

Guinalle looked up at him, squinting slightly into the sun.

'Thank you, Esquire,' she said gravely, but Temar had an uncomfortable feeling a smile was hiding behind those full lips.

He walked briskly back along the quay, growing busy again as people hurried to complete their tasks. There was an air of expectation now. The moons would soon be sending a double tide to speed them on their quest and the ships had to be ready to reach the unknown lands with as much summer as possible left to them.

'Temar!'

'Not now, Vahil.' Temar's step did not falter as he continued on his way.

'Oh, come on, let's find a drink.' Vahil matched Temar's stride and looked around with lively interest. 'These inns must have done more trade since Equinox than they've had in the last generation,' he observed with a laugh. 'So, what are the bawdy-houses like? Where does a fisherman go to plant his anchor round here?'

'I'd stay well clear, if I were you,' advised Temar, his expression serious. 'You'll end up with a dose of the itch or crotch lice the size of blackbeetles.'

'You're not serious?' Vahil's square jaw fell slightly, his hazel eyes dismayed.

'No, I'm not.' Temar shook his head with a grin. 'I've no idea what the brothels are like; I've not been looking for whores.'

'Plenty of girls looking to start their adventures before they set sail?'

'I wouldn't advise that either; it'll only lead to inappropriate expectations or misunderstandings.' Temar kept any tremor out of his voice but was glad Vahil kept looking in the other direction until he felt the faint wash of colour ebb from his face.

'What's a man to do for excitement then?' Vahil turned and his expression of broad good humour faded a little. 'The road's too bad to get to the Gulf side of the city and back in an evening, and Mother will raise three kinds of riot if I stay out all night.'

He stared back up the long slope where a tree-lined track wound up to the low saddle of land that broke the line of mountains marching down to the Cape of Winds. Temar looked too; tempted by the thought of a night sampling the entertainments offered by the larger part of the town on the far side of the isthmus.

'I only came over to bring Mother a message from Elsire and now Father's saying I should stay until we sail.' Vahil was grumbling, but Temar's thoughts had already moved on.

'Someone'll have to do something about making up that roadway when the colony really takes off,' he said slowly. 'Hauling sleds full of fish up gravel is all very well, but we'll really need a decent footing for carts and mules, proper cobbles at very least.'

'Saedrin save me, you really are taking this seriously!' Vahil laughed in disbelief.

'It wouldn't hurt you to do the same,' replied Temar, nettled. 'This colony's going to be the future of your House, isn't it?'

'Oh, my father takes care of all that,' Vahil said airily. 'Come on, let's get a drink, there must be game of runes going somewhere.'

He draped a long arm round Temar's shoulders, who shook it off in sudden irritation.

'I've got work to do; I'm the only one there is, since Saedrin saw fit to find his keys for my father and uncles.'

Vahil stood dismayed, contrition in his rough-skinned face. 'I'm sorry, singing out of tune again, you know me. All right then, what can I do to help?'

'Pick up that bale?' Temar suggested with a suspicion of malice.

Vahil's brows rose as he hefted the weight awkwardly on to one shoulder and followed Temar down the quayside.

'Put it in the forehold.' Temar pulled out his lists and began giving concise instructions to the men who were drifting back from their break. Vahil looked at him for a long moment, shrugged, shed his precisely cut and satin-trimmed jerkin and joined the line of porters moving the stacks of cargo steadily on to the vessels.

'I'll want you as a witness,' he warned Temar after a while, taking a pause to wipe sweat from his blunt-featured face. 'You're to swear to my parents that I put in a day's honest work, vows to Misaen and everything, if necessary.'

'Half a day, if you see it through,' Temar corrected him with a wicked grin.

'I see I should have got involved in this sooner,' Vahil shouted back as he lifted one of the dwindling number of bundles on the cobbles, 'then I could be the one sitting there chewing my pen-holder.'

'Get on with it, or I'll dock your pay.' Temar waved his list in a fine gesture of dismissiveness.

This sort of by-play kept the other workers amused and Temar was pleased to see the day's cargo loaded and securely stowed before the sun started sinking into the mountains that dipped down to the isthmus before rising again to form the savage cliffs and reefs around the Cape of Winds.

'You can't say I haven't earned a drink now?' Vahil looked ruefully at his reddened hands as Temar dismissed the dockers with thanks and instructions for the morning.

'I'll buy,' nodded Temar.

Vahil slung his jerkin over one shoulder and they made their way to an ale-house. 'I am interested in this colony idea, you know,' he said abruptly. 'The Empire needs something like this, to give people hope, something positive to work for and to build upon, now that our respected Emperor, Nemith the Witless, has managed to lose us the provinces. My father says the land out there is good for crops and stock, there are metals and even gems to be had, everything we need. That's where our future's going to be, Temar, and it's going to be more than we could ever imagine, I'd lay coin on it.'

'With your luck at wagers lately, that's not much encouragement.' Temar pushed a mug across the sticky table-top.

'Do I hear the mule criticising the ass for his ears?' Vahil raised his thick eyebrows. 'Remind me, just how much was it you lost in that brothel game last time we went to Toremal together?'

Temar's reply was lost as Vahil turned to a messenger who tapped him on the shoulder.

'You are expected to dine with your parents, Esquire, and the D'Alsennin too.' The lackey nodded a quick reverence to Temar.

'Dast's teeth, that's what I came to tell you. I clean forgot, we were having such a lovely time hauling your sacks around for you.' Vahil hastily drained his tankard and stood, wrenching his jerkin on with a nasty sound of snapping stitches. 'Come on, I think we've got a guest coming, niece of Den Fellaemion's or something.'

'You really are hopeless, you know that!' Temar fumbled in his belt-pouch for his hair clasp as they hurried through the town after the servant. He tugged at his jerkin to try to lose some of the creases and folded back the cuffs of his shirt to hide the worst of the grime.

'Vahil!' Messire Den Rannion was waiting on the step of the

modest house he was renting, displeasure plain on his usually genial face.

'I was helping Temar with loading his cargo.' Vahil was unabashed. 'It's a marvellous way to work up an appetite! Just let me have a quick wash and we'll be right down.'

'Lend Temar a clean shirt!' his father shouted up the stairs.

'Take your time, dear.' Maitresse Den Rannion's placid voice followed them. 'It's all right, Ancel,' she reassured her husband. 'I allowed time for them to be late when I gave Cook the menu.'

It never ceased to amaze Temar that someone as persistently disorganised as Vahil could be born of two such efficient and capable parents. He grabbed the ewer and took possession of the washstand with scant apology.

'Find some clean linen, will you?' he demanded.

'Yes, Messire, at once, Messire, anything else, Messire?' Vahil pulled open a drawer and tossed a couple of shirts on to the bed.

Temar shivered, bare-chested as he reached for one of them. He pulled it on and grimaced at his reflection in the inadequate glass; he'd have to wear his work-soiled jerkin to hide the fact the shirt was both too short in the body and too wide in the shoulder. At least it was clean and, with luck, the quality would be more noticeable than the fit.

'Come on.'

Vahil was sorting through a tray of oddments with unhurried good humour. 'Just a moment, where did I put the cursed thing? Ah!' He pulled a scrap of leather thong out of his hair and snapped a rather florid gold clasp into his wiry, chestnut locks. 'The perfect gentleman!'

Temar smiled, shaking his head. Vahil took great pleasure in assailing the heights of fashion, unbothered by his incongruous stoutness or the pockmarks pitting his cheerful face.

A bell rang and they hurried downstairs to find Messire Den Rannion enjoying a quiet glass of wine by the fireside with his guest.

'This is Guinalle, Demoiselle Tor Priminal.' He rose and bowed to her, Temar and Vahil doing the same with the instincts borne of childhood training. Guinalle answered with an elegant curtsey, spreading her flame-coloured skirts in a rustle of silk.

'I gather you have already met, D'Alsennin?' Den Rannion passed Temar a fine glass goblet of richly fragrant red wine.

'We have.' Temar was heartened to see a friendly answering smile on Guinalle's face.

'I don't see much point in Imperial ceremony when we're eating in the parlour; do sit yourselves down.' Maitresse Den Rannion swept in ahead of several servants with laden trays; for all her claims to informality, she was splendid in a full-skirted sapphire gown, silver combs glinting in an immaculate coiffure.

'Demoiselle.'

Temar watched with some irritation as Vahil managed to offer his arm first and escort Guinalle to a seat at a comfortable distance from the hearth. Temar took the chair across from her, despite the warmth of the fire on his back.

'So, my dear, you are recently arrived from Sarrat, I hear?' The Maitresse's eyes were wide in her plump, powdered face.

'Two days since.' Guinalle smiled politely as she reached for a dish of spiced beans and served herself a modest portion.

Temar passed her a plate of cheeses lightly fried in herbs and noted that the table bore an unusually wide choice of meatless delicacies. The Maitresse had always enjoyed a reputation among other women for being remarkably well informed, although at the cost of being dismissed as an inveterate gossip by men such as his grandfather.

'Your uncle and I are extremely grateful that you agreed to leave your studies and join us.' Messire Den Rannion regarded a glazed onion tartlet with some suspicion and took a slice of bloody beef instead. 'We are sorely in need of expertise in the higher techniques of Artifice.'

Temar managed not to drop the plate of baked beets he was trying to offer Guinalle but it was a close run thing. He cleared his throat and tried not to stare at her as he took a drink of water.

'I thought you'd said you had plenty of message-takers and the like?' Vahil commented as he skewered a couple of slices of peppered lamb with his knife point.

'Indeed?' Guinalle's attention sharpened slightly. 'What manner of people are they, Messire?'

'Oh, mainly clerks, stewards and the like, people with sufficient instruction to send messages to another trained mind, but little beyond that.' Messire began pouring everyone more wine. 'Many of them have been displaced as the Empire draws in and, frankly, there is less need for such accomplishments these days.'

'Just how far can one send a message using Artifice?' Vahil looked expectantly at Guinalle.

'As yet we have discovered no limit in terms of distance,' replied Guinalle easily. 'The attainments of the practitioner are what determine how far and with what clarity he or she can reach another's mind.'

'We will have people with the expertise to send messages across the ocean, won't we?' A faint shadow of concern flickered in the Maitresse's eyes as she looked to her husband. 'We shan't be cut off from home? That's what you told me, Ancel.'

'That is one thing that my uncle has requested I ascertain.' Guinalle smiled with serene confidence as she reached for a tray of stuffed apples.

Temar passed her a bowl of onion sauce. 'You're not actually joining the colony, then?' Of course, it would be stupid to expect such a well-connected and evidently well-educated girl to give up all her advantages.

'Oh, I am,' Guinalle assured him. 'It's a tremendous opportunity for me.'

'How so?' Vahil looked intrigued.

Guinalle wiped her fingers on her napkin before continuing. 'These days, Artifice is mainly used to send messages, to find those lost or absconded, for truth-saying in the Justiciary, things like that. All of this is essential work and in recent generations has been vital in maintaining the Empire. Don't think I don't value those trained in such skills, I do, but there are far more uses of Artifice that we simply have no need for in the present day. Joining your colony should give me opportunities to test their efficacy.'

Temar got the impression this was a speech she had given before.

'What sort of thing are you talking about.' Vahil leaned his elbows on the table, intrigued, waving away his mother's offer of a portion of chicken.

'Well, for instance, there are ways to understand the speech of people who don't know your tongue; how are we to try those when everyone this side of Solura speaks Tormalin? Even the Forest Folk and Mountain Men use it as the language of commerce and learning these days.'

'There has been no trace of people living in Kel Ar'Ayen, the land across the Ocean.' Messire Den Rannion looked up from his plate, faint concern in his eyes.

Guinalle smiled demurely. 'That's merely one example. Would you find it useful if I could tell you exactly where game was hiding in a thicket? If we find predators there, wolves and the like, would you like me to hide your trail from them, set wards to keep them clear of your stock?'

'You could do that?' Temar began to feel Vahil was over-doing the keen interest just a little.

'Talagrin granting,' Guinalle nodded confidently. 'There are ways to request that Saedrin open the way between the worlds and to travel from place to place or to move goods, covering many leagues in little more than a breath. One can request Maewelin to quit her rights of decay in food, to purify water, to hasten the rotting of waste to put fresh heart into soil. The correct incantations to Ostrin can staunch mortal wounds or fell a beast painlessly in its stall for the butcher. Drianon's care can keep women from conceiving and then ease them into child-bed at the time of their choosing; Larasion's mercies will keep frost from tender crops or send rain in time of drought. Artifice gives us the means to call upon such bounties.'

She looked at the awed faces round the table and Temar saw a faint blush on her cheekbones as she helped herself to some salt.

'I had no idea.' Maitresse was plainly astounded, social graces notwithstanding.

'These days medicine and good husbandry mean we have practical remedies for such things,' shrugged Guinalle. 'In many ways that is preferable.'

'And anyone can learn how to do these things you mention?' Vahil was gaping, his meal forgotten.

'Misaen marks some folk for his own, for some reason, and they cannot; but most people can learn the lesser tricks of Artifice, if they care to.' There was a serious undercurrent to Guinalle's light tone. 'It is a question of scholarship, of applying oneself. The demands become greater the more complex the tasks that are undertaken and so, inevitably, fewer people find they have the mental aptitude for such rigorous study.'

'But you do.' Temar looked at her, wondering if she ever stepped down from the lofty heights of such learning to tread a measure in everyday dances.

'I have found so.' There was appropriate modesty in Guinalle's reply but no hint of apology. Her eyes met Temar's across the candles with a hint of a challenge.

He smiled at her, sufficiently intrigued not to be daunted by her talents or her relations. 'I think you will be a valuable addition to our expedition, as well as one of its leading ornaments.' He raised his glass gallantly.

'You'd better not let my sister hear you saying that!' Vahil laughed robustly. 'Elsire's determined she's going to be the leader of beauty and fashion; I reckon it's the only reason she's coming, to get away from the competition at court.'

'Never mind that,' Maitresse Den Rannion looked round the table. 'If everyone's served, let us eat.'

The House of Mellitha Esterlin, Relshaz, 28th of Aft-Spring

It must have been the touch of salt in the air, muddy though it was; I realised I had been dreaming of home when a servant's discreet knock woke me the following morning. It was a strange dream, though; something felt not quite right about the city, but as I opened my eyes the thought evaporated. I smiled as I shaved at an elegant marble washstand; my father would certainly be impressed with the quality of Relshazri stonecutting, for all that the city was largely built on little better than a mire.

'Good morning.'

I turned to see Livak watching me, fresh in a pale-lemon linen tunic over a loose divided skirt in something like the Aldabreshi style that was fashionable in the summer seasons last year back home. The soft folds paradoxically revealed her shapely legs in a more tempting fashion than her usual breeches and the colour set off her red hair nicely.

'You look very elegant,' I said approvingly.

Livak smiled briefly then wandered over to the window where she began to finger the ornaments catching the early sunlight. She looked unusually ill at ease and I began to feel a little concerned. Mellitha, a woman of tact as well as discernment, had given us rooms not only adjacent but with their own connecting door; when I had woken alone, I had simply assumed Livak had returned to her own bed.

'Who's Guinalle?' she asked abruptly.

'Who?' This meaningless question was a complete surprise.

Livak turned a searching emerald stare on me. 'Who is

Guinalle? That's a Tormalin name isn't it? You were muttering in your sleep last night, I heard you mention her.'

I shook my head before realising I still had my razor in my hand and cursed as I nicked myself.

'Yes, it's a Tormalin name, but I don't know anyone called that.' I hastily ransacked my memory; it rang of the sort of outdated elegance a whore might fancy as a working name. No, I couldn't remember any past conquest or purchase calling herself that.

Livak shrugged. 'No matter, then.'

I was not so sanguine. 'Really, I don't know anyone called Guinalle.'

Livak dropped her eyes. 'I couldn't remember what your sister's name had been.'

I caught my breath on a sudden memory of that face, twelve years burned on her pyre but still vivid in my mind. 'No,' I said shortly. 'Her name was Kitria.'

'So why would you be talking about someone called Guinalle?'

I was relieved to hear the taint of jealousy in Livak's tone turn to puzzlement.

'It must have been a dream.' I shook my head, the razor held at a safe distance this time.

We both stood still at that remark and our eyes met again in mutual uncertainty. This time it was me who turned away, pulling my shirt over my head, not wanting to pursue the implications of that idea.

'Don't mention it to Shiv,' I warned Livak. 'I honestly don't remember anything and I'm not at all sure I want any aetheric magic getting inside my head again, Archmage's orders or no.'

'He won't hear about it from me.' Livak slipped her hand in mine as we went down the stairs, sympathy in her comforting grip. She knew better than anyone else what a foul invasion that cursed sorcery could be. Shiv, being unconscious for much of our captivity by the Elietimm, had escaped having his memory turned inside out by the bastards but, as Livak had memorably commented, no bodily rape could ever equal that violation of the mind.

Mellitha was working her way through a stack of letters at the breakfast table, smiling with satisfaction over some, frowning at others in a manner that I suspected promised retribution of special significance. She was dressed today in the sober style befitting her position, formidable in dark-blue linen, high-necked and firmly laced.

'I sent someone out to make enquiries yesterday,' she announced without preamble as Shiv entered the room. 'It'll take a couple of days to weave the whole tapestry, but I have heard the market in Tormalin antiquities is unusually busy; prices are rising and dealers are starting to look around for anything connected to the House of Nemith the Last. I've let it be known I'd like to be made aware of anyone who's buying and of anyone new in the city who's selling.'

'You're sure no one will think it strange that you're asking questions about these people?' Viltred was evidently still worried.

'I'm putting together a tender for a new contract at the moment,' Mellitha reassured him. 'Everyone in the business will be asking questions about anyone and everything.'

'We can ask around as well.' Livak looked at Halice, who nodded her agreement, temporarily silenced by a mouthful of excellent, soft white bread and glossy cherry preserve.

'No, we don't want to draw attention to ourselves,' frowned Shiv, his fingers busy reducing a sweet roll to an inedible heap of sticky fragments. 'I don't want anyone going off on their own just yet, either.'

Livak scowled. 'I thought the whole point of my being here was getting Viltred's little trinkets back! I've got the contacts to track down the Elietimm for you and I'm the one who'll be cracking the shutters to get them back. If I'm risking my neck for Planir again, I'm the one who's going to be cracking the whip as well.'

'When we're looking at trying to take back the goods, then of course you'll be the one to do the planning.' Shiv pushed away his plate. 'There's someone I want to talk to before then, someone who might be able to help in other ways.'

'I take it you mean Kerrit Osier?' Mellitha finished her meal and her hand hovered over the silver bell by her glass. 'He'll be in the Temple today. He's got an appointment with the priestess of Maewelin.'

Shiv stared at her. 'How did you know who I meant?'

Mellitha stood up and pulled an ochre silk shawl over her shoulders, the splash of colour adding an interesting touch to her outfit.

'I keep a weather eye on mages visiting the city,' she smiled at Shiv with complacent superiority. 'I like to know what stones they're turning up, just in case something interesting comes to light. He's been here since Equinox, going through the Archive and talking to the older priests.'

She looked round the table, including us all in her commanding gaze. 'Tell the servants if you want anything; I will be in my offices until the noon chime and then I have meetings with some of the magistrates. I will be dining out but I should be back around sunset to dress and I'll let you know what I've found out.'

She departed with a swirl of her lace-trimmed underskirt and the rest of us turned to Shiv, who looked back defensively.

'So what are our orders?'

I couldn't tell if there was a taint of sarcasm in Halice's words or if I was just imagining it. No matter; from Livak's expression, which she was not even bothering to conceal, Shiv was spending from a very lean purse if he was expecting that pair to continue taking orders from him without question. I would have to find time to talk to them each about it before our fragile alliance was grounded on disagreement.

'So who is this Kerrit?' I passed Livak some fruit and handed Shiv a fresh roll.

'He's been investigating magic in the Tormalin Empire for Planir. I don't know much about that side of the work, but Kerrit's been visiting all the major temples that survived the Chaos. He's been looking into what the priests call miracles since that seems to be the only survival of aetheric magic that we have on this side of the ocean.'

'Sideshow chicanery,' sniffed Viltred.

Shiv ignored him. 'He may be able to explain why we can't scry for the Elietimm; he may know how to rework the spells to get round the aetheric influence.'

I could see that Livak looked completely unconvinced, but as she went to argue I laid my hand on her thigh under the table. She closed her mouth to give me a quick glance of warning before opening it again to say what she intended to Shiv.

'We'll see what this Kerrit has to say for himself, but after that I'm going to contact some of my own acquaintances, to get a scent on the Elietimm for myself. We can't waste time like this, Shiv; for all we know they could be planning to leave today and then what will you have to tell Planir?'

From Shiv's unhappy expression, that shot certainly struck home.

'Let's get moving, then,' he snapped uncharacteristically. 'I'll meet you at the gates.'

Halice rang the little silver bell and servants appeared to clear the table. We all dispersed to our rooms; I filled my purse and then stood, the sheathed sword in my hand, wondering whether or not to belt it on.

'Ready?' Livak appeared in the doorway.

'Does one wear a sword before noon in Relshaz?' I tried to make light of my indecision.

'This one does.' Livak tapped the short sword on her own waist. 'She also keeps plenty of daggers about her person as a rule, but I'm not usually paying calls around the Temple so I'm keeping it to two this morning.'

I answered her grin with a half-smile of my own and buckled the sword-belt, following her down the broad marble stairs. I was letting this whole business with the sword unnerve me unnecessarily, I decided; it wasn't as if I could remember any of these cursed dreams anyway. Planir had been wasting his time, trying to manipulate Messire and myself. If it drew the Elietimm to us, well, what could happen in broad daylight with half a hundred people within arm's length? At least we would have found them and I couldn't see Livak or Halice losing their scent, given such a chance.

We made our way through the swarming city, now thronged with people trying to go about their morning business and we were soon separated, Shiv escorting Viltred and the rest of us tailing some way behind, Halice finding it slow going with her crutch in such a crowd. I was enjoying the sights and sounds of the city, but I could see Shiv was chafing at the frequent delays as we were held up by traffic, the sheer press of bodies around the footbridges over the canals and, somewhat to my surprise, old acquaintances of Viltred's greeting him. Livak and I took the opportunity of one such delay to buy a handful of chicken bits from an old man with a cook-pot bubbling on a charcoal brazier; the taste of green oil was a welcome reminder of home after a season or more eating food fried in mutton fat or worse. I glared at a woman as she rammed me in the ribs with a basket and I nearly dropped the rough reed paper wrapped around the meat, but all I got was a dismissive sneer in thick Relshazri for a reply.

'Where do all these people live?' I muttered to Livak as we were halted yet again and I picked the last of the chicken from the wrapping.

'The landlords pack them in like salted fish.' She licked her fingers and pointed down a side alley, where a double line of tenements were tall enough to close the sunlight from the cobbles.

I blinked as I counted six levels of windows. 'That's only mud brick and wood, isn't it?' I shook my head. 'My father wouldn't risk building that high with the finest Bremilayne stone.'

Halice confirmed my suspicions with an acid comment. 'Some people certainly end up as flat as a stock-fish; there'll be a major collapse a couple of times a year, fires too if they're unlucky.'

I shook my head but I shouldn't have been surprised; it's all too often the way in these cities where elected rulers are only really concerned with their own profits. Commerce is everything in Relshaz, goods from a hundred leagues away or more bought, sold or turned into finished wares by gangs labouring in garrets, never seeing a tenth of the price the woodwork, bronzes or glassware sells for.

'Your father's a stonemason, then?' enquired Livak as we were halted by a donkey deciding to be difficult in the middle of a narrow bridge.

I looked at her in some surprise. 'You knew that, didn't you?'

She shook her head. 'I'd no idea.'

'I must have mentioned it; he's in business with two of my elder brothers. The next eldest to me, Mistal, is in Toremal, training to be an advocate in the Justiciary.'

'You mentioned him, that I remember,' allowed Livak.

The traffic moved on and the moment passed, but as we went further through the city I found myself thinking just how little Livak and I really knew about each other, about our families and the ties that held us, or not in her case, to home. What would this mean for any chance of a future we might have together? I was still pondering rather fruitlessly on these questions when the cluster of people ahead of us suddenly melted away and we stood, awe-struck, as the sight caught us unawares.

The road opened into a great expanse of flagstones. I squinted against the glare of the sun and realised we had reached the far side of the city now. A massive white marble edifice faced us, framed against the sparkling sapphire of the sunlit sea. I was staring like a shepherd fresh off his mountain, I'm not ashamed to admit it. After the destruction of most of the major temples in the Chaos, shrines in Lescar and Caladhria are invariably small places, served by virtual hermits and I suppose I'd expected something fairly modest, for all the size of the city.

This opulent building wouldn't have looked out of place in the centre of Toremal, though I have to say our Emperors have generally had more taste in their architecture. Massive stone pillars with extravagently decorated capitals held up a long pediment adorned with a frieze of improbable leaves, statues above showing the gods in scenes from myth and legend beneath a roof of ceramic tiles, startling colours woven into garish patterns. The entrances between the pillars were twice the height of a man, each door loaded with bronze and carving, the metal polished and gleaming. A broad flight of white stone steps ran the width of the building, drawing in the crowds from the square.

This temple certainly seemed to have as many people crowding around its steps as any Imperial Palace I've ever seen; ragged beggars, citizens pushing through, presumably to their devotions, suspiciously prosperous-looking priests accosting all and sundry. As we drew nearer pedlars approached with trays of votive offerings and sticks of incense, waving handfuls in our faces, voices rising as they tried to outbid each other. Their clamour mingled with the exhortations of a sizeable group of Rationalists intercepting those trying to get to a fountain for a drink and having little luck in trying to persuade the thirsty people to debate their theories on the irrelevance of the gods in the modern age. It was with some surprise that I realised these were the first Rationalists I'd seen since leaving eastern Lescar; their complicated philosophies must be finding few takers amongst the perennially unimaginative Caladhrians.

'I hope we can find Kerrit in all this foolery.' Viltred looked hot and aggravated and I couldn't say I blamed him. Relshaz seemed a remarkably windless city for a port and the heat of the sun was reminding me how far south we had travelled. We were still a fair way north of home, but in Zyoutessela we have the ocean breezes to keep us cool.

'Let's try inside,' I suggested. 'Mellitha mentioned the shrine of Maewelin, didn't she?'

I pushed a way past the insistent pedlars, the others tucking in behind me as we went up the broad steps. The cool of the interior raised sudden gooseflesh on my arms and it took a few moments for my eyes to get used to the gloom. The haze of candle smoke was mingled with incense and for a moment

I thought I was going to sneeze, a problem I frequently encountered in temples and always a grave embarrassment to my mother.

Shrines at home are individually dedicated to a single deity, but the Relshazri seemed content to pack their gods and goddesses in like their tenement classes. The temple had a multitude of small chapels, each with its own icon watched over by a few sharp-eyed priests. This left the broad expanse of the floor to the crowds of people patiently queuing to make their intercessions, and even here they were harried by persistent beggars. The priests were dressed in well-cut robes belted with braided silk cords, jewelled amulets around their necks. The quiet murmur of prayers was accompanied by the steady chink of coins. I shook my head; the destitute go to Tormalin shrines for alms from the priests, not to try to beat them to a share of suppliants' coin.

Shiv was scanning faces. Viltred followed closely, doing the same. Since I had no idea who we were searching for, I looked for Maewelin among the dedications written above the shrines. The archaic Tormalin script was not easy to read, long obscured by candle soot and fading into the darkening limestone. I frowned. Dastennin, Master of Storms? That wasn't a title I had seen before. Raeponin, that was easy enough, the Judge. Pol'Drion, Lord of Light, that was a very ancient style for the Ferryman. Relshazri religion seemed to have taken a few turns of its own since the fall of the Empire, I concluded. At home Ostrin's domain is husbandry, hospitality and care of the sick; here he was merely a fat and jolly figure cast in bronze, vine leaves in his hair, wine skin in hand. Next to him Talagrin stood severe, crowned with horns of black Aldabreshi wood, a hunter with bow and quiver, his care and dominion of the wild places forgotten.

One statue that did not have any worshippers caught my eye and I moved for a closer look. It was an emaciated youth, wretched in a ragged loincloth, badly carved in poor stone: Dren Setarion. Child of Famines? The prosperous-looking priest moved towards me and rattled his offertory dish; I gave him a rather hostile stare.

'What is this? How can you worship a god of starvation?'

'All powers were honoured by the ancient Tormalins, who first discovered how to move them with supplication and offering. As their Empire spread, so they brought enlightenment to the conquered and all people learned to pray for help and favour in the difficulties of life.'

The fat man's complacency irritated me; I know the rote of the gods as well as anyone else, but that was irrelevant here. 'This was no cult of the Empire!'

The priest was unperturbed. 'Much wisdom was lost when the dark ages of Chaos came, but people are making their way back to the truth. Have you ever seen such hunger, when babies die at their mother's breast for lack of milk? Famine is a great power in many lands and we try to reach that power so that it will not visit its dreadful destruction on our people.'

I could not think what to say to that, so I moved on with a snort of disgust. With priests taking this kind of opportunist attitude, maybe Rationalism would find adherents in Relshaz after all.

'There've been several poor harvests in Ensaimin lately,' commented Halice. 'That sort of thing always leads to new cults. They don't last.'

We crossed to the other side of the vast hall and found the same mix of the familiar and the strange in the ranks of the female deities. Here a weeping Arimelin was somehow the Mother of Sorrow, not the Weaver of Dreams, which effectively stifled my sudden urge to light some incense with a plea to have Planir's schemes frustrated. We moved on and I saw that Larasion was carved in red-brown heartwood and crowned with a garland of wheat, styled Mahladin, Harvest Queen. Drianon's role seemed limited to the supplications of pregnant women, while presumably unmarried girls were queuing in front of the icily remote Halcarion in her more traditional guise of the Moon Maiden. She looked to the beams with a blank marble stare while, next to her, grandmothers waited patiently to bring their entreaties to Ahd Maewelin, the Winter Hag, an ancient slab of oak bearing a primitive image with sharp, quelling features.

'There he is!' sighed Shiv with relief, pushing through the throng towards a stout man with a pale face and stooped shoulders. As we drew nearer I was a little startled to realise this Kerrit was scarcely a handful of years older than myself or Shiv, rather than half a generation as I had first thought. He was deep in conversation with a mild-faced little man in a rather dusty and faded robe; I wondered how this ancient acolyte managed to avoid being forcibly taken to a tailor by the other elegantly turned-out priests.

'Shivvalan!' Kerrit smiled at our mage with broad recognition. 'I'll be with you in a moment.'

He turned to bid the old priest a sincere farewell and to tuck a sheaf of notes into a smart leather satchel slung over one shoulder.

'So, what brings you to the delta city?' He made his way through the press of people, pushing without compunction or apology.

'Can we talk somewhere a little more private?'

I glanced at Shiv in some surprise; anyone trying to eavesdrop on us here would either have to be standing under our noses or rely on us shouting at the tops of our voices.

'This way.' Kerrit led us to a comparatively quiet corner behind a representation of Saedrin at the door between the worlds. This offered excellent cover for anyone who might want to creep up and overhear our discussions, but before I could move to watch the approach Halice had stepped forward to deal with it. I added this to the growing list of things I was going to have to discuss with Shiv before he drove the rest of us demented with his growing paranoia.

'So, do you have a letter from Planir for me?' Kerrit's eyes were still on the icon of Maewelin, his mind clearly busy elsewhere.

'No. We're here on the trail of some Ice Islanders who've stolen some artefacts,' said Shiv baldly.

That got Kerrit's undivided attention. 'They're here, in the city?'

Shiv nodded. 'But they're using some kind of aetheric influence to evade our scrying.'

'Are they now?' Kerrit breathed, eyes bright. 'That's something I'd—'

'Can you help Shiv get round it?' interrupted Livak as she saw the bookish mage's expression grew remote with speculation.

'Pardon? No, not as such, my dear. You see, being mage-born myself, aetheric incantations are ineffective when I try them.'

I could see that Livak's patience, never very long, was rapidly shortening.

'Do you have any knowledge that one of *us* could use to try to counter whatever it is they are doing?' I had some difficulty keeping my own tone level.

A slight frown wrinkled Kerrit's bland forehead. 'I'd need to see what they were doing, really, but I think there are a few things we could try.'

'Can you come with us?' asked Shiv politely.

'It's not really very convenient.' Kerrit looked distinctly put out. 'You see that old priest, he has six of what he calls miracles that he claims he can use to heal illness, old wounds, even some birth defects. I really must get some more details from him, try to—'

'What about broken bones?' Halice broke in suddenly. I felt a pang as I saw the desperate hope on her plain face.

Kerrit looked momentarily puzzled until he registered her twisted leg and crutch. 'He didn't say so. The thing is, Shiv, he seems to be able to make effective incantations on every attempt. I really do need to find out more about him, discover what he's doing, examine some of his cures and see how valid they are.'

'He's something special, then, the old man?' Livak's curiosity was inevitably getting the better of her. At least that was keeping her temper reined in.

'Oh yes,' Kerrit assured her, his expression animated. 'You could take ten priests from here and ask them all to perform the same rite and you'd have anything from five to ten different results. I'm trying to find out why.'

'I appreciate that's important—' began Shiv.

'I don't suppose the old priest is going anywhere,' I spoke over him firmly. 'The Elietimm might well do so. I'm sure you can spare us the rest of the day to help with something so crucial to Planir's work.'

The idea that he might find himself answering to the Archmage evidently weighed a coin or two with Kerrit. 'Very true, very true.'

'Let's go then.'

I stepped forward to help Halice force a way towards the doors. As I did so a disturbance in the corner of my eye made me turn my head. Some way off in the press of people a tall man in a dark cloak was caught up with a fat woman who seemed determined to prevent him getting ahead of her. As Viltred looked, the man stared past me, straight at the old wizard, recognition evident and expression hostile. He pushed the fat woman aside, ignoring her cries, and headed straight for Viltred.

'Viltred, do you know that man?' I nodded my head in what I hoped wasn't too obvious a gesture.

'No,' Viltred frowned and fear flared in his faded eyes, 'I've never seen him before.'

I saw the grey-cloaked man looking to his left and right as he came towards us; following his gaze with growing apprehension, I saw that he was not alone. I spotted three more of the grey-clad men and as one forced his way past a group of children, his cloak was swept back to reveal a familiar black livery.

'Elietimm,' I concluded tersely. 'We need to get out of here now.'

'This way.' Kerrit turned and hurried along behind the line of icons, leading the five of us to a small door presumably for the use of the priests.

I found a knot of fear was tying itself in my stomach and fought to calm my suddenly ragged breathing. Silently cursing the memory of Elietimm magic that could reduce me to this, I glanced at Livak and was at least a little comforted to see she too was unnaturally pale and gripping her sword hilt with white knuckles.

'Can you hide us?' I snapped at Shiv.

'Give me a moment.' He paused and I caught a flicker of blue light between his fingers as he closed his eyes in concentration. 'Viltred, can you help me?'

The mages stood, working together with some difficulty as they had to conceal the magelight that manipulating the elements usually called forth. I watched with Livak and Halice as the grey-cloaked men began to move in a line down the length of the temple, searching for us like beaters springing game for a hawk.

'There, that should shield us.'

The air around us shimmered, like haze on sun-scorched sand, and we moved cautiously into the open, heading for the open door. I held my breath as a thin-faced Elietimm scanned the crowd encircling us, his eyes passing over the wizards. I was about to breathe a sigh of relief when the man's gaze returned to us; he started visibly and evidently saw right through the concealing spell. The Elietimm looked round for his colleagues and caught the gaze of one. I felt certain some sort of communication must have passed between them; the second man started to push his way unerringly in our direction, despite having had no clear sight of us because of the statues in the way.

'They've seen us. Move.' My hand hovered over my sword hilt but I really didn't want to draw a blade in here, not knowing how the priests would react. The last thing we needed was to be held up by an outraged religious rabble.

'Curse it.' Shiv dropped his spell with a muttered handful of obscenities and began forcing a path to the door. Seeing him abandon stealth, the grey-cloaked men did the same. Taking the rear guard I heard gasps of outrage and then screams as one of the Elietimm answered a priest's remonstrance with the metallic rasp of a drawn sword. Looking back I saw people hurrying to get out of the way, but the crowd was sufficiently thick that we still made it to the door ahead of our would-be captors.

'Run!' I commanded as we ran down a flight of steps into the comparatively open expanse of the temple square. Livak caught Halice under one arm and they half ran, half hopped together. I tried to stifle my irritation. This was just the sort of situation I had feared, where a cripple must either be abandoned or put everyone in danger.

We put a fountain between us and the temple and I snatched a glance backwards. The grey-cloaked men had fanned out, drawing a cordon through the crowd. I turned and looked at the far side of the square; if these were the beaters, where was the hawker? Putting my hand to my sword, my senses suddenly swam. Dizziness threatened to overwhelm me and I clapped one hand to my head, cursing. When I opened my eyes I gasped and real panic threatened to stifle me. I was no longer in the midst of a crowded city square but standing in some wilderness, thickets all around me, tussocks underfoot, placid birdsong and skeins of mist replacing the bustle of the Relshaz morning.

'Get a grip on yourself,' I cursed viciously, gripping my sword hilt. I thought I heard a soft sigh behind me and spun round, sword drawn in an instant, but there was no one there. I gritted my teeth and concentrated on my rage rather than my fear and the world dissolved around me again, my sight clearing to reveal Livak staring at me with dismay naked in her own eyes. I swallowed on a sudden rush of nausea and felt sweat beaded cold between my shoulder blades.

'Your eyes, Rysh, your eyes! They went completely blue!'

Our gazes locked, frozen on the memory of the black pits that had been Aiten's eyes when the Elietimm sorcerers had reached inside his mind and taken over his body to try to kill us all.

'There is someone using aetheric magic on us again, Shiv!'

Livak's voice was shrill as she looked over my shoulder and I turned to see the pursuit was drawing closer.

Sudden memory spurred me to action. 'The gorgets! Shiv, Viltred, their magicians wore gorgets at their necks. Can you see one?'

We halted suddenly in the midst of the bustling crowd, looking all ways, Halice and Livak ready with their daggers, my hand on my sword.

'There!'

I turned to look where Shiv was pointing and my heart sank as I picked out a handful of Elietimm on the far side of the square, gold bright at the throat of the central figure. The hunter evidently had his fowling dogs with him, as well as his beaters.

Viltred drew a deep breath and his eyes lost their focus as he began to draw power into himself.

'Getting out of this is going to take direct action, I think,' he murmured. He flung his hands at the enemy in an abrupt gesture. I saw the air in front of the man's eyes glow and shimmer, effectively blinding him. A man next to him stumbled and fell and, even at this distance, I could see confusion reflected in his colleagues' faces.

'Rope of air?' Kerrit asked in genial enquiry.

'Round their feet,' confirmed Shiv with a grim face.

'Can we discuss the finer points of magecraft later?' Livak snapped with understandable irritation.

I spoke in almost the same breath. 'Come on!'

We moved fast, Shiv forcing a path through the crowd with scant apology. When he saw another grey cloak ahead of us Viltred sent a sudden blow that stunned the man like a clubbed fish. As his colleague fell, a second hunter broke from the line and headed for the spot. We hurried for the gap in the cordon, shoving people aside with increasing force.

The old wizard suddenly doubled up, gasping for breath; Halice and Livak grabbed him and I looked around for the source of the attack. One of the grey-clad men had climbed on to the fountain's pedestal and was staring at us, mouth moving, a silver sheen at his collar. Shiv wasted no breath on curses but green light glittered in his fingers as a long arm of sparkling water snatched the enchanter and held him down in the basin. Water splashed high above the pedestal as a despairing hand rose and was dragged down again by greedy splashes, soaking the bystanders. People began to move away from the fountain, exclamations of confusion rising sharply above the murmur of the square.

I tried to move but Kerrit was in my way, staring in confusion.

'For all the elements revealed, that man was working no magic at all.' He sounded positively affronted and turned to rummage in his satchel for paper and ink.

'Later,' I snapped, grabbing his arm. 'Viltred?'

'I'm all right.' He didn't look at all well, with a bluish tinge around his lips and incipient panic mingled with the pain in his eyes.

'Shiv!' Livak's gasp pulled all our heads round and the throng parted for a breath to show us a gorget-wearer thrusting bodies aside as he headed directly for us. All three wizards spat incoherent exclamations at the Elietimm and he exploded in a scatter of azure and scarlet light. Shock scattered the crowd away from the smouldering corpse and sudden panic began to race through the square. Where people had pushed, they began to land blows; where they had been jesting, they began to curse and shout abuse. The sound began to turn ugly and screams rose from the centre of the growing stampede, rising with the dust above the accelerating smack of boot soles on the flagstones. We were buffeted from all sides, tossed like crab-boats caught in a winter squall; I struggled to keep my footing.

'We have to stay together.'

I grabbed Kerrit's tunic and reached for Livak, who was in turn linking her arm with Halice, who was using her crutch on nearby shins to clear a path as Shiv dragged Viltred over to us. Viltred was struggling, fruitlessly trying to resist the force of the crowd.

'Let yourself be carried along, we have to go with the flow,' I yelled at him.

The last thing I wanted was to be noticeable in this mob; there was going to be no question but magic had started the panic and I didn't want to be caught on the streets with three wizards when the local Watch or whoever came looking for a culprit. A riot like this was going to leave bodies in its wake and the Relshazri would want someone to blame. When a city elects its officials, keeping the mob happy tends to be more important than justice and I wasn't about to have my head clamped in a pillory just for having a Tormalin accent.

Since we had been heading for a side street anyway, the tide of fleeing Relshazri soon washed us into a dank alley between an inn and a gaming-house. I looked round to make sure we were all all right, but I wasn't too reassured; Viltred was still recovering from the assault he'd suffered and Livak was supporting Halice, who'd lost her crutch in the crush by now.

'Wait here.'

I moved cautiously back down the muddy street, taking full advantage of any cover offered by doorways and a few abandoned vehicles and hand-carts. The square was largely clear by now, save for two knots of weeping women clustered around prone bodies and a few dazed individuals staggering to their feet. Black-headed gulls were wheeling overhead and a few of the bolder birds were already pecking at fallen fruit, an abandoned loaf of bread, a peddler's tray of sweetmeats scattered in the dust; others looked speculatively at a motionless body in a huddle of soiled rags. Their thin cries were suddenly lost beneath a child screaming hysterically on the temple steps, flailing thin arms as a red-robed priestess tried ineffectually to calm it. I looked for grey cloaks and saw at least one of our pursuers had been trampled, unable to rise as his feet were still caught in Shiv's spell I realised with some satisfaction.

'Rope of air is a cantrip any novice could dispel.'

I turned to see that Kerrit had followed me, pen in his mouth as he fumbled with the lid of his ink-horn.

'It should have presented no problem to someone able to see through a complex illusion or to send a direct attack over such a range,' he mumbled, rifling through his notes for a clean page.

'Come on.' I grabbed him with rising irritation, ignoring his protests as ink spilled down the front of his breeches as I dragged him back to the others. Was I ever going to meet a wizard with the sense to run a whelk stall?

'Shiv, do everything you can to hide us. We need to get back to Mellitha's at once!'

Shiv nodded, and the air around us began to shimmer again as the air wove itself to conceal us.

'I've something here which is supposed to hide a trail,' Kerrit piped up.

'Do it then!' I snapped.

'Well, I can't; you see, it's an aetheric incantation. I'm fairly sure it should work though; if my notes are correct, it should prevent them using their magic to find us.'

Kerrit beamed and held out a page of precisely written syllables. I reached for it but sudden qualms stayed my hand in mid-air.

'Livak? You did some of these before, didn't you? You said something about the rhythms?'

I could see my own reluctance reflected in her grass-green eyes as our gazes locked for a still moment.

'Give it here.' Livak suddenly snatched the paper and spat out the words, a Forest cadence in her voice.

'Ar mel sidith, ranel marclenae.'

As far as I was concerned, we had no way of knowing if it would do any good. I would rely on the methods I've used before.

'Viltred, do you know a way to Mellitha's, using the back streets?'

The old mage dragged a weary hand across his face and nodded. 'This way.'

No one stopped us as we made our way back across the city, more slowly than I would have liked in order to maintain the spells woven around us. The Arril streets were as quiet as any-where in Relshaz and since the people were going about their business, unconcerned, we all began to breathe a little easier. I was starting to think I recognised some of the houses when Viltred stopped abruptly and I nearly trod on his heels.

'I'm not going back to Mellitha's house until I'm sure we're not being pursued,' he said brusquely. 'I'm not risking leading people like that to her door.'

His lined face was set with grim determination. I had to concede he had a point.

'Let's find an inn then.'

I shook my head at Shiv to quell his protest and we made our way to a nearby inn where we sat under a vine-laced portico, sipping an aromatic Ferl River white wine until noon had come and long gone. Viltred's colour had improved by then and Halice's eyes were no longer so shadowed with the pain from her leg. The sixth chime of the day was carried across the city on a sequence of bells and I caught Livak's eye.

'If they had followed us, they'd have us by now.' She drained her glass and did not refill it. 'There's been no sign of anyone; trust me, I'd have seen them.'

Shiv nodded, sweeping aside a pool of seemingly accidentally spilled wine that he'd been staring into intently. 'I've been scrying all the neighbouring streets and everything's clear and safe.'

'I suppose that will have to do,' Viltred yielded with ill grace. 'Though they could still be spying on us from some-where else.'

I nodded to the wine waiter and dropped some coins on the table. 'If they are, there's nothing we can do about it. Come on.'

As we entered the courtyard, Mellitha strode out of the porter's room. She wasted no time in greeting or questions, but hurried us into a precisely organised office.

'I heard what happened by the temple; I arrived to find half my meetings cancelled and the Magistracy in an uproar. What's been going on?'

I looked at Viltred, who glanced at Shiv, who looked round for Kerrit, so I spoke up with a rapid summary of events.

'So now you're the hunted, not the hunters,' observed Mellitha dryly as she opened a calfskin folder on her desk. 'I've had some interesting reports back, though I don't know quite how they will further your cause. There seem to be two groups of these foreigners in the city. As far as anyone can tell me, they're not working together. The first lot arrived just before the last lesser full moon and they have been trading in Tormalin antiquities. No one's quite sure where they're from; I've several different guesses, they're dressed in local cloth but no one can place their accent. The majority opinion is that they're from Mandarkin.'

'In other words, from a place so far north and west, no one here is going to have ever seen anyone from there, let alone have heard the accent,' I said sourly.

'Quite so,' Mellitha continued placidly. 'They've also been seen spending a lot of time in the temples, talking to the priests, but I can't find out why. They seem to have plenty of money and are paying good prices, so no one's too bothered about them. The second group arrived four days ago, and I think they could be the ones who are giving you trouble. People are steering clear of them; they're soldiers by the look of them, all black leather and doing everything by the five-count.'

Mellitha looked up with an impish smile. 'They must be sweating like colts round a brood mare, wearing leather like that in this climate. Anyway, their leader has put round the word that he's looking for a pair of thieves and, wouldn't you know it, he's giving out a very good description of Livak and Halice.'

They exchanged a rueful glance.

'It's not the first time,' sighed Halice. 'Are they offering a reward?'

'I've not heard so far, but I've sent out an enquiry.' Mellitha's eyes sparkled. 'I wonder how much it might be.'

'I can dye my hair, I suppose,' said Livak with some asperity. 'You're going to be stuck in here unless we hire you a carry-chair, Halice. That leg's just too cursed noticeable.'

Mellitha smiled at them. 'You're supposed to have stolen a valuable weapon, by the way, an Empire long sword with a green-figured scabbard and gilt filigree work on the pommel.'

Viltred cursed. 'It's valuable all right, Toremal-work made by Delathan. It's the one Ryshad here is wearing.'

'So they've given themselves an excuse to seize us on the street,' I said grimly.

'I don't think the magistrates would look too favourably on that,' frowned Mellitha.

I was not so convinced; enough coins in a handshake usually removes any objections an elected official might raise.

'I imagine they want the sword for itself; we know it's tied into the lost colony somehow.' Shiv glanced a little apologetically at me.

'Delathan was working in the reign of Nemith the Seafarer, wasn't he?' Mellitha looked thoughtful.

'At the end of his reign and in the early years of Nemith the Reckless. Why?' enquired Viltred.

'These foreigners dealing in antiquities are concentrating on that period too. In fact it's the only common factor in their trading,' explained Mellitha. 'I mean, most people concentrate on buying jewellery or silverware, something like that, and worry about reign marks later. These people are trading earlier pieces worth much more for quite small items from the decades just before the Empire fell. That's what's been pushing up the price, but they don't seem at all concerned about that.'

Shiv cursed with exasperation. 'All we come up with are more questions. I need some answers.'

'Can you lay information with these magistrates of yours without having to reveal your source?' I asked Mellitha.

'Of course,' she nodded. 'My unsupported word's good enough; it has to be if they want their ledgers passed without too much scrutiny.'

'Let them know the foreigners who are looking for the sword are the ones who started the riot outside the temple, the black-leathered troop. At least one of them was trampled and there should be some witnesses who can support your information.'

'Do I know why they are after you?' Mellitha made a note on a clean, square-cut leaf of reed paper. 'These people aren't exactly making themselves popular but the Watch aren't too inclined to arbitrate in private quarrels.'

'I'd rather you didn't mention us at all,' objected Shiv.

I certainly agreed with that. 'Don't involve us. Just say they were out for robbery, rape, stirring up trouble to discredit the current authorities, whatever you think will be most unpopular and get them stamped on as soon as they show their faces again.'

Mellitha smiled. 'We've got elections due at greater full moon. I think I can hint they might be in the pay of a couple of people with a vested interest in unnerving the populace.'

'That should hobble them for a while.' Viltred's expression lightened with malevolent satisfaction.

'A round of chimes should be all we need.' Livak's impatience drove her to her feet; she crossed to stare out of the window into the courtyard. 'Mellitha, do you think you could send a maid out to get me a herbal rinse? Black or brown, I don't mind.'

'I want everyone to stay here and do nothing until I've contacted Planir,' said Shiv with some heat.

'So go and bespeak him.' Livak stared at him, challenge in her cold green eyes.

'Viltred, Kerrit, come with me.'

The older mages followed Shiv with unexpected docility; Livak ignored them as she bent over a letter, paper and ink taken from Mellitha's desk without apology or request. She finished her writing and double-folded it, looking around a little blankly until Mellitha passed her a wax wafer to seal it.

'Thank you.' Livak scribbled a quick direction on the outside. 'Can you send another servant out with this?'

Mellitha raised one exquisitely plucked eyebrow as she read the address. 'I think one of my less reliable grooms will probably know this tavern.'

Livak grinned despite herself. 'That sounds about right.'

Mellitha rose. 'I'll see to it directly.'

I folded my arms and looked sternly at Livak, who met my gaze with untroubled assurance.

'Who were you writing to?'

'Someone I can trust to put around the word that it'll be worth more to keep quiet about Halice and me being in the city than it will to try turning a coin from these Elietimm,' she smiled grimly. 'Shiv had better be ready to spend some of Planir's coin closing a few mouths with decent wine.'

I half shook my head doubtfully. 'We've only been here a day.'

'And at least a handful of people we know will have seen us by now,' Halice spoke up from her chair on the far side of the room. 'If they don't hear otherwise they'll see no harm in trying to take the Ice Islanders' coin.'

'I need to get out on my own and start doing things my way,' Livak warned me. 'If they're after us, the quicker we find their nest and lift Viltred's trinkets, the better. The sooner I can let the local shutter-crackers know I'm interested in these bastards, the sooner someone will chalk their door-post for us.'

I sighed. 'Can't you wait until Shiv's contacted Planir?'

'I'll give him till morning and see what he has to say,' Livak conceded slowly, seeing the appeal in my eyes. 'But if he wants me to go thieving for him, he has to let me set things up my way, using people I know. I'm not risking a swing on the gibbet because those three wizards come up with some daft plan.'

'If Shiv doesn't want our help, we'll see if we can't get a scent of Arle Cordainer's trail. I'd say that's starting to look like being a cursed sight more profitable than staying with you lot.' Halice's tone was uncompromising as she stared at me, defying me to mention or even glance at her leg.

CHAPTER FOUR

Taken from the Magistrate's Court-Rolls, Charlaril District, Relshaz, Spring Assizes, the 3rd year of Emperor Perinal the Bold in Toremal, the 15th year of the reign of Queen Mirella of Solura.

To Zindan Ar Willan, Medlar Lane

Sir,
Further to your protests as to the likely penalties your son will face, may I remind you that as theft is a crime against property, rather than person, he will not be subject to physical penalties or execution. However, since the value of the goods stolen is estimated as in excess of 500 Crowns (Tormalin minting), the plaintiff is fully entitled to recover his losses against the body of your son if the charge is proved and the property is not recovered. In that eventuality, you cannot compel the plaintiff to sell your son in open market if he chooses to sell him to the city for service in the galleys or at the ferry-capstans. I appreciate this threat must be very distressing for your wife, but it is not directly relevant to this case; if you wish to lodge an accusation of harassment with this office, it will be treated as an entirely separate matter.
The theft case will be heard at the Hall of Justice on the day of the greater full moon. If your son denies the charge absolutely, you may either retain an advocate or argue the case yourself. If your son admits the offence but contests the amount stolen, you will be required to present the property in question to the Magistracy for valuation and submit to a

search of your household for the disputed items. The plaintiff
will of course have to agree to a similar search and prove
ownership of said items to the satisfaction of the Magistracy.
If your son admits the offence and the full value of the theft,
you will have the chance to offer the plaintiff compensation
in lieu of the price of your son, who will then be banished
from the city. I should warn you that the plaintiff is entirely
at liberty to refuse such an offer.

I return herewith the affidavits concerning your son's
presence at a private party on the night in question. You
may call witnesses with any pertinent information when the
case comes to the Hall of Justice. A jury will be empanelled
from the voting lists on the morning of the sitting and I
must remind you that any attempt to influence witnesses
or jurors, by either defendant or plaintiff, will result in
immediate forfeiture of the case.

May I remind you that you only have five days remaining
in which to lodge your hundred Marks with the Magistracy
as Surety of Conduct. Please do not hesitate to contact me
if you require any further information.

Trusting in Raeponin's justice,
Magrin Colarene,
Clerk to the Magistrate

The House of Mellitha Esterlin, Relshaz, 29th of Aft-Spring

I woke from a fitful sleep, startled to realise it was much later than was usual for me, and I hurried to wash and shave. Livak's mood hadn't improved much during the previous evening. When we'd made our way upstairs after a rather strained dinner and I'd paused on my threshold with an enquiring smile, she'd simply pulled a sealed packet from one pocket and held it up to me.

'I'm dyeing my hair.' Her smile was an uneasy mixture of defiance and triumph and she whisked past me into her own room with a swiftness that left my desire as effectively snuffed as my candle. I didn't bother to try the connecting door.

The house seemed unusually quiet as I made my way downstairs. An elegant breakfast selection was laid out in the morning salon but, from the used plates and glasses stacked neatly on a side-table, I looked to be the last to rise. I shrugged and made a good meal before going in search of the others. Most sound was coming from the kitchen, so I peered round the door, courteous apology ready on my lips from long experience of Messire's fiercely territorial cooks.

'Sir?' A maid bobbed a nervous curtsey and looked round anxiously for reassurance.

'Morning, Ryshad.'

I was a little surprised to see Halice in a window seat, carefully examining knives, oil and whetstone to hand. She looked entirely at her ease and I realised she had that same talent of fitting in almost anywhere short of a children's dame-school that had made Aiten such an effective enquiry agent for Messire. I made a mental note to find out later what she might discover from a morning's ostensibly idle chat among the servants. There might well be something I could include in the letter to Messire that was to be my next priority, I reminded myself.

'Where is everyone?'

'Mellitha's gone out to rearrange the meetings she had cancelled, Viltred and Kerrit are scrying or some such, Shiv's waiting for Planir to contact him with instructions.' Halice tested the edge of a particularly vicious carver with a cautious thumb.

'Livak?' I asked with a sinking feeling.

'Gone out.' Halice looked up, her expression unreadable. 'Shiv couldn't say when he might hear from Planir, so Livak said she couldn't wait.'

I must have been deeply asleep to miss that exchange; half the street had probably heard it.

'Where's Shiv?' There was no point me falling out with Halice over the issue.

'The garden room, end of the corridor past the dining room.'

I nodded a polite farewell to the curious maids and scullions and left Halice to see what she could elicit with sharp knives and sharper ears.

Shiv was sitting by a linden wood game-table, moodily rearranging the pieces of one of the finest White Raven sets I have seen outside an Imperial residence.

'Good morning,' I ventured brightly.

Shiv shrugged and made some indeterminate reply. I moved round the room to the window for a clearer view of his face and saw weariness clouding his eyes.

'What are you doing?'

'Waiting for Planir to deign to contact me with instructions and trying to decide what to do for the best,' snapped Shiv with an irritation I was glad was not directed at me personally.

He smacked the alabaster raven piece down in the centre of the board with a force that made me wince; that is too soft a stone to appreciate such treatment.

'Want some company, or do you have something else more useful I could be doing?' I smiled as he looked at me for the first time.

'I reckon I could do with someone to talk to,' he admitted, pushing with an aimless finger at one of the softly swirling malachite trees standing around the board inlaid on the table top. 'Planir said he should have instructions for me before noon. I'd appreciate your thoughts on what he has to tell us.'

I relaxed on a velvet-upholstered chair and picked up one of the crow pieces, admiring the exquisite workmanship; jet's difficult stone to carve, according to my father.

'Livak's gone out,' said Shiv abruptly, closing the circle of trees around the raven with an irritated gesture.

'Halice told me,' I replied mildly. 'Still, she knows the city better than either of us; I'd say she'll be able to keep herself out of trouble.'

Shiv looked up with a ghost of a smile; I hadn't been able to keep the chagrin out of my voice.

'You don't think she'll need either of us riding in at the end of the fifth verse to rescue her like some maiden in a bad Soluran ballad, then?'

I shook my head. 'A knight-protector is the last thing Livak's ever going to want or require.' My voice must have betrayed me.

'So where does that leave you?' asked Shiv with a genuine concern that surprised me a little.

'A sworn man, whose oath is supposed to come before any other consideration?' I set the crow down carefully next to a golden agate owl. 'I'll settle for whatever she's willing to give, just at the moment, as long as she's willing to let me keep my oaths. As for anything more, I don't even know if she wants a future with me, so I'll worry about selling that skin when I've caught the bear.'

Shiv nodded his understanding. 'Pered and I took quite some time to work out a way of living together, what with him not being a mage. It became quite difficult when I started

working for the Council, but we managed to find a balance.'
His gaze lengthened as he stared seaward out of the window.
'I do miss him.'

I wasn't quite sure what to say to that; I'd been a little
surprised to find that Shiv preferred to dance with his own
side of the set, but as I was confident he'd be keeping his
hand off my shirt tails I didn't give the matter much thought.
It wasn't something I particularly wanted to discuss, however.
I'm no Rationalist, I don't subscribe to their theories about
the determining logic of nature's pattern – meaning one man,
one woman and no alternatives; still, enough Tormalins take
on Rational ideas while observing the rituals and holy days of
less censorious traditions to make any of my acquaintance who
felt inclined to scent his handkerchiefs do so very discreetly.
I liked Shiv, I respected him as a man and a mage, and I
certainly didn't want to offend him by saying the wrong thing
or revealing my own ignorance, come to that.

'How about a game of Raven while we wait?' I carefully
replaced the pieces in their niches on either side of the table.

Shiv looked at the board as if only just registering it was
there. 'No, thanks, I don't play as a rule.'

That made sense, since the whole game is based on the pre-
mise of birds driving out the one born different to the majority.

I opened a drawer in a small cabinet. 'A few hands of
runes?'

'Yes, all right.' Shiv stretched his long arms over his head
and his expression lightened a little.

I took out a velvet bag and closed the drawer. 'You know,
if we find ourselves up to our hips in horseshit over all this
and paid off in Lescari Marks, we ought to think about
tax-contracting.'

'It certainly looks to pay well enough,' Shiv agreed, his
grin broadening as he turned the table-top over to reveal the
velvet-lined face for rune play.

I spread the nine finely made sea-ivory rods on the table-top
and Shiv gave them rather more than the customary examina-
tion, dark brows meeting above curious eyes.

'Is this inlay gold or bronze?' He picked up one of the bones and turned it slowly, looking at the three faces, the angular sigils that were the ancient symbols for the Deer, the Oak and the Forest. I'm more used to the ornamental sets used in Tormalin, little pictures painted on each rune.

'Gold,' I confirmed. 'So, what are we playing?'

'Three runes, three throws?' suggested Shiv, tossing the heaven rune to give us the sun and the lesser moon either side on the uppermost faces.

'Male runes strong, then,' I nodded. 'Are we counting points or pence?'

Shiv smiled and this was a wide, guileless smile that made me wonder how much he played. 'Pence, I'd say, just to keep it interesting.'

I swept the bones back into the bag and held it out so Shiv could draw three. The first few plays were certainly interesting; Shiv consistently passed up modest combinations of runes from his first throws in favour of trying for higher scoring patterns. He showed no nervousness and was soon winning more than he was losing. I could almost have suspected him of weighting the game when he threw the Wolf and the Storm first toss when all I could come up with was the Reed and the Harp, and that on my third throw. Just as I was thinking the odds were starting to favour me, I drew the heaven rune and it landed with both moons up, ending the hand.

'Have you got something to keep score on over there?' Shiv grinned at me. I shook my head in mock disgust as I rummaged in the cabinet drawer.

There were several sticks of charcoal in elegant silver holders and some off-cuts of reed paper which I drew out. I glanced at the backs but they were blank; Mellitha evidently didn't risk unfriendly eyes seeing even the most innocuous memoranda from her office.

'You don't seem to have a problem deciding what to do when you're playing,' I winced as I totted up my losses. Would things improve now female runes were dominant? Knowing my luck, I'd be drawing the Mountain and the Drum in every hand instead.

Shiv paused in casting idle trios of bones, hand against hand. 'It's easy enough to be bold and reckless when the worst that'll happen is losing your boots to pay your debts.'

'You were quick-witted enough when we were trying to find a way out of that Elietimm dungeon,' I shook my head with a friendly smile, choosing my words carefully. 'Don't take me wrong, but you've been like a cat wanting fish but afraid to wet his paws on this trip.'

Shiv's expression hardened a little. 'I'm sorry if I'm a little hesitant; it's not so easy finding a way to do what Planir wants that I can be sure will keep us all out of Elietimm hands.'

He shoved the runes into the bag with unnecessary force and promptly threw the Eagle, the Sea and the Zephyr first toss.

'Is Planir baying at your heels, then?' I barely bothered calculating the meagre score I got from the Calm, the Pine and the Broom, deciding I wouldn't be playing Livak for anything important until my luck improved dramatically.

Shiv shook his head. 'No, not at all. He lets you know where your task ranks on the scale of things and generally you know how long you have to get results, but he'll always listen to reason and give you leeway when you need it. I trust him; he's got all the reins firmly in his hands.'

'He sounds like Messire.' I threw then rerolled all three bones with a mutter of disgust. 'So if Planir isn't going to savage you for following a few false scents, why are you keeping Livak on such a tight leash? Let her do some of the work for you; you know she's got the nose for something like this.'

Shiv returned the runes to the bag, drew his three and sat fingering them with a pensive expression.

'It was easier, last year, taking chances, when I didn't know what we might run up against. Now I know what kind of snares we could run ourselves into. I may not have had all my birds on the board after that knock on the head I took, but I saw what those bastards did to you and Livak.' He looked at me. 'See, you've gone pale just at the mention of it.'

I wasn't about to deny it; Shiv threw his runes with an explosive gesture of anger.

'Geris' death was bad enough; torturing him like that went beyond any questioning or punishment. Whoever did that did it because he enjoyed it. I don't want to end up in his hands; I wouldn't wish it on my worst enemy. Aiten's death was the worst, though, because it was magic that took his mind, and it's a magic I can't sense, I can't counter, I can't even begin to understand it.' Frustration edged his voice. 'I might as well try casting the runes like my grandmother looking for answers by the fireside. If I could remember half of what she used to do, I'd give it a go. I'm that desperate!'

I laughed but bit it short when I saw Shiv was more than a little serious. He stared at me. 'Don't you cast the runes for fortunes in Tormalin? You must draw birth runes, if nothing else?'

I struggled for an answer. 'I think my father's mother did that when we were babies.' I sorted through the bones until one sparked a faint flicker of memory. 'This would be it, yes, this one. The Calm, the Drum and the Earth, though I've no idea what it's supposed to mean for me.'

Shiv gave a perfunctory nod but his thoughts had moved on. 'I'm a mage and I'm a good one; I work for Planir because I think that's where I can do most good, but if I wanted to turn my talents to studying my element, I could get elected to the Council inside a year on my own merits. Set me against these bastards from the far side of the winter storms and I'm as scared of their cursed sorcery as some lackwit peasant seeing fire conjured for the first time. I hate it, Rysh, I just hate it!'

'I'd be worried if you weren't scared.' I said with a shrug. 'Just thinking about having one of those bastards inside my mind again makes me feel like wetting my breeches. The thing is, though, you can't let that hobble you or you're giving them another advantage.'

'I do know that,' said Shiv with some sarcasm. 'It's just that's the way I feel.'

'So don't feel.' I leaned forward, sweeping the disregarded runes aside. 'Lock it in a box in the back of your mind and don't get it out again until you've got the time for it. As for the rest of it, why are you trying to square this circle all on your own? Halice and Livak know this town, they know a lot of people here; I spend every other season looking out information for Messire. There's a double handful of things we could be doing instead of sitting here with our thumbs up our arses waiting for the Archmage to give us the self-same orders.'

'Livak seems to have decided that for herself.' Shiv's tone was sour.

'Are you surprised? Now, I reckon she'll concentrate on the black-leather troop; I don't think she takes kindly to people putting a price on her pelt. I've been wondering about this second group, the ones who are trying to blend in a bit more thoroughly. How about I take this sword round a few of the dealers, see if anyone can point me in their direction? I'd like to know where they are, just for my own peace of mind. You never know, we might be able to use them against the other lot.'

'That's a possibility.' Shiv looked thoughtful.

I stood up. 'Right, then. I'll see if I can get a scent.'

'Don't forget what you owe me for this game,' Shiv called after me.

Viltred came bustling out of an open door as I headed for the outer yard. 'Where are you going?' he demanded.

'To get a haircut,' I said mildly; I didn't answer to him and besides, my curls definitely needed a trim if we were going to be spending much more time in this city. Just the thought of the vermin that would relish such a tightly packed population made my scalp itch. I could look for a barber while I made my way to the eastern wharves, I decided, where I should be able to find a merchant willing to ferry a letter to the Despatch in return for an appropriate coin or two. It felt good to be out on the streets, on my own; the sun was bright on the whitewashed buildings but a faint breeze was bringing in high clouds from the seas of the Gulf today. I've always hated inactivity; I'd drive my mother nearly demented on wet days when I was a child, according to my father. Walking down the streets I kept my eyes and ears open but not worrying overly much. Relshaz was an unfamiliar city to me, but I've seen enough new places in my years working for Messire. The garbage in the gutters is usually much the same.

My letter could wait until I had some news worth sending, I decided. Making my way to the goldsmiths' quarter, I began looking for a likely dealer to interest in the sword. It would have been easier if Mellitha had been available to ask for advice but I was confident I could manage. When a treacherous little voice whispered at the back of my mind, 'You could always have waited,' I locked it back in that box I'd been telling Shiv about.

A couple of brawny lads propping up the door-posts of an auction house suggested there was more than silver-gilt behind the stout grilles on the unshuttered windows. I walked up the street, stopping every so often to admire the wares on display in each shop frontage and found that theirs was indeed the richest array for a galley-length in any direction. More importantly, they seemed to deal in any and every type of merchandise. I didn't meet the intimidating stare of the guards, not wanting to get them up on their hind legs and barking; I simply went in and waited for someone to come and persuade me to part with some coin.. After scarcely a breath, a dapper little man in watered blue silk sidled up to me.

'Can I be of assistance? Are you buying or selling?'

'I was just passing and you know, I was wondering what you could tell me about this sword?' I smiled at him and did my best imitation of Camarl D'Olbriot's countless generations of good blood and better education.

'A pleasure, sir.' The man had the pleasant knack of being effusive without being ingratiating. His eyes gleamed as I unbuckled the sword and handed it over.

'Now this is very interesting.' He actually sounded as if he meant it. 'This insignia, it's the House D'Alsennin.'

His Tormalin was flawlessly accented; it was a shame I'd never heard of the House in question.

'How very odd,' I registered aristocratic embarrassment.

The little man ran a finger over the crest embossed in the leather of the scabbard. 'The House fell in the collapse of the Empire; it was extinct in the principal line some time before then, I believe, and what remained of the property reverted to a cadet succession of Tor Alder.'

A frisson ran through me that I couldn't explain. Was Tor Alder an ancestral connection of Messire's? I knew the family had several links to Houses that styled themselves 'Tor' to show they had once held the Imperial Throne, but I didn't think that was one of them.

I realised the evaluator was talking about the engraving on the sword.

'Delathan, yes, that would certainly fit, he was a smith working in the last years of the Empire. Tell me, Esquire, is this a family heirloom?'

'Of sorts, from a collateral line.' I repossessed the sword and made sufficient business of buckling it on and settling it on my hip again to avoid the little man's eye. He couldn't bring himself to stoop to further vulgar inquiry.

'What would it make at auction, just out of interest?'

He was polite enough to take me at my word, despite my distinctly unaristocratic appearance. 'I would expect you would get offers upwards of two thousand Crowns. We could sell it for you, should you wish to part with it for any reason, but I'm honour bound to say we don't deal in swords as a rule, so you might well get a better price elsewhere. We don't really have clients looking for such things. If you take the second turn after the fountain on the Gulf side, you'll find dealers who specialise in blades,' he added a little reluctantly.

'Many thanks.' Waving an airy farewell, I sauntered off along the street, following his directions. Satisfaction warmed me as I discovered a cluster of merchants dealing in everything from ivory-handled daggers for ladies to efficient glaives to keep watchmen at a suitable distance from anyone trying to do them damage. I would look for a nice little blade to take back for Livak, I decided, doing a little business would give me better reason for being here. I'd been wanting to get her a present for some while now.

I rejected a long salesroom whose two open doorways were thronged with a lively clientele of fashionable youths trying out impractical rapiers. The place looked too busy and would most likely be too honest to do more than tell me what I already knew about the blade. A more subdued establishment off the main thoroughfare looked more promising until I saw an ill-shaved handful idling the morning away in an alley opposite. As a customer left with a friendly pat on the shoulder from the pockmarked craftsman, one detached himself from the group and sauntered purposefully after the heedless merchant. I made a note of the name above the counter-front to pass on to Mellitha; I was sure she could use the information to earn a few Marks of goodwill with the Watch. Lying a hand negligently but noticeably on my sword hilt, I continued on my way past.

Back on the busy carriageway, I paused and wondered which way to go; my initial ebullience was fading a little. I felt a sudden familiar pang of loss, missing having Aiten waiting in a doorway for me, watching my back before taking his turn with the questions and chat while I looked out for anyone taking too much interest in him. This was a job for two and, with Halice tied by her leg and none of the wizards more reliable than a wax rune, perhaps I should have waited for Livak. 'Then you'd have nothing to match her with, when she comes back with the name of the inn where the Elietimm are staying and tells you what they ate for breakfast.'

I tried to laugh at myself but I could not shake off a growing feeling of unease. I turned abruptly down an alley and cut across a back entry to take another on to a side street. A mercer's cart provided some handy cover and I waited for a long moment to see if anyone came out of the alley looking for me. No one did but I couldn't shake off a prickling at the back of my neck.

'Anyone would think you'd had an Eldritch man tread on your shadow,' I mocked myself with some irritation.

This street had a choice of more workaday metalworkers. I crossed to one whose shutters stood open to reveal a display of old as well as new blades in a wide range of styles. Pausing to rumple my overlong hair across my eyes and pull the laces of my jerkin askew, I went in, rounding my shoulders and ducking my head.

'Good mornin',' I drawled in the tones of the dock urchins my mother had spent my childhood warning me about.

'Noon chime's been and gone, friend. Good afternoon.' The smith was a thick-set man, muscled arms scarred with the burns of his craft and his black eyes had all the warmth of wet coal.

'I was wondering what you could tell me about this sword?' I gave him a slack-jawed smile and shuffled my feet in the dust of the floor.

He reached for the blade and turned down the corners of his mouth, unimpressed. 'Where'd you get it from?'

'Borrowed it off my brother,' I snickered, remembering a time I had helped myself to a rather lewd carving Mistal had been cherishing, concealed, as he had thought, inside his toolbag in our father's workshop.

'These leaves graved on the metal, that's Delathan's style, but this isn't Old Empire.' The smith shrugged, his tone dismissive. ' 'Tis a good copy though, I'll give you two hundred Crowns for it, Tormalin minted.'

'That's a deal of money,' I grinned vacantly. 'I'm not after selling it just yet, though.'

The smith scowled and shoved the blade back towards me. 'Why are you wasting my time then?'

I hunched my shoulders and shuffled my feet some more. 'Well, a man never knows when he might need some spare coin, not in a city like this.'

I snickered some more with a suggestive grin and the smith smiled back broadly.

'True enough. If you're looking for a nice clean girl, try the Hole in the Wall, off the Lantern Way.'

I nodded with unnecessary enthusiasm. 'Thanks for the tip.'

The smith made a creditable try at registering a sudden thought. 'You know, I might have a customer who'd be interested in making you an offer. Where was it you said you were lodging?'

'Plume of Feathers,' I told him readily. 'Thanks again.'

I shambled out of the workshop and made my way round a handy corner before straightening up. That had certainly started a hare or two but I realised with some frustration that this was going to be hard game to course. If I'd had Aiten with me, I could have set him to watching the friendly metal-beater while I kept an eye on the Plume of Feathers. Livak might be able to take Ait's place, if she hadn't come up with any leads, but I wasn't any too keen on the idea of her hanging round this neighbourhood on her own. I couldn't very well stay with her, not without risking suspicion, even if we could somehow get Halice to keep watch at the Plume of Feathers. It wasn't that I didn't think Livak could take care of herself, as I knew only too well that she could; the problem was I didn't want to risk any Elietimm spotting her, dyed hair or not.

I was getting uneasy again. I turned back to the end of the alley, looking back at the smithy, wondering what to do for the best. My wits seemed to be unravelling, and I swallowed on a suddenly dry throat. It was a warm day, sure enough, but I hadn't been that long without a drink. I scrubbed a hand across my face but that seemed to make things worse. My eyes began to blur and the noises of the street around me became oddly distorted, echoing round my ears then lost in a sound like crashing waves. Cold sweat began to pour from me, my shirt clung stickily to my back as I crumpled against a wall, legs suddenly unable to support my weight. The blood was pounding in my head like the beat from Misaen's own anvil and my breath was catching in my chest as I fought off the panic that threatened to choke me.

I heard a footstep on my off hand and gripped the hilt of the sword with nerveless fingers; as I did so, Saedrin opened the shades to swallow me.

*The outer court of Wellery's Hall,
in the hidden island city of Hadrumal,
30th of Aft-Spring*

He was an imposing figure; tall, dressed in black velvet with a subtle embroidery of scarlet and gold flames at the neck, indicating his mastery of fire to even the most untutored apprentice. A ruby glowed on his breast, clasped in the jaws of a sinuous dragon brooch, the red gold of his ring of office catching the sunlight as he raised his hand to adjust the hang of his maroon cloak. This and the excellent cut of his gown happily concealed much of his bulk, but regretfully the current fashion in high, tight collars was cruelly unflattering to his thickly jowled neck. Several apprentices hastily removed themselves from his path as he strode through the courtyard, an expression of extreme displeasure on his flushed face.

'Archmage!'

A slimly built man in dark, workaday broadcloth turned his head, an unremarkable figure were it not for his air of absolute confidence.

'Hearth-Master.' Planir inclined his head in a nicely calculated acknowledgement then turned back to the trio of nervous novice wizards.

Kalion had no choice but to wait for the Archmage to conclude his conversation. He stood, feet planted firmly on the cobbles, brows knitting as his already high colour deepened to beetroot, which clashed unpleasantly with his opulent attire.

'It's been a pleasure; remember, my door is always open.' Planir's warm smile deepened the fine creases around his eyes, which lingered a little on the slim back and fine ankles of one of the girls. The apprentices quickly retreated from Kalion's forbidding gaze.

'Good morning, Hearth-Master.' Planir ran a hand over his close-cut black hair and turned to Kalion. 'Let's use your study, shall we? It's closest.'

Before the fire mage could reply, Planir led the way briskly out of the courtyard and down the flagged sidewalk of Hadrumal's high road. Kalion swept after the Archmage, his lips narrow with barely concealed irritation by the time they turned into a second courtyard of pale stone buildings and he took out a key to open the door to a slender tower whose pinnacles were carved into tongues of stone fire.

'I am very much perturbed by what I have just learned—' he began as they climbed the stairs.

'That much is evident,' said Planir without heat. 'Which is why I feel we should discuss your concerns in the privacy of your rooms.'

Kalion's heavy boots rang on the oak of the stairs as he stamped his way up to his luxuriously appointed accommodations.

'What has happened to this man Ryshad?' he demanded without preamble, shoving the door closed behind Planir and dumping his cloak unceremoniously, half on to a sumptuous brocade chair, half on the floor.

'Shivvalan is attempting to find out, Hearth-Master,' replied Planir mildly, retrieving the cloak and hanging it precisely on its customary hook.

'Attempting sounds more than a little vague,' Kalion sniffed. 'Do these Ice Islanders have the man or not?'

Planir spread his hands in an eloquent gesture. 'As yet, we do not know.'

'We need to find out,' stated Kalion firmly. 'The matter must be raised with the Relshazri magistrates at once; I have contacts in the city with sufficient status to do so. I should have an answer for you within a few days at most.'

'Thank you, Hearth-Master, but I don't believe that will be necessary, just at present.' There was steel wrapped in the velvet of Planir's courtesy.

Kalion stared at him, undaunted. 'Your man, Shivvalan, has

managed to lose perhaps the most significant of all the artefacts we have discovered pertaining to this lost colony, and you don't think urgent measures are necessary? That sword is one of the few items we can absolutely place in the possession of a man we know without doubt to have sailed with Den Fellaemion to Dastennin only knows where and then vanished.'

'I prefer to give Shivvalan some time to discover Ryshad's whereabouts discreetly.' Planir made himself comfortable on a leather upholstered settle. 'I don't particularly want the Relshazri asking questions about this man's significance or wondering just what our interest in him might be. It is my decision to make, Kalion.'

The Archmage's tone was smooth but implacable. Kalion turned to busy himself at a sideboard where a crystal decanter stood in a circle of red-stemmed glasses.

'Cordial?'

'A little of the damson liqueur, thank you.'

Planir took the glass with a warm smile and Kalion sat down in a high backed, ornately carved chair, arranging the skirts of his robe with some care.

'If the Elietimm have taken the man, it'll be because they have the talents to unlock the mysteries the sword is concealing.' Kalion leaned forward, his expression intent. 'We must be prepared; we have to know what we are dealing with. I have said time and again that we should make a more active search of the libraries on the mainland, demand access to the archives of the remaining temples, perhaps even bodies such as Merchant Venturers' associations, the Caladhrian Parliament. We need to know if they have information we can use and this slow accumulation of reports from itinerant scholars is simply not good enough.'

'I am sure that we are learning what we need as fast as is consistent with discretion.' Planir wiped a bead of moisture from the foot of his empty glass and placed it carefully on the top of a highly polished wine cooler. 'Still, tell me Hearth-Master, what do you propose to tell the Merchant Venturers of Col, for example, when you demand access to their confidential archive? What would be your explanation?'

'I would assume such a request, with the authority of the Archmage behind it, would need no explanation.' Kalion clearly thought the question nonsensical.

Planir nodded, pursing his lips. 'And then, how would you counter the subsequent flocks of rumours taking flight clear across the Old Empire and probably right through the Great Forest and into Solura as well. That some secret plot is being hatched among all powerful wizards, hidden among the enchanted mists of their island city, guarded as they are by spell-wrought demons? What would you give me better odds upon; a plan to foist a mage-born King on to the throne of Lescar or some scheme to take control of, say, the Aldabreshi diamond trade?'

Kalion looked at the Archmage, puzzlement wrinkling his pudgy brow.

'Never underestimate the power of ignorant people in sufficiently large numbers, Hearth-Master,' said Planir crisply. 'When people do not know the reason for something, they will supply their own. I have no intention of telling anyone outside the Council and our other contacts about the dangers the eastern lands might be facing.'

'We have to do something.' Kalion raised one hand in an impotent gesture of frustration. 'I have spent both halves of the last season trying to come up with an application of the elements to this cursed aetheric gimmickry and I might as well be trying to catch the moon's reflection with a spoon.'

Planir permitted himself a slight smile at the nursery tale image. 'Your efforts may not have been rewarded but that in itself adds significantly to our knowledge. If you, the senior Hearth-Master, with one of the strongest affinities on record, cannot find an application of fire in the aetheric methods of kindling flame, no one can.'

His tone was entirely sincere and Kalion acknowledged the truth of this with a grunt. 'That's all very well, Archmage, but if we can't counter these unholy magicians, the threat they pose becomes even greater.'

'We will find the means to combat them with their own methods,' Planir said firmly. 'If we mages cannot use these incantations to access this aetheric power, whatever it might be, there are intelligent, trustworthy minds among the non-mage-born that we can enlist. The answers are there to be found and I am confident many of them are somehow carried in these artefacts from the end of the Empire. There are many secrets held in these dreams.'

'How are you to reach them?' Kalion looked at him, unsmiling. 'Your record to date is none too reassuring, Archmage. Tell me, has that girl from Vanam recovered her senses yet? Sending her into such a deep sleep may well have given her dreams holding all we could wish to know, but as long as she remains comatose, we cannot tell.'

Planir's expression remained unchanged. 'We are hopeful that we will find a means to revive her. The indications are promising and she remains healthy in her sleep, thus far.'

'So your quest for knowledge is split now; searching for a means to control aetheric magic, on the one hand, and the means to cure those whose wits unravel when your experiments go wrong, on the other.' Kalion's tone was unforgiving. 'Surely that makes it more urgent to find the relevant material more speedily?'

'I think that haste has played its own significant part in those few tragedies that you are, of course, quite right to remind me about.' Planir rose and refilled his glass. 'More cordial?'

Kalion left his own drink untouched. 'So you are going to continue as you are? Do my concerns count for nothing? What of the Council?'

Planir relaxed against the deep crimson of the leather upholstery and smiled reassuringly.

'Until the Elietimm make an overt move, either against ourselves or in attempting to establish a presence on the mainland, the greatest danger from aetheric magic stems from our attempts to wield it with imprecise knowledge. Our most complete information, such as it is, has come from the dreams of those students we have recruited from the Universities of Vanam and Col, and most particularly from those who are most closely matched, as far as we can estimate, to the original owners of the artefacts. I am confident the Council will understand that this is a long, drawn-out process. We know it takes time for the dreams to assert themselves and we have more artefacts than we have suitable volunteers for this project, since we cannot, by definition, use mages. We are doing all we can to interest suitable scholars, but any overt recruitment will only start more rumours, probably about ambitious wizards seducing innocents into arcane rituals, probably as a cover for unbridled carnality, knowing the sort of things cloistered academics dream up about us.'

Kalion could not restrain a bark of laughter at that remark. 'That's all very well, Archmage, but—'

Planir raised a hand. 'You cannot deny that such things have happened in the past, Kalion. Remember the stories that are still told about Lauder the Benefactor. Think how much worse they would be if the mages of the day had not managed to conceal his worst excesses.'

Kalion shuddered with unfeigned horror and Planir continued before the stout wizard regained his composure.

'You have spent long hours in the Council, Kalion, making a very persuasive case that the time has come for wizardry to take a role in the wider world. I agree with you; you know that. Therefore, I would hate to see some ill-judged move as we attempt to deal with this puzzle of the Elietimm lead to a renewal of all the old prejudices and fears that drove some of my predecessors to a frankly excessive insularity.'

The Hearth-Master sighed. 'There was enough of that when we were apprentices, wasn't there? When the Cloud-Master of New Hall had to clear up that mess Azazir and his clique made with the weather in Caladhria.'

Planir nodded and got to his feet. 'I appreciate your concerns, Kalion, I really do, but you have to understand I have a great many pots in the hearth at once. If one boils over, all the alchemy's ruined.'

Kalion looked up. 'I've always said earth-mages shouldn't

play with fire,' he commented with a touch of heavy-handed humour.

'Do come and see me if you feel you need to.' Planir left the room without ceremony and strode back through Hadrumal to his own domain, high in an ancient tower overlooking the roofs of the various Halls, old and new, strung out along the long high road as it wound down to the harbour. He did not appear to be hurrying, but he covered the distance more rapidly than most would have done. The Archmage climbed the dark stairs two and three at a time without any excessive effort and slammed the heavy door of his study back without preamble. A young man leaped to his feet, very nearly upsetting the parchment-covered desk he had been working at and only just managing to save a broad silver bowl from flying headlong. An amber gleam faded from the swirling waters within it.

'Where's D'Olbriot's man, Usara?' demanded Planir, his eyes gleaming. 'More to the point, where's that cursed sword?'

'I don't know.' The pale mage's voice was under control but he couldn't restrain the tide of colour that swept up from his ink-stained collar to shine through his sparse hair.

'If you can't manage the scrying, get Shannet to do it. It's her specialism.' Planir's tone was unforgiving.

'I can't see how that would help; she doesn't know the man any more than I do and we don't have any of his possessions to give us a focus. At least I met him on the boat coming back from the ocean last year,' said Usara defiantly.

'We need to find him, 'Sar, and fast!' Planir's warning was unmistakable.

'I know.' The younger man squared his rather thin shoulders. 'I bespoke Shiv a while ago and he's persuaded Mellitha to call in any favour that might give them a lead. It'll cost her a lot of goodwill but she's confident she should get a result.'

The Archmage scowled. 'Spending her goodwill means costing me coin. At least tell me she's got the sense not to make it mage business? If people start thinking of her as a wizard instead of a tax-contractor she's no use to us any more.'

'Give her some credit. By the way, there's a letter here for you, came in with one of the ships from Col.' Usara turned to a side-table and held out a thick package with several ornate seals. 'That's the D'Olbriot crest, isn't it?'

'Yes, thank you, 'Sar, I think it might very well be.' Planir looked at the letter for a long moment and groaned with exasperation, tapping the creamy parchment against one palm. 'So what do I tell the good Sieur? How exactly do I explain to him that we've lost his heirloom sword and have no idea where it has got to?'

'I think he might be a little more concerned about the loss of his sworn man.' Usara avoided Planir's eyes but his voice held a mild rebuke.

'That too.' Planir granted him a perfunctory nod. 'When does the ship sail? Do you know if they're expecting a reply?'

'They are,' confirmed Usara. 'The courier said he had authority to hold the vessel for as long as you needed.'

'I think I'll write to Camarl,' Planir said thoughtfully. 'He has the Sieur's ear and can be trusted to be discreet. Tell me—'

His question was lost as the studded door swung open to crash against its hinges. A sharp-faced old man leaned against the door jamb and heaved a rattling sigh.

'Get me a drink, 'Sar, and clear away some of those bloody papers so I can sit down.'

'Good morning, Cloud-Master Otrick. May I say how delighted I am that you honour us with your company.' Planir's tone was sarcastic but he offered the old man his arm while Usara hastily grabbed a sheaf of documents off a chair.

'Don't get lippy with me, you jumped-up coal-heaver, or I'll turn you into a rabbit. Thank you, 'Sar.'

Otrick drained the glass of white brandy and coughed with a penetration that rang a faint echo from Usara's scrying bowl. The deeply carved lines in his face told of a long life, lived hard but his vivid blue eyes were as alert as either of the men in the room.

'So, what's the latest?' demanded the old wizard.

'If we don't come up with some results and fast, I'm going to be spending some long evenings persuading Council members not to back Kalion's demands for an all-out assault on every library with more than three books to its catalogue,' Planir said grimly.

'For a man who wants to see wizardry raised to a position of influence, he doesn't seem too clear on the consequences of that, does he?' Otrick shook his head in disgust. 'Perhaps we should just send an envoy to the Elietimm: "Please don't attack us just yet; you see, we have no idea how to combat your magic and that really wouldn't be fair, would it?"'

'I can think of a few others who would be interested to learn that the fabled Archmage isn't omniscient,' commented Usara, glancing through his documents. 'Summertime ambitions in Lescar and parts of Ensaimin could get distinctly out of hand.'

'I'd like Kalion to come up with that idea for himself,' Planir mused. 'Do you think you could accidentally encounter Allin, that apprentice of the Hearth-Master's, 'Sar?'

'Do you mean the mouthy piece from Selerima with the unlikely hair or that timid little lass from Lescar with the fire affinity?' Usara looked up for a moment.

'The latter,' confirmed Planir. 'She'll answer any questions Kalion puts to her, I'd imagine.'

'I'm surprised Kalion lets her associate with the likes of you, 'Sar,' Otrick laughed suggestively.

Usara ignored the old wizard. 'I'll discuss a few minor worries with her,' he said to Planir. 'By the time she's carried them back to Kalion and he's had a chance to think it all through I imagine he'll see the way the birds are flying well enough.'

Otrick growled something obscene under his breath and held out his glass to Usara.

'So how are your experiments going, 'Sar? What wonders of aetheric mystery have your sad little collection of bookworms managed today?'

Usara refilled the glass, his hand steady despite a faint tint rising on his high cheekbones at Otrick's words. 'I am pleased to report, Cloud-Master, that we now have the incantations perfected to send a message clear across the island.'

Otrick's eyes widened and his jaw dropped. 'And that must be all of six leagues!'

'I don't think sarcasm is particularly helpful, old man.' Planir reached for the brandy himself, his tone a little acid. 'Unless you have something constructive to follow it, that is?'

Otrick frowned and his face became serious, his angular features forbidding. 'We are agreed that we need people with knowledge of aetheric enchantments to combat the Elietimm – when, mark you, when, not if – they decide that the mainland offers more than those wind-scoured islands of theirs. I know you're working those scholars hard, Usara, and yes, some means for non-mage-born to communicate over distance could be vital, especially if it comes to a full-scale war. The thing is, we know these ancient sorcerers could do so much more; finding a path, confusing pursuit, taking information out of hostile minds—'

'Do you teach goodwives to spin their distaffs in your spare time, Otrick?' Planir enquired. 'We know all this.'

'All I know is we need to find out how this magic works, the basis of it. Only then can we work out how to stop the bastards.' Usara's shoulders drooped and weariness clouded his face.

'The ancients who sailed to Kel Ar'Ayen knew. That's what they called that colony of theirs, that much I can tell you.' Otrick leaned forward in his chair, his eyes bright sapphire. 'They knew enough to disrupt the basis for aetheric magic so thoroughly that the Elietimm have been chained to their barren rocks for thirty generations or more. They must have been masters of it; they'd been using this mysterious power to stitch the Empire together across thousands of leagues for twenty generations! They would hardly have sent people clear across the ocean without the very best magical support they could muster. We need to know what they knew, so let's find this colony of theirs and see if they left any records, any clues, some helpful tome covering aetheric magic right from its first principles, whatever there might be!'

Planir drew a sudden breath and leaned back in his tall chair, long fingers laced together in front of his smoothly shaven jaw. 'You might have an idea worth study there, Cloud-Master.'

'You mean I've got something else to try to tease out of this ever increasing tangle of half-remembered dreams and reveries,' groaned Usara.

'It can't be that difficult.' Otrick's tone was dismissive.

'Would you care to work out the rules for White Raven, working from a set with half the pieces missing and no board?' the younger mage retorted with spirit.

'Who can we spare for a search of the Archives?' demanded Planir abruptly. 'We'll start by collating all the references to this lost colony in the existing record; that should give you some idea which thread to pull to unravel the weave, 'Sar.'

'Casuel Devoir,' Usara replied almost before Planir had finished speaking. 'He has the talents for it, Misaen only knows, and it'll keep him out of my hair for a good long while with any luck.'

'He's a real kiss-breeches, that one, isn't he?' commented Otrick contemptuously. 'Still, he has an eye for detail, I'll give him that. So where are the best records likely to be held?'

'I've been thinking about sending a mage to wait upon Messire D'Olbriot,' Planir said thoughtfully. 'Devoir's Tormalin born, isn't he? He'll know the steps of the dances there well enough to be a credible choice for an envoy and he could make a discreet survey of any contemporary records, while he was there.'

'It'll be a long job.' Usara shook his head.

'Well, if the Elietimm turn up before we've discovered some more elegant way of frustrating their magic, we'll just have to blast them into the Otherworld with traditional fire and flood.' The old wizard grinned like a death's head.

'That would certainly give Kalion something useful to do,' remarked Planir dryly.

The Barracoons,
Magistrates' House of Correction, Relshaz,
30th of Aft-Spring

I can't say I woke up; rather the chaos inside my skull finally subsided enough for me to become aware of my surroundings and myself again. Once I had the measure of it all, I almost wished I hadn't bothered.

My arms and legs ached as if I'd been trampled by a dray team and for one heart-stopping moment I thought I couldn't move any of my limbs. The frozen panic of that idea eased when I found I could just about force my sword hand towards my eyes but it felt as if I were drowning in treacle, it took so much effort, so I gave it up once I had seen my fingers with my own eyes.

That wasn't particularly easy either; blood, mud or both was thickly smeared across my face and my eyelids pulled painfully at my lashes as I forced them open. I blinked to try and clear the worst but it did little good. To my feeble annoyance an unbidden tear of frustration escaped me, and I winced as it stung a raw graze across the bridge of my nose. That at least did not seem to have been broken again and I managed to mumble a rather incoherent blessing to Dastennin for that minor mercy. If my nose had been broken I would probably have suffocated on my own blood, never to waken.

Insidious fears came creeping out of the back of my mind. How had I come to collapse like that? Was this falling-sickness? There wasn't any history of it in my family, not that I knew of, but you never could tell. Perhaps that Elietimm enchanter rampaging through my mind had done some damage that was only now becoming apparent. Was this the start of some awful disease; was I going to lose my legs, my sight, my wits, end up drooling into my gruel like the old man who had lived with his daughter at the end of our street, worms eating away his brain? Was I going mad?

I gradually became aware that I was lying face down on a dirt floor, coarse straw pricking painfully into my naked skin. This did not augur well. I drew a deep breath, preparing to try to get myself to my hands and knees, but the stench of the place seized me by the throat: a potent mix of old urine, rank sweat, rotting food and soiled straw. I was racked by merciless coughing until I retched up a sour mouthful of bile. That started such vicious cramps in my gut, they would have floored me if I hadn't already had my nose in the ratshit.

I had taken an unholy beating; that much was becoming apparent. Who had done it, and, in Dast's name, why? I lay in the filth, wished helplessly for some water and waited for the fire in my lungs to subside, the iron constriction around my chest to ease. In the meantime, I tried to lash my debilitated wits into action to at least make sense of the sounds around me, since that took no effort that could cause me more pain.

There was a low murmur of voices, mostly male, some that could either be lads or women. A bark of rapid Relshazri came from somewhere and caused a shuffle of bare feet on the earth and straw of the floor. Someone laughed, a vicious cackle and leather whistled and snapped on naked skin, the crack followed by a strangled whimper. Whoever was laughing carried on merrily, clearly having the whip hand in more ways than one. Somewhere at a little distance, an argument erupted, the words lost in snarls and obscenities. Fists smacked on flesh and a surge of encouragement from all sides urged the combatants on until a metal door clanged and booted feet stamped in to break up the brawl. I opened my eyes and squinted at the figures silhouetted against the meagre light from a grille set high in a wall, watching as clubs forced the fighters apart, landing indiscriminate blows on any of the cowering, filthy bodies within reach, just for good measure.

I was in a lock-up. That was better than being in an Elietimm cell or at the mercy of Relshazri street robbers, I was forced to conclude, but how in the name of all that's holy had I got here? I forced myself to try to knit my wits back together; I'd collapsed for some reason I couldn't guess at and the implications of that were enough to start shivers running up and down my spine like blackbeetles. Given the place I was in, who knows, it could have been actual blackbeetles. I forced myself to concentrate, no easy task given my exhaustion and the multitude of aches distracting me.

'You're a Tormalin, a sworn man; get a grip on yourself,' I berated myself silently. 'Lying in a heap of filth feeling sorry for yourself will get you nowhere.'

If I'd been found collapsed on the street, some kind citizen could have rung the Watch bell on me, couldn't they? If that had happened, the Watch would most likely assume I was drunk. From what I'd seen of Relshaz, it seemed to be a city where soaks would probably be left where they lay, but if I'd been blocking some wealthy man's gate perhaps the Watch would have dumped me in a cell to sober up. All this sounded reasonable enough, but what had I done to deserve a kicking like this? I narrowed my eyes with some effort and deciphered the pattern of boot nails on my forearm. I had hardly been in a state to stand, let alone fight back, so why beat me even further senseless?

A groan escaped me. I shut my eyes, black despair threatening, despite all my efforts to fight it. My head swam and, as I felt myself slipping back to the shades, I didn't even try to fight it.

Waking again, briefly, I saw faint stars dotting the midnight blue of the sky as the lesser moon rode high, alone and unreachable behind the stark black bars of the window grille. Chilled to the bone but too stiff to move, even assuming there would have been anywhere to go for warmth, I stared hungrily at the distant lights until my eyes slid shut once more.

'Ryshad Tathel!'

The sound of my own name, bellowed in a harsh Relshazri accent, stung me to life more effectively than any lash.

My first attempt at reply died on my dry tongue and cracked lips. I swallowed, winced at the truly foul taste in my mouth and coughed, gasping as all my bruises awoke at once and fought to outdo each other with stabs of agony.

'Here!' I managed to croak, getting painfully to my feet. 'This way.'

I scrubbed hastily at my face to clear my vision and blinked at a burly man in a coarse, stained livery who was standing in a doorway. Morning light came through the grille in the wall and showed me a wide room, stone walls and sloping floor carrying the worst of the ordure to an open drain. The stench was enough to choke a cat. Men were slumped against the walls, some sleeping on jealously hoarded piles of straw, most stripped, a few in rags and all with wounds and bruises in varying stages of healing. If I looked like any of them, I was in a worse state than I had realised.

'Come on, move!' The guard growled and gestured menacingly with a short stave. I didn't need telling again and followed him meekly, stumbling on knees weak as wet wool, determined not to give him the excuse to hit me that he was clearly looking for.

He crossed a narrow courtyard and shoved me into a stark, whitewashed room, closing the door behind him and leaning on it, curiosity alive among the boils on his face as he stared greedily at my visitor.

'Good morning, Ryshad.'

Mellitha was seated on a crude bench, her skirts gathered neatly around her ankles, no lace on her petticoats today and stout boots laced against the filth underfoot. She had a closely woven and lidded reed basket beside her and looked entirely at her ease.

'Good morning, my lady.' I lifted my chin and ignored the fact that I was standing there with my stones swinging in the breeze. At least the muck on my face would conceal any blushes that might escape me.

'Do sit down. Now, what in Trimon's name do you think you were doing?' Anger sparked in her stormy grey eyes as she spoke in a rapid Toremal dialect, which evidently left the guard struggling to keep up.

'I have no idea what you are talking about,' I said flatly.

Faint puzzlement deepened the laughter lines around her eyes.

'The last thing I remember is passing out in a street in the metalsmiths' quarter,' I hissed. 'What got me here?'

'The fact that you attempted to steal a valuable antique arm-ring from a antiquarian's salesroom.' Mellitha shook her head, as if not quite believing it herself. 'Apparently you simply walked in, picked it up and tried to leave. When the man tried to stop you, you fought with him but by then his assistant had sent for the Watch. It took five of them to subdue you, apparently. How badly are you hurt?'

'No bones broken,' I was glad to realise this as I answered. 'Whoever gave me a beating knew just what they were doing.'

Mellitha surveyed my various bruises and lacerations and then reached into her basket.

'Yarrow ointment,' she said crisply, pressing a small pot into my hand.

I ignored it. 'This makes no sense. I wouldn't try to rob someone in broad daylight. Why should I when Shiv's got a bag of coin heavy enough to buy up whatever he fancies?'

'There has to be an explanation.' Mellitha looked at me speculatively. 'What about the Elietimm? They might want you off the board for some reason. You've some experience of them attacking your mind; could this be one of their tricks?'

I shook my head decisively before stopping to think properly about what she was suggesting.

'No,' I said slowly after a long moment. 'The Ice Islanders, that was definitely an assault from outside, someone forcing their way into your head and seizing your wits. This was—' I shrugged. 'This was just losing myself, everything coming apart at the seams—' I shook involuntarily at the horror of the memory and Mellitha reached out to take my hand, leaning forward.

'It's all right; I'm here now.' Her words were those of a

mother soothing away a nightmare, but her grip was strong and reassuring, somehow passing me a measure of strength.

'How did you find me?' I managed to ask.

'Not easily.' A shade of a smile lightened the concern in her eyes.

'How soon can you get me out?' I was starting to get a grip on the essentials at last.

'I can't,' said Mellitha grimly. 'Not today, anyway.'

I stared at her. 'You must know who to pay off, surely?'

'It's not as simple as that.' Irritation coloured her voice. 'We have elections at the next greater full moon; several of the candidates have been making a lot of noise about excessive profiteering by the sitting magistrates, so no one's taking so much as a consideration until the votes are counted.'

'You're telling me an elected official doesn't want to take a bribe?' I shook my head in disbelief. 'Don't Relshazri dogs eat free sausage? Just offer more money; Messire will honour the debt.'

'It simply isn't a question of money these days.' Mellitha's tone was sharp. 'Despite what you Tormalin may think, our elections do sometimes produce dedicated and honest magistrates. We certainly find it preferable to nailing everyone into place with clientship and patronage for the benefit of those lucky enough to born to the right parents. That's one thing I do think the Rationalists have got right.'

'I'm sorry.' I shut my eyes for a moment to get myself in hand. Just for the present Mellitha was the only help I had and it would do me no good at all to alienate her. What was I thinking, losing my grip like this? 'So, what is going to happen to me?'

'You'll be sold at the open slave auction, the day after tomorrow.' Mellitha lifted the lid on her basket. 'Now, I have some clothes for you and some food and water. I've paid the jailer to get you into a better cell as well. There's some coin inside the cheese, in case you need to pay anyone else off or buy food before I can send more in to you. Now, where's the salve? Oh, yes, I gave it to you . . .' She continued talking but her words faded to a meaningless jumble as I stared at the opposite wall. This is probably going to seem really stupid, but I hadn't even given a thought to the trade that is, after all, one of the principal foundations of Relshazri wealth: the buying and selling of slaves.

We don't trade in slaves in Tormalin, not for the last handful of generations; we've progressed beyond such things. Caladhrian Lords, on the other hand, are only too happy to take a bond against a debtor's body and even against his wife's and children's, in some cases. Defaulters can wake one morning to find themselves being measured for an iron collar and either sold to an erstwhile neighbour to work the fields or stumbling down the road to Relshaz, depending on the prices. Lescari Dukes are often in the market for a couple of hundred warm bodies, trying to get a quick crop of wine or grain out of any land that has escaped the fighting for a couple of seasons, to sell for sound Tormalin Crowns or Caladhrian Stars. On the other side of the coin, they're only too happy to recoup some of their costs at the end of the fighting seasons by selling off any prisoners they've managed to seize, the poor bastards who don't have relatives willing or wealthy enough to pay a ransom. Relshaz takes them all and sells them on at a profit, usually to the Aldabreshi where by all accounts they live a few wretched years chained in a galley or worked to death on some island, Trimon only knows where.

'You have to pay whatever it takes to get me out at the sale,' I broke in on Mellitha's detailed explanation of her agreement with the jailer.

'Of course, I'll do my very best—' she began, a little affronted.

'Bid whatever you need to,' I insisted. 'Messire will repay you, trust me.'

'Of course. Try not to worry. Once you're out of here, we can sort out what happened, find some answers.' Mellitha sounded just like my mother, consoling me over a lost hound-puppy. I wasn't reassured. That hadn't turned out at all well either;

the poor little scrap had gone scavenging round the crab-boats, fallen into the harbour and drowned.

The guard snapped something at Mellitha and she responded with a curt rebuke. She still got to her feet however, pressing a bundle into my arms. 'Just keep out of trouble in here and we'll get you out at the sale.'

'See if Shiv has any ideas,' I called over my shoulder as the guard hustled me out with his stave jabbing painfully into my kidneys.

The rank-smelling turnkey led me through a couple of courtyards to a different wing of the lock-up. Mellitha's coin had bought me a pallet lumpily stuffed with coarse husks in a wooden-floored, second-storey room with a couple of handful of others. I sat down carefully, my back to the wall, and unwrapped the bundle, the outermost layer proving to be a plain linen shirt and a pair of old breeches. Judging from the garb of my companions that was evidently the most clothing anyone here was allowed. A threadbare towel was rolled around a leather water bottle, some fresh bread and a creamy yellow cheese. The sharp scent made me realise I was actually starting to feel a little hungry again. I dampened the corner of the towel and cleaned the worst of the filth from my hands and face but gave up on the rest; the water would be more valuable in keeping me from the risk of prison fever lurking in whatever the turnkeys gave us to drink. Eating half of the bread put more heart into me and I certainly felt less vulnerable with some clothes on.

A few of the others in the long room were staring with a greater or lesser degree of curiosity. I met their gazes without a challenge but with enough intensity to make them drop their eyes first. Once I was satisfied that I was unobserved, I discreetly removed the wax-paper package moulded into the cheese and tucked it down the front of my breeches. That done, I made my own survey of my fellow would-be slaves, making sure I didn't catch anyone's eye or look at any one of them for too long. The last thing I wanted was to get myself into a fight. The other men were slumped on their pallets or staring idly out of the barred window; most were a little older than myself, well enough fed, and about half had the weathered faces of an outdoor life. No one was talking so I had no means of identifying their origins, but since I was only going to be here for a short while I didn't see any benefit in striking up a conversation with anyone.

A couple of younger men were coughing persistently, a soft but repetitive sound that was already becoming tiresome. It looked as if they had been forced to the far end of the cell, my pallet and another vacant place separating them from the other prisoners. I glanced at them and wondered how far over I could move myself before my neighbour on the other side would object.

'Sit tight, be patient and Mellitha will get you out,' I told myself sternly. If I kept myself to myself and didn't share a cup or anything, I shouldn't be at too much risk of contagion.

To my considerable surprise only the second chime of the day came ringing in through the unglazed window, from a timepiece quite close by, from the sound of it. I sighed; it was evidently going to be a long and tedious couple of days.

Noon came and went, a shower of rain pattered softly down on the roof tiles and a different turnkey appeared with a tray of wooden bowls of barley-meal, all unpleasantly crusted with the remains of old meals and with flies hovering eagerly above them. I left mine untouched, soothing my growling stomach with a little more bread.

'Hungry's better than risking the squits,' I advised myself firmly. Besides, the less I ate, the less I would have to visit the reeking crocks standing against the far wall; one for excrement to sell for manure, one for urine to sell for bleach, I assumed wryly. Trust the Relshazri to find a way of turning coin from every situation.

That was about the most humorous aspect of the day. The afternoon's entertainment came when we were herded to the window by a couple of guards with whips in order to watch a man being garrotted in the courtyard below. It took ten men to drag the heavy-set criminal out and lash him to the execution frame; he screamed obscenities at them until a leather gag stopped his mouth. At that point tears began to stream down his brutish face, already red and suffused with blood even before the guards drew lots to see who would turn the ratchet to crush the sad bastard's throat.

I didn't bother watching; there are no more lessons I can learn by seeing men die. Instead I looked at the other windows in the tall blocks ranged around the courtyard. The bottom-most levels were evidently cells of the kind I'd woken up in; gaunt and filthy faces with matted hair were pressed to the bars, too many all too eager to see the spectacle. At the higher levels, men and women in decent garb looked down, some reluctantly, some with horrified fascination. I wondered how much they were paying for decent food and cleanliness; probably more than they would had they been lodging in the costliest inn the city boasted.

As soon as the guards allowed us, I returned to my pallet.

'What did he do?' one of the others asked, rubbing a hand over his ashen face.

The guard scowled. 'Raped and murdered little girls.'

I was pleased to see everyone in the room grimace or spit with honest revulsion; perhaps it would be safe to risk going to sleep in here after all.

By the time evening came I was bored out of my mind. I'd tried doing some basic stretches to loosen up my bruised limbs but that attracted everyone's attention, so I soon stopped. I ate the rest of the bread and cheese, reasoning it would probably be stolen while I slept if I didn't. The window faced west, so we caught the last of the sunlight as the rain clouds passed and I watched the black shadows of the bars slowly crawl across the chipped and stained plaster as I dozed. I can't have gone to sleep so early since the summer evenings when my mother would herd Mistal, Kitria and myself to our beds as we all protested that it was still light and it wasn't fair, why were Hansey and Ridner allowed to stay up?

I woke in the dawn cool of the following morning with a nagging sense that something was not quite right. With a sudden shock I realised the coughing had stopped. Sitting sharply upright, I looked over to see one of the sick men lying rigid and silent, his glazed eyes staring blankly at the ceiling, lips blackened in an ashen face. His companion was prostrate opposite, skin pale and tainted with blue, his chest still moving slightly, a pulse hammering in his neck as the breath bubbled moistly in his lungs.

My abrupt movement had woken a couple of the others; one went to hammer on the door and bellow for the turnkey. When two surly jailers arrived, they dragged the corpse and the sick man away, treating both with equal indifference and leaving the stained pallets behind. I shuddered and hoped that no one had died on mine recently, certainly not of anything contagious.

If anything, that day was harder to endure than the first. I've never taken well to inactivity and although I continued to tell myself not to let it rile me – that Dastennin sends fish to the patient, anyway, that I'd been in worse places than this – it was all wearing a little thin by the end of the day. The only worse place I could think of was the Elietimm dungeon and at least I'd had people I could talk to in there, Aiten's support, Shiv's magic and Livak's talents with locks as a basis for plans for escape. That started me thinking about the others, hoping they had some plan to secure my purchase at the auction, worrying in case the Elietimm had made some move while I was stuck in here. I finally concluded that what I hated most about my current situation was not the place I found myself in but the fact that I was having to rely on other people to get me out. That realisation did nothing to improve my mood.

I was trying to remember all the verses to one of those interminable Soluran ballads about some brainless noble rescuing an idiot girl with more hair than wit when the door swung open to reveal a couple of guards and a well-dressed man with a ledger under one arm and in the other hand a pomander that he kept lifted to his nostrils. I envied him that more than his well-polished boots. The book-keeper looked round the room and then started with the closest to the door, which happened to be me. Looking me up and down, he nodded to the nearest guard.

'Strip him.'

I ripped off my shirt and breeches myself, giving the guard a warning glare and trying to tuck Mellitha's coin under the clothes unseen. The man with the pomander scrutinised me closely from head to toe and then nodded again; this time the guard seized my jaw and held it down so the man could see my teeth. The turnkey's hand stank and I swallowed against an urge to gag, opening my mouth wide so the bastard wouldn't have a reason to put a filthy finger in my mouth. If he had I'd probably have bitten it off, whatever it cost me.

The clerk counted my teeth, nodded, made a note in his ledger and then looked me in the eye.

'Do you have any skills?' he asked in passable Tormalin.

I wondered quickly what to say for the best; I didn't want to push my price up too high for Mellitha, but equally I didn't fancy being sold as part of a yoke of ten field slaves to the first bidder.

'Swordsman,' I said firmly.

He shrugged, made another note and moved on to the next man. I won a warning glare from the turnkey as I reached for my clothes, so I simply sat down to wait and see what would happen next, listening as the book-keeper went round the room. It seemed I was in the company of a couple of dockers, a mercer's runner, a clerk, two rent collectors, a potter and a stockman. Dastennin only knows how they had ended up here. With this interrogation complete, we were herded, still naked, out of our cell and down to the end of a long line of other unfortunates waiting to enter a long, low building at the far end of the compound. A second line was forming, evidently drawn from the female cells, which made the wait a little less tedious. I felt sorry for some of the women, probably here through no fault of their own, vainly trying to cover their nakedness with hands and hair, often with children clinging to their thighs, eyes hollow with distress. Others had clearly been through this before, challenging the men with bold stares, pointing and giggling, hand gestures leaving little of their conversation to the imagination. One bold piece caught my eye and gave me a long, slow wink, but I caught sight of the brand on her palm marking her as a whore who stole from her customers so she didn't get a response from me.

The line moved on. We were shoved through a door by guards with ungentle clubs. I found myself facing a long, deep bath, for all the world like the one on Messire's hill country estate that they use for washing the sheep. The guards were using their staves like shepherd's staffs, so I jumped in rather than wait to be pushed. The water was scummy and foul with soiled straw but I didn't care, scrubbing at myself to get the worst of the filth off, ignoring the sting of my cuts and grazes that were now joined by numerous bites from nameless vermin. When I emerged at the far end, a man in a long tunic forced me on to a bench with impersonal hands and took a pair of clippers to my head. All in all, I now had a fair idea of what it felt like to be a ram being readied for market.

The air was cold on my shorn scalp as we were herded through another door. It was one way of getting a haircut for free, but on balance I would rather have paid the coin to a barber and had a decent shave into the bargain. I rubbed a hand over the bristles on my chin, now at the aggravating stage where they were both sharp and itchy, and I doubted my own mother would recognise me at that moment.

Stock brought down off the mountains for sale at home gets cleaned if it's lucky, then it gets weighed while the water in the wool is still adding to the burden. The Relshazri evidently worked the same way; this line moved slowly towards the kind of balance I was used to see weighing sacks on at the harbour side. A couple of men were manhandling the hefty bullion weights on and off the scales while another checked the arithmetic, consulted a ledger and scrawled something on to labels, which were tied round the neck of each piece of merchandise. I tried to squint at mine but it was tied too short, tucked under my chin. For some reason I found that irritating me more than anything else that had happened so far.

On the way back to our cell a guard handed me a bundle which proved to come from Mellitha. It had obviously been opened but she'd put in enough bread and cheese to leave me a decent meal after the guards had taken what they wanted. That was the highlight of the day; my money had vanished from my pallet and, as the sun faded from the window, I found myself struggling to keep my spirits up. Despite all my efforts to distance myself from events I had no hope of controlling, I could not help feeling humiliated. It wasn't the nakedness, the impersonal handling like a piece of merchandise. It was the way my mind had been invaded again.

Something had been done to me to make me lose my senses, to make me do something so out of character and worse it was something I couldn't even remember. If I'd known who to blame, I could at least have been angry with them, but I couldn't even be certain about that. Was it the Elietimm? If so, what were they trying to achieve? As I wondered, I began to worry about it happening again, despite all my determination to stay calm. Losing control like that, my wits lost in the shades, my body at the mercy of whoever might be passing, the danger of being robbed, even killed; I found myself shaking at the thought and with a real effort forced myself to drive it out of my mind.

Fighting sleep as the night darkened outside the bars, I tasted faint salt on the breeze, reminding me of home. How was I going to explain this to Messire? However I told the tale, I was going to look incompetent. I've never favoured explanations for failing in a duty that begin 'I couldn't help it but . . .' and frustration welled up in me as I tried in vain to come up with something better. My pride was going to take a worse beating than my body when I had to make my report. My hopes of making the step from sworn man to chosen man would fall right down the privy, I realised gloomily.

I looked out at the stars. Livak was a girl who could count the beans in a handful; she wouldn't blame me for what had happened but I still didn't like the idea of looking such a masquerade fool in front of her. I cursed under my breath and sighed, looking in vain for the first glimmer of dawn lightening the sky. This would never have happened to me if those cursed wizards hadn't dragged Messire into their half-witted schemes; I scowled into the darkness. Surely Shiv, Mellitha and Viltred could have come up with some way of getting me out of here? If you believed any of the ballads that kept minstrels fed, couldn't wizards do things like walking themselves through walls, turning things invisible, sending guards to sleep? What were they doing while I was stuck in here, at risk of anything from a ramming up the arse to jail fever?

'There's no more point in them magicking you away than there is in you finding a way to break out of here,' I told myself sternly. 'Think sense, fool. The Watch would have the ferries tied up and be turning the city inside out before we'd gone round the chimes.'

I awoke with a sudden start to find guards busily rousting us all to our feet, herding us down the stairs to the courtyard where I saw manacles were to be clamped around our wrists, a chain threaded through to link us all together. The thought of being chained like a common criminal filled me with sudden rage. Without thinking, I pulled my hands away, cursing. A stinging slap from the guard split my lip. I reached for the bastard, only to be felled by a numbing blow to the meat of my thigh from the blunt end of a stave. The pain of that brought me to my senses. When I could stand, I gritted my teeth and submitted meekly to the fetters.

'Get yourself reined in, imbecile,' I rebuked myself. 'You'll be out of here by the end of the morning and then you can go looking for the bastard who had you slung in here.'

That idea warmed my blood and I began to take more notice of what was happening, realising too that the worst of the stiffness from the beating had passed, unnoticed, over those idle couple of days. I found myself behind the clerk as we were marched along a series of foul alleys, the guards laughing and joking, wagers being made as to who would fetch the best price. The sun was barely climbing above the ruddy tiled roofs and we were all glad to move briskly in the morning cool.

'No one knows what to make of you,' the clerk commented, looking back over his shoulder.

I shrugged. 'They seem to think you'll go for a decent weight of coin.'

The man smiled. 'Yes, I should do, if the auctioneer gives me a chance to speak for myself. It did the trick last time.'

'You've been sold before?' I had no idea what usually happened to slaves and this seemed the ideal time to start learning.

'Twice,' he confirmed. 'First owner died and we were all sold to clear his debts; second was only interested in getting a couple of seasons' work for a deal with some Aldabreshi warlord.'

'So what happens to you now?'

'If I'm lucky, I'll go to a decent merchant who'll let me earn a coin or two at the back gate, so I'll have something put by to keep me out of the gutter. It won't be too much longer before I get too old to be worth my bed and bread and they set me free.' The skinny man's face grew solemn.

The jingling column reached a broad market square with a high platform on one side. We were herded unceremoniously into a pen behind it; to my frustration, I could see none of the crowd. All I could hear was the noise and it sounded as if there was a good turn-out, eager to buy the servants, field workers and labourers who made up most of the early lots.

The sun was riding high in the sky by the time the sale reached the skilled men like myself and my companion. It was hot and airless in the slave pen and I shouldered my way forward when a lad with a bucket and ladle walked down the lines, dipping stale water into eagerly cupped hands.

'Come on.' A guard unchained the clerk and he stepped eagerly on to the platform.

'I am a clerk and book-keeper, fluent in Tormalin, Caladhrian and the western Aldabreshi dialects. I am honest and accurate and I have worked in this city for fifteen years; you will get a loyal servant and the benefit of my knowledge and contacts. I know the bronze trade, shipping and exchange, the tax systems of every port from Col to Toremal and can advise on contracts drawn under either Soluran or Tormalin law codes.'

His confident voice rang back from tall buildings on the far side of the square. After a moment's pause, bidding started briskly. He went for a thousand and five Crowns and judging by his smiles as he came down from the auction block, that was a good price.

My manacles were removed and I walked slowly up the steps, a hollow feeling in my stomach; I hoped swordsmen went for less than book-keepers as I really didn't want to be responsible for landing Messire with that kind of debt to a wizard.

The square below me was thronged with people, faces turned up and eager. I looked for Mellitha, fighting the threat of panic as I initially failed to find her. The auctioneer was rattling off something behind me but I ignored him, waiting desperately for the bidding to start so I could get a sight of Mellitha.

The first offer came from a burly man in dark brown and for one moment of complete confusion I thought it was Nyle. A second glance told me I was wrong but he was a similar type and I decided the heavy-set men standing behind him were swords for hire. How keen was he going to be to add me to his stable? For fifty Crowns, not very, it would appear.

Relief flooded me as I heard Mellitha's clear tones ringing across the heads of the crowd to top the previous bid. She was almost hidden behind a group of giggling girls, who must have simply been there to ogle half-naked men. A hundred and fifty Crowns sounded like a fair opening offer.

My satisfaction was short-lived as Mellitha's bid was rapidly countered by a stout matron with a vicious nose and at least two hundred Crowns to spend, and then by a fat man in blue velvet whose hand rested on the shoulder of a painted youth in rose silks.

A bid of three hundred Crowns came from the back of the crowd and a chill hand gripped my stones as I saw a black-clad arm raised above a corn-coloured head. I looked frantically at Mellitha, not daring to signal to her, not wanting to risk identifying her to the Elietimm. Squinting at the Ice Islander,

I saw it was not one of the liveried troop but an older man dressed in a plain Caladhrian style. Gold at his neck showed he wore the gorget of a magic-wielder, however, and I found my breath coming faster and faster as the pace of the bidding increased, soon passing five hundred Crowns. That meant all my savings would have to be offered to Messire when I returned home, if only for honour's sake.

The goodwife was clearly keen to have me, for reasons I couldn't imagine, but dropped out first at six hundred, yielding to the sack-arse whose interest in me was only too easy to imagine. I glared in his direction, trying to look as unappealing as possible and, to my intense relief, he dropped out at six hundred and fifty, relief unmistakable in his companion's face as he draped himself over the older man's shoulder. The sword-master was still pushing up the price with an air of unconcern and I looked anxiously at Mellitha as the numbers climbed steadily. It was hard to judge her expression at this distance, but her voice remained steady as she countered each offer. A thin man bent down to whisper in her ear and she nodded, raising her bids from ten to twenty-five Crown increments, which rapidly drove the sword-master to retreat at eight hundred, shaking his head with disgust. My heart began thudding in my chest as I realised the man with Mellitha was Shiv, his black hair oiled and curled, a clerk's tunic flapping around his knees.

The Elietimm was still in the game, topping each offer Mellitha made. I clenched my hand in impotent anguish as the auctioneer kept taking bids from each of them. A sudden stir at the back of the crowd abruptly interrupted the to and fro and I swore under my breath as a flurry of activity hid the Elietimm from me and I lost Mellitha in a surge of bodies. Shiv moved rapidly across the square and vanished from sight.

'Two thousand Crowns.'

A harshly accented voice bellowed across the market place and silenced every voice there. Half the faces turned to see who had made such an outrageously extravagant bid and the rest looked to see what the auctioneer would do.

Before anyone could react, the bastard slammed his hammer down. 'Sold.'

The market erupted in a frenzy of speculation and astonishment, Mellitha was nowhere to be seen in the sudden bustle and I struggled against the pull of the guards, desperate to try to find her neat figure in the throng.

'Move.' A smack across the back of my legs sent me sprawling down the steps and I struggled to find my feet as I was hauled round to the far side of the sales block.

'No, listen—' I shoved the guard in the chest with my manacled hands, fury welling up inside me.

A lash came curling round from behind me, wrapping a coil of fire around my chest, tying my arms to my sides. As I gasped and bent involuntarily, two thick-set men grabbed me by the upper arms and hauled me off.

'Here he is, bought and paid for.'

I looked up to see a bored Relshazri stamping a closely written parchment. He reached over and tore the label from my neck, the cord leaving a stinging weal under my ragged collar. I ignored the pain, staring open-mouthed at the woman clutching my bill of sale.

She was slightly built, with coppery skin and thick black hair with a curious blue tint coiled high on her head. A gauzy mantle of gossamer silk was draped over her shoulders, open at the front to reveal a low-cut dress of emerald silk, closely tailored to outline full breasts and slim hips, all accentuated further with gem-studded chains of gold and silver. She looked as if she might be the same age as Livak but it was hard to tell, given the bright paints that decorated her pointed face, which was alight with mischief.

A burly man of about the same age as my father stood next to her, studying me thoughtfully down a hooked nose, eyes keen under thick black brows. He wore a flowing silk tunic of vivid green, belted with a black sash over loose black trousers tied at the ankle. His skin was considerably darker than the woman's and his long, greying hair and beard were slicked back with aromatic oil; an emperor's ransom in jewels glittered in his earrings and around fingers and wrists. A thin-faced man in fine chainmail waited behind the pair, his hands tucked into a jewelled belt bearing two swords and a multitude of daggers. He looked at me with an expression of profound boredom.

Beyond realising there was absolutely no point in any more resistance, I couldn't summon a rational thought. I'd been bought by an Aldabreshi Warlord. Viltred's piss-poor magic hadn't shown any of us that, had it?

The man in the mail-shirt gestured towards me and I fell in beside him numbly as the three Aldabreshi walked happily away from the slave sales, the woman hanging on the Warlord's arm, evidently thanking him, laughing with a delight that started to make me seriously worried. My only consolation was that all the passers-by were so busy staring at the wealth dripping off the exotic couple that they had no time to spare for the mundane sight of a slave in chains stumbling along behind as we walked briskly through the city.

Pausing at a footbridge, I tried to look around for Mellitha or Shiv but that earned me a growl from the man with the swords. I glared back at him but, when he put a hand to a dagger hilt, I dropped my eyes. If he wanted to be cock of the dunghill, I wasn't about to challenge him, not just yet, anyway, not until I had a blade in my hand. Once I had a sword, we could find out if the reputation of Aldabreshi swordsmen was all it claimed.

We turned between two lofty warehouses and I found myself on a dock facing the open gulf. This was a far cry from the grimy wharves that took in the trade from Caladhria and Lescar; here the quays were swept clean by urchins standing ready with their brooms, pale stone bright in the sunlight. Tall buildings with private apartments above the storerooms looked down on a bustle of activity, laden hand-carts and porters carrying bolts of silk, bales of linen cloth, barrels of wines, small iron-bound caskets closely guarded and larger chests treated with lesser concern.

Massive breakwaters reached far out into the deep waters of the Gulf here, tides or storms no more than a passing inconvenience as the sweeping arms of the great harbour offered sanctuary from the open seas. Immense galleys bobbed gently, tethered to the jetties, their vast holds ready to receive every luxury that Relshaz could offer in return for Aldabreshi gemstones. Men in flowing silks and stern expressions stood in intense conversation, jewels at waist and wrist catching fire in the sunlight, women with painted faces and seductive dresses chatted and laughed, tall men in shining mail expressionless beside them, each with enough weapons to outfit half a troop of mercenaries. Voices chattered harshly all around me and I realised with a sudden shock that I couldn't understand a word anyone was saying.

I found myself buffeted and shoved but the throng opened itself instantly before my new owner and his lady, anxious faces bowing low in reverence, hands spread wide. The Warlord passed by, aloof, but the woman turned this way and that with a brilliant smile and a negligent scatter of silver from a pouch at her waist. We reached a high-sided ship, one of the few with three banks of oars and a bright green pennant at the masthead bearing an abstract, angular design in broad black strokes. The Warlord paused, spoke rapidly to the swordsman and then escorted the woman up one of the two gang-planks.

I raised my eyebrows at my companion in mute question. He shrugged, slight confusion in his copper-coloured eyes and walked down the dockside to the other gang-plank. I hesitated for half a breath but a quick glance around made it clear I'd have twenty Aldabreshi after me like dogs on a rat if I tried to run. I sighed and followed obediently, my expression calm but my mind racing around in fruitless circles, like a mouse trapped in a bucket by a squeamish maid. Dastennin help me, how was I going to get out of this?

Once on the deck of the ship, the man with all the blades simply pointed to a space between two bales and turned his back on me. I watched him enter a door at the rear of the vessel and, hardly able to believe that I was left unguarded, I took a couple of rapid steps towards the gang-plank. A handful of dark faces immediately turned towards me, sailors and porters all halting in their tasks to stare at me with unfriendly eyes. I returned to my assigned spot and tried to look harmless; just a piece of self-loading cargo, that was me.

A ripple ran through the organised bustle on the quayside and I looked desperately to find its origin, hoping for a sight of Shiv's dark head or Mellitha's blue cloak. Instead I saw the crowd parting for a troop of black-liveried men whose yellow heads stood out like beacons among the dark Aldabreshi. My breath came hard and fast as I stood, helpless, watching as they drew closer and closer, a gleam of gold at the neck of the leading man the only touch of colour in his garb. Relief swept over me like a breaking fever when they passed the galley. I watched, heart pounding, as they halted at a distant berth, the leader accosted by a slim Aldabreshi woman with russet hair and eloquent, gesturing hands.

A sudden stillness all around me turned my head. I looked warily to see if I had done something to provoke it. I found I was completely ignored as all eyes were fixed on the Warlord, now standing in the prow of the vessel, in conversation with the woman. He took a small withy cage from her and opened it to release a white sea bird, its wings edged with blue and black. Everyone but me seemed to be holding their breath as the bird rose skywards, circled the mast for a moment, then winged its way south on urgent wings.

The stillness was broken by unmistakable cries of pleasure and relief from the Aldabreshi. The deck lurched beneath my feet and I watched in horror as scurrying sailors cast off the chains that held the galley to the dock. With a sudden shout the oars crashed into the dimpled water and I heard the muffled beat of the pace drum beneath my feet. Unregarded now, I moved to the rail, gripping it with desperate hands, finally spotting Shiv's lanky figure in animated debate with some Aldabreshi in a vivid emerald tunic. I looked hastily for the Elietimm and saw he was moving down the dockside, his men obediently falling into step behind him, heading towards Shiv, who was oblivious, still arguing with the warlord's man.

'Shiv!' I bellowed frantically but my lone voice was no match for the slap and flurry of the oars, the creak of the timbers and the shouts of the sailors as the massive galley made its careful way out of the busy harbour. The great vessel wheeled round and another ship glided past, hiding the dock from me.

I stood and swore in impotent fury, only registering a peremptory tap on my shoulder when it was repeated. I turned, an oath dying on my lips, to see the man with the swords looking at me with expressionless eyes. He unlocked my manacles and tossed them disdainfully into the sea before turning, beckoning me to follow.

CHAPTER FIVE

*A letter found in the Receipt and Commonplace Book of
Sidra, Lady Metril, Attar Bay, Caladhria, dated to the
10th year of Emperor Leoril the Dullard.*

My dearest Sidra,

*I have the most exciting news imaginable! Herist is newly
home from his voyage and he has done it! As I write, we
have rows of little spice plants all flourishing in our glass
houses. Is it not wonderful? Better still, our head gardener
is confident he should be able to grow them outside once
they are big enough. Herist is not sure how long it will be
before the bushes will bear berries, but once they do we will
be able to sell all manner of spices and make our fortunes. I
am sure people will much rather deal with us; after all, we
will be happy to take properly minted gold and silver and not
bother with endless arguments over barter and exchange. As
long as the island savages cannot understand the concept of
coin, I do not see how they can hope to compete, not when
we have no shipping costs, neither.*

*Herist has a wondrous store of tales about his adventures
among the barbarians. He travelled widely and was welcomed most warmly; they seem to be quite naive, almost
child-like in some ways. Since Misaen in his unfathomable
wisdom has seen fit to grant their islands vast riches in
gemstones, fine jewels are to be seen on all the men and
women, even those of quite inferior status. Yet they swap
such things among themselves, in the manner of children
exchanging baubles at a Solstice fair. Herist has brought
me home pearls that will make you quite sick with envy,*

my dear, and acquired merely for a couple of old swords and a bag of nails.

   Their rulers are all old men, gross from indulgence in every luxury of life. When I pressed him, Herist acknowledged their appetites are not merely for food and wine. Each has a flock of women kept at hand; they call themselves wives but I would rather describe them as concubines, from all Herist says. They dress themselves in the most scandalous style, all paint and adornments, and they have no other purpose in life than satisfying the lusts of whatever men will have them, it would seem. One can only assume they know no better, untutored and ungodly as they are. Herist assures me he did not succumb to temptation, though it seems the more depraved customarily offer travellers the choice of their doxies.

   They seem to have no idea of kingship or proper government; each Warlord simply holds whatever islands he can seize by force of arms. They set great store in skills with sword and bow, knowing no other means of solving disputes beyond the exercise of brute strength. Accordingly, Herist had to be most circumspect in obtaining the seeds for the spice plants, since his life would not have been worth a penny's purchase if the poor ignorant barbarians had had an inkling of his plans. Still, as he says, a bull is only dangerous if you rouse it, so he was quite able to elude their slower wits.

   You must come and pay a lengthy visit, my dear. I long to show you my new jewels and all the other things Herist brought back for me, silks, curios and some carvings that I swear will bring a blush to the most liberal cheek.

   Written the 11th day of Aft-Spring, at our Derret Chase lodge.

   Trini, Lady Arbel

The galley of Shek Kul, sailing the Gulf of Lescar, 33rd of Aft-Spring

I walked obediently behind the swordsman, who led me to a cabin at the stern of the ship. Faint sympathy flared in his eyes as he opened the door and gestured me through. I entered warily, ducking my head and trying to look as harmless as possible, not difficult given my bruises and prison-stained rags. My mind, meanwhile, was racing furiously; what was happening on the dockside?

The woman responsible for my present predicament was sitting on a heap of bright cushions, a complex embroidery in her hands as she matched silks with a critical eye. She glanced up and I didn't trust the expression of malicious amusement on her sharp face for a moment. She called out something in a sweetly inviting tone and a younger woman swept through a second door, her expression of excitement turning rapidly to one of horror when she saw me.

The first woman was studying an intricate flower with a serene expression as the other girl gave me a scathing glance of contempt and stormed over to her. I watched with intense frustration as the woman sewing calmly replied to the newcomer's tirade in tones of sweet unconcern. Finally the combination of rage and injured pride overcame the girl and she burst into furious tears as she flounced out of the cabin.

Left standing there without any idea what I should do, I forced myself to put aside the question of Shiv and the Elietimm, to lock it away in that box in the back of my mind. The others would have to look after themselves; they were together, they had allies in Relshaz, above all Livak was no fool. My first duty was to myself now; I had to concentrate on staying alive here until I could somehow return to the mainland. I was on my own and, I judged, in no little danger.

I looked at the woman but she was concentrating on her embroidery, a slight curve to her carefully painted lips and satisfaction in her almond-shaped eyes. A gesture from the swordsman caught my eye. Watching his mistress warily, he pointed to the door through which the weeping girl had fled. Keeping my face carefully expressionless, I went through the slatted door, which was still swinging on its pins from the fury of the girl's passage.

I found myself in a large airy cabin whose long shutters opened on to a small private deck at the rear of the ship. The girl was no longer weeping but the hot tears were still wet on her face, ruining her intricate makeup. A blush swept up her cheeks and her lips narrowed. Embarrassment warred with fury in her stormy brown eyes as she took a deep breath. I judged it prudent to keep my expression as noncommittal as I could.

After a few minutes the girl shrugged with an enigmatic sigh, pushed a long curl of black hair off her face and sat on a pile of cushions, her elegant amber gown hitched above jewel-clasped ankles. They were nice ankles, though I noticed she had incongruously toughened feet. In fact she was a luscious blossom all together, about as tall as my chin, rounded hips and a plump bosom barely concealed by the loose, sleeveless silk. Her angry frown looked inappropriate on her round face but I could believe her full lips were used to pouting prettily. She pointed to the floor with a curt instruction, hitching her dress back on to one smooth brown shoulder.

It seemed the Aldabreshi didn't believe in chairs, so I sat on the floor and tried for an ingratiating smile. 'I'm sorry, I don't understand the Aldabreshi tongue.'

The girl frowned and tried again in Relshazri; I shrugged in mute apology. This was a new problem for me; in those few instances when I find myself dealing with a backwoods peasant who has no Tormalin, I have enough Caladhrian and Dalasorian to fall back on if pressed. I had never imagined I would need to learn the language of the Archipelago. I couldn't even think of anyone I knew who could have taught me.

'You are Tormalin?' the girl asked after a few moments, her words hesitant and thickened by a strong Aldabreshi accent.

I bowed awkwardly from the waist, not knowing what else to do. 'My name is Ryshad.'

She repeated it a few times to herself, splitting the syllables and colouring them with an Aldabreshi intonation. 'Rhya Shad.'

I'd better get used to answering to that then, until I found some way out of this maze.

The girl nodded with satisfaction and then pointed to herself.

'I am Laio Shek, fourth wife to Shek Kul and manager of his weavers.'

I bowed again, making as low a reverence as I could; I know precisely the etiquette required when meeting the Sieur of a House, his heirs and ladies, how to address a Lescari Duke or an Ensaimin Lord, but I had absolutely no idea of the courtesies usual between owner and slave. I had imagined any exchanges were largely made with the tongue of a whip and had no desire to have her resort to that; I'd rather look an idiot and scrape my nose on the floorboards. I'd have no chance of getting away if I were to be injured.

There was an awkward silence, so I looked around the cabin. The wooden walls were painted in a pale yellow and furnished with delicate, silken embroideries. The floor was polished and a low bed was set against the far wall, heaped with silken quilts. Several dresses were tossed carelessly on it and a tray of makeup perched perilously close to the edge.

'You stink,' Laio said abruptly. 'You will wash before you attend to your duties.'

'What exactly are my duties?' I asked cautiously.

Laio's lips narrowed and she drew a swift breath of irritation in through her finely shaped nostrils.

'Pour me wine.' She pointing to a flagon on a low side-table by the shutters. I fetched a glassful, looking round in vain for a tray or a salver. Laio nodded approvingly but a faint frown still wrinkled her forehead.

'Take some yourself and be seated,' she said unexpectedly.

As I did so, unimpressed by its thin taste and weakness, she finished her own drink and sat twirling the narrow-stemmed glass in her hands, the nails brightly varnished. 'You are a mainlander from the lands of the east, is that correct?'

'Yes, from Zyoutessela, in southern Tormalin.'

Laio dismissed this with a wave of her hand. 'A mainlander, you know nothing of our islands?'

Not much, other than there were supposed to be about a hundred bloodthirsty Warlords; each ruling one major island and any number of smaller ones with an iron fist, blood and terror. I thought of the various lurid tales I'd heard over the years.

'No, nothing,' I lied firmly.

Laio looked at me with speculative eyes. 'I see. How long have you been a slave?'

'Shek Kul is my first owner,' I coughed as the words threatened to stick in my throat.

Laio frowned again and muttered something petulant in Aldabreshi but I got the impression her anger was not directed at me.

'I do not know how Gar Shek managed to persuade Shek Kul to buy you, but I am sure she expects you to make a poor slave. Since the quality of a body slave reflects on his owner, she hopes you will humiliate me. I am not going to let that happen, I have already given her too much satisfaction with my reaction.'

She gestured with her glass and I hastened to refill it. 'What do you think your duties here are?'

I ran through the various rumours I'd heard about the personal slaves of Aldabreshi women and opted for the least lewd.

'I am to protect you from other men, to keep you safe for your husband?' I hazarded.

A faint look of distaste flickered across Laio's face. 'Do

your mainlander women submit to being guarded like fowl
in a garden? You are not my husband's slave, you are mine,
do you understand?'

I nodded, understanding almost nothing so far.

'You are to defend me, that is true,' continued Laio, 'Not
for my husband's sake, but for mine. If I order it, you will fight
whomsoever I say, even Shek Kul. In the Islands, no husband
has rights over his wife's body.'

It would be truly astounding if that were true, I thought
sarcastically. The Toremal law codes are the only ones I know
that will deny a man his marriage bed, and that only happens
when the wife can bring three independent witnesses to the
Justiciary to swear they've seen him abusing her. However, I
schooled my face to an impassive blank as I listened to Laio's
clipped accents.

'Now, listen to me; you must learn fast and I am not going
to instruct you a second time. In Aldabreshi, a wife has both
status and duties in her own right; we manage our husband's
property and give him children, if we so choose, in return
for his protection and favour. Profitable wives are a credit
to a man, marriage is a binding alliance and alliances mean
power in the Archipelago. Shek Kul has alliances with his
neighbours and with two of the central Lords through his
wives; he is considered a powerful man. His domain is in the
south of the Archipelago.'

That meant I was going even further south than the Cape
of Winds; I thought with some distaste of the Archipelago's
reputedly hot and sticky climate. Laio was speaking slowly
now, to make sure I understood her and I listened obediently.
The more I knew about the set-up, the sooner I could work
out how to get clear of this mess. I realised with a sudden,
inappropriate surge of relief that at least I was on my own
here; without wizards to obey or someone else's plans to
take into account. Certainly Messire would have no means
of sending me aid, even if it occurred to Planir to warn him
of my plight. The House of D'Olbriot's only dealings with the
Archipelago are to chase off the occasional raiders who risk the

storm-tossed eastern crossing to prey on the ships that ply the Gulf coast.

'Shek Kul's First Wife manages his gems and his household. She is called Kaeska Shek, born Kaeska Danak. The Second Wife is Mahli Shek, born Mahli Kaasik, and she has charge of the farms on Shek Kul's islands, dealing with the overseers and the free Islanders as well as trading the produce. The Third Wife is Gar Shek who was born Gar Gaska, from the north-west; she has developed a trade in fine embroideries. It has given her great status and that reflects well on Shek Kul, which is why she gets her own way so often at the moment.'

A rather smug smile lit up Laio's face for an instant. 'That won't last for much longer; Mahli is pregnant and when her baby is born she will become First Wife and keep Gar in her place. I am Fourth Wife, I was born Laio Sazac in the west-central islands and married Shek Kul just over a year ago. As the most junior wife at present, I have charge of the cotton weavers, I oversee their work and trade the finished cloth. I travel all over Shek Kul's islands and to those of Kaasik Rai at least three times a year. I also receive visitors and agents from other domains. You will see to all my needs and those of my guests when I meet with them. Is that clear?'

'Quite clear, my lady.'

So it was looking as if all those lurid tales of Aldabreshi ladies kept isolated and caged like decorative birds, waiting only to satisfy their husbands' exotic lusts, were more than a little inaccurate.

'You will obey my orders without question in public. You will not argue with me and you will not answer back. If you do not understand something, wait until we are alone and then ask, but I will not answer any questions in front of Shek Kul or Gar. You may take orders from Mahli but not from Gar or Kaeska. They have no right to get you to do things for them and they know it.'

I couldn't see the haughty Gar Shek taking kindly to defiance but it was clear from Laio's scowl that this was not open to debate. I also realised Gar would be easily able to hear Laio's words from the next room and the girl was telling the other woman just where the runes lay as well as me.

'I will arrange for you to spend as much time as we can spare with Grival, who belongs to Mahli; you will learn everything he has to tell you about a body slave's duties. Sezarre is Gar's body slave; he is an excellent swordsman so he can train you to an acceptable standard. You can also use your time with him to learn what you can about Gar's plans. You will have to learn to speak Aldabreshin; I cannot be doing with your barbarian tongue all the time. You will be fluent by the end of the season.'

This was also clearly not open to debate and I wondered uneasily how hard it would be. All the Aldabreshi I'd heard sounded as if they were trying to spit while chewing nails.

Laio wiped a hand across her face and frowned at the smear of rouge.

'Fetch me some cream to clean all this off.' She gestured to a heavily inlaid coffer standing in a corner.

I rose and opened it to find a tray holding rough scraps of cloth, a fine porcelain, lidded bowl of thin lotion and a blue bottle of Relshazri glass that contained something smelling faintly astringent. Laio nodded approvingly and I knelt, feeling quite superfluous, as she stripped the cosmetics from her lips, eyes and cheeks. Looking at her naked face, I was startled to realise that she was no more than seventeen or eighteen years old; given her poise and evident ease with her status as a Warlord's wife, I'd have put at least five years on that.

A knock on the door made Laio pause; at her impatient gesture, I opened it to reveal a heavily pregnant woman in a plain cream robe, much my own height, who leaned against the door-post and smiled at Laio. She asked something in Aldabreshi, her low husky voice softening the harsh language. Laio laughed and pointed at me with a dramatic gesture of helplessness. That decided me; I was going to learn this tongue, even if it did make me sound like a dog being sick. No chit of a girl nearly half my age was going to be able to make jokes at my expense without me understanding them.

I studied the newcomer as the women talked. She was

tall and, even allowing for her condition, was a heavily built woman. Where Laio had long black tresses tumbling down her back, this lady had short hair, growing in strange, tight curls that dotted her head like peppercorns. Her skin was the darkest I'd seen yet, an unnerving reminder of how different the Aldabreshi could be. I was somewhat reassured by the good nature in her wide, deep-brown eyes, set above broad cheekbones with laughter lines at their corners. Laio said something that made Mahli burst into peals of laughter and then stood up, a smile brightening her own expression.

'I will spend some time with Mahli now,' she announced. 'Clear up in here and then go and find Sezarre. We will talk again later.'

She left the room in a perfumed rustle of silk and I stood up, rubbing my knees. I was certainly not looking forward to spending so much time scrambling around on the floor and wondered if the Aldabreshi went in for more furniture when they were on dry land. I looked around at the chaos it seemed Laio habitually created and recalled my mother threatening to drill Kitria into neatness with a willow switch. Some things were common to all young girls, it would seem.

Something in me rebelled as I reached for a slippery, silk gown and looked round for a coffer or somesuch to stow it in. Incandescent with instant rage, I hovered on a knife edge of temptation, longing to rip the flimsy thing to shreds and see how the bossy little blossom liked that. My grip tightened on the delicate cloth but I suddenly found myself laughing instead at such uncharacteristic and ill-considered anger. I was certainly adrift with no hope of wind at the moment, but I had to stay calm if I was going to paddle my way out of this.

'From sworn man to maidservant! Well, Ryshad, you've certainly done well for yourself.'

Laio could call me a slave all she wanted; no one could make me think of myself as one. I could play the part though, the same way I'd played the half-wit with no more sense than his dung fork for half a season in order to unravel a fraud in Messire's shearing sheds. I gathered up the discarded dresses and found their allotted chest, rapidly restoring the room to order before going in search of the man who'd escorted me to the ship – Sezarre, that was his name, I remembered.

I found him on deck, conferring with an impressively muscled man with a shaven head and hard, black eyes. They were both stripped to the waist and sweating freely, a blunted blade in each hand. Nodding agreement, they resumed their contest and I stepped back hurriedly out of their way. The other tales I'd heard of the Archipelago might turn out to be false, but it soon looked as if the reputation of their swordsmen was if anything underestimated. The swords might be a hand's width or so shorter than I was accustomed to, but using them in pairs, rather than with a dagger or shield for the off hand, any Aldabreshin was going to make up in damage for anything he lacked in reach. I whistled soundlessly as the two of them went at each other with a flurry of strokes, blades clashing and smacking together, only breaking when Sezarre took a stinging slice to one shoulder.

I winced as I saw the red line darkened to an instant bruise; his eyes caught mine and he rubbed at it with a rueful grin. The other one said something and picked up the practice blades, sliding them into a canvas bag. He had to be Grival.

'We wash,' Sezarre said in halting Tormalin.

I nodded and followed him to the side of the ship where Grival was already hauling up buckets of sea water. Both the other body slaves stripped naked, unconcerned and attracting no notice from the sailors busy about the business of ship. I joined them, happy to discard the memories of the Relshaz lock-up along with the rags and relishing the sting of the clean, clear water. I started slightly when Grival took a washcloth to my back but reminded myself of all the times Aiten and I had done each other such a service. I shut my eyes on the sting of sudden grief, all the more searing in my present uncertainty.

'Here.' Sezarre handed me a bowl of thin, liquid soap and I scrubbed myself clean eagerly.

Grival said something and rummaged in a bag, passing

me a small pot of ointment. I wondered if he spoke any Tormalin at all.

'For the skin.' Sezarre took the pot and rubbed a fingerful on to his own bruise.

I nodded and began the lengthy task of anointing all my own scrapes and swellings. The stuff stung but smelled wholesome enough and the simple fact of being clean again and tending my injuries did wonders for my spirits.

Grival made a comment to Sezarre that had both of them laughing as they looked at me; I smiled and swallowed my indignation. I needed allies here, it was time to start making myself one of the lads.

'He says you look like a dog he once owned, all patches of brown and white,' Sezarre explained with a wide smile.

I looked down at myself and saw the lines marking my sun-darkened arms and face from the paler skin of my chest and thighs. Nodding and forcing a smile to show I understood the joke, I realised that I was the lightest-skinned person on the ship, as far as I could tell. Grival was the colour of old leather from head to toe, and while Sezarre's arms were about the same shade as mine it was evidently the natural tone of his skin, not the touch of the sun. It felt distinctly strange to stand out like this; going north for Messire, I am more used to people commenting on the darkness of my hair and complexion. The deck rocked beneath my feet, reminding me of my uncertain footing here.

I mimed scraping my face with a blade. 'Razor?'

Sezarre frowned and said something to Grival who looked startled.

'No,' Sezarre shook his head emphatically. 'Not now you are an Islander.'

I looked round the boat and realised that I couldn't see a clean chin anywhere. I smiled and nodded to Sezarre, sighing inwardly at the prospect of having to wear a beard. I've done it a few times, by way of a disguise, and as far as I'm concerned there are few pleasures to compare with shaving the cursed thing off. Unfortunately, from what I'd already seen of my so-called mistress, I couldn't see her agreeing to let me ignore a current fashion for hairy faces.

Grival passed me a clean if well-worn shirt while Sezarre found a spare pair of trousers, both of soft, unbleached cotton. Fingering the unfamiliar cloth, I couldn't restrain a smile; this was an expensive stuff, back home. I looked round for some footwear.

'Boots?' I enquired hopefully.

Sezarre shook his head. 'Not in the Islands. Feet will rot.'

That explained the puzzle of the fine ladies with their calloused feet.

Grival muttered something to Sezarre, not looking at me.

'He says you are not born a slave?' asked Sezarre, hesitation warring with curiosity in his voice.

'No.' I gave him a friendly smile; one of these men might have that crucial piece of information that would get me out of here; the most compelling reason I could think of to learn to speak their language.

'What do you do, before?'

I could see the questions hovering in his eyes and I couldn't blame him; I'd be wary if someone suddenly foisted a potential criminal on my watch roster.

'I was a sworn man to a great lord, a swordsman, a man at arms.' I'd been a lot more than that but this was hardly the time to try explaining notions of oath and duty to these people.

'Now you serve the wife of Shek Kul, our Great Lord,' Sezarre smiled broadly at me, apparently expecting me to share in his delight at the prospect.

I nodded and remembered an Aldabreshi carving Lady Channis kept in her salon; look at it one way, and it was a tree, but from another angle, it was a face. That would be a good enough way to cope with my situation, for the time being at least, looking at slavery as another form of service. I couldn't change what was done, so I had to concentrate on making things go my way in future.

Before I could pursue that thought, Grival clapped a hand to his forehead with a sudden exclamation and rapidly crossed the deck to a pile of bundles. He tossed something to me and I caught it in a reflex action, wondering what it could be.

It was my sword. I stared stupidly at the gleaming green leather of the scabbard.

'Good blade,' said Sezarre approvingly, face expectant as he held out a hand.

So, buyers at the Relshaz slave markets got their stock complete with harness, I thought sardonically. Well, well; how civilised. I passed the sword over and watched as he sent the shining steel whirling round his head and shoulders in a glittering series of arcs and passes that made me glad I hadn't tried my luck against him earlier.

Still, it would be good to have the blade with me, a constant reminder of my true master, my service given freely, the oaths that protected my honour. Those oaths meant Messire would be doing all he could to trace me too, as long as those cursed wizards let him know I'd been taken. I'd rather get myself out of this mess but the remembrance that others would be busy on my behalf was a comforting one.

A bell rang. Sezarre and Grival hastily packed their gear and I followed their lead to the galley. It seemed we were to serve the ladies their lunch; I copied the others as they each loaded a tray with plates of a pale yellow, steamed meal and things chopped up in bowls and covered with a wide variety of sauces. From the amount Grival took from the galley, the woman Mahli must be eating for a litter of six, never mind one baby. Sezarre seemed to think Gar must have hollow legs.

I soon discovered my mistake when I realised that a body slave's meals were his lady's leavings. I couldn't follow the women's conversation but from the tone of it and their expressions, you would have thought they were all the closest of friends. Watching gloomily, my stomach protesting, I saw that Laio's curves stemmed from a hearty appetite. We served more of the weak wine and fruit and eventually Mahli took herself off for a rest, Gar returned to her embroideries and I was surprised to see Laio ensconce herself on some cushions with a writing case and a stack of correspondence, close-written on fine reed paper.

'We eat.' Sezarre nodded to the door and I followed him and Grival to what appeared to be our accustomed spot on deck.

Grival laughed, not unkindly, and passed me a couple of bowls from his own, largely untouched tray. I smiled my thanks and looked cautiously at their contents. I passed over something that looked like a nest of tiny innards and poked a finger at a heap of wilted green leaves.

'Called "Turil".' Sezarre passed me a strange sort of spoon; it had a flattened bowl and two prongs at the end of the handle, like a tiny hayfork. I watched as he mimed scooping and spearing food and understood why everything was cut into such small pieces.

'No hands, very bad.' He shook his head firmly. 'Not clean, mainlander habits.'

I sighed and forked up a mouthful of the leaves. For one appalling moment, I thought I'd bitten a wasp; given I could see flowers in several dishes, it was the only answer I could imagine for the searing pain in my mouth.

'Mountain plant,' Sezarre passed me some fruit juice, 'very hot.'

Eyes watering, I washed away the worst of the taste and played safe with a mouthful of the creamy cereal. It was a little gritty in texture, the tiny grains tending to stick to my teeth and palette, but while it had a strange, sour quality, it was not unpleasant.

Grival offered me a little plate with pieces of dark meat in a dark red sauce.

'Very good,' Sezarre nodded approvingly.

I managed a weak smile and touched a little of the sauce to my lips. To my surprise, it was sweet, almost honeyed with a hint of aromatic spices. At least I wouldn't starve here, I thought as I emptied the dish hungrily.

'What became of my lady's slave before me?' I asked.

Sezarre shrugged with an air of resignation. 'Bone fever, very bad.'

I looked at my plate. I might not starve but there were a myriad other dangers that could leave me dead in the Archipelago.

A narrow strait between two steeply forested islands set in the heart of the far ocean

Temar woke with a sudden start, disorientation clouding his senses, dense blackness pressing down on him. He shoved the stifling blanket off his head in a convulsive heave, blinked and the world returned to normal, the lantern of the unhurried sentry circling the camp a swinging pin-prick of light, soft noises of other sleepers all around him. Temar sat up and put his hands on the cool grass either side of him, taking a deep breath as the sensation of still being aboard a swaying ship gradually faded. He looked up at the increasingly unfamiliar stars and wondered how long it would be before dawn broke.

'Not long enough, at any rate,' he smiled to himself and rolled himself up to get as much rest as he could before facing the demands of another busy day. This was certainly no pleasure cruise, he mused as he drifted easily off to sleep.

The clatter of cooking pots and a rising murmur of conversation stirred him next. The sun was climbing over the dense trees on a spit of land at the far end of the strait and the camp was busying itself with breakfast, fires dotted across the grassy strip separating the water from the dense scrub. Temar sniffed appreciatively at the smell of biscuits on griddles mingling with the lush green scents of the anchorage.

'Good morning.' Vahil shoved his head out of a tangle of blankets, wiry hair sticking up in all directions, a thick crease printed across one ruddy cheek.

Temar yawned and reached for his boots, checking them for opportunist crawlers before putting them on, wincing at the clammy touch of the damp leather. 'I'm going for a wash,' he announced, heading for the brook that wound its way across the sward down to the shingle beach.

Cold water did much to drive the lingering sleep out of Temar's eyes and he began to take in some of the details of the scene around him. His gaze fixed on Guinalle as she sat braiding her hair in front of a tent, face pink from her own ablutions, a thick shawl over her crisp linen shift.

'Feeling better for a night on dry land?' enquired Temar, pausing to clip back his own hair with his father's silver clasp, now tarnished from salt and spray.

Guinalle managed a faint smile. 'Yes, thank you. I must admit, I didn't think it would take me so long to get my sea legs.'

'Do you know how long we'll be stopping here?' he asked.

'We need to take on water, any fresh food we can find, make some repairs,' Guinalle grimaced. 'I'd say we'll be here just long enough for me to get used to being ashore again, so I can spend another handful of days with my head in a bowl once we set sail again, Larasion grant me strength.'

Temar smiled at her, thinking how even more attractive she was with her enviable self-possession just a little dented like this. 'Shall we find some breakfast?'

'Not just at the moment.' Guinalle shook her head with a theatrical shudder. She pushed her braid back over her shoulder and reached for her gown, laid ready on a stool. 'Could you lace me up? Elsire's not up yet and the maids are busy.'

Temar watched with carefully concealed appreciation as Guinalle pulled the sensible brown gown over her head and settled it on her hips before turning her back to him. He pulled the laces tight and breathed in the scent of the pennymint she used in her linen as he tied them off securely.

'Do you know where Messire Den Fellaemion is?' Guinalle was all business now, dignity put on along with her clothes.

'Let's see.' Temar scanned the camp. 'There, by that stack of water casks.'

Guinalle stood on tiptoe and squinted uncertainly. 'Oh yes, I see him.'

With a touch of regret Temar watched her go and then turned to look for some food, waving off a tenant who was heading his way with a disgruntled expression and a waterskin clutched in one hand.

Breakfast was all too soon over and Temar found himself scooping the last of his porridge out of his bowl as he took a seat at a rough trestle table where his ship's steward was waiting with an array of ledgers and wax tablets. The sun had climbed high over the glassy waters of the strait, burning the morning mists from the trees, by the time Temar had an up-to-date record of stores remaining, water required and all the various minor injuries and disputes on the five ships that were carrying D'Alsennin tenants to their new home.

'Do you have a report for me?'

Temar looked up to see Messire Den Fellaemion pulling up a stool. The commander had a definite touch of colour on his thin cheeks and his eyes were bright, the rough clothes of a sailor suiting him far more than the elegant dress he had worn in Zyoutessela.

'I should have it written up in a chime or so.' Temar hastily drew his scribbled notes together and reached for an ink-pot.

'That will be fine,' Den Fellaemion nodded easily. 'After that, if you've no other calls on your time, you might like to see what game you can find for the cook-pots tonight. Take young Den Rannion with you.'

Temar couldn't restrain a surprised smile and the older man laughed. 'I think you've both earned a little recreation and since we're going to be here for a handful of days, everyone would appreciate some fresh meat.'

'How long is the second half of the crossing?' Temar looked up, pen poised.

'With good winds, another twenty days or so.' Den Fellaemion rose. 'We've done the worst of it.'

Temar nodded at the memory of some of the foul weather the ships had had to contend with.

'These islands are certainly a blessing from Dastennin,

Messire,' he commented a little hesitantly. 'I don't recall you mentioning them before we set sail.'

Den Fellaemion grinned down at the younger man. 'No, I didn't. I'd rather any other would-be explorers continued to put my ability to cross the ocean down to my consummate seamanship and Dastennin's particular favour. Once we have the colony established, we can set up a permanent settlement here; that'll be time enough to let the secret be known.'

'My compliments on your wisdom, Messire.' Temar sketched a ceremonious bow and the commander chuckled.

'My gratitude for your appreciation, Esquire,' he replied in the same mock formal tone before striding off to consult with the captain of one of the other vessels.

Temar bent to his notes with renewed zeal and finished his report in less time than he had anticipated. Carefully sanding the document and checking the ink was dry, he folded it neatly and tucked it in the breast of his jerkin before going in search of Den Fellaemion. The commander was standing by the stack of water casks again, deep in conversation with Guinalle and two of the ships' captains.

'Thank you, Temar,' he said as he reached for the proffered parchment. 'I think that's all we need, Guinalle; why don't you take some time for yourself this afternoon? You've been so busy lately, what with taking sightings and keeping the charts. Make the most of the stop, before we take ship again.'

'Thank you, Uncle.' Guinalle looked a little surprised. 'I'll just see to that milch cow, though.'

'Anything I can do to help?' asked Temar quickly.

'Perhaps; come on.' Guinalle led the way to a sturdy corral on the far side of the camp where the expedition's precious livestock was securely confined.

'There you are, my lady.' One of the stockmen bustled up, relief palpable on his blunt face. 'We're all ready for you.'

Temar followed Guinalle to a pen of rough hurdles set some distance from the other beasts, his curiosity rising. A brindled cow with a white stripe down her back was lying there, eyes glazed and jaw slack, flanks heaving. One of her forelegs was crudely splinted with canvas and a broken spar.

'Give a hand on the ropes, lad.' The stockman evidently didn't recognise Temar, giving him a gentle shove towards the waiting gang on the far side of a sturdy frame, lashed up of rough-cut green wood.

'Are you ready?' A faint frown creased Guinalle's brow as she concentrated on the cow, starting a soft incantation that raised the hairs on the back of Temar's neck.

The cow's eyes rolled up in her head and her laboured breathing rattled harshly.

'Quickly!' The gang hauled on the ropes to raise the beast on the frame as the stockman rapidly sliced through the great vessels on either side of her neck, the rich blood gushing into a cauldron waiting ready with oatmeal, herbs and dry fat.

Guinalle sighed and turned away as the men waiting to butcher the carcass moved in with long knives; nothing was going to go to waste, not if they could help it.

'Are you all right?' asked Temar with some concern at the sadness in Guinalle's eyes.

'Oh, yes.' Guinalle rubbed a hand over her eyes. 'It's just that I could have mended that leg, given the chance, but I didn't have the time to spare, not with keeping track of the currents and the winds. I can't say I liked just keeping the poor beast alive and insensible until she could be slaughtered here.'

'Oh.' Temar couldn't really think of anything to say to that, but Guinalle didn't seem to notice. He tried to stifle his own guilty pleasure at the thought of blood sausage, something he had developed quite a taste for, even if it was peasant food.

'The problem is that, we just don't have enough people with skills in Artifice, at least not beyond the very basic levels.' Guinalle shook her head determinedly. 'That's going to be one of the first things I remedy when we land.'

'Good,' nodded Temar. Guinalle looked up at him, a touch of humour returning to her expression.

'I'm glad that meets with your approval, Esquire.'

Temar swept a florid bow. 'Your wisdom is only excelled by your beauty, Demoiselle.'

Guinalle laughed with a little more amusement than Temar would have liked, but at least the sadness lifted from her eyes.

'So what are you going to do with your afternoon?' he asked genially.

Guinalle let slip a look of slight disdain. 'Probably listen to Elsire complaining about the effect of sea water on her hair and lamenting the limited space she has for her wardrobe.'

Temar chuckled. 'That sounds about right.'

Guinalle looked at him consideringly. 'Do you think you could find an excuse to show her around one of your ships, let her see how most people are spending their time on this voyage?'

'Why?'

'She seems to think she's being terribly brave and is really suffering nobly, having to share a cabin and a maid with me. With Messire and her mother aboard with their personal servants, we are enjoying rather better treatment than I imagine you are. I certainly can't make Elsire understand that everyone else on the other ships is packed in like herring in a barrel, that a lot of them are out on deck in all weathers and she's cursed lucky to have room for more than a couple of changes of linen.'

'All right.' Temar had always had a soft spot for Elsire. 'Her airs and graces don't fool me, you know, I remember her when she was a gap-toothed nuisance with torn petticoats and muddy shoes.' Besides, if he got Elsire on her own, there was always the chance of stealing a taste of honey from her petal-soft lips. She was a girl who knew exactly where to step in the dances.

'Temar!' Vahil's hearty shout echoed around the steep heights on either side of the inlet. Temar stifled a touch of irritation as his friend loped across the grass, a crossbow in one hand and a hunting bag slung over his shoulder.

'Den Fellaemion said we had leave to see what kind of game's hiding in these woods.' Vahil slapped Temar on the back. 'That's the kind of order I'm happy to take. Go on, man, get your bow and let's get out of here before someone thinks up some real work for us to do.'

Temar hesitated, tempted but equally unwilling to pass up the chance of some free time with Guinalle.

'Can I come?'

'I'm sorry?' Her question took him by surprise.

'I'd like to see some more of these islands and I'm quite a good shot with a short bow.' Guinalle's eyes were wide with mute appeal.

'Absolutely,' said Temar emphatically. 'Of course, we'd be glad to have you along.'

'I'll get changed.' Guinalle ran over to her tent and Vahil groaned.

'I'll allow she's a pretty flower, Temar, but she's not exactly ripe for plucking, is she? Now we'll be hanging around for the best part of a chime while she decides which dress will go most tastefully with the undergrowth.'

'She's not Elsire,' Temar shook his head. 'Half a Mark says she's back here before I am.'

He didn't exactly tarry over finding his short bow and quiver but the boots he had been wearing would probably have been sufficiently stout for the hillsides, though he decided to change them anyway. At any rate, Temar was pleased to see Guinalle heading for the waiting Vahil at much the same time as he finished lacing the tops of his hunting boots. She was wearing a close-cut divided skirt in a dull green and a long-sleeved tan jerkin and her own flat-heeled boots had clearly seen plenty of wear. A long knife was belted at her neat waist and she carried a short bow with the ease of familiarity.

'There should be a game trail coming down to the water.' Vahil led the way, his usual good humour well in evidence once more.

Temar and Guinalle followed him, the sounds of the camp soon fading as they climbed into the dense green of the moist forest, where the clouds clung to the high trees. Temar paused to give her a hand over a rocky stretch of path, the stones slick and damp with the warm mist.

'Isn't it nice to get away!' he commented appreciatively. 'No one asking you to sort out their tenth quarrel over baggage space or expecting you to have the answers to everything from homesickness to colicky babies.'

'That's what you've been doing, is it?' Vahil was clearly amused.

'That and consoling the cook, who's been planning something with eggs but the hens have gone off lay, convincing people they can manage on their water ration if they don't use it for laundering their linen and dealing with a handful of petty disputes a day.' Guinalle shared a rueful glance with Temar.

'I leave that kind of thing to my father,' laughed Vahil. 'My main problem's boredom.'

Temar was not displeased to see faint vexation in Guinalle's eyes, but felt honour bound to support his friend to some extent.

'I know I'll be glad when we make a landfall and we can get on with the business of setting up the colony. You'll have plenty to do then, Vahil.'

'True enough,' groaned Vahil with mock dread. 'Look, there's a trail heading through that dip; with any luck the noise of the camp won't have spooked the game through there.'

'You'd better go in the middle,' Temar gestured to Guinalle. 'I don't suppose there are beasts of any size on a place like this but we might as well be careful.'

'Thank you, Esquire,' she said demurely, pushing carefully through the bushes after Vahil who was showing just how quietly he could move when he chose to.

Temar followed, his shirt soon damp from the moisture on the leaves and with sweat from the warmth of the day. They passed through the dip and began a careful descent into shallow valley, rich with strange, glossy-leafed plants in a myriad shades of green and dotted with a few spicily scented blooms.

'There's a clearing ahead.' Vahil paused to speak softly to Guinalle, who passed the word back.

Temar had to restrain an impulse to brush a sticky tendril from her damp forehead but happily answered Guinalle's smile of frank enjoyment with one of his own.

'There!' Guinalle froze and sank down, taking an arrow from her quiver and nocking it carefully.

Temar and Vahil followed her gaze and saw a scatter of furry creatures grazing peaceably on the long grass in the centre of the clearing. They exchanged a nod and moved stealthily to take up positions for themselves. Temar glanced across to Guinalle and, when she gave the nod, let fly. His second arrow found its target as well, but by then all the animals had vanished into the concealing forest, a few shaking leaves the only sign of their panicked flight. They rose and crossed to see what quarry they had taken.

'What do you suppose these are?' Vahil shook his head in mystification as he expertly removed his quarrel from the expiring creature.

Temar used his knife to open the mouth of his kill, cautious in case it was not quite dead. 'It's got teeth for grass and fruit, I'd say, so it should be good eating.'

'It's certainly heavy enough, for the size of it.' Guinalle had pulled back the blunt-nosed, squarish head to slit the throat of the one that Temar's second arrow had not quite killed clean. 'I'd say it's a hare that has ambitions to be a deer.'

Temar laughed. 'That sounds about right.'

'Let's find somewhere else to gut them,' Vahil suggested. 'We could try waiting for the rest of them again tomorrow, if we don't leave too much blood.'

Five of the densely muscled beasts between them was no slight burden and Temar was glad to let the two he carried slide from his shoulders when Guinalle sat down on a scatter of rocks a little way above the stream running through the base of the valley.

'I'll cut some poles.' Vahil headed for a stand of springy young growth and Temar began gutting his animals, pleasantly surprised to see Guinalle doing the same with reasonable skill, if not the speed of any long practice. They worked in companionable silence until all the prey was cleaned, the entrails buried to baffle the flies and Vahil had uncorked the wineskin he had thoughtfully picked up before leaving the camp. Temar coughed at the smell of blood clogging his nostrils and picked some sprigs of a low-growing, purple-tinged thyme. He handed one to Guinalle, who accepted it with a composed smile, faint colour kissing her cheeks.

'Den Fellaemion said he'll be looking to set up a permanent anchorage on these islands, you know, when the colony's established,' Temar observed, looking idly round to stop himself gazing too obviously at Guinalle.

'I can think of worse places to live,' commented Vahil. 'Nice climate, plenty of timber, game for hunting and room for farming.'

'You won't be the first, if you do settle here,' said Guinalle unexpectedly.

'No, there are no people here.' Vahil shook his head. 'Den Fellaemion told me; they checked all five of the islands when they first found them and they've been back several times since. There's been no sign of anyone living here; he wouldn't have let us go off like this, if he wasn't certain.'

'Yes, I know.' Guinalle's tone betrayed a certain irritation. 'I spent most of yesterday using Artifice to make absolutely sure. What I'm saying is that there were people here once.'

Vahil opened his mouth to argue but Temar waved him down. 'How do you know?'

'Look around you.' Guinalle rose from her seat on a boulder and swept round, arm outstretched. 'There were huts here; can't you see the circles, where the hearths were?'

Temar looked but with the best will in the world couldn't see what she was indicating.

'Here.' Guinalle paced around a wide circle and suddenly Temar saw it, an almost invisible depression in the rough grasses with a clump of spite-nettle in the centre.

'Yes, I see.' He looked at her, a little daunted but still impressed. 'You have good eyes!'

Guinalle shook her head with a deprecating smile. 'Well, I did get a clue from this.'

She held up a shard of crude pottery and tossed it to Temar. He turned it in his hands; black on one side from use in a fire, it was coarse and gritty stuff, still bearing the thumbprints of its maker.

'They were an uncultured people, I think. They hunted in the forests, gathered fruit in season, that kind of thing, not farmers in any real sense, as we understand it. They had music though, pipes and drums and story tellers; they weren't complete savages.'

'A bit of broken pot can't tell you that much, surely.' Vahil was trying politely to hide his scepticism, Temar could tell, but merely sounded patronising.

'Artifice can.' Guinalle's eyes were distant as she turned another potsherd over and over in her hands. 'I can pick up echoes, sort of, from things like this. It was a long time ago, though.'

'What happened to them?' Temar was fascinated.

'I can't tell.' Guinalle frowned slightly. 'There are flames in the destruction of this pot, distress too.'

'That could just mean some woman dropped it in the fire and ruined the dinner,' laughed Vahil. 'Either that or she threw it at her husband and missed!'

'It's more than that.' Guinalle looked more than a little piqued but Vahil seemed oblivious as he finished the wine.

'Just what sort of things can you tell from something like this?' Temar held out a hand and tried to fit the two pieces of weathered crock together without success.

'It depends on many different factors – on how old something is, how valued it was by its owner, the strength of emotions involved.' Guinalle's tone became slightly didactic. 'Of course Artifice can be used to deliberately instil memories in an item as well, visions that an Adept can retrieve.'

'Saedrin's stones,' said Temar without thinking, wondering what possible use that sort of thing could have.

Guinalle didn't seem to notice the vulgarism. 'It's a difficult thing to achieve, and it's something that has been subject to misuse in the past. It can have rather unexpected effects on some people,' she sighed. 'I'm afraid certain Masters of Artifice haven't always been as scrupulous about the use they have made of their talents.'

'I bet they haven't!' Vahil grinned with inappropriate humour as he reached for the carrying pole. 'Come on, let's get this meat back to camp in time for dinner. Even if there's no time to hang it properly, no one will thank us for it if it gets flyblown.'

Guinalle followed closely behind Temar as they followed the narrow game trail back down to the shore, but carrying the laden pole made it impossible for him to talk to her.

'You know, I would like to know more about Artifice,' he puffed when they reached the camp and he was able to hand over his load. 'Could you tell me about it?'

'I could, if you are serious in your interest.' Guinalle's expression was one of good-humoured scepticism.

'Oh, I am. I think it could be very valuable for the colony.' Temar realised somewhat to his surprise that he meant what he said. Not that the thought of spending time alone with Guinalle wasn't a considerable inducement, but if he was going to be responsible for a crowd of clients he would need all the resources he could muster.

'I am a little surprised that you haven't had some basic instruction,' commented Guinalle, her eyes softening a little.

Temar shrugged. 'My family was very hard hit by the Crusted Pox,' he said shortly. 'My grandfather rather lost any confidence he might have had in healers and acolytes after that.'

'I am so sorry.' Guinalle laid a gentle hand on Temar's arm, her face concerned.

He slapped his hands together briskly. 'Look, I stink of blood and dirt. I must get a bath before dinner. I'll see you later.'

CHAPTER SIX

A letter discovered amongst the effects salvaged from an Aldabreshin galley wrecked in the Gulf of Peorle, in the 278th Year of the Freedom of the City of Col.

Segalo Ria greets Imir Sazac with loving respect by the hand of her body slave Cathu,

We are all curious to learn of your trip to the mainlanders at Col and cordially invite you to visit us upon your return. If these foreigners are any less predatory than the vermin of the Relshaz mud flats, the dangers of such a voyage will be worthwhile. It is a matter of no little concern to us that you had scant opportunity to deal with mainlanders before the grievous passing of the esteemed Iru Sazac elevated you to the honour of First Wife. Please allow us to impart some of the experience we have garnered over recent years.

You are accustomed to hear all mainlanders stigmatised as thieves. This is not merely based upon the recurrent thefts of spice plants and the subsequent dishonourable diversion of that trade by the men of the leeward coasts. You will find all plead to be allowed to visit your domains and, should you allow this, they will ask repeatedly who owns every item in your residence. Although such a question is meaningless to a person with any honour, reply that everything is the personal possession of Sazac Dega, otherwise these mainlanders purloin anything not actually nailed down.

Make sure that your triremes are well in evidence when your galleys reach Col, a visible display of Sazac Dega's might. Leave them in no doubt that any attempts at incursion into your domain will leave their boats burned to the waterline, else you will find their clumsy vessels sniffing round your lands, stealing your crops and slaves, attempting to inveigle themselves into your trade.

There is no place for beauty or honour in their notions of exchange. All they want to do is assign a number of little metal tokens to any and every object and then attempt to trade for as few of these as possible. Do not, for example, agree a trade and then offer an additional, superior gem to show your appreciation of politeness, as you would with an Islander. These mainlanders will not understand this, merely taking it as a sign to attempt to extort further gems from you. Also, do not give them any sizeable or noteworthy jewels; they will cut up and facet whatever they get, having no appreciation of the natural forms of the stones.

Be extremely careful to assess the quality of the gold and silver they offer you. Much is badly adulterated with base metals, but you have to understand this is so commonplace as to be openly accepted and not the disgrace it would be among a civilised people. The best metals are worth keeping for turning over to your jewellers and craftsmen but much of the rest is only fit for ballast. All you can do is use it to simplify trading for slaves, which does at least get it off your hands.

Make sure you keep Denil with you at all times and that he knows to keep his blades sharp. Mainlanders virtually leash and muzzle their females and feel entitled to offer insult to any woman not so constrained. We would certainly advise you not to seek recreation with any mainlander; they have simply no idea how to conduct themselves. Their customary use of liquors and narcotics curdles any sense of decency.

Nevertheless, we await news of your trip with great eagerness and wish you every success.

The Palace of Shek Kul,
the Aldabreshin Archipelago,
5th of For–Summer

I stood, leaning against the wall for as much support as I dared, and felt the sweat trickling down between my shoulder blades. Although I was trying not to move, I must have somehow betrayed my discomfort and that earned me a swift glance of displeasure from Laio's dark eyes. I tried to concentrate instead on the rhythms of the little fountain playing in a broad ceramic basin set into the middle of the white marble floor. An insect whined somewhere and I tried to spot it, not wanting the bastard to add to my already impressive collection of itching bites.

'So you see, my lady, there is no consistency to the thread. It jams on the loom or breaks, the quality of the cloth shames me greatly.'

The weaver was an old man, white-haired and skinny, wearing only a crisply laundered loincloth, kneeling in abject supplication in front of this girl young enough to be his granddaughter.

Lucky bastard, I thought, my shoulders aching viciously from most of a day spent standing around in chainmail, doing nothing more useful than looking war-like for the benefit of Laio's workers. Still, at least I was standing upright.

'I understand your problems and there will be no penalties,' Laio interrupted the old man's complaints, as well she might. We'd been hearing the same thing all day in various forms; I could have told her myself what he was going to say.

Her brisk and efficient manner still struck me as incongruous, as she sat there in a filmy silk dress that left few of her charms to the imagination. Bright paints all but obscured her face and she was adorned with more jewels than the entire House of D'Olbriot at a Sieur's wedding.

I closed my ears to their conversation and stared out of the open shutters, across the lush grounds of Shek Kul's palace compound. Precisely tended gardens surrounded the central residence, slaves' dwellings beyond them and, looming over those, the high black walls patrolled day and night by keen-eyed sentries, always with double-curved short bows to hand. I looked at the green pennant lazily flickering in the breeze above the tower over the main gate and, in the far distance, the dark green hills of the next island in the domain, hazy in the moist heat. So far I'd found as little prospect of getting beyond those gates alone as stepping through a rainbow to meet an Eldritch-man.

Dark clouds were boiling up above the steep conical peaks of the far islands and I wondered when the rains that Laio had been promising for days would actually arrive. Would it get any cooler? I was just about getting used to being covered in a permanent film of sweat. As long as there was some breeze, it was tolerable, unless I was wearing this cursed hauberk, that was. On those days or when the air hung still and heavy, I felt as if I were walking around wrapped in a warm, wet blanket and I found myself dreaming about fresh, salt-scented winds off the ocean at home.

A knock on the door brought me back to my present duties. I opened it to reveal Gar Shek, her golden eyes dancing with delight, Sezarre impassive as always behind her.

'Laio, my dear, I have some wonderful news for you,' Gar smiled sweetly, her customary expression concealing whatever mischief she was trying to foment. 'The pigeon-master has just brought me a message from Kaeska. She arrives home on the afternoon tide. Isn't that perfect; she'll be here for the birth!'

Laio looked up with a wide smile of untroubled pleasure. 'Thank you for letting me know so quickly.' She glanced at the complicated arrangement of toothed and interlocking metal wheels that I had been startled to learn served her as some kind of calendar. The senior wife, Kaeska, hadn't been due back for a couple of days.

Gar nodded and then looked at the weaver, who was kneeling, forehead to the floor, in what I had learned was the appropriate manner and very hard on the knees.

'Are your workers still having trouble with that yarn you traded from Tani Kaasik?' asked Gar, all innocent concern and missing no opportunity to remind Laio of her lapse.

Laio shrugged. 'It's of no consequence and I had to do something for the poor girl. With that amount of overproduction, she was at her wit's end.'

Perhaps, but the youngest Kaasik wife had still had the wit to offload the poorest quality cotton on to Laio. I recalled the meeting where Laio's eagerness to increase her own production and reap the attendant benefits had got the better of her good sense. She had failed to check the yarn for herself and I had garnered a severe slapping when Laio had discovered her error and come looking for an outlet for her frustrations.

'I'm sure you will find a way to resolve the situation,' smiled Gar warmly.

'I have a market in mind for the cloth,' Laio assured her confidently. I would have been completely convinced if I had not seen her storming round her chambers the previous day, volubly lamenting the fact that she had no such thing.

Gar smiled sweetly once again, turned on her heel and swept lightly down the corridor, Sezarre clinking softly behind her. For all that she never missed a chance to needle Laio, I had recently heard Gar assuring some noble visitor that Laio had known exactly what she was doing, generously helping the hapless Tani Kaasik out of the difficulties stemming from the girl's deplorable inexperience. In the course of a day, I reckoned an Aldabreshi lady wore more different faces than an actor in a Soluran masquerade.

'You are all dismissed!' Laio nodded at the weaver and the line of others waiting patiently in the corridor. They dispersed without a murmur and I looked after them with no little disdain.

'You are looking puzzled. What is it?' demanded Laio as we climbed the stairs to her apartments on the top floor of the palace. I should have remembered that Laio had a talent for spotting every nuance of expression or tone that would even put a professional gambler like Livak to shame; years of training for the complicated life of a Warlord's wife, no doubt.

'Your slaves, the weavers, they are very obedient,' I said, somewhat lamely.

Laio clicked her tongue in exasperation. 'They are not slaves, they are free Islanders. You must learn these things. A slave is one who has been purchased from the mainland or traded from another domain.'

Personally I would call anyone a slave who was entirely dependent on a Warlord and his wives to trade the product of his labours, to keep a roof over his head and to give him permission to marry, raise children or do pretty much anything beyond eat, sleep and breathe. I nodded obediently and added this to the ever growing list of things I had to remember. We reached the top floor and I hurried to open the door to Laio's bedroom. She was already stripping off her dress as she crossed the threshold, dropping it carelessly on the polished and patterned wooden floor. I had seen her naked too often to react much by now, and simply went to the stairs to send one of the ubiquitous pages for some hot water.

Laio was cleaning off her face paints in the tiled bathroom when I returned with a steaming jug.

'Come here,' she commanded. 'I need to speak to you.'

I emptied the ewer into a broad basin and Laio waited while I mixed in some cold water.

'Kaeska is a very clever woman but her power will end with the birth of Mahli's child. Accordingly, it is entirely possible that she will make some attempt to injure Mahli or the baby.'

I had no trouble believing that; for all their endless courteous dances round each other, I had already seen ample evidence of Aldabreshin ruthlessness. The breeze coming through the open windows still carried a faint hint of ash, carried from a neighbouring domain where an island struck by one of the foul pestilences peculiar to the Archipelago had been quite deliberately burned clear down to the black earth, utterly destroying homes, plants, animals and inhabitants to contain the disease.

Laio scowled as she briskly lathered her face. 'You are to remain vigilant at all times. We will dine as a family tonight, so you are not to shame me in the slightest fashion. You will speak only in Aldabreshin and only when directly addressed. You will not draw attention to yourself, no matter what is said.'

The soap bubbles rather spoiled the effect of Laio's stern look, but as I had no desire to feel her cane switch on my back again I stifled my desire to laugh.

'What dress will you wear?' I could manage that much in passable Aldabreshin by now, as well as a few other useful phrases, but it looked as if I was going to spend the evening largely silent. That did not bother me; I may still have been having trouble speaking the language, even though it had proved far simpler to learn than I had feared, but I was finding I could understand more and more, something I took pains to conceal from everyone around me. What I really wanted was to overhear something that would get me out of this compound, past the guards and down to the harbour on my own. I was increasingly certain that waiting for any wizard to rescue me was a waste of time.

Laio paused as she soaped her body vigorously. 'The red and gold. Do you agree?'

I thought for a moment. 'I'd have said the cream and gold, especially if Mahli's going to be wearing yellow. Gar has that new red gown, remember?'

Laio nodded. 'That should remind Kaeska that Mahli is much supported here.' She tilted her head back and tipped a bowl of cold water over her face. She shuddered, glistening in a very distracting manner as the water curled away down the drain in the sloping floor.

I left her to her ablutions and fetched the dress in question, adding a choice of pearl-studded ornaments of yellow gold for ankles, wrists, neck, waist and hair. I was getting positively casual about handling enough wealth to buy up half of Zyoutessela by now. Laio had cases of the stuff and, quite evidently, no real idea of just what she owned. I could quite easily have purloined a ring, an ear-stud or two, a fine chain perhaps, jewels that would have paid my passage clean across the Old Empire at home. Here they wouldn't get me past the first gates of the compound, since no one apart from the nobility had any understanding of the value of such things. The irony could have been quite amusing, if it hadn't been so galling. Her jewel case was an odd mixture too; some pieces of workmanship so fine an Emperor would have coveted them, some plain pieces with huge gems simply polished in their natural shape, for all the world looking like oddly coloured pebbles rather than wealth enough to buy every slave in Relshaz.

'My hair will suffice. Do my face,' commanded Laio, settling the folds of her draperies to her satisfaction.

I found the paints and looked for a judicious choice of colours. Whatever else I'd imagined I might learn from an Aldabreshi swordsman like Sezarre, it hadn't included mixing cosmetics. However, the duties of an Aldabreshi lady's body slave were proving to be a most peculiar mixture of guard, personal dresser, spy and footman. Luckily, before my father and I had agreed that masonry wasn't for me, I'd served sufficient apprenticeship to give me a good eye and a steady hand. It could have been worse; the indigo Gar used to tint her hair left Grival with permanently blue nails, from what I had seen.

A brazen scream of horns came from the harbour, startling me so much that I nearly stabbed Laio in the cheek with a silver-laden brush.

She spat something that just had to be an obscenity. 'That's Kaeska's ship; she's early of course. Hurry up! Wash your face as well, I won't have you looking like that!'

I complied, and almost before I was finished Laio was on her feet and out of the door. I followed, trying to ease the screaming pain in my shoulder muscles and wondering when

I might have a chance for a cooling wash myself. The best I could do was to tighten my belt, to try to settle as much of the weight of the armour on my hips as I could.

'I don't think we need hurry, my dear.'

As we emerged from the main door of the keep, we found Shek Kul waiting on the broad steps of polished black stone, his long beard lustrous with oil, looking the complete masquerade barbarian in loose trousers and overtunic of lavishly embroidered white silk studded with gems, still more jewels on his wrists and fingers. His hair was scraped back off his face with more oil, braided and laced with gold chains, the first time I had seen it done so. A gold mounted fly whisk of iridescent feathers added the final touch to his air of ease.

'We will wait for Mahli,' he smiled at Laio, taking her hand with a fond squeeze.

'Of course,' she beamed up at him and I wondered if I would be taking my cotton-stuffed pallet out into the corridor again that night, rather than sleeping at the foot of Laio's bed like a house dog as I had been forced to become accustomed.

'Trust Kaeska to be early!' Mahli came cautiously down the steps, leaning heavily on Grival's arm.

Sezarre and I were seeing less and less of him these days; with Mahli scant days away from child-bed, he was hovering round her like an old bitch with one pup. Personally, I was starting to wonder about his fondness for her but was careful to keep my speculations to myself.

'Let us go and greet our wife,' commanded Shek Kul, his steps crunching down the pebble path that wound through the vivid and richly scented blooms filling the gardens. Laio took Mahli's arm and Grival fell in beside me. I heard the door behind us swing open, but as I went to turn my head to look Grival shot me a forbidding frown. I kept my eyes ahead and my face carefully impassive as Gar hurried past us in a flurry of scarlet silk and Sezarre took his place at my sword hand, the three of us marching in step. I'd been relieved to find that outside the palace buildings everyone wore open leather sandals, but even though my feet were toughening up I could still feel every pebble through the thin soles.

I schooled my expression as we approached the gates of the compound, but could not help a quiver of anticipation deep in my belly. We'd arrived at night and gone straight to the palace, so there had been no chance for me to see the harbour, to get some idea of what boats were available and assess how closely things were guarded or patrolled.

What I saw now did not encourage me. A rough lane snaked down to the broad curve of the bay, clusters of single-roomed houses on either side, broad shutters open to show people washing, cooking, weaving, spinning, going about their daily lives unconcerned at observation from all sides. At the water's edge a broad, square building of harsh, grey stone stood sternly above the tide line, watchmen on its roof walk, windows no more than slits for arrows, the only double door a massive barrier of wood, studs and iron. It was a fair wager that it was a hollow square, like so many of the palace buildings, built for defence on the outside, all amenities facing inward. The great doors of black wood stood open, meek Islanders carrying in loads deposited on the dark sand of the beach by the flotilla of little boats that were ferrying in considerable amounts of cargo from the galleys anchored in the centre of the bay. Even if I had a chance to steal one of those skiffs, I wouldn't want to risk it in anything more than a stiff breeze, with its shallow draught and triangular, coastal sail. I sighed inwardly. Was I ever going to find a workable plan of escape?

I looked at the ships bringing home the spoils from what must have been a lengthy trading trip by Kaeska Shek. Two were the same style of galley as the one that had carried me here; broad in the beam, square-rigged for a following wind, far more massively built than those that plied the coast of the Gulf of Lescar. Each rower on the benches had his own oar, rather than all three pulling on the same one in the Tormalin style and I knew the Aldabreshi had long made sure that no one else experimented with this technique by sinking any other vessel they saw with more than one rank of oars. Since the Warlords were the ones with all the gemstones, mainland mariners tended to let them have their own way on this issue.

The third ship was a bird of a different feather altogether; lean, narrow, its three ranks of oars set one on top of each other, armed men lining its rails and a fleck of foam betraying the long ram cutting the waves just below the waterline. This was a warship, one of the more compelling reasons why the galleys that ply the coasts from Col to Relshaz and on to Toremal keep close to their own shores and do not venture into the Archipelago without a very specific invitation and the flags to fly to prove it. Two of these vessels had joined our galley as soon as we had left the outer Relshazri anchorages. On our lengthy progress down through the Islands, I had learned that Shek Kul had treaties with other Warlords that allowed his vessels to land each day on certain tiny islets to take on food and water and to rest the rowers. At all of these halts, we had seen more such predatory shapes standing off at sea, shadowing us until we left the waters of that particular domain. I had come to the conclusion that Dastennin has indeed favoured us southern Tormalins with the violent weather than screams round the Cape of Winds and keeps the Aldabreshi out of our waters for the most part. At least the prevalent atmosphere within the Archipelago was one of armed truce at the moment and I sincerely hoped peace would hold until I got myself out of there.

A little boat was leaving the warship's side, rowers bending to their oars, three figures seated in the stern. One was bright in flame-coloured silks fluttering in the breeze; sat beside her was a man all in solemn black, close-cropped white hair vivid in the sunlight. He was little taller than the woman next to him but broad in the shoulder and deep in the chest. I had seen such men before, the previous year and in Shiv's scrying as the heart of the Empire was consumed by flames. I watched the boat draw nearer, a mounting dread stifling my instinctive denials. That man was an Elietimm, I'd wager my oath fee on it.

'Kaeska, my beloved!' Shek Kul walked on to the beach to help Kaeska down himself, oblivious to the wavelets lapping at his ankles.

'My revered husband.' Kaeska's tones were warm with affection as she embraced him. 'Mahli, my dearest, you should have waited in the gardens, in the shade; it's too hot for you to be walking so far, so close to your blessing.'

'I had to welcome you properly, you've been away so long.' Mahli kissed Kaeska's immaculate cheek with every appearance of sincerity as Laio and Gar stepped forward to embrace the new arrival.

After all the tales I'd heard from Laio about Kaeska's manipulative, cunning and vengeful nature, I'd been expecting something a little more impressive than a small-boned, doe-eyed woman with neat ankles and a pert figure. Her skin and hair were a little lighter than the other women, there was a distinct tint of red in the curls artfully coiled round her head. I judged her about my own age.

'What a delightful dress, Laio my sweet.' Kaeska held her at arm's length to get a better look. 'Your face too; what an unusual style.'

'Laio has a new body slave,' Gar chipped in, beaming with pleasure.

'Oh yes!' Laio was all girlish excitement. 'It was so clever of Gar to chose me a mainlander. Can you believe it, he knows nothing of our ways, not even how to talk? It has been such fun, training him up from nothing!'

I stood and stared straight ahead, trying to look as if their rapid chatter was beyond my understanding. Nevertheless, I caught a fleeting glance exchanged between Gar and Kaeska, the former looking for approval, the latter giving it with a glint of satisfaction in her hazel eyes. So there was something they had woven between them, was there?

'You have brought us a guest?' Shek Kul turned to study the white-haired man with frank appraisal.

'This is Kra Misak.' Kaeska turned her head to acknowledge her companion with a brief nod. 'He comes from a land far to the north and wishes to investigate the opportunities for trade here.'

I ran the name through my mind; Kramisak, it would be on a civilised tongue, but it had an unfamiliar ring to me, no echo of the Empire anywhere.

'You are welcome to my domain.' Shek Kul did not bow or offer a hand, but the Elietimm was not discomposed, evidently well briefed on what to expect.

'I will respect your hospitality.' The man ducked his head in a show of nicely gauged homage; his face was honest and open, his stance one of ease masking slight intimidation. He had definitely been very well advised; it had taken me days to work out the precise bows required for the different levels of nobility. My shoulders still smarted under my chainmail at the memory of Laio's displeasure after I had embarrassed her in front of a visiting friend.

The Elietimm ran a swift glance over Grival, Sezarre and myself, the three of us standing like statues on a shrine front, all alike with our armour, weapons and close-trimmed beards. I kept my eyes motionless, holding the blank expression that Laio's switch had drilled into me. The man's eyes were ice blue and austere but gave nothing away as he offered Kaeska his arm and we all began the ascent to the palace compound, Mahli's laborious pace slowing the rest.

I stared at this Kramisak's back, sure I was missing something here. Kaeska was talking to him, laughing and smiling. As she turned towards him, I felt suddenly cold, despite the heat of the day. I recognised her in that tilt of her head, in her profile. She was the woman I had seen on the dock at Relshaz, talking to the Elietimm who had been at the slave auction. This wasn't the same man, the would-be purchaser had been younger, a little taller, that much I was sure of, but there had to be a connection. However I had fallen into that Relshazri lock-up, the Elietimm had known enough to be ready to try to take advantage, hadn't they? If Kaeska had encompassed my purchase through Gar, what did that signify? I wondered at the Elietimm's lack of any insignia; all the Ice Islanders I'd seen the previous year had worn a badge to proclaim their loyalty to one or other of the bitterly contested fiefdoms. Why was this Kramisak so anonymous?

Before I could pursue that thought, Sezarre deliberately knocked his elbow against mine. That was unusual enough to get my undivided attention. I slid my eyes sideways to catch his and saw a faint frown darkening his face. He tilted his head a fraction towards Grival, who immediately stumbled for a pace to allow me sight of Kaeska's body slave, who had fallen into line on his far side.

The man stared straight ahead, one eye darkened by a livid bruise that overlay the fading discoloration of an older injury. His beard was raggedly trimmed, uneven and clotted with dried blood under the ear that I could see. His shoulders were square under his chainmail, but the tension in him was brittle with fear rather than ready for action. His hands were striped red with weals from a whip or a cane and I wondered what other injuries we would see when he was stripped for exercise with the rest of us. His skin was pale, paler than my own tan, and though his hair had the tight black curls of Aldabreshi blood, the cast of his features was distinctly Caladhrian. If he were mixed race, I wondered if he retained any attachment to the mainland that I might use to my benefit, especially given Kaeska was so clearly mistreating him. I didn't hold out much hope of that; his eyes were as dead as those of a dog whipped too often and too long.

Our progress back to the palace was slowed as the so-called free Islanders came out of their houses to bow low before Shek Kul, press flowers on the ladies and often to lay a gentle hand on Mahli's distended belly, taking a liberty that rather surprised me. I noticed Mahli seemed to be getting the most and the choicest blooms, and although Kaeska nodded, smiled and laughed to all sides, threading a long stem of golden blossoms through her hair, her eyes were hard and calculating.

The press of people separated the nobles from us body guards and I saw Grival tap Kaeska's slave on one arm. 'How was the trip, Irith?'

The man Irith shook his head, not meeting Grival's eyes. Sezarre frowned and moved closer. I followed.

'Are you sick?' enquired Sezarre in an undertone, his concern plain.

Irith shook his head again, still staring at his feet, this time making a faint grunt.

Grival glanced warily in Kaeska's direction but she was absorbed in examining a spray of crimson flowers. 'Have you offended our mistress?'

The man grimaced as if in sudden agony and turned to present his open mouth to Grival who recoiled with an expression of naked horror.

'What is it?' hissed Sezarre, but the path suddenly cleared and we had to resume our measured pace behind the nobles.

Grival muttered a word I did not know to Sezarre and I saw the same startled revulsion flare in his dark eyes.

'Sezarre?' I glanced at him as the curve of the path allowed me to turn my head.

'Irith has no tongue now,' he replied with a finality that forbade further enquiry.

As we were halted by another group hurrying up to make their obeisances, I noticed the Elietimm was staring, not directly at me but rather at my sword. That brought me up short as I realised it would almost certainly identify me to him, beard and armour notwithstanding. It may sound silly, but I had been concentrating so hard on learning the rules of this new situation, where the slightest mistake led to a thrashing, that I had hardly given the sword a thought since I'd got here. I certainly hadn't been troubled by dreams that I was aware of; my main problem sleeping stemmed from the fact that Laio snored worse than Shiv. Keeping my face expressionless and making sure I did not look directly at the Ice Islander, I decided I had better talk to Laio about this as soon as we were alone. If I suggested Kaeska was plotting somehow, I knew I would have Laio's instant interest.

As we entered the palace compound, one of the underlings came to escort the Ice Islander, presumably to a guest room.

I watched him go with relief and wondered maliciously if the slave, who seemed to be what we would call an understeward in Tormalin, would misinterpret the white-haired man's lack of a beard. I had soon realised why Sezarre had warned me against shaving after I had noted the nightly visits of a couple of sleek-eyed boys to the smooth-cheeked steward's quarters. At least as a fighting man I was expected to keep my beard close-trimmed, offering no handhold to an enemy, but it still itched abominably in this sultry climate.

'Dinner will be served shortly,' Mahli smiled at Kaeska as she seated herself under a shady tree with visible relief.

'I congratulate you on having everything so well organised.' Kaeska's tones dripped pure honey. 'Especially when you had no real idea of when I would arrive.'

'You need not be so modest.' Mahli shook her head in mock reproof. 'I've learned so much from watching you over the years. I've had a watcher at the north of the island, ready to send a signal down the flag-line as soon as your pennant was sighted.'

'All the flag stations and beacons are manned.' Shek Kul clasped Mahli's hand warmly. 'Everyone is awaiting news of our child.'

'I have some lovely things for the babe.' Kaeska's expression grew more animated and she took a seat between Gar and Laio. 'I have been right round the windward domains.'

The conversation grew more rapid and increasingly idiomatic as the five of them talked about people and places that meant nothing to me. The one thing I did notice was that Kaeska made no mention of visiting Relshaz at all. I wondered how Laio would take my assertion that Kaeska had been there at the same time as the rest of them.

I stopped trying to follow what they were saying and let my thoughts drift as I looked idly round the gardens. A few of the ever present gardeners were trimming the luxuriant shrubs, removing spent blooms, tidying the paths. Eventually a chime sounded from the far side of the central residence and Grival nodded to the rest of us. We escorted our ladies and the Warlord into the long and airy dining room where marble channels carried water around the edge of the room and then cascaded into a central ornamental pool that was home to some distinctly odd-looking lizards. Small censers set to give off faint columns of scented smoke were a welcome sight, since I was starting to think one of my minor roles here was to decoy the cursed insects into biting me rather than the Aldabreshi, who didn't seem nearly so troubled by them as I was.

I realised this was going to be as long and tedious an evening as the ones when Laio was entertaining visitors from the domain of Kaasik Rai. The only good thing was there was no sign of the Elietimm; I wanted to keep out of his way as much as possible until I had some idea of what he wanted here. I was certainly curious to know just what he might be up to while everyone was dining, but my duties waiting on Laio kept me too busy to worry about it just for the present. A succession of courses came and went, my own hunger increasingly gnawing at my belly since Laio had neglected to eat at noon, too preoccupied with the complaints of her weavers. So I fetched, served, hungered and listened.

When at last the conversation turned to Kaeska's unexpected guest, I pricked up my ears like the good hound I was spending so much of my time emulating lately.

'Where is he from?' enquired Gar innocently, abandoning her attempts to hold Shek Kul's attentions.

Kaeska swallowed a mouthful of sour pickled fish. 'The north somewhere.'

Laio looked thoughtful but did not say anything. She had been asking me about the precise geography of the Old Empire recently, but everyone else seemed happy to treat the mainland as one undistinguished lump, for all that they could describe every reef and islet of the Archipelago and name its owner besides.

'A mainlander,' Shek Kul's expression was somewhere between pity and contempt, 'they are all the same.'

Kaeska tilted her head in a rather feline gesture. 'His people live on islands; I do not find him as uncouth as most.'

'What does he have to trade?' Mahli looked up from her plate. 'Are his people interested in proper barter or do they reduce everything to metal bits and paltry gems like the rest of them?'

Kaeska shrugged. 'The north has long been a source of metals, timber, leather, has it not?'

I couldn't decide if she was speaking from genuine ignorance or deliberately being vague. I would have to make sure Laio knew the Ice Islands had none of these resources, to my certain knowledge.

'Let me know when you find out what he wishes to trade for.' Mahli laid a negligent hand on her abdomen as she smiled fondly at Kaeska. 'Gar and Laio have been making up their accounts for me and I have been assessing the treasury.'

'Have you examined those sapphires I had from Rath Tek, my dear?' Shek Kul spoke through a mouthful of spiky green stems. 'I think you should be able to do very well with them the next time we visit Relshaz.'

Kaeska's expression froze at this unusually unsubtle exchange and I even saw Laio blink a little at the realisation that Mahli had been taking on so many of Kaeska's duties even before the birth of her child.

'If this man is from a northern land, perhaps he might trade for that cloth of yours, Laio,' Gar rushed to fill the awkward silence, her eyes betraying an unaccustomed confusion. 'It's too thick for anyone in the Islands to want it, even if it were not such poor quality.'

'Oh dear, Laio,' Kaeska's face was instantly sisterly concern. 'Are you in difficulties with your weavers?'

Laio hastily denied any such thing and began to explain how she had only been looking to help the foolish Tani Kaasik. Kaeska nodded and sympathised, but every time Laio looked to be coming out ahead, Gar innocently sank another barbed comment into the sensitive conversation. I was surprised to see Mahli remain aloof from the fencing but she concentrated on discussing household matters with Shek Kul, which seemed to keep Kaeska all the more determined to pursue the issue of Laio's mistakes.

As the night deepened beyond past the slatted shutters, I saw the greater moon rise above the battlements, not yet quite at the half as it waned, with the lesser moon just showing an edge above the trees. I tried to remember when I'd last seen an Almanac and how many days the Emperor's Chronicler had decreed for Aft-Spring this year. As far as I could estimate, from what I remembered of the charted phases of the two moons, we would be in the early days of For-Summer, around the 5th or 6th.

Soft-footed house slaves answered Shek Kul's abrupt summons with small lamps and I hastily gathered my wits. Delighted to realise this interminable evening was about to end, I saw my own relief trebled in Laio's eyes. Gar and Kaeska linked hands in high good humour and led the way up the broad central stairs though I saw the satisfaction on Kaeska's face falter when she turned and realised Shek Kul was giving Mahli the support of his own arm. When Shek Kul did not leave his wives at the landing to go to his own apartments on the floor below, Kaeska abruptly dropped Gar's hand with a theatrical yawn.

'Do forgive me, I am so tired.' She turned away almost instantly towards her own suite. 'Irith!'

The poor wretch hastened up the remaining stairs like a beaten hound and Kaeska swept through the opened door to her own apartments without a backward glance.

Shek Kul muttered something I did not catch as he was embracing Mahli at the time. She laughed loudly as she took Grival's arm down the corridor, a sound that would have carried clearly through the louvered doors of Kaeska's apartments as she passed.

'To bed!' Shek Kul kissed Gar briskly and then turned to catch Laio round the waist with a swiftness that caught everyone by surprise. He swept her off her feet and planted a smacking kiss on the exposed swell of her bosom. Laio giggled with delight. At her nod I hurried to open the door to her bedroom. As I stood to let the Warlord and his wriggling armful past, I saw Gar's face, scarlet and a suspicion of tears in her eyes. She turned on her heel and strode down the far corridor towards her own rooms.

Beyond hoping that she didn't take her chagrin out on Sezarre with a cane switch, I had no time to worry about Gar's feelings. Shek Kul had Laio's dress off her shoulders and down to her waist, hands cupping her ripe breasts, by the time I had dragged my pallet out into the corridor and fetched the canvas bag that held all the possessions I was allowed.

At times like this it was nigh on impossible to pretend to myself that I was a servant, not a slave. I was weary and ravenous, my back and shoulders were knotted with pain and, for all anyone cared, I might as well have been a door-post. Shek Kul's falcons were treated better than us body slaves sometimes. I cursed softly to myself, loosened the thongs on my chainmail and bent over, arms outstretched to shrug it off over my head. The crash it made hitting the polished wood of the floor seemed to echo all around the silent corridors and I froze for a moment, half expecting a rebuke from Laio. I need not have worried; there was scarcely a pause in the sounds of rising passion coming through the flimsy door.

Getting the weight off my shoulders was some improvement, but my aching muscles still screamed their indignation. If I'd been able to go and find Sezarre or Grival, we could have helped each other out with some of the remarkably effective rubbing oils the Aldabreshi favoured, but I now knew that once a Warlord's lady has retired to her rooms for the night her slave is expected to stay with her. Unless he is sitting on his bed in the corridor like a hound that can't be trusted with the furniture, that is. I couldn't even hope for a proper bathtub for a hot soak in the morning. Laio had told me in no uncertain terms that only mainlanders wallowed in their own filth, while decent people rinsed themselves clean with fresh water. Rubbing my own shoulders as best I could, I tried to ignore the clamorous demands of my stomach. I hadn't been this hungry since Laio had arbitrarily kept me without food for a day and a half as punishment for some mealtime transgression that I had never fully understood.

Shek Kul's wordless expressions of pleasure were settling into a regular rhythm behind the door of Laio's room and her uninhibited responses were answering him enthusiastically, accelerating to moans of rapture. I knew from previous nights that, when it came to chasing a snake through the undergrowth, the Warlord was a man of considerable stamina for his age, so I padded stealthily away on bare feet. The pages who spent their days in a lobby off the stairwell were always provided with water and I reckoned I should at least be able to get a drink to stave off the worst pangs of hunger.

The stairwell was at the corner of the hollow square that formed the central keep of the Warlord's residence. Each wife's suite of rooms ran along one inner side of the square, overlooking a central garden that had some special significance I had yet to fathom. The staircase was at the corner, where Kaeska's rooms met Laio's. I moved cautiously, not wanting to alert Kaeska to the fact that I had left my station. As I reached the stairs, I saw bars of light on the dark wooden floor, revealing a lamp was still lit in Kaeska's sitting room. I swore silently to myself and crouched low, not wanting to risk being found crossing to the pages' room.

'So what are you going to do to help me?'

Kaéska's low words drove all thoughts of thirst clean out of my head. Apart from anything else, she was speaking in passable Tormalin. The blood started to pound in my veins, almost deafening me, and I fought to curb my racing heartbeat.

'Whatever I do for you will depend entirely on what you are able to do for me.' The Elietimm accent was unmistakable, for all that his Tormalin was better than Kaeska's. His tone was uncompromisingly harsh.

'Of course, I will do all I can.' Kaeska was abject, pleading. 'Haven't I already done well? You said you were pleased with me, you said you could reward me—'

'The Queen of the Moonless Night must be properly venerated if she is to answer your prayers.' The Elietimm sounded contemptuous. 'She must have worshippers in every domain.'

I forced myself to breathe slowly and evenly, to concentrate on getting every word. I had certainly never heard of this Queen he was talking about. How often do you see a clear night with no trace of either moon, anyway? Maybe once in a handful of years?

'I will travel, I will spread your teachings. I have done your bidding, have I not? I told Gar to secure that slave for Laio—' Kaeska's voice rose in something approaching panic and was cut short with what could only be a slap.

What hold did this man have over her that he dared lay a hand on a Warlord's wife without losing it in the next breath to her body slave's sword?

I moved to the corner with agonising care, lying prone until I could edge my way forward and look into the room through the lowest slats of the door. Kaeska and the Elietimm were sitting on cushions, facing each other from either side of a low table where a candle flickered under some kind of incense burner. This was no mere scent to deter insects; a chance draught wafted a taste of the smoke in my direction and I recognised the acrid, seductive tang of smouldering thassin leaves. I caught my breath, and not just from the fumes. Chewing thassin nuts is one thing; it's a habit that's hard to break, but beyond dulling your senses and staining your teeth, it won't do you too much harm, not taken in moderation anyway. Taking the smoke is quite another matter; any sworn man who started that would soon find himself paid off with a Lescari cut-piece for his oath fee. No one is going to trust a swordsman who might turn his blade on imaginary three-headed monsters at any moment.

Kaeska's eyes were dark and glazed, her intricate makeup smeared, disregarded. Sweat beaded her forehead and she wiped it away with a clumsy gesture, heedless of the trickle of blood at one corner of her mouth.

'Show me my son,' she pleaded in a hoarse whisper.

The Elietimm shook his head, a cruel satisfaction curling his lip. He was sitting cross-legged, straight-backed, stripped to the waist but for a gold gorget bright at his throat. Strange sigils were dark on his pale skin, on his chest and down his arms to his outspread hands. They must have been painted on; I was certain I hadn't seen anything on his palms earlier. Even in the dim light of the candle, the man's eyes were clear and focused; the smoke wasn't curdling his senses at all and I wondered just why that might be. I was already getting enough to be risking a light head and exotic dreams and I was keeping my face to the floor and breathing as shallow as I dared. Who was this man and what was he doing here with his cursed aetheric enchantments?

'Please . . .' Kaeska held out shaking hands in abject supplication.

'If I do, you must do something in return. The Queen of the Moonless Night demands balance in all things.' The man pretended to think, but I could see right through his false hesitation. He knew exactly what he wanted.

'Anything.' Kaeska's eyes were wide and vacant by now, her jaw slack, but she still looked at the Elietimm as if he held Saedrin's keys to the Otherworld.

'That slave of the woman Laio's,' the Ice Islander leaned forward, his expression all cold intent, 'he and his kind are enemies of my Queen. I will need to counter his powers if I am to get you with child. Trade something for him; if he is yours, we can take him with us when we leave and I can deal with him fittingly.'

'Once the child is born, Mahli will be First Wife.' Concern wrinkled Kaeska's brow with visible effort. 'It will be her business to make such trades.'

'So do it before the child arrives.' The Elietimm's voice was harsh. 'I can dispose of this garbage tonight, if necessary. Crush a few more berries on his gums and he won't even wake up.'

He shoved a foot at what I had taken to be a pile of cushions and coverlets. It wasn't; it was Irith who groaned feebly and rolled away from the kick. He came to rest facing me, eyes rolling half open, bloodshot even in the feeble light and a trickle of dark slime oozing from his lips.

'Shek will not be pleased,' Kaeska whimpered. 'Disciplining

a slave is one thing, using tahn on him like this is quite another.'

The bastards, the shit-sucking, pox-ridden bastards. I clenched my fists and fought to contain my revulsion. Anger wouldn't help Irith, it didn't look as if anything could now, but I needed to hear as much of this plot as possible, to take to Laio for certain and, if at all possible, to use to my own ends.

'If you swear to me that you will do it, I will show you your son again.' The Ice Islander's voice was as sweet and seductive as honeyed wine.

'I swear.' Kaeska's voice was all but inaudible, a trembling whisper, her eyes fixed on the blue wisps rising from the burner as the drug stirred her senses into chaos.

The Elietimm began a low chant and the hairs on the back of my neck bristled like a hound who's caught a hated scent. The strange words and rhythms echoed those of Kerrit's paltry cantrips but power rang in this man's voice, confidence and real, unchallenged power. An unbidden memory of my time as a captive in those distant, barren islands came crawling out of the back of my mind, incantations like this ringing over me as I lay paralysed, naked and seemingly bound hand and foot. Only later had I discovered that the fetters had never even existed, a delusion wrought inside my head by the one we had called the Ice-man.

The smoke from the censer began to coil in on itself and thicken oddly, a plume rising straight up in defiance of the evening breeze and then twisting into a vortex. Without a pause in the chant, the Elietimm placed something small on the table. It glinted as the candle flared to an unearthly brilliance. It was a belt buckle in a high, antique Tormalin style, and something about it teased at my memory, though for the life of me I couldn't recall ever having seen it before.

The vortex evaporated abruptly and the faintest outline of a face appeared, wrought from the smoke and the light. But this was nothing like the magics I had seen Shiv or Viltred working. As the thassin fumes wove around my head, for all my shallow breaths I could feel the enchantment hovering around my mind, curious fingers picking at the edges of my wits. Luckily for me, the Elietimm was totally focused on Kaeska and the feeling passed before I somehow betrayed myself. As I watched Kaeska's breathing quicken like a woman in the throes of passion, I felt sure the sorcery was feeding on her fears and desires in some way I couldn't fathom. The face grew clearer, more distinct. I frowned, almost risking an attempt to rub the fog from my eyes but holding my hand back at the last moment, remembering the mortal dangers of the slightest noise. This was no more an Aldabreshin face than the belt buckle was Island-made. I could see a youthful face through the skeins of smoke, probably a boy, but perhaps a girl on the verge of womanhood. The hair was reddish, sandy blond, and freckles dusted pale skin; as the pitch of the chant shifted, the unearthly apparition opened its eyes. Even at this distance, I could see they were pale, blue or green, I was unable to tell. Kaeska's eyes were fixed greedily, insanely on the figure, her breath coming in low, animal pants.

'My son, mine and Shek's,' she whispered, 'heir to the domain and my future.'

The smoke may have been dulling my wits but I've bred enough dogs to make me confident that Kaeska and the War-lord wouldn't produce a child with a face from the Bremilayne hill country if she netted the old ram's horns every other night and bore a child each Summer Solstice on the strength of it. I can't say why but I was suddenly convinced that, whatever I was seeing, Kaeska was looking at something quite different.

'And you will bear him in due season. Your rights as First Wife will therefore be restored and you will rise high above the women of the other domains as your trade with my people brings you metals and timber to build Shek Kul's power still further. You will not need to deal with the thieves and savages of the mainland at all, but with an island people like your own, who understand the value of beauty and honour in trade. You will bring your husband a powerful alliance, place him first among the Warlords as the Islands find friends to defend them against the depredations of mainland pirates and swindlers.'

The Elietimm leaned forward, his eyes fixed on Kaeska. 'And your son will inherit all of this. He will grow and thrive while your rival's child sickens and dies, just as long as the Queen receives her due and you obey her priest without question.'

Meaning him, no doubt. I shook my head slowly, keeping my eyes on Kaeska as the apparition dissolved into smudges of smoke carried off on the night breeze. The eager light faded from her eyes and she clawed at the last wisps with despairing fingers, a sob strangling in her throat.

'Show some dignity.' The Elietimm spat a curt command and the candle guttered, the last tendril of smoke coiling to vanish in the darkness. He climbed to his feet and sneered down at Kaeska as she sprawled across the table, shoulders shaking in silent anguish. He stalked off toward a far door and as soon as he had left the room, I made my way back to my pallet at Laio's door as fast as I could. I found I had to actively concentrate on walking quietly; my co-ordination was definitely affected by the smoke I had been unable to avoid. Glad to lay my head on the cool, soft cotton, I closed my eyes as the floor seemed to dip and sway beneath me, the scent of the drugs still tantalising me.

The Kel Ar'Ayen settlement,
Autumn Equinox, Year One of the Colony

Temar strode purposefully through the crowded market-place, his optimistic mood buoyed with simple pride at the raw yellow of new stonework gleaming here and there in the deepening dusk. It was deeply satisfying to see such tangible proof of his success in locating those quarry sites. Elsewhere the gloom was being held back by the light of flambeaux and braziers set around the dancing floor where determined revel-lers were already forming lines for round-dances. Temar noted with some surprise that some of the craftsmen and traders who had marked out these first lines of their new settlement had still found the time to plant up odd-sized half-barrels and battered kettles. Bright with flowers, the improvised gardens masked the worst deficiencies of the wooden houses and halls that had sheltered the colony through that first summer, giving the place a suitably festive air.

It might be a primitive celebration by D'Alsennin standards, Temar decided, but judging from the noise already echoing around the broad estuary, the colonists were intending to make this a holiday to remember, regardless of what they might be lacking. He nodded as people passed him, waving at half-remembered faces from the voyage and hoping a warm smile would suffice instead of the coin he was used to distrib-uting on the streets at such times of year. The wealth he was carrying tonight was intended for only one recipient.

Temar took a deep breath and paused at the gateway of Messire Den Rannion's steading, checking that no wisps of hair had escaped their clasp and brushing at the worn patch on his jerkin in a futile gesture. He lifted his chin and set his jaw; it wasn't as if he was going to be the only one wearing last year's finery, was it?

'Temar!' A hefty slap on the back caught him completely unawares and nearly sent him sprawling on the beaten earth of the roadway. 'Hold on, I've got you!'

'Vahil, you idiot!' Temar shook off the hand that had saved him from the fall, tugged at his belt and straightened his shirt, checking the pocket with a hasty pat.

'Come on in.' Vahil's good humour was undiminished as he hammered on the pale wood of the gate with the hilt of his belt knife. 'Everyone's longing to see you.'

The gate-ward opened to them and Vahil breezed past him with a cheery greeting that surprised Temar. 'Drianon's favour to you,' he muttered a little awkwardly to the man as he passed him.

'And to you, Esquire!' The gate-ward raised his tankard to Temar in an affable salute.

Temar moved to one side of the entrance and looked curiously at the changes made in the season and a half that he had been away. The steading was still surrounded by a fence rather than a decent stone wall, but the gardens were starting to take shape. Lanterns glowed among spindly fruit trees planted in a sparse avenue and vines were endeavouring to soften the rough-cut wood of the palings. The formal patterns of a herb garden were waiting for the plants to start spreading themselves in their new beds, but faint scent was already rising from the little clumps of bee-balm, meadowsweet and mothbane. Temar wondered in passing where the shingle that crunched underfoot had come from to make the paths, and then he remembered the heap of ballast down by the wharf.

'Your steward's been busy!' he noted with approval.

Vahil shook his head. 'This is all Mother's work. Come on, let's find a drink!' He strode purposefully in the direction of the wine standing on a trestle table under a rather scrawny arbour of climbing plants with startling scarlet flowers. 'Well, Mother and Jaes, the porter.' He waved an arm in the direction of the gate.

'Since when have you been on first-name terms with the outdoor servants?' Temar helped himself to a modest goblet of golden wine since there didn't appear to be any servitors doing the usual duties.

Vahil paused and then shrugged as he found himself a flagon of red. 'I don't know really. It just seemed a bit silly to keep everything so formal. Things are a bit different here, somehow, don't you find?'

Temar nodded as he sipped his drink, blinking a little at its unrefined newness. 'I suppose so. It was certainly like that up river, all of us getting on with the tasks to be done. You caught me a bit by surprise, that's all.'

'We've been too busy breaking and planting enough land and getting the harvests in to worry about making sure the right people sit below the salt.' Vahil's expression turned fleetingly sombre. 'After losing those ships at sea, we've needed to set every pair of hands to work.'

'We?' Temar raised a quizzical eyebrow.

'That's right.' Vahil met the challenge in Temar's expression with a direct gaze and unmistakable emphasis on his words. 'We have a great deal to be proud of and we can look forward to a secure winter.'

'So what exactly have you' – Temar stressed the question lightly – 'been doing?'

Vahil took a pace backwards and swept an extravagant bow. 'I have the honour to represent the Secretariat on the First Council of Kel Ar'Ayen. Oh, sorry!' He raised an apologetic hand to the passing man whom he had narrowly missed in spilling his wine. 'Yes, Temar, give me a couple of chimes and I could show the records of everything that's been planted, plucked or poleaxed since we made landfall here.'

'Vahil den Rannion, bonniest buck in a brothel turned bean counter? I don't believe it!' Temar laughed to cover his astonishment.

'You wouldn't be alone there.' Messire den Rannion appeared at Temar's shoulder, an unmistakable note of pride in his voice as he looked at his son. A harder edge replaced it however.

'You're late, Vahil. Your mother has been wondering where you were.'

Vahil bowed low, neatly avoiding answering. 'I'll go and make my apologies.' He walked rapidly away and his father watched him go with a faint sigh.

'Come, Temar,' The Messire briskly dismissed whatever was concerning him. 'There are some people here very eager to hear your news.'

Temar quickly checked the pocket in his shirt again through the breast of his jerkin. 'Is Demoiselle Tor Priminale here?'

He found he was speaking to Messire den Rannion's departing back and remembered that the older man was more than a little deaf. Temar shrugged and followed obediently towards a knot of stern-faced men deep in discussion.

'D'Alsennin!' One took a step forward to greet Temar with a brief bow. 'It's good to see you again.'

'Master Grethist,' Temar smiled broadly. 'How's the *Eagle*?'

'Safely high and dry on the mud flats,' the mariner assured him. 'Those rocks didn't do as much damage as we feared, in any case.'

'That's as may be, but if that cataract can't be navigated, we can't use the river to get to the interior.' A thin man with tired eyes folded his arms in a gesture of finality.

'I've heard the ship needs the best part of a season's work on it if it's to be seaworthy again.' A taller man with a receding hairline sank his beaked nose into his goblet and took a long swallow.

Grethist shrugged and winked at Temar. 'What else would sailors be doing over the winter? There aren't any brothels hereabouts as yet, are there? I shan't have too much trouble keeping the lads at their caulking if there's nowhere for them to soften a stiff rope.'

'We will be sending expeditions along the coasts in the spring, Master Dessmar,' Den Rannion addressed the thin man seriously. 'Messire den Fellaemion's charts from the original voyages show several estuaries which warrant exploration. It will be some seasons before people are ready to strike out on their own from here and by then we will have navigable rivers and good sites to offer them.'

Dessmar nodded, lips pursed. 'Perhaps they'll find some trace of the ships that were scattered by that appalling storm.'

The balding man continued as if no one else had spoken. 'It's all very well saying the *Eagle* can be repaired, but more than half the vessels that reached this land need beaching and cleaning now. A goodly number of ropes and sails are in need of repair and materials are severely limited. I hate to think what state the timbers are going to be in by next spring.'

'Finding suitable woods for the shipwrights was one of the reasons for D'Alsennin's expedition up the river, Master Suttler.' Messire den Rannion's tone was relaxed but Temar caught a calculating light in his eye.

'Indeed,' Temar nodded firmly. 'We found some excellent stands of mature timber, didn't we, Master Grethist?'

'We'll start felling once the growing season ends and the undergrowth dies back,' the sailor confirmed. 'I've already set those that can be spared from the mines to digging out a dock so we can get a keel laid and work started over the winter.'

'You see, Master Suttler, we'll have new boats busy along the coasts and up the rivers long before the present fleet are spent.' Den Rannion nodded his discreet approval to Temar. 'The larger ships are still in good repair, in any case.'

'We'll only need ocean ships if we have something worth-while to send them home with.' A ruddy-faced individual had been following the exchange with an impatient expression. 'So, Esquire, what are these mines like? If we're to get any more interest in this venture, it's vital that we prove it's not simply a singularly ill-timed drain on the Empire's resources.'

'We have found significant outcroppings of copper in the tributary valleys leading down to the main river, Master Daryn,' stated Temar confidently. 'Some of the men with Gidestan experience made a short trip into the plateau and think there is an excellent chance of tin as well.'

'Useful but not exactly news to set all Toremal talking.' The man frowned a little and looked thoughtfully into his wine cup.

'Come on, Sawney, it's early days yet,' Messire den Rannion encouraged Master Daryn with a familiar slap on the shoulder. 'Who knows what Temar and his men will find over the next hill come the spring.'

'How soon will we know the quality of this ore?' asked Master Daryn.

'The initial assays were promising.' Temar hesitated a little. 'I'm afraid it's not a craft I know much about, but the miners were looking very pleased.' He wondered if he should show these men what he had secure in his shirt pocket but decided against it; Guinalle should see it first.

'So we'll be able to send ingots home in the spring?' demanded Daryn. 'Something to encourage a second fleet, more settlers?'

'I'm sure of it,' Temar replied. 'You'll have excellent news to convey.'

'You wait and see,' Messire Den Rannion smiled broadly. 'It's just as we told you; we will supply the craftsmen at home with all the materials they can desire while as our settlements here spread, those same goods will find an eager market among our people. Our fellows at home will soon need spend no more effort struggling to sell to rebellious Caladhrians and the like.'

'It might not be gold and silver but the Empire could be grateful soon enough for copper and tin,' Master Suttler observed dourly. 'Things were going from bad to worse in Gidesta before we left, weren't they? His Imperial Uselessness could have been driven back clear over the Dalas by now.'

'Has that lass of Den Fellaemion's had any information for you recently?' Sawney Daryn turned to Den Rannion. 'It's all very well having Artificers along but I can't say I've noticed her putting herself about much.'

'Demoiselle Tor Priminale has been busy looking for plants and herbs to replenish the stores and find alternatives for medicaments.' Temar realised he had spoken a little too quickly and certainly too forcefully.

Messire Den Rannion moved smoothly to gloss over the

awkward moment. 'You know my wife's sister, Avila? She brought their grandmother's old still-room manuals with her and the women have been trying to remedy their new situation on the far side of the ocean from their favourite apothecary!'

'Trust the ladies to see to their own comforts first!' Master Suttler lifted his beak of a nose above a mocking smile.

Temar laughed with the rest but remembered what Guinalle had told him. He wondered what these men would think if they found themselves lacking soaps for their linen, out of mugwort to dissuade the lice and moth from their gowns, with no bay leaves to keep the weevils out of the flour. He caught Messire den Rannion's elbow as Master Dessmar began interrogating Grethist about the precise nature of sailing conditions up river.

'Is Guinalle here?' he asked, hoping he didn't look too eager.

'I believe so.' Den Rannion looked speculatively at Temar. 'Avila told me your expedition met up with one of their foraging trips in Aft-Summer. She was concerned that they had delayed you unnecessarily when you escorted them back to their vessels.'

Temar turned his head to look around the throng, hoping no blush would betray him. 'I was not going to risk having to answer to Den Fellaemion for the loss of his favourite niece.'

'Quite so.' Messire Den Rannion inclined his head. 'I believe she was with my wife when I last saw her.'

'I'll go and pay my respects then.' Temar was surprised to see a grin on Messire den Rannion's face.

'Go on, my boy. Oh, and tell my wife I think it might be a good idea for her to spend some time with Mistress Daryn, would you?'

Temar nodded and walked quickly across the garden towards the new stone hall that was rising from a framework of scaffolding poles.

'Esquire D'Alsennin, isn't it? Fair festival to you!' A delicate hand on his arm forced Temar to halt and he turned to find a vaguely familiar and undeniably pretty face smiling at him.

Golden hair was coiled high above old jewellery decorating rather more shoulder and bosom than he was used to seeing a Tormalin lady display.

'Drianon's blessings.' Temar bowed low, desperately trying to remember the woman's name. He rose with a relieved smile. 'Mairenne, isn't it?'

'That's right, and I shall call you Temar, shall I?' Unmistakable flirtation lit periwinkle eyes set above a pert nose and full, reddened lips. This was one lady who was not running short of cosmetics, Temar noted.

'Temar, there you are.' Vahil appeared at his shoulder. 'My mother wishes to speak to you. Excuse us, Mistress Suttler.' He caught Temar's elbow and wheeled him round with a perfunctory bow of farewell.

Temar shook Vahil's arm off, more amused than irritated. 'How does old Suttler get to put his knife away in a casket like that?'

'Mairenne gave him the key in return for several steps up the ladder.' Vahil strode purposefully in the direction of the hall. 'She was on the *Reedsong*, the two-master that wrecked on the sandbars, and her husband was drowned. He was a tanner, from D'Istrac lands, I believe, but Mairenne keeps very quiet about her origins now she's a merchant's wife. Stay away from her, Temar, she's on the look-out for a gently born prospect in case something carries off old Suttler over the winter.'

'Don't worry, I wouldn't take her if I found her naked in my bed,' laughed Temar. 'I know trouble when I see it. Anyway, you're not the only one who's a reformed character.'

'Glad to hear it.' A smile softened Vahil's words. 'Things are rather different from home, with everyone living in each other's pockets like this.'

They reached the steps of the hall and went in, Temar blinking a little as smoke in the air made his eyes smart.

'Obviously this central hearth is only temporary, the chimneys will be built next.' Maitresse den Rannion was showing a gaggle of avid visitors around the skeleton of her new domain.

'The mason is confident they can continue working well into Aft-Autumn; the climate here is so clement, compared to home.'

'Drianon's blessings on you.' Temar started to bow as the Maitresse turned to him but she stepped forward to catch him by the shoulders and kiss him warmly, rather to his confusion. 'Temar, my dear, how delightful to see you. When did you arrive?'

'This afternoon. We had to wait for the ebb tide to bring us down river,' Temar explained. He took a pace backwards and looked the ladies up and down, hands spread in a gesture of admiration. 'I feel I should apologise for my appearance, seeing you all so elegant in your new style.'

Several of the women blushed and giggled. Maitresse Den Rannion smoothed the close-cut bodice of her narrow-skirted grey gown, its neckline more decorous than Mairenne's but still considerably lower than Toremal fashions had been dictating when the fleet sailed.

'Elsire is proving to have quite a talent for dressmaking and design,' she explained with a suggestion of a smile dimpling one cheek, 'since she realised that she would have to get two gowns out of every dress-length if she was to maintain her customary variety in her wardrobe.'

'You won't catch my sister in the same gown twice at a festival,' interrupted Vahil, a broad grin on his face. 'What's this I hear about her bargaining for furs?'

'She intends to make herself a fortune by first tantalising the ladies of Toremal with the exotic pelts the trappers have been bringing in and then by making sure they stay very exclusive.' Temar wondered if he was imagining the hint of tension in the Maitresse's voice.

'You're allowing her to go into trade?' One of the ladies with a figure most unflattered by the new style hovered between astonishment and envy.

'It's a different life on this side if the ocean, isn't it? So much has changed, why not this?' Maitresse Den Rannion shrugged airily. 'Now then, come and see where we've marked out the east wing. It's only pegs and line at the moment, but you'll be able to get the idea. I'll see you later, Temar.'

'I'd like to see Elsire in a dress like that,' Temar remarked to Vahil as the women departed, neat ankles glimpsed through hems short enough to keep clear of the dirt floors.

'There you are,' Vahil gestured with his glass. Temar saw Elsire standing beside a scaffold supporting an open doorway decorated with festival garlands of unfamiliar flowers. He caught his breath as his heart seemed to skip a beat and then start racing like a spurred horse. Elsire was talking to Guinalle.

Elsire's dress was a vibrant green, the silk shot through with a russet weave that echoed the glossy auburn of her hair. The close tailoring showed off her narrow waist and full bosom to superb advantage, an heirloom necklace of gold and amber bright against the pale skin of her neck. Temar nodded his approval to Vahil and then grinned wickedly. 'She's still got those freckles, though, hasn't she?'

'A price we colonists have to pay for our labours in the heat of the day,' Vahil mimicked his sister, not unkindly, and Temar laughed.

'Guinalle's looking well,' observed Vahil with a sideways glance at Temar. 'We've been seeing quite a lot of her, since she's been working with Aunt Avila on those old concoctions of Great-Grandmama's.'

Temar nodded, not trusting himself to speak, gazing at Guinalle as he approached her. She had added her own touch to the new style of gown, deep pleats faced with a darker blue than the rest of the skirt, a colour echoed in the trim of the bodice. She wore a modest tippet of lace around her shoulders, pinned across her bosom with a sapphire brooch. Temar shivered involuntarily at a sudden memory of those soft and milk-white breasts naked under a tracery of leaves through summer sunlight.

'I said, Guinalle told us you were interested in continuing your studies of Artifice with her over the winter,' Vahil repeated himself with some amusement.

'What?' Temar hastily reined in his wits. 'Yes, that's right. I think it could be useful, especially when we are planning next season's explorations.'

'Temar!' Elsire greeted him with a shriek of delight that silenced people in all directions. 'How lovely to see you!' She embraced him, delicately scented and warm beneath his hands. 'When did you get back? I want to hear all about it, everything, all the details. You'll be staying with us, won't you? Have you spoken to Mother?'

'Hello, Guinalle,' Temar looked over Elsire's shoulder at her, hoping his eyes were speaking the words he could not.

'Fair festival to you, Temar.' Guinalle's self-possession was secure as always, but Temar was pleased to see a faint blush highlighting her cheekbones.

'I need another drink,' began Vahil, 'how about you ladies—'

'I was simply saying that this colony is not turning the profit I was led to expect.' A harsh voice rang through a lull in the general buzz of conversation and heads turned to see Messire Den Rannion standing squarely opposed to a thick-set man in an ostentatious gown of purple velvet.

'It was made clear from the outset that the rewards of this venture would depend on hard work.' Den Rannion's tone was icily polite. 'The hard work of each individual, that is.'

'I served my apprenticeship too long ago to take up my tools again.' The sturdy man planted his hands either side of an ample waist. 'I am entitled to take a commission from my artisans when I am the one advancing them materials, buying in their goods, arranging carriage for their wares back to Zyoutessela. It's only right!'

'No one is going to give you licence to sit idly by and simply levy a percentage to make yourself rich, Master Swire.'

'Father, let's just enjoy the evening. Don't talk business at festival time.' A plain-faced girl tugged ineffectually at his elbow, her long blonde hair unflatteringly dressed in coiled braids that only served to emphasis the length of her neck and nose. 'Everyone's staring!'

'I'll have this out at Council.' The man ignored his daughter, leaning forward to raise a hectoring finger to Messire Den Rannion.

'Council has already established that every artisan is free to deal directly with whomsoever he pleases, whatever his previous status as tenant or journeyman may have been.' Messire Den Rannion's tone remained courteous, but his face was starting to betray his contempt. 'Tell me, Master Swire, you were obligated to Den Muret, were you not, before your Sieur granted you permission to join this venture? Will you be sending a due tithe to that House on the spring sailing?'

'Elsire, can you get Kindra out of there?' Temar was startled by the desperation in Vahil's voice and looked again at the girl. She was a gawky piece in her lavender gown, thin-hipped and bony, no more bosom than a lampstand.

'Of course.' A combative light glinted in Elsire's green eyes. 'She shouldn't have to suffer for her father again.'

'I'll come with you.' Guinalle took a pace forward, to Temar's consternation, but Elsire raised a hand to stop her. 'No, you know how nervous you make her.'

Temar watched Vahil wringing his hands as the argument became further bogged down into what seemed to be a familiar rut, astonished at his friend's agitation.

'I think you should be preparing to defend your own position before Council rather than making complaint against me,' Messire den Rannion was saying, lips thin with growing anger. 'You might care to explain why you have been trying to buy food and fodder far in excess of your household's needs for the winter. I will be interested to hear how that sits with the testimony of some of those artisans formerly obligated to you, who have been finding surprising conditions attached to your so-called gifts.'

'Kindra, my dear, do come and see what one of the trappers brought me today,' Elsire gushed heedlessly over Swire's intemperate reply. 'It's so soft, white as miniver, but the pelts are far bigger, you'll simply love it. You'll have to tell me what you think, whether it's fine enough to use to trim a gown or whether we should keep it for hoods and muffs and the like, not that we're likely to need them here, not unless the winter turns very harsh, but think about the winters in Toremal and up near Orelwood. Do you know that area at all?'

Temar saw people all around smiling at Elsire as she tucked Kindra's arm under her own and escorted her away in a manner more suited to a herd-dog cutting out a calf than a supposedly polite festival party. Now that her interruption had effectively driven Master Swire's complaints onto the shoals, everyone turned back to their own discussions and laughter began to lift the murmur of conversation again.

'I'm going to see how Kindra is.' Vahil shot a hasty glance in his father's direction. 'Stall the old man for me, can you?'

'What's going on there?' Temar raised enquiring eyebrows at Guinalle as Vahil headed for the shadows of the fences and a circuitous route towards Elsire, who was showing something to a clutch of exclaiming girls.

'Vahil has managed to fall desperately in love with the one girl whose father has been an unmitigated pest to both Messires since before we made landfall.' Guinalle's reply was dry but not unsympathetic.

'She's not to his taste, far too mousy. He must just be garter-chasing.' Temar spoke without thinking, his mind full of the flamboyant doxies Vahil had been wont to squire around Toremal.

'That's a sport you excel in, isn't it?'

Temar could have kicked himself but was immeasurably relieved to see Guinalle smiling at him. He felt heat in his face as it was his turn to try to stifle a blush.

'Not any more, not since I met you.' His heart was racing again. 'Not since we found each other this summer—'

'Temar, about that—' Guinalle raised a hand and Temar wondered at the sudden shadow in her eyes.

'Guinalle!' Before she could continue, Maitresse Den Rannion came in through the open doorway. 'Have you seen Vahil?'

'I think he was thirsty.' Guinalle looked towards the wine table, a slight frown wrinkling her brow.

'Oh dear,' Maitresse den Rannion sighed as she looked over at Elsire and her companions, Kindra's fair head no longer visible. 'I'm sure she's a sweet girl and I know it's silly of me to worry about rank and such like, now we're all setting a hand to the same wheel, but I do think he could do better for himself, quite apart from the trouble it's making for him with his father.'

'I'll see if I can find him for you,' offered Guinalle.

'Thank you, my dear, it's just that now that horrid man has spoiled Ancel's evening, he'll be absolutely furious if he find Vahil's been disobeying him and speaking to her.'

Maitresse den Rannion suddenly noticed some new arrivals and hurried to usher them in the direction of food and wine. Guinalle turned to go but Temar caught her hand. 'I just want a moment, can we find somewhere a little more private?'

Guinalle nodded. 'Just for a moment, we do need to talk.'

She led him around the outside of the hall and into a shadowy corner in the angle of two walls. Temar reached for her, desperate to kiss her, but Guinalle held him away, a hand on his chest, looking around in case they had been observed.

'This isn't the back end of some wildwood, Temar, with Avila turning a blind eye,' she chided him. 'People will talk and gossip spreads faster than fire in a thatch round here.'

Temar pressed her fingers to his lips, his own hand trembling with passion. 'Let them talk. Anyway, what's to gossip about when we're betrothed.' He reached into his shirt and pressed the precious parcel of linen into Guinalle's hands, closing her fingers around the silken ribbons.

He heard her catch her breath as she untied the gift and held the gemstone up, the moonlight sparking blue fire from its facets.

'I know the chain's not much, there wasn't a lot of loose gold in the streams, but that diamond should have every girl this side of the ocean chewing their hair until they get one.' Temar could not restrain his glee, stumbling over his words in his eagerness. 'I asked one of the miners to make it for me;

there were only a handful of us on the trip into the hills and I'm
to get them a charter from Council to make sure our rights are
protected. You'll be marrying a man wealthy enough to satisfy
your family, no question. We announce our betrothal tonight,
and then we can be married at Solstice. We'll travel back to
Tormalin next spring, if you like, to visit your family. As long
as you're not pregnant by then, of course.'

'Oh, Temar.'

Temar wasn't sure what he had expected to hear in Guinalle's
voice – excitement, delight, devotion? – but he certainly hadn't
anticipated a mixture of regret and rebuke. 'What?'

'I wish you'd spoken to me before making all these plans.'
There was a definite edge of annoyance in her tone. 'You
haven't thought this through.'

Temar was instantly contrite. 'I'm sorry, my love. I suppose
I should have made more of a ceremony of it, but after the
summer I didn't think you'd need me to send a designate to
ask for your hand. I thought we'd left all that kind of thing
behind us.'

'Temar, listen to me, I beg of you. I'm not about to marry
you or anyone else!'

Temar blinked and shook his head to clear his confusion.
'What are you saying?'

'I have no intention of getting married for quite some years,
if at all.' Guinalle tried to give Temar back the necklace, but
he refused to take it.

'Halcarion save us, why not?' Temar felt a hollow spreading
in his gut.

'I have too much to do here, too many responsibilities, too
many people depending on me. I can't just drop everything
to keep your hearth warm for you. My uncle needs me—'

'He can't stop you marrying me, I won't have it.' This made
no sense to Temar. 'You can still practise your Artifice, if that's
what's worrying you. Haven't I been studying what you taught
me on the voyage, getting the tricks of it?'

'Artifice is much more complicated than you imagine,' said
Guinalle tartly. She took a deep breath and spoke more calmly

again. 'That's beside the point. Please try to understand. You say you want to marry me? You want me to bear your children?'

'I love you,' Temar protested. 'I want to make a family with you. What's wrong with that?'

'Are you planning to stay by the fireside and rock the cradle when my duties call me away? What if I die in child-bed?' Guinalle folded her arms, her face unreadable in the shadows as she pulled away from him. 'This isn't Toremal, with maid-servants and wet-nurses for hire at every festival fair. Have you had much to do with babies and little children? Do you know the amount of work they are? Three of my sisters have families – I tell you, it's not something I'm going to take on before I'm good and ready, not while every spare hand this side of the ocean has three tasks to do and four on market day!'

'I'll help.' Temar was starting to get irritated now. 'Anyway, you said in the summer that you could use Artifice to keep you from conceiving. We can still be married; I'll wait for children, if you insist.'

'And have everyone counting the seasons and waiting for my waist to thicken? Whispering in corners when it doesn't? No, thank you! For your information, I have better uses for my skills. Oh, Temar, please try to see it from my side of the river. I take it you're planning to continue to lead the explorations for my uncle and Messire Den Rannion?'

'Of course, that's my duty.'

'And what am I supposed to do if you get yourself killed on one of these expeditions? I was there when my uncle got news of that rock fall, when Frinn and Eusel were killed, Temar; I know the sort of risks you've been running. Saedrin save me, this is a dangerous enough place for the people staying by the shore.' Guinalle's breath was coming quicker now though her tone stayed mostly level. 'This colony can't support any more widows and orphans and I'll be cursed before I'll be packed off back to a proxy marriage with your grandfather as your only male relative. I can't waste a year sitting around in mourning to make sure I'm not carrying your child before I'm free again.'

'No one would make you do that.' Temar's voice rose and he quelled it with an effort. 'You're being ridiculous.'

'I don't think so. You're the last of your line. In any case, my family do insist on the traditional observances, whatever you might choose to do.'

'Is this about family? Is that it?' Temar could not hide his outrage. 'My Name isn't good enough for you? You know very well D'Alsennin is an ancient house and—'

'If I wanted to marry some well-groomed stud from an impressive bloodline, I'd have my choice ten times over in Toremal.' Guinalle interrupted Temar acidly. 'I've had fortune hunters after my father's coin and rank since Drianon blooded me. Why do you think I study Artifice? Why do you think I asked to join my uncle here?'

A nasty suspicion reared its head at the back of Temar's mind and grabbed his tongue before he could stamp it down. 'You keep bringing your uncle into this? You're not related by blood, are you, only marriage. He's not planning to salvage the Den Fellaemion bloodline with a judicious marriage, is he? That would be very traditional.'

Guinalle gave Temar's face a stinging slap. 'Don't be disgusting. You just can't accept it, can you? You're so full of yourself that you cannot imagine a girl not falling over herself to marry you!'

'You were quick enough to lie down with me this summer!' Temar scowled as he heard the pain in his own words, suddenly glad of the darkness hiding his face.

'That was different, that was fun, it was delightful,' Guinalle's anger softened with contrition, 'but I would never have done it if I had thought you would make so much of it. I'm sorry.'

Astonishment drove all other feelings out of Temar's head. 'Are you telling me it wasn't your first time?'

'Oh Temar, I'm the youngest daughter of a long family. My older sisters were the ones who had to make sure they could stain their wedding sheets convincingly.' A faint giggle escaped

Guinalle and a glimpse of moonlight betrayed a smile on her face. 'You've obviously had little experience of virgins.'

'I wouldn't have thought it of you,' spat Temar angrily. 'How could you?'

'Oh really?' Guinalle took a pace towards him. 'Tell me, what right have you to judge me? Temar D'Alsennin, the Esquire every chaperone warns their girls not to let get them behind a curtain? You accused Vahil of garter hunting, didn't you? What was your score last Winter Solstice? That was what you would get the girls to wager, wasn't it? Against your hitting a rune bone with a throwing dagger at twenty paces? According to my brothers, you had the best collection in the cohorts and a fair few girls let you pluck their petals when you claimed your prize didn't they? Your reputation precedes you, Temar, didn't you know that? At least I'm discreet!'

Temar stood amid the wreckage of his hopes, furious with Guinalle, with himself, with everything. He opened his mouth but, before he could speak, Maitresse Den Rannion rounded the corner and halted abruptly at the sight of them.

'Maitresse, I'm sorry, I was just about to—' Guinalle lifted a hand towards her mouth before realising she still had the necklace twined around her fingers.

'My dear, whatever is that?' The Maitresse reached for Guinalle's hand and lifted it towards a lantern.

'Why, Temar, how splendid!' Her eyes were alight with curiosity. 'Are you celebrating Drianon's festival with something important?'

'Temar was telling me of the discoveries his expedition made.' Guinalle tried to pass the necklace back to Temar but he stuck his hands stubbornly through his belt.

'It's a birth festival gift for Guinalle.' He forced a semblance of a smile. 'You were an Aft-Summer baby, weren't you, demoiselle?'

Maitresse Den Rannion turned to him, open-mouthed. 'Now isn't that just typical! I was asking Messire Den Fellaemion if any of his household would be celebrating their year at the festival and he told me Guinalle was born in For-Winter!

Here, my dear, let me take your lace, you must show off a jewel like that!' She unpinned Guinalle's tippet before the girl could find a plausible objection and clasped the necklace around her throat. The gem shone rich and brilliant on the soft hollow of her throat. 'What a handsome present to make, Temar.'

'I think the Messire is looking for you, Maitresse.' Temar pointed through the arch of an empty window to where Messire Den Rannion was waiting by the hearth, head turning this way and that.

'Oh, yes, I think you're right.' The Maitresse tucked Guinalle's lace briskly around her own neckline. 'I'd better see what he wants.'

'I'll go and find Vahil.' Guinalle began hastily to walk away from him but Temar followed.

'You do that, my lady. I'll get Elsire away from those silly girls, shall I? The music's started so if I dance with her all evening that should give the gossips plenty to go on, shouldn't it? That should protect your reputation, Guinalle. Don't worry, I won't tell anyone how hollow it really is!'

Temar strode past, outpacing her with his long legs, catching Elsire around the waist and making her an extravagant bow, keeping his back firmly turned on Guinalle as he swept Elsire into a closer embrace than was quite appropriate for that particular dance.

The Palace of Shek Kul,
the Aldabreshin Archipelago,
6th of For-Summer

I woke with an image vivid in my mind, a dream so clear I could recall every detail. A young man, black hair drawn back in a silver clasp of wrought leaves and dressed in the style of Messire's ancestral portraits. So this was Temar D'Alsennin, last scion of a lost line and the man whose sword I now possessed. But this was more than an image, more than a dream. I shook my head at the thought of his conflicting hopes and apprehension for the future, reason yielding to an overwhelming need to make a family to replace the one he had lost in his childhood. I felt his pain at Guinalle's intransigence, his confusion, sympathised with his blatant flirtation with Elsire, just to let Guinalle know she wasn't the only squab in the dovecote. In many ways he reminded me of myself twelve years gone. I recognised that impulsiveness, the confidence that had led me into the toils of chewing thassin, above all the intensity of youthful emotion unblunted by more mature experience.

I shook my head with a faint smile over Temar's difficulties with Guinalle; at least Livak and I only had ourselves to please when we finally worked out what we wanted from each other and the future, if we ever did. I wondered fleetingly what Livak was doing at that moment.

It had been a strange dream, mostly seen through Temar's eyes, but at the same time I had felt separate from him. I was an outsider yet seeing direct into his ambitions and fears in that curious fashion. Above all I was most startled to realise that if I'd met him on the road I would have sworn Temar was the man who had awakened me when the bandits had attacked us on Prosain Heath. What had that been all about? That must have been a dream as well, mustn't it? I'd recognised that belt buckle too, the one that Elietimm priest or whatever he called himself had been weaving his spells around for Kaeska. It had belonged to Temar; what could that signify? Had it been Temar's passion erupting into my mind that had sent me insensible in Relshaz? I had no logical reason to think so but felt convinced of it nevertheless.

I sat up on my pallet and leaned against the wall. This early in the morning the air was still cool and the sounds of birdsong in the gardens filtered through the light shutters, no insects to torment me. I savoured the peace and quiet, only broken by the sounds of stealthy house slaves going about their duties far below. Was this recollection of the long-passed festival the sort of memory that Planir the Archmage had been hoping the sword would pass to me? If so I could not for the life of me see any significance in it, other than perhaps as an object lesson in the many paradoxical ways people can find to fall out with those they love. I looked at the sword. If this was aetheric magic, it seemed no more than a curiosity, a far cry from the vicious enchantments of the Elietimm.

I had not long come to the conclusion that one of the most irritating things of the many galling facts of life as a slave was the way I hardly ever had a moment to myself to think my own thoughts. Sure enough, just as I was trying to address these mysteries, the door behind me opened and Shek Kul emerged, bare-chested, trousers loosely tied and his tunic slung carelessly over one shoulder. Despite his lack of gems and adornment, the Warlord looked no less intimidating, formidably muscled for a man of his age, self-possession in every fibre of him. He nodded to me, his smile broad with satisfaction, and he padded softly down the corridor, whistling softly under his breath. I watched him go, partly envious of his good fortune and partly resenting him and all his kind, with their unchallenged power over the likes of me.

I looked through the partly open door to see Laio fast asleep, lying on her stomach in a soft tumble of silken quilts, face child-like in sleep with a lock of hair over her eyes, her nakedness inviting a caressing beam of sunlight that reached through the louvres to finger her smooth thigh. The morning breeze stirred the air in the room, heavy with perfume and the scents of sex.

Stifling a churlish desire to drag my pallet noisily inside and start a thorough tidy-up, preferably with a rasping floor brush, I pulled the door to and began looking through my clothes for a clean tunic. A booted footfall at the far end of the corridor startled me and I looked up to see the Elietimm priest looking at me, an unpleasant anticipation in his eyes. The man was dressed in plain, inconspicuous clothes, a black tunic and trousers, well washed and somewhat faded, looking no threat to anyone, a supplicant for honest trade. Only those eyes gave him away as far as I was concerned, dangerous as a dog trained only to understand the lash and brutality.

'Let me see that sword,' he commanded abruptly.

I looked at him blankly, summoning the expression of polite incomprehension I had been perfecting on Gar.

'I know who you are, Tormalin man.' The priest halted, hands on his hips, looking down at me with disdain. 'You are nothing. All I want is the sword. Let me have that and I will let you live.'

I stood up, the scabbard in my hand. The priest was no fool; he was staying just out of the reach of the blade. I put my hand to the hilt and saw an odd mixture of apprehension and anticipation in those light-blue eyes, cold as the winter sky.

'I will have that blade and you as well,' he sneered, my continuing silence evidently needling him. 'You will be at my mercy. Before I am done you will be weeping like a whipped child.'

'I think that it is my place to chastise my own property.' Laio opened the door with a swift movement and stared haughtily at the Elietimm, her eyes hard. Her queenly manner was not diminished in the slightest by the fact that she was inadequately clad in a gossamer undertunic. 'Your behaviour is hardly respectful, for a guest of Shek Kul,' she added with unmistakable emphasis.

The Elietimm's face was wiped clean of expression in an instant and he bowed low to Laio before turning on his heel and stalking rapidly back down the corridor.

'What a peculiar man.' Laio shook her head in puzzlement. 'What is Kaeska thinking of, bringing him here?'

I seized the moment. 'I can tell you exactly what she is planning. I overheard them talking last night.'

Laio's eyes brightened. 'Excellent. I knew you would learn to be a good slave eventually. Get something for us to eat and you can tell me all about it.'

She opened the long shutters to the balcony and found a plain, loose dress among the jumble of clothes on a bench, the fact that she was doing things for herself the best evidence that she was seriously interested in what I had to say. I hurried to fetch a plentiful breakfast of unleavened bread, cheese, fruit and juice. I was still ravenous and, anyway, I had learned to make a hearty breakfast whenever I could, it being the meal least likely to spring a nasty surprise on me.

'So, what did you hear,' Laio demanded, settling herself on a cushion and reaching for some berries. 'Tell me everything.'

I hesitated, wondering exactly where to start. I couldn't see the whole business of the sword being of any interest to Laio; I had to tell her something directly relevant to her own ambitions and interests. 'Well, to start with, I know where that man comes from. It is a group of islands far to the east and north, in the heart of the great ocean. The thing is, they are very poor lands, they have no metal, no wood, no beasts to give them fine leathers. He is lying to Kaeska about the trade he can offer her.'

Laio shrugged, but I could see satisfaction in her eyes. 'Then she will look extremely foolish when she can achieve nothing and she will lose even more status. Go on, and eat something as well. I've got things I want to do this morning.'

'The promises of trade are only an excuse.' I took a hasty drink. 'He is telling Kaeska that he will help her bear a child and regain her place as First Wife.'

To my surprise, Laio laughed heartily. 'Then he is as much
a fool as she is. Kaeska is barren, we all know that.'

I chose my next words with extreme care. 'She might be
barren with Shek Kul but what if she were to take this man
as a lover and pass off his child as the Warlord's?'

Laio frowned at me. 'Shek Kul has no difficulty getting
children – women in several domains can attest to that; Mahli
took particular care to make sure her first child was of his blood
as well. Anyway, if it was only a matter of finding a fertile man,
Kaeska would have been pregnant years ago.'

Now it was my turn to look puzzled. 'Wouldn't Shek Kul
have objected?'

'I keep forgetting how ignorant you can be. Do see sense;
the wind may sow the seeds but the farmer who tends the
seedlings reaps the harvest.' Laio sighed and shook her head.
'It is a wife's duty to bear children for her husband but it
is her business who begets them. After all, some wives are
closely related to their husbands, some men cannot get women
pregnant, others prefer to go clean-shaven. In any case, we are
an island people; bringing new blood to a domain is always
beneficial. It's understood that a good wife will do that with
at least one of her children. If we always bred to our own, we
would all be three measures tall with six fingers by now.'

She tossed the stripped berry stem on to the floor and took a
spoon to a dark green pod of milky seeds. I drizzled honey on a
piece of the leathery flatbread and rolled it around a little white
cheese, cramming my mouth full while she was busy talking.

'Kaeska is definitely barren,' Laio stated firmly through
her mouthful. 'She has been married to Shek Kul for nearly
twenty years and in all that time has never even quickened.
If she would only acknowledge the fact she could quite easily
retain her status as first wife, trade for a baby from an Islander
and rear it herself, for instance. There is no shame in being
infertile among civilized people. The whole problem is that
Kaeska won't admit it. She stays away from the domain as
much as possible and lets it be rumoured that is why she
doesn't conceive; she has been making herself and Shek Kul

ridiculous for years, but he has had to indulge her in order to protect his treaty with her brothers, who dote on her as well as benefiting from her rank. She also does everything she can to provoke him into doing something that would entitle her to divorce him, but he's too clever to let her get away with that. Still, now that her brothers have been ousted from the Danak domains, Shek Kul does not need to protect her status as First Wife any longer. That alliance is as dead as yesterday's fish. Now our husband can finally get himself some heirs.'

Laio giggled sunnily. 'He and Mahli were busy before Danak Mir's blood was dry on the sand. I will be next and once Gar has recovered from Kaeska's demotion, I imagine she will want a child as well. Our husband hasn't decided yet how long he will keep from her bed, just to make sure she understands he knows about her plots with Kaeska, but I imagine Sezarre will be capable of doing his duty.'

Nailing his owner was one of a body slave's duties? I didn't want to jostle that basket of crabs! 'What will happen to Kaeska?'

'She will end up as Fourth Wife, unless she does something stupid enough to give Shek Kul an excuse to divorce her.' Laio leaned forward, suddenly intent. 'Just what is this foreigner promising her? Do you think she might over-reach herself?'

'I'm not sure,' I replied cautiously, swallowing my mouthful. 'He is definitely promising her a child and I know he is using drugs to addle her wits on the subject.'

'Drugs?' Laio looked thoughtful. 'I could do much to discredit Kaeska if I let it be known she was indulging in filthy mainlander habits like that. Her negotiations will soon suffer as well. What about distilled liquor? Did you see any sign of that?'

I shook my head. 'Would that be worse?'

Laio opened her mouth in exasperation then tossed her head with a sudden smile. 'You mainlanders! Of course it would be. Narcotics and strong spirits dull the wits and rot the body; any domain that permits their use soon finds itself with troops on its beaches.' She frowned. 'It's not really enough to get Kaeska divorced though. Is there anything else I can use against her?'

'She's been using tahn berries on Irith,' I volunteered.

'What's that?' Laio looked mildly curious.

'It's a plant; physicians steep its leaves to get a tisane that dulls pain but the berries are very addictive, narcotic, deadly after a while.'

Laio shrugged. 'If Kaeska wants to poison her body slave, that's her business. If she makes a habit of it, Shek Kul will be entitled to rebuke her for the wasted trade, but other than that he has no rights in the matter.'

'She's had the poor bastard's tongue cut out!' I objected with some heat.

Laio arched her finely plucked eyebrows. 'How odd. Mutes haven't been fashionable since before I was born. Still, we're getting away from the point. How does this foreign man propose to get Kaeska with child?'

I forced myself to ignore these further unpleasant sidelights on Aldabreshin life. 'I imagine he is going to use magic. He has all the signs of being a sorcerer of some kind.'

'Magic!' Laio breathed, eyes bright with exultation, clasping her hands to her face.

'Can Shek Kul divorce Kaeska for that?'

'He can execute her!' Laio looked like a child who's woken to find Solstice come a season early. 'You will get a substantial reward for this, for enabling us to get rid of her permanently, for such a crime!'

'Magic is punished by death?' I swallowed my mouthful with difficulty, almost choking on my incredulity, but Laio was too pleased to even get annoyed with my ignorance.

'Oh yes, it is absolutely forbidden. The elements are holy, they give us life and nurture us all. Interference with the balance is a desecration only redeemed with the lives of those involved.'

I breathed a silent prayer of heartfelt gratitude to Dastennin that I had not yet mentioned my own connections with wizardry or magic. 'The man has been using thassin smoke on

Kaeska,' I reminded Laio. 'He's turning her own senses until they betray her and using her desperation for a child to help him dupe her.'

Laio shrugged again, a favourite gesture of hers. 'More fool her. Ignorance is no defence to bring before Shek Kul's justice.'

'What will happen?'

'I will accuse her, Shek Kul will sit in judgement and weigh your evidence against her denials.' Laio bit into a juicy red fruit and licked her sticky fingers. 'Then they'll both be executed.'

This all sounded a little too easy but I tried to keep my disbelief out of my voice. 'The Warlord will take the word of a mainlander slave against his own First Wife?'

'You are an Islander now, you really must remember that,' Laio reminded me sternly. 'Your word is as good as Kaeska's.'

'When will you accuse her?' I remembered I had my own reasons for speeding up this plot, especially now I didn't want to have to explain the Elietimm's interest in my sword in any way.

'I will have to pick my time carefully.' Laio's eyes darkened with cunning, focused on some point in the middle distance. 'I think we should isolate Kaeska first. If we let Gar and Mahli know what she has been up to, Gar will want to get clear of her plots at once or risk being executed herself. That should net us some valuable information.'

'When will you tell Gar?'

Laio turned her gaze on me, irritated. 'I will not tell Gar. You will tell Sezarre, who will tell her, so that she can come to us of her own accord and make it clear she is acting on her own suspicions and behaving as a good wife.'

I should have seen that coming. 'All right. The thing is, that man, the Elietimm priest, he wants Kaeska to make a trade to get me as her body slave. He's dangerous and if you want me alive and with enough of a grip on my wits to give evidence, you had better not delay too long.'

'What does he want of you?' Laio frowned, then laughed

like a greenjay. 'Perhaps Kaeska wants you to father this child of hers!'

That notion rocked me back on my heels; could the vision really have been Kaeska's child after all? I shook my head firmly. No, the Elietimm wanted the sword, he had made that clear enough.

Laio wiped happy tears from her eyes. 'So, what does this man want of you?'

I took my time chewing a mouthful of fruit before answering. Telling Laio that this man wanted to possess an enchanted sword, somehow mystically linked to me, probably in order to frustrate the magical plans of the wizards of Hadrumal, now sounded like a very bad idea.

'I imagine he knows that I can expose him, tell you all how barren his islands are, how little he has to trade.'

Luckily Laio was still so full of the notion of getting rid of Kaeska that she let this rather meagre explanation slide past her. I realised that the Aldabreshin obsession with trade would make this sound perfectly reasonable to her, as would the notion that all the Ice Islander sought was an entry to commerce with the Archipelago.

A knock on the inner door startled us both and I scrambled to my feet to answer it. Grival stood on the threshold, looking more agitated than I could recall seeing him.

'The child, it comes.' He managed a rather forced smile. 'Mahli wants you with her, my lady.'

'Tell her I'm on my way.' Laio ran her hands through her hair and tied it back all anyhow with a convenient scarf. She turned to me on her way out. 'Keep yourself out of mischief and I think you might like to have that conversation with Sezarre today.'

I bowed low and watched her run lightly down the corridor, Grival striding purposefully beside her.

CHAPTER SEVEN

A letter written by the Archmage Holarin of Imat River in the 3rd year of Emperor Aleonne the Valiant (original held in the Archive of the Archmage, Trydek's Library, Hadrumal).

Dear Dretten,

I note with interest your news of increased Relshazri trade with the Islanders from the Aldabreshin Archipelago. Now that you are living in the city, it is important that you understand somewhat of the basis of their hostility to magic, if only for your own protection. Most will tell you this antipathy stems simply from blind prejudice; this may be true in some cases but the origins of such a prevalent bias go much deeper. I will attempt to explain, given the limits of our present knowledge.

Although the Aldabreshi do not worship the gods as we do, it is a mistake to dismiss them as unthinking barbarians. The complex philosophies of the Archipelago are spun from their observations of the natural world, the behaviour of animals, the seasons of flower and fruit, the shifting patterns of the stars and moons. More than this, the Aldabreshi believe in a wide range of unseen forces at work in the world about them. They have no concept of the Otherworld, rather believing that the essence, the spirit of a dead person, remains an intangible part of their household, their family. Do not mistake my meaning; they do not worship their ancestors like the barbarians of the far west, but see both the deceased and the still unborn as continuously linked to the living. Imagine, if you will, a tree felled by a storm later sending up a shoot that blossoms, death, growth and the prospect of new life all contained within the one plant.

*The Aldabreshi believe that all things, material and
intangible, seen and unseen, are linked and interdependent,
hence their many and varied methods of divination, practised
freely by all levels of their society. A Warlord will quite
literally hold or commit his forces to battle depending on his
interpretation of the flight of a flock of birds. His prospects
when hoping to take a wife will stand or fall on the movement
of precious stones placed on a hot sheet of metal. Aldabreshin
astronomy has reached heights of sophistication that we can
only envy; they believe actions at a time of eclipse can benefit
an individual enormously or, conversely, promote an enemy's
ruin. Day-to-day life is influenced in countless minor ways by
the most trivial events, while major events such as eruptions
or tempests can lead to warfare, reconciliation or some other
entirely unexpected conclusion. There seem to be few fixed
rules; if there are, we have yet to discover them.*

*Putting such store in random events may seem whimsical
and even futile to ourselves, with our generations of more
sophisticated learning and debate, but that is not my point.
This principle of belief is central to Aldabreshin life and holds
the key to their hatred of magic. To see the elements that make
up all living matter deliberately manipulated and altered by a
wizard is at once obscene and supremely menacing in their eyes.
Magic is a chaotic, destructive force; it is inconceivable that it
could be used for good. Whatever temporary advantage might
accrue would be as nothing compared to the damage done. One
might just as well set light to the corner of a tapestry in an
attempt to illuminate the whole.*

*You will understand therefore, when I advise you to steer
well clear of Aldabreshi traders. Their hostility will remain
implacable and any attempt to win them over will only place
you in peril. Remember the foul torments reserved for those
convicted of practising magic in the islands of Archipelago.*

The Palace of Shek Kul,
the Aldabreshin Archipelago,
6th of For-Summer

I looked at the mess that Laio invariably managed to create and hurried through a perfunctory tidy-up, not about to waste the only chance I'd had so far of exploring the compound on my own. Strapping on my sword in case the Ice Islander came snooping, I left my armour rolled in its corner. Wearing it without being in attendance on Laio would simply make me too noticeable. Walking briskly down the stairs, head high and confident, I nodded to the pages who were bent over some incomprehensible game of coloured stones in their little vestibule.

Once outside, I walked purposefully in the direction of the main gate, racking my brains for some excuse to give at the gate that might get me down to see what else the foreshore might offer as a means of escape. I might have a chance if some of the younger guards were on duty, all cocksure arrogance in freshly burnished chainmail, the type I remembered only too well from my days training Messire's militia levies. Would there be any possibility of stowing away on a galley from another domain? What good would it do me if I could?

The path turned a corner around a glossy tree whose razor-edged leaves I had learned to respect and I took a hasty step backward into its cover as Kaeska Shek entered the compound. She was plainly dressed in white cotton, a long scarf worn up over her head, which she hastily removed as she entered. Pausing to look behind her before she crossed the threshold, she said no word to the guards as they opened and closed the tall black gates for her. Her hands were clasped at her midriff, holding something close.

'And where have you been, my lady, while Mahli's laid up in child-bed?' I wondered.

I looked at the gate guards; a trio of hard-faced men a handful of years older than myself with a generation more experience of guile and deception, if Laio was any guide to life in the Archipelago. Abandoning any hope of getting outside the compound, I listened to the soft sounds of Kaeska's stealthy steps on the stony path instead. The more evidence I could get against the woman, the safer I would be. I took a path between dense stands of a ubiquitous berry-plant that thrived on the rich black soil, its dark leaves providing excellent cover. Advancing slowly, I saw Kaeska's bright hair through the foliage and after a moment's thought realised she was sitting on the stone edge of a fountain basin where a motley collection of fish lived their lives in aimless circles.

I couldn't see exactly what she was doing and stood stock still, burning with frustration until she rose and walked briskly in the direction of the main residence. I followed after allowing her a suitable distance, glancing briefly at the fountain as I passed. What I saw stopped me in my tracks. Several of the dull, bluish fish were floating on the surface of the water, their pale bellies stark, fins flapping feebly and in one instance not at all.

I quickened my step, determined not to lose sight of Kaeska as I tried to work out what play she was setting the board for this time. There were various fountains with fish in them around the compound and she visited them all in her apparent wanderings. Her path also took her through the section of the grounds where each wife had an aviary where she kept a variety of birds, some bright and tuneful, others with no apparent virtue unless they tasted better than they looked. As Kaeska mounted the steps to the main residence, I wondered if she was heading for those creepy lizards in the dining hall. All these animals had some significance that I had yet to determine. All I had established so far was that the first thing Laio did each morning was release a bird from her balcony and study its flight intently. What it chose to do could significantly affect her mood for anything up to the rest of the day; I had already learned to be wary on the mornings the stupid creature headed for the mountain that dominated the centre of the island.

Was Kaeska poisoning the fish an end in itself? Was she testing the efficacy of whatever it was she had concealed inside her gown before slipping someone else a dose? I had better warn Laio and Grival too, I decided. He would be able to keep Kaeska from getting too near the baby, wouldn't he? Newborn babes must be even more vulnerable than usual in this pestilential climate and Kaeska might be hoping to pass its death off as a natural tragedy.

I walked briskly back to the residence and hurried up the stairs, pleased to hear voices above. As I reached the top floor, Mahli turned the corner, leaning heavily on Shek Kul's arm, Grival offering support on her other side. She looked at me without apparent recognition as some spasm seized her and wrenched a hoarse groan from the very depths of her being. Laio and Gar appeared, wiping her forehead, murmuring encouragement, rubbing her back until the torment passed. Mahli began her ungainly progress again, muttering a start-ling selection of Grival's practice-ground obscenities under her breath. The woman looked to be in extremis to me but the midwife was smiling and nodding and, since no one else was either panicking or shouting, I had to suppose they knew what they were doing. I certainly didn't, childbirth being an exclusively female mystery in decent Tormalin households.

I stepped forward, hoping to speak to Laio, but she waved me off with a scowl and an unmistakable dismissal. I moved backwards again, frustrated but not about to risk pressing the issue given the tension knotting Laio's brows. I went down the stairs, increasing my pace somewhat when Mahli let loose a gut-wrenching yell which I swear rattled the shutters as I passed them.

Turning a corner on the ground floor, I came face to face with the Elietimm. This time, rather than challenging me, he looked startled, almost frightened and turned instantly on his

heel, running down a white-tiled passage that I knew led to the
suites of reception rooms each wife commanded. I was about
to head in the opposite direction when intense curiosity seized
me and I found myself following the man into the labyrinth
that made up the lower level of the residence. Apprehension
warred with a sudden, iron determination to find out what
that precious pair were up to, but I locked the warning away
in the back of my mind, dimly thinking how Aiten would
have mocked such uncharacteristic behaviour but dismissing
the notion.

The sound of a door shutting drove all such considerations
out of my head. It was the main entrance to Kaeska's reception
rooms and I could hear a faint murmur of voices, which set
my frustration fully alight. Moving slowly, bare feet silent on
the marble floor, I edged towards the door, but I could still
hear nothing clearly. Well, with the penalties for using magic
around here, she was hardly going to be chanting sorceries at
the top of her voice. I caught my breath as I heard a low-voiced
murmur, cursing silently to myself as I saw that a muffling
curtain had been drawn across the inside of the door, scarlet
silk bright against the black wooden slats.

'When the child is born, you will take this message to my
cousin, Danak Nyl. He will tell you—'

Who was Kaeska talking to?

'*Behind you!*'

In the instant that voice sounded inside my head a shadow
fell across the wall in front of me and I looked back to see
the Elietimm priest, arm raised as he brought down a mace
to spill out my brains across the patterned tiles. I launched
myself forward, crashing straight through the flimsy louvres
of the door, saving my skull but taking an agonising strike on
one thigh. I found myself face to face with a startled Kaeska;
she was on her own and with a shock of understanding I cursed
myself for an imbecile, taking their bait like that.

'Seize him!' The Elietimm was ripping the tattered drape
aside as Kaeska fluttered like a startled cage-bird. She made
a futile grab for me and squealed with a mixture of outrage

and fear when I put both hands around her narrow waist and threw her bodily at her enchanter. They went clashing to the floor and I ran for the shutters that opened to the gardens, vaulting over a day-bed in my haste to get away. Excruciating pain in my leg felled me like a poleaxed beast as I landed and lost my footing. I rolled around, screaming, clutching my thigh where the mace had landed. When I could blink the tears of agony from my eyes, I looked down to see ivory shards of bone sticking through a ruin of bloody flesh, torn rags of skin. Dast's teeth, how had he done that much damage with just the one glancing blow? As I whimpered with the torment of it, the bastard came to gloat over me, a mocking cadence to the incantation he was running under his breath.

'More fool you, dungface,' I thought savagely, using the last of my strength and will to kick out with my sound foot, catching the priest in the side of the kneecap with a strike I'd used to disable bigger men than him. Sure enough, he fell like cut timber, screeching as the fine-turned legs of the day-bed splintered under his weight. I caught a mean kick in the kidneys from Kaeska for my trouble, but that hardly bothered me. As soon as the priest's incantation had unravelled, the agony in my thigh vanished, my hands were gripping bruised but otherwise unbloodied flesh and I scrambled to my feet, shaking with a combination of rage and terror. The bastard was messing with my mind again, scrambling my own wits to trick and betray me. Shoving Kaeska full in the belly, I sent her clean off her feet into a rack of delicate vases, which shattered beneath her. I spared a scant breath to hope she collected a good few shards in her arse, the vicious bitch.

I looked swiftly towards the corridor to see if the uproar had brought any slaves to offer me unintentional protection, but that faint hope proved worthless. I dragged a hand across my eyes and swore vilely as all sense of direction dissolved beneath the insistent pulse of another enchantment in my ears, the meaningless words rebounding from the walls as the room swum before my unfocused eyes. I swung round to face the priest, hands reaching for his blurred form, but he had somehow recovered his mace. I backed off as he hefted it with worrying expertise. He drew a dagger from his belt with his off hand and tossed it to Kaeska. 'Hamstring him.'

'You just try it, you slack-arsed whore,' I snarled, not taking my eyes off the Elietimm. He just smiled. I felt the blood start to pound in my head, temples throbbing, my vision darkening and my feet stumbling numbly as the earth seemed to tilt beneath me. As my senses dissolved, I groped blindly for the hilt of my sword and as I laid nerveless fingers on the pommel I heard Guinalle's precise tones inside my head.

'Of course, a simple ward can be very effective. Try this – "Tur-ryal, tur-ryal, tur-ryal".'

I heard a voice that was not my own echoing the meaningless syllables, using my lips in this strange trick of memory. The girl spoke again. *'You see, I can't make your feet cold now, can I?'*

I blinked as my sight cleared and drew a breath of release deep into my lungs as I saw the priest's jaw drop with horrified astonishment.

'You swore they had no true magic,' he spat, his eyes shifting to a point over my off shoulder. That told me where Kaeska was, so I tore my sword free of its scabbard, sweeping it round in a glittering arc. If I had to answer to Shek Kul for gutting her, so be it; I had to get myself free of this snare first. Kaeska squealed and I heard her scuttle backwards, the dagger clattering to the floor. I brought the sword to the front and moved swiftly towards the priest, who was between me and my escape to the gardens. Now he was the one backing away but he began another complicated pattern of words and I felt a chill of confusion hover around me, greedy fingers of enchantment ripping away whatever frail shield that strange incantation had given my mind. I couldn't win this fight, not on these terms.

Yelling a full-throated curse at the bastard, I raised my sword high above my head, both hands on the hilts as I charged at him. Not surprisingly, he recoiled, stumbling over a low stool. I shoved him aside with my shoulder as I brought my sword down on the flimsy latch of the shutters, sending them swinging wildly as I fled to the uncertain safety of the gardens. Running past several startled gardeners, I headed for the practice ground the body slaves shared with the guards, tucked behind the slave quarters. To my intense relief, Sezarre was there, sitting and brooding over a grid drawn in the dirt as he played some solo variant of the Aldabreshi stone game.

'Your leg—' he frowned, abandoning his puzzle as he saw my torn trousers and darkening bruises.

'Kaeska and her visitor, the white-headed man,' I said succinctly, dropping to a bench with a shuddering sigh of relief. Sezarre moved with the instincts of long training to strip away the tattered cloth and wipe down the rapidly swelling and badly scored thigh with an astringent that made me hiss through my teeth. For all that, I realised well enough I was lucky not to have taken the full force of the blow; the bastard could have broken the bone in reality if he'd caught me right, not just crippled me with an illusion woven inside my mind.

'What is this about?' Sezarre asked urgently as he rubbed a salve into the deep scratches, something I'd done for him and Grival often enough since arriving here.

'Kaeska is plotting to kill Mahli and the baby – she is convinced she can then have a child of her own and become First Wife again.'

Sezarre shook his head with a wordless exclamation of contempt.

'The man is not here to trade, he has come to help Kaeska by using magic against Mahli and Shek Kul.'

Sezarre's hands halted at that and he looked up at me, eyes wide, mouth half open in astonishment.

'I swear this is the truth.' I held his gaze with mine. 'I have seen such men as these at work before. Their enchantments killed a friend of mine, closer than my brother. This magic stole his mind and turned his blade against me.'

The pain in my voice as I talked of Aiten more than made up for my remaining deficiencies in the Aldabreshin tongue; Sezarre was convinced, no question of it.

'You have told Laio?'

I nodded. 'She wished Gar to know before Kaeska is accused to Shek Kul.'

Relief was plain on Sezarre's face. 'Gar would not be involved in any such scheme, you must know this for certain,' he insisted. 'Not magic, of all things, and never to harm the child.'

'Of course,' I assured him. 'Laio never imagined that she would.'

'Magic,' he repeated with an expression of revulsion. 'That Kaeska would stoop so low . . .' Words failed him and he shook his head again.

'They know that I can expose them,' I gestured at my bruises. 'They will kill me if they can.'

'Not while I am with you,' replied Sezarre grimly. The thought of his sword arm at my side was certainly a reassuring one. 'Can you walk?'

I nodded, stood and followed Sezarre as he walked rapidly to the main gate and summoned the commander of the guard, a thick-set, dark-skinned Aldabreshi I was used to seeing deep in discussion with Shek Kul. I couldn't follow much of their conversation but the gist was plain enough when the guard on the gate was doubled and liveried retainers with drawn swords went out, four by four, to quarter the grounds of the compound.

'Will they detain Kaeska if they find her?' I asked Sezarre as he strode towards the main residence, face stern, hand on his sword hilt.

'She will be required to explain herself to Shek Kul,' he answered in tones of unmistakable threat.

We went to Kaeska's reception rooms, where the torn silk curtain flapped forlornly in the breeze and the wreckage of the room gave its own mute testimony.

'Why would she do this?' Sezarre shook his head. 'Who is this man that he has such a hold over her.'

'He's an enchanter who can get inside minds and twist them to his will.' In all justice, I felt I had to keep reminding these people how Kaeska was being manipulated by that bastard Ice Islander.

We left the room through the doors to the garden and watched as the guard commander met a couple of troopers, their shaking heads making it clear there was no sign of the quarry.

'And Kaeska has been killing the fish as well,' I remembered abruptly. 'Why would she do that?'

Sezarre reacted with a surprising display of horror at this news. 'She wishes to make bad omens for the child,' he spat with disgust. 'Show me!'

I lead the way swiftly to the poisoned fountain and Sezarre stared at the handfuls of dead fish that now littered the water.

'We will deal with this,' he said with a determined nod.

Seconding a startled gardener with a few brisk words, Sezarre set about getting the fountain emptied and scalded clean while he and I checked the other fish, birds and animals. I couldn't have told if the lizards were ailing as they sat glassy-eyed and impassive on their rocks and tree branches, but Sezarre was confident they were unharmed, explaining that they had some significance for the Warlord that I have to confess escaped me. Dead song-birds were easier to spot and Sezarre went straight to the steward who soon had a lad picking the sad little corpses from the floor of the aviaries belonging to Laio and Mahli. From the seriousness of the expressions all around me, I gathered this went beyond mere malice towards the other women's pets on Kaeska's part, but no one seemed to want to discuss it further.

The steward went to speak to the gate guards and I followed Sezarre to a wrinkled old man who wailed aloud at the tale, his voluble lamentations only shocked to silence when Sezarre told him about Kaeska bringing an enchanter to the island. As more people became involved in frustrating Kaeska's mean and paltry plot with the animals, the word of her conspiring with a sorcerer spread and with some apprehension I wondered how Laio would react to this. She wasn't going to be best pleased to learn that the best rune in her hand had already been played without her consent.

On the other side of the scales, I soon realised I had inadvertently earned a good measure of approval among the general household, receiving nods and smiles and incomprehensible remarks that nevertheless carried unmistakable overtones of gratitude and approbation. I even managed to go outside the gates, carrying a basket of dead birds and fish that we spread on a stretch of crab-infested beach. I was discreetly looking around to see if any possibilities that might lead to an escape plan were apparent, when shouts of excitement erupted all around me, everyone looking at the sea with expressions of delight while at the same time backing hurriedly away to the tree line. Caught unawares by this, I found myself alone on the sand, staring at the monstrous form undulating slowly down the narrow strait.

It was a sea serpent. All my mother's childhood assurances that there were no such things, that they were only tales like the Eldritch kin, went for nothing as I watched the massive, leathery coils rise and fall, a long glaucous fin running the length of the beast, scattering a shining shower of droplets as it broke the surface of the sea. It was not scaly, like a snake or even a fish; its skin was dull and rough textured, oily-looking as water streamed off it in twisted rivulets. An immense head rose above the turbid waters for an instant, long and blunt-nosed, as thick as the huge body with no suggestion of a neck; a vast mouth filled with yellow needle-like teeth gaped for an instant, tiny black eyes almost invisible against the darkness of its skin. Questing, head raised for a moment as the Islanders fell silent in frozen awe, the great beast abruptly disappeared beneath the roiling waters, the last flick of its tail slapping across the strait.

The excitement all around me was as nothing I had ever experienced, cheers and shouting ringing in my ears, the commotion spreading as the crowd carried me back towards the residence, word spreading in all directions. Still half disbelieving what I had just seen, all I could think was that if

I got off this island it wasn't going to be by swimming.

'What is all this about?' I demanded of Sezarre when I was able to fight my way through the throng to his side.

'To see Rek-a-nul – that is a omen of the strongest kind, a great mark of the day,' he assured me, smiling broadly. 'You will have great good luck.'

I'd believe that if I survived all this without my own involvement with magic being revealed or finding an Elietimm knife in my back.

For the rest of that day Sezarre stayed so close to me you'd have thought I was carrying his purse. There was no sign of Kaeska or the Elietimm, to my profound relief. As we made repeated circuits of the gardens, fountains and aviaries, there were no more deaths among the hurriedly replaced birds and fish, brought from Talagrin knows where by a succession of shocked-looking islanders. Mahli continued to labour in child-bed; we heard intermittent cries from the top floor of the residence when our paths took us periodically under the high walls and in an exchange of glances that needed no translation shared our rather guilty relief that neither of us would ever be called upon to bear a child . Finally, as the sun was hovering orange and massive on the horizon, a thin, high wail pierced the expectant silence that had descended over the entire compound. The place erupted with cheers and shouting as more people than I had imagined lived there emerged from every doorway.

I followed Sezarre as he forced a way through the throng towards the residence. A question was shouted at him from all sides and he laughed as he nodded his acquiescence. I saw pottery shards being exchanged in all directions and suddenly understood. The Aldabreshi may not drink anything stronger than their piss-poor wine or take smoke or leaf, but they are the keenest gamblers I've ever come across. One evening, not so long before, I'd caught Laio and Mahli betting a fortune in gems on the tiny yellow lizards that were climbing the walls of the dining room.

'Boy or girl?' I pulled at Sezarre's shirt.

'I say boy,' he grinned at me. 'I wager five days of taking dishes back to the kitchen.'

I laughed and took the scrap of earthenware he passed me, the token covered in looping Aldabreshin script.

Laio and Gar were standing together in the corridor when we reached the top floor of the residence. Both looked drained and dishevelled, heedless of bloody smears on their clothing. Gar stepped forward to embrace Sezarre in a surprising display of emotion, tears glistening on her cheeks. I looked uncertainly at Laio, who seemed to be on the verge of crying herself. She shook herself like a kitten caught in a shower of rain and clutched at my hand. 'Come and see our new son.'

So I was in for five days of manoeuvring overloaded trays down the stairs and corridors while Sezarre took life a little easier. Smiling nonetheless and shaking my head at him as he grinned over Gar's head, I followed Laio to Mahli's rooms where the new mother lay in a bed of fresh quilts, reclining against Shek Kul's shoulder. She was cradling a tiny bundle of snuffling cotton swaddling topped with a tuft of thick black hair that certainly suggested he was Shek Kul's child. Mahli smiled at me and I managed to smile back, although I don't think I've ever seen anyone look quite so exhausted and still remain conscious.

Shek Kul looked over her head at me and addressed me directly for the first time since I was caught up in this whole mess.

'This is my son, Shek Nai. You will protect him as if he were blood of your blood.'

I looked at the tiny, fragile face, eyes screwed shut against the strangeness of the world, and nodded; that much was no hardship, no threat to any other allegiance I held. I looked round for Laio, wondering how soon she was going to act to remove the threat of Kaeska's malice that was hanging over this infant life. She must have read this in my face, a faint frown marring her brow as she gestured me out of the room with a shake of her head.

'Is Mahli all right?' I asked as we headed for Laio's apartments, walking the customary pace behind her. I only have a hazy notion of the sorts of things that can go wrong for women in child-bed but I've seen a handful too many men of my acquaintance sobbing as they place a crimson urn in a shrine to Drianon.

'She's come through it very well. The midwife is delighted,' Laio nodded. 'The aspects of the heavens are highly propitious as well. We must make sure the stars are fully recorded.' She looked upwards, her mind clearly occupied elsewhere. I couldn't help that.

'When are you going to tell Shek Kul about Kaeska and her magician?' I demanded.

'What are you talking about?' Laio turned from pouring herself a drink from a jug of fruit juice. 'You mainlanders only make a note of the sun or which moon is uppermost, don't you? Do you know the time of your birth? We could chart your stars if you do—'

Of all the irrelevancies I could imagine her wanting to discuss, the fact that I was born under the lesser moon seemed the most pointless.

'Kaeska and the magician attacked me today, look at my leg. I could have been killed. She has been using poisons; she has tried to kill the fish and the birds.' I wondered with a cold horror where the bitch had been creeping while Sezarre and I frustrated her plans in the gardens. Any standing drink could have been fouled. I dashed the porcelain cup from Laio's hands; it shattered on the floor, sticky juice splashing us both. Laio was too taken aback even to rebuke me.

I knelt with a curse as my bruised leg protested and touched a finger to a puddle of juice, smearing it on my lip and waiting tensely for any burning or numbness that would betray any taint. Laio listened, astounded as I told her about my eventful day.

'I will get you a fresh drink from the kitchens,' I told her firmly. 'So we can be sure it's safe.' I strode off, determined that Laio should denounce Kaeska as soon as possible, refusing to countenance this degree of uncertainty and fear.

On my return, I found Laio in the bathroom, stripping off her bloodied and juice-spattered clothing. I handed a cup and retreated in some confusion. It had been easy enough to ignore her tempting form when I had thought any hand laid on her would be instantly hacked off by an outraged Warlord. It seemed her earlier revelations had removed that particular chain on my desires and the old dog was up and barking. To my relief this appeared to be one nuance of our relationship that Laio was failing to comprehend as she emerged, hair tied up in a silken scarf, a loose yellow chamber robe belted negligently over her nakedness. Her expression was still thoughtful.

'When you find a moment, ask Sezarre for some green oil, will you? I want some of the first pressing, do you understand? I know Gar has some and that's the best.'

Wondering why the topic of conversation had suddenly turned to condiments, I nodded my understanding nevertheless, turning to find something else to look at. 'The flavour is so much better.'

'Ryshad!' Laio half laughed and half gasped. I looked round to see her blushing, unmistakable even given her complexion. 'I didn't think you mainlanders went in for that kind of thing!'

I looked at her uncertainly. 'What do you mean?'

Laio rubbed a hand over her mouth, smiling now though her eyes were still startled. 'What do you mean?'

We looked at each other for a moment, the noise of the revelry below invading the silence of the room.

'We prefer the first pressing of green oil for dressing fresh vegetables,' I said cautiously. 'What do you use it for?'

'Keeping ourselves from pregnancy!' Laio giggled, hands cupping her face. 'I want a bit more time to think about having a child now I've seen what Mahli's had to go through!'

Caught off guard like that it was my turn to blush and I cursed as I felt the heat in my cheeks.

'So what do mainlander women do,' Laio's eyes were bright with mischief, 'to keep themselves without child?'

I ran a hasty hand through my hair. 'I don't know.' I quelled a sudden memory of the pot of salted cedar resin my father had given me in his workshop, together with some very straight talking, the day after I had laid my first whiskers on Misaen's altar.

Laio moved closer and laid a hand on the bare skin of my arm. The hairs rose like a hound's at her touch. 'Come to that,' she purred, 'what do you mainlanders do—'

A loud knock interrupted her and Sezarre stuck his head round the door. 'The tree-planting will be done at moonrise,' he said to Laio before ducking out again.

The thread between us snapped. 'I'll want the blue gown with the feather-patterned wrap,' she instructed me briskly. 'I'm going to wash my hair.'

Not sure whether I should be cursing Sezarre or blessing him, I obeyed and was pleasantly surprised to find I was also allowed plenty of time to wash and dress myself in a new green tunic and trousers that Grival brought by, a gift from Mahli apparently.

As the last half of the greater moon rose over the distant horizon, the black stone of the keep grim in the cold, bluish light, I followed Laio down the stairs and into the inner garden at the heart of the residence. I kept close to her, alert for instruction or reprimand as the air was thick with expectation and a sense of ritual, slaves from the household lining the walls, silent and respectful. Laio moved to stand next to Gar and I exchanged a fleeting glance with Sezarre. He tilted his head a finger's width and I saw Kaeska on the far side of the garden, Irith standing behind her, swaying slightly, mouth slack, no spark of life in his eyes. The Elietimm stood next to her, hair startlingly white in the night, his jaw set as he stared at me, unmistakable hatred crackling across the distance that separated us. I touched Laio's shoulder and leaned forward slightly.

'I know,' she murmured. 'Wait.'

A stir ran through the waiting assembly as a far door opened and Shek Kul entered the garden, Grival beside him carrying a silver bowl draped with a silken cloth.

Laio tilted her head back a little to whisper to me. 'That is the—' she struggled for the right words in Tormalin, 'it comes with the baby, nourishes it in the womb.'

'Afterbirth.' I was very glad I was not Grival; my determination to be long gone from here before Laio found herself brought to child-bed instantly doubled.

Shek Kul was dressed in a plain green tunic and, working without ceremony, he dug a deep hole in the rich earth in the middle of a stand of five trees of varying heights. Grival emptied his burden into it and then one of the gardeners brought a new sapling, which Shek Kul planted with a surprising air of competence, firming down the black soil with a large foot. The gardener bowed low and spoke to the Warlord, who shot a startled and unfriendly glance at Kaeska. Her eyes were fixed firmly on the ground and I saw Laio bridle as she observed this exchange.

Gar turned her head to catch my eye. 'The growth of the tree will guide us as to the health and nature of the child. Its leaves will be used in divination.'

I nodded, hardly about to say I'd seldom heard anything so improbable.

Laio stirred again and as Shek Kul wiped his hands on a towel proffered by the steward, she took a pace forward. A discreet ripple of surprise ran through the assembly and Laio lifted her chin, by every measure a Warlord's lady.

'My husband, just as you do your duty to protect our new son, the hope of the domain, I must act to counter a grave peril that nests in our midst like a venomous snake.'

Her clear voice echoed around the tall stone walls and Kaeska's head snapped upwards, her eyes wide, whites stark in the pitiless moonlight as she stared at Laio in horror.

'I accuse Kaeska Danak of suborning sorcery, to further her plans to kill our son and to regain her status as First Wife with a child born of enchantments.'

There was no triumph in Laio's voice, none of her earlier glee, simply an implacable ring of truth. The hiss of indrawn breath all around us was followed by murmurs of consternation from all directions.

Shek Kul raised a hand and the throng were silent as a grave. 'These are capital charges that you bring.' He spoke directly to Laio as if no one else were present. 'What is your proof?'

Laio gestured backwards over one shoulder. 'The word of my body slave.'

All eyes were instantly upon me and I stood, motionless, expressionless, as my mind raced, wondering what would happen next.

Shek Kul looked back at Kaeska and then studied me as the entire gathering held its collective breath.

'I will hear this case at sunset tomorrow,' he announced finally, tossing the towel to Grival and striding back inside the residence as the crowd erupted into a frenzy of speculation. I struggled to keep Kaeska in view as Laio led the way back to the stairwell. This was not at all what I had expected.

'What happens to Kaeska?' I looked around in vain for guards or household slaves. 'Where will she be held? Where is the Warlord's dungeon?'

Laio halted on the stairs and turned to look down at me. 'Kaeska will not be detained in any way.' Her tone was puzzled. 'The household guard will be on alert, that will be sufficient to dissuade her from anything foolish.'

'Why ever not?' I demanded. 'What is Shek Kul thinking of? Now she knows we're on to her, she has a night and a day to work whatever malice she wants!'

'Not with every eye on her, knowing she is accused,' commented Sezarre, rather to my surprise. 'Anyway, Shek Kul is hearing the case as soon as possible, at the very start of the day following the accusation.'

Of course, one of the many peculiarities of Aldabreshin life is the way they measure each day from sunset to sunset.

'Even the lowest slave is entitled to know of what they are

accused, to be given time to prepare a defence,' Laio said tartly, 'in the Islands, at least.'

'It may be that she takes her chance to flee.' Gar was looking thoughtful. 'That might be preferable.'

Not from where I was looking, it wasn't. I cursed under my breath in exasperation as I followed Laio up the stairs. There was just too much I didn't know about this unholy place, their bizarre customs and peculiar notions. I was going to have to rely on Laio's guidance and I didn't like that idea one little bit.

'What is the form of the trial?' I demanded. 'Do you have an advocate to speak for you? Will Kaeska have someone to argue her innocence? What exactly do you want me to say?'

'Aldabreshin justice is swift and sure,' answered Laio crisply. 'Shek Kul will call you to stand before him and tell your tale. Kaeska will respond and you can argue the details out where necessary. Shek Kul will listen for as long as he wishes and then give his judgement. We do not hide behind intercessors and contention, like the mainlanders. The truth is not some dead beast to be picked over by carrion birds and weasel words.'

I'd have to remember that line to use against Mistal one day. So this court was going to have all the validity of a barrack-room assize, as far as I could see; my best hope had to be that the legendary blood-thirstiness of the Aldabreshi would carry the day against Kaeska, regardless.

'What about the fish and the birds? When are you going to tell Shek Kul about that?'

'I'm not and neither are you.' Laio opened the bedroom door with a vindictive shove. 'Kaeska will only deny it and once we acknowledge the fact of the deaths there will always be the suspicion that it was a valid omen.'

And if no one mentions the lizard sitting in the middle of the dining table, presumably it doesn't exist either.

'I don't want you mentioning this attack you say they made on you either, not since there were no witnesses,' Laio continued. 'They'll only use that to muddy the waters by arguing some personal conflict between you and this foreigner, that your accusations are simply malicious.'

Laio forbade any further discussion with a wave of her hand and readied herself for bed with her usual routine, soon asleep and snoring with an insouciance that I could only envy. I lay on my pallet, naked sword ready to hand, unable to sleep as my ears seized on every slightest noise as the long night deepened, darkened and paled into day.

The Palace of Shek Kul,
the Aldabreshin Archipelago,
7th of For-Summer

I was standing on the balcony, watching as the sunlight spilled the golden promise of a new dawn across the dark green flanks of the mountain when I heard Laio stir behind me. Stifling a yawn, I turned to see her emerge from her silken cocoon of quilts, eyes unfocused, her soft face betraying her girlhood. As her gaze lit on me, her expression hardened.

'You look dreadful!' She tossed her coverlets aside. 'Have you been awake all night?'

'I know what Kaeska's been up to. I've dealt with these cursed Elietimm before,' I snapped, exhaustion hitting me like a slap in the face now I had to start thinking and talking again. 'I wasn't about to have her come in and slit our throats in the middle of the night!'

'Oh don't be so ridiculous,' Laio said with no little contempt as she dragged on a old crimson tunic and ran a hand through her hair. If I hadn't been so spent, I would probably have managed some cutting retort; as it was all I could do was scowl.

'I need you awake and alert to give your evidence against Kaeska this evening,' she continued, her voice taut with irritation. 'Get in.' She pulled aside a quilt on the bed.

'What?' I blinked, too tired to bother with niceties.

'Get some sleep, you idiot.' There was precious little patience remaining in her tone and her foot was tapping ominously.

I moved to the bed, consoling myself with the realisation that Sezarre and Grival would be awake by now and the residence guard would have been changed at dawn. They would be more than a match for Kaeska and her sorcerer in a straight fight. Now the plot had been exposed, for the Elietimm to use magic would be to condemn the pair of them out of hand. My sluggish thoughts had just reached this conclusion when the silken pillow touched my cheek with a seductive caress. I was lost and asleep even before Laio's warmth and lingering scent in the bed could stir my tired senses.

I was borne upwards from the depths of sleep by a swelling tide of noise in the compound below Laio's apartments. Opening my eyes, I was just trying to identify the individual elements in the mix when the door opened. I sat bolt upright, heart racing, only to see Laio standing looking at me, her expression a blend of concern and irritation.

'Are you going to be able to tell a coherent tale without falling asleep in the middle of it?' Her foot was tapping again and I realised belatedly how much of her own prestige Laio was investing in my word.

'Yes,' I said simply. 'You were right, I did need to sleep.' If I had expected my admission would soften her mood, I was wrong.

'Of course I was,' snapped Laio. 'Get up, get washed and fetch something to eat.'

I hurried to comply; having Laio standing in the middle of the floor, arms folded and eyes hooded with annoyance didn't encourage any lingering in bed. Stifling a fleeting wish that I could have a decent shave for once, I headed down to the kitchens, pausing at the half-landing to open a shutter and check the time by the sun. It proved to be late afternoon, but I barely spared the sun a glance when I saw the activity in the gardens. I'd thought the place was crowded when the news of the baby's birth has spread but that was nothing compared to the scene below me. It looked as if half the domain had somehow made its way here; I couldn't believe all these people lived on this one island. A tremor of nervousness threatened to unsettle me and I slapped a passing insect with unnecessary venom.

'Get a grip on the reins, Rysh,' I muttered to myself. 'The only one you need to convince is Shek Kul. Imagine he's the Sieur in a difficult mood.'

. The problem with that was not only did I know the Sieur and his disposition while Shek Kul was largely still an untold tale to me, but I could also rely on the protection of oaths that the Sieur had made when offering me his commission. I realised that I had no idea just what Shek Kul might do to me if he decided for some arcane reason that my words were a malicious fabrication. I made haste to fetch Laio's meal and waited impatiently for her to eat her fill.

'What will happen if Kaeska is not judged guilty?' I asked abruptly, not bothering to ask permission as I began to eat, trying to see if some food would settle the qualms gathering in my gut.

Laio shook herself as she rose and began pacing along the balcony. 'You don't need to concern yourself with that,' she replied in a haughty tone that nevertheless rang a little hollow to my ears. 'Tell the tale as you gave it to me and she will not be able to excuse herself.'

There was a distinct edge of nervousness in her voice, which struck answering echoes from the doubts starting to gather around my mind. I stared at the flatbread in my hand, appetite failing me.

'Will you hurry up!' Laio suddenly snapped. 'I need to dress and make ready.'

As I shoved the tray aside, I forced the tumult of doubt and apprehension into the back of my mind and slammed a door on it. If I betrayed any nervousness, I could see Laio's poise would desert her and then we would both be in trouble. I might have the evidence that would condemn Kaeska but Laio was the one who knew how this so-called system of justice worked, which arguments would be most likely to sway Shek Kul, how Kaeska's mind would be working as she tried to evade her fate. I needed Laio calm and confident, all her wits sharp, honed to perfection as she cut through the intricacies of life in a Warlord's household. Well, that at least was something I had some control over.

Accordingly, I dressed her in a flamboyant golden gown, the silk shot through with a vivid bankfisher blue, answering fire caught from an Emperor's ransom in sapphires and diamonds around her neck, her wrists and her ankles. I drew her hair up with jewelled clips and pins, piling it high to give her an illusion of greater tallness, the style encouraging her to carry her head high, shoulders back. She sat still as a statue, expressionless, as I painted her face in the intricate mask of an Aldabreshin noblewoman, outlining her eyes and brows with black, a sweep of azure and gold carried out from her lashes to her hairline, cheekbones highlighted to dramatic effect and lips full with a rich red tint that promised untold delights. As her mouth yielded to the soft kiss of the brush, my hand halted and our eyes met.

'This is more than rivalry between wives or Shek Kul ridding himself of an inconvenience,' said Laio sombrely. 'The practice of magic is a foul offence and it must be punished. I would be doing this if it had been Mahli you had overheard, you must understand this.'

I understood that Laio meant every word, whatever I might think of the so-called crime. 'You are doing your duty to Shek Kul and to the domain,' I replied with equal gravity. 'I will do everything in my power to support you.'

Laio drew in a long breath and, after a moment, released it slowly. Moving to look out across the straits to the distant hills, oblivious to the milling crowds below, she stood in silence, preparing herself. I looked at her, wondered if I should try talking to her further, but decided against it and addressed myself to my own appearance. Taking a brush to burnish my hauberk, I scoured it to a silver brilliance before scrubbing the resulting grime from my hands. Once I was clean I dressed in the green and black silk arming jacket that proclaimed the domain when I was on show to visiting nobles. Settling the armour on my shoulders and hips, I was about to buckle on my belt when Laio stirred.

'There's a coffer by the door,' she said, almost absently, her eyes still fixed on the far distant heights.

I looked round and found a small casket of reddish-brown wood bound with bronze. Opening it I found a broad belt rich with silver-mounted stones, jet and malachite, arrogant in their size and cut. Clasping similarly ornamented bracers around my forearms, I lifted out an Aldabreshin war helm, something I had not worn to this point. Shaped close to the skull, it had a veil of fine chainmail to protect the neck and shoulders and a sliding nasal bar. Chased silver bands around and across it were inlaid with curling enamel lines of Aldabreshin script and I put it on with an odd sense of foreboding, wondering just what I had written above my eyes.

'Now you are an Islander.' Laio nodded her approval.

I managed a faint smile. I certainly looked the part but I would have to convince everyone present that I was truly Laio's man at this masquerade of a trial, loyal to her, Shek Kul and the domain in that order. How could I do that when I did not believe it myself? My oath had been given long before I had been brought here and I was the only one who could take it back and give it elsewhere. My loyalties to Laio or Shek Kul weren't worth a Lescari cut-piece; I spent every spare moment racking my brains for a way to escape them. Was I forsworn by this pretence? Where was the virtue in standing on my honour if that would only get me killed?

What of my immediate situation? My quarrel was with the Elietimm, with him and his kind who had somehow encompassed my slavery here; I wasn't doing this for Laio or the domain, I wanted some measure of vengeance for my own predicament, even if that hapless slut Kaeska was going to suffer Dastennin only knew what torments if I succeeded. I caught my breath on a sudden memory of the visions Viltred had shown me; these Elietimm were a threat to all that held my oath, weren't they? That alone should validate my actions here, shouldn't it?

Would I be any closer to escaping and returning to the duties I had chosen of my own free will? If I did, would Kaeska's death be a price I was prepared to accept, a consequence I could defend to Saedrin when the time came? Too late for these questions; I was committed now. It was time to act and deal with the consequences as the runes fell, the moment any good soldier learns to recognise if he's to live beyond his first season in the militia.

I moved to stand at Laio's shoulder and stared out towards the hidden seas, wondering what Livak was doing at this moment, watching the shadows lengthen as the sun sank inexorably to the horizon. A rising note swelled above us from a deep-throated horn I had not heard give tongue before. In the gathering dusk I saw bright flowers of flame blossom along a line of beacons, answering points of light identifying islands far distant. Whatever happened here tonight clearly involved the entire domain.

'Come.' Laio turned and led the way, back straight, head held high, her poise impeccable. I drew myself up as straight as if I had been granted a private audience with the Emperor and kept pace at her heel. As we reached the stairs, Gar and Sezarre emerged, equally resplendent, faces equally grave. Side by side and everyone in step, we descended to the compound where the throng parted before us in silent waves of obeisance before sweeping round to follow like a gathering sea at our backs. Crossing the compound, we entered a great hall that I had not been in before and it took all my training to remain impassive as I took in my surroundings.

This was Shek Kul's audience chamber, the heart of the domain, the seat of his authority. It was a lofty, pillared hall with walls of shining black marble inlaid with false arches of a green, veined stone, bracketed with torches scattering golden light from their faceted and mirrored niches. Shutters high above our heads had been opened and a breeze stirred the array of pennants hanging from the central arch of the roof. The snap and flutter of the silk could clearly be heard above the faint sounds of the expectant crowd. Censers filled the air with their perfume and the soft whisper of fly-whisks sounded on all sides.

Our steps echoed on the floor, the sound vanishing into the masses already gathered along the walls, more pressing in at the wide double doorway. We proceeded up the central aisle to stand in the centre of a vast abstract design in green marble set into the floor at the foot of a flight of three broad steps. Shek Kul looked down from the dais, seated squarely on a black wood throne inlaid with silver and precious stones. In a dramatic contrast to ourselves, the Warlord was dressed in plain white silk, hair and beard unornamented, his only gem a great emerald set in a heavy gold chain around his neck. He waved Laio and Gar to seats at his off hand with an economical gesture, his grave expression unchanging.

I took my stand at Laio's shoulder, wanting to share a glance with Sezarre but unable to do so without moving my head. Before I had time to grow concerned about the possible implications of Shek Kul's dress, a low murmur swept towards us through the expectant crowd and the guards at the doorway stood aside to let Kaeska Shek enter. I heard a note of sympathy, which gave me something new to worry about.

Kaeska was a forlorn figure, tiny in the vastness of the hall, bare feet silent on the cold marble as she walked up the central aisle towards judgement. Her hair was bound in a simple braid down her back, face naked and vulnerable, and she wore only a plain dress of unbleached cotton. I managed to keep my own contempt out of my face, but couldn't help glancing at Shek Kul to see how he was reacting to this display of penitence. To my relief I was sure I saw a gleam of cynicism to answer my own in his dark eyes. Looking for the Elietimm priest, I saw he was following Kaeska, his distance nicely judged not to distract the onlookers from her portrayal of humble duty.

My thoughts were interrupted by the heavy slam of the far doors, the bar falling across with a thud that made me feel as trapped as Kaeska, the feverish scent of anticipation replacing the fragrant aroma of the night-time gardens. I drew a deep breath as Shek Kul rose to his feet, looking down at Kaeska with hard eyes.

'You are accused of suborning sorcery in my domain, woman. How do you answer?'

'I deny the act.' Kaeska's reply was little more than a whisper, catching on a half-stifled sob that elicited a ripple of sympathy from the closest spectators. Shek Kul looked unmoved.

'I will hear the accusation.' He looked at me and I thought I saw some hint of encouragement in a softening of his expression.

'Stand next to Kaeska,' Laio murmured through barely parted lips and I marched briskly down the steps, pleased to see faint distress in Kaeska's eyes as I towered over her, armoured in all the regalia of the domain. Wreathed with the coils of the inlaid design, I have to confess that I felt uncomfortably exposed to the probing gazes all around.

'Speak only the truth or suffer the consequences.' Shek Kul looked even more forbidding from here.

I took a soldier's stance and began my tale, drawing on all my knowledge of the Aldabreshin tongue, forcing myself to speak slowly and clearly, repressing any hint of emotion, trusting that the facts alone would condemn the woman. Murmurs among the crowd rose, died back and swelled again as I continued my recital, but I kept my eyes fixed on Shek Kul, speaking to him as if we were alone in the windswept centre of the Dalasorian plains. When I fell silent, the tension in the air would have blunted steel.

'What say you?' Shek Kul demanded of Kaeska.

'I confess—' She collapsed to her knees, face hidden in her hands, her sobs ripping through the shocked silence of the great hall.

'You—' Shek Kul was startled to his feet for an instant before he regained his poise. I looked at Laio and saw she had gone so pale beneath her complexion and her face paints that I thought she would faint.

'Not to the sorcery!' Kaeska's head snapped up and, for all her tears, her eyes were clear and calculating. 'Never to the magic but, oh, my lord, I—' she choked on a shuddering breath. 'I confess to fatal weakness, mortal foolishness, to succumbing to the lure of the mainlander smoke. I have sought for so long for a cure for the pain that twists in my heart, that I have been unable to bear children, that my blood falls barren, not to nourish the domain—'

Her eyes closed in anguish, she clasped her hands to her

breast, mouth working but no words emerging. She could certainly weave a pretty sentence for a woman in such dire distress, I thought sourly.

'In my travels and trade, as I sought to serve the domain in the only way I could, I heard mention of these mainlander smokes, of the way they can lighten the heaviest burdens. I was tempted but I resisted, you must believe me, I resisted until I heard that Mahli was to bring the blessing on the domain where I had failed. The anguish, the envy, the mean and petty jealousy that clawed at me, oh my lord, I hated myself for the foulness of my thoughts when I should have been rejoicing – I could live with the pain of my empty womb but I could not face the repellent creature I had become. I took to the smoke to escape myself, the rending of my conscience, the corruption that festered within me!' Her voice, rising through this increasingly frantic speech, fell and shattered into hysterical crying, Kaeska prostrate on shining floor, hands clinging to the unyielding stone.

I kept my stance, expressionless but I could assess all too well from the faces I could see the impact of the tableau the pair of us were presenting; Kaeska, tiny, undefended, baring the shameful secrets of her heart as I loomed over her, armoured, ostentatious in my finery, eyes hooded by the helm, my sword hanging over her naked neck.

Rapid chatter scurried round the assembled islanders, the volume increasing until it was abruptly silenced as Shek Kul rose and descended the steps with a measured tread.

'Calm yourself.' His soft words reached to the furthest corners of the hall as he knelt beside the weeping woman and she fell silent. Taking one of Kaeska's hands, he raised her to her knees and used a soft silk square to gently wipe the tears from her face.

'So why does this slave accuse you of sorcery?' I breathed a shallow sigh of relief at the firmness of Shek Kul's question.

Kaeska spread her hands in a helpless gesture. 'I do not know. I cannot say – my lord, forgive my foolishness, my failing! I have spent long days of anguish repenting my weakness, I will be a good wife to you – raise Laio and Gar above me and I will take my place as the least of your women. My transgressions have been grievous but I have seen the error of my ways – let me make a new start just as the birth of our son marks a fresh opening for the domain. Crown this joyous time with the shining jewel of mercy.'

'If this slave did not see sorcery, what did he see?' Shek Kul stood and looked down at Kaeska, arms folded, face stern, his manner subtly directing the mood in the hall.

'May I speak?'

The Ice Islander's halting words shocked a hiss from the assembly but I saw Shek Kul's eyes were unsurprised. 'I will hear you.'

The Elietimm moved from the shadow of a pillar where he had been waiting and stepped into the light at the edge of the great marble insignia. 'I must apologise most humbly for my part in this affair.' He paused, a nicely calculated shake of his head as he looked at the kneeling Kaeska. 'It is I who supplied your wife with the smoke. I had obtained the leaves to take home; our holy men use it to open their minds to a higher realm of being. I did not understand the powerful reasons the Aldabreshi have for keeping such things from your islands and sought only to relieve the lady's dire distress by lifting her perceptions beyond her immediate sorrows. I did not know that I transgressed against your customs and for that I am heartily sorry.'

So his was the pattern of words I had been hearing in Kaeska's impassioned laments.

'The slave was listening at the door, was he not?' The snake wasn't even looking at me. 'The shutters were open to catch the breeze and the door was uncurtained, as I recall. I suggest the air carried the smoke to the slave and worked on his mind to weave a hallucination. It is not an uncommon effect of the drug on an unprepared mind; I blame myself for not ensuring the smoke did not drift.'

Shek Kul looked at me. 'How say you?'

I bit down my instinctive rebuttal and took a slow count of three before replying. 'No, it was no hallucination.' The approval in Shek Kul's eyes at my considered response heartened me further.

'Forgive me,' the Ice Islander's words were courteous, but I hoped Shek Kul could see the hostility in the man's eyes as he turned his gaze towards me, 'but how can you be so sure? The very nature of an hallucination is to mimic reality in every particular.'

'I had experience of taking smoke in my youth.' I kept my voice level and unemotional. 'This was completely unlike that feeling.'

'Of course,' the Elietimm nodded, 'you are a mainlander, are you not?'

I could tell this reminder was not lost on the watching islanders and saw that Shek Kul was looking thoughtful.

'I am body slave to the Warlord's lady, Laio Shek,' I stated firmly. That much was simple fact, and no forswearing.

'The question of the effect of the drug aside,' the Ice Islander moved on smoothly, 'your accusation of sorcery, of magic, stems from what exactly? From the rites you say you saw and heard? From the words I spoke in what you yourself said was a tongue unknown to you?'

I nodded, not about to risk a snare in his tangled argument. He inclined his head with a satisfied air and turned to Shek Kul.

'As I explained, the holy men of my people use the smoke to open their minds to the higher states of awareness. I have some grounding in what is a complex procedure, not without risk, and we use chants to focus ourselves. This is what the slave heard and did not understand; it is not magic in any sense.'

'What I saw being practised was sorcery.' I raised my voice above his tone of level reasonableness and was gratified by the whisper that ran around the hall.

'Again, I ask, how can this man be sure?' The Elietimm kept his eyes on Shek Kul.

'I have seen magic worked before—'

'The mainlander practices of charlatans and those whose very blood is tainted with enchantment – are you saying you are familiar with such men?' The priest's eagerness to discredit me betrayed him.

'I have seen this magic worked by men of your race, on the islands you inhabit in the far ocean,' I stated baldly.

The bastard knew I had scored a hit with that stroke and looked for a recovery. 'You say you have visited my homeland? How did you come to be there? What were you doing in the deep ocean?'

'I was on a fishing vessel that was carried far off its course by wind and current.' What did the fool think I was going to say? That I had been on a spying trip working with a wizard of Hadrumal who reported directly to the Archmage?

'So you don't know exactly where you were?'

I had to concede that, given the circumstances.

'Did you see much of the island you arrived at? How long were you there?'

'Enough to know your islands have none of the resources you are offering to trade – no wood, no metals, no leathers,' I said crisply. 'Long enough to be greeted with hostility and attacked with magic.'

'You are no fisherman, surely? What were you doing on a fisher vessel?'

This change of tack momentarily threw me off balance. Aware that I had hesitated, if only for a breath, I opted for the truth. 'As a sworn man to the House of D'Olbriot, I was seeking revenge for cowardly and magical assaults on members of my master's family.'

That came out more forcefully than I had intended. I mentally kicked myself as I felt a shift of disapproval in the air of the hall.

'It would seem your mistress has still to beat those old loyalties out of you, Tormalin man.' The Elietimm fixed me with a challenging eye for a moment but then shrugged helplessly. 'I believe I know the islands that you speak of, but I can assure you I am not of their race.'

'You are of the appearance of the enchanters, you speak their tongue,' I insisted, aware this was now my word against his. 'I have also seen your kind of magic worked on the mainland, used in foul assaults on the weak and helpless, to maim and to rob.' I couldn't keep the anger out of my voice as I remembered Messire's nephew, blinded and bleeding after these scum had beaten him senseless. If this bastard was going to remind everyone I was a mainlander, I'd do my best to reverse that rune for him.

Shek Kul raised a hand and returned to the dais, all eyes on him, my heart quickening.

'I do not find this matter either truly proved or satisfactorily refuted,' he declared, his deep voice ringing through the hush of the hall. 'A grave crime is alleged and this must be resolved. The truth will be tested in single combat, at noon tomorrow, on the person of this body slave who brings the accusation.'

I looked blankly at Laio, only to see a look of total shock on her face. She jumped to her feet, silencing the buzz of speculation running rife on every side.

'Where is the body slave to Kaeska Shek, that her veracity may be defended?'

'Yes, where is Irith?' Shek Kul looked at Kaeska who was unable to restrain a fleeting smug expression before collapsing once more with piercing wails of distress. 'He is dead, my faithful servant, he is lost because of my stupidity. As well as the smoke, I acquired some berries to numb my mind, but whereas I knew they should only be eaten one at a time and seldom, Irith found them and ate them all!'

'The commander of the guard will examine the body.' Shek Kul's uncompromising pronouncement shocked Kaeska to silence and she stared up with no little dismay. I couldn't see what she had to worry about; tahn poisoning is tahn poisoning and I couldn't see there being any trace to prove whose hand had been behind it.

The Elietimm stepped forward to divert attention from Kaeska, all humble solicitude. 'Since it is my ill-considered actions that have exposed the lady to these accusations, may I make some reparation by defending her honour. I am no swordsman but I have some small skill with a mace, if that would be allowed.'

Shek Kul looked at him, contempt plain on his face now he had given his judgement. 'That would seem entirely fitting.'

I bit down hard on my protests as I caught a frantic look of appeal from Laio. Fuming, I waited as first Shek Kul then the two wives descended from the dais, Kaeska taking her place beside Gar, a spring in her step proof against the venomous glance she received from Laio. Sezarre moved to put himself between me and the Elietimm, a good thing because I was so furious I was sorely tempted to put a length of sharp steel through the bastard's guts there and then. Kaeska and the enchanter must have been working to this end all along. We returned to the residence, my anger driving me on so fast that Laio was only able to keep her position in front of me by half running at times.

I turned on her as soon as we were inside her apartment, not caring who heard what through the flimsy walls and shutters. 'What's this about a single combat? You never said anything about that! You were so cursed sure Shek Kul would leap at the chance to get rid of that bitch, he'd hardly pause for breath! What's going on?' I ripped off my helm and bracers, dropping them anyhow, heedless as a gem bounced loose from its mounting.

'It's hardly ever done, I never thought Shek Kul would opt for testing the truth like that.' Laio was visibly upset, but I had more important things to worry me as I stripped off my chainmail.

'Where's the cursed justice in a single combat, Dast help me? I could have taken Irith, no question, whether Kaeska was innocent or guilty – that's probably why they finished the poor bastard off! Now I have to fight that cursed enchanter, who's not only handy-looking with a mace but I'll lay sound coin he will be using magic on me as well!'

Laio was struggling to follow my rapid and impassioned Tormalin. 'He wouldn't dare,' she objected.

'Who's going to know? Who's to say his little chant isn't some kind of battle cry? Is Shek Kul going to stop the fight when I back off and say the bastard is messing with my mind? How exactly does this test of truth work?' I was sweating profusely and shrugged myself out of my padded jerkin with an oath.

'It's a fight, two men, each with a weapon and armour, to the death.' Laio looked on the edge of tears. 'Once the word is given, it cannot be stopped, not until one is dead. Anyone backing out is deemed guilty and executed.'

'Either party? If I back out, all of a sudden, I'm looking at a sunset trip with Poldrion?'

Laio's hands hovered in confusion as my meaning escaped her. 'The test is a serious matter, Shek Kul would not call for one unless he thought it was necessary. You are telling the truth, so you are bound to win!'

I looked at her and cursed myself as a gurry-eating fool for relying on her like that, seeing her extreme youth with new eyes. I'd been so far adrift out here, I'd taken the first thing I'd been offered for a bearing, only to find I'd been setting a course by a cloud bank.

'Shek Kul wants rid of Kaeska, but he doesn't want her blood on his hands, does he? This isn't about truth or justice, it's about Shek Kul avoiding condemning her outright himself!' I was as angry with myself as I was at Laio; I'd been in such a hurry to draw the Elietimm's teeth that I hadn't stopped to think all of this through myself. That didn't stop me taking my fury out on Laio though.

'You were so pleased with yourself weren't you? Now I have to go up against a cursed sorcerer who'll be able to pickle my wits and pick me off at leisure. Well, I hope you're pleased with yourself; this time tomorrow, I'll be dead and Kaeska will be judged pure as spring water and free to poison whoever she wants. Still, look on the bright side – you and Gar can plan a nice trip to Relshaz to buy yourself a new slave. Try to take better care of the next one. With luck Mahli and the baby might still be alive when you get back!'

'You're making a lot of fuss—' Laio began tremulously.

'No, pigeon, I'm not!' I caught her chin as she went to turn away and looked her straight in the eye. 'I'll take on any man you want in fair fight – Grival, Sezarre, the captain of the guard. I'll trust my skills and take the runes as they fall. This is different; this is magic. And not just honest magic – air, earth, fire and water. This is enchantment that gets inside your own mind and turns it against you.' I laid a heavy hand on Laio's head to emphasise the point and felt her quail beneath it. 'I've had one of these bastards loose in my skull before. I've tried to fight it and I know that I can't!'

'For this man to use magic would be to condemn himself and Kaeska—' Laio began, a tear trickling unheeded down one cheek.

'I'll be dead before anyone notices!' I pulled my hands away and looked round the room. A pitcher of weak Aldabreshin wine stood on a side-table and I began to pour before abruptly heaving the jug at the wall. 'I can't even get a decent pissing drink in this shit-hole!'

The crash of the shattering pitcher shocked Laio into full-blown sobbing but it brought me to my senses, my rage as effectively in pieces as the earthenware jug. I shook my head; Laio was so very young, she couldn't expect to play for the same stakes as Kaeska and win. I should have known that.

'Come on, stop crying.' I put a hand on Laio's shuddering shoulder. She turned to fling herself against my chest, her tears hot through the thin silk of my undertunic.

'I'm so sorry,' she sobbed. 'It seemed like such a good idea, such a good way to get rid of Kaeska. I thought Shek would be so pleased, it might make up for me not wanting a child just yet, I don't want to do it, not just yet, not after yesterday, and I've got myself into such a mess with the cotton, but if Gar was to help, I could sort it out, as long as Kaeska wasn't here to make trouble, and Nai is so lovely, I couldn't bear it if anything happened to him or to Mahli and it would be all my fault, if I knew Kaeska was planning something and I didn't do something to stop her—'

She choked as she ran out of breath and coughed on her tears. I sighed and gave her a hug, a little startled to feel her cling to me like a drowning kitten. 'Hush, what's done is done, after all.' I didn't feel that sanguine, but if I was going to have any chance against the sorcerer I needed sleep, not to spend half the night soothing Laio's hysterics. 'Let's just go to bed.'

Laio lifted her tear-stained face, a puzzled expression fleeting across her brow. 'All right, if you want to.' Standing on tip-toe, she kissed me full on the lips, pressing herself against me. That met an instant reaction as my body received the message half a breath ahead of my wits. Before I could say anything to correct this misunderstanding, Laio twined her arms around the back of my neck to draw me closer, her mouth open and inviting. Abruptly I kissed her back, hard, a challenge in my lips and tongue, knowing this was almost certainly an inappropriate thing to be doing, but equally only too aware that I would be fighting for my life tomorrow, with a lame leg, against a sorcerer who would have me just where he wanted me. Laio evidently felt the shift in my weathervane and pressed her thigh into me, my scruples weakening as my ardour hardened. Dast take it, I could be dead by sunset tomorrow, and if the condemned man wasn't going to get a hearty meal I'd take what was on offer. Sliding my hand down, I teased her breast through the fine silk of her dress and felt her nipple rise to my touch.

Things moved more quickly after that, neither of us stopping to think, just concentrating on losing ourselves in sensation. Laio knew some tricks that made me wonder just where Aldabreshi girls got their education once I had my breath back, but there was nothing of the practised whore about her, just a frank and sensual delight in her body and mine. As a sexual experience, it was quite remarkable. Afterwards, a long while afterwards, as we lay in the rumpled chaos of the bed, the sweat drying slowly on our bodies, I pulled a quilt over us to keep out the chill and so we drifted off to sleep. Although Laio had been a unique delight, I smiled as I realised that despite everything my last thoughts were still of Livak.

The chamber of Planir the Great,
the hidden island city of Hadrumal,
7th of For-Summer

'Don't worry, I know exactly where Ryshad is. We have everything in hand to rescue him.' Planir spoke confidently at Shiv's image, tiny and gold-tinted in a steel mirror lit by a single candle flame. 'How are you getting on?' The Archmage was in shirt sleeves, seated at a polished table in his panelled study, the evening sun sinking behind the towers of Hadrumal just visible through the tall lancets of the window next to him.

'I'm afraid Viltred is being difficult.' Exasperation was clear in Shiv's muffled, tiny sounding voice. *'All he wants is to get to Hadrumal as soon as possible; he doesn't feel safe anywhere else, not after Ryshad disappeared like that.'*

'Tell him not to worry about Ryshad,' Planir repeated himself, clenching a fist beneath the table where the spell would not be carrying his image to Shiv. 'We need Viltred to persuade Lord Finvar to let us have the records of that shrine. I'm counting on the man having some respect for his old tutor; nothing else we've tried has succeeded thus far.'

'I can't see Viltred inspiring respect in anyone just at present,' responded Shiv dourly. *'He's old and tired and running scared of everything from Elietimm to Eldritch-men. There must be someone else you can send.'*

'Casuel? He's on his way to Toremal, to help Esquire Camarl look for any material on this lost colony. Other than that, no, Shiv, I can't send anyone just at present.' The undertone of authority in Planir's voice forbade further argument.

'If Cas is the only alternative, I suppose Viltred will have to do.' Shiv scowled and leaned back in his chair, running both

hands through his hair, a pause as he laced his hands behind his head eloquent of his frustration.

'Please just ask Viltred to do what he can, tell him it's a special request from me to him, personally. I appreciate his situation and as soon as you have the archive, I'll arrange a nexus of power for you to link to and translocate here directly.' Planir's tone was warm and amiable but his fingers were drumming silently on his worn and faded breeches.

'I'll do my best but Saedrin save me from nurse-maiding any more senile old wizards,' sighed Shiv. *'We're in Claithe at the moment; we'll be on the road as soon as we can get Livak's horse shod. It's no more than a couple of days to Lord Finvar's fiefdom from here in good weather.'*

'You've still got those women with you?' Planir frowned. 'Why?'

'They're not about to leave until they know what's happened to Ryshad and seen for themselves that you're doing everything you can to get him back.' Shiv's image showed a tiny, rueful smile. *'Would you believe Livak is actually offering to steal the books for us, if Lord Finvar really digs his heels in? That's on the understanding the entire Council turns its talents to finding Ryshad though. We might have another advantage as well; Halice reckons she knows the captain of his guard from her mercenary days. We'll get those records for you one way or another, Archmage.'*

Planir shook his head with a grin. 'I'm glad to see you're showing a bit of initiative, Shiv. Mind you, only let Livak loose if there's no other option. That one's services come expensive, as I remember!"

Shiv laughed as the spell dissolved the image, and Planir snuffed the candle with an absent-minded word of command. The Archmage ran a hand over his face and rubbed the back of his neck with a muttered oath as a knock sounded on the oak of his door.

'Enter.'

'Are we any closer to getting that Arimelin archive from Finvar yet?' Usara enquired without ceremony. While a pale complexion was to be expected with his sandy hair, the scholarly mage was looking almost grey with fatigue.

'Are you any closer to scrying out that unholy sword?' countered Planir, rising from his chair and crossing the room to a sideboard of elegantly simple design. 'Cordial?'

'Thank you, a little of the mint.' Usara dropped into a deeply upholstered chair with an explosive sigh of frustration, lifting his dirty boots heedlessly on to a low table heaped with documents. 'No, since you ask, we still can't get any kind of a fix on the cursed thing.'

'You know, I'm starting to think it might be better if D'Olbriot's man got himself killed after all,' said Planir grimly. 'We might get a lead on the sword if that happened.'

'Only if it's the man being shielded, not the weapon. Remember what Mellitha had to tell us, and there's what Shannet said about the time she and Viltred were looking for islands in the deep ocean to try and prove Azazir's stories.' Usara sipped his drink with a small murmur of pleasure. 'Anyway, I can't see D'Olbriot continuing to support you in Toremal if all he gets to show for it is another man dead with an unredeemed oath fee and an heirloom sword lost and presumably in the hands of an unknown enemy.'

'No, I don't suppose he will.' Planir stared into the depths of his own glass. 'Do you suppose Viltred might have anything useful to add? On the scrying? And get your feet off Kalion's proposals for remodelling the conduits to the bath-houses, will you, 'Sar?'

'A few creases'll make it look as if you've read them.' The younger wizard was unrepentant. 'No, I can't see Viltred having anything to contribute at all; he was a guttered candle before he went off to the arse end of Caladhria and I don't suppose a handful of years conversing with peasants will have restored him much. Still, he'll have done more service than he knows if he can get that cursed archive for us. We must find a key to unlock these unholy dreams, to give us some means of controlling them, opening things up once that initial sympathy with the artefact has been established. Has Otrick located any other shrines to Arimelin that might predate the Chaos, or is this still the only one?'

'Sorry? What did you say?' Planir's gaze had been fixed on the thick sheaf of parchments under Usara's feet. 'I tell you, 'Sar, there are times when I'm tempted to let Kalion loose, let him take all his petty wrangles and pompous plans to restore the authority of wizardry to the Council. I could just say, "All right, I yield. You take over as Archmage, Hearth-Master, until a proper vote can be convened and Misaen help you!"' The wizard stretched out a hand and studied the heavy golden ring of his office, the central diamond mysterious in the fading sunlight, catching and mingling the colours of the four gems set around it, sapphire, amber, ruby and emerald. 'Air, earth, fire and water; we can do what we like with them, can't we, 'Sar? That's what all the mundane populace think, anyway. I'm the Archmage, you know, most powerful man on an island of wizards with untold powers over the very elements of the world around us. It all counts for nothing, does it, not now we have to find a way to face powers we can't even start to explain.'

'I'm sure the information will be out there, somewhere. Knowledge is rarely lost, just misplaced or misinterpreted.' Usara went to refill his glass, offering the decanter to Planir, who shook his head. Usara took his seat again before continuing. 'Saedrin only send we find it before the Elietimm put their first pieces on the board and start the game in earnest. Oh, by the way, about Shannet – she and Troanna are at each other's throats over who exactly offered that lad Corian a pupillage first. I'm not going to get any sense out of either of them until they settle it.'

Planir groaned. 'He's that opinionated youth from Dusgate? For such venerable and respected mages, those two can be sillier than first-season apprentices at times. Where will I find Shannet tomorrow, do you know?'

'She'll be working with Otrick over at New Hall in the morning,' replied Usara after a moment's thought. 'They're giving a lecture on air and water conflicts.'

'If I get a chance, I'll just happen to drop in on Troanna too; after all, as senior Flood-Mistress I should consult her about Kalion's desires to mess about with the water supply, shouldn't I?' A spark of humour reanimated Planir's countenance.

Usara laughed. 'Absolutely, o revered Archmage.'

Planir began pacing in front of the empty fireplace, renewed vitality driving the tiredness from his face and lifting a generation's burden of years from his shoulders. 'And when I've sorted that precious pair out, what can I do to stall D'Olbriot, keep him happy until I've found out exactly what's happened to his man?'

'Do you really think you can find Ryshad?' There was surprise rather than doubt in Usara's question.

'Oh yes, 'Sar. Why? Don't you have unquestioning faith in your Archmage after all?' Planir smiled, his teeth gleaming white and even in the gathering dusk. He snapped his fingers and candles all around the room leaped to brilliant life. 'You should know more than most, the power of this office is based on a great deal more than a gaudy ring and its promises of sorcery. I should have news of Ryshad inside a couple of handful days.'

'Then all you'll have to worry about is Kalion.' The lines furrowing Usara's brow were smoothed away as his expression lightened.

'You know, I think the same scent may well divert them both, if we lay it carefully.' Planir paused to look out of the window. 'Kalion wants to know why we're working round the chimes with nothing to show for it; I think I'll take him into my confidence about the complex Elietimm plots that are frustrating our every move, tying up all our effort just in countering them. I'll send the Sieur D'Olbriot a despatch too, with just enough dark hints and evasions to give him something more urgent to worry about than his missing hound.'

'Just what plots would these be, exactly?' enquired Usara, a smile spreading across his face nevertheless.

Planir spread his hands in a vague gesture. 'I think that'll be too complicated to explain, don't you? How about we hint

that these Elietimm were somehow responsible for Ryshad's
arrest in Relshaz?'

'Do you think they did?' Usara blinked in some surprise.

'No, not really, I think they just took advantage of the situation. From what Mellitha says I imagine whatever sympathy
he's developed with D'Alsennin betrayed him somehow; she
identified the arm ring he was trying to take as an old piece
with Den Rannion's crest. No, the truth of it's not important,
'Sar. You just tell Kalion what I told you about Ryshad when
he comes asking, as long as you swear him to secrecy of course
– tell him to keep it closer than the lid on an urn! We suspect
these cursed Ice Islanders had some hand in his disappearance
into the Archipelago, if nothing else, and it's certainly this
pestilential aetheric magic that's hiding him after all. Kalion
will tell Ely and Galen, in strictest confidence obviously, and
once they start spreading their version the rumour mill will find
its own grist. That should give us some time to concentrate on
getting Ryshad back and by then, Arimelin willing, we should
have that archive and some clue as to how to start turning these
dreams to our advantage.' The Archmage poured himself a
second larger measure of white brandy and raised his glass to
the younger mage in high good humour.

'Arimelin willing,' echoed Usara, draining his own drink.
'I'm still worried about what might be happening to Ryshad,
though,' he added soberly.

Planir nodded. 'The Archipelago's a dangerous place,' he
agreed, his eyes dark. 'Dastennin grant he's not being too
badly treated, not starved nor beaten nor worked in chains.
That's probably the best we can hope for.'

CHAPTER EIGHT

Taken from the Family Archive of the House Tor Alder, Toremal, from the Records of the 35th Year of Emperor Aleonne the Gallant.

> *Compliments to Dardier, Esquire Tor Alder, from his brother Caprel, Sieur of that House.*
>
> *I am pleased to tell you that Carrey continues to recover well from his injuries. This comes as a great relief to his mother and myself, one's last son being no less precious than any of the others after all. Forgive my feeble attempt at levity, it stems from disordered nerves, I confess it.*
>
> *We have had no success tracing the brigands who attacked the boy and his companions in such an underhand manner; I suppose that would have been too much to hope for at this late date. Nevertheless I still remain concerned that by all accounts an organised and liveried troop of men could commit such an outrage on the Emperor's highways and vanish so thoroughly. I can only surmise that their appearance was a calculated disguise, wigs and liveries discarded as soon as their work was done. Perhaps they wanted to throw suspicion on to the Men of the Mountains since they are generally fair of head and visage, but few are trading so far from home at this season so I am not inclined to suspect them.*
>
> *Carrey's greatest concern is the loss of his sword, an heirloom admittedly but one of little significance for the House after all. His mother is anxious lest this distress lead to a return of that disorder of sleep and nightmare that plagued the boy last year, and I confess I share her worry. There has been no recurrence of such trouble as he has*

convalesced and I would not wish to see it visited upon him again. Accordingly, could you alert your sergeants-at-arms and ask them to spread the word among their fellows in other Houses in case the weapon should be offered for sale to any such. If we can recover the blade, so be it but my main concern is to reassure Carrey that no blame for its loss attaches to him. Since you are due to visit us soon, if you could find a way of broaching the subject in private converse with him, I would be most grateful.

The Palace of Shek Kul,
the Aldabreshin Archipelago,
8th of For-Summer

I checked the sun again; it seemed to have been hanging directly overhead for what would have been nearly a full chime at home, but we hadn't heard the signal horn yet.

'More water.' Sezarre passed me a beaker and I drank obediently. The sun was striking up from the sandy surface of the practice floor like the blast from a roasting hearth, even though we were sitting in the shade of the bath-house.

'There, that is good.' Grival gave the sword blade one last wipe with an oiled rag and laid his whetstone aside. I should say it was; I could have shaved with the edge he had put on it had that been allowed.

'Thank you.' I hadn't been looking for Grival to turn up, expecting he would be staying close to Mahli and little Nai, but he had appeared without ceremony and taken it upon himself to check all my weapons and armour. He placed the sword next to my mail-shirt; I wasn't about to put that on until the very last moment possible.

'This man, he is older than you by some years. The heat, the armour, losing much sweat, all of this will tire him the sooner,' remarked Grival thoughtfully. 'You could use that to your advantage.'

'If this was a fair fight, then yes, I would look to draw him out, keep him moving until he tired.' I scowled at the circle marked on the white sand in charcoal. 'But I still think he will find a way to use magic. Can you appeal to Shek Kul for me, ask him to forbid the chanting?'

'I will denounce him myself and ask it as a boon,' Sezarre nodded. 'You look to finish him as soon as possible?'

'How stiff is your leg? You need to be able to move against a mace.' Grival wiped moisture from his own brow. 'A blade may glance off a hauberk but that mace will leave a bruise wherever it lands. That could hamper you if he lands too many blows.'

'I'll be looking to cut him as early as I can,' I said grimly. 'He's going to bleed freely with the exertion and the heat. I want him to weaken quickly; with luck that'll stop his magic as well.'

Sezarre and Grival nodded as one, their faces grim at the thought of enchantment polluting this fight. 'Try not to shed his blood outside the circle,' warned Grival solemnly. 'You are here to protect the domain as well as assert the truth.'

I wondered exactly what he meant by that and looked up at the sky again; the sun didn't appear to have moved any further on. 'Have either of you ever fought like this, as a test of truth?'

Sezarre shook his head. 'It is very rare. I can understand why Laio did not expect such an outcome.'

I grimaced a little at his implied rebuke, only too aware that he and Gar must have heard all my dealings with Laio the previous night. To my relief everyone was continuing to treat me just as they always had, and anyway I was too preoccupied with this forthcoming fight to feel particularly self-conscious.

'I saw such a test in the domain of Lys Izat.' Grival looked up from wrapping his sword-cleaning kit in its cotton bag. 'It was to resolve an accusation of murder, but that was three years ago.'

'Why do you think Shek Kul chose to do this?' I was curious to know what they thought.

'It will send a message through all the domains,' stated Sezarre with considerable satisfaction. 'That magic will not be tolerated, in any form.'

'If these enchanters are looking to worm their way into our lands, I don't suppose Kaeska is the only fool they have seduced,' Grival added. 'Her fate will give any others who are tempted pause for thought.' I liked the certainty in his tone, his confidence that Kaeska's doom was already sealed. I wondered if he was right – were other Elietimm trying to suborn those with influence among the Aldabreshi and, if so, just what was their plan? I tucked the question away, one more to address after I had met this present challenge.

'Do you fight like this on the mainland at all, one to one? Have you experience that will help you?' Sezarre's hesitant question surprised me, given how much effort he and Grival always put in to reminding me I was supposedly an Islander now, all past life as surely lost as the morning mists off the mountain.

I leaned back against the wall of the bath-house and shut my eyes for a moment, trying to summon up a memory of the fresh frosts of a Toremal winter amidst the heavy and humid heat of the Archipelago. 'We fight one man against another as a test of skill sometimes, when all the Great Lords gather to make treaties with each other.' That was going to be about as much explanation as Grival and Sezarre would understand of the Convocation of Princes at Winter Solstice. 'Each Lord puts forward his best men and a contest decides the finest.' Aiten had won the last time we'd both attended and carried off a heavy purse, soon lightened by our celebrations. Esquire Camarl, Messire's nephew, had asked me privately if I had wanted to compete this time and understood instantly when I told him I hadn't the heart for it.

I opened my eyes abruptly. This wasn't the time to be dwelling on memories of home, though I made a mental note to watch for the bastard striking at my head. Such strokes were banned in the formal contests I was used to and I didn't want to be caught unawares, lulled into expecting the same rules to apply.

'You have killed before?' Grival was clearly expecting that I had.

'Yes, when I have had to.' My unemotional reply won satisfied nods from them both.

The signal horn sounded and we all started. I rose to my feet and began some stretching exercises, determined to meet this challenge with every possible preparation. People began filing into the practice ground, the early arrivals taking the best spots under the broad-leafed trees. Some eager youngsters decided to forsake shade in the hopes of a better view and climbed on to the roof of the bath-house, sharing pockets of nuts and waterskins. As I looked round I realised most of the free Islanders were here; another occasion when the main gates would be standing open, thronged with people, while I had no chance of slipping out unnoticed. I discarded the irrelevance as Sezarre and Grival began to armour me, focusing my mind entirely on the contest to come.

A rise in the level of sound all around alerted us to the arrival of Shek Kul and his wives. Three chairs had been set below a broad canopy on the far side of the practice ground and Gar and Laio took their seats composedly, tucking their silk skirts around their ankles. Each was dressed in a modest, everyday dress, scant makeup and limited jewels. Laio raised her hand in a half-wave and I nodded to her, noting her calm face and posture. For all her abandoned passion last night, her manner to me this morning had been the same as it ever was, something I had to admit came as a relief.

Shek Kul was standing in the centre of the charcoal circle, robed in much the same style as the women, a slave at his elbow carrying a carved and pierced gourd. The Warlord took it and released a lizard from it, all eyes on the scaly creature as it darted this way and that before finally dashing for the cover of a bush laden with blossoms. A murmur of approval ran around the crowd and I was pleased to see Grival and Sezarre nodding and smiling at me. Whatever the nonsense signified, it seemed to be working in my favour.

The crowd then lost interest in the bush and parted to admit Kaeska and the Ice Islander. Kaeska wore a similar dress to Laio and Gar but had a long and quite dense veil covering her face, secured with an ornate arrangement of hairpins. I looked across the killing ground to see Laio and Gar exchange a questioning look and a shrug of incomprehension.

'Why has she covered her face?' I asked Grival as he laced

my hauberk tight to my hips. 'Is that usual?' I hauled my belt in another notch and then loosened it again, finding it constricted my breathing too much.

Grival looked puzzled. 'No, not as I understand the rite.' He shrugged. 'May be she is worried that something in her looks will give her away.'

As good as his word, Sezarre had crossed the circle to speak to Shek Kul. The Warlord inclined his head and nodded with a serious expression; his gaze followed Sezarre's hand, outstretched towards the Elietimm. Shek Kul summoned the priest with an imperious wave of his hand and spoke to him sternly, emphasising his words with a series of sharp gestures. The Elietimm bowed his head in acquiescence, nodding humbly, too readily for my peace of mind, given enchantment had to be part of his strategy somehow. Moving slowly to the place marked for me inside the dark circle, I wondered what the bastard was going to try first as I flexed my fingers inside my close-fitting gloves.

His face gave me no hint, barely visible beneath a helm that reached down to his neck and curved round to guard his cheeks. I studied his armour; laced mail plates protected his shoulders and gut over what looked to be a boiled leather base. With the padding I could see under it, he was going to be sweating like a dray horse, but then so was I, so that would balance the runes. My beard was already soaked with perspiration, but I ignored the unpleasant sensation. This was no time to give way to petty distractions. A flexible leather cuirass covered the priest's thighs above steel greaves. As always, that left his knees the most vulnerable point. All in all, I had more protection from my mail and helm, especially with the studded leather leggings Grival had produced from somewhere, but I was carrying much more weight and in this heat, with the water we would be sweating away, that was going to count if the fight went on too long. More than ever, I decided to finish this as fast as I could, settling my helm firmly on my head and sliding the nasal bar down to lock it in position.

With us both in position, Shek Kul took his place between

Gar and Laio, Kaeska seated to one side on a low stool, head bowed beneath her veil. I drew a deep breath and focused on the Elietimm to the exclusion of all else as the Warlord clapped his hands together, the abrupt sound echoing back from the surrounding buildings. For a long moment neither of us moved then the Elietimm took a cautious pace sideways and the fight was begun.

I moved slowly, sword at the ready, assessing what I was facing. He was using a long mace, a foot soldier's weapon, the flanged metal head with a collar of spikes on a haft of black wood reinforced with strips of steel. No chance of simply hacking through that, then. I wasn't used to seeing such a complex guard on a mace though; it almost enveloped his hand and gave his knuckles unassailable protection. I noted the poniard at his belt as well and resolved to spare what attention I could for his off hand, also protected by a heavy plated gauntlet, which would at least make drawing that dagger a clumsy task.

We continued to circle, just out of each other's reach, feet scuffing up the sand, sweat already beading our faces. I wanted to go for his knees but wasn't about to risk lowering my stance and catching that mace on the side of my head, helm or no helm. He made a move, a darting step towards me and I took a rapid pace backwards, sword at the ready. He didn't follow it up, instead shaking his head at me with a mocking smile. Let him grin; I wasn't some first-season recruit about to let any taunt distract me. I'd spit in his face, if I got the chance; see how he liked that. Lost temper kills more men than lost swords – I reminded myself of the sergeant-at-arms' words back home.

I stopped the circling and swayed from side to side, transferring my weight from one foot to the other, assessing his balance and stance. A backhanded downward sweep nearly reached him, but he caught my blade with the head of his mace, circling it up and around, trying to catch the blade in the sword-breaking spikes as I fought equally hard to free it up. I pulled the blade loose and the priest leaped backwards just in time to escape a blow to the gap between shoulder and helm that would have taken his head off if I'd landed it. The bastard caught my blade again, putting all his effort into denying me another stroke until I ripped the sword free. Taking a pace backwards myself, I looked for the next opportunity. Against another sword I'd have aimed to trade a flurry of blows, sending the killing stroke through any hesitation in the response. This was clearly not going to be an option here, not against a mace used like this; I was starting to think the Ice Islander was looking to draw the fight out until the heat and the weight of my armour started to slow me down. I could tell already that my reactions were just that little bit faster than his, my blows just that little bit harder, my feet just that little bit lighter in the dry sand. I reminded myself not to grow overconfident.

I lunged, he parried, I got my sword back fast for a round, high swing, he swept it aside and as my blade slide down the mace's shaft, I leaned into it, shoving him backwards, nearly taking him off his feet. I followed up my advantage, hitting him with rapid strokes that he could only defend against, giving him no chance to tie up my blade again. A feint deceived him and I got a full-bodied blow in on his side, the finely honed blade gouging into the black leather, the weight of the stroke punishing his ribs sorely. As he retreated around the circle, I looked for a chance at his knees, sending him jumping backwards with a low sweep before dodging back myself to avoid his riposte.

That was when I first felt it: a scratching; a tapping; insistent fingers running along the edges of the doors to my mind. I set my jaw and went for the bastard, sending fast, short feints to either side until his guard faltered and I thrust for his guts. He turned sideways just in time as my step took me forward; we stood there, helmets almost touching, hands trapped between our bodies and I saw his lips were motionless inside his concealing cheek guards. No words from him were raising whatever demon had escaped Poldrion's vigilance to pick away at my consciousness. As I thought this, the gnawing sensation redoubled.

I threw the Elietimm away from me but he came back with renewed vigour. Now I had no time to spare to wonder who was working this cursed enchantment as I dodged and shifted, fighting to turn every defensive move into a chance to regain the initiative. All the while the feeling of being undermined, that my defences were crumbling, grew stronger and stronger. In a burst of desperation I unleashed a storm of blows on him, sacrificing my own protection in an all-out assault, taking a few bruising blows myself but managing to leave some telling cuts on the priest's arms and legs. I withdrew, satisfied, careful to avoid the treacherous patches of blood-stained sand, happy to let the Elietimm go back on the defensive now he had bleeding injuries to drain his strength.

A ripping noise tore through my head. Cold talons dug themselves into my mind and clenched themselves, sending my senses reeling. The hot sunlight faded before my eyes, and I could feel nothing beneath my feet. The sounds of the crowd died to nothing as I gasped and stumbled, knees as weak as water, head swimming. Some instinct pulled me away from a mace stroke that would have sent my brains rattling in my skull, but I could only watch the bastard prepare for his next stroke, unable to move as the black iron flanges came hammering in towards my blurring eyes, wrestling as I was with the grasping hatred that was clawing at my wits.

My sword met the stroke, turning it fluently aside. My feet followed up the move, spreading my weight, light and balanced, as my hands launched a series of piercing thrusts. I could only look on in astonishment, locked in a frantic struggle for possession of my own mind, as some other intelligence took over my body and defended it against everything the Ice Islander could do. I was dimly aware of a long, shadowy hand overlaying my own work-hardened fingers as they wrapped around the sword hilt, the great blue stone of a signet ring catching the sunlight. My mind was stumbling a step or two behind my body, struggling as I was with the clutching hands of the magic trying to drag me down into the blackness. Someone else's emotions were running through my veins, stiffening my sinews, guiding my every move. I could feel an eagerness, a resolution, a youthful energy and above all an implacable

hatred of the Elietimm and all his kind, but somehow I was
isolated from it, as if I were lost in a fever dream.

The priest went down, stumbling on a sticky patch of sand,
weakened by the punishment he had taken. I watched from
some distant corner of my mind as the long hands sent blow
after hammering blow down on the Elietimm's back, head and
shoulders as he rolled, this way and that, feet kicking, mace
flailing, trying to evade the razor-sharp blade as it gouged into
his armour, his skin and the raw red flesh beneath, his blood
running freely. A voice that was not my own came from my
lips, Tormalin words ringing with an archaic cadence I had
only ever heard in poetry and law courts.

*'Go back to your master and tell him this land is ours. We will
hold what we have won from the wilderness to the last man!'*

The priest looked up in startled horror, his face paling
beneath the mask of blood and sweat. He gabbled an incantation
and was suddenly no longer there, leaving only a welter of
blood-stained sand before my eyes.

The place erupted with noise, but all I could hear was the
frantic shouting inside my head.

'What is this? Who are you? Where am I?'

I sank to my knees, ripping off my helm, my gauntlets,
clutching my head as I summoned every measure of strength
I possessed to force that panic-stricken presence out of my
mind. With a suddenness that left me gasping, it was gone,
leaving my skull echoing with a hollow silence in the midst
of the deafening uproar. I looked at my hands; they were my
own again, no shadows blurring them, but I saw that I bore a
pale mark and a dent in the flesh around the long finger of
my sword hand. Anyone would say that I habitually wore a
broad ring with one central stone, now somehow lost.

'Ry-shad, where are you hurt?' I looked up to see the captain
of the guard peering at me with wide-eyed concern.

'I'm bruised but I'll be fine.' I turned my head to try to find
Grival and Sezarre, wondering why they had not been first to
my side. I was more than satisfied with what I saw. Grival had
Kaeska face down in the dirt, kneeling on her thighs as he tied

her hands securely behind her back. Sezarre was using that cursed veil of hers to gag her securely, pulling her head up at a cruel angle with a hand twisted hard in her hair. The bitch, the whoring, murderous bitch; that poisonous enchantment had to have been her work. No wonder she'd been veiled. Too bad her tame sorcerer had fled his fate, leaving her condemned before all the Islanders to suffer who only knew what fate.

'Ryshad!' Shek Kul's abrupt summons silenced the assembled Islanders so thoroughly I could hear the heedless chirping of the birds in a distant tree. Getting to my feet, stumbling slightly as my knees still seemed to be looking for someone else to give their instructions, I crossed the bloody sand to stand before him.

'The truth condemns the woman Kaeska and she will pay the price,' said the Warlord in an unemotional voice. 'You are vindicated, but I find much to trouble me in this matter. This magician has singled you out and you say there has been much strife between his people and those that were yours before you came to this place.' Shek Kul's voice grew a little louder, to carry his words unmistakably to the outer reaches of the avid crowd. 'I truly believe that you are innocent of any taint of magic, the omen of Rek-a-nul declares this. However, there is a very real danger that these men will seek you out, to avenge their comrade. I cannot keep you here, to risk bringing such pollution to the domain.'

Laio stirred in her seat, subsiding as Shek Kul's head moved as if about to turn and look at her. I stared at the man, wondering what in Dastennin's name he was saying. Shek Kul folded his arms as he studied me. 'You will leave this place as soon as the execution is complete.'

Turning on his heel, the Warlord strode from the practice ground, Gar catching Laio under the elbow to force her along, Grival and Sezarre hauling Kaeska between them, cruel hands gripping her shoulders, not even allowing her to regain her feet when she stumbled, but dragging her along to score her knees on the gravel of the path. A hand from somewhere thrust a waterskin at me and I emptied it in a handful of parched gulps before taking a cup of thin wine from the steward whose wide smile was belied by the fear in his eyes.

'Come.' I followed the captain of the guard numbly to the barracks, where I stripped and washed in a quiet corner, my mind in turmoil at this unexpected turn of events. Finding everyone else keeping a constant arm's length away from me, I was anointing my various bruises and scrapes with a selection of Sezarre's ointments when a murmur of surprise made me look round. I turned to find that the guards had all melted away. Shek Kul was standing there, looking at me thoughtfully.

'Let me.' He held out a hand and I gave him the pot of salve, not knowing what else to do. Obeying his gesture, I turned and felt him rubbing the pungent balm into a vicious bruise on my shoulder.

'You have done me a great service, in many ways, by ridding me of Kaeska,' he remarked. 'I always knew she would become ever more dangerous when her brother was killed. Once I no longer needed the alliance of her marriage she knew I would get the domain an heir and stop indulging her nonsense. In many ways, you are a very good slave. I know Laio thinks so and there would be much you could teach her, given time. Yet you remind me of a hawk I once had, taken wild too late and only trained with harshness. He was a fine bird, brave and fearless, swift to fly but always slow to return to the lure.' Shek Kul handed the little jar over my shoulder and I turned to face him.

'I could always see that bird looking for the mountain heights,' said the Warlord simply, 'even when he was hooded and leashed in the mews. In the end, I untied his jesses myself and let him fly. I think this is the only reward I can give you that would mean anything to you.'

I opened my mouth but he silenced me with an upraised hand. 'That would not be enough in itself to persuade me but there is the magic to consider.' His eyes were hard, searching my own. 'There was something wrong in that fight, something ill omened hanging round you. I cannot say what it was, but were you any other man, had the great serpent not appeared when you stood alone on the sands, I would have you killed under suspicion of sorcery. As it is I am content to let you go, provided you swear on whatever you consider most holy that you will not return.'

I swallowed on a suddenly dry mouth. 'I swear; may Dastennin drown me to cast me naked on the shore if I prove false.'

Shek Kul nodded, apparently satisfied. 'This token will guarantee you safe passage across the Archipelago.' He handed me a gold and jewelled medallion that would pretty much guarantee me a safe retirement if I ever brought it home.

'My thanks,' I said, quite unable to think of anything else.

'Now dress and we will deal with the traitor,' the warlord said grimly. 'As her accuser, your responsibility only ends with her death.'

I dragged on my clothes and followed obediently at his heels, wondering with a sick sensation exactly what I was about to witness as we left the compound and headed for the foreshore. Kaeska was lying on a wide wooden platform fixed to stakes at the high-tide mark, her hands and feet spread and tied. I tried hard not to react when I saw her eyes and mouth had been sealed with wax, burns scoring her skin. Her nostrils flared as she drew what frantic breaths she could. Shek Kul regarded her impassively for a moment then picked a large stone from the black sand of the beach and placed it firmly on Kaeska's breast bone. She flinched as if it had been a burning coal but could not dislodge it, pinioned as she was. As Shek Kul nodded to me, I reluctantly found a fist-sized rock and laid it next to his, averting my eyes from Kaeska's blind grimaces.

'You stay until she is dead.' Shek Kul strode away without a backward glance and I found myself standing there as a succession of Islanders came to add their weight to Kaeska's punishment, some in tears, some openly gloating, but all adding to the load that was slowly pressing her to death.

Gar came towards the middle of the afternoon as Kaeska was labouring to draw every breath, her colour sickly.

'Are you all right?' she asked, coming to stand next to me in the shade of the shoreline after laying her own middling sized stone with a sombre face.

I nodded. 'Tell me, what is the purpose of all this?' I was struggling with the measured cruelty of the execution. 'Why not just let me cut her head off.'

'Her blood would pollute the ground,' Gar shook her head soberly. 'Her mouth is closed so that she cannot curse anyone and her eyes are shut so that her gaze cannot contaminate anything it falls upon. Kaeska has committed a high crime against the domain, against the people and the land, and in this execution all share in her death. When she is dead, all her belongings will be piled on the corpse and burned, to destroy everything that has ever linked her to this place. The sea will carry away the ashes and the defilement with them.' She sighed. 'I know how you mainlanders speak of us, as bloodthirsty savages, always at war with each other. In truth, we value life, we value it highly, so when we have to take a life like this, we make sure the nature of that death makes its own statement.'

Gar, like Shek, did not look back as she left the beach, making her way back to the residence through the Islanders who continued to come to share in this incomprehensible rite. Laio came some while later as the line was thinning out somewhat. She was carrying a large stone that took her all her strength and both hands and it must have come from somewhere in the residence. Panting as she raised it in front of her chest, she dropped it hard on the heap now covering Kaeska's torso. A feeble whimper escaped the tormented woman and Laio leaped backwards as if she'd been bitten by a snake, looking round wildly. Seeing me, she came to sit on the dry sand beneath the fringed trees.

'I wanted to end it for her,' she murmured softly.

'That will have helped,' I assured her.

'Where will you go?' Laio's voice shook. I reached for her little hand, giving it a comforting squeeze, not caring if this was inappropriate.

'I'll be fine, once I'm out of the Islands. I'll go back to my old master.' I managed a rather bleak smile.

Laio pointed at the harbour where several large galleys were swinging at anchor, more heading in down the channel between the islands. 'That crimson pennant, that is the mark of Sazac Joa. If I speak to the captain, he'll give you passage. I will make sure that all your belongings are loaded aboard.' Laio lifted her chin to quell a trembling lip.

'That's very good of you.'

'Not really,' admitted Laio with a shadow of her old manner. 'Shek Kul told me to make sure you left nothing behind that might taint the domain.'

That made sense. Laio rose to her feet and brushed sand from her dress. 'I'll send Sezarre down with some food,' she promised over her shoulder.

'Thank you,' I called as I steeled myself to check the pulse in Kaeska's neck again. Her skin was clammy to the touch but the faint beat of her life still pushed against my fingers. I sighed and sat down again to wait out this grim vigil.

Kaeska took three long days and nights to die.

*The coast east of the settlement, Kel Ar'Ayen,
34th of Aft-Spring, Year Two of the Colony*

'How's the river bed, captain?' Temar looked up from making painstaking notations in his journal as the weather-beaten seaman stood before him, wide stance secure on the deck as the ship rode the gentle swell.

'Sound enough, the anchor will hold. The old *Eagle* will nest safe enough here for a while.' The thick-set sailor patted the mast with affectionate satisfaction, a smile creasing his leathery face and softening the scowl moulded from his bushy brows by a lifetime squinting in the sun and wind. 'I've set Meig to keep an eye on the tide and the run of the river.'

'Good.' Temar got up from his seat beside the lateen-rigged aft-mast and stretched his cramped shoulders, half inclined to shed his stout hide jerkin in the strengthening sunshine. He looked around the broad estuary, thickly forested hills dropping sharply to an open beach of shingle and scrub, winding away inland on the banks of a wide, brownish river that offered tempting access to the mysteries of the hidden interior. The fitful breeze brought an alluring fragrance from the burgeoning woodlands. Temar took a deep breath of the scent of spring. 'They would surely have put in here to take on supplies, wouldn't they, Master Grethist?'

The captain nodded. 'They had fair copies of the Sieur's charts, just the same as us, the ones he made when he was exploring the coastline with the Seafarer and they're good for another six days' sailing beyond here. This place is marked clear enough as a good anchorage with game and fresh water to be had.'

Temar moved and leaned over the rail of the stern, sighing.

'So where are they? Could they have come to grief? I suppose things will have changed, sandbars and the like, those charts must be what, eighteen or nineteen years old by now.'

'I know Master Halowis,' the mariner folded his arms as he too gazed at the shoreline. 'He knows to take care sailing in strange waters. In any case, if they'd come to grief, we'd have seen sign of it. We found the wreck of the *Windchime* and she was lost on the crossing last year, wasn't she? That was still plain enough, even after a whole winter of high seas tearing it up – her cargo was scattered all along the strand.'

'I suppose a storm could have hit them,' mused Temar. 'They did set out barely halfway through For-Spring, but no one was prepared to wait until the Equinox, given the weather seemed set fair.'

'It would have to be some storm for all three ships to founder without at least one making it to land and no survivors washed ashore.' Grethist shook his head stubbornly. 'We'd have seen sign of weather that severe as well, uprooted trees and the like.'

Temar shrugged. 'So what do you suppose befell them? Sickness, disease, falling prey to beasts when they put ashore? We're talking about eighty-some men, Dastennin help them!'

'I'll get the longboat launched.' The captain set his square, grey-bearded jaw. 'If they made landfall here, there'll be fire-pits and such, some sign, and we should be able to get some idea of when they landed, how many they were. That should give us something to work on. Maybe they've headed up this river, it looks as if it should be navigable a fair way inland. Wasn't that something they were supposed to be doing?'

'You're probably right.' Temar nodded, the tension in the back of his mind easing at this eminently reasonable suggestion. 'Still, we don't know what's prowling these forests, do we? Make sure the rowers take weapons with them, swords for those that have them and the ship's axes for those that don't. Let's not take any chances.'

He stood with Grethist and watched as the crew lowered the shallow ship's boat down to the glassy surface of the estuary, oars hitting the water with a crack that echoed back from the distant hills.

'Can I speak with you for a moment, Temar?'

'Demoiselle.' Temar turned and bowed to Guinalle with precisely calculated courtesy.

She ignored the faint provocation in his greeting but swept him an ironic curtsey more suited to a silken robe than the practical grey woollen dress she was wearing. 'There's something wrong,' she stated abruptly. 'I can feel something peculiar, just hovering beyond my comprehension, a threat of some kind.'

'Quietly, please.' Temar looked round to see if anyone had overheard this unnerving pronouncement, relieved to see the remaining sailors absorbed in watching the longboat make its slow way inshore. 'What exactly are you telling me?'

'I don't exactly know,' admitted Guinalle, her frustration plain to see as she tucked her hands inelegantly through her braided leather girdle. 'I can't put my finger on it but something's wrong. Avila and I have been reaching out to see if we can find anyone to contact; the expedition may have been lost, but I can't believe no one survived.'

'But you can't find anyone?' interrupted Temar.

'It's not that, exactly.' Guinalle frowned. 'It's more as if I'm trying to look through a fog. Avila says it's like trying to shout when you're wearing a veil.'

'You were saying yourself that working Artifice from a ship was causing some odd effects,' Temar reminded her, a suspicion of satisfaction in his voice. 'Perhaps things work differently on this side of the ocean. There was that business when the far-seeing to the mines went all wrong, wasn't there?'

'That was seldom-used Artifice in barely trained hands,' insisted Guinalle. 'I am arguably one of the best practitioners anywhere in the Empire and this is a skill I mastered long ago. This is different, Temar, you have to believe me. There's a danger out there and everyone needs to be alert for a sign of it. Avila feels it too, just a little but enough to convince me it's real.'

Temar raised a hand to silence her, frowning. 'All right, I take your word for it. What do you want me to do? You say we're in peril, but you can't tell me how or why. Look around you, these men are tense enough; they had friends, brothers aboard the ships we're searching for. They're already worried enough about still failing to find any trace of them.' He realised his words were sounding harder than he intended and tried to soften his tone. 'Please understand me; it's not that I don't believe you, I do, honestly. It's just that I'm simply not prepared to make a potentially bad situation worse by giving out some vague warning of danger when I can't answer the first question that anyone puts to me about it. When you have something definite to tell me, something I can explain to the crew, I will act. Until then, please keep this quiet; we have enough problems to handle without adding unfounded fears.'

Guinalle's lips were thin with irritation and a faint flush of anger reddened her cheeks. 'Of course, Esquire, my duty to you. I'll do what I can.' She turned on her heel and strode briskly away, neck and shoulders stiff with annoyance, soft shoes hissing across the polished decking.

Temar watched her go with a sinking feeling compounded of contrition and exasperation. When would he be able to have a conversation with Guinalle without one or other of them giving or taking offence in some way? He was doing his best to avoid her, since she'd made it clear she wanted no part of him, Saedrin curse it, but given the seriousness of this situation, Den Fellaemion had insisted on putting Guinalle and her deftest pupils aboard.

'Did the Demoiselle have some word for you?' Master Grethist's curt enquiry pushed Temar's personal turmoil aside.

'Not as such, nothing important.' Temar smiled in what he hoped was a convincing manner.

The sailor took a pouch from the pocket of his rough, sailcloth tunic, helping himself to chewing leaf before offering Temar some as an afterthought. 'Setting out this way, finding no answers, the lads are starting to ask questions.

Have you heard how the other expedition fared, the one that headed south?'

'Yes, of course.' Temar shook his head at the offer of leaf and at his own stupidity for not sharing his news. 'I should have told you, I'm sorry. From what they've reported, it seems that coast runs pretty well due south for a hundred and sixty leagues or so, and then it curves round back to run east and north, up a long sound fed by a massive river, about eighty, ninety leagues inland overall. It's excellent land for running cattle on by all accounts, not nearly so much timber as these northern and eastern reaches.'

The captain's eyes brightened. 'That sounds promising, somewhere to think about taking the young stock calved this year.'

'It's looking very good,' agreed Temar. 'Messire Den Rannion is already talking about founding a new settlement there before the turn of the year. As far as he can judge, it'll only be a scant hundred leagues from the port overland, less from the mines.'

'Maybe so, but that'll be over some vicious, steep ground, won't it?' Grethist laughed nevertheless. 'I'll take sail to see it, until they build a decent high road.'

Temar smiled. 'I'll hitch a ride with you, Master.'

A shout from above turned the mariner's head and Temar turned his attention back to his journal, leafing through it to find the news of the southern expedition that Guinalle had relayed to him just after they had set out on this voyage. That had come from one of Guinalle's most recently trained Adepts, hadn't it? Artifice had kept that other flotilla firmly linked to the port, information passed back every second or third day. What had befallen this northern expedition, what had happened to the ships they were now seeking, that they had vanished so thoroughly without even a hint from the Adepts aboard? What sort of things might have affected the use of Artifice? How well skilled had the Adepts been who had joined the expedition? Temar stifled a regret at his ill-tempered decision to abandon his own studies of Artifice during the

winter seasons, unable to stand being in such close contact
with Guinalle on a daily basis.

'Sail ho!'

Temar's head snapped round at the look-out's bellow, jaw
dropping in disbelief. Jostled by eager sailors, he forced his way
to the rail to see a three-masted ship round the far headland, a
full load of sail rigged.

'Who is it?' a voice rang out from behind, frustrated at not
being able to see.

'Looks like the *Salmon*!' came the reply, supported by noises
of agreement and delight all round. Temar squinted at the
fast approaching vessel, looking for the rune at its bow, all
but obscured by flying foam, cheers all around as the sailors
waved and whistled.

'Temar! Temar!' Guinalle's frantic shout dragged Temar
back away from the side of the ship. He pushed his way up the
steps to the stern where Guinalle stood wringing her hands next
to the captain. The sailor was starting to frown, a hand shading
his deep-set eyes as he peered at the rapidly closing ship.

'They're not flying any flag at all, not even their pennant. I'd
expect a signal too, given the situation,' Grethist murmured,
doubt colouring his tone.

'I can't reach them, Temar,' Guinalle caught at his sleeve,
'something's desperately wrong on board that ship!"

Temar looked past her towards the captain. 'I can see our
lads, plain enough,' Grethist went on slowly, 'but they're not
working the lines, nor managing their sail.'

'Every mind on that ship is closed to me, Temar,' Guinalle
insisted. 'I know some of that crew, I should be able to reach
them from here!'

'Run a signal, Meig!' bellowed the captain suddenly. 'Can't
they see we're at anchor?'

A flurry of disquiet ran through the waiting crew as the
long looked-for ship continued to come up the estuary at a
reckless pace.

'Temar!' Guinalle shook his arm, a gesture of fear and
frustration in equal measure.

'They're going to broadside us, if they—' The mariner shook his grizzled head in disbelief. 'Meig, cut the anchor! All of you, get some sail aloft, we've got to get underway – brace yourself, my lady.'

The captain jumped down from the aftcastle as the crew scrambled to get their ship moving, the second vessel swooping down on her with predatory intent. Temar grabbed at the rail with one hand, reaching for Guinalle with the other as the ships collided with a shattering crash. Guinalle was knocked clean off her feet and Temar to his knees, and several men went plummeting from the rigging into the foaming waters, yells of shock lost in the mounting clamour in deck. Temar struggled to his feet as the boats swung apart, tossing wildly, sails flapping in confusion. As he looked for any explanation of this turn of events he saw the men of the *Salmon* dropping like clubbed beasts, other forms leaping up from the waist of the ship to cast grapnels and ropes across the gap, hauling the vessels together. A sailor clinging desperately to the rail was crushed between the tall wooden walls, his scream of agony lost as howling figures in black leather leaped across the rails, short swords and axes naked in their hands. The sailors grabbed whatever was at hand to defend themselves with, belaying pins and rope spikes, belt knives raised in desperation.

Temar vaulted over the rail of the aftcastle, drawing his long sword and catching several of the invaders unawares, their blood making the decking treacherous beneath his feet as they fell beneath his wrathful blade. The others drew back a little, cold blue eyes assessing him as Temar looked for his own opening, glaring at flaxen heads pale above studded leather armour. These were soldiers, Temar realised belatedly. Where were they from?

'Cut the ropes!' Grethist's bellow lifted above the tumult, a roar to rise above the direst of storms. Temar darted forward to protect a handful of sailors as they sawed desperately at the taut hemp holding the clinging irons fast, jumping to avoid an attacker falling at his feet in agony, a rope spike embedded in one eye. Temar sent the metal deep into the man's skull with a heavy stamp of his boot and kicked the corpse aside. As more assailants pressed on over the rail, Temar dodged and weaved, skills born of long practice saving him from anything worse than a stinging scratch to one arm as a blade ripped through the linen of his sleeve. That reminder of his lack of protection sobered Temar a little, though with his leather jerkin and buff breeches, he was still better off than the sailors in their sailcloth tunics and trews. Even a spent blow could rip through the fabric and every bleeding cut would weaken.

He hacked at a questing axe, shoving the haft aside to open the man's defences. With a deft thrust he caught the unbalanced soldier at the angle of neck and shoulder, the keen blade contemptuous of studded leather, biting deep into bone and flesh. The axe fell to the deck, the clatter lost in the uproar as the man stumbled blindly to fall over the side.

'Ware feet!' Temar yelled as he kicked the loose weapon backwards to arm any sailor who could grab it. As his next victim fell away in a flurry of gore, legs cut from beneath him, two more came at Temar abreast but he had the reach on them with his longer blade and soon felled them for an eager pair of sailors to finish with their belt knives. Further assault broke and faltered on a rapidly improvised barrier of spars and captured weapons as the crew rallied to support Temar, bringing all the savagery of dockside brawls to bear in the battle, kicking, gouging, spitting, biting as the sailors dodged to get inside the reach of swords and axes and bring their own crude weapons to bear with devastating effect. A shudder ran through the vessels as the *Eagle* fought to pull free.

A yell from behind hauled Temar's head round. One sailor had managed to free a grapnel, gouging his hand grievously in the process. Now he dropped to his knees, screaming as he clutched at his head, eyes stark with terror and pain. A second fell, convulsing, howling. Temar spared them a horrified glance before looking round wildly for any explanation of this unexpected turn of events.

'Temar!' Guinalle's shout tore through the chaos. He found her instantly, on her knees on the stern deck, skirts all stained and bloodied to the elbows as she tried to help a dying sailor. Temar looked frantically for any black-clad figure threatening her but could see none.

'It's him, that man, up in the prow. He's the one with the Artifice!' Guinalle shouted, her voice hoarse with effort. She shrieked abruptly, her own hands rising to claw at her eyes before she managed to control them. Falling forward, she lay there, panting for a moment that seemed an eternity to Temar before dragging herself upright again, jaw set, eyes huge in her white face. 'Kill him!' she screamed, shrill as a stricken hawk.

Temar looked at the motionless figure high in the prow of the entangled *Salmon* and took a breath to assess their situation. The crew of the *Eagle* were holding their line, the air thick with curses. A flutter of colour overhead caught Temar's eye. Aloft in the rigging, Meig and a couple of others were raising a signal to bring the longboat back with reinforcements and weapons. The bastards, Temar realised with sudden, impotent fury; they had been standing off behind that headland, waiting until the *Eagle* was weakened by the departure of half her complement. Guinalle might not have been able to see them but somehow that bastard in the long cloak had been spying on the Tormalin ship as he held the strings of the marionettes he had made of the innocent colonists. Just as Temar thought this a hapless figure fell headlong from the ropes above his head, Meig making no move to save himself with nerveless hands as he crashed to the deck to lie motionless in a broken huddle.

Temar lifted one foot on to the swaying rail, one hand reaching up for a rope as the ships struggled against each other, planks splintering, lines creaking under the strain, canvas snapping overhead. His sword was ready in his other hand, the razor-sharp edge showing silver through the clotting blood choking the fuller.

'Who's with me?' he yelled, all the while judging the narrowing gap as the *Salmon* swung back into the battered side of the *Eagle*. Satisfied with the bloodthirsty howls at his back, Temar leaped, putting every effort he possessed into his jump, falling to his hands and knees on the far deck, sword nevertheless poised and ready. Thuds behind him announced the arrival of a handful of the *Eagle*'s crew, eager to make use of their captured weaponry.

'Ramsen!' Temar saw one of his men drop his guard as he gaped at a figure rolled this way and that by the plunging motion of the trapped vessels. 'They're lost!' Temar shouted harshly, his own stomach hollow as he recognised a face slack and white among the fallen crew of the *Salmon*. 'Watch yourselves!'

The enemy were quick to react to this unexpected counter-attack and a close-knit detachment was making its way down the deck, blades raised. Temar steadied himself, his longer sword at the ready to defend and to rend, but half an eye spared for the tall figure in the forecastle, blond hair blowing in the breeze, a gold gorget bright at his throat as he focused all his attention and skills on the attack on the other ship.

An axe came scything in at Temar's head but he blocked the blow with ease, following up to force the man backwards. Taking a pace forward but careful not to outstrip the others behind him, Temar cut and sliced, feinted and parried, less to kill than to gradually force those opposing him into a gradual retreat up the ship. He focused all his efforts on the men before him, trusting the sailors at his back and the stout defence of the ship's rail to his off hand. Step by step, Temar and his men drew closer to the enemy Artificer, who abruptly turned to face them, arms raised, hands spread, hatred twisting his face as he spat at them in an unknown, harsh-accented tongue.

The air before Temar seemed to shimmer and ripple, the faces before him distorted as if seen through poor glass. The deck beneath his feet suddenly felt rough and broken, like a rocky road. Temar took a pace forward but his footing shifted and slipped, snarls as of wild beasts echoing all around him, greedy and eager for blood. The hair on Temar's neck rose as every instinct told him to flee and he heard cries of dismay and terror from the men behind him. Temar shook his head in frenzied denial and furiously ransacked his memory for the wards and defences that Guinalle had been teaching him before their friendship had foundered.

'Tur ryal myn ammel,' he yelled, screwing his eyes shut for a scant breath to put every effort he could summon into throwing the Artificer's touch from his mind. Panting, he opened his eyes and found his gaze was clear again, more than that, the sailors at his back seemed to have recovered. Temar spared a moment to wonder just what the incantation he had half remembered was actually supposed to do.

The shouts of the enemy back aboard the *Eagle* grew suddenly louder, but now they were ringing with consternation rather than victory. A dull tremor shivered through the deck and rolled the lifeless body of another crewman at Temar's feet, threatening to trip him until he steeled himself to kick it aside. Tormalin voices suddenly rose in shouts of triumph from the other ship, taunts mingled with obscenities and curses. Temar spared a glance to see several of the black-clad invaders dropping their weapons to struggle, screaming, with some unseen threat, scrambling backward to escape some horror only they could see, one tumbling over the rail to vanish into the turbid waters as the ships swung apart and crashed back together. The soldiers facing Temar and his men fell back to the steps leading up to the aftcastle, weapons now ready to defend rather than to attack.

Temar looked back to the enemy Artificer and saw consternation mingled with hatred on the thin, lined face as the man stared at Guinalle, now standing on the aft deck, a circle of sailors defending her as she wrought unseen destruction on the attackers. As Temar watched a handful hurled themselves yelling towards her, felled even before they could bring blade to bear on the ring of wood and iron. The Artificer raised a hand, the threat in the gesture unmistakable, but a sudden lurch of the deck threw him off balance. Temar grabbed at the rail himself but a bark of humourless laughter escaped him nevertheless.

'The longboat!' One of the sailors shook Temar's shoulder and he nodded with grim satisfaction as he saw the returning

crew of the rowing-boat scrambling up over the distant rail
of the *Eagle*, weapons raised, fresh wrath pouring over the
attackers like a breaking sea, sweeping the black-clad figures
aside like so much flotsam. The deck swung beneath Temar's
feet again and he realised nearly all of the grappling irons had
been unhooked.

'We need to get back to the *Eagle*!' he shouted over his
shoulder, loud agreement coming from the sailors. They
retreated, slowly, weapons raised, alert for any sudden rush
from the enemy. Several of the black-clad assailants paced
them down the deck, just out of reach, taunts clear in their
unintelligible tongue. 'Ignore them.' Temar shook his head at
a sailor whose backwards steps had halted, captured axe eager
to rejoin the fray.

Temar felt inside the breast of his jerkin for his throwing
dagger. Retreating like this was all very well, but it was too slow.
As the ships writhed in the snapping toils of the ropes, he could
hear the snap and whistle of breaking hemp, every movement
as the wind tugged at the *Eagle*'s sails putting intolerable strain
on the remaining lines. He palmed the dagger as they drew level
with the remaining grapnels, relieved to hear eager shouts from
the *Eagle*'s deck, hands and ropes offering assistance.

'Make ready to go,' he commanded sternly, judging distance
and wind, wondering if he could do this.

'When?' demanded a sailor at his elbow.

'Now!' yelled Temar. He took a pace forward and brought
his hand up and back in one fluid movement, sending the
bright blade shooting the length of the vessel, a flash of silver
in the sunlight as it buried itself in the Artificer's chest. His
yell of agony halted the troops on deck who were just about
to fling themselves on the sailors desperately scrambling back
over the rails of the two ships, unable to defend themselves
adequately. As blond heads turned this way and that, Temar
and his men seized the moment of indecision to escape to the
Eagle, where waiting knives hacked through the last fibres of
the entangling ropes to free the vessel.

'Make sail and head for open water!' Captain Grethist

roared, his voice sending sailors scrambling into the rigging, hands still sticky with gore, clothing stained with their own blood and that of others. The *Eagle* moved on rising wings of white canvas to pull away from the *Salmon*, now drifting away at the mercy of wind and current as dark figures struggled with her ropes.

'We can't just abandon the *Salmon*!' a voice protested.

'How do we go about retaking her?' demanded Grethist scornfully, but his own outrage was plain on his twisted face as he moved to instruct the helmsman. 'No, we'll let those bastards look after her for a little while, just as long as it takes us to get back to port, raise a flotilla and come back to send every last fancy whore's son straight to Dastennin's feet!'

This prediction raised a general shout of agreement and defiance, insults hurled from every side as the *Salmon* finally got under way and lurched towards the distant headland.

'D'Alsennin!'

Temar looked towards the stern of the ship, trying to place the unfamiliar voice. He saw the tall, spare figure of Avila Tor Arrial on the aft-deck, struggling to support a fainting Guinalle.

'Here, let me,' Temar shoved his way through to the aftcastle and swept Guinalle up in his arms, alarmed by her extreme pallor.

'Let's get her to our cabin.' Avila silenced the startled questions of the sailors with an imperious look and hurried to open the doors to the accommodation in the rear of the ship. Temar laid Guinalle gently down on the narrow cot and clenched his hands in unconscious dismay as Avila deftly untied Guinalle's girdle, unlacing the high neck of her gown to check the pulse in her neck. The older woman bent her head close to Guinalle's, a grunt of satisfaction as she felt the girl's breath on her cheek.

'She'll do well enough. She's just exhausted herself.' Avila laid a fond hand on Guinalle's forehead, herb-stained fingers brown against the white skin.

Temar didn't know whether to be more relieved or furious

with Guinalle for giving him such a fright. 'She always thinks she can do everything herself,' he burst out. 'Is this the first time she's over-reached herself like this? Why can't she pace herself better?'

Avila was pouring water into a shallow bowl and paused, a linen cloth in her hand. 'The reason Guinalle has to do so much is the lack of other trained hands to lift the burden from her,' she said crisply. 'If enough people would come forward to be trained in Artifice, her life would be a great deal easier. The problem is that so many of those that start give up as soon as the studies become at all demanding.' She didn't bother concealing the contempt in her voice or in her eyes as she looked across the cramped cabin at Temar, brushing a wisp of greying hair back from her broad brow with the back of her hand.

'I had my reasons and I have my own duties,' Temar snapped. He looked at Guinalle again, a faint flush of pink starting to soften her cheeks again. 'Messire Den Fellaemion asks too much of her,' he said reluctantly, hating himself for the disloyalty.

'Messire Den Fellaemion is ill.' Avila sprinkled an aromatic oil from a tiny bottle and laid the dampened cloth across Guinalle's forehead. 'Guinalle's Artifice is just about the only thing keeping him on his feet some days.'

Temar gaped at her. 'You're not serious?'

'As plague spots, Esquire!' snapped Avila, wiping her hands heedlessly on her plain brown gown. 'If it weren't for Guinalle, he wouldn't see out the year. So she has to spend her time and strength on him as well as on all the other duties laid on her.'

'What am I supposed to do about it?' Temar demanded, more to defend himself than expecting any answer.

Avila gave him one nevertheless. 'Stop finding every excuse to leave the port to take your sulks about Guinalle off with you,' she glared at him. 'You're Den Fellaemion's obvious successor, boy! Stay and learn from him, take over some of the real work of the colony, stop gallivanting off up river and inland whenever someone offers you the chance. If Den Fellaemion has less to do, he will need to demand less of Guinalle, and she might have a chance to stop spending from the bottom of her purse all the time. Get yourself in hand, D'Alsennin! I've been watching how you behave towards Guinalle. Drianon save me, you're not the only boy who ever got turned down. Guinalle's not the first woman to see more important paths lying before her than just being a wife and mother!'

Pent-up grievance escaped Temar before he could restrain his tongue. 'And I have you to thank that she's taken them, haven't I? Guinalle kept mentioning your name when I was trying to find out what turned her against me. Just because you chose not to wed, I don't see you have the right to meddle in other people's happiness.'

Avila regarded him steadily, but her blue eyes were bright with a suspicion of tears. 'I would have wed, D'Alsennin, had my betrothed not died of that same Crusted Pox that took so many of your House to the Otherworld. My father died too and my mother was left an invalid; it fell to me to nurse her for the next four years, youngest and unlooked for daughter as I was. By then, with so many dead, any chance I had to marry had passed me by. But you're right, I did advise Guinalle to think very carefully before hampering herself with a husband, children and all the expectations of society. It's not as if there is any middle way, not now, not here. Guinalle has had education and opportunities I could only have ever dreamed of, and I would hate to see her cast them aside for a self-centred boy who has so much growing up left to do!'

Guinalle stirred in the bunk, a vague hand reaching for her forehead. Temar looked at her for a long moment, then, not trusting himself to speak, turned on his heel and slammed out of the cabin.

A trading islet in the domain of Sazac Joa,
the Aldabreshin Archipelago,
20th of For-Summer

I stepped out of the skiff on to the sand, hauling my baggage
out without any hand raised to help me. 'My thanks,' I said
curtly, but no one responded and I walked away without a
backward glance. It was hard to feel angry with the Aldabreshi
though, despite their lack of courtesy. However they sent their
messages with their flags and beacons, word of Kaeska's fate
had spread through the Archipelago like fire through dry brush
and Shek Kul's token, while securing me passage on whatever
vessel I wanted, also clearly identified me as the mainlander
who'd started the whole business. It was no real surprise that
wherever I went I found myself about as welcome as someone
who's lost their nose and half their fingers to creeping scab. I
walked slowly along the beach, looking at the signal pennants
flying at each masthead, trying to find the yellow and crimson
pattern the last galley-master had grudgingly shown me, identifying the next domain I needed to cross on this painfully slow
progress up the Archipelago. I sighed. The sun was sinking
behind a rocky island to the west and I didn't fancy another
night sleeping fitfully in a hollow of sand, hoping no one would
rob or knife me before I woke.

'You're a long way from home, Tormalin man.'

This unexpected greeting was sufficiently friendly that I
didn't reach instantly for my sword. In any case, given my
recent experiences, I was starting to feel rather wary of using
that blade for anything short of outright assault by a full detachment of Elietimm. I turned to see a short, coppery-skinned man
in a shabby tunic grinning at me. He was beardless and bald
as an egg, pate gleaming in the afternoon sun, but with the

right clothes and some hair he could have stepped off any dock anywhere along the coast of the Gulf of Lescar. There was a distinctly Lescari touch to his mongrel Tormalin as well.

'I could say the same of you, couldn't I?' I watched his dark eyes to judge the sincerity of his reply.

'Perhaps but I don't really have a home these days, not beyond my ship, anyway. That's her, the *Amigal*!' He waved a proud arm at one of the smaller vessels anchored in the narrow strait. Despite the Aldabreshin rigging and unfamiliar arrangement of mast and sail, it looked about the same size as the boats that ply the rivers and coasts on the Gulf coast of Tormalin, carrying a good weight of cargo but only needing a couple of men to manage it. That was interesting in itself, given the preponderance of massive galleys all around us, but more intriguing still was the array of white-bordered pennants strung down a long line from the top of the mast. This little ship and its unknown master had permission to trade their way through a double handful of domains.

I looked down impassively at the man, whose broad smile did not falter, and folded my arms. 'What do you want with me?' I demanded with just enough challenge to deter casual conversation.

'I'd have thought you'd be looking to do some business with me,' he replied with an engaging grin. 'I know who you are, Tormalin man. You're the slave to young Laio Shek, that helped her put that bitch Kaeska out to sea in ashes.' He wiped a hand over his mouth in an unconscious gesture I'd seen all too often lately, as people around me realised who I was. 'I'd say you'd pay handsomely for a quick passage home, instead of spending the next season hopping from galley to galley and hoping no one tips you overboard, just in case you're really tainted with magic.'

I wondered how he made a living, if this was his idea of negotiation. Sadly, he was essentially correct. 'Where could you take me?' I demanded, no smile to answer his as yet.

'Close enough to the mainland for you to get a passage to a Caladhrian port, Attar or Claithe, choose how you will.'

I considered this. The most northerly Aldabreshi Warlord had pushed the Caladhrians out of the coastal islands nearly a generation previously and, from all I'd heard, reasonably peaceful trade had resumed a handful or so years ago. Attar or Claithe were entirely the wrong end of the Gulf of Lescar, as far as I was concerned, but did I really want to try to cross the width of the Archipelago in this haphazard fashion and then hunt around for one of the few ships that risked the perilous, if profitable crossing to Zyoutessela, beating against the winds and currents that coiled round the Cape? If I reached Caladhria it would be a long way home, especially now the fighting season in Lescar would be in full bloody flow. Still, I would at least be able to send a letter to Messire via the Despatch and there was always the chance of a direct passage across the Gulf from Relshaz to Toremal. I remembered the haul of gems I had found at the bottom of my kit bag, a parting gift from Laio. I could buy my own cursed galley if I wanted to, if only I could get back to somewhere civilised.

I looked at the little man and wondered what his idea of me paying handsomely might be. 'What's your name?' I asked, relaxing my stance a little.

'Dev.' He held out his hand palm up, an unmistakably Lescari gesture, that being a country where proving you've not got a dagger up your sleeve is reckoned a courtesy.

I shook his hand. 'Glad to meet you, Dev. I'm Ryshad.' I looked around the beach, thronged with people and goods as the little skiffs ferried cargo and passengers to and from the waiting galleys. The scent of cooking came from little fires and braziers set up at intervals along the tree line and my stomach rumbled.

'I'm also hungry, that bastard of a captain insisted on putting me ashore before the crew ate.' That had happened to me all too often on this uncomfortable trip and, with no one in this benighted society understanding the notion of simply paying for a service, I had had no way of purchasing a meal, no matter how much food was being prepared around me, the wealth in my bag a taunting irrelevance.

'Come on then, you can eat with me.' Dev led the way to a shelter woven of tree fronds where a fat woman was deftly pouring batter on a sizzling skillet, folding the resulting pancakes around a spoonful of whatever mixture was requested from a row of pots bubbling on the rim of her broad brazier.

'Which is least spiced?' I asked Dev cautiously, watching as he asked for a helping of meat laced with what I now knew to be scorching red pods. Wherever he'd come from, he'd obviously been in and around the Archipelago long enough to have his tongue tanned like old leather.

'The fish, I'd say.' Dev laughed, not unkindly. He told the woman the name of his ship and she nodded with satisfaction as she noted the pennants at the masthead.

'So what's an amigal?' I asked, biting cautiously into my meal and finding it reasonably edible to my relief, though I still couldn't understand why the Aldabreshi couldn't just eat fish plain.

'It's a bird of the islands,' replied Dev, mouth full as he ate in rapid bites. 'Spends half the year heading south and the rest of the time coming back again, daft creature.'

'Is that what you do?'

'Pretty much, though I don't go much beyond the domain of Neku Riss.' Dev swallowed his last mouthful and signalled to the woman for another pancake. 'So, how did you end up solving Shek Kul's oldest problem for him then?'

That raised heads all around us, people recognising the name and enough having sufficient Tormalin to get the gist of Dev's enquiry. Leaves on the ground rustled as those closest edged away, a reaction I was also well used to by now. I started to give him a concise account of events, thinking it would be no bad thing to spread as much suspicion and fear of the Elietimm throughout the Archipelago as I could. As I mentioned Kaeska for the first time, Dev laid a hand on my wrist.

'Wipe the taint from your lips when you mention that name,' he warned me in an undertone, 'and never call her Kaeska Shek; she has no link to any domain now.'

I nodded and complied, wondering angrily how much

additional offence and suspicion had gathered around me on my journey so far simply because I hadn't known any of this. That made up my mind for me; whatever Dev wanted by way of payment, if I had it, it was his. I wanted to be free of these unholy islands and their merciless people as soon as I could.

'So how did you end up in a Relshazri slave auction anyway?' enquired Dev, eyes keen as I finished my tale.

'I was in Relshaz on business for my patron,' I replied with a shrug of bemusement. 'I was set upon, street robbers I suppose they must have been. One of them managed to fell me from behind and I woke up in the lock-up, witnesses all swearing to Saedrin that I'd robbed some poxed merchant I'd never even seen. The greedy bastards can't have been satisfied with what I had in my purse and thought they'd see what my hide would fetch.'

'I wouldn't have thought a sworn man would get caught like that,' Dev shook his head with a chuckle.

'You're not the only one.' I had no difficulty feigning disgust with myself. 'The patron might be prepared to overlook it but the rest of the barracks will be reminding me about it till I'm old and grey.'

'Come on.' Dev got to his feet and we headed for a little boat drawn up on the shore, a lad leaning on its single oar, rammed into the sand to hold it fast. Dev turned to me and shoved his hands through the frayed length of rope that was serving him for a belt.

'What are you offering for your passage then, Tormalin man?' he asked, head cocked to one side.

'What are you asking?' I countered.

'What about that little bauble?' His eyes fixed greedily on the gold and emerald token that Shek Kul had given me, prominently displayed on my chest as I had soon discovered was only prudent if I wanted to keep my hide intact.

I scowled and hissed sharply through my teeth. 'This is my only safeguard as long as I'm in the islands,' I protested. 'My life's not worth a spent candle without it.'

'You'll be safe enough with me,' insisted Dev, his eyes not wavering from the gleaming gemstone.

'How about I give it to you once I'm safely ashore or aboard a Caladhrian ship?' I offered reluctantly after a lengthy pause.

Dev grimaced as he considered this. 'Your word on it?' he demanded eventually.

'My word on it, Dastennin drown me if I break it,' I confirmed. 'And if Dastennin doesn't work his vengeance on me, my patron is Messire D'Olbriot. You know of him, don't you? I'm hardly going to risk playing you false and having to answer to him, am I?'

Dev's expression cleared. 'True enough. Come on then.'

I was glad that we were both satisfied; Dev that he would get what he assumed was my only possession of value, myself that I had not had to reveal the existence of the random trawl through her jewel cases that Laio had rolled inside an old tunic when she'd been packing my kit-bag for me. We reached Dev's ship and I followed him over the rail, looking round in vain for any other crew.

Dev laughed. 'It's just you and me, Tormalin man. My partner got himself knifed in a fight a while back. You'll be working your passage home; you must know your way around a boat if you're from Zyoutessela.'

'Doesn't that mean you should be paying me?' I protested with a half-smile.

'The deal's done now, no going back on it.'

I let him enjoy his little triumph. 'If you say so.'

'Let's get a drink.' Dev lifted a hatch in the prow of the ship to reveal a cramped storage space packed with small barrels. Dropping down a ladder, he lifted one up to me and we made our way to an equally confined cabin at the stern of the ship where I rolled my bag inside the hammock Dev indicated. This ship was evidently fitted out to carry the maximum amount of cargo and if I was going to help sail her, it didn't look as if I was going to have much time to spare.

Dev dragged a stool out from beneath the folded-down table as he tapped the little cask with a practised hand. I took the cup he offered and emptied it thirstily, choking as it proved to contain something like dark brandy rather than the feeble Aldabreshin wine I had been expecting.

'I'll wager it's been a good while since you had a real drink,' laughed Dev as I wiped the tears from my eyes.

'What is this stuff?' I gasped, trying not to cough and taking a more cautious sip.

'It's made from honeycane.' Dev poured himself a second drink but I waved his hand away from my cup. There are precious few people I trust enough to get drunk with, and Dev wasn't even close to making the bottom of the list. Still, it was undeniably pleasant to feel the bite of real liquor again.

'I thought all the Aldabreshi drank was that horse-piss they call wine.'

'There's always a market for what's forbidden,' chuckled Dev but I can't say I saw the joke particularly, none too keen to find myself on a boat laden with what could only be called contraband.

'Aren't you treading a rather fine line?' I asked.

'I watch my footing,' he replied airily.

I took another drink; I'd just have to hope he didn't make a misstep while I was on board. If he did, well, I still had Shek Kul's token and I'd be off this little ship at the first sign of trouble to take my chances on my own.

'Right, you can keep watch. I'm off ashore to do a little trading,' said Dev briskly.

I followed him up on deck and looked for a comfortable spot in the shelter of the mast as he hailed a ferry-boy.

'When should I expect you back?' I called as the lad worked his oar to turn his cockleshell boat around.

Dev looked at the stars beginning to shine in the darkening sky. 'Midnight or thereabouts.'

I waved and settled myself on the deck. I wasn't about to relax, but my spirits were certainly rising and not only because of the encouragement from the liquor. Wrapping my arms around my knees, I sat and watched the business of the anchorage all around me, lamps casting long yellow fingers across the dark waters, voices sounding from the various ships, in debate, dispute and as the night drew in, more frequently in song. The stars turned slowly above my head, the moons carried themselves on their stately progress, greater waxing behind lesser, which was scant days off the full. Gradually the galleys fell dark and silent, fires on the shore left to burn down to dim red embers and most of the ferrymen finally hauling their little boats up above the tide line.

I caught my breath as I heard a low noise beneath my feet. I listened and it came again, a scrape and a knock, not from the hold but from the rear cabin. On any other ship I'd have dismissed it as rats but I'd seen the extreme measures the Aldabreshi took to keep vermin from getting on to their islands and didn't think Dev would still be trading, liquor or no liquor, if a rat showed so much as a whisker over his rails. The next sound made up my mind for me; rats may be cursed intelligent for scaly-tailed rodents but I'll wager none have yet worked out how to open a drawer. I slipped my sandals off my feet and moved to the hatch, silent as a hunting cat. Drawing a thin Aldabreshi dagger from my belt, I gripped the rope handle of the trap door, ripping it open and dropping into the cabin in one movement.

I had been ready for grappling whoever it was in darkness but a feeble candle stub showed me a girl, all skin and bone, eyes like great dark bruises in her pale face, unwashed hair straggling over her narrow shoulders in dark rats' tails. I gripped her by the throat all the same; the bitch had my bag open at her feet, various of my possessions strewn on the floor. I raised my dagger so she could see it and shook her hard.

'Dast seize you, what are you at?'

Her eyes focused on the bright blade with difficulty and followed it, her expression blank, slack-mouthed, the taint of thassin bitter on her breath. I frowned and waved the knife deliberately to and fro. Her muddy, bloodshot eyes rolled as she tried to keep up with the rapid movement. I let her go and wondered just what her addled mind was making of this, what phantasms her imagination was conjuring up in my place, hoping she didn't suddenly decide I was a two-headed dog and start screaming.

'Don't worry about Repi, she's harmless enough. She's looking for thassin, tahn, anything, chewing leaf if you've got it.' Dev's voice startled me and I scowled up the hatch at his unconcerned face. 'She hasn't the wit to think about robbing you of anything else.'

'Curse it, Dev, you should have said something,' I protested. 'I could have killed her.'

'I don't suppose she'd have noticed for a while.' Dev slid down the ladder and snapped his fingers in front of the girl's vacant face. 'Bed,' he snapped, opening the door to the main hold, manner and tone much as I would have used to an errant hound. The girl made it through the doorway on the second attempt, clumsily rubbing her arm where she had banged it cruelly on the jamb. Dev's expression remained contemptuous as Repi stumbled into a tangle of blankets against the far bulkhead.

'What's she? An advertisement for your other wares?' I snapped at Dev.

'Something like that.' He pulled off his tunic and climbed deftly into his hammock, unconcerned. 'She's quite good on her back as well, as long as you give her some sapsalt to wake her up a bit. Help yourself if you like, she'll do anything you want if she thinks there's a trip to the shades in it for her.'

I couldn't even begin to reply to that, so I thrust my belongings back in my bag, tying the lace at the neck in a secure knot before hanging the whole thing on the high hook of my hammock. Settling myself to sleep, I forced myself to concentrate on the fact that this unsavoury vessel was still my fastest hope of leaving these pestilential islands.

We weighed anchor just after dawn and Dev steered us expertly through the crowded strait into more open waters. Whatever I might think of him, he was certainly a proficient sailor. I worked the ropes as instructed and took over what cooking there was to be done when I realised Dev's taste for hot spices extended to even the simplest of meals and Repi was rarely in a state to be trusted near a naked flame. I rolled up my mail and stowed it at the bottom of my kit, my gems securely tied in the middle of the metal. Dressed in simple cotton, I kept my head down and concentrated on looking as unremarkable as I could, Shek Kul's token hidden beneath my tunic, as much to ensure Dev didn't get his hands on it too early as anything else. I didn't figure it would take too many reminders of temptation for him to decide to slit my throat one night. As it was, I always waited for him to sleep before I did and woke myself early with the tricks of a soldier's training.

As we worked our way up the long chain of the Archipelago, we made landfall in various anchorages, some the busy trading straits like the one where I had met Dev, others secluded coves where furtive men in shallow rowing boats drew alongside to bargain with Dev. I stayed out of it all, only going ashore to eat when necessary and on the not infrequent occasions when Dev brought one or more eager men aboard to get Repi below decks and take their pleasure with her.

All in all, I was seeing a very different picture of life in the Archipelago to the one Laio had painted for me. Well, her advice hadn't exactly proved entirely trustworthy, had it? Every so often, I wondered how she was, her and Gar, Mahli and the baby. Having spent ten years and more in Messire's service, I have had to get used to visiting places and making friends, only to leave them after a season or so, often never to see them again. Still, I knew I would always remember Laio with fondness, and not only for the gifts of her body and her jewellery. I wondered idly if she had any idea of the real worth of the trinkets she had bestowed on me. Different though her beliefs might be, I reckoned I'd be burning incense at a shrine to Drianon for Laio, to keep her safe through child-bed; for Grival and Sezarre too, though I couldn't quite decide whether Trimon or Talagrin would be the most appropriate deity to watch over them.

I turned my thoughts to such considerations whenever life

on the little ship threatened to be too distasteful, slamming a firm door on any impulse to try to shelter Repi from Dev's abuses. Some days this was harder than others, especially when some islander who'd paid for a turn with her had shown a taste for violence.

'Why don't you give the poor bitch a chance to recover?' I snapped one day as Dev knelt beside her, lifting her unresponsive head to blow some smoke into her nostrils, a great bruise purpling one side of her face. The smell of the smouldering leaves was making me edgy as well; I was more than a little concerned that catching too much of it might let those voices loose inside my head again. I was finding I was having enough trouble with the increasingly vivid and powerful dreams I was having about young D'Alsennin. I'd be cursed if I'd unleash him into my waking mind again, having finally recognised his as the voice I had heard when fighting the Ice Islander priest. If I'd thought I had any chance of picking up another decent blade, I'd have been sorely tempted to drop D'Alsennin's sword into the sea some night and face answering to the Sieur for so dishonouring his gift. Unfortunately, common sense reminded me that the Archipelago was no place to be travelling without a weapon.

Dev scowled and dropped Repi's head to the deck with a sickening thud. 'Silly poult, she's been mixing tahn and liquor again. No wonder Ful lost his temper with her; it must have been like ramming a rag doll.'

I bit down hard on the words that were hammering at the inside of my teeth and stared over the rail at the shoreline. We were anchored in a secure cove with no other ships and I noticed the trees were sparser here, more akin to the ones you'd see in southern Caladhria. With any luck I'd be off this ship in a few days if my rough calculations as to our course were anything like correct.

'Smoke? I can't rouse Repi and I don't fancy spitting dead meat, so we might as well get glazed.' Dev blew on the embers of his censer and added a few more leaves, taking a deep breath before offering me the little metal bowl in its horn holder.

I shook my head abruptly, moving out of the way of the drifting scent.

'You want it, though, don't you?' Dev laughed, his own eyes growing wide and dark as the intoxication spread through him.

I didn't bother replying. In any case it was true. Catching the scent so often lately had reawakened all the cravings that I thought I'd left so far behind me. I kept catching myself finding justifications for just a little smoke, taking a little thassin to chew or some leaf, there was plenty on offer after all. The notion of losing myself just for a little while was just so tempting, stealing an evening free of the memories of Kaeska's appalling death, my apprehension over how Messire was going to judge my recent experiences, my struggle to decide whether I would admit to these dreams of D'Alsennin and his lost colony and sink myself deeper into some wizards' plotting or lie through my teeth and deny it all, forfeiting my oath though none but me would know it. Some nights just about the only thing holding me back was the fear that relinquishing control like that would let loose whatever shade of D'Alsennin remained tied to his sword and was currently locked firmly away in the back of my mind, for the moment at least.

Dev showed no after effects of the smoke the following day and got us moving in a high good humour. 'We're heading out away into open waters today,' he announced over breakfast. 'It'll be rougher and we'll need to watch the winds.'

'Keep Repi below decks then,' I said shortly, 'or tie a line to her.'

Dev laughed as if I had just made an excellent jest, so I turned my back on him and addressed myself to the business of sailing the little ship, which was not really built for the seas we faced as we left the shelter of the Archipelago, alone on the empty expanse of the waters.

'Take the tiller and turn her into the wind!' Dev shouted to me. I hurried to comply as he left the stern and the ship rocked alarmingly. I grabbed for the arm of the rudder but missed as I saw a complex tangle of red light swirl around his fingers, the ruby glow sparking arcane reflections in his dark eyes.

'You're a pissing wizard!' I gasped, reaching for the tiller and just managing to grab it this time to steady the ship.

'Reporting to the Archmage and a seat on the Council any time I want it,' Dev confirmed as he spread his hands and sent a column of fire high into the sky above our heads. 'Not that I do want it, not just yet. Sailing the islands like this, in my line of trade, it's a fine life. If I can earn some credit in Hadrumal with what I discover, so much the better. I'll be wintering there this year, though. You're a fine prize for me to bring in.' He laughed at my shocked expression. 'I've been hunting for you ever since Shek Kul set sail from Relshaz. What did you think? The Archmage was going to let you loose in the Archipelago and forget about you? Not with what I think you've got in your head, not when those Elietimm are spending so much time and trouble to get their hands on you and that sword.'

He was openly gloating now. If we'd been within sight of land, I'd have been over the rail and swimming for shore to take my chances with whatever lurked beneath the waters. As it was I took a step towards the smirking man before the lurch of the ship brought me to my senses.

'I'm a Tormalin sworn man, I answer to my patron and no one else, you bastard,' I told Dev in no uncertain terms. 'If Planir wants me, he'll answer to Messire D'Olbriot first!'

'Already signed and sealed,' Dev laughed. 'You've been handed over as surely as when you were sold in Relshaz!'

I might really have hit him then had a sail not appeared on the horizon. Square-rigged and three-masted, it was a Tormalin ship, the type I had seen all my life in the oceanside harbour at Zyoutessela. Squinting into the sun, I struggled to identify the flag at the masthead, desperately hoping to see the D'Olbriot insignia. Let the mages try and get me off one of Messire's ships against my will; I couldn't believe Dev's tale, that the patron would transfer me to another's orders without my consent, especially not to the Archmage.

The three-master closed with us rapidly with the winds at her stern. I ignored Dev's protests as I abandoned the rudder to him and collected my gear. I was ready to catch a line thrown from the taller ship as soon as she drew alongside and tied my kit-bag securely to it, waving a hand to the sailor who hauled it aboard for me. A rope ladder snaked down to me and I looked for the right moment to catch it.

'Don't you owe me for your passage?' Dev shouted, half angry, half taunting. I looped my arm through the ladder and got my feet on to it before turning to glare at him.

'You really think so?'

'I can do a lot for the Archmage with a token like that,' he insisted, face serious for once. 'Besides, you swore it to me.'

And I wasn't about to forswear myself, just for the sake of poking this little filth in the eye. I spat on to his deck before ripping the medallion from my neck and tossing it over, watching with contempt as Dev scrambled for the shining disc. Fury goading me to unexpected violence, I decided it would be best to leave before I killed him and climbed rapidly aboard the three-master. A genial mariner helped me over the rail, the master of the ship by his dress and manner.

'You and Dev not the best of friends then?' he enquired, evidently amused.

'The man's privy slime!' I wasn't about to change my mind on that in a hurry.

'You know the legend about the masquerader whose mask stuck to his face when he abused Ostrin's hospitality without knowing it?' The sailor nodded towards Dev's retreating boat. 'That's Dev's problem; he's spent so long playing the part to keep himself from being skinned alive for magecraft.'

I watched the little vessel move swiftly away in defiance of wind and wave. No need for concealment excused Repi's plight, as far as I was concerned. Still, there was nothing I or anyone could do to help her and at least I was free of Dev now. I turned to the captain.

'Where are we headed? Relshaz or Col? I'm not quite clear which side of the Cape of Caladhria we are.'

The sailor laughed. 'Sorry, friend, we're bound for Hadrumal, full sail and best speed.'

'Hadrumal can wait; I'm a sworn man to Messire D'Olbriot, my duty is to him.' I thought about the fortune I had concealed in my gear. 'I can make it worth your while to set me ashore on the mainland, I'll pay a full charter fee.'

'I'm not crossing the Archmage for all the gems in Aldabreshi.' The mariner shook his head firmly. 'You're going to Hadrumal, friend, like it or not.'

CHAPTER NINE

Taken from the Archive of the Guild of Master Mariners, Peorle, a letter written by Master Obrim Eschale to his son, in the 10th year of Emperor Inshol the Curt.

> *Dastennin send his blessings on you, Pennel, and all who sail with you.*
>
> *I am gravely concerned to hear that you are intending to attempt a voyage to Hadrumal on the spring tides. I would tell you to steer a course well clear of that accursed isle, were I not confident that you will never make landfall there. You fool, don't you realise that the mages who have made that place their own will only allow those boats they wish to find them? You will never even see the hidden island, let alone navigate the magical defences wrought around the harbour. All you are doing is risking being lost at sea, along with your crew and hull in a futile quest for a moon's reflection.*
>
> *I have spoken with various mariners who have taken the Archmage's coin to ferry hapless youths to their so-called apprenticeships in the service of those ancient wizards and none of their stories agree. Some have sailed for days beyond the sight of land, only to find themselves surrounded by fog, which hangs proof against the strongest winds. Then the mist magically clears to reveal the island they are seeking. Others tell of enchanted currents seizing their vessels, carrying them this way and that, proof against all pull of wind and sail, to bring them suddenly to an unexpected landfall. No two ships spend the same time on the journey, no two captains' records agree but for the one incontrovertible fact that, once a ship has taken the Archmage's coin and set sail for Hadrumal,*

the sun cannot be seen after the first three days at sea. There is daylight, do not mistake me, but the sun is lost behind a haze of shifting magic, so that no readings or calculations of position may be made.

These wizards do not want to be found, my son. Respect their wishes or risk their wrath. You have heard the tales as well as I of the savage vengeance taken by mages on those that defy them; do you want your eyes blasted from your head? Do you want unquenchable fire burning your ship to the waterline? Why do you think these people were driven into the sea in the first place, if not to save us all from their inhuman powers and unbridled lust for domination? Do not be dazzled by the glitter of the Archmage's gold, my boy, do not let it blind you to the dangers that ring Hadrumal, more perilous than any reef or shoal.

What is the point of such a voyage? These wizards have no interest in the lives of ordinary folk. There is no trade to be done, no cargo to ferry, beyond those few foolhardy enough to risk their lives in a search for unholy powers. I would call it wiser to sail blindly into the Archipelago and hope not to be ripped apart by the brazen fangs of barbarian warships. Have you learned so little, in all the years I have struggled to teach you wisdom? What is your mother going to say?

The hidden island city of Hadrumal,
29th of For-Summer

Hadrumal was bigger than I expected. Not that I could have said exactly what I was expecting; some bleak and rocky islet, aloof above inaccessible cliffs, storm-tossed and lost in clouds of brooding spray? Possibly, perhaps, certainly not a long island of shelving beaches and wooded lowlands, a swell of green downs rising away to run down its length, unmistakably dotted with livestock of some kind. As the ship with me as its unwilling passenger turned down the narrowing estuary of a little river, I saw docks and quays, warehouses and boatyards, such as you might find anywhere along the coast from Col to Toremal, where a seaside Lord has turned his own modest anchorage into a handy base for passing ships. It was quiet in the noonday heat of a summer's day, the few people about ready enough to help with line and gangway when the master of the ship drew the vessel deftly alongside the timber piles of the dockside.

I was leaning on the rail, my thoughts grim, when I heard a familiar voice.

'Ryshad, over here!'

I'd been glad to see Shiv the last time he had hailed me like that. I looked for him, unsmiling, and returned his enthusiastic waves with a single desultory gesture.

'Thank you for the passage, Master,' I bowed with bitter irony to the captain of the ship as I passed him on my way to collect my baggage. 'Where are you bound for next?'

'Col,' he shrugged, unconcerned.

'Please pass this on to the Imperial Despatch.' I slipped a

folded and twice-sealed parchment into his hand, 'It's a letter for my mother.'

He nodded. 'I'll be glad to.'

That was one weight off my mind at least. I'd wondered about writing to Messire or better yet to Camarl, who might just be more sympathetic to my sorry tale, but I had decided against it. These wizards could make themselves useful and send any communication I had a mind to make once I had the measure of this new situation.

'I can't say how relieved I am to see you again!' Shiv clapped his hand against my shoulder. 'Come on, I'm to take you straight to Planir.'

'Why?' I was going to make it clear from the start that my days as anyone's slave were over. There had been no point in taking out my frustrations on the captain of the ship; he had been simply doing as he was ordered and I had to respect that. Now I felt slow anger building within me; if Planir thought he had bought me, body or mind, he was going to find he'd got more than he bargained for.

'He wants to meet you, congratulate you, hear all you have to say,' replied Shiv. 'There's much your experiences can tell us, information we can use against the Elietimm. Planir needs that straight away.'

I nodded. All right; I had no problem with letting Planir know just where I stood right at the outset. If he wanted to argue about it, he'd have a fight on his hands and that didn't worry me in the slightest. The sooner everything was clear, the sooner I could leave this cursed place and get back to my own life. I wondered fleetingly where Livak might be. Turning to Shiv, I was about to ask him, but something in his expression deterred me.

The doubts and diffidence that had been so marked in Shiv last time I had seen him were strikingly absent. He was looking far more confident and assured and, as a result, far more distant than I remembered him, his dark hair cut level at jaw length, a formal gown belted in with a tooled leather strap. Not at all sure I'd find him my ally now his feet were firmly on

Hadrumal's soil, I decided I could wait to find out where Livak was. Shrugging my bag on to my shoulder, I followed Shiv up the dock to a boggy pool of the river where a bridge marched across on stout foundations towards a road Misaen himself would have been proud of. Close-laid stones were laid on a solid foundation, ditches at either side to carry the run-off from the curved surface. I tried not to be too impressed as I saw the city of the wizards for the first time. After all, compared to somewhere like Toremal, or even Zyoutessela, it was no bigger than a middling market town.

The road curled away across a broad, shallow plain, great halls of the soft grey stone standing four-square at intervals along it, long and lofty roofs rising above quadrangles of lesser buildings, in each case the whole surrounded by purposeful walls, towers at their corners looking out and around like careful sentries. The overriding impression that Hadrumal gave was of watching and waiting; the tall buildings seemed to loom above me as I came closer. The sun emerged from behind a cloud and, in a sudden alchemy, the stone glowed gold and inviting for a moment, glazed windows shining like jewels. The moment passed and I could see where smaller houses, workshops, stores and the like had filled in the gaps between the forbidding, implacable fortresses of arcane learning. There was no wall around the city as a whole to protect these lesser folk, I noted; what was there to defend them in time of danger? The arts of the wizards, presumably, and I wondered how sure a protection that might be.

I slowed my pace unconsciously, finding myself falling further behind Shiv, who had to stand and wait, his expression startled when he turned to find himself so far outstripping me. I took my time catching him up, wiping sweat from my forehead and swapping my kit-bag to my other shoulder. The street was busy; men and women of all ages and styles of dress walking this way and that, their only common feature an air of self-absorption and an unconscious arrogance in their carriage.

'This way.' Shiv led me through an archway of ancient

stonework and across a flagstoned court where my sandals scuffed uneasily on the hollowed stones. Pushing open a door, Shiv ran lightly up the flights of dark oak stairs, eagerness in his every move. I followed slowly, deliberately placing each step on the polished boards, trying to decide what I was going to say to this Archmage of Shiv's.

'Ryshad Tathel, how pleased I am to see you again.' Planir had been seated, poring over a leather-bound book when Shiv pushed open the heavy door without any particular request for admittance and he sprang to his feet, hand outstretched in welcome.

I nodded an acknowledgement. Planir looked much the same as when we'd met before; tall, dark, fine-featured and at first sight younger than you eventually realised he must be. His eyes were as opaque as ever, his schemes and motives as hidden as the far side of the lesser moon. He was plainly dressed in an indeterminate style, neither Tormalin or Soluran, neither overtly rich or incongruously commonplace. I was not impressed, having seen various noblemen try the tactic of putting the soldiery at ease by dressing down to them. Most fail with it.

'I was most concerned when I learned what had befallen you, but everyone assured me that if anyone could rise above such challenging circumstances, you were the man to do it.' Planir smiled broadly at me and gestured towards an elegant array of crystal and decanters. 'Can I offer you any refreshment.'

I was tempted to ask for ale, just to see his reaction. 'No, thank you.' He could keep his flattery as well.

'Please, be seated.' Planir took his own chair again and leaned forward on one arm, a friendly smile on his face. 'You've done sound work, there, Ryshad. We weren't even sure if there was an Elietimm threat in Aldabreshi, though we had our suspicions, given the information you helped recover last year. We have good reason to be grateful to you again, have we not? As soon as we realise the Elietimm are worming their way in, before we've even begun to form a plan to counter them, you discredit the bastards in a storm of scandal that will carry from one end of the Archipelago to the other before Solstice. Saedrin will lose his keys before they secure any base or alliance among the Aldabreshi now!'

'It was all entirely accidental.' I took a seat, but only because my bag was weighing heavy on my shoulder. 'Incidental to keeping myself alive, since I had no illusions that anyone would be helping me out of there.'

Planir leaned back in his chair, his smile vanishing. 'I can understand that you might feel abandoned,' he said seriously, 'but that was by no means the case. Dev is far from my only agent in the islands.'

I didn't respond, unconcerned whether he took the contempt in my face for Dev personally or not.

'Right then, let's hear your tale,' Planir said briskly, rising to his feet and striding to a table set under the tall windows looking out across the towers of Hadrumal.

'I was sold in Relshaz, made slave to a Warlord's lady and found I had to denounce another in order to save my own skin.' I folded my arms and waited for the Archmage's reaction, ignoring Shiv who was frowning at me as he leaned on the mantel above the fireless hearth.

'There's much more to it than that and you know it, man!' Planir folded his arms and abandoned his attempts at flattery, which was one relief. 'We suspect the Elietimm were responsible both for your enslavement and for your purchase by Shek Kul's women. It's the sword, Ryshad. We thought it would be important and the degree of sympathy you've established with it is beyond anything else we've seen. Even without that, the Elietimm have betrayed its importance. They wanted that sword so desperately that they broke cover and exposed themselves completely.'

I was not at all convinced of that, rather suspecting that young D'Alsennin had been somehow roused in Relshaz, the Elietimm only taking advantage of the situation. These wizards were looking to do much the same, weren't they? 'So I was the goat tethered to draw the wolves out of the wildwood?'

'Not intentionally, but I'll grant you the effect was the same.'

Planir nodded, unperturbed. 'Now we need to know just why they were prepared to run such risks to get their hands on that blade.'

'You want the sword, it's yours.' I shrugged again. Messire wouldn't take offence, not when he heard my side of this sorry tale. 'You can find someone else to dream D'Alsennin's dreams for you.'

Planir shook his head with a half-smile. 'I'm afraid it doesn't work like that, Ryshad. Once a sympathy has been established there is no going back, no handing it on. No one else will be able to hear the echoes of D'Alsennin's life but you, not if we pass the sword round every man in the cohorts.'

I looked at him, stony-faced.

'Nor will disposing of the sword relieve you of his presence in your sleeping mind,' continued Planir. 'As I say, this can be no more undone than an egg can be unbroken.'

I shot Shiv a grim glance that promised a reckoning between us and he coloured, looking down at his notes.

'So, we can all move on and learn what we may from this.' Planir broke the tense silence. 'What have you learned about the man who owned the blade, what can you tell us about the colony and its fate?'

'Very little.' I shrugged, keeping my face expressionless.

Planir leafed through a handful of documents to find a sealed letter, which he handed to me without further word. I set my jaw as I recognised the imprint and scribe of Messire D'Olbriot on the outer surface. Cracking the wax, I was surprised to find only a handful of lines in Messire's own, unpractised hand:

Dastennin send that you receive this, Ryshad, that you have come safely out of the perils of the Archipelago. I do not pretend to understand all that I have been told about lost magics and mysteries hidden in dreams but know this; the Men of the Ice are enemies, to my House and to our Empire. This is a peril we cannot counter with swords or the strength of our arms and resolve. The Archmage is our best hope of defence at present and I charge you, on the oath that binds

us, to tell him all you can and to spend all your efforts in
his service, even to the hazard of your life. You are sworn
to my service and so I command you.

So Dev had been wrong when he taunted me about being
sold to the wizards. This was far worse; my honour was
being held before me as a challenge. I stifled a disloyal anger
towards Messire, that he would lay such a burden on me
with no certainty of its weight or the length of the journey
he was sending me on. Then I remembered the vision of the
Elietimm flaunting the Emperor's head on a pike and sighed
heavily.

'I hope you are not going to prove Messire D'Olbriot's
word false, when he gave me his personal assurance of your
co-operation and good faith, Ryshad,' said Planir crisply as
he spread a yellowing chart over his highly polished table,
anchoring its corners with books, an empty goblet and a
random lump of rust-coloured stone. 'Tell me about your
dreams before you were separated from Shiv, all of them,
especially the night you were attacked.'

I crushed Messire's letter in my hand, fixing my eyes on
a distant weathervane and began my report, as detailed and
dispassionate as any I had ever given Messire. Shiv motioned to
me to slow down a little; as he took rapid notes, I remembered
the time I had been sent to find the truth of a massacre of camp
followers on the Lescari border where it abuts D'Olbriot lands.
That hadn't been a pleasant task, but it had to be done, and
I had drawn the reversed rune. A sworn man had his orders
to follow and his oath to protect him – that was the way of
things, wasn't it?

I talked and talked; Planir asked many questions, some so
obvious as to be irritating, others obscure in the extreme.
I didn't notice him or Shiv ring for wine and bread, but
drank and ate gratefully when sustenance arrived, snatching
mouthfuls between answering yet more questions as we went
over what had happened a second time.

'There's more, isn't there?' Planir was leaning over his chart, measuring something. He threw his rule down and turned on me, eyes bright.

'How do you mean?' I wasn't about to give him a touch-by-touch account of my night with Laio, if that was what he was after.

'The dreams, Ryshad, the dreams,' said Planir softly. 'Tell me about the waking dreams.'

I took a deep breath but could not bring myself to answer, not wanting to discuss the echoing sensations that kept trying to pick their way out of the back of my mind of late, if I ever let my guard slip.

'You see, I can help you with that,' Planir lifted a book from a neat pile on the window ledge. 'We've recovered an ancient archive from a shrine sacred to Arimelin and learned a great deal about the dream lore of the ancients. We have a way to close your waking mind, to let us reach those dreams and learn all we want directly. Once we wake you from the trance the dreams will be gone and we won't need to make any more demands on you. You will be free to go and you won't be troubled any longer by dreams or visions.'

That was an offer so tempting there just had to be a hook in it somewhere, especially with the Archmage on the other end of the line.

'Just what exactly would you hope to learn?' I asked, puzzled. 'I've told you everything I can remember and to be frank, none of that has seemed especially important. Anyway, the venture failed, didn't it?'

'It was certainly lost, that's true, but we still want to locate this colony, not just hear about it. We're not simply trying to fill in the gaps in the archives to satisfy the scholars.' Planir poured himself some wine and offered a glass to Shiv, who closed his inkwell and folded up his notes. 'If we are to counter the Elietimm threat, we need to know more about this aetheric magic, these powers the Ancients called Artifice. From what you have already told us, it's clear people were being trained in these skills at this colony. There might be records, archives, even training regimes and instructions possibly.'

'Keep your coin to buy a pie!' I scoffed. 'When was this? Twenty-six generations past? Anything they left will be rotted to dust and dirt by now!'

'Perhaps, perhaps not.' Planir was unbothered by my unrestrained scorn. 'We can do much with air and fire, the sympathies of earth and water, to restore even the most damaged and stained parchments. Don't forget the resources I have to call on, Ryshad; the finest minds of wizardry are to be found in Hadrumal. Anyway, finding nothing is a risk I'm prepared to take. You, on the other hand, would find yourself central to finding a lost land of considerable resources. I know full well your patron has already spent a great deal of coin and effort tracing every reference and record concerning Den Fellaemion's expedition and would dearly love to reclaim that colony for the D'Olbriot name. Performing a service like that would go far to raising you to chosen man, wouldn't it?'

There were a whole string of hooks nicely baited on this lure, weren't there? No, for a man reputed to be someone you wouldn't play at Raven for a bet, the Archmage was being about as subtle as a farmer tethering a mare in season to fetch a wild stallion into stud. Did he think I was stupid?

'You've done this? With other people you've foisted these artefacts on?'

'It's not without its risks,' Shiv spoke up from his corner, his face sombre. 'We've been unable to rouse one girl from her sleeping state.'

'There's no denying it can be perilous,' agreed Planir gravely. 'I blame myself. We undertook the experiment with her before we had recovered the archive and had all the information we needed. Obviously you'll need to think very carefully before any such undertaking, though, of course, since you say young D'Alsennin had some initial training in aetheric magic, it might be that we find some clue to restoring the poor girl to her wits.'

So if temptation didn't bring me into his hands, the Archmage wasn't going to leave me with a way out that didn't make me feel lower than a louse's stones, was he? I shook my head as

I drained my glass and the eighth chime of the day rang out across the city, startling a bevy of mottled fowl from the leaded roof opposite Planir's tower. After my time in the Archipelago, it was an incongruously familiar sound, especially in these unnerving surroundings.

'You need time to think about it.' Planir took a gown from a hook on the back of his door and pulled it over his simple shirt and breeches. I have to admit the transformation set me back on my heels a little. It was not a gaudy robe, neatly cut of matte black silk, but the close collar lifted Planir's chin to give him an imperious gaze. The breadth of his shoulders was more apparent beneath square tailored cloth than soft linen, and as he strode from the room the fabric swept around him like half-bated wings, his questing face hawklike in its intensity.

I looked at Shiv. 'Planir wouldn't get very far in a Convocation of Princes, if that's his idea of sweet-talking someone.'

'You can stick all the roses you want in a pile of horseshit, it'll still stink,' shrugged Shiv. 'Planir knows you've been round the provinces, Rysh. Trust me, you should take plain speaking from the Archmage as a compliment. Come on.'

Shiv picked up my bag and his tone carried something more like the friendship I had first looked for, which weakened my defences more effectively than any of the Archmage's sallies. I followed him down the stairs and out into the court where the stone buildings overhung me on every side, oppressive and confining, the shadows dark and chill. A woman crossed the court, her eyes turning towards me, and two youths coming out of a doorway halted their conversation to stare for a moment before hurrying away. For a city built so close to the water, there was precious little scent of the sea in Hadrumal and I felt the dust of dry and ancient stone catch in my throat.

'I don't suppose you want to stay in the hall, so I told Pered you'd be stopping with us.' Shiv was talking blithely as he led the way out along the main street, heading inland where I was relieved to see the lofty halls give way to more normal row houses of pitted grey stone and tile-hung roofs. I began to notice all the other businesses that kept these wizards free to pursue their arcane studies; scribes, booksellers, apothecaries and not a few tisane houses where younger mages laid aside their parchments and robes to gossip with their fellows over a cup of steeping herbs. Wizards had to eat as well, it seemed; shopfronts had their shutters laid down to form counters laden with summer fruit and plump vegetables where canny-eyed women were doing their marketing and catching up on gossip with their cronies. Children hung at their skirts and a more venturesome group scampered in the roadway with a rag ball. There was a light drift of debris around a barrel fallen into a gutter and two men were arguing over who exactly had let it fall from their handcart. Hadrumal began to seem less outlandish, but I warned myself not to let apparent familiarity breed carelessness.

'We prefer to live down here; most of the other mages don't give a cut-piece whether someone's sleeping with a man, a woman or a donkey but there are always a few who are Rationalist enough to make themselves offensive. You remember Casuel, don't you? Anyway, we find it's better this way; nails that stick up get hammered down, after all.'

Shiv's back was to me as he stepped ahead through the gap between two carts. I allowed myself a grimace. Still, unsure as I might be about meeting Shiv's partner, anything had to be better than lodging in one of those grim halls with a covey of wizards staring at me from every side like crows waiting out a dying beast. I got on well enough with Shiv, didn't I? A more urgent consideration that had been tugging at my cloak since I landed now seized my attention and held it.

'Where's Livak?' I enquired, stepping off the kerb to draw level as Shiv made his way along the crowded walkway.

'She went to see Halice. There are some Soluran scholars here who are trying to improve her leg. Some aetheric magic has remained in their healing traditions, but you knew that, didn't you?'

I have to confess I'd hardly given Halice and her problems a passing thought since we'd been separated. Mentally shaking myself, I determined to stop dwelling on my recent experiences and get a grip on the reins again. Would there be some magic that could mend so severe a wound, and one now several seasons mended and healed? That would certainly be something to see and, more importantly, something to bring to Messire's attention. I've not seen too many men left with only stumps of leg or arm in order to save them from green rot, but hearing one screaming, weeping, pleading with the surgeons to no avail had been enough for me when Aiten and I had been working for Messire along the Lescari border. The reminder that I was not the only one with troubles was salutory as well.

'What about Viltred?'

'He's back in his old hall, catching up with whoever he trained with who isn't dead yet.' Shiv's tone was nevertheless affectionate. 'Here we are.'

He opened a stout door to usher me into a modest abode in the centre of a well-weathered terrace. I blinked as my eyes adjusted after the sunlight outside and I saw the front of the lower rooms was laid out as a workplace, a sloping desk set to catch the best of the light, parchment, pigments and binding agents neatly arranged, ready for use. I vaguely recalled hearing that Shiv's partner was a copyist or an illuminator, something of that kind, certainly not a wizard, which was the most significant thing to me.

'Pered!' Shiv stepped into the rear room and then shouted up the tight curve of the boxed staircase. 'No, he must be out, probably getting some food in. Look, make yourself at home, there's wine in the kitchen or you can have a tisane. I have a few things I need to do but I'll be back soon.'

Before I could protest he was out of the door, pulling it to behind him with an emphatic slam. Not wanting to upset anything in the study, I went through into the kitchen, a little surprised to find a modern charcoal stove standing in the fender of the hearth where a damped-down fire was making the room stuffy in the summer heat. Other than that it was an unremarkable place apart from a collection of wildly differing and highly decorative herb jars with a shelf to themselves on the far wall. I opened a couple, sniffed, stoked up the fire and put a kettle on to boil, but then decided I didn't really want a tisane after all, took the kettle off again and went out into the narrow yard at the back. Shiv's neighbours evidently kept chickens and on one side a pig, as you might expect, but the sty and run in this yard were swept bare and empty. I poked around a bit, finding a handful of stones and tried my hand at hitting a large, pale stone high on the wall of the piggery. Striking it every time, I was about to look for more missiles when I heard the door behind me open.

'You should follow a plough and earn yourself some coin stoning the crows. That's some skill,' a cheerful voice complimented me.

'It is, but it's not my own,' I said without thinking.

'That sounds like a line from a bad ballad! You must be Ryshad, I'm Pered.'

I turned to see what manner of man Shiv had returned to so fondly. As with the island of Hadrumal itself, I couldn't have told you what I was expecting. I had the sense not to be looking for a masquerade matron, all feathers and flamboyant gestures, but perhaps I was anticipating something a little more obvious than a stocky, blunt-featured man with curly brown-blond hair and hazel eyes. His Tormalin was excellent, his accent that of Col and I recalled that city's reputation for letting folk follow their own path.

'Go on then, tell me the tale.' Pered sat himself in a bench to enjoy the sunshine, arms folded, muscular legs outstretched at his ease.

I hurled my last stone and struck a chip of rock from my target. 'I have a fair eye but this particular talent belongs to a man many generations dead whose memories are somehow cluttering up my dreams.' It sounded rather improbable put like that, but Pered didn't look surprised.

'So our revered Archmage has entangled you in one of his schemes, has he?'

I liked the almost total absence of respect in his voice and thought that Pered and I could probably be friends.

'Like a fly in a web,' I nodded.

'This is all to do with some lost colony and this unknown magic that has all the mages fluttering like doves with a cat in the cot, is it?' Pered shook his head. 'Good thing too, if you ask me. It's nice to see some of them learning a little humility for a change.'

No, I decided, we were definitely going to be friends. 'Shiv's told you about it?'

'Enough,' shrugged Pered. 'So, what's he like?'

'Sorry?'

'This lad who's wrecking your nights, the one with the throwing eye, what's he like?'

I looked at Pered and found myself at a loss for words. The Archmage had asked so many things, teased out so much detail about the colony, found far more information that I had realised I knew, but he hadn't once asked about young D'Alsennin himself.

'He's not a bad lad. He still has an unholy amount to learn about women but he's growing up fast, squaring up to his responsibilities all right. He has plenty of character but it needs tempering, polishing up.' It seemed strange to be talking about Temar like this.

'What does he look like? Can you describe him?' Pered pulled a scrap of reed paper from the breast pocket of his shirt and found a broken length of charcoal in his breeches pocket.

I closed my eyes to picture Temar more clearly and Pered sketched swiftly as I spoke, charcoal deft in his stubby fingers. 'He's a skinny lad,' I concluded. 'He'll fill out a bit in a few years, but he's outgrown himself just at the moment. I suppose you'd call it a wolf's face, long jaw, thin lips, angular, if you know what I mean. He certainly has a wolf's eyes, really intense light blue, which is strange when you consider he has black hair.'

'How does he wear it?'

'Long, straight, mostly tied back.'

'Anything like this?' Pered turned his sketch towards me and I smiled involuntarily.

'Are you sure you're not a mage? Actually, his nose isn't that prominent and his brows are finer but that's a better likeness than many a portrait I've seen. You're wasted in a copy-house.'

It was strange, seeing that picture, imperfect as it was, the face of a youth so alive in my dreams and reveries but so long lost on the far side of the pitiless ocean. I felt an odd tug of affection, almost. Besides, I owed the boy, didn't I? He'd saved my stones against Kaeska's enchanter.

'As my father said when he apprenticed me, it's a fair trade and it keeps bread on the table,' grinned Pered. 'I'll turn my hand to proper portraiture when Shiv finally gets fed up with being ordered about by Planir and we find ourselves hurrying for the next ship to somewhere different. Until then I'll bide my time and mix my inks.'

'Don't you mind the way Shiv has to go running every time Planir tugs his leash?' I asked curiously.

'Yes,' said Pered simply, 'but that's Shiv's choice and I have to respect that if we're to be together. The trick is making sure Shiv himself comes out ahead when all the runes are drawn, whatever game the Archmage is playing. That's what you need to do, trust me.'

This struck me as an unusually intense conversation to be having with someone I'd only just met. 'You seem very well informed. Shiv must have told you more than you're saying.'

Pered shook his head. 'Not Shiv, Livak. Anyway, what you need to work out first is just what you want. Then make sure whatever Planir tries to talk you into works for you as well as for him. Watch your step if he's being all honest and open with you as well – there'll be a barb in the honeycake, mark my words.'

I heaved a sigh. 'I just want to get clear of all this, have ordinary, nonsensical dreams about swimming through deep water with talking fish or whatever; to be allowed to go and pick up the threads of my own life again.'

'Then keep your eye on that target and don't let Planir or anyone else distract your throw.' Pered raised a hand and stood up. 'I think I heard the street door.'

We went into the kitchen, the inner door opened and Shiv came in, moving to one side to reveal Livak, who stepped directly into my arms, tucking her tousled auburn head under my chin. I breathed in the scent of her as I kissed her hair and felt her arms tighten around me. Holding her close like that was a feeling worth more than a season in Laio Shek's embraces. I could have stayed like that for ever if Shiv hadn't needed to get to the range to put the kettle on the heat.

'What's for dinner, Shiv?' Livak peered into a basket full of vegetables that was standing on the scrubbed table-top.

It proved to be a sturdy pottage that had been simmering away in a cook-pot on a tripod in the hearth and only awaited the addition of the vegetables. Shiv skimmed the fat and thickened the mix with the marrow from the bones while the rest of us peeled and chopped.

I caught Livak looking thoughtfully at me and raised an enquiring eyebrow.

'Are you planning to keep the beard?' she asked with a faint smile.

'Do you like it?' I did hope she was going to say no.

She tilted her head to one side, considering this. 'It definitely makes a difference but—'

That was good enough for me. 'Shiv, do you have a razor I can borrow?'

Shiv laughed. 'Certainly but I'd wait a bit before you use it. Shave a beard like that off in high summer, especially after spending time in the Archipelago, and you'll have a piebald face. Your chin will catch the sun too, unless you're careful. Trust me, I've done it!'

Pered's artist's imagination was instantly caught by this picture. 'When did you wear a beard?' he asked, intrigued.

'Soon after I came to Hadrumal,' replied Shiv. 'I thought it would make me look older and force some of the senior wizards to take me a bit more seriously.'

'Didn't it work?' Livak asked with a wicked smile.

'No,' Shiv shook his head ruefully. 'The only thing that impresses master mages is how you handle your element.'

In very little time we were sitting down to an extremely satisfying dinner. Whatever the mages might be doing, someone with more practical skills was raising very good beef on Hadrumal, and while I couldn't identify the wine it was of a quality I associate with feasts and festival days. Best of all, we spent the entire meal talking about everything and anything and nothing to do with Planir, arcane dreams or lost colonies. It was almost as if my life were turning normal again.

As Shiv eventually rose to stack the plates in the sink, Pered looked out at the night. 'You might as well stay, Livak. There's no point in you heading back to the hall now and Halice will be asleep, if she's anything like as tired as she was after the last session with those Solurans mauling her leg about. So, am I making up the bed in the garret as well or will the one in the back bedroom suffice?' he enquired with the first trace of archness I had seen in him.

I looked at Livak, who hid a smile in her wine goblet. 'One bed will do, I wouldn't want to put you to too much trouble.'

'You two can wash up then.' Shiv tossed me a dishcloth and he disappeared up the narrow stairs with Pered.

'You wash, I'll wipe,' said Livak, taking firm possession of the towel.

'Thanks,' I replied dryly, before taking the kettle from the hearth to pour scalding water on to the crocks and blinking in the steam. 'You and Pered seem to get on well.'

'We do,' agreed Livak. 'Halice likes him as well.'

'How is she?' I asked belatedly.

'Better,' Livak's nod was emphatic. 'Much better.'

'Shiv was as good as his word then.' I was glad something positive seemed to be coming out of all this, for Halice's sake as much as anything, though a part of me was also selfishly glad that Livak would be freed of that particular burden.

'By the time we arrived, he didn't have a lot of choice,' laughed Livak, evidently well satisfied with something.

'How so?' I was intrigued, pausing in my work to look at her.

'Well, there was this archive Planir was desperate to have,' Livak began, her expression gleeful.

'From a shrine to Arimelin?'

'That's right. Well, Lord Finvar, the old greyhair who had it, was absolutely dead set against giving it up. He'd got it into his addled head that wizards dealing in natural science is only one step away from Rationalism and he wasn't about to hand over sacred texts to godless mages and risk who knows what wrath from an outraged deity.' Livak's eyes gleamed wickedly.

'What changed his mind?' I was smiling myself now.

'There were a whole series of portents, strangely enough.' Livak shook her head in mock perplexity. 'The old boy would wake up and find things in his bedchamber had been moved around while he slept. He kept finding an ancient set of runes laid out on his reading desk, up in his study, with something he was convinced was a mystical message. All his staff and retainers were questioned and, of course, the first people he suspected were Shiv and Viltred but the captain of his guard kept them under constant watch and they couldn't possibly have been responsible.'

'Of course not.' I nodded solemnly. 'So what finally convinced him?'

'Oh, waking to find his own birth runes laid out in the middle of the floor when he was sleeping in a high bedchamber with only one, inaccessible window.'

'Inaccessible?' I couldn't restrain a chuckle.

'That's right,' confirmed Livak, pulling up a sleeve to examine a long graze, now nicely healing. 'Inaccessible and cursed narrow as well.'

We both burst out laughing but then fell into an awkward silence, broken only by the clatter of crockery and the sounds of shifting furniture on the floorboards above our heads.

'I thought I'd lost you, you know,' Livak said abruptly, a faint hint of red beneath her summer freckles as she stared blindly out of the window into the darkness.

'Not so easily done,' I said as lightly as I could manage. 'I'm just glad to find you here. I wouldn't have wanted to go all the way back to Relshaz to search for you again.'

Our eyes met for a long moment until Livak turned to lay a plate on the table. 'I've been thinking – if the offer's still open, I could come back to Zyoutessela with you for a while. Whatever the Solurans are doing for Halice's leg, it's going to take a long time, at least into Aft-Autumn, that's what they were saying, anyway.'

'I'd like that,' I said, carefully keeping my tone even.

'I mean, I'm not making any promises and I shan't be growing my hair just yet,' Livak continued hurriedly, 'but we could see how things went, though of course, you're still a sworn man—'

'For the moment,' I said, surprised to hear the curt note in my own voice. 'I'm thinking about that. It may be time to hand back my oath fee and take charge of my own life again.' Now I had actually said it, put into words the impulse that had been growing slowly and inexorably within me.

Livak gaped. 'What will you do?'

'Come to see what Vanam's like?' I'd never been to Livak's home city.

'What will you do for coin?' Livak was frowning now. 'Don't say you're thinking of going for a mercenary in Lescar?' It was a feeble jest and I could see real concern in her eyes.

'Coin won't be a problem.' I grinned at her and went to recover my kit bag. As I spread Laio Shek's largesse on the table-top, Livak's eyes grew as round and as bright as the emeralds in the bracelet she first picked up.

'Just what sort of services were you rendering to earn this kind of pay-off?' she giggled.

I winked at her. 'I'll show you when we're in bed.'

Livak laughed and ran a wondering hand over some of the more choice pieces. Her eyes were keen as she looked up at me. 'With what you have here we could take ship tomorrow and disappear. I know people who'd give us a good rate to turn this into sound coin and I reckon we could take a chance on the mages not finding us. I have friends who'd hide us. You don't need to do whatever it is that Planir's asking; you could just walk away from it all.'

'I know, and I've thought about doing it,' I admitted. 'But then it wouldn't be finished, would it? There would always be questions – what if, if only. No, I want to be able to walk away on my own terms, leave no one with a claim on me.'

As I spoke, I realised this had to mean letting Planir and his scholars work their ritual over my dreams of Temar D'Alsennin. The thought of aetheric magic loose inside my head, breaking down all my defences, was a chilling one but if it was the price for getting rid of these echoes from the past or whatever they were, I'd have to pay it. I looked at the wealth spread all over the table-top and shook my head at the irony of it all.

I looked up to see Livak regarding me intently. 'Do you mind?' I asked her. 'I need to finish this once and for all.'

She nodded. 'I knew you would,' she said simply. 'That's the kind of man you are. I suppose if I were honest I wouldn't have you any other way.'

I drew her to me in a close embrace. 'Planir has some scheme for sending me into a half-sleep, a ritual to reach these cursed dreams directly.' I shivered involuntarily. 'Once that's done we should be able to leave.'

Livak's arms tightened round my chest. 'I'll stay, I'll be there with you if anyone wants to mess with your mind. Anyway,' her tone brightened, 'there are good pickings to be had here in Hadrumal. There are wizards here who might be able to talk to each other a thousand leagues apart but haven't the first idea of reading the run of the runes. Give me half a season and I'll probably be able to match your little treasure trove.'

'Planir will definitely want to get rid of us then.'

Up river, south of the settlement, Kel Ar'Ayen,
12th of Aft-Spring, Year Three of the Colony

'So that's it; we've no hope of a breakout that's any better than suicide.' Den Fellaemion's tone was as cold and passionless as a winter snow field. 'Is every ship sunk?'

'They were cut to pieces, all of them.' Avila's voice shook as she rubbed her temples with trembling hands, eyes tight shut as she recovered herself from the far-seeing. 'The invaders have blocked the mouth of the river completely.'

Temar could stand it no longer, shoving his stool back as he began to pace across the narrow alcove in the damp rock of the cave wall. 'Why are they waiting? Why don't they just come and finish it? We're caught like rabbits in a warren just waiting for the ferrets.' The walls of the cave seemed to press in on him and he clasped his hands together so hard they hurt. Misaen's truth, he hated to be confined like this.

'Why should they hurry?' Messire Den Fellaemion scrubbed a bone-thin hand across his bloodless face. 'They can take their time, rest and feed their men; we're not going anywhere, are we?' The dry note in his commander's voice was threatening to take on the hollow ring of defeat to Temar's ears.

'Perhaps we might. I know it's reaching for a single rune but we should explore the caves further,' he urged, stifling his own qualms at the prospect of going still deeper under the earth. 'We should start at once, widen some of the fissures and see where they take us. We know that at least one river travels through plunge pools as it comes down the gorge. If water made these caves, it must have found its way in somehow, and in some force. There could be a way right through the high ground, out to the far side, out of sight of these bastards.

Then we could strike out for the new port, where the stockmen have been building these last seasons. They've seen no sign of the invaders, have they, Avila? You said so yourself.' Temar bit his lip in frustration and sat down again, seeing that his words were going unheeded as Den Fellaemion turned his attention to Vahil's approach, a sheaf of crumpled parchments clutched desperately in the younger man's hand.

'Our supplies are very limited, Messire, no more than will give short rations for a scant handful of days. We have bread enough for several meals, cheeses and the like that people managed to grab as they fled, but many came empty-handed. We managed to salvage some sacks of meal from the ships and some small store of vegetables, but no meat or wine to speak of, and there's precious little means of cooking anything. It is far too dangerous to send people out for fuel or foraging.' Vahil's normally robust voice was as colourless as his face. 'With the attack coming at dawn like that, few were in a position to take more than themselves and their families, if they were to escape at all. A good number are still in their night-gowns or simply their linen. We have some blankets, but nowhere near enough, especially for the wounded. There are still twelve children separated from their parents,' Vahil reported bleakly and now his voice was raw with grief. 'I think we have to assume they are lost, the parents that is.'

Temar closed his eyes on his own anguished remembrance, the sight of Messire Den Rannion lying in a welter of blood, guts spilled across the muddy ground, sword still clutched in the hand that had been hacked clean from his wrist as he fought frantically to protect his people. The gems of his rings had shone in the dawn light, a detail of memory that confused Temar until he realised that the invaders were too set on bloodshed to bother with looting their victims. Worse yet was the other hand Temar had seen reaching blindly for the fallen Den Rannion, that of the Maitresse, her white hair trampled bloody into the earth, that shrewd and kindly face destroyed utterly by the pitiless boss of a shield sweeping her aside with vicious disdain, boot prints plain on the fabric of her night-gown where she had been trampled heedlessly underfoot.

'Avila, why don't you take Vahil and get him something warm to drink?'

Temar opened his eyes at Guinalle's soft words, forcing away the horrid image.

'No, there are others in greater need than I—' Vahil began to object uncertainly, but he followed Avila meekly enough when she took his hand, forcing a smile on to her own worn and tear-stained features.

Den Fellaemion looked up at Guinalle from his seat on a low rock ledge. In the dim light filtering through the greenery fringing the cave's mouth, he looked almost as grey as the rocks around him. 'What have you to tell me, my dear?'

The blend of love and grief in Guinalle's eyes as she gazed at her uncle tore at Temar's heart when he could not have imagined any more emotion could have been wrung from him.

'We have tended the wounded as best we can, with Artifice and with what medicaments we were able to salvage.' Guinalle unconsciously pushed a blood-stained sleeve back above one elbow. 'Most are settled and, Ostrin be thanked, most of the injuries are relatively minor. Still, there are a number whom we simply dare not move, not for some days, if we are not to send them straight to Saedrin's mercy.'

'Have you determined how many of your Adepts escaped?' Temar wondered at the urgency in Den Fellaemion's question.

'Nearly all.' Guinalle's answer was bitter with irony. 'We were so much better able to defend ourselves when the invaders started using that Artifice of their own.'

Temar's urge to demand aid from Guinalle and her students in surveying the caves died on his lips as he was suddenly overwhelmed by remembrance of the horror of the previous sunrise. Waking from a contented sleep to the sound of screaming, pure terror ripping through the air, horrid shrieks rising to be cut off by merciless blades as black-liveried invaders poured from ships driven high on to the mud flats to fall upon the undefended colonists. Temar's hand groped for empty air at the memory of grabbing his sword, rushing from his bed in Den Rannion's steading, only to see fires raging all around, women and children fleeing in desperation from the flames only to die on the greedy tongues of swords flashing bright as the building inferno struck a false dawn from the glowering clouds.

Temar's heart began to race, anguish twisting within him as he tried to think what he could have done different, how else he might have succeeded in rallying the men who appeared, whatever weapons they might find in hand, desperate to gather in some concerted defence of the frail wooden gate. Cold fingers gripped Temar's heart, cold sweat beading on the back of his neck as he heard again the echo of their screams, flinching from his own memories of the evil Artifice that had robbed so many of their wits and will, leaving them standing dumbly like beasts awaiting the poleaxe to die under the black metal weapons of the invaders. A tear trickled unheeded down one cheek and he looked down to see his knuckles shining white in a very death grip on his sword.

'You had to flee when you did, Temar.' Den Fellaemion laid his own desiccated hand over the younger man's. 'Saedrin be thanked that you had some little Artifice of your own to defend you, or we would have lost you as well.'

Temar could not trust himself to speak but neither could he resist a guilty glance at Guinalle. He saw only understanding and sympathy in her eyes, and for an instant that made everything even worse.

'Who are these cursed people?' he demanded hoarsely. 'Why are they doing this?'

'Since any attempt at a parley has ended with our envoys meeting a hail of missiles, it's a little hard to tell.' Messire Den Fellaemion's mirthless smile would not have looked out of place on a deathmask. 'I can't see us resolving this by negotiation.'

'I have some idea of where they might be from,' began Guinalle hesitantly.

'What?' Temar and Den Fellaemion demanded in the same breath. 'How?'

'When I was repelling their attacks, I made an unexpected contact with someone imperfectly practised in their Artifice.' Guinalle looked uncharacteristically defensive. 'Last night, when I was sure the youth was asleep, I used that touch to look into his memories.'

'The risks—' Temar drew breath to remonstrate with her but subsided at the Messire's warning glance.

'What can you tell us, my dear?'

'They come from a place far to the north of here, small, barren islands locked together in the heart of the ocean.' Guinalle's eyes grew distant as she looked again on the images she had stolen. 'It's a cold place, pitiless, few trees and bleak, grey rocks all around. They have very little, and what they have they steal from each other, counting blood well spent for a few measures of land. Lives are renewed in due season but land ends at the water's edge.' Her voice deepened and took on a harsher inflection. 'Artifice is used to keep the priests as rulers of the people. They can sniff out disloyalty in the sleeping mind and kill with a thought. Unity is everything when both nature and culture surrounds you with perils, foes always armed against you.'

She caught her breath on a sudden shiver and her expression and tone returned to normal. 'They have discovered what they see as an endless land of unimaginable riches and will not share it with anyone, no matter what,' she concluded softly.

Before Temar could speak, Den Fellaemion rose and gathered Guinalle in a close embrace. 'My dearest child, such insights may be valuable but you are more precious still.' A hint of rebuke stiffened his words. 'Your skills are our only defence against the evil of their Artifice and we cannot risk you in this way. You are not to attempt such a contact again.'

'He would only have thought he was dreaming of home,' protested Guinalle, but her expression was chastened nevertheless.

Temar interrupted as an urgent thought demanded immediate

speech. 'Have you managed to contact home – Zyoutessela, Toremal, anywhere that might be able to send us aid?'

Guinalle shook her head unhappily. 'I have been trying, but something is preventing me, some kind of smothering that is limiting the range of my Artifice.'

'Have you tried working with some of the others?' Den Fellaemion looked up from studying the rocky floor of the cavern.

'I have and that was even worse; we found ourselves harried on all sides by hostile Artificers.' Guinalle shuddered at the memory. 'We barely broke free of entanglement, Larasion blight their seed!'

'So we have only ourselves to rely on,' said the Messire softly, grimly.

'We're well into the sailing season,' Temar protested half-heartedly. 'There will be the new ships on the way who can break through the blockade, if we can only hold out for half a season, maybe less. How close would they have to be for you to contact them, Guinalle, without making yourself a target?' he added hastily.

Den Fellaemion sighed. 'There will be no ships, Temar, in this season or any other.'

Temar could only stare, first at Den Fellaemion and then at Guinalle, who coloured and hung her head. 'What do you mean?'

'There will be no new colonists this year, Temar.' Den Fellaemion could not keep the bitterness out of his voice. 'We had precious few last year, didn't we? The last ships of the season brought me several letters, from my House and from others, all saying the same thing. Nemith is running the Empire into the sands on all fronts, hamstringing his troops with lack of resources at the same time as driving them on like a madman with a metal flailed whip. No one has men or coin to spare to venture overseas; all the provinces are going up in flames. We are on our own here.'

'You've known this all winter?' Temar stared at Den

Fellaemion's pallid face, the sunken eyes still steady and stern.

'What difference would it have made to spread such news?' demanded the older man. 'What benefit would there have been to stir up despondency and doubts when we were doing so well, had gathered a bountiful harvest, Drianon be blessed? We were set fair to spend a busy winter making ready to spread our wings further in due season. From all I could see around me, we had no need of further men and women from Tormalin, if none should choose to come.'

Temar opened his mouth to protest but shut it again, feeling foolish as the force of Den Fellaemion's words struck home. 'And I was so sure we had driven off whatever sortie these invaders had sent against us,' he remembered bitterly. 'That the loss of the *Salmon* was the end of it.'

'We all were,' Guinalle spoke up, her face sombre. 'It's as much my failing as anyone's, Temar.'

'We cannot simply sit here like rats in a trap, waiting for someone to put in our skulls with a club!' Temar sprang to his feet again and ripped a handful of ferns from the rocky wall, peering up hungrily at a distant patch of uncaring blue sky far above. A wisp of cloud was tinged with gold, mute evidence of the unseen sun sinking towards evening.

'There is an alternative, Temar,' Guinalle began hesitantly, her eyes sliding sideways to her uncle who gave her an encouraging nod. 'There is a way we can use Artifice to hide us all in the caves until help can be summoned from Tormalin itself. We can be concealed from any search the invaders might attempt.'

Temar blinked, startled. 'How? But even if you can conceal us, how will we survive? You heard what Vahil said about our lack of supplies. Curse it, Guinalle, there must be close to a thousand people here by now, and more will find their way in before nightfall, Talagrin willing, if they escape the invaders' hounds. I'm none too happy about the water supply and think how cold it was last night. To send a vessel to Toremal and wait for rescue, you're looking at the best part of a full season,

maybe more if things at home are as bad as Messire thinks!'
He shook his head with fresh determination, ignoring the fear
of confinement in the caves that was clamouring in the back of
his mind. 'No, whatever the risks, we must find a way out
of here and try to make it overland to the new settlement.
Use your Artifice to conceal us while we're doing that, to
stop these murdering bastards hunting us down and cutting
us to pieces again.'

'Even if we could find a way out undetected, half these
people would be dead before you'd crossed the first range of
mountains, Temar.' Den Fellaemion looked down the rough-
cut steps crudely hacked into the rock to give access to the
main body of the cave. Temar followed his gaze, to the knots
of families huddled together over a few meagre possessions
salvaged from the nightmare, at the individuals sitting isolated
in the horror of their memories, at the still ranks of wounded,
laid carefully on beds improvised from cloaks, blankets and in
not a few cases leafy branches and sacking. The oppressive
silence had a dull, defeated quality, broken only occasionally by
a child's whimper or a low sob of pain, mental or physical.

'We can't just give up!' protested Temar, fighting to shore
up his own determination.

'We can hide ourselves in a sleep woven of Artifice,' Guinalle
said softly, boundless pity in her soft eyes as she looked down
at the ragged remnant of the once optimistic colonists. 'We
can give these people respite, all life and thought suspended,
Arimelin willing, until help can come to drive away these
invaders.'

'How?' demanded Temar, incredulous.

'There is a way to separate mind and body.' Guinalle
shook the loose hair back from her face and fumbled in
a pocket for something to tie it back. 'It is a rarely used
technique . . .' her voice faltered for an instant, 'only considered in times of grave illness, as a rule. The mind, the
consciousness, the essence of the person, is bound into something they value, something they have an attachment to. With
the mind removed and in stasis within the artefact, the body

is held uncorrupted in an enchantment until the two are reunited.'

'And how would you propose to do that, even supposing you manage to do this with so many people?' Temar stared at her, absently handing her a scrap of leather thong pulled from the trim of his jerkin.

'This is where sending a small detachment overland to the new settlement becomes a valid plan. You're right, Temar, there is a way through the caves; some of the miners found it a while back. It's difficult and narrow, underwater in places but it's passable with care and Misaen's favour.' Animation brought a false hint of colour to Den Fellaemion's wasted cheeks. 'We send a picked band, fighting men, good in the wilds, to get past the invaders undetected, with the aid of Artifice if we can spare someone. They can take these valuables, wherever the minds of these folk left behind reside.'

'To tell the stockmen to strike back, to mount a rescue?' Temar's doubts warred with gathering hope in his voice.

'No.' Den Fellaemion shook his head decisively. 'To tell them to take ship and flee, Dastennin guard them. Curse it, Temar, you've served your House in the Cohorts; how could farmers and stockmen hope to take on greater numbers of trained troops, secure in a defended position, even without the complications of Artifice? No, my orders will be absolutely clear; they must make all speed back to Zyoutessela while the weather is favourable. Then they must enlist the aid of every House that has blood or tenants here in gathering a fleet to come in force and drive these white-haired demons back to their barren islands.'

'You think the help will come in time?' asked Temar, struggling to absorb this astounding proposal. 'Could force enough be rallied to cross the ocean before the autumn sets in?'

'Could the Sieur of any House deny his support, given tokens that contain the very life-essence of his people to hold in his hand? Could he face his brothers and sons knowing he was condemning those minds to for ever remain frozen and insensible, far from their bodies sleeping in a distant cavern for all eternity?' Den Fellaemion's voice was soft, but his eyes were as keen as steel.

'I see what you mean,' said Temar faintly. 'How could they refuse?'

'So will you help us?' Guinalle asked, her eyes pleading with Temar. 'We need to persuade our people here that this is their only hope. We have to call on all the ingrained loyalties to each Name that we bear, give them just enough information to convince them to do this. Without their belief in the plan, it cannot work.'

Temar nodded, his mind already searching the plan for any flaw or opportunity. 'So who will you be sending overland,' he asked Den Fellaemion, 'those with families in the new settlement might be best—'

'They will be the first to submit to Guinalle's ministrations,' Den Fellaemion said sternly. 'Use your wits, Temar, these people have been through a waking nightmare and I am only going to put demands on them where I must.'

'I don't understand,' frowned Temar.

'Think about it, lad,' the Messire rubbed a weary hand over his bloodless lips. 'If we are sending people away from horror and death, towards safety and their loved ones, if danger threatens, who among them is going to struggle to protect a burden, however precious they have been told it might be? I don't mean to condemn our people as cowards, but be realistic, Temar, we need to send men who will lose their lives before they lose these valuables. More than that, we need to give the settlers at the new port every incentive to get home, to rouse a riot if need be, to summon aid and bring help to restore their own loved ones to life again.'

Temar could see Guinalle was as shaken by this uncompromising argument as he was.

'It can only be a matter of time before these invaders follow the coast south and find the new settlement. There's more to this than simply protecting our own lives, you know,' Den Fellaemion continued, his pale eyes distant. 'I do not understand how these murdering bastards came to this land but

I will not leave them our great ships to steal, to cross the ocean with and fall upon an unsuspecting Empire, especially if the chaos that we have heard of is worsening. I bless Dastennin that they were all sent south for refitting in those more sheltered waters. If we must die here, so be it, but I spend my life in defence of my honour to my House, even if my Emperor is a wastrel and a fool.'

Guinalle and Temar exchanged an uncertain look. He stifled the qualms gnawing at his empty belly and squared his shoulders.

'I won't fail you, Messire,' said Temar formally, resolutely banishing his own terror at the prospect of a journey through cramped and dangerous caves. 'You may lay this burden on me.'

'Guinalle, could you go and help Avila, make a start on getting a meal inside these people. Warm food, however little, will put some heart into them.'

Guinalle blinked, evidently surprised at this albeit gentle dismissal, but rose obediently from her damp seat and made her way carefully down the slick steps into the cave.

'You won't be leading the expedition overland, Temar,' Den Fellaemion said crisply.

'You cannot be thinking of going yourself, Messire—' protested Temar hotly.

'No, I am not, I know I haven't the strength left.' Den Fellaemion shook his head. 'This throw of the runes falls to Vahil.'

'But surely—'

'Hear me out, Esquire.' Den Fellaemion folded his arms over his narrow chest and looked steadily at Temar. 'Vahil has Elsire at the new settlement and, yes, I know what I said about choosing those who would go, but this is a special case. The thought of rescuing Elsire is just about all that is keeping Vahil on his feet at present, all that is stopping him succumbing to the shock of seeing his parents slaughtered before him. I'm not going to remove that prop and, more importantly, I need Vahil and especially Elsire to demand aid from the Empire.

As nephew and niece to the Sieur of arguably the mightiest
Name in the south, their demands will not go unmet, I'm sure
of it. Their uncle will get things moving, he will have to or be
forever dishonoured.'

'And D'Alsennin is a fallen House with little or no influence, is that it?' Temar could not keep the bitterness out of
his voice.

'Hardly. Your grandfather will take Nemith himself by
the ears to shake some sense into the sot, if need be,' Den
Fellaemion smiled faintly. 'No, it's rather that I want you
here, at Guinalle's side, just in case of the unexpected.'

'How do you mean?' Temar looked up, a little heartened.

Den Fellaemion drew a sigh deep into his thin frame.
'Guinalle is confident that this extraordinary idea will work
and, more, that she will be able to conceal all traces of the cave
where you are hidden. I have to confess I still have concerns.
We do not know just what Artifice these invaders are capable
of and I am worried lest they find you all and somehow revive
you. Guinalle has had to admit that in theory the body might
be used to summon the mind from afar. In any case, whatever
she chooses to contain her mind will have to remain with her
body, since she has to be the last awake to seal you all in.' He
looked after Guinalle, small in the vastness of the cavern as
she knelt beside a weeping child.

'Of course, she swears that were she to wake to find herself
in the hands of the invaders, she would use the last of her
skills to warn the Empire then to stop her own heart, but I
am concerned that if these savages have the Artifice to wake
her they might also have the skills to take her will from her
and bend her to their purpose. Should that happen, Temar,
I would want you here above anyone else, to defend Guinalle
and to find a way to salvage something from the wreckage
of our colony, even if it is only spending your life in killing
whoever has the Artifice to defeat Guinalle's enchantments.
I know I can rely on you for that, D'Alsennin. I can think of
no other I could call upon.'

Temar could not find any words in the confusion of emotions

within him until one question above all others demanded an answer. 'But you will be here, Messire, surely?'

'No, Temar, I shall not.' Den Fellaemion moved to the edge of the alcove and looked out at the dark-green secrets of the gorge below them, the shadows deepening. 'Walk a little with me, Esquire. We can check on the look-outs.'

Temar drew a deep breath of the fragrant air as they made their careful way along the ledge at the front of the cavern, slippery with returning dew where the sunlight had never reached the stone. Coming out of the shadow, Temar turned his face to the meagre warmth, the chill of the rocks seemingly sunk into his bones. Den Fellaemion rubbed his thin hands together, the hooked nails almost blue against the papery skin.

'I'm dying, Temar,' he said simply. 'The whole reason Guinalle started to research this arcane ritual was in a desperate hope that I would agree to be sent back to Bremilayne in such a sleep, to the shrine of Ostrin where the Adepts might have the skill to destroy the canker that's eating away at my vitals.' He smiled, this time with fondness. 'The dear girl does so hate to be beaten. Anyway, that's how all this started,' he continued briskly, 'but by now there is no likelihood that I could be revived, even if the enchantment did not kill me outright. In any case, knowing that Saedrin waits just beyond the door for me, I cannot see the virtue in sleeping awhile, only to waken to die. I intend to spend my life to some purpose at the last; I am going to take a ship, the rails lined with the fallen, and attempt to run the blockade myself.'

'That's suicide,' said Temar faintly.

'It's a diversion,' Den Fellaemion contradicted him with a glint in his eye. 'I will cast off the day after Vahil has set off through the caves. That should tie up these invaders just as he should be reaching the way out and it ought to keep them from getting curious about the far valley. I will greet Saedrin with a sword in my hand and an oath to Dastennin on my lips, Temar; I don't think he will rebuke me for the waste of a life.'

'More likely Poldrion will give you passage to the Otherworld for free.' Temar blinked away hot tears and scowled at an inoffensive bush.

As leaves behind them rustled, both turned to see Guinalle picking a cautious path through the undergrowth. 'If we are to do this, we have to do it soon,' she said firmly as she approached. 'At present, most of them are still so shocked by what has befallen, I don't think they will argue, even with such a bizarre proposal.' She smiled with a brief flash of humour. 'If we leave it much longer, people are going to become more aware of their situation. Either panic will set in or you'll be dealing with a handful of separate schemes to break out of here. I'm also worried about some of the more frail and the wounded. They may not survive the trials of the night here.'

Den Fellaemion nodded. 'There's nothing to be gained by delay. We'll feed them as best we can then I will speak. Temar, go and help Vahil. Guinalle, get your Artificers together and work out how best to combine your efforts in such a task. Oh, and do what you can to make sure no one is using Artifice to eavesdrop on us, if you would be so good. I don't want to find myself telling these invaders where to find us all like fish stunned for the pot.'

A more immediate concern struck Temar. 'How are we to be reawakened, when help comes?'

'The adepts at the Shrine of Ostrin, where I studied, they will know what to do,' Guinalle stated confidently. 'We will tell all those leaving to make sure the word gets through.'

'Has something like this ever been done before?' enquired Temar, curiosity getting a nose ahead of his instinctive dread.

Guinalle shrugged. 'Not that I know of, but I don't see why that should dissuade us from the attempt.'

'That's the spirit that put the House of Priminale on the Imperial throne!' Den Fellaemion laughed and hugged Guinalle to him as they walked back into the cavern, though now Temar could see the support the older man was taking from Guinalle's slender shoulders.

Temar left them talking to Avila and went to help Vahil, who was giving orders in a listless monotone to women and children whose movements were no less dull and unthinking. However, a hot meal, sparse though it was, did seem to put heart into the gathering. As the noise level rose through the cavern Temar saw the force of Guinalle's argument that the enchantment had to be worked quickly as he began to hear questions and even disputes on all sides.

'My friends!' Den Fellaemion's voice rang through the cavern, silencing the tumult of voices so that an expectant hush hung in the dim air. 'You all know that our situation is grave and I have still more grievous news to give you. Those valiant enough to remain with the boats that brought us here attempted to strike down river this morning in the hopes of breaking through to the open sea and summoning help. I cannot lie to you, my friends, they have failed.' The Messire lifted his voice above sudden weeping and laments from distant corners of the great cave. 'They spent their lives in our defence and Saedrin will speed them to the Otherworld with all due honour, do not doubt it. However, this means that for the present we are trapped with little food or fuel to sustain us, or so our enemies would have us believe and so despair.'

Temar looked around and saw faces raised, questioning this obscure pronouncement, wondering at the new ring of defiance in the Messire's voice, searching for hope or reassurance.

'We have all seen the dark use these invaders have made of Artifice.' Contempt sounded harsh in Den Fellaemion's words. 'What they do not know is that we have Artifice of our own to defeat their foul purposes. We may be trapped for the moment, but we have the means to summon help and it will come, never fear. While we wait, I have decided that Artifice will protect us from all that we lack. Demoiselle Guinalle and her adepts are to give us an enchanted sleep, a respite by the grace of Arimelin, where our grief and wounds will be healed, keeping us safe from all detection until the full wrath of the Empire falls upon these savages and makes them rue the day they ever set foot on our new lands!'

A murmur of startled questions began to circulate around the gathering. Den Fellaemion let it grow for a moment until raising his hand once more for silence. 'As we sleep, Esquire Den Rannion will lead a hand-picked team through the caves and out to the far valley, marching thence to the new settlement in the south. He will take your reassurances to your friends and family there, then use the ocean ships to take everyone far from any chance of harm and to summon the help that will drive these worthless midden-dogs from the lands we have worked so hard to tame.'

A ragged scatter of applause greeted this announcement. Temar saw a faint spark of life relit in his friend's eyes, new determination forcing Vahil's head up and his shoulders back.

'These carrion crows can scavenge on the hollow bones of their victory for the present, but I swear to you they will soon be put to flight. Enjoy your meal, my friends, my apologies that it is so humble, and then we will settle ourselves to wait out this siege in peace and contentment. When we wake, I promise you a better feast, something to look forward to before we start to rebuild our colony.' The total confidence that rang through Den Fellaemion's words was having its effect on the shocked and demoralised people, Temar saw. He heard questions on all sides, over what such sleep might be like, what they might find when they woke, but no one was disputing the proposal itself.

'Will you be with Esquire Den Rannion?' A stout woman whom Temar vaguely recognised as a former tenant caught at his arm.

'No,' he shook his head, forcing confidence into his voice. 'There's no need. I shall wait here with you all, to make sure there's someone ready to give a full account to our rescuers. If you've finished your food, I suggest you make ready. Wrap up warmly if you can.'

The woman nodded, familiar obedience to authority something to cling to in the midst of the catastrophe that had befallen them all, Temar realised. He pushed his way through the crowd, those adept in Artifice surrounded on all sides by questions and demands for more information, Guinalle in particular at the centre of a vociferous knot of people.

'All you need concern yourself over is choosing something precious to you, to focus your mind on while I work the enchantment.' Guinalle was soothing a young mother perilously close to tears as she clutched her three children to her.

'If we all need something, I have so little, my husband—' the girl's lip quivered and her eyes filled, her distress visibly infecting her children and many of those closest to her.

'We can manage easily enough.' Guinalle's voice was warm with reassurance. 'You keep that ring, and why don't we give your necklace to your eldest daughter?'

The girl brought a trembling hand to her throat. 'My mother gave me this on my wedding day. I always wear it. I was going to—'

'She can have the chain, and here, let's put the pendant on this ribbon,' Guinalle broke in briskly. She suited her actions to her words, unfastening the necklace with gentle hands and unthreading a length of braided silk from the purse at her own waist. 'The little one can have that. It's a good choice, too. If the girls are used to seeing you wearing this, it will hold their attention so much better, excellent for the workings of the Artifice.'

She raised her voice a little to address those gathered closest. 'This is the kind of thing you should be looking for, a small trinket that has particular meaning for you and yours.'

Guinalle's confident tone wavered just a little as her gaze fell on the oldest child. She looked round and Temar saw a mute appeal in her eyes. He stepped forward to kneel beside the boy, a lithe lad with coppery blond hair and wide eyes, blue as a spring sky, with a sprinkling of freckles over his snub nose.

'Would you like this, so the lady can work her enchantment over you?' Temar unbelted his tunic and wrapped the leather strap twice around the skinny waist as the boy nodded silently, eyes huge in his pale face. 'Now, you concentrate on this buckle,' he commanded. 'This is an heirloom of the House D'Alsennin. If you can do this, take care of it for me, when you wake up I'll make you my page and you can keep it. Do you agree?'

The lad nodded again, a faint smile on his lips, and Temar looked up at the mother. 'You see, we can easily find something if we all help each other out. After all, it's only something to centre the Artifice upon.'

'The children are so tired, I think it would only be right to let them sleep as soon as possible.' Guinalle led the feebly protesting woman towards Avila. 'Let the demoiselle help you settle them.'

Temar caught Guinalle's hand and gave it an encouraging squeeze, which won a faint smile from her to warm his heart. 'The trick to success here is going to be getting it done fast,' she said with determination.

'Then let's get started,' replied Temar, setting his face to the daunting task.

He settled the boy between his two little sisters and wrapped all three children securely together in a warm woollen cloak. 'Lie back now,' he instructed them softly, tucking a coarse blanket around them with gentle hands.

'All you have to do is close your eyes and think about your special thing.' Guinalle knelt beside the children with an encouraging smile. 'Do you all have something to hold on to?'

The children nodded, wide eyed, and the smallest girl wriggled one hand free to solemnly proffer an enamelled silver flower on its silken cord.

'That's very pretty.' Guinalle stroked shut the eyes of the little lass with one hand, doing the same for her sister with the other. At her nod, Temar tousled the lad's hair before similarly closing that beseeching gaze.

Guinalle softly chanted the complex words of the Artifice. Her low tones were echoed from points all round the vast cavern as Temar watched the Adepts begin the lengthy process of settling the colonists to this frozen rest. He looked back to the children, now motionless, not in the relaxation of sleep but stiff in the grip of the enchantment, no hint of breath to be seen, the colour fled from their cheeks to leave them waxen-faced.

Temar trembled at a sudden memory of childhood horror. It had been the morning he had finally summoned up the courage to return to the playroom, in those dreadful days when he had wandered the house, confused and alone, unable to comprehend how his father, his brothers and sisters had all been taken from him. Opening the door, the blank, painted faces of his sisters' dolls had confronted him, silent, still, never again to be brought to life by happy hands and bright imagination.

'I can't—' Temar choked on his words, but as he raised his head he caught Avila's piercing stare as she carefully laid down the children's motionless mother. The warning and contempt mingled in her eyes cut him to the quick. Temar held out his hand to help Guinalle to her feet. 'Who is to be next?'

In the event it went more quickly than he might have imagined. Temar stood looking across the great cavern as the last of the daylight hung around the alcove at the entrance. He could see rows of motionless bodies lost in the shadows, neatly laid out, hands clasped at their chests like – no, they were not bodies, not like corpses – they were sleeping, taking a respite from the horror that had befallen them, sojourning in the Otherworld by Arimelin's grace, to recover and restore themselves.

'Will I dream?' Temar turned to Guinalle as she lifted her hands from Avila's forehead, the older woman now frozen in the grip of Artifice, her hands clasped around a richly ornamented cloak pin. She was the last of the Adepts to lay herself down, all now exhausted by their efforts.

'What?' Guinalle looked at Temar with eyes barely focusing on him.

'Never mind.' Temar caught Guinalle to him, feeling her trembling uncontrollably with fatigue. 'Are you sure you can do this? Do you want a rest before you go on?' Part of him desperately wanted to delay being locked into sleep only to be buried beneath the earth.

Guinalle was breathing with some difficulty, a pulse in her throat fluttering. 'I think we had better go as fast as we can,' she stammered. 'There's something interfering with the Artifice, everything's going awry. I don't know how much longer I can hold the enchantment together before I have to submit myself to it, otherwise it will all unravel.'

'She knows what she's doing, Temar. Come on, you're the last to take your rest.'

Temar looked round to see Vahil standing behind them, his face grim and drawn, dressed in old leather for the gruelling trip through the caves. The small band going with him were busy packing the miscellany of possessions, safeguarding the unknowing, unconscious minds of the colonists, into a series of leather packs.

'What will you focus on?' asked Guinalle, her voice stronger now.

Temar unbuckled his sword. 'This.' He looked at the blade, at the engraving, rammed it home into the scabbard and gripped the hilt to quell the trembling in his hands.

'Lie down then.' Guinalle knelt beside the pile of cloaks prepared for him and Temar forced himself to comply, gritting his teeth but unable to prevent himself starting at the touch of Guinalle's icy hands on his forehead.

'I'll see you soon, Temar,' Vahil's voice seemed to come from somewhere far distant as insidious tendrils of sleep began to coil themselves around Temar's waking mind.

'Don't fight it, my dearest,' he heard Guinalle murmur, her words distorted as all sensation of the rocks beneath him was lost in a giddying feeling of falling, spinning, his breath coming rapidly, panic burning in his throat, numbness seizing his legs, his chest, his arms, his head, choking him, stifling him.

The hidden island city of Hadrumal,
30th of For-Summer

I was dying. I was suffocating; pressure tight as an iron hand was crushing my chest. As I struggled in a futile effort to draw a last breath, eyes blind, my hearing somehow still clinging to life, I struggled to make sense of the words echoing over my head.

'Push some air into him, Otrick, curse you. 'Sar, warm his blood before we lose him completely.'

The constriction slackened a little and the spiralling dizziness abated somewhat, just enough for me to feel a damp, shaking hand on my forehead. I tried to toss it off, but found I could not move my head. Worse, I could not move my arms or legs; any effort dissolved in confusion. I tried to speak, to swear at these people, whoever they might be, but I could not even raise a groan. At least I could hear; that had to mean I wasn't dead yet, didn't it?

'Planir, I think we have it now, let me—'

A jumble of nonsense words in another voice that I vaguely registered as unfamiliar rang inside my head, scattering the unremembered nightmares that were trying to shred my sanity. Just as I realised this, I managed to move my hand, although with no more control than a day-old babe. Exhaustion overwhelmed me and I let myself drift into the welcoming embrace of helpless stupor.

'No! Don't let him go, don't let him go!'

Some bastard stuck something sharp into my hand and I managed a feeble moan of protest, only wanting all this confusion to go away, to sleep and to sleep again, more deeply.

'Breathe, curse you, Ryshad, breathe!' Now the swine was

slapping my face, and I forced my eyes open to look up at a blurred face, all angles and confusing movement. It gradually coalesced into a man of middle years, close-cropped brown hair surrounding a plump face with dark eyes too close set above a sharp nose. A gleam of silver on his hand caught my feeble curiosity for a moment, but identifying it was simply too much effort, so I just closed my eyes again.

'Ryshad!' That voice was familiar, that one I recognised and that notion distracted me from the seductive lure of slumber. Who was she, I wondered drowsily? She sounded upset. That roused me a little. Whoever she was, she was upset with me. What had I done wrong?

'Wake up, Ryshad, come back to us.' The first voice was getting distinctly annoyed, so I opened my eyes again and a face slowly swam into focus, hair the colour of autumn, eyes of summer leaves. This was the face of the familiar voice, I decided somehow. I coughed and found my breathing easier, my wits slowly piecing themselves back together.

'Livak?' That was her name, I remembered now; I tried to speak but my mind seemed somehow disconnected from my voice. Trying again, I managed a faint croak but was rewarded by a squeeze to my numb hand, a welcome sensation even if it felt as if I were wearing three thicknesses of winter gloves.

'Ryshad, are you with us?' That was the first voice and, after a little effort, I placed it. Planir; it was that bastard Archmage, the one who had landed me in this in the first place. The surge of hot anger that followed on the heels of that thought must have set my wits alight and, in an instant, I knew who and where I was.

I coughed again and smelled the distinctive reek of thassin. 'I said no narcotics, mage.' I rolled my head to glare at him accusingly, still unable to lift it to my intense frustration.

'We found we needed them.' Planir was unapologetic, which came as no real surprise. 'Tonin found your defences against his ritual were simply too strong to break down without it.'

'I'm sorry, I know what I said, but you have to remember this is all untested ground.' This voice did sound genuinely contrite and, with its Soluran lilt, I remembered hearing it moments before. Tonin, that was his name, the scholar and mentor from the University of Vanam who was in Hadrumal, along with his students, to study the few enchantments of aetheric magic so far discovered.

'Did you get what you needed, mage?' I demanded hoarsely, not daring to try to remember for myself in case I fell into that smothering turmoil of sorcery again.

'Oh yes, Ryshad, most certainly.' My wits were still woolly, I realised; the exultation in the Archmage's voice didn't fill me with nearly the dread that my reason told me it should.

'Thank you, thank you very much indeed,' continued the wizard, pulling a plain black robe over his shirt sleeves as he spoke. 'You have been more help than you can possibly imagine. Now, if you will excuse me, I have a great deal to do and you will need time to recover. Otrick, Usara – with me, if you please.'

The three mages swept out of the room without further courtesy and I found myself alone with Tonin and Livak. I managed to get myself on to my side, propped on one elbow, trembling with an exhaustion that for the life of me I couldn't understand. Livak was sitting on a stool by the bed where I lay, rubbing her hands, which I could see had been crushed white and numb in a fierce grip. An angry red line betrayed the bite of a broad ring band into her finger.

'Did I do that?' I asked, aghast.

'You or that D'Alsennin, I'm not sure,' she replied, a faint smile doing nothing to lighten the shock in her eyes, green as deep water and about as revealing.

'Was it very bad?' I managed to keep my voice level, which was some achievement, given the circumstances.

Livak shuddered involuntarily. 'It was so strange,' she said slowly after a long moment's silence. 'It simply wasn't you. There was nothing of you, of Ryshad, in what you said, how you acted, how you moved even. It was all that lad, the D'Alsennin boy, wearing your skin and looking out of your eyes.' She clasped her hands to her face in remembered shock. 'Your eyes, Rysh, they went completely blue, pale as ice and less alive. Arimelin save me, but it was foul!'

I reached for her hand and after a hesitation, a breath only but unmistakably reluctant, she gave it to me. I clung to her like a drowning man as we shared a look and remembered Aiten's death together.

'I'm so very sorry we had to put you through that,' Tonin began hesitantly, plucking absently at the slashed sleeves of his purple jerkin, the latest Ensaimin style from the north, which he wore with none of the required bravado. 'I'll admit I was hoping for a rather more revealing contact than we have had with other subjects, given the extraordinary sympathy you've established with the D'Alsennin sword, but that turned out to be dramatic beyond anything I expected. I certainly had no idea it would be quite so dangerous. I cannot explain it, though I'll address myself to the question at once, obviously.'

The shock in his voice made me realise I had been through something even more traumatic that I had realised, still dazed as I was. I looked at Livak again. 'At least it's all over now. No more dreams, no more voices in my head.'

She looked over at Tonin and I followed her gaze to see him looking first startled then guilty. 'It is over, isn't it?' she demanded in a dangerous tone.

'Well . . .' Tonin clasped his notes nervously to his barrel of a chest and I remembered thinking before that he was somewhat overtimid, both for a man of his size and of such standing in his learned community. His hands were soft too, never toughened by anything more demanding than paper or pen.

'Has Planir lied to me?' I managed to sit up and looked round instinctively for my sword. Still reasoning too slowly, I was thinking I might be using it on the Archmage, before remembering the cursed blade was what had run me into his snares in the first place.

'No one has told you untruths, not deliberately anyway,' Tonin moved closer, his voice more confident. 'It's just that we didn't realise what we were dealing with. We have all been misled by only having such partial information. We all thought these dreams were echoes of the past, carried by the artefacts. Now we know better, it's clear the actual consciousness of the original owner is held in the item and communicating with the unconscious mind of whoever possesses it in the present. That can never have been foreseen, or intended, for that matter.'

'Temar's been doing a cursed sight more than communicate with my unconscious mind,' I just managed not to snarl. 'Are you telling me I still have him lurking in the back of my head?'

'For the moment, I'm afraid so,' sighed Tonin with unfeigned regret. 'I'll set to work at once, go through all the references and that Arimelin archive, see what I can do for you.'

I was tempted to let my mounting fury find its target in him for an instant, but simple justice held me back. It wasn't Tonin's fault and, if he could be believed, it wasn't even Planir's, not really. Besides, I was starting to think that the uncharacteristic rages I had been feeling were not my own, but Temar's. A wave of black depression swept over me as I managed to swing my feet to the floor, my legs feeling as weak as if I'd been lying abed with a four-day fever. 'So I risked my life and my sanity for no purpose?'

'Not at all!' Tonin looked most concerned. 'Now we know what happened to the colonists in Kel Ar'Ayen—'

As he spoke the image of the great cavern full of silent figures came sweeping over me. I gasped and clutched at the bed, hearing the linen rip beneath my fingers as my heart raced, blood pulsing in my head until I managed to slam a door shut on the vision.

'Ryshad?' I hated to hear the uncertainty in Livak's tone.

'Yes.' I managed to open my eyes and squint at her, attempting a reassuring smile and evidently failing miserably.

'Saedrin save us, I hate this!' she burst out, the fury in her voice a dim echo on my own wrath. I clung to that bright anger in a vain attempt to ward off the dark surges of despair threatened me on all sides.

door opened. 'Is he all right?'

'Come in, Shiv,' I said wearily. 'I'm upright and conscious, which is about as good as it's going to get for the moment.'

Whatever Shiv saw in my face evidently shook him, which perversely cheered me up a little. He looked guiltily at Livak, who glared at him, expression fierce.

'I came to see if you wanted to come home with me, if you feel ready,' Shiv glanced at Tonin, 'but if you need to stay here—'

'I'll come.' I got unsteadily to my feet and Livak tucked herself under my arm to give me what support she could.

'It might be better if you waited a while . . .' protested Tonin weakly as we made our way towards to the door.

'No, thank you.' I drew a deep breath and gripped the door handle as much for support as to open it. 'Just find a way to throw Temar D'Alsennin out of my head once and for all.'

Outside I was startled to realise the noonday sun was riding high in the cloud-strewn sky. Hadn't we started this nonsense just after breakfast? I'd sent Shiv with a message, telling Planir to be ready at the second chime of the day and I duly arrived to sit and concentrate obediently on Tonin's incomprehensible, archaic chants. I had certainly been expecting an unpleasant experience, but never to lose myself so completely as I evidently had. If young D'Alsennin had had the run of my head for that amount of time, no wonder I was feeling so peculiar.

'Come on.' Shiv took my other arm. Leaning heavily on the pair of them, I stumbled along towards the dubious sanctuary of Shiv's little house. Given the dramatic events still echoing around in my memory, it was rather incongruous to see women with their market baskets, men delivering faggots of firewood, children skipping through a rope tied to a horse-rail, normal life going on all around me. We certainly attracted some curious glances; people must have thought I was a drunk making an early start, but that was the least of my concerns as I struggled with Temar's increasingly intrusive recollections. I kept seeing Avila trying to hold up Guinalle when she fainted on the boat, Den Fellaemion leaning on Guinalle at a meeting in the settlement, Vahil supporting a wounded man in the frantic flight from the Elietimm invasion. The summer sun was warm on my back but the chill of that distant and long forgotten cavern seemed to have bitten deep into my bones, gnawing at me despite the heat of Hadrumal. By the time Pered opened the door to us, I was shaking again, and not just from fatigue.

Pered took one look at me and shot an accusing glance at Shiv. 'I hope Planir's good and satisfied now,' he said curtly. 'Bring him into the kitchen.'

Half lying, half sitting on a settle padded with blankets, I began to feel a little better, a process speedily aided by a large measure of white brandy. As the warmth of the liquor spread through me I wondered for a moment whether this was entirely wise, but I honestly couldn't see how it could make anything worse by this stage. Forcing myself to take slow, deep breaths, I reminded myself how tedious convalescence from any fever or wound can be. It was all a matter of finding the right attitude, wasn't it? This was simply a different kind of injury, and I would deal with it. Losing my temper was pointless when there was no gain to be had from it; hadn't I learned that long ago? Enough; I had sworn to myself that I would be taking the tiller to control the direction of my life from now on, and this was as good a place to start as any. Brave words, as long as there was only me to hear them. I shut my eyes and set my jaw against any hint of memory.

Shiv vanished upstairs for a while, reappearing in a formal robe of green broadcloth over close-tailored breeches and clean linen. Pered straightened the collar for him with brisk hands, but his eyes were still unforgiving, even as they shared a brief embrace.

'So what happens now, Shiv?' demanded Livak, her eyes like a stormy sea.

'Planir is calling a full session of the Council for this afternoon,' replied Shiv, which effectively silenced us all. 'He wants you there, Ryshad.'

'He's in no condition to speak,' Pered objected heatedly.

'Not to speak, just to listen, to comment if he wants to,'

said Shiv placatingly. 'To learn what Planir intends. It's just that you're so deeply involved in all of this, Rysh, that Planir feels it's only right you should have the chance to participate in any decision-making.'

'What do you think?' I looked at Livak.

'I hate it,' she said simply. 'I don't trust wizards, I'm sorry, Shiv, but I never have.'

'I have to see this through,' I reminded her, 'if I'm to be able to hand back my oath with any measure of honour left to me.'

Livak gritted her teeth audibly. 'I know, but it still makes my skin crawl.'

'Believe me, I understand.' I closed my eyes wearily.

'Does anyone want something to eat?' asked Pered, more for something to say than anything else.

We ate a desultory meal, largely in silence, Shiv awkward in his finery. I picked at some bread, but found I was still somewhat nauseous, shoving it away with relief when a great bell tolled out over the city and Shiv jumped to his feet.

'That's the Council summons,' he said tensely. 'Come on.'

Livak and I exchanged a glance and followed Shiv to the door.

'I'll see you soon.' Pered waved after us, his expression one of concern warring with irritation as he looked after his partner, already a way down the street ahead of us.

I was immeasurably relieved to find the strength returning to my legs; I wasn't about to appear before this Council leaning on Livak, however badly Planir might want me there. We walked slowly down to the hall, finding Shiv hovering anxiously in the archway.

'It's this way,' he said unnecessarily, leading the way to a forbidding door banded with enough iron to stop a fully manned battering ram. This gave on to a short flight of stairs, topped by another grim portal, deep sigils carved into the wood, iron bolts tying in the metal reinforcements. I did not allow myself to be too overawed; I've stood before the Emperor's throne in the Imperial audience chamber of Toremal more than once. My step faltered at that notion as I remembered the destruction I had seen the Elietimm visit upon the place, if only in augury.

The Council chamber itself was impressive, that I have to admit. It took me a moment to realise there were no windows, the illumination inside was so intense. It was not sunlight, but came from a ball of pure radiance hanging in the centre of the vaulted ceiling, a visible display of the magic that had its focus here. The room was circular, dark oaken chairs of varying ages and styles arranged all around the walls, each with a niche moulded into the soft yellow stonework. In the middle an empty circular dais was positioned directly under the ball of light and I wondered who would be standing there, every eye on him. Not me, that was for certain.

Mages of every age and appearance were filing into the great chamber: aged, youthful, ragged, prosperous, placid, alert, some moving swiftly, faces preoccupied, others more slowly, a couple looking frankly vague – and they were two of the younger ones. Some were dressed in finery fit for the Emperor's court, some looked as if they had just stepped out of a tisane house, with every style of dress between to be seen around the room. Not everyone took a seat at first; here and there knots of men and women stood in close conversation, heads close together, glances darting to either side as they exchanged opinions.

'Here.' Shiv led us to three plain seats to the immediate side of the great door. I leaned back in my chair, observing the scene, looking for any clues to which way the tides would be running. All conversation halted for a moment as Planir swept in, Otrick and Usara in his train, all dressed in formal robes of shining silk. I remembered the old wizard, Otrick, from our voyage back from the Ice Islands when he had looked no better than a pirate, braiding the winds in his hands to destroy the Elietimm ships pursuing us. Now he looked every measure the mage as he strode briskly across the yellow flagstones, an azure gown resplendent with embroidery, the sinuous shape of a dragon just apparent amid the design of clouds, if you knew to look it out.

Usara was wearing an amber robe rather than the undistinguished brown I had always seen him in previously. Silver thread was worked down the front to frame gemstones highlighting a complex pattern of angled lines. For a man who usually seemed so diffident there was no trace of hesitation in his step; he carried his head high, a fine rod of white gold in one hand. Planir reached his seat and turned in his heel to survey the waiting wizards, drawing all eyes irresistibly to him. He was all in black, the cut of his robe impeccable, discreet ebony embroidery on the darkness, a touch of sable at the collar for a hint of luxury, hair close-cropped and face clean-shaven, eyes bright and dangerous. He put me in mind of a raven, watching and waiting, ready to fly through a rainbow carrying tidings to the Eldritch Kin, their concerns beyond mortal ken. As their Archmage stood there, silent, expectant, the various mages rapidly found their places, the last to seat himself in a highly polished and canopied chair, a fat man in an overelaborate mantle of red velvet flames.

Planir raised a hand and I expected him to speak, but instead a metallic whisper at my side made me turn my head to the door. As I watched, the great straps of iron that bound the wood spread themselves, shimmering and running into each other and over the door jambs to seal the entrance with a solid sheet of metal. Livak and I exchanged a dubious glance.

'So, you have all had a report of what Mentor Tonin's rites have discovered for us, through the D'Alsennin sword and the courage of Ryshad Tathel.' I kept my face impassive as Planir nodded a brief acknowledgement in my direction before continuing briskly. 'I do not propose to reiterate this information; time is pressing, so I will open the floor to debate.'

Wizards on all sides looked at each other; this was clearly some departure from established practice. I was not surprised to see the fat man in red was the first on his feet, his expression eager.

'I think, Archmage, that these researches are now quite

clearly complete. You have been telling us for several seasons now that your aim is to establish the fate of this colony, and now you have your answer. While it is always interesting to be able to put such a firm conclusion to a question of historical record and, I will allow, it is a rare achievement, there is now nothing more to be said on the subject. The colony failed, these people are lost and now we must turn our minds to more pressing matters.'

The wizard adopted a lordly pose, one plump and lavishly beringed hand resting on his chest. 'It is time wizardry began to play an active role in the affairs of the mainland and I can see no more opportune time when we have clear evidence of such a threat causing such concern to the Princes of Tormalin. We have been keeping our peace at your insistence while Mentor Tonin and his scholars attempted to complete their researches, but now we must act. I know your modesty will not permit you to take all the credit, Planir, but this Council should know that you, in your office as Archmage, have taken considerable pains to locate and trace the movements of the envoys from these Ice Islands who are even now attempting to undermine the security of Tormalin and the ocean coast. The business of this Council must be to decide how we are to rid the mainland of these insidious vermin. In doing so, not only will we put paid to their schemes in short order but we will also demonstrate our undoubted right to participate in the decisions of the ruling classes, wherever they may be.'

'You are very confident of your ability to drive out these Elietimm, Kalion.' A sturdy woman in crimson with a no-nonsense expression spoke, rising from a chair on the far side of the sealed door from me. 'May I ask how you propose to combat a magic we patently still fail to understand?'

'I remain to be convinced that this aetheric artifice is such a threat as has been suggested.' Kalion's reply was patronising enough to set my teeth on edge; he had barely sat long enough for his broad arse to dent his cushion before getting to his feet again. 'The scholars who have been researching it for many seasons now have little more to show for their pains than festival tricks and curiosities.'

Livak stirred beside me and I knew she was remembering the savage sorcery that the Elietimm had wielded to such dire effect on our trip to their cursed islands. I blinked on a sudden memory that had to be Temar's; of the ship, the *Eagle*, her rails lined with the mindless bodies of her crew, and I struggled to conceal a shiver of apprehension.

'I rather think you're missing the point, Kalion.' The woman was unbothered by the big man's superior attitude. 'The question is not what we can achieve with this enchantment, it is rather what these Elietimm can do.'

'Surely the Archmage's information makes such questions irrelevant?' Kalion flicked his hand in a throw-away gesture. 'The basis for this magic was destroyed along with the Empire, if his conjectures are correct, as I am sure they are.'

'What about all this nonsense in the Archipelago, this cult of the Dark Queen or whatever it was?' objected a mage with a Lescari accent, looking up from a handful of notes. 'Isn't that a clear attempt by the Elietimm to create a focus of belief so as to provide themselves with a source of power?'

'You know, I've been wondering about that,' his neighbour said eagerly. 'Do you think this means there is a limit on the distance over which they can draw on this aetheric potential? Are they in any sense cut off from the power vested in their home islands when they are on the mainland?'

I kept my face expressionless as several others joined the discussion and Kalion seated himself reluctantly, still leaning forward, ready to be first to his feet again. If the Convocation ran their debates in Toremal like this, the great Houses would never have risen anew above the Chaos. Shouldn't one of the Archmage's roles be to conduct this Council? I looked at Planir as I was thinking this but, seeing the keenness in his eyes, concluded things were indeed taking just the course he wanted.

'I have a more pertinent question regarding the collapse of this aetheric magic.' A short but sturdy man in blue rose to his feet on the far side of the chamber. 'This new tale takes us up to the loss of the colony but I still do not see how the Artifice, aetheric magic, call it what you will, was in fact destroyed. I thought the whole purpose of these highly risky proceedings was to discover this very thing? What progress has been made on this issue?'

'We have been giving the matter our closest attention, Rafrid,' Usara spoke up and walked swiftly to the centre of the room, rod in hand. 'We contend that it is all a matter of balance. I would remind you all that such concepts of harmony and symmetry were central to Ancient Tormalin religious practice, albeit those ideas have been largely obscured in later liturgy.' As he spoke, he lifted the rod to a level with his eyes and then removed his hand, leaving the gleaming metal bar hanging in the empty air. 'The scholar Geris Armiger established, I think beyond argument, that this aetheric magic draws its power from the unconscious potential of the mind, a capacity greatly enhanced when those minds are focused on a common loyalty or belief. Forgive me, I know you will all have read the relevant dissertation.'

A glance round the room soon told me who had and who either had not or was a wizard to avoid meeting over a game of runes or Raven. I saw a faint smile in Usara's eyes as he looked around the room, halting briefly at Planir, bowing slightly before continuing.

'Mentor Tonin's researches suggest that this potential is a collective phenomenon, a reservoir of power without defined boundaries. I am sure he will be only to happy to go through the evidence if any of you wish to consult him later. For the moment, it is sufficient to say that two groups wielding aetheric magic may oppose each other absolutely, be convinced of radically different philosophies or ambitions, yet remain linked by the underlying principle.'

With a wave of his hand, Usara's bar became the beam of a balance, a pan on either end heaped high, one with black crystals, one with white.

'The Lady Guinalle was certainly learned in the practical

applications of her Artifice but I get no sense that she, or indeed any of her teachers, fully understood the fundamentals of the power they were using. Her youth alone suggests no lengthy period of study. Our contention is this: in removing such a large number of people from the equation, including a disproportionate element trained in focusing the aether or as they called it Artifice, Guinalle inadvertently unbalanced the entire supporting structure of that power.'

Usara snapped his fingers. The white crystals cascaded towards the floor to be followed by the black as the balance swung wildly up and down. He bowed at the faint ripple of applause and amusement running around the room and picked the rod out of the air, crystals and scale pans disappearing with a flash.

'That is all very interesting but we should address ourselves to the Tormalin—' the wizard Kalion was up in the next instant, struggling to hide a scowl as Usara's theatrics diverted the attention of the gathering from his intended purpose for the debate.

'Kindly allow the rest of us to participate in this discussion, Hearth-Master.' A tiny, wrinkled woman in a crumpled leaf-green robe stood with some effort, leaning heavily on a carved, crooked stick. Nevertheless her voice cut through the room like a hot blade through wax. She fixed Usara with a glittering eye, keen as a dagger. 'Young man, I find it very hard to believe that these people, with all the tradition of scholarship of which we have been told, had so little understanding of the fundamentals of their art that such a mistake could be made. No mage here would make such an error; few apprentices beyond their first season's training could!'

One of the younger wizards in grey with a discreet scarlet trim to his tunic stood, his expression thoughtful and his manner assured despite his lack of years in such a company. 'I think, Shannet, that it would be more accurate to say that no apprentice would have the opportunity to make such an error these days. Here in Hadrumal, we have twenty genera-tions of research and scholarship to support us, a thorough understanding of the laws of magic as they pertain to the elements. Yet we have all read the diaries of those who first came to this island with the founding Archmage Trydek, have we not? Those early wizards were working with purely empirical knowledge, mere fragments of the understanding we now have. What little learning those mages came with was garnered from widely differing traditions, acquired in an entirely haphazard manner. The early history of Hadrumal is one of experimentation, trial and error, is it not? Magic was used extensively for many generations with a very imperfect understanding of its nature. I see no reason why these Ancients should not have been using their Artifice with as little basis of true wisdom.'

'Given they believed their power was god-given, why would they have felt the need to explain its origins anyway?' a wizard similar enough in age and appearance to the first to be his brother chipped in, not bothering to stand.

'Who's to say it was an error, anyway?' A tall, spare man in ochre robes got briefly to his feet. 'This girl may have known exactly what she was doing, killing two birds with the one stone as it were; saving her folk and striking at the enemy in the one enchantment.'

The immediate doubt in my mind at this proposal was unmistakably tinged with Temar's reactions.

'But what of the effect on the Empire in Tormalin?' protested a motherly-looking woman. 'Granted Nemith the Last's misrule had seriously undermined Tormalin power by that point, but it was the collapse of the magic that precipitated the final downfall!'

'I think you will find all the writings on harmony and balance date from the generations immediately after the Chaos,' a nervous-looking young man near Usara bobbed up to speak. He looked as if he had more to say, but he lost his nerve and sat again.

I gritted my teeth and ignored the stray thoughts trying to hook my attention, concentrating hard on the increasingly wide-ranging debate as further wizards discussed the nature of the scholarship of magic. Most of it went completely over my head, so I watched Planir and Kalion instead, the former silent and poised like a waiting hawk, the latter visibly irritated at his inability to steer the meeting in his chosen direction. I can't be sure but I think I saw a brief glance exchanged by Planir and the mage Rafrid before the latter rose to speak again.

'I think we can agree to accept Usara's contention as a working hypothesis until more compelling evidence emerges to refute it, can't we?' said Rafrid mildly. 'Interesting though this debate has become, I would like to know what those scholars working with Mentor Tonin feel their next step should be?'

All eyes turned to Tonin, who got slowly to his feet, a sheaf of parchments in one hand betraying him with a faint fluttering. 'Now that we have the Arimelin archive from Claithe to complement the records of the Dimaerion traditions in eastern Solura, I am hopeful that we could attempt to reunite the minds and persons of these ancient Tormalins, were we able to bring the artefacts and bodies together. We have increased our understanding of the lesser uses of the aetheric principles in recent seasons and I am hopeful that we have identified rites that would reunite that which Artifice presently keeps separate.'

My own surge of hope at Tonin's quiet words was echoed by an answering desire ringing through the back of my mind. I was suddenly convinced Temar was as eager to be free of me as I was to be rid of him.

Rafrid stood patiently as a surge of speculation ran round the room, eventually subsiding as the assembled mages looked at each other and finally back at him. He looked round the room. 'Should we consider doing this?'

'Of course,' said the woman who had first answered Kalion. 'Think of the information they could give us, about this aetheric magic, about all the mysteries of the Ancients that were lost in the Chaos.' She shot a hard glance at the fat wizard. 'Then we will know exactly what we are facing in these Elietimm and their peculiar magic.'

'These people have been lost for, what, twenty-five generations or more?' scoffed a balding man in brown, 'and you are proposing to restore them to life again? Their families are long gone, any land or possessions scattered to the four winds, in every sense that matters, these people are as good as dead. I appreciate there are many scholars curious about the fall of the Tormalin Empire, but I hardly think it reasonable to thrust these unfortunates into our world, when so many changes have happened, when so little from their own age has survived, just to satisfy an intellectual curiosity. What's done is done. These people should remain at rest. Nothing will be gained by such an attempt at rescue so long after the event.'

'Oh, I don't know about that,' one of the younger mages spoke up, again without standing. 'Read the primary sources, Galen. Look at the language and ideas. Consider the vast amount of knowledge lost in the Chaos. I'd say we of this generation have more in common with the people of the last days of the Empire than with almost any generation in between.'

'I don't necessarily agree with that, Reis, but am I right in thinking the dreams that these artefacts have been provoking indicate these people are far from at rest?' A severe-looking man in his middle years looked at Tonin. 'Is that not so?'

'I would certainly argue that the intensity and detail of the dreams reflects the desires of the subject to be free of the enchantment,' nodded Tonin, his voice confident. I could definitely confirm that, I thought grimly.

'Surely, now that we have this knowledge, we have a duty to rescue these individuals from this undeath?' a plain young woman in a modest rose dress spoke up suddenly, blushing at her own daring. 'We cannot condemn them to an eternity in the shades, neither in this world or the other, at the mercy of Poldrion's demons. Such a fate should only befall the worst of people, not innocents such as these.'

From the expressions around the room, I gathered traditional religious beliefs were not common among the wizardry. The girl sat down again, ducking her head and clutching a shawl to her. I realised I remembered her from a brief meeting the previous year – Allin, I recalled her name was.

'You say this restoration is something you could attempt?' A petite woman in an expensively cut turquoise gown stood, fine-boned hands clasped together, head tilted, birdlike as she looked at Tonin. 'You are not certain of your rites, as I understand it; rather you have been piecing them together from various traditions and sources of lore?'

'I am confident that we have sufficient reason to make the attempt,' replied Tonin carefully. 'I would argue that our priority should be the woman Guinalle. Her skills would then supplement our own knowledge and aid us in reviving the remaining colonists.'

'But what if there is some flaw in your ritual, some vital piece of information missing?' persisted the elegant mage. 'What will happen then? Does failure risk the irretrievable loss of this suspended mind? Are you prepared for such consequences?'

'Ely has a point. Have all the potential sources of information been exhausted?' enquired a nearby wizard thoughtfully. 'Perhaps we should wait a season or so, make sure all the knowledge available has been gathered?'

'We have already sent word to Bremilayne,' the scholar interjected hastily, 'to see what can be learned from the Shrine of Ostrin, since D'Alsennin's tale makes such significant mention of it.'

'What about that girl whom you still can't revive, Mentor Tonin? What of her fate?' demanded a voice from somewhere. I saw Tonin flush miserably.

'May I make a point?' A mage in a workaday jerkin of no significant colour and buff breeches raised a hand. 'If this rite requires both the body and the artefact, any discussion of whether we should do this remains entirely academic until we have located the cave in question. This discussion is irrelevant until we have some idea of where to look. Are you proposing that we cross the ocean in search of this unknown land, Archmage?'

Planir remained seated as he looked at the wizard posing

the question. 'Clearly that would be essential, Herion, should the Council decide to pursue this. However, that is not such a startling proposal as it might seem. With the assistance of the House of D'Olbriot, we have found copies of the original charts made by Den Fellaemion's early expeditions. Given we sailed deep into the ocean last year to rescue Messire D'Olbriot's man over there from the Ice Islands, Cloud-Master Otrick is now well acquainted with the currents and wind systems prevailing in the eastern waters. Moreover, now that the tale of this colony has been uncovered, albeit in part, both Messire D'Olbriot and the Emperor Tadriol himself have expressed an interest in finding the lands in question and offered all aid at their disposal.'

I saw the fat wizard Kalion's eyes grow shrewd as he worked that fact into his calculations.

A burly man of middle height stood, waving one hand in an urgent demand for attention. 'In which case, we should wait until these Tormalins have made the attempt and see what they discover. What is to be gained by running such risks ourselves when for all we know these bodies may have rotted away entirely, been crushed in a rock fall, been eaten by wild beasts?'

'Mentor Tonin tells us that the ability of the artefact to promote dreams is linked to the continued existence of the body itself!' An untidily dressed female of uncertain age sprang to her feet, her tone scornful. 'As you would know had you read his submission properly, Edlow.'

This exchange sparked a more heated debate on a wider front. The noise grew as several separate arguments raged, the flames fanned by discourtesy on all sides, from those supporting the rescue of the colonists as well as from those dismissing the whole idea.

'What happens now?' I asked Shiv, leaning close to make myself heard over the hubbub.

'Watch Planir,' he advised, a smile in his eyes, if not on his carefully neutral face.

As I looked, the Archmage exchanged a few words with

both Otrick and Usara and then walked swiftly to the dais in the centre of the room. Silence fell and Planir swept a low bow to the assembled wizards, his back to me.

'The wizard Viltred Sern wishes to speak. I would ask that you give his words serious consideration.' Unmistakable authority rang through the Archmage's voice as Viltred, whom I had not even noticed sitting quietly on the far side of the room, made his way to the central dais. The old wizard was leaning on a slim cane but his colour was better than I remembered it, his clothes no longer threadbare but newly made of stout gentian broadcloth. When he spoke, his voice was calm and assured, the old man seeming to gain in stature as he surveyed the gathering.

'You are debating whether you should or should not attempt to raise the lost settlers of Kel Ar'Ayen to life again as if it were some scholarly exercise, as if you had all the time in the world to come to a decision or to do yet more research in a bid to guarantee success.'

His faded gaze swept round the seated wizards and his voice grew more cutting.

'Drag your heads out of your close-written scrolls and sheltered researches for a moment. Consider what is happening in the real world, even as we speak. The Archmage has told you what his agents have been reporting to him, has he not? These Men of the Ice, these Elietimm, have been appearing among the Aldabreshi since the turn of the year before last, and now we know why. They are spreading this cult, this worship of the Queen of the Dark Moon. What is their purpose? Now we know; these Elietimm are creating a reserve of aetheric power to fuel their sorcery, which grows stronger with each convert to this new cult. Do not imagine that conversions will cease; the worship of a powerful female deity will find many takers among the Aldabreshi Warlords' women folk, whatever their other philosophies.'

Viltred paused for a moment and shook his head. 'Set aside the questions of magic for a moment; what else are these so-called priests doing? The experiences of D'Olbriot's sworn man make it clear that these Elietimm are actively working to spread their influence in the Archipelago and shrink from little in their determination to do so; imagine the man assaulting a Warlord's wife with complete disregard for the consequences, no less! Am I the only one concerned at the prospect of a hostile race gaining a hold over those who contribute so much to the decisions the Warlords make? Look to the future; what if holding a cult in common has the effect of unifying the domains? Where will Aldabreshin eyes turn then, if they are no longer watching each other so closely?' Viltred walked round the edge of the circular dais as he spoke, his words lashing the assembled wizards.

'Another question: what power did this priest have that gave him the confidence to ignore the might of an Aldabreshi Warlord in his very encampment? Evidently he had sufficient capabilities to remove himself bodily from peril when his sorcery failed to overcome Ryshad's will. Let us think about that for a moment; we can all translocate ourselves if need be, but what of this dominance over the mind? This aetheric magic has facets we cannot match, however strong our own enchantments in other spheres. We know these Elietimm retain their knowledge of the old sorcery, despite having lost their original source of power. Consider the implications of what you are being told! The Elietimm have crossed the ocean again, a feat that we know requires magical aid from whatever discipline, aetheric or elemental. Quite clearly they have somehow restored themselves; they are now able to apply that knowledge and take to the open seas for the first time in twenty or more generations! They are working from a position of strength, do not doubt it.'

The mage took a pace backward, to the centre of the dais where the magelight overhead grew faintly tinted with blue under the force of his passion.

'We are not here to debate the rights and wrongs of an erudite moral dilemma! We are facing very real dangers. These men who are even now spreading their lies among the Aldabreshi are of the same race as those who attacked and defeated the Kel Ar'Ayen settlements with savagery, madness and death by sorcery. Read the tale that D'Olbriot's man has brought you, of the last days of D'Alsennin and his attempts to defend those beleaguered colonists. Ask yourselves how you would counter the magics that were used if you should find them raised against Hadrumal? Remember no matter how much we may learn about this magic of the mind and matter, we cannot use it. Not one of the weakest mage-born has been able to master the simplest cantrips of an illiterate Lescari hermit. Our magic is powerful, but I prefer to fight fire with my own fire. The finest sword in the world is little use if your enemy is using a pike or a crossbow!'

Viltred turned and spread his hands in a dismissive gesture. 'Not that these Elietimm will be interested in Hadrumal of course, not when far richer and more helpless game grazes all unsuspecting for their arrows. If these Elietimm wage war against Tormalin now, what is there to resist them? With all due respect to Mentor Tonin and his scholars, aetheric magic these days is reduced to little more than a meaningless jumble of superstition and half-remembered incantations. Our practitioners of aetheric enchantments certainly cannot meet the Elietimm on anything approaching level ground. Can we mages defeat them with our own magics? Perhaps, but I do not share Hearth-Master Kalion's certainty. More to the point, would we be allowed to? Can anyone here seriously imagine the Emperor allowing the wizards of Hadrumal free rein with fire, flood and storm, even if it is to defend his lands? I do not see that happening before the situation is utterly desperate. How long do you think it would take these sorcerers to gain a hold on the mainland if they really want to?'

Viltred gripped his cane in one thin hand and shook his fist at the assembled mages. 'Whatever the risks, whatever the dangers of drowning ourselves in the far ocean or condemning these unfortunates trapped in enchanted sleep to madness or darkness, I tell you that we should not be debating whether we can afford to try to revive these people! Rather the question is can we afford not to, can we afford to face the threat of this Elietimm sorcery without some true knowledge of aetheric magic, without at least one person who knows these people and what they are capable of? Make no mistake, this threat is real and it is not going to go away. We know they are already covertly attacking our ability to resist them; you have all been told of their attacks on Tormalin shrines over the winter seasons. Why else would they do this, if not to destroy the last vestiges of aetheric lore remaining to us? I am here myself, forced into flight to escape torture and death at Elietimm hands, leaving them free to steal some few things from the lost colony that I recovered on my voyage with Azazir.'

Viltred paused for a moment, struggling with an understandable desire to remind the Council of the derision that had always greeted the tales of that journey. To his credit, the old wizard rose above the urge, continuing his challenge in a harsh voice.

'There's another question! Ryshad's testimony shows the extent of Elietimm interest in these artefacts from Kel Ar'Ayen, even more than my own experiences. Possessing the D'Alsennin sword was so important to this so-called priest that he was prepared to risk not only doing murder but working his enchantments in the very heart of the Archipelago, with all the dangers that entailed. How important would a quest have to be before any of you would risk the torments the Warlords reserve for the crime of magic? Ask yourselves – why do these Elietimm want these artefacts for themselves? I don't know but I'll wager a pennyweight to a pack-load that it bodes ill for the colonists if we do not rescue them! In all conscience and logic, how can we do anything else?'

The room erupted into chaos as the mages all tried to speak at once, shouting each other down with scant regard for the formalities of debate, leaping to their feet on all sides. Viltred returned to his seat and sat down, arms folded tight, breathing hard, passion burning in his fierce eyes. Planir sat on his plainly carved chair, face calm but a spark of cunning deep in his eyes. There was an alertness to his relaxed posture that reminded me of a hunting heron, ready to strike when the moment was right.

I couldn't see what signalled that moment but Planir suddenly sprang to his feet, a carved ebony staff appearing in his hand from the empty air. The foot of the stave came down on the flagstones with a ringing strike that silenced the chamber. As the mages stood motionless, cut off in mid-pronouncement, Planir strode to the dais.

'Be seated. This debate has lasted long enough. We have a clear choice before us. Do we act or not? Do we take what knowledge we have and try to rescue the settlers of Kel Ar'Ayen, or do we do nothing, simply continuing our researches despite the Elietimm threat?' He struck the dais with the staff, the hollow boom echoing round the great chamber as the wizards hurried to their seats. 'Those for action?'

Mages all around the room raised their hands, some with papers clutched in them, some with staff or rods. Beams of radiance streamed from them and gathered in the centre of the room, coalescing in a brilliant pattern of coruscating light, cyan, saffron and rose flickering on the very edge of sight.

'Those against?' Planir demanded.

The remaining wizards summoned their powers and sent tendrils of shadow into the shifting luminescence, strands of darkness weaving into the light and dimming it, softening the lustre with shades of jade, vermilion and indigo. The pattern hung in the air, the colours twisting around each other in a dizzying confusion. I blinked and leaned toward Shiv, careful not to risk touching the stream of emerald light rising from his outspread hands.

'What's the purpose of this?'

Shiv's eyes did not leave the twisting and tangled rainbow above our heads. 'The Council does not make its judgements on mere numbers but on the strength of will shown by those called to give judgement,' he said softly. 'Watch.'

I watched as the colours writhed and fought, casting strange reflections on the upturned faces all around the room. The shadows grew, thickened and dimmed the radiance but could

not put it out, suddenly fading as colour as intense as sunlight
striking off gemstones burned through the darkness.

'Enough.' Planir banged his staff a third time and the colours
vanished, leaving blinding white radiance that scoured the eyes.
'The decision of the Council is for action. So be it!'

CHAPTER TEN

Taken from the correspondence of Leorn Den Lirel, last Governor of Caladhria in the 7th year of Emperor Nemith the Reckless; held at the Archive of the Temple at Col.

Solstice salutations from Leorn to his brother Jahon.

I do not know how long this letter will take to reach you but I feel sure the Imperial Despatch will still fight their way through, no matter what calamities befall the rest of us. I don't know what reports you've had of the situation here, but you can take the worst and double all the figures. It's bloody chaos and without any support from home, there's not a thing I can do about it, so I've given up trying. Don't worry, I have a ship standing by and will sail for home as soon as the fighting comes south of the Ferl River. Amille insists on celebrating Solstice here but I'm sending her and the children home immediately afterwards. The damp may have got into my library, but not into my wits! Please tell Mother to expect them anytime around the turn of Afi-Summer; we'll have to stay with her until we can move our tenants out, so make sure you give them notice to quit as soon as you receive this.

As I'm sure you can imagine, this is not how I had hoped my appointment would turn out, but with the Emperor withdrawing the Cohorts for his mad plan to conquer Gidesta I simply do not see how I am supposed to maintain Imperial rule here. None of the locals have paid their due taxes since Equinox and I can't even get the records to make a fresh assessment. My officials are showing remarkable ingenuity when it comes to finding reasons for staying inside

the Governor's Compound rather than risking themselves on
any of their duties in the countryside. I cannot say I blame
them and I am certainly not going to send them out to battle
with brigands and scavengers armed only with quill-case
and inks. Most of them are spending their time drawing
up highly dubious claims to supposed ancestral lands and
planning how to go about seizing them when Tormalin rule
officially ends.

I suggest you start liquidating your investments here,
discreetly but rapidly; there are no profits in Caladhria
any more. It might be worth keeping an eye open for
opportunities in Lescar; Governor D'Evoir's murder will
mean panic selling and there should be bargains to be had.
From what I hear, the Reeves are planning to set themselves
up in their old tax districts and work together to enforce their
own rule. I don't suppose they'll be swearing allegiance to
that wine-soak that calls himself Emperor these days, but
frankly I don't see why that should concern us if you
see a likely chance to turn up some coin. Nemith's idiot
ambitions must have cost our House his own weight in
white gold by now, and the sooner Poldrion ferries him
to the Otherworld the better as far as I'm concerned. I'm
planning to drop his Imperial Majesty's statue down the
privy pit when I leave.

I nearly forgot; no, I have no idea what Den Fellaemion
was up to when he sailed last. In all the confusion that
surrounds us these days, I couldn't even tell you how many
years ago it was. I can't think of anyone else who might
either. I think Den Rannion was somehow involved, but the
present Sieur seems very keen to hush it up, so I can only
suppose it came to naught.

The lost settlement of Kel'Ar Ayen,
42nd of Aft-Summer

'This is rather different to our little excursion last year,' I observed to Shiv as the wizards' ship swung slowly at anchor in the broad estuary. It was a relief to be out of the gales that scythed across the open ocean and I turned to the warmth of the late summer sun, noticeably hotter here than I would expect at home this end of the season. I smiled with pleasure at the sensation of the sun on my clean-shaven face.

'If I have to cross the ocean, I'd rather do it in a well-built three-master with the mightiest of the Council subduing wind and wave, I have to admit,' Shiv grinned back at me. 'It's a sight better than that fishing boat, isn't it? Even Livak only got a little seasick.'

I didn't want to discuss Livak at the moment. 'When will the rest of us be going ashore?' I nodded at the ship's row-boat, which was unloading a group of mercenaries on the nearby beach.

Shiv frowned. 'There still seems to be some disagreement about that. Most of the mages want to stay aboard for a while, let Halice and her – er – "associates" scout out the terrain first.'

'Surely the search would get done faster and more effectively with magic to help?' I turned to Shiv, puzzled.

He shook his head ruefully. 'I think it's going to take a while for my esteemed colleagues to become used to working co-operatively with fighting men, whatever Planir may require of them.'

I looked along the rail, to where Halice stood with the commander of the mercenary force, a massive man called

Arest with an uncompromising attitude and an ill-educated Dalasorian accent. Lack of education didn't mean lack of intelligence however; his narrow eyes were alert with practical cunning, and from what Livak had told me he'd been a major player in the endless games of the Lescari wars for a good few years. More importantly he had no problem treating Halice as an equal, leaning his blunt head close to hers as they discussed their next moves. I wondered briefly if they might have been lovers at some stage; they had that air of familiarity about them but discarded the notion as irrelevant. I looked at Halice's leg, now much straighter and able to bear some weight, though still far short of being fully healed. I wondered what part she would be playing in this particular game.

When Planir had got his decision from the Council and instantly set about organising this voyage, he had been momentarily wrong-footed by the discovery that all his own most valued agents, men whose skills and sword arms were retained for his use by liberal amounts of coin, were absent on other commissions. It had been Halice who had suggested looking for mercenaries spending the Summer Solstice in the Carifate. It seemed the battles of Aft-Spring and For-Summer between Parnilesse and Triolle had been bloody, vicious and inconclusive, hardly a surprise in itself, and the self-declared neutral region around Carif had been full of the disgruntled remnants of scattered corps, looking around for a hire that offered them a better than even chance of ending the summer with coin in their hands, instead of as ashes in an urn.

Halice had made herself extremely useful to the Archmage, using her many contacts to weld together a troop of hardened fighters sharp enough to have seen the way the fish were running and get clear of the futile slaughter that was overwhelming the central dukedoms. The roll of Raeponin's runes had brought bloody chaos back to Lescar once more after a few years of comparative peace. I spared a thought for Aiten's family, hoping Messire's gold was giving them either a measure of security or the means to flee.

Shiv and I watched a second group of fighting men and

women getting their gear together, tightening straps and adjusting sword-belts. The mercenaries were a battered lot, I had to admit, which was probably what was disconcerting the wizards. Nearly all bore scars on faces and hands, old and white as well as new and purple, some ugly and puckered, betraying a lack of the skilled treatment a sworn man can justifiably expect. Their clothes were mostly leather, black and brown with only rare touches of colour, covered with cloaks of fur and crudely tanned skins rather than the good broadcloth that a true patron provides. I stifled a pang of muted sorrow, remembering Aiten arriving to take service with Messire in similar rough attire.

'Halice was saying these are among the best she could hope to find.' Shiv smoothed his own immaculate tunic unconsciously and adjusted the ornate silver belt buckle that Pered had given him before we left. 'It doesn't look as if they spend much of their loot on clothes, does it?'

'Who needs to look smart to fight? I reckon their money goes into their swords.' The quality of the weapons each warrior carried had been the first thing I had looked for. 'Workmanship like that doesn't come cheap.' The ragged and stained garments worn by the mercenaries contrasted sharply with their armour and weaponry, ready for anything they might discover in this untrodden land. Most wore two swords as well as daggers in belts and in boot tops, while many carried bows, a mace or a spear and more besides. Well-honed metal scattered bright reflections from the hot sun, in sharp contrast to the dull sheen of plate and chainmail, newly scoured free of the biting rust that had gnawed at the metal on the long voyage, fed by the damp, salt air. I was having to burnish the steel of my mirror almost daily if I wanted to shave without cutting myself, but at least my own armour required little maintenance.

Arest started down the ladder into the ship's boat and Shiv and I both involuntarily held our breath as rope and wood creaked with protest under his weight; the man wore a full hauberk and coif, grieves and vambraces, as well as carrying swords, a shield and a pack. He reached the boat and sat on a bending thwart without mishap and we breathed a sigh of relief.

'I wouldn't fancy anyone's chances of dragging that lot off the river bed if he went in!' Livak said cheerfully as she came to lean on the rail next to us. I turned to her with a smile. I'd seen precious little of her on this voyage as she'd rapidly allied herself with the mercenaries, leaving me tied by my oath to continued attendance on Planir.

'What do you reckon then? Do they look as if they'd be useful in a fight?' she asked me, a tentative smile on her face.

'I'd say so.' I had been watching the warriors covertly on the voyage, wanting to make sure of the quality of help I'd have at my back, if need be. Most had the cock-on-a-dunghill arrogance that any mercenary picks up along with a sword paid for by the season, but the intensity of the regular drills and exercises they had undertaken with unspoken consent during the crossing had won a measure of my respect. I certainly felt more comfortable with them than I would have with the Archmage's agents, if the man Darni whom we'd met the previous year was anything to go by. Learning that individual was employing his abrasive arrogance in Solura to further Planir's ambitions had been no loss. 'They look as if they could take on most things and force a draw, if not an outright win. So, what's the plan?'

'Let's ask her,' Livak whistled sharply. Halice looked round, raising a hand in acknowledgement as two female mercenaries stopped her with some question. Both were shorter than Halice, one slightly built with masses of curly chestnut hair and a delicate, heart-shaped face curiously at odds with her chainmail vest and crested helmet. The other was one of the few mercenaries not in armour of some kind, wearing stained and patched leathers with a surprising number of daggers about her person. Black-haired and with an open, friendly expression, she looked as if she should be running a market stall or a busy household rather than hiring out her services to the high-est bidder.

Halice disposed of their query briskly and came down the

deck to join us. Her gait was more even but still unbalanced, and I wondered again about the extent that her injury had been healed. Was this as good as her leg was to get? If so, her future looked as if it would be in organising a corps rather than fighting with it. Perhaps this was her start in that line of work.

'So what's the plan?' asked Shiv at once.

'Rosarn takes her scouts and begins quartering the ruins, trying to get a line on major landmarks and buildings, to get ourselves oriented correctly.' Halice waved at the woman in leathers who was now poring over a freshly pale parchment with a lad I recognised as one of Mentor Tonin's pupils, called Parril or something similar. 'Minare and his lads are to clear the wharf, try to get an anchorage prepared so we can bring the ship in close and not have to ferry people on and off with the boats all the time.' She looked sharply at Shiv. 'That would be a cursed sight quicker and easier with some help from you mages, you know.'

I cursed and clutched at the ship's rail as my vision suddenly swam and shifted, thickets of matted vegetation vanishing to show me stout wharves of dressed stone where now a crumbled bank slid crookedly into the water, sturdy houses lined up around a flagged market square, unsuspecting people busy about their everyday lives, all unaware of the approaching Elietimm threat.

'What is it?' Livak was watching me warily.

'D'Alsennin,' I said curtly, making a conscious effort to loosen my whitened knuckles. 'I'm remembering things he knew here.'

A fleeting look of unhappiness came and went in Livak's eyes.

'You really don't like this, do you?' I challenged her, knowing it was probably a mistake but sick of the way she had been avoiding me.

'What do you think?' she spat back. 'I know it's not your fault and I'm sorry for it, but that aetheric magic killed Geris, and it killed Aiten. One of those Elietimm bastards got inside my head and nearly pushed me into madness as well. Just the thought of someone else's mind lurking inside yours makes my skin crawl.'

'I have it under control,' I replied, just about managing not to raise my voice in frustration and anger.

'I don't think so.' Livak shook her head, her face pale beneath the freckles raised by sun and wind. 'Last time we shared a bed, when you melted in passion, your eyes changed and you called me Guinalle again. I keep seeing someone else looking at me through your eyes, especially when you're tired.'

I managed to hold my tongue, getting a firm grip on the outraged denial that had to be Temar's, but that very realisation brought the truth of Livak's words home to me. I saw tears standing in her emerald eyes, belying the firm set of her jaw. I took a deep breath, knowing any more argument between us would be as destructive to us both as two eagles locking their talons in battle only to crash together on to the rocks below. A tremor threatened my composure as I realised I could not say whether the memory of such a sight in boyhood was Temar's or my own.

Drawing a deep breath, I looked at Shiv, who was shifting from one foot to the other, looking acutely embarrassed. Halice's expression was unreadable as always.

'Arest will be going with Lessay and his troop,' she continued, as if there had been no interruption. 'We want to find some defensible position, somewhere with a vantage point on the shoreline would be best.'

'You want Den Rannion's steading.' The words were out of my mouth before I could help myself and I gritted my teeth.

Halice looked at me, keen speculation in her hard eyes. 'Where's that? What's it like?'

I looked landward but the unfamiliar lines of river and shore meant I could not place any of Temar's memories. 'So much has changed,' I frowned.

'The lay of the land shifts over the generations,' said Shiv thoughtfully. 'It won't be so marked on the ocean coast, where you come from, Rysh, but big rivers like this carve the land over time and the sea carries sand along the shoreline with every season.'

I ignored him. 'It was a good stone-built hall by the end, with a sound perimeter wall and a gate-house. Even if the roof's come in, I'd say the masonry should still be standing.' I blinked as judgements learned at my father's elbow mingled oddly with Temar's memories of Den Rannion's sturdily built home. 'It was on the other side of an inlet from the main wharf, with its own river access.'

'Let's see if we can find it.' Halice turned and waved to Lessay, the third of Arest's troop commanders. He headed for us without further ado, nailed boots ringing on the decking. About a full hand's width taller even than me, he was thin as a rail, long blond hair pulled back into a ratty braid with humorous blue eyes and an indeterminate accent dominated by recent years in Lescar. I was still finding it hard to see how he and Arest managed to work together so well, given the contrast between the commander's uncompromising use of his authority to achieve things and the way Lessay accomplished his results with good-humoured jokes and encouragement.

'Ryshad thinks he knows somewhere that might make a secure encampment,' Halice explained.

'Go on,' Lessay urged us to elaborate.

I was grateful he was prepared to take Halice's word at face value; Arest was the sort to test word or coin in every way short of melting it down. Taking a deep breath, I tried to look at the river bank through Temar's eyes, or was that wrong? Should he be looking through my eyes? I shook my head absently, searching my memory for any dreams of the settlement that Temar had inflicted on me. The scene before me melted abruptly away and the daylight faded to be replaced by a winter's dusk. Bright radiance put the darkness to flight, warm orange flames denying the chill of the year's end. The stiffening wind carried the scents of incense and perfumed woods burning on braziers, while more purposeful fires sent the savour of roasting meat into the air. Laughter and snatches of music rebounded from the stony heights to carry the festival to the ships. I flinched as a gust threw a handful of sleet into my eyes, but when I raised my hand I found my face was dry.

'Ryshad?' asked Livak gently.

I looked down at my fingers, the nails blued with cold, now fading fast in the hot still warmth of the morning as Livak laid her own hand over mine in mute reassurance.

'It's over there,' I looked at the view with new eyes, Temar's memories overlaying the indistinguishable hummocks and thickets to show me houses and alleys in a disconcerting manner that I didn't want to examine too closely. 'Do you see that crag on the skyline? Take a line down from there – see where the rock outcrops at the water's edge. The inlet used to run pretty much from that lone tree to the thing with the yellow blossoms. The steading should be just about in the middle of those stands of that long grassy stuff.'

'Let's get to it.' Lessay let loose another of those piercing whistles the mercenaries used among themselves and waved in the rowing-boat from the shore. 'Maraide, Jervice, fetch some axes and the like.'

The longboat was uncomfortably laden when we pushed off from the ship, with entirely too little freeboard for my peace of mind. We landed without mishap, however, and gathered some more help from Minare's troop, who were only to glad to leave off wrestling with fallen blocks of masonry knee deep in the mud. I led the way confidently across the hidden remnants of the settlement towards Den Rannion's steading, my feet on oddly familiar ground. My boot heel rang on stone and I halted, looking down to see the flagstones of the marketplace, broken and tilted at odd angles.

'Watch your footing,' I called back over my shoulder, moving more cautiously and testing any slab before I put my weight on it. A curse from behind made me turn and I saw one of the mercenaries up to his shin in a hidden pit of dirty water. Arest drew level with me, sword in hand as he scanned the increasingly dense undergrowth on all sides. A large bird with ͟ ͟ ͟ious twisted beak burst out of a nearby bush, squawking ͟ ͟ sh alarm.

'That's it.' I raised a hand to sketch the outline of the ivy-covered walls, almost invisible against the dense leaves of the close-set trees all around, blurred by the man-high grasses that clumped thickly where the flagstones were absent underfoot.

Arest nodded slowly. 'Where's the main gate?'

I pointed with my off hand. 'Round past that bush with all the purple fruit on it.'

As we drew closer, the outlines of the steading became clearer and I had to fight to keep Temar's memories from overwhelming me. I drew a deep breath and concentrated on seeing it as it had been, without letting the waves of sorrow and regret that were hammering at the doors of my mind sweep over me.

'Here's the gate-house!' The mercenary Minare, a short but thick-set man of unquenchable optimism with the reddish hair of some old Forest blood in his line, waved his billhook to summon help. Standing back to let the others hack down the vines and bushes, I saw the still intact arch of the doorway, now low enough to touch as the generations of windblown soil had suffocated the entrance, raising the ground level. The stout hardwood of the gate was still there, now dark and immovable, tied close with creepers and debris.

'Should we put it in?' Minare's usually cheerful face was doubtful as he hefted his sturdy billhook.

'Not just yet,' Arest mused as he looked up to scan the walls thoughtfully, still well above our heads in their shroud of greenery. 'We might want it intact. Is there another way in? There's no point in putting a hole in our own defences if we don't have to.'

About to ask what he thought he might be defending against, I blinked away Temar's recollection of the Elietimm attack. I thought carefully. 'There was a sally port on the off side of the hall.'

Arest took a pace backwards and studied the long curve of the wall. 'I'd like to know what's inside,' he murmured to himself.

'Let me.' Livak pushed past a mercenary who was examining a scratched hand with an expression of distaste. She gave the finger-thick vines an experimental tug and grinned at us. 'If I start yelling, just blast that door in, will you, Shiv?'

'Be careful,' I stifled a protective urge that had to be Temar's; I knew well enough how Livak could take care of herself, didn't I?

'Of course,' she said dismissively as she climbed deftly up the obscured stonework, gloved hands finding fingerholds with the ease of long practice, albeit at getting into other people's houses uninvited. Reaching the top, she peered over before swinging herself cautiously down to what remained of the walkway.

'This looks a bit doubtful,' she commented. 'I think I'll climb down.'

I glanced round to see a ripe mixture of frustration and anticipation on the upturned faces of the mercenaries all around me as we waited in silence, long moments sliding past like the sluggish waters of the broad river.

'Come on, lads, let's try to find that sally port.' Minare laid his billhook on his broad shoulder, looking to Arest for his approval. At the big man's nod, he and a handful of others began slashing down the undergrowth to carve a path round the base of the wall.

'If we're to get any anchorage cleared, we're going to need help from you mages.' Arest turned to Shiv abruptly, looming over the slighter man in a frankly intimidating manner. 'It's plain stupid to have my lads exhausting themselves when you could do a better job in half the time. We don't mind doing the hard work – that's what we're being paid for – but there is a limit to what I'll ask of the troops.'

'I see your point. I'll speak to Planir,' answered Shiv hurriedly.

'Is anyone still out there?' Livak's voice was muffled by the blocked doorway, but her irritation came through clearly enough. 'Didn't you hear me calling?'

'What have you found?' I shouted hastily.

'That sally port, for a start,' came the reply. 'Minare and his lads are clearing it at the moment.'

'Let's go,' Arest slapped his hands together in a decisive gesture and everyone moved, hurrying down the newly hacked and trampled path around the base of the wall.

I had to duck my head to enter the sally port, looking doubtfully at the crumbling stonework of the lintel. The courtyard was surprisingly clear of undergrowth; the pale lines of the shingle paths showed faintly through a blur of low level weeds. As I crushed them underfoot the scents of thyme and pennymint rose sharply around me, dizzying me with the ever present threat of D'Alsennin's memories. The roof of the hall had fallen in but the walls still stood four square and defiant, fine-dressed stone still visible through the stains of age and decay. I took a deep breath to clear my mind of the shadowy image of the place as it had been.

The hall's tall, stone-mullioned windows had been glowing with lamplight when Temar had last seen them, the harmonies of the Maitresse's harp floating above the noise of the courtyard, guests' horses being stabled now the colony had sufficient beasts to let people ride the young stock. The kitchens, set to one side of the hall, had been bustling with activity, the two new maids busy fetching and carrying through the covered walkway, giving as good as they got when the outdoor men had whistled and teased them, begging for a mouthful or, better yet, a taste of honey from their lips. Workshops either side of the gate-house were idle now, tools laid aside after the day's labour and neatly stowed. The tall gates, newly black with pitch, stood hospitably open, the gate-wards resting on their bench, greeting everyone by name.

Now all was silent apart from the heavy tread of the mercenaries as they began efficiently clearing the enclosure. Odd words grew into low-voiced conversations as more people arrived.

'How secure is the wall?' Arest's voice startled me from Temar's reverie and I looked round to see him shouting at Minare. 'Any breaches worth worrying about?'

'Not so far!' the mercenary replied, not looking round as he and his lads continued cutting their way through the clinging vines, bright scarlet flowers masking vicious thorns.

'I think I can determine that for you,' Planir's voice turned heads all round the enclave. The Archmage stooped through the sally port and laid one long-fingered hand on the dark stone of the jamb. A crackle of amber light danced round his fingers and seemed to vanish into the masonry. 'There,' Planir pointed to a section of the wall obscured by masses of leaves hanging down over the top. 'A tree has disturbed the foundations and the whole wall is cracked. It'll probably come down if a heavy-footed owl lands on it.'

I looked round for Livak at this and saw her auburn hair catching the sun as she clambered over the tangle of fallen beams and timbers that choked the hall. She saw me, waving with a satisfied smile as she looked down on mercenaries too heavily armoured and too clumsy to follow her.

'How are we going to clear this lot, wizard?' she shouted to Planir.

'Let me show you.' Otrick appeared from somewhere and a swirl of blue radiance gathered up Livak to carry her bodily through the air and deposit her neatly at my side. White beneath her tan, she clutched at me to steady herself and I was glad of the excuse to put an arm round her and draw her close.

'Stuffing wizards,' she muttered shakily, glaring at Otrick with something closer to outright dislike than the wary amusement he usually elicited from her.

The same azure light was now coming from a couple of other mages as more people crowded into this decayed sanctuary. I realised I was standing with my mouth open as massive balks of rotting wood were lifted out of the hollow hall, floating impossibly to stack themselves neatly beside the weak point Planir had identified in the wall. I was not the only one; all the mercenaries halted to gape at the spectacle and exchange startled looks.

'Do you reckon any of this lot would take a hire with a decent corps?' Arest jested with a creditable attempt at maintaining his poise. 'We could put whoever we liked on the Lescari throne with that kind of help!'

I made a mental note to try to keep the mercenary commander apart from Kalion, though I had the impression the Hearth-Master would be more inclined to want to deal with Dukes and Princes than the men who kept them in their positions of power. Dressed for once in voluminous breeches, more practical than his usual florid robes, the fat mage was directing one of Tonin's pupils to lay out his bed roll beneath an awning that two others were erecting with some difficulty. As I watched a couple of mercenaries took the canvas and ropes from the scholars and had the shelter securely rigged inside a handful of moments.

'The first thing we need is to determine the layout of the town,' Arest turned to address the Archmage in tones that brooked no argument. 'We could spend the next couple of seasons clearing thickets and piles of fallen stones and barely scratch the surface.'

Planir looked at me, grey eyes as unfathomable as the night seas. 'You could save us a great deal of time here, Ryshad. Shiv tells me you've been seeing the place as Temar knew it.'

I shot an irritated glare at Shiv, who coloured faintly. 'I'm sorry, but the Archmage needs to know,' he said apologetically.

'That might help some, I suppose—' Arest's scepticism would have annoyed me intensely in any other circumstances, but this was not the time to force any kind of trial of strength or will.

'I'm not prepared to let D'Alsennin loose inside my head if that's what you're hoping, Archmage,' I said curtly. I was having enough difficulty keeping Temar's intrusive recollections barred securely at the back of my mind as it was.

Arest continued as if I hadn't spoken, '—but I'd rather rely on proven magic. We need you wizards to give us the lay of the land as it was when this place was built, to do whatever you can to identify key buildings and places – the market, for instance.

That's where we might find metalwork, even gems, valuables that will have withstood Maewelin's teeth. You did say we would be entitled to any spoils we found.' The challenge in his demand was unmistakable.

'I have been telling my colleagues much the same,' agreed Planir peaceably. 'Obviously, a priority is the scrying in support of the information Mentor Tonin has culled from his researches; we must locate this cavern as soon as possible, after all, but we will make sure you get every assistance from the mages not directly required at present.'

'I could help, Archmage, I'm not needed for scrying.' I looked round to see one of the younger wizards, a man a few seasons younger than myself. Dressed in grey with a red-trimmed collar to his jerkin, I recognised him from the Council meeting.

'Thank you, Naldeth, that would be most helpful.' Planir bowed briefly. 'Please excuse me.'

I followed Naldeth's eyes and saw he was studying Maraide, the lass with all the glossy brown curls. 'Do you know if she's a follower for anyone in particular?' he asked me, his gaze covetous.

I have to admit I was finding the reactions of the wizards to the mercenaries more amusing than anything else. The ship had been rife with increasingly lurid speculations in avid undertones as we had sailed to Carif and I recalled Naldeth had been the source of some of the wilder tales of turbulent adventure and limitless wealth, far removed from the truths of life as a sword for hire, as Aiten had told it to me. He'd have found all this highly entertaining, that much I was certain.

'None of the women in this troop are followers for the foot soldiers or courtesans for the commanders either,' I told the mage firmly. 'They're here for their fighting skills and if you're interested in anything more I suggest you wait for the lady to indicate an interest. Put a hand wrong and I imagine you'll be served your stones on a skewer.'

'Oh,' Naldeth's face fell, to my relief. That kind of disturbance would do little for the harmony of this expedition and, besides, I'd seen Maraide leaving Planir's cabin with a discreet air of satisfaction on more than one occasion on the long voyage, when the menace of Temar's memories had made sleep impossible. Even that passing thought brought new visions of Den Rannion's steading to the fore, the past and the lost hemming me in on all sides. I blinked and tried to rub away the tenseness in my neck, driving the encroaching recollections away with increasing difficulty.

A series of whistles alerted Rosarn's troop and I saw them gathering at the sally port, axes and long knives to hand.

'If you want to help, now's your chance,' I said to him crisply. 'Come on, I want to have a look round for myself.'

What I really wanted was to quit this place before I lost my grip on present reality all together. As I walked rapidly across the enclosure, Livak hurried to meet us, slipping her hand in mine as she slid me a sideways glance of concern. I squeezed her hand with a reassurance I did not really feel as we listened to Rosarn's crisp instructions. I stifled a brief longing for the simpler days, when Aiten and I had stood taking our orders with a similar lack of question or personal involvement in our tasks.

'I want to know exactly where this town starts and ends, and I want to know what state the buildings are in. Look out for snakes and stingers. We'll all need to know if you see anything so remember colour and size. I imagine anything bigger will move itself sharpish once we start making a noise, but be careful in case anything's laired up in a hollow somewhere. Big Thorfi, you take your section over the way, Clever Thorfi, keep the road to your off hand.'

'All right if we come along?' I raised a polite hand, trying not to laugh at Rosarn's distinction between the two men, which was clearly familiar to all the mercenaries. 'This is Naldeth, a mage who would like to help.'

Rosarn nodded. 'You'd better come with me, wizard. You're a sworn man, aren't you, Ryshad? Then you can pick your own path, but watch your step.'

We followed the mercenaries out of the crumbling circle

of the walls and looked at a seemingly impenetrable mass of plant life smothering the remains of the colony, more shades of green than I could have imagined were possible. To my relief my vision stayed steady, firmly rooted in the present.

'You two, over there.' Rosarn looked back and waved us to the far side of a creeper-covered hummock as the rest of her troop spread out to examine similar anonymous shapes shrouded in vegetation. Livak drew her sword and slid it under the knotted stems, slicing away a great swathe of glossy green to expose the dull grey of weathered stone. At home I would have called it ivy, but here the leaves were long and smooth, dark and secretive. I reached for my own blade then thought better of it; I could do without making any more contact with Temar's imprisoned mind than I had to.

'We're doing this at the wrong time of year,' she commented. 'It'd be a lot easier if we could wait until all this died back.'

'The growing season goes on well into Aft-Autumn here,' I said absently as I reached for a stick to poke into a tangle of orange flowering bushes.

'Oh.' Livak glanced at me, her eyes uncertain again, before she hacked down another snarl of smothering leaves. I tried to reassure her with a smile and made myself a silent vow to talk to Mentor Tonin when we returned to the encampment. Dast's teeth, I simply had to get this under control for the sake of my own sanity and any lasting relationship I might have with Livak, never mind Planir's arcane schemes.

A strange little slate-coloured bird with an odd, fluting cry came fluttering out of the bush, startling us both as its calls of alarm roused its fellows from their perches and the air was suddenly full of flapping bluish wings.

'Do you think this is a building?' asked Livak when the commotion had died down, her voice determinedly matter-of-fact as she looked at the largely smooth stone face she had uncovered, shockingly pale against the dark green of the vines.

I rammed my stick into the leaves and it rapped hard on rock. Moving along, I repeated the strike until I was rewarded with a dull, damp thud.

'I'd say that's a door or a shutter,' I nodded.

Livak began cutting away the dense creeper as I looked round to see how the others were doing. Several groups were trying to uncover stonework in much the same way as we were, and the simple sight of decent, dressed masonry, albeit stained and deeply weathered, was starting to make the place look as if there might have once been a town here, even without the benefit of Temar's memories.

'It's a door all right,' said Livak with some satisfaction.

I tapped the ancient and wormy wood with my stick and felt it give slightly. The handle and hinges were dark stains of corrosion on the wood and windblown soil obscured the bottom edge of the door. This was never going to open again, not while Dastennin was ruling the oceans. Taking a step backwards, I lifted my boot and kicked it in, bracing myself on the stonework on either side, not wanting to enter before anything else chose to leave.

'Shit!' Livak leaped to one side as a flurry of blackbeetles scurried in all directions and I stamped hard on something with far too many legs for my peace of mind.

'What's the problem?' shouted Rosarn abruptly from somewhere beyond a nearby thicket.

'Crawlers,' I yelled. 'Nothing to worry about.'

Livak and I exchanged a rueful grin and peered cautiously into the dim interior, blinking at the contrast to the bright sunlight.

'There's a shutter over there,' observed Livak, and I walked round the outside to hammer the crumbling wood inwards with my useful stick. This gave some more light, enough to see the ominous downwards bulge of what remained of the ceiling and the massive crack running down the back wall.

'Stay by the door,' I warned Livak as she moved cautiously inside. 'That lot could come down at any time.'

'It's been there a while. I don't suppose it'll choose to fall down today,' she said scornfully as she poked her sword inquisitively among the debris thickly littering the floor.

I tried to see what she was prodding. 'What have you got?'

'Barrel staves, I'd say, hoops, nails, something that might have been hinges a handful of generations ago. I'd say it was a store of some kind.'

I frowned and looked round again at the lie of the land. Surely the warehouses had all been closer to the sea as well as to the docks?

'Anything of interest?' Rosarn appeared at my shoulder and I stood back to let her peer in through the window.

'Not really,' Livak coughed and a passing breeze carried the damp smells of rot and decay out to us.

'How about you?' I asked.

Rosarn held up a small spotted animal, blood clotting its frozen snarl. 'Well, if I find a few more of these, I might get a new pair of gloves out of this job, but no, all we're finding is empty walls and rubbish like this. What I came to tell you is that wizard reckons there are caves in that outcrop over there.' Rosarn looked at me with the faintest suggestion of a teasing smile. 'They don't seem to be big enough to be this cavern you're looking for but I thought we might make sure there's nothing dangerous lurking in the bushes. Why don't you two come with me and we'll do a little reconnaissance. Maybe I'll find some more of these,' she added, hanging her scrawny prize on a handy branch.

Livak grinned at her and after a quick look at the crumbling stonework of the window took the longer way out of the door and around to join us.

I had no option but to draw my sword to cut down the burgeoning plants as we worked our way beneath the cool shadow of the crag, but to my relief Temar remained locked quiescent in the back of my mind.

'Here's something.' Naldeth ducked under a low branch and vanished into a hollow of darkness, Rosarn following him hastily with an oath. 'It's certainly a cave of some sort,' the mage's voice came back to us, muffled and echoing.

I pulled the branch aside impatiently, cursing as it sprang back, lashing me with thorny tendrils. 'How far back does it go?'

Livak was ahead of me, slipping past the obstructive tree and reaching into her belt-pouch for her firesteel and a stub of misshapen candle. The yellow light flared in the blackness and showed us a shallow cavern in the rock face. I slapped down Temar's dislike of such places with an irritated thought.

'What's this?' Naldeth spun a ball of magelight around his hand and moved to the far side of the cave where the reddish illumination struck a whitish gleam out of the gloom. 'Bones?'

My heart started pounding in my chest despite all my efforts to tell myself this could be nothing of significance. I closed my eyes and suddenly saw the last dawn of the colony again, people running, screaming, fleeing the pitiless blades of the Elietimm as they came out of nowhere, gold heads catching the faint sunlight, cutting down the hapless colonists like corn beneath a sickle. Had we left someone behind, taking desperate shelter in a hidden cranny in the rock face, only to die of wounds or thirst?

'It's an animal, but I couldn't tell you what kind,' said Rosarn, mystified.

My eyes snapped open and the image of slaughter faded into the darkness of the cave.

'Look at this,' Livak's tone was one of wonder as she lifted a broad, bulging skull in both hands, as wide as a bull's but far more rounded. I looked more closely and ran a tentative finger around the one, huge hollow in the middle of the brow.

'I've never seen anything like it,' I shook my head. 'Rosarn?'

The mercenary woman looked up as she knelt, sorting through the pile of stained and broken bones. 'No, never. I'll tell you something, though. This is a den of some kind. Look, these are chewed, you can see the teeth marks where they've been cracked open for the marrow.'

Livak turned the great skull thoughtfully in her hands. 'What size would you say something would have to be to bring down a beast this big?'

'Big enough that I don't want to meet it,' said Rosarn briskly. 'Let's go.'

'Is there anything other than bone?' Naldeth was stirring a heap of fragments with a foot. 'If we can find a pot or something, I can try to use fire to make it reflect its origins. It's something I've been working on and Planir said—'

'You shine magelight on it or some such?' Rosarn sounded politely sceptical.

Naldeth shook his head impatiently. 'No, you set it afire and the magelight sometimes reflects things of interest before it consumes the object.'

I felt suddenly sick. 'Tell me you haven't been doing this with any of the colony artefacts?'

'What? No, no, we did consider it but Planir forbade it until I had more consistent results.' Naldeth smiled sunnily. 'It's a good thing, he did, really, isn't it?'

'There's no fresh spoor,' Livak pointed out. 'I'd say whatever's lived here is long gone by now.' She poked at a smaller skull, pointed with a central ridge. I would have called it a badger at home but the teeth were all wrong.

'There are other caves we could explore,' said Naldeth eagerly.

'Maybe so, when we've checked with the scholars. Otherwise all we're going to do is raise more pointless questions.' Rosarn shook her head firmly.

'But we're supposed to be looking for this cavern, for the colonists,' objected Naldeth.

'It's not here,' I said, stopping to wonder at the certainty with which I spoke.

'Then where is it?' demanded Rosarn.

All I could do was shake my head helplessly. 'I don't know, not yet.'

We all blinked, rubbing our eyes when we left the cave for the bright sunlight outside.

'Right, you two carry on over yonder.' Rosarn strode briskly away to deal with a couple of mercenaries who were taunting some creature cowering in the angle of two collapsed walls.

Livak looked at me and shrugged. We continued hacking down the all-pervasive vines to reveal nothing more exciting than more empty and broken buildings. I was becoming tired, thirsty and frustrated when Livak stood abruptly upright and pointed.

'Smoke!'

I turned to see the thin blue spiral of a camp fire twisting upwards into the still air and realised that the sun was high in a noonday sky. As I did so, we heard Rosarn shouting to us.

'Food! Everyone back to the camp!'

We pushed our way back through the increasingly battered undergrowth and entered the walls of the Den Rannion steading to see a well-organised encampment taking shape.

'So who's got something to tell?' Halice was asking as she took her belt-knife to a row of small creatures spitted and browning nicely over a good fire. Livak and I joined the line to get our share.

'Lots of nothing special,' one of the older mercenaries said as he stripped a mouthful of meat off the leg he held. 'All empty.'

'That's a bit off, if you ask me.' A thin-faced man who had dealt with receding hair by shaving his head clean was passing rough flatbread from a linen sack. 'This place was supposed to have been sacked, wasn't it? Dawn attack, lots of people killed in their night-gowns, that kind of thing?'

I nodded as he looked enquiringly at me, not trusting myself to speak as I held the doors to Temar's memories firmly shut.

'So where are the bones?' the bald-headed man asked, looking around the circle of mercenaries. 'All right, so there'd have been scavengers and I know it was a long time ago, but Saedrin's stones, you'd have thought we'd have found some bones, inside these buildings maybe, certainly in the ones that were burned out.'

'Scavengers would have scattered bones but they'd still be around. Carrion feeders eat where they find a meal,' one of the older women agreed, gnawing unconcernedly on her meat.

'That is a shame,' frowned a middle-aged man in the robes of a scholar. 'If you could find us a skull, there are some necromantic rituals we might try. I'd have liked to see what that would raise.'

That silenced everyone for a long moment.

'Never mind the bones, what about other things?' A burly man looked over his shoulder since he was sitting with his back to the circle, facing towards the entrance in case of unexpected threats. 'I was at Thurscate when the Draximal retook it, four years back. Now that had fallen close on a generation before and not been touched since, and there was all manner of stuff everywhere. Lots of things will rot, granted, but not pots, coin and suchlike. I reckon this place was stripped, not just abandoned.'

'Who would have done that?' I was curious to see how far these supposedly untutored warriors would pursue these questions. They'd clearly been keeping their ears open on the voyage over the ocean.

Rosarn passed me a joint of meat from the fire which I split with Livak. 'We were talking the other evening about what could have happened to those Elietimm that were here when the old magic failed,' she mused, 'me and Lessay. They'd not have been able to return home, not without their magic. It doesn't look as if they set up here, so where did they go?'

'Does it matter?' Livak said indistinctly, licking hot fat from her fingers. 'They were all men, weren't they? They'd all have been dead inside a couple of generations, no matter how many of them took to dancing on the other side of the floor.'

That raised smiles all round and the talk turned to more general matters as the other groups of mercenaries drifted in, summoned by the tempting smell of roasting meat. I noticed Livak looking pensive as she stared into the impenetrable forest and I tapped her on the shoulder to offer her some more of the unleavened bread.

'Oh, thank you.' She tore off a mouthful and chewed, still looking thoughtful.

'Misaen borrowing your wits for something?' I asked lightly.

'What? Oh, it's just that I was wondering how far this land goes. Do you know?'

I shook my head, 'No, no one had the time to find out before the colony was lost.'

'I mean, I like being out in the country well enough, for all that I'm city-bred, as long as it's farms or forest,' continued Livak, 'but I've never been anywhere like this, where there are no roads no matter how far you travel, no villages or towns to get a bed and a bath when you really need one, nothing but wilderness in every direction. It's worse than Dalasor.' She sounded more intrigued than dubious and I followed her gaze into the mysterious forest, distant heights rising beyond it leading to Misaen alone knew where. Where had the forge god and the lord of the sea settled on dividing this land? How far was it before Dastennin's realm took over once more and some as yet unseen ocean lapped against an untrodden shore?

'That's why they came here, the colonists, to find empty land, enough for all those dispossessed as the Empire contracted.' I settled myself against a convenient fallen tree and took a long drink of well-watered wine from my belt flask. 'I suppose that's why the Elietimm wanted it so badly too, you remember how poor and cramped their islands are.'

I offered Livak the bottle, and she looked as if she were about to say something more but Arest's harsh voice overrode her.

'Right, let's get on with it. Listen for my horn at sunset.'

There were a fair number of reluctant glances as we all stood up, and the kind of muttering that any competent sergeant at arms would quell with a look or, in Messire's militia, his baton. Sworn men would never dream of tarnishing their oaths by voicing such dissent either. I sighed; all of that was starting to seem increasingly irrelevant given my own concerns. Arest simply ignored the murmurs and no overt protest arose as everyone returned to the tedious and ultimately fruitless task. As the afternoon wore on I found it increasingly hard to maintain either concentration or patience, venting my annoyance with long and complex muttered curses on Temar, Planir and even Messire for getting me into this mire. For all my efforts, I only seemed to get bogged further and further down. But of course the first thing you're told about getting out of a marsh is not to struggle, to wait for help. Where did that leave me? Who was going to pull me out of this morass but myself? Planir was more likely to use my sunken head as a support for a walkway if it suited his purposes, and Messire had given me over entirely to the Archmage's use, hadn't he? What price our oaths now?

'Enough!' The ringing note of Arest's horn and the bellow that followed it were the most welcome sounds I could recall hearing in a long season. Tossing aside a hefty branch that I'd been using to hammer down yet another blocked and rotting door to reveal little more than garbage, I made my way rapidly down to the foreshore below the steading, where the mercenaries had tapped a barrel of weak beer. They were drinking thirstily, eating odd remnants of meat and bread and shaking their heads over the unproductive day. Many were stripping to wash the sweat and dirt of the day away in the slowly coiling waters of the estuary. That seemed like a cursed good idea and I began making a neat bundle of my gear, securing it with my sword-belt.

'Take this back, will you?' I called to Livak, acknowledging her consent with a wave as I took a running dive into the murky waters and struck out with scything strokes. It was nothing like swimming in the clean, clear seas of home, but there was enough salt in the river this far down to give it a welcome tang on my lips. I pulled myself through the water with a punishing stroke, channelling all my frustrations into physical exertion, letting go of all restraint as I concentrated solely on speed and breathing, finding a release from the mental struggles I had been wrestling with for so long in the pure, uncomplicated demands on my body. As I rolled my head to take a breath, I thought I saw someone else, trying to make a race of it, dark hair sleek in the corner of my eye. I redoubled my efforts, but when I had to rest, lest I exhaust myself, I found myself alone in the water. I'd been competing against some shadow from the mysteries locked in the back of my mind. Fresh memories swirled slowly inside my head as I floated, limp for a moment.

I clenched my fists in impotent anger and swam slowly back, walking reluctantly into the embrace of the walls, tired limbs trembling slightly.

'That's quite some swim.' Shiv handed me a towel and I dried myself roughly, covering myself with the shirt he offered next, rapidly dragging clinging breeches over my still damp thighs.

'Where's Planir?' I demanded.

'Talking with Arest, over there,' replied Shiv, eyes widening at my brusque manner.

I looked blindly at him for a moment. There was something wrong, wasn't there? An elusive memory teased me, fragile as a shade. I screwed my eyes shut to try to capture it. The scents of the summer came to me on a wisp of breeze and I smelled the richness of the forest, the sharpness of the dew-damp stone, the faintest suggestion of salt and weed from the exposed mud flats down river.

Forcing a smile to reassure Shiv, I took a deep breath, running a hand through my wet hair, now just about long enough again to curl and tangle. I interrupted the Archmage's conversation with scant ceremony.

'Ryshad,' Planir greeted me politely enough, but I could see the questions in his eyes while Arest glared at me with frank annoyance.

'It's not here, it's not anywhere close,' I said abruptly. 'There was never any smell of the sea by the cavern. The forest was different too, more resinous, more aromatic. We're looking in the wrong place!'

I was nearly shouting as uncharacteristic rage filled me – rage with myself for not realising sooner, with Temar for taking the tattered remnants of the colony so far afield before finding sanctuary, at all these cursed scholars and wizards for not working things out more readily. It was so obvious, wasn't it? Heads turned all around and a voice called out from the wall walk, the sentry quickly reassured by Arest.

'Where are they then?' Planir demanded, arms folded, authority undiminished by his breeches and shirt sleeves.

'The mines, that's where they fled, up river to the sanctuary of the caves up there.' I shook off Temar's clinging memories and turned to Shiv. 'Can you scry at that kind of distance?'

'I can try,' he set his jaw.

Planir raised a hand. 'No, Shiv, not this evening.'

We both stared at him, open-mouthed. 'It's late, everyone is tired,' said Planir firmly. 'If the colonists have slept for so many generations, a day's delay to make sure everyone is fresh will hardly make a difference.'

I opened my mouth to object heatedly but Livak slid herself inside the circle of my arm. 'Come on,' she said abruptly. 'He's right. We've all done enough today. Lend us a hand in the hall and then we can make sure we pick a good spot to sleep in.'

'That would probably be best,' Shiv admitted with ill grace. 'I am pretty well drained after helping clear that anchorage.'

I yielded reluctantly, only a little cheered to find Livak taking my hand as we crossed the now busy courtyard. I vented some of my anger in driving uncounted generations of crawlers out of the corners of the ruined hall, but I was still seething inside.

'I think we'll stake our claim here,' Livak announced, planting her light pack and the heavy bundle of my armour either side of the low remnant of an interior wall that would give us some semblance of shelter and privacy. 'This will do us fine.'

'Good.' Fighting for calm, I looked around to see if anything was being done about food and saw Halice handing out bread and stew with her usual air of efficiency.

'So who made you quarter master?' Livak enquired with a grin as we took our place in the line.

Halice greeted us with a thin smile. 'This cursed leg has to be good for something.'

I took a hungry mouthful of excellent stew and nodded to Halice. 'You certainly have a talent for it.'

'It's how I got started in the mercenary trade,' she remarked, rather to my surprise. 'I hired out as a cook, to a merchant train first of all and later to a corps. That's where I learned to fight.' She smiled at me, more at ease than I could remember her, and not just for having two sound feet again. 'What did you think? I just picked up a sword and went looking for adventure? The only thing that'll get you is dead in a ditch or chained in a brothel.'

That raised chuckles of agreement on all sides. 'At least it's keeping me clear of the real work,' Halice continued with a broader grin. 'It's not bad, taking my ease for a change.'

'How are the scholars doing?' I tried not to envy her contentment too much and looked for distraction towards the intense huddle around Tonin's fire.

'They seem very pleased with themselves,' Halice replied with a touch of amusement. 'Tonin has been drilling Parrail in the incantations they're hoping to use to revive the sleeping colonists.'

Livak blew through a hot mouthful of meat and vegetables, wincing as she swallowed it. 'So now we have to wait until morning?' she asked in a resigned tone. 'Before we can finally get all this sorted out?'

'Just so, we wait,' confirmed Halice, her own impatience clear in her furrowed brow.

I stifled a sour desire to ask what in Dastennin's name they had to worry about with a spoonful of stew. I was the one with an ancient Tormalin lurking all too wakeful in the back of my head, wasn't I? It was getting so I couldn't think of anything else, fighting a growing, cumulative exhaustion along with Temar's increasingly intrusive personality.

Darkness, broken only by piecemeal dreams

At first there was nothing, no sensation, no light, no sound. It seemed that he had never known any existence but this dark enchanted sleep. Painfully, agonising as warm blood pulsing in a dead limb, awareness returned, old dread, new dismay. Once known and recognised, emotion coursed sluggishly down old paths. Temar awoke to nothingness, blackness pressing down on him. Terror began to scratch at the corners of his mind, gnawing at his determination to withstand this trial. Uncertainty began to grow, spurred on by the sudden realisation that he could feel nothing, nothing at all. There was no release in an accelerating heartbeat sending fire into his blood, to kindle a fury to fight off whatever was threatening him. No sweat beaded his brow to cool him, no ancient instinct was raising his hackles to warn of impending danger. He floated, bodiless in the featureless void, and when the urge to cry out could no longer be denied he lost himself in sickened terror at the realisation that he had no mouth to shout with, no voice to raise. Pure horror overwhelmed him, screaming soundlessly out to be lost in the suffocating enchantment.

Guilt tormented him, to be swept aside by the motion of a violent sea, tossing and swamping a vessel caught in the teeth of a rending storm. Lightning flashed overhead, sparking eerie phosphorescence from the timbers and lashed-up rig of a skiff with no business out on the open ocean. A man wrestled with the tiller, himself tied to the thwarts with a knot of thick rope; Temar heard the desperate mariner's thoughts clearly. He would fight his way clear of the storm or sink with the ship; if he could not save his precious cargo, both living and that held in unknowing, enchanted sleep, Dastennin could cast him to drown for eternity with Poldrion's demons in the river of shades. It was Vahil, Temar realised, some measure of awareness returning to him just before it slid from the feeble grasp of his mind.

The echo of steps in a lofty hall was the next thing he knew, a purposeful stride, crisp with determination.

'Have you considered our petition?' A female voice rang out from some unseen direction, Temar struggling to register anything beyond a dull greyness swirling all around.

'Do you have any idea what you are asking?' It was a Sieur's reply, confident enough to make a refusal with comforting eloquence. 'Even if such an expedition could be organised, we could not sail before the latter half of spring, and Saedrin only knows what we will find. With the Empire falling asunder on all sides, you are asking me to risk men and material on a quest to find a new and most dangerous foe, doing nothing more in all likelihood than giving these marauders fresh encouragement to sail to encompass our own destruction!'

'We cannot leave them like this!' Elsire was weeping now, Temar realised distantly, a longing to comfort her welling up inside him.

'May we have your permission to contact the Shrine of Ostrin in Bremilayne?' Vahil's voice was rough with emotion, his pain a bright goad in the leaden mists that wreathed around Temar.

'You may, of course,' the Sieur replied wearily. 'The Healer grant that they might be able to help you, though I should warn you they have troubles enough of their own just at present.'

Temar's awareness shied away from the heavy weight of the Sieur's despair and dissolved into the dullness of the haze.

The scent of thyme crushed under the hooves of a galloping horse mingled with the acrid dust of the road and the sharp reek of the beast's sweat. A scream rang out and Temar heard foul curses spat from all directions as the clash of swords struck sparks from his sleeping mind. Harness rattled and creaked, the swish and snap of a whip with its promise of pain to spur on the already desperate. A dire sense of urgency possessed him, a desperation mingled with an arrogance that soon shifted to fear, uncertainty and pain. The bite of the sword was as deep in the mind as into the body and Temar struggled in a futile effort to rid himself of the panic that was flooding him, its tendrils dragging him down as surely as weeds would drown a swimmer. Sudden agony overwhelmed him to be replaced by an emptiness even more horrible, until the darkness claimed him once more.

'So what exactly are you and how do I unlock your secrets?'

Temar awoke with a start to see a hawk-faced man with flaxen hair stooping over him. Terror filled him but in that same instant he realised the man with the piercing blue eyes was not looking at him but at something to one side. He was himself still disembodied, no more than a shade crying to Poldrion for passage to the Otherworld, Temar realised. Who was this man? Memory struggled to knit together the tangled skeins of recollection and a distant echo of pain and terror sounded dimly in Temar's reason. Pale heads in the dawn sunlight flashed across his mind's eye and a terrible sense of danger began to build in Temar as the blond, cold-eyed man began a low murmur of enchantment, a tainted miasma overlying the image Temar was seeing. This time Temar reached desperately for the mists of the enchantment that concealed him, diving into the concealing depths to evade the poisonous touch of the sorcerer.

Light seared him like a burning brand.

'Come on, Viltred, move! They're nearly on us!'

In a gateway, the speaker stood, intense eyes in a pale face, reddish hair streaked with white swirling in the biting wind. His companion hurried after him, burdened with a motley collection of jewellery, weapons and trinkets. The first man ran, long legs spurning the short grass while his companion, shorter and more sturdy, dark of hair and beard, plunged after him, the long skirts of his azure surcoat threatening to trip him at every stride. Temar was silent in helpless anguish as trifles slipped from his grasp to be lost in the uneven ground.

Quarrels thudded into the turf on all sides, but as Temar despaired of the two men ever escaping the arrows were snatched out of the air by unseen hands, blue light streaming from the bearded man's hands, brilliance startling against the overcast.

'Here, Azazir, it's here!' Suddenly they were at a cliff's edge, black basalt columns forming a perilous stair to a tiny coracle, which bobbed seemingly untethered in the tumultuous foam of the breaking seas.

'Watch your step,' the red-headed man shouted, an insane exultation in his voice as he skipped lightly down the treacherous rocks, sure-footed as a cat. The younger man picked his way down more carefully, testing his footing at every step. Spray lashed him, bitter cold biting deep into flesh and bones as he made the long and hazardous descent.

Yells from aloft signalled the arrival of pursuit but as black-clad warriors gathered at the cliff-top and a few bolder than the rest began to edge down the slick and treacherous rocks, the red-headed man reached the flimsy leather boat. Standing easily in the frail craft, he raised his hands and green light gathered around him, casting an unearthly light on his thin face. Where the sea spray landed on the rocks, it began to cling, to pool, to draw together, drops making rivulets that joined to stream down the black stones, pushing at feet and hands. As the younger man reached the sanctuary of the tiny craft, he dumped his burden and wove his own skein of blue light, gusts of wind snatching at heads and shoulders, sharp blasts of icy air tugging at legs and feet. The first to fall shrieked in utter terror as he fell to his fate in the icy foam, the second clawed frantically at his neighbour, only to drag him down too, smashed on the unforgiving rocks before the seas claimed the bodies as their own. A wild exultation filled Temar, but before he could seize it the swirling mists swept over him as surely as the icy seas of his vision.

A longing filled Temar with an intensity beyond anything he had known. Guinalle. She was gone, not lost but hidden, a jewel buried deep in the earth as surely as the finest gem Misaen ever minted, not rough and unpolished but sleeping in peerless beauty, waiting only to be revealed to those that sought her. He shook off a sudden image of green eyes, dark with passion against unbleached linen in a tumble of auburn hair and determination filled him. He had to escape this, whatever this was, to reach out and find some way to rescue Guinalle. Nothing less would do.

The ruins of the Den Rannion steading,
Kel Ar'Ayen,
43rd of Aft–Summer

'Are you awake?' Livak propped herself on one elbow to look curiously at me, her eyes huge in the light of the moons, greater waning from the half, lesser waxing scant days from the full that would signify the arrival of For-Autumn.

I nodded and heaved a long sigh. 'I am now.'

'You've been dreaming?' she asked with that uncertainty that I was truly coming to hate in her voice.

'Dreaming someone else's dreams, as far as I can make out.' I sat and stretched to work the stiffness out of my shoulders. Temar might have suffered terrors made worse by his bodilessness, I thought to myself, but I'd wager I was suffering enough for the pair of us with the knots his memories were tying my sleeping muscles into. 'I think I've been seeing something of what Temar's been perceiving over the generations, when someone's emotions have been running sufficiently strong to make some kind of connection with him, if that makes any sense.'

Even in the modest moonlight, I could see Livak looking both dubious and confused. A qualm of fear chilled me in the midst of the warmth of the night as it occurred to me to wonder what might happen when Temar's dreams included me. Would I see myself through his eyes? Sitting up, I looked across the gloomy enclosure to see a faint green glow betraying Shiv's magelight. I ruffled Livak's unbraided hair with an affectionate hand. 'I don't think I'll be able to sleep again for a while,' I whispered. 'I'm going to stretch my legs.'

'Have one for me,' she said sleepily, voice muffled by her blanket.

When I drew closer to Shiv, I saw he was talking in a low voice with Tonin. The mentor had a small chest between his outstretched legs and I caught an unmistakable glint of gold in the magelight.

'Rysh,' Shiv looked up with a welcoming smile. 'Can't you sleep?'

'Not without my uninvited guest taking over my dreams,' I replied as lightly as I could.

'We've been discussing how to go about the scrying in the morning,' explained Shiv.

'Did you say you'd been dreaming of the colony again?' Tonin looked up, expression inquisitive, so I reached into his casket to forestall further questions.

'What are these?' I picked out a small brooch, dropping it instantly as a shock like the spark from cat's fur stung my fingers.

'Some of the colony's artefacts.' Tonin retrieved a ring with careful fingers and rolled it lovingly in a scrap of silk.

'What we need now is to find the people they belong to,' said Shiv, frustration lifting his voice loud enough to raise a few heads from their blankets.

'Do you think we could have a little less disturbance?' A waspish request came from a dark bundle and I identified it with some surprise as Viltred. I'd have thought the old wizard would have stayed on the ship, given a choice.

'Does anything strike a chord with you?' Tonin offered me the casket and I reached hesitantly for a plain gold ring, the kind that men at home still give their wives to mark their child's first steps. Resting it in the palm of my hand, I tentatively loosened my hold on the bars that held Temar behind closed doors. Nothing resulted, leaving me feeling absurdly disappointed. I shook my head, more than a little mystified.

Tonin removed the ring and laid a chatelaine across my hand, the long chains jingling softly as the keys, knife and purse swung to and fro. Still feeling nothing, I handed it back and took the casket from Tonin. For the most part, it contained rings, some plain, others ornamented with enamel or engraving, a few heavy cabochons and more seals that must have been worn for generations before crossing the ocean in hopes of reaffirming their ownership. Faceted gems on rings and other jewellery shone soft and secretive in the fugitive moonlight. I reached down to find a slim dagger in an ivory sheath. A smear of brazing showed where the hilt had been repaired after that scuffle with Vahil, I noted, but otherwise the trifle that had betrayed Den Domesin's noble birth was still an elegant piece. I smiled at the memory of Albarn's chagrin when his pose as a yeoman's son orphaned in the retreat from Dalasor had been so easily unmasked.

The fleeting moment was shattered as Viltred was seized with a paroxysm of coughing and Tonin turned to him hurriedly, helping him to sit upright.

'Viltred, are you all right?'

I looked round to see Tonin laying a concerned hand on the old wizard's brow. Even in this dim light, his colour struck me as unhealthy.

'What do you think?' The aged mage struck Tonin's hand away crossly but was seized by a further fit of coughing that left him gasping, clutching his arms to himself.

'Take this.' Tonin ignored the old man's irascible reply and held a small vial to his pallid lips. 'Trust me, it was studying healing that first took me into investigating aetheric magic. I was to be initiated into the Daemarion conventual life until my father decided I should see a little more of the world before making such an important decision. I found I liked Vanam, you know, never seemed to find the right time to leave, got my silver ring, then the next project came along . . .'

The Mentor's inconsequential chat made it impossible for Viltred to interrupt. Whatever was in the potion certainly eased the old wizard's breathing and the knot of pain between his brows gradually loosened.

'I think we'd all better get some sleep,' said Tonin apologetically, repacking his casket with deft hands.

Shiv yawned and nodded. 'I'll see you in the morning, Rysh.'

I nodded and turned on my heel but did not return to my niche with Livak in the great hall. There was no way I could risk sleep again, not with every memory Temar had of this place awake and clamouring for my attention. I picked my way carefully through the sleeping figures and climbed up the wall to a ledge where I could rest my feet on an old and weathered corbel. Only I could also see it as it had been, a cheeky likeness of Den Rannion's steward, his beak of a nose now reduced to a faint stump, hooded eyes mere blind hollows in the pitted stone. I drew a deep breath and settled myself to wait for morning. That would bring some surcease from all this, I swore to myself, else Planir would be facing questions on the point of my sword. Only it's not your sword, I rebuked myself, it's that lad Temar's, and demanding answers with threats is his style, not yours. I hoped that was true, it was starting to become difficult to tell.

As the night wore on, I found some small measure of comfort in the regular pacing of the sentries and their quiet exchanges as the duties were swapped. Eventually the sun came up with the rapidity Misaen had thought fit for this strange land and, from my vantage point, the daylight showed me our little troop gathered within the sheltering walls, surrounded on all sides by skeins of milky mist. Huddled shapes began to stir, crawling out of blankets to go to relieve themselves, to share a drink and low-voiced chat over a mouthful of flatbread. The last of the night watch rolled themselves gratefully in their cloaks, with hoods over eyes and genial curses for those talking too loudly nearby.

Jumping down from my perch, I headed for the Archmage as soon as he emerged from his tent, waving aside an offer of food from Halice as I passed her.

'How soon can you scry for these mines, Planir?' I asked without preamble.

'Just as soon as the necessary wizards have woken and broken their fast,' replied the Archmage with the faintest hint of surprise at my early appearance.

'Who do you need?' I was determined to get this masquerade on the stage as soon as all the fiddlers were together.

'Wake Viltred, somebody, please,' Planir commanded over his shoulder, his own eyes fixed on mine.

'I'm already awake, Archmage,' the old wizard said crossly, a steaming tisane in one hand as he rubbed the knotted fingers of the other against his arm if they pained him. 'What do you want me to do?'

'Scrying,' replied Planir tersely. ''Sar, where are you?'

'Here,' Usara yawned fit to crack his jaw and grimaced as he scrubbed at his eyes with a shaking hand. 'Sorry, I rather overdid it yesterday, clearing that channel in the river bed.' He nodded a casual greeting to me but started visibly when I looked up to return it.

'What are you staring at?' I snapped.

'I think most of us find it rather disconcerting to watch the colour of your eyes flickering like that,' Planir answered for Usara in level tones that nevertheless effectively silenced me.

'It is certainly an effect I've never come across in the written record, but then there was never any hint about this whole business with the dreams, either.' Mentor Tonin arrived at my shoulder, busily lacing his ink-smeared jerkin before accepting an armful of parchments from an attentive pupil whom I identified as his protégé, Parrail, a wiry-haired Ensaimin lad I'd have thought was scarcely old enough to be halfway through an apprenticeship, let alone wearing the silver seal ring that Vanam bestowed on its scholars. 'Thank you for agreeing to undertake this scrying so early, Archmage. I very much appreciate the courtesy.'

'Where's Naldeth?' Viltred looked round crossly and the brisk young mage pushed his way through the warriors with scant apology.

'Where do you want me?'

'I'll need you to join the nexus.' Planir rolled up his sleeves as Shiv set a broad silver bowl nearly an arm's length wide on a rough wooden table lashed from green timber. He poured plain river water from a skin and, with a snap of his fingers, the silver bowl was full of emerald light, the radiance illuminating a gathering circle of awed faces as the mercenaries looked on silently. I stifled an ill-tempered desire to tell them to lose themselves and take their ignorant curiosity elsewhere.

Viltred laid a hand on the rim of the bowl and now it shimmered with mingled blue and green light. Usara nodded to Planir, laying his own hands on the sides of the bowl and the circle of colours developed a yellowish undertone. Naldeth stretched out his hands, palm down over the water, and a reddish tint warmed the swirling pattern. The waters circled faster and faster, a vortex plaiting the liquid light in a dizzying spiral until Planir dipped both his hands into the centre of the well and the bowl rang with a chime like a great temple bell. I could hear the watching mercenaries stir and murmur behind me but Planir's steel grey eyes held my gaze in a vicelike grip.

'Watch and tell me what you recognise.' The Archmage spread his hands and an image rose from them, a circle in the empty air, edged with an ever changing pattern of the colours of wizardry, the clarity of the vision startling in the midst of the early morning mists. The picture moved and swooped, circling until I saw the placid expanse of the estuary, the wizard's ship at anchor. I blinked as my eyes swore every oath they knew to tell me I was moving, while my ears denied them absolutely, leaving my stomach churning violently somewhere in the middle. I've never suffered from seasickness but now I made a mental note to be more understanding to those, like Livak, who do.

The river sped away beneath the magical mirror, the banks on either side narrowing, growing more steep, white water now breaking the swirling greens of the current, the flatter grasslands of the coastal plain shrinking as the forest marched down to the water's edge. I found myself swaying and tilting as my vision convinced me I was somehow travelling over this landscape, high as a bird but effortless in this enchanted flight. Peering in a futile attempt to see round the corner of the image and completely caught up in the spectacular improbability of the experience, I nearly missed it.

'There, back a little, on the near side, that's the entrance to the gorge!' I struggled with the words as Temar's memories came clamouring out of confinement and an urgency I could not explain filled me with dread.

Planir closed his eyes for a moment and the image wheeled round, whispers on all sides telling me I wasn't the only one finding this more than a little hard on the gut. The sunlight in the spell shone down on a narrow defile, ferns and wiry stems of opportunist bushes very nearly concealing it completely as a small torrent bubbled its way over a rocky bed to lose itself in the main flow.

'Where exactly is this?' Planir demanded, looking intently at the vision from his own side.

'It's a little way upriver from the mining settlement.' I had the answer before I realised I knew it. 'Temar and Den Fellaemion managed to get the survivors away on the boats and then marched them to the mines to get them away from the moorings.' A flood of recollection threatened to overwhelm me, the shouts, the weeping, the outburst of anger as frustrated people with nothing more to lose save their lives rounded on those driving them so hard for the sake of their salvation.

'Do we know where that is, 'Sar?' The Archmage rounded on the younger wizard, whose face was grim with effort as he poured his power into the spell.

'Yes,' he said shortly.

Planir clapped his hands and the unearthly vision was gone, leaving only a bright pattern lingering inside my eyes, shooting across the pale morning light as I rubbed them. The mercenaries began to drift away, curiosity and misgivings in their low-voiced conversations, a few stumbling over unseen obstacles with attention momentarily elsewhere.

'Archmage!' Kalion pushed his way towards us, an expression of intense annoyance creasing his fat jowls.

'Hearth-Master,' Planir greeted him with smooth courtesy.

'Why was I not wakened for this scrying? I would have thought I was the obvious choice for anchoring the nexus and—'

'Archmage!' The urgency in Shiv's voice turned every head

towards him. He was still leaning over the broad silver bowl, scrying alone now. 'It occurred to me to trace down the river on other side of the watershed, to see if it offered a better route from the coast. Just look what I've found!'

We crowded round to look down into the shining water. The bowl showed three ships riding easily on the calmer waters of the coastal reaches, anchored just off an inlet that I recognised from Temar's encounter with the stolen *Salmon*. I looked up to see every face grim.

'That's where the Elietimm attacked the colony's ships,' I told Tonin, who nodded thoughtfully, checking a much folded piece of parchment.

At this size, each boat looked more like a child's toy than a real vessel. Still, no child's toy would have tiny figures moving around the decks and rigging; well, not outside Hadrumal certainly.

'Could this be a deception?' I asked suddenly, remembering the illusions the Ice Islanders had wielded to such deadly effect before.

'I don't see why it should be,' said Planir thoughtfully. 'They have no reason to know we're here, after all.'

'Are you sure of that?' Otrick elbowed his way to the Archmage's side. 'Haven't they followed us here?'

'I don't think so,' mused Planir. 'Could you expand the radius a little, Shiv, show me some of the coast? No, there, that camp looks well established. That's a base for exploring the interior, I'd say. Back to the ships, if you'd be so kind, thank you. Look, that sail's been jury-rigged, and you can see a season's fouling on the bottom of that ship riding high in the water.'

The Archmage looked up at the circle around the bowl. 'I'd say that's an expedition that's spent the summer here, charting and surveying. However, I would certainly say it suggests Elietimm interest here is at least as urgent as ours.' He looked over at me. 'If Messire D'Olbriot is looking to re-establish a colony here, I think he might have to evict some sitting tenants.'

'That's a service I think we could very well look to render the Sieur,' Kalion mused, expression intent.

'That's the enemy, is it?' Arest pushed Kalion aside to loom over the bowl, scowling darkly as the fat mage attempted to recover his position before thinking better of it.

'Thank you for joining us,' Planir greeted the warrior with a trace of irony.

'So what are you going to do about them?' demanded the big mercenary. 'They've got four or five times our number, given the size of those ships. If they find us we're dead and booking passage with Poldrion. You either have to kill or capture them.'

'How far away are they?' Planir enquired of Shiv thoughtfully.

'No more than a handful of days' sail.'

'Too close,' the Archmage grimaced and shook his head. 'I think you're right, corps-master. We cannot afford to risk having them at our back, or them getting wind of what we're doing.'

'You're simply going to kill them?' Tonin's expression was aghast.

'Give me one good reason why not?' challenged Arest. 'They'll kill us without a second glance at the runes if they find us!' The scholar subsided in unhappy confusion.

'Taking such decisions is part of the price for taking a place at the highest tables.' Kalion did not look in the least distressed at the prospect. 'It's a matter of statecraft, mentor.'

'I'll soon knock the bastards out of this game.' Otrick's eyes sparked blue fire as he spread his hands over the bowl.

'I don't want to alert them unnecessarily.' Planir laid a warning hand on Otrick's arm. 'Use wind and wave, work with Shiv and simply drive the ships onto those rocks. That will suffice for the present.'

'No dragons?' scowled Otrick, glaring up at the taller wizard like a terrier about to take on a mastiff.

'No dragons,' the Archmage confirmed in a tone that brooked no argument.

Livak slid in beside me as we all watched, unashamedly avid as the two mages bent their heads over the water, Otrick's grizzled and tousled, Shiv's black and neatly braided for a change, in the manner I'd seen on several of the mercenaries.

The sky above the tiny ships began to darken; clouds swept in from the ocean in swirls of white, then grey, then forbidding black. Piling high on top of one another, lightning began to flash within the dark towers of vapour, an odd thing to see without the sound of thunder following. Where the waters had been placid and blue, green swirls of current now began tugging at the anchor ropes, the ships shifting and bucking, white teeth of breaking foam nipping at them, harrying them. The tiny figures on the decks were moving busily now, reefing sail and wrestling with flailing ropes. We saw them flinch from something, a hard rain of hail punishing them with icy blows, dimpling the waters all around but not quelling the gathering waves now ripping the vessels from their grip on the sea floor, driving them inexorably into the savage embrace of the rocky shoreline.

I felt Livak shift her footing beside me

'Move aside, trollop.' Viltred's harsh words startled me and as I looked up, three things happened inside the space of half a breath.

Livak drew a dagger from her belt and lunged at the old mage, only to be sent headlong backwards with a stunning flash of red fire from Kalion. Viltred ignored them both to fasten his skinny hands around Otrick's equally scrawny neck, his rushing charge sending table, bowl and water flying. The Relshazri wizard was not big, but he was big enough, Otrick's robust personality residing as it did in a small if wiry frame. Viltred had him down in an instant, leaning all his weight into crushing the Cloud-Master's throat.

I looked for Livak, to see her wringing her scorched hands, expression dazed.

'Are you all right?'

'His eyes, Rysh, his eyes!'

At her scarcely coherent words, I moved to grab a handful

of Viltred's hair, wrenching his head back to show me sockets filled with featureless black.

'Elietimm magic!' I yelled, barely getting it out before a shattering pain numbed my hands, next smashing upwards into my head and dropping me to my knees. A flash of amber light snapped audibly through the air and I looked up through tears of agony to see Viltred wrestling in toils of enchantment woven by Planir, the backlash flinging me aside.

'Tonin, do something!' the Archmage shouted angrily, cursing under his breath as Viltred struggled in his bonds, blue flames crackling down the golden beams to set Planir's sleeves alight. The Archmage grimaced in pain but his concentration did not waver.

The mentor spilled his parchments on the dewy grass, tossing them aside until Parrail snatched one from the litter and the pair of them began an faltering incantation. Livak reached for me and I helped her to her feet, scarcely more steady myself. I noticed distantly that Shiv and Naldeth were tending to the fallen Otrick while Kalion was weaving a circle of unearthly, crimson flame around the Archmage and Viltred, still frantically struggling against the confines of the wizardry. A cry that sent birds fleeing their roosts all around ripped through the morning mists and Viltred suddenly collapsed, all the magic vanishing to leave a smell of burning and a riot of startled questions shouted on all sides.

Planir ran to gather the fallen Viltred in his arms. The killing anger in his face contrasted with his gentle hands as he searched for pulse or breath. Mentor Tonin rummaged frantically in a pocket, but when he found his little vial saw there was no longer a need for his medicaments.

'Did we do it? Did we restore him before his heart gave out?' the scholar wondered fruitlessly, more to himself than to anyone else.

Planir just shook his head, eyes steely with an awesome wrath.

'*Ware the invaders!*' Temar's voice sounded inside my head so loudly I could not believe the rest of the encampment hadn't heard it too. Startled, I sprang to my feet, abandoning questions over Viltred's fate.

'Ware Elietimm,' I bellowed, a bare breath before black-liveried shapes leaped out of the empty air, swords naked and hungry, pale steel soon running with the blood of startled victims. The mercenaries, caught on the back foot, ran to meet this unexpected challenge but took a moment to realise that the invading Elietimm were sweeping past anyone with a blade to cut down scholars and wizards with indiscriminate butchery.

I ran to Planir, Livak at my side, mercenaries led by Minare dashing toward us, all of us desperate to protect the wizards gathered in a tense circle around the Archmage. Tonin tried frantically to run to one of his pupils, a young woman, harebell eyes glazed and lifeless as they stared blindly at the brightening sky, the pallor of death shrouding her young face, but two mercenaries tripped him with merciless force and dragged him bodily with them.

'Get behind me, you imbecile,' Minare cursed the weeping mentor, thrusting him into Parrail's startled arms. 'She's dead meat and you need to save yourselves!'

Minare's lads formed themselves into an angry ring of steel around the mages, blades outwards, hacking down the invaders, who were throwing themselves forward again and again, taking blows from behind without heeding them as they spent their lives in a single-minded attempt at killing the wizards.

I parried a scything stroke to my knees and swept my own blade upwards to take the man's hand off at the wrist. Our eyes met in that instant and I saw only madness and hatred in that ice-blue, white-rimmed gaze. His life bleeding out from the wound, the Ice Islander still ripped a dagger from his belt and lunged past me, reaching over my shoulder in a suicidal bid to stab at Shiv. As I wrestled with him, feet slipping on the bloody ground, Livak slid a careful hand inside this foul embrace to stab him once in the vitals. The Elietimm stiffened in my arms, head jerked backwards as foam bubbled from his bloodless lips. I flung his corpse from me, dead before it hit the ground.

A great gout of flame reached for the distant sun and I saw Kalion ignite the ground all around him, a knot of panicked scholars clinging to the tails of his jerkin as the fires greedily licked at their boots. The handful of Elietimm who escaped immolation circled the inferno, seeking any flaw only to die at the hands of Lessay and his warriors coming up behind them, eager to channel their own fury and chagrin into killing those who had taken them so badly by surprise.

In what could only have been a matter of moments, Arest's harsh voice was echoing around the encampment, the stone now betrayed as such an inadequate defence, as little use to us as it had been to Den Rannion. 'Any enemy still alive? No? Make sure!'

'My lads, get your arses on to the walls!' Outrage thickened Minare's yell.

Lessay's shout came hard on the heels of Arest's. 'Find your pairs, check who's wounded and count the dead!'

Voices harsh with the accents of Lescar came from all directions in turn, other mercenaries hurrying to fetch water, bandages and salve as calls came from the wounded. I hugged Livak close once she had sheathed her daggers and we looked round for Halice and Shiv. They were together, Shiv pale as Halice ripped away a bloody sleeve in one brisk movement.

'I have tunics I've put fewer stitches in than you, wizard,' she remarked with rough sympathy as she washed the gore from a ragged slice above his wrist. 'Whoever taught you to use a blade left a nasty hole in your defences; I'm going to have to give you a few lessons!'

'Leave that! Shiv, here, with me!' Planir caught the dented silver bowl from the ground as he strode towards us, the rim now an irregular ellipse. The Archmage swept a hand over and across it, the last remnants of the morning mist sucked down to coalesce into a feeble puddle in the mud-smeared base.

'Your hand.' Planir caught Shiv's fingers, still slippery with blood, the burns on his own wrist raw and angry beneath the scorched linen of his shirt.

A flash of multi-hued light struck an image from the surface of the water, the inlet where the Elietimm had anchored, the rocky arm reaching out into the surf, the trees of the forest gently tossed by no more than a breeze, no sign of either camp or vessels.

'Pox on it!' spat the Archmage. 'Tonin, get over here!'

The still trembling mentor peered into the bowl and shook his head slowly in mystification, wringing his hands.

'Are they still there and somehow hiding themselves, or have they gone elsewhere?' demanded Planir.

Tonin shook his head again. 'I have no way to tell, Archmage.'

'We've three dead and a handful wounded, two badly, out of the fighting force,' Arest declared, striding up. 'What of the scholars?'

Parrail peered unhappily round Tonin's shoulder, tears carving pale streaks through grime on his face. 'They killed Keir and Levia, Mentor—'

'How many of your number are wounded?' demanded Arest.

'Six,' Parrail drew a long, shuddering breath and tried to straighten his shoulders. 'And two others dead, Alery and Mera.'

I winced; by my count, that meant two of every three of the scholars were fallen or injured. I was relying on them and their learning to free me from Temar's insidious tyranny.

'What of the wizards?' Arest looked round and cursed. I looked after him to see Kalion kneeling by a motionless figure, one of the two cloak carriers who had attended him so assiduously on board ship, a youngish wizard whose name I had never quite caught. When the fat wizard stood, his face was swollen and purple with a fury that promised dreadful retribution.

'Get Shannet and that lass of hers off the ship,' Planir ordered, dropping both Shiv's hand and the scrying bowl. 'Arest, deploy your troops to give us a secure perimeter while we work. Kalion, over here, if you please. Kindly work with Shannet to construct both a barrier and concealment over this place; you can draw on everyone save myself, Usara and Shiv.'

Kalion nodded, eyes burning with determination now he had a task on which to focus. 'The only thing that will get past me will be embers blown on the wind!'

'I'll provide that,' croaked Otrick hoarsely, rubbing darkly purple bruises on his throat with a shaking hand.

The Archmage spun on his heel to fix Tonin with a challenging eye.

'Mentor, who is your most adept pupil still unharmed?'

'That would have to be Parrail,' Tonin quavered.

'Then work with all the others, wounded or not, to weave whatever enchantment you think might conceal or protect us from aetheric magic,' the Archmage commanded him crisply. 'Get to it at once, if you would be so good.'

'What do you want with the lad?' asked Tonin, shuffling through his parchments nonetheless.

'You're going up river, scholar,' Planir turned from the gaping lad to me. 'Ryshad, we need to find that cavern and fast. You and Shiv, take the boat, take 'Sar and as many troops as Arest can spare you. The Elietimm will be here as soon as they can. If they've crossed the ocean, they almost certainly have magic to work against the weather, so it could be any time. Otrick, Kalion and I will be able to hold the river mouth for a good while, but the faster you find the colonists, the happier we'll all be!'

I could feel Temar's exultation echoing round the back of my mind. 'Of course, Archmage,' I replied with some difficulty.

'I can scout for you and we'll ask Minare for some of his lads.' Livak spoke up from where she was holding Shiv's arm secure for Halice's needle. 'Go on, Rysh, find him while we finish up here.'

I did as I was instructed and we had the ship manned and rigged for river sailing before the sun was halfway across the morning sky. I stood on deck, looking up at the Den Rannion steading, no heads visible against the greenery although I knew full well archers now waited patiently on every trustworthy section of the wall walk, ready to send a deadly rain of arrows down from the battlements. Equally unseen, Kalion's magic was enclosing the whole area in defences of elemental fire, Shiv assured me, while Planir's power stalked beneath our feet and Otrick's skills rode high on the winds above. Parrail had tested the aetheric barriers with repeated attempts to contact his colleagues, each failure perversely boosting his confidence.

'Are you sure you're doing it right?' Livak demanded a breath before I could come up with a more tactful version of the same question, but Parrail was not affronted by this.

'Quite sure, my lady,' he replied in the cultured tones of Selerima, one of the great trading cities of western Ensaimin. 'I am one of the most well-versed practitioners of these arts, as we so far understand them,' he added with simple pride.

'Do you know what you have to do to revive these colonists?' I asked, trying not to let my desperation show. At least Parrail was proving older than I had first thought, being a rather baby-faced youth with softly curling brown hair above a snub and freckled nose. His rueful hazel eyes told me he was well used to this kind of reaction, as he nodded, clutching Tonin's ornately inlaid casket to his chest.

'I will continue to study our theories as we travel,' he assured me earnestly.

The word theory had a worrying lack of certainty about it, but there was nothing I could do about that. The boy had earned the silver ring to prove his scholarship, hadn't he? I waved to Halice, who nodded to the mercenaries waiting with her on the wharf side. They cast the ropes securing the boat into the water. Raising a hand, I signalled to Shiv who was standing by the captain of the ship at the tiller. Defying both current and tide, masts and spars bare of canvas, rails lined with mercenaries, bows at the ready, the boat moved upstream, slowly at first and then more rapidly, a spur of foam at her prow frothing with green light.

'Now we should see an end to this, Arimelin willing,' muttered Livak, coming to stand beside me, offering a cup of tisane.

I took a sip of the steaming liquid, feeling the bracing bite of herbs at the back of my throat. 'You're sure you want to do

this? I'd understand if you wanted to steer well clear of any
aetheric magic—'

'And stay with Planir? To risk being skewered by an
Elietimm who thinks he's an Eldritch-man or get myself
fried by Kalion getting over enthusiastic?' Livak shook her
head. 'I'd sooner challenge one of Poldrion's demons to a
draw of the runes for free passage to the Otherworld!'

'That's a cheery thought,' I grimaced as I took another sip
of tisane. 'I'm glad to have you with me though, after the way
you avoided me on the voyage here.'

'I had a lot of thinking to do.' Livak fixed her gaze on the
curve of the river as it narrowed towards a bend. 'I had to
decide if I wanted you badly enough to put up with all that
comes with you just at present.'

'And you do?'

'For the moment.' Livak's eyes remained hard. 'And I'll be
making sure every cursed thing possible gets done to empty
that D'Alsennin out of your head, once and for all.'

Despite the seriousness of our situation, I felt absurdly
happy. As I watched the river banks slide past, at once both
unknown to me and familiar to Temar, I could not agree with
her more, finding it harder and harder to batten down the
defences in the back of my mind.

We reached the mouth of the gorge just as the sun slid
down behind the grim and mossy crags of the high ground
above us. The captain guided the ship cautiously into a limpid
pool, frowning as gravel scraped noisily beneath the hull.

'Where to now, Shiv?' I asked as both wizards and Parrail
came to join me and Livak at the rail.

'I've no idea. I mean it's the right place, sure enough, but
I can't locate a cave.' He shook his head. 'I've been scrying
and there's nothing, nothing at all.'

'There's something preventing me from searching beneath
the surface on the far side of that ravine,' Usara looked
thoughtful. 'That must mean something.'

'Parrail?' I turned to the young scholar who clutched a
parchment defensively to his chest, eyes wide.

'I'm sorry,' he stammered, 'I'm sorry but I can't find anything out of the ordinary.'

'Which is what we'd expect if this place was supposed to be shielded from aetheric magic,' Livak managed to damp down most of the scorn in her voice. 'Let's follow Usara's lead. Buril and Tavie, you're with us.'

It seemed Halice's word was good enough to give Livak a measure of authority over the mercenaries and the two she named climbed down readily into the ship's boat, the rest remaining alert and guarding the ship. I followed more slowly, my feelings increasingly confused, reluctant to risk making contact with this ancient magic, desperate to rid myself of Temar and constantly struggling to keep him from laying his shadowy presence over my eyes and my hands. I was starting to feel quite light-headed as we reached a rocky ledge, where a stunted tree offered a handy place to tie up. The feeling worsened as my feet made contact with the ground and with every step we took up that narrow ravine, my senses reeling as the jagged walls of the defile seemed to be pressing in on me, frozen in time but ready to topple down on me at any moment.

'It's no good, I can't find any kind of entrance to a cave,' said Usara with marked irritation.

'There's no sign along here,' called one of the mercenaries, a bull-necked man with blunt features marred by a thoroughly broken nose.

'Nor here,' confirmed his mate, Tavie, I think it was, a burly bruiser with a gut on him like a two-season child-belly.

Livak looked down from where she was exploring a narrow ledge, sure-footed as a mountain goat. 'This all looks as if it's been undisturbed since Misaen made it,' she commented. 'Shiv?'

'What?' the wizard looked up from a puddle in a rocky hollow where he had been working magic. 'No, there's nothing I can see that's of any use.' He turned to me, face deathly serious. 'The only one who's going to be able to find that cave is Temar D'Alsennin.'

My first instinct was to reach for my sword but I managed to stick my hands through my belt instead. 'What do you mean?'

'You have to let Temar show us the way.' Usara folded his arms. 'It's the only way, Ryshad.'

I shook my head slowly, wanting to shout my denial but unable to find the words. Livak slid down a convenient tree and reached up to lay her hands on side of my face, drawing my gaze to her.

'Look at me, Rysh,' she said softly. 'Arimelin save us, I don't want to see this again, but finding this cave is the only way you're going to be rid of him, isn't it? Saedrin's stones, I know what we're asking of you, better than anyone else, but you have to do this, to save yourself.'

She was right, curse her, curse the day Messire had ever given me this unholy sword. What choice did I have? Death? If I could leave this Temar D'Alsennin behind to make his own deal with Saedrin, would it be so very bad to cross over to the Otherworld and see what a new life there had to offer? I was so tired, so very tired, exhausted by the now incessant struggle to keep myself intact, to maintain my crumbling defences against Temar. I was not even sure I even knew myself anymore, so much had changed in me over the seasons. Could I trust myself? Not really, but one thing I knew – I could trust Livak. I reached up with one trembling hand to bring her slim fingers to my lips in a bone-dry kiss. Shutting my eyes, I laid the other hand to the sword-hilt and lost myself in a bottomless pit of darkness.

The mining settlement of Kel Ar'Ayen, 43rd of Aft-Summer

Temar blinked and stumbled, disconcerted to find himself standing upright and putting out a hand to save himself by grabbing a tree branch. How was it that he had woken up here? Or was this just one more of the tormenting dreams that the enchantment had wrapped around him, only to rip away the illusion of normality to leave him alone in the dark once more? No, this was real; it was daylight. He could feel the uneven rocks beneath his feet, wet leaves in his clutching hand. He could smell the green freshness of the flowers and bushes all around and he drew a deep breath of the warm, moist air down into his lungs. This was real, no vision of a forbidden reality to tempt him into madness. That first exultation of sensation faded to be replaced by a lurking headache and treacherous weakness in his limbs. Had he been ill, he wondered, vaguely recalling childhood fever. No, better not to think of that, of the way he had woken from delirium to find father and siblings lost to him for ever, never to know each other again, even if they should meet by chance in the Otherworld.

A voice spoke hesitantly beside him and Temar frowned, unable to make sense of the rapid, oddly phrased sentence. Who was this man? Obviously he was from some distant land with a different tongue. He looked to be ten or so years older than Temar, somewhat taller with long black hair and a sallow complexion. He was dressed in curiously cut and tailored clothes, a blood-stained bandage grimy beneath the tattered remnants of what had once been a good linen shirt of leaf green.

'Temar D'Alsennin?' the man tried again, slowly. While the accent remained hard on the ear, Temar could at least recognise his own name. He nodded, cautiously and asked his own most immediate question. 'Who are you?'

The man frowned then tapped himself on the chest, speaking slowly. 'Shiv.'

Temar did not think that much of a reply and wondered why the foreigner was looking so uneasy. He closed his eyes for a moment and ran rapidly through his memories, ruthlessly shoving aside the chaos of his dreams in a desperate search for his last moments before the enchantment had taken his wits from him. That was it, he had been sent into a sleep woven of Artifice to remain safe until rescue could come. Eyes snapping open, Temar took a step towards the man in green, clear challenge in his words.

'How do I come to be here?'

The man shrugged helplessly and looked past Temar to someone at his back. Angry at himself for allowing them to take him unawares like this, Temar swung rapidly round to find himself outnumbered and took a pace sideways to get the solid rock of the gorge to defend his back.

'We are here to help you,' a lad some few years younger than Temar spoke up, snub-nosed face pale with tension beneath a thatch of coarse brown hair, a small book in one hand, crammed with odd notes and scraps of parchment. 'My name is Parrail and I have some knowledge of enchantment.' His words were spoken with painstaking care and his sincerity was evident. 'What you know as Artifice,' he added hastily.

That was all very well, but Temar was more concerned about the other people he could see. Two men, guardsmen by his guess, were further up the gorge, looking at him with frank curiosity, while a tempting blossom with tousled red hair was standing rather closer, arms folded and an expression close to hatred burning in her grass green eyes. Temar found himself recoiling from this a little, unable to think how he might have offended the lady, though her claim to such a courtesy looked rather doubtful, given her immodest breeches and manlike jerkin. The last member of this band of brigands was a quiet man of no more than usual height with thinning sandy hair and shrewd eyes, dressed in some kind of long robe with no weapons that Temar could see. Was he a priest of some kind? Temar looked round again and realised with some relief that only the retainers and the woman looked to be carrying weapons. If it came to a fight, the runes were not too heavily weighted against him.

He laid a hand to his own hip, reassured by the familiar feel of his own sword and glanced down instinctively. What he saw chilled him to the bone. This was not his hand; it was older, broader, tanned with oil ingrained around the nails, small scars pale in a lattice around the knuckles, a hard-worked hand with its fellow matching it. Temar spread both hands before him, unable to stop them shaking, mouth agape in consternation. These were an artisan's hands, no noble bloodline bore these sturdy workmanlike fingers. The great sapphire that had been his father's was gone too, but a deep indentation marked the flesh of the central finger, for all the world like the mark from the band of a ring.

Was this madness? Had he finally succumbed to the insanity that had tormented him through the smothering darkness of the enchantment? Terror threatened to overwhelm him. Stumbling, he fell to his knees, heedless of the pain of the sharp rocks. The scene before him shifted and altered, everything distorted as if he were looking through cheap and flawed glass.

'Come on,' the man called Shiv caught him under the arms and helped him stand. Temar's vision cleared but his confusion grew as he realised he now stood taller than this man, not shorter. He looked down to see long, muscular legs encased in stained leather breeches running down to boots far wider and longer than they should have been. Temar was certain he had never owned such garments or footwear. What had happened to him?

The scribe or whatever he was hurried to Temar's other side. 'You are under an enchantment, a sorcery, laid upon you by the

Lady Guinalle. We are here to restore you and your fellows if we can only find the cavern where you are hidden.'

Guinalle! All Temar's alarm for himself receded as he picked that name out of the man's slow words. He clung to the thought. Guinalle – she would help him, she would know why he was so fearfully transformed, she could answer all the questions that were crowding round him, threatening, taunting.

'Where is Guinalle?' The man with the bandage seemed almost to be hearing his thoughts.

Temar shook off his hands and scowled, sensation returning to his nerveless hands and feet. 'What do you want with her?'

'We wish to restore her to herself, to awaken her,' the lad with the parchments said hesitantly.

'We need her aid to defend ourselves against invaders from the sea,' the thoughtful man in brown spoke up, picking his halting words with evident care, his accent still strange to Temar's ear. The red-headed girl said something fast and furious that escaped Temar completely, her speech an incomprehensible gabble.

The lad rummaged in a pocket and held out a ring to Temar, a tarnished and battered circle of bronze whose engraved crest was worn to little more than a shadow. It was the crest of Den Rannion's house, the ring a retainer would wear to show his allegiance and status.

'Vahil!' Memory came hurrying back to Temar and a frail hope reached past the taunts of delusion. 'Vahil returned home? He has sent you?'

The one called Parrail hesitated, but the two unarmed men answered as one: 'He has.' 'To seek your help against the men from the sea.'

Sudden recollection of the invaders' assault shook Temar. 'They are here?'

'Not yet, but they are coming,' replied the man in green.

'We need to find the cavern before they arrive,' added the man in brown, hushing the lad, who was looking more and more confused.

Temar shut his eyes for a moment and rubbed a hand over his aching head, stopping in consternation to feel a mass of short curls. That should tell him something, he knew, but what?

'What has happened to me?' he asked, more in anguish than in any hope of answer.

The redhead spat something at him but the man in green snapped back at her in words too rapid and oddly spoken for Temar to understand.

'Guinalle will be able to restore you.' The brown-robed man took a step forward and offered a pale-skinned hand. 'We mean no harm to any of you. We only wish to help.'

Temar reached out one trembling, unfamiliar hand and clutched the man's thin fingers. Contact with another living being steadied him; this was certainly no dream, no delusion wrought of fear and tangled memory.

'Where is Guinalle?' the man asked, eyes intent despite his friendly expression.

She would have the answers, Temar realised at once. Guinalle would know what to do; she might even know these people, whomever it was that Vahil had sent, from whatever distant land. He had to find Guinalle!

Turning, he surveyed the gorge, dismayed to find it narrower and deeper, the bottom choked with stones and clinging ferns as the foaming water splashed and bubbled its way through to the river. Was this the right place? Low oaks clung grimly to crevices in the rocks, twisted branches reaching upwards to the light. Finer branches of ash and hazel dappled the ground with shifting shadow. Winter storms must have sent landslides or floods or something to reshape the land so drastically, Temar concluded desperately. Struggling along the treacherous stream bed with no little difficulty, he scanned the sides of the defile frantically for any sign of the cavern's entrance. Chest heaving with burgeoning panic, Temar halted, turning abruptly to see these strange visitors watching him, waiting, expressions wary.

'Search, curse you,' he shouted, suddenly enraged. 'Help me!'

'What do we seek?' the lad Parrail called after an awkward moment of still silence.

'A narrow ledge, leading to rock-cut steps, a walk down into a small cave that gives on to a larger.' Temar looked around helplessly. 'I cannot tell where it might be.'

'Think of Guinalle,' the wounded man urged as he made his way through the jumble of broken rock. 'Let your instincts lead you to her.'

As the man spoke Temar felt an irresistible conviction that Guinalle was somewhere close. He turned and turned again, head going from side to side like a hound searching for a windblown scent. Moving rapidly, eyes unseeing, he let this unfamiliar body stumble through the chattering stream until he was brought up hard against the treacherous surface of a long, sliding scree of shattered rock. Blinking through blurred vision, temples throbbing, Temar looked up to see a familiar series of hills far distant, sharp profiles against the clear blue sky, backdrop to the raw and broken stones blocking the entrance to the cavern.

'She's here,' Temar said helplessly.

The red-headed girl moved quickly along the narrow and treacherous ledges, hands and feet deft as she moved out on to the shifting surface of the scree. One of the swordsmen tried to follow her, lost his footing, tumbled and gained only scrapes and bruises for his trouble. The girl spat what could only be curses at him and he coloured uncomfortably, turning to quench his hurts in the cool waters of the stream. The girl moved slowly up the long slope, everyone else watching in a tense silence broken only by the skittering of loose stones dislodged by her careful movements. Pausing, she wedged her feet securely against some larger stones and looked down, calling the first thing Temar had understood from her.

'Mind your heads!'

She began tossing stones down into the water, ringing splashes echoing down the rocky angles of the gorge. Soon a black patch of darkness showed against the grey of the rock face, a hole in the side of the hidden valley.

'Be careful, Livak!' the one called Shiv yelled as the redhead swung her legs slowly round and eased herself through the narrow gap. Temar stood, looking upwards along with all the rest, silent while the sounds of the chattering stream, the woodland birds singing all around, went unheeded.

'Yes! It's here!' The girl Livak's face reappeared in the breach, pale but triumphant, her voice somehow easier now on Temar's ear.

'Get yourself out of the way and I'll clear the entrance!' The man in brown robes shouted upwards, rolling his sleeves up in a purposeful fashion. The girl nodded and scrambled with some alacrity to a ledge above the opening.

Temar watched, open-mouthed, as the man laid a hand on the boulders at his feet and an unearthly golden glow swept up through the scree, bright beneath the dull grey of the weathered and stained stones. With a whisper at first, building to a full throated growl, the very rocks themselves flowed like water, swept sideways like wind-tossed waves, sliding downwards to leave the black hollow that led to the cavern open to the sunlight. A final ripple clattered back down through the scree, running its length to toss a few stones gently at Temar's feet as the amber light faded and vanished.

He stared at the man. 'What are you?'

'My name is Usara,' the man smiled and bowed abruptly from the waist. 'I am a wizard.'

Temar shook his head in mystification.

'I work magic, but not as the Lady Guinalle does it. My colleague Shiv and I follow a different path.'

'Come on.' Livak, the redhead, was glaring at Temar again with that unwarranted dislike. 'Let's get this done!'

The broken and treacherous rocks were now transformed into a firm pathway and Temar found himself hurrying ever faster to reach the entrance to the cavern. He paused on the threshold, squinting into the darkness, any old fear of such places irrelevant in the face of his urgency to find Guinalle. A glow at his shoulder made him turn to reach for a torch, but he took an involuntary step backwards when he saw a pale yellow flame burning insouciantly in the centre of the magic-wielder's palm.

'Don't worry about it.' The other one, Shiv, raised his own hand to create a greenish light, seemingly reflected from the very rocks. 'Just help us find Guinalle.'

Temar needed no further urging to move away from these strange people with their peculiar talents. He hurried down the rough-hewn steps, the arcane light pursuing him as the others followed. At the foot of the uneven stair, he paused and looked round the huge expanse of the cave, heart pounding in his chest but strength and courage returning to him with every pulse of his blood.

The cavern had been much enlarged by the miners, Temar recalled, hewn out of the living rock, angles and facets marking the stroke of axe and pick on the walls. The roof was jagged and uneven, dipping and rising in a series of frozen waves. The silent air was motionless, not over-cold but the absolute stillness made him shiver nonetheless. He forced himself to take another step as his unwanted companions crowded at his back. As they moved out into the cave as one, their footsteps rang harshly in the hushed calm.

Unnerved, the younger lad stood close to Temar and glanced around for guidance while the guardsmen exchanged wondering glances, looking back up to the circle of leafy daylight at the head of the stair. The two men with their unnatural light growing to reach the furthest reaches of the cavern moved out to either side. No one entered the body of the cave, Temar noted with surprise, leaving that to the girl, Livak. She took a careful step forward, then another, a thief's tread silent on the sandy floor as she picked her way through pallets and mattresses, rough beds of cloaks and blankets packed close together, a pale light of enchantment hovering over her head to show her a motionless figure in every space — men and women, unformed youths, bearded artisans, staid matrons, fresh-faced maidens, children curled in unconscious memory of that first, short, dream-filled sleep within their mother's belly. Temar watched as the green-eyed girl moved slowly between the motionless figures, his scalp prickling with apprehension.

Most looked peaceful, as if they merely slept, but others wore frowns, faces twisted with fear and sorrow, a crystal tear glinted in the corner of an eye, a mouth half open on a final protest. Some wore bandages, old blood staining the linen black and brown. These people were not asleep however. The warm flush of natural rest was nowhere to be seen. It was replaced on all sides by a cold pallor, an unnatural stiffness. Livak put a tentative hand to a young man's cheek and shuddered.

'It's like touching a marble statue,' she said softly, an echo carrying her words whispering round the cave, spiralling up into the darkness of the roof.

'Where will Guinalle be?' Parrail plucked hesitantly at Temar's sleeve, eyes huge and black in the dim light.

Temar frowned. 'I'm not sure. She would have been the last, so she could seal the cave, along with the Artifice, so . . .' His words trailed off as he looked around, gaze drawn to a low pallet set a little aside from the serried ranks stretching out into the cavern. He hurried towards it, the boy at his side, desperate hope taunting him, tears starting at a sudden pain behind his eyes.

'She's beautiful,' the lad breathed and Temar could not find any words to answer him as he looked down on Guinalle's motionless form. Clad in simple cream linen under an undyed woollen gown, her rich chestnut hair provided a single note of colour, frozen in soft wisps against a face as remote and colourless as the more distant moon. A crystal vial with a silver lid shone between her breasts and a tightly furled parchment rested beneath her clasped hands. Temar stroked her hair, which was stiff and unresponsive under his fingers where it had once flowed, sensuous as silk.

'If this is her, get on with it,' Livak startled both of them as she appeared on silent feet to lean down and pull the document from Guinalle's helpless hands. 'Come on, Parrail, this is where you're supposed to make yourself useful.' She spared Temar a glance, venomous with that peculiar dislike, and he felt a sudden shock of pain through his temples again.

The boy, Parrail, leafed through his book hastily, lips moving silently as he ran a finger over something. 'Right,' he sniffed, and ran a trembling hand over his mouth. 'I think I can do it.' He took the crystal vial and wrapped Guinalle's white fingers tightly around it. Unrolling the parchment, he squinted uncertainly at the flowing script before clearing his throat and starting to read.

'Ais margan arsteli sestrinet . . .'

His faltering words echoed round the great cave and a terrible weakness overwhelmed Temar, dropping him helpless to hands and knees. Face close to Guinalle's he saw her white pallor sicken and grey and, for one terrible moment, he saw the skull lying in wait, shining beneath her flawless skin. Something in the depths of Temar's mind was screaming in anguish and rage, that lone, tormented voice drowned in the next instant by howls of disembodied anguish battering him from all sides. A foul charnel air choked him and he struggled for breath.

'No,' he gasped, 'no, stop, you're killing us!'

'Have you no sense of rhythm in you? Trimon curse you for a tone-deaf fool!' Livak snatched the parchment from Parrail as she cursed him.

'Ais marghan, ar stelhi, sess thrinet torre . . .' Her musical voice rang high and clear in the emptiness as she chanted the cadence of an ancient tongue and Temar blinked the desperate tears from his eyes to became aware of another sound. Slight and hesitant at first, the sigh of breath rose from Guinalle's sleeping form and he saw the first kiss of life soften her lips to a living rose. A blush warmed her pale cheeks and the unnatural stiffness left her body and clothes, the folds of her gown relaxing in a soft fall around her frame and wisps of her long hair moving slightly as her breath caught them.

She shivered suddenly and opened her eyes, wondering and curious as she saw the faces above her. No one spoke. Guinalle frowned slightly, puzzled. She reached out and touched Temar's face as he knelt there, heart too full of emotion to speak.

'Are you real? I dreamed of you, in a distant land, far from family and friends. Is this another dream?'

Temar clasped her delicate hand in his to warm it between his palms. 'This is no dream. You are awake now, Guinalle. Vahil sent help to rescue us all!'

Guinalle sat up abruptly, her eyes confused. As she did so, the crystal vial rolled down her skirts to shatter on the stone floor. The strong scent of perfume made her gasp, 'I remember, I remember! The sleep, the cave—' She looked round, eyes wide and face distressed, snatching her hand away.

'Guinalle.' Temar's voice was choked with tears and he reached for her. The look of consternation she gave him cut him like a knife.

'Who are you?' she asked, suddenly wary, drawing away unconsciously. 'What do you want with me?'

'It's me, Temar.' He did not understand this, why did she not recognise him?

'D'Alsennin has somehow been revived within the body of one of our companions,' Livak spoke to Guinalle, forcing herself to speak slowly and clearly, sparing Temar only a fleeting look of naked hatred. 'That sword has something to do with it, I don't fully understand how. You must send Temar back to himself and pray to Arimelin that our friend survives unharmed!'

Guinalle was rubbing her eyes, as if she sought to wipe away the lingering effects of her long enchantment. Raising her head, she studied Temar closely, frowning.

'Yes, I see it now – the eyes, the gestures, all that I know, but the face, the body, no wonder I did not recognise you, Temar.'

'What are you saying?' Now it was his turn to retreat in instinctive defence. 'I know I am somewhat changed, but the enchantment—'

'Look at me.' Guinalle studied his eyes and he saw wonder

in her face. 'Look at your hands,' she said, 'feel your hair.' She reached to run her fingers through the tight curls.

'What are you doing?' Temar snapped. 'Don't you know me?'

'I know you, Temar D'Alsennin, none better, but not in this guise,' Guinalle said with a touch of her old manner. 'You must let this man return, and go back to your sleep until we can revive you properly. You have fought the Artifice and twisted it, broken through it to invade an innocent man's mind and steal his body! That was never intended.'

Temar could not meet her gaze. He looked back down at his hands to see those tanned and scratched artisan's fingers instead of the thin aristocratic hands of a nobleman, the sapphire seal ring of his house missing. Fear clutched at him, his own cowardice appalling him.

'I can't, I can't go through that again,' he whispered, remembering the sickening, smothering sensation, the feeling of drowning, of choking, the soft claws of enchantment stealing his mind away. 'I can't do it, don't ask it of me!'

'So will you stay as a thief in this man's body?' Guinalle's hazel eyes were hard in the unearthly green light, her tone uncompromising. 'Where will you go? There will be no place on either side of the ocean for the abomination you will have become!'

Temar gasped under the lash of her words and tears started to his eyes. 'How can you say that?'

Guinalle rose cautiously to her feet and held out her hand. 'Come with me, whoever you are.'

She picked her way unsteadily through the rows of silent sleepers, the strangers who had accompanied Temar to this place following at a distance, the red-haired woman fumbling in a belt-pouch, face dangerous as she rested her other hand on a dagger at her belt. Guinalle came to a lone figure by a hollow, laid out on its back, hands meeting on its chest, fingers circled round empty air. Temar looked down at himself, at his lean, angular face, bloodless lips, thin black brows startling against the pallor of his skin, harsh lines above closed, blind eyes.

'We brought you down here after we wrought the Artifice,' murmured Guinalle, eyes distant. 'Vahil took your sword, he and Den Fellaemion bade me farewell, and then I laid myself down to sleep with you all.' She gazed round the cavern and sighed. 'I felt so alone, so very alone.'

'I'm here now,' Temar blinked away angry tears.

'No, you're not, you're no more than an evil dream tormenting this man. You cannot live in his body without both of you going mad.' Guinalle shook her head with absolute conviction. 'Temar, listen to me, trust me. You must go back under the bonds of the Artifice, until I can return you to yourself.'

'I won't! I can't!' shouted Temar. 'How can you ask that of me?' He seized her, rage filling him, struggling with a furious impulse to shake some understanding into her.

'For the sake of the love we once shared,' replied Guinalle softly as the echoes of his outburst died away. 'This isn't you, Temar, is it?'

Temar stared at her aghast and then at the strange hands he was using to clutch Guinalle's shoulders, his own familiar hands empty and still beside them. A sudden howling fury rang silently through his head, an enraged demand for release hammering against the inside of his skull, sending his senses reeling, blinded, deafened. The moment passed but he staggered under its impact.

'I can't face the darkness again,' he pleaded, unable to help himself.

'Trust me.' Guinalle laid her cool hands on his temples and the pain coursing through his head eased a little.

'Place the sword back in your own hands,' she said calmly. 'It's going to be all right, my dearest.' Her eyes left Temar's for an instant, to convey her reassurances to the silent knot of strangers watching, still, intent.

Temar unbuckled the sword with clumsy fingers, sliding it into the unfeeling hands of the body that had once been his. Weakness overcame him again and he knelt, all strength in his legs deserting him as Guinalle began a low-voiced incantation, her own voice roughened with tears.

The scream of terror and desolation that ripped from his throat set Temar's blood racing in his veins, but as he tried blindly to climb to his feet he pitched forward – and knew no more.

Kel Ar'Ayen,
43rd of Aft-Summer

I came to myself lying across a body that was as cold and immobile as stone. Pushing myself backwards in horror, I found I was as weak as a half-drowned kitten and able to make about as much sense as I struggled to speak. I gasped and hugged my arms to myself, nausea surging up within me, threatening to choke me. A flush like sudden fever left me sweating and dizzy, head ringing like a new-struck bell. I swallowed on a throat ripped raw by the screams of another man's anguish.

'Hush, let me.' Livak was at my side, dragging me away, to prop me sitting against the rough wall of the cave. She knelt before me and gripped my shoulders with both hands, staring deep into my eyes. 'Ryshad?'

I nodded and she held me tight, burying her face in my neck where I felt her hot tears of relief. I wrapped my own arms around her, feebly at first then with growing strength. The urge to vomit passed and I felt the sweat cooling on my body in the dimness of the cavern.

'Are you all right?' I recognised Guinalle at once, but where I had always heard her voice clear and comprehensible in my dreams now I found it hard to understand her slow and lilting words.

'I am, thank you,' I nodded as best I could with Livak's red hair half smothering me.

'Do you remember . . .' Guinalle began hesitantly.

I raised a hand to silence her. 'Yes,' I replied curtly. 'No matter, I don't want to speak of it.'

She managed a half-smile of guilty relief and turned to Temar. Disentangling myself from Livak's embrace, I managed to get to my feet and looked down on the physical body of the man I'd spent so long struggling against inside my head. Livak came to join me, wrapping an arm around my waist as she tucked herself under my arm. Temar looked very young and I realised with an overwhelming relief that I was free of his uncertainties, his ill-governed emotions, all the ills of youth that I had thought I had left behind long since. Not that this whole foul experience hadn't left me with a few quandaries of my own, but I would address them in my own time, I decided. For the present, it was enough to know I was sole master of my own head once more.

Guinalle laid a fond hand on Temar's waxen forehead and I shivered as unseen fingers touched my own skin in a shadowy echo.

'Are you all right?' Livak moved to look at me, face concerned, and as she did so her foot knocked against a dagger on the floor. I recognised it as hers and reached down to pick it up.

'Careful with that.' Livak took it from me hastily and plunged the blade repeatedly into a patch of damp earth until the blade gleamed, cleaned of the oily salve it had carried.

'What were you planning to do with that?' I stared at her, startled.

'His lordship over there was none too keen on giving up your warm body to return to that cold one yonder,' Livak glowered at Temar's unconscious form. 'I was just about ready to make his decision for him, when he yielded. Let him argue the fall of the runes with a dose of tahn in his blood.'

I hugged Livak to me. 'Thanks for the thought, but don't blame the lad too much.' I closed my eyes on a brief memory of that appalling sensation of being locked away in endless darkness, cut off from all sensation. 'After a taste of what he's been going through, I can't say I would have done any different.' Seeing the world through Temar's eyes had been a salutory reminder of the power of the emotions of youth, the mixture of fear and impetuousness that had driven me in my turn first to the excesses of thassin and then to service with Messire.

Livak snorted and muttered something under her breath as Shiv and the others approached cautiously, the mercenaries in particular looking extremely unsettled. 'What do we do now?' Tavie demanded truculently, folding muscular arms over his rounded gut, a scowl lifting his lip to show teeth like a row of burned-out houses. 'We came to find this cave and now we've done it. What next?'

I looked at Shiv and Usara who turned to Parrail. 'Well, I have as many of the small items as we thought promising with me,' he offered. 'Shall we see who we can revive?' He looked questioningly at Guinalle, whose head had turned at his words.

'Let me see.' She held out her hands and Parrail gave her the casket with alacrity, kneeling beside her to open it. As Guinalle examined the rings and trinkets with tentative hands, she looked up at us, eyes wide. 'How long have we slept?'

I exchanged an uncertain glance with Shiv and Usara, but Parrail spoke up eagerly. 'Close on twenty-four generations, as far as we can tell.'

Guinalle's jaw dropped and she gaped at the lad. 'What? How? I mean . . .' The multitude of questions defeated her and she buried her face in her hands, Parrail putting a helpless arm around her in a futile attempt at comfort.

'We have come to find you, to seek your assistance against that same enemy that destroyed your colony here.' Usara knelt before Guinalle and took her hands in his, holding her tearful gaze. 'There will be answers to all your questions in time, but just at present we need your aid. Your Artifice has long been lost to our people and the Elietimm, the men who attacked you, they are using it against us. Will you help us?'

Guinalle struggled for an answer. 'I . . .'

'Leave the rest of it for another time, just consider that one thing,' Usara's voice was calm and soothing but I could hear the urgency behind his words. 'We need your help, otherwise more people will die at the hands of these invaders.'

Guinalle blinked and rubbed away her tears with a trembling hand. 'Whatever I can do, I will,' she faltered.

'Should we be doing this?' Parrail looked round the great cavern, uncertainty wrinkling his brow. 'I mean, the theory sounded all very well, but—'

'What else are we going to do, now we've come this far?' Shiv took a parchment from Parrail's book. 'I hardly think we can leave Guinalle all alone? Now, is this a list of the people you think owned these artefacts?'

Parrail scrambled to his feet hastily. 'It's what we compiled from the dreams, the most common images that were seen. You see, that one there, the chatelaine, all the evidence suggests it belongs to a mature woman with rather noticeable pock marks and—'

Shiv thrust the list at the scholar. 'You read it out. Tavie and Buril, come with me and see if you can find anyone matching his descriptions.'

The mercenaries shared an uncertain look before joining Shiv and then Usara in slowly quartering the cave as Parrail read out brief and often unflattering descriptions of the people they sought.

'Oh dear,' Guinalle stifled a hesitant smile. 'Mistress Cullam always preferred to be called robust or sturdy rather than fat.'

'Are you up to doing this?' Livak was looking at Guinalle with open scepticism.

The slender woman lifted her chin and a spark of determination lit her eye. 'I am, but first we should revive as many Adepts in Artifice as we may. They will be able to support me in restoring the others.'

'Can you identify them for us?' I took a step towards the others.

'In a moment.' Guinalle turned to Temar's motionless form. 'I cannot leave him in the darkness any longer.'

She knelt to lay her hands on Temar's own, where they clasped the hilts of the sword. I gripped Livak's fingers so hard that she flinched. Again I felt that shadowy touch, like a breath of cold air, but it passed and I felt a curious sense of release as Temar drew a first, long shuddering breath. As he opened his eyes Guinalle drew him close to her and, by unspoken agreement, Livak and I turned to leave the pair of them alone.

'How are you getting on?'

Shiv looked up from a child's tiny form at my question, an enamelled silver flower on a bracelet in his hand. 'Pretty well, but we've artefacts for fewer than a third all told, even with those still back in Hadrumal.' He shook his head. 'We'd better be careful whom we chose to revive. I hope Guinalle can identify people for us; I don't fancy finding I've woken a child whose mother is still no better than dead.'

I looked back over my shoulder to Guinalle and Temar, still clinging to whatever reassurance they could give each other.

'She says we should try and revive any adept in Artifice,' I commented.

'Can you,' Shiv hesitated. 'I mean, do you think—'

'I can still remember the dreams, if that's what you're trying to ask.' I managed a weak grin, but in fact when I looked through my memories the dread that had coloured the images for so long was absent. I could still remember, but now it was like recalling a story, a tale I'd heard, something that had happened to someone else, if it had ever happened at all. I walked a little way and pointed to a long-boned woman with a smear of old blood dark against the white of her frozen hands. 'This is Avila; I'm pretty sure she chose a brooch, set with rubies and little pinkish diamonds.'

'It's a cloak pin and has an inscription on the underside,' said Guinalle, coming towards us, hugging herself and shivering slightly. 'It was from her betrothed, an Esquire Tor Sylarre.'

'You remember that kind of detail?' Parrail wrapped his cloak around Guinalle's shoulders and she thanked him absently.

'Of course,' she replied with a faint smile. 'It was only yesterday, after all.'

I felt a presence at my shoulder and turned to see Temar waiting. Livak stirred under my arm and I held her close to silence her.

'I must apologise for my conduct,' the young man began

stiffly; I sympathised with his struggle between pride and embarrassment, but I shook my head.

'No, you weren't to know,' I said firmly. 'I bear you no ill will.' I was relieved to find I meant it too, if a little surprised at myself. Having had the smallest taste of imprisonment within my own head, I found I simply could not blame the boy.

'I should make some recompense,' Temar's jaw jutted obstinately. 'You should keep the sword, it is the only thing of value I possess.' His eyes looked lost, clinging to this hollow notion of honour.

I shook my head in absolute refusal. 'No, I'm sorry but I cannot accept it.' A tremor in my voice showed me I was not yet so secure as I thought.

'I insist—' Temar tried to lay the scabbard in my hands, so I put them behind my back.

'It was never mine,' I told him firmly this time. 'I don't want it!'

Something in my voice must have convinced him; he coloured and belted the weapon on without another word. I watched him look round for Guinalle and hurry towards her, now on the far side of the cavern, Parrail attentive at her side.

'Your Messire gave you that sword,' commented Livak, her hard eyes still following Temar.

'He did and look where it got me,' I said grimly. A gasping cry echoed round the vast expanse of the cavern and we saw Guinalle embracing Avila, the older woman rubbing at her eyes with one trembling hand, the other clasping her brooch as if it were the only constant thing in her world.

Shiv joined them, concern plain in his stance, while Parrail hovered, uncertain and unsure in the face of some abrupt challenge from Temar. Avila struggled to her feet, still shaking, and, thrusting aside Shiv's offer of support, made her way to a woman lying next to three children swaddled together under a rough blanket. Her words were lost at this distance but I watched with growing dismay as Shiv shook his head, pointing first to one of the children, then to another, something bright glinting between his fingers. Parrail stepped forward and rummaged in his coffer, but finally shook his head in a helpless gesture over the tiny middle figure and the woman.

Blood drummed in my ears as I remembered the belt buckle that Kramisak had used to weave his snares around Kaeska. I'd had no notion of its significance – how could I have – but now guilt seared me. If only I had retrieved it. When would this little family be reunited once more in the sunlight, not left still and cold in their rocky tomb? Avila's sudden sobs shattered the silence until she stifled them in her hands as Guinalle desperately sought to comfort her, tears now streaming down her own cheeks.

'I want no more of this!' I turned blindly to escape the gloom of the cavern.

'Let's get out of here,' agreed Livak abruptly. 'We should let them know on the ship what's going on, and get some food organised for when they start waking these people up.'

'I hadn't thought of that,' I confessed.

'Halice did,' grinned Livak, the fear and strain finally leaving her eyes soft as new leaves in the sun. I followed her readily back up towards the fresh daylight and out into the warmth of the living sun. I had done my duty by my patron, the wizards and the lost colonists of Kel Ar'Ayen, I decided. Someone else could answer the questions, make the decisions and deal with the problems, for a while at least. Livak and I got the mercenaries who had remained on board ship busy gathering firewood, flushing game from the surrounding woods and preparing to feed whoever emerged from the cavern. We left them to it and found our own secluded glade, where I proved to Livak that she now had my undivided attention any time she wanted it.

I woke the next morning feeling more fully rested than I could remember in seasons. Leaving Livak curled in the nest of blankets we had shared, I went down to the riverside to wash the sleep from my face and found Shiv frowning over a cup of water.

'Caught a worm or something?' I asked with a grin.

'Morning, Rysh.' Shiv looked up. 'How are you feeling, in yourself?'

He winced as he heard his own words and I laughed. 'Pretty much my old self. It's nice not having a lodger inside my skull. So, what are you doing?'

'Trying to scry the settlement.' Shiv shook his head. 'Only Kalion's put up such a strong barrier that I can't hold the focus together. Oh well, I'm sure they'd summon us fast enough if there was trouble.'

I nodded. 'How many have you revived all together?'

'Close on five hundred, as you would know if you hadn't managed to lose yourself so thoroughly last night,' replied Shiv with a strained smile. 'It was no Festival Fair, I can tell you, trying to explain what had happened to them all, in terms that would make even the slightest sense.'

I looked at the ship, straining at its moorings in the current. 'You're going to have to make several trips and you'll still be packing them in like salted herring,' I commented.

'Most will be staying here – they're too confused to do anything else at present.' Shiv emptied his cup into the river. 'Some of the mercenaries too, to defend the cavern if need be, while we take some of the Artificers down river to meet Planir and help decide what to do next.'

'Shivvalan!' We both looked round to see Guinalle hurrying towards us.

'Is there a problem?'

'What were you doing, just then?' Guinalle looked startled, flushed with haste.

Shiv looked down at his cup. 'It's called scrying. I believe you can work something you call a far-seeing? It's similar but I believe we reach rather further—'

'You also lay your minds open to any attack an Adept might care to make!' Guinalle shook her head. 'I was weaving my own spell, making sure no invaders were anywhere near and I found you at once, defenceless as a newborn babe.'

Shiv grimaced. 'That's how they got to Viltred then.'

'Who? Never mind,' Guinalle frowned, irritated. 'The thing is, I can sense a considerable working of Artifice along the coast. I can't tell its purpose, not yet, but it has to be the invaders, from what Parrail was telling me last night.'

'We'd better get back to the settlement as fast as we can.' I stood up, my respite clearly over for the moment. 'Make sure there are enough here to defend the cavern, but we'll need all the troops and magic we can spare if Planir's facing trouble.'

Shiv nodded. ''Sar and I were talking about this yesterday evening, looking at routes here if the Elietimm have somehow got wind of what we've done. That other river's the only fast way in, so we started work early to block it a good way downstream.'

'How did you do that?' enquired Guinalle.

''Sar did the rocks, I did the water,' Shiv grinned, 'you see—'

'You can tell her when we're on the boat.' I paused, disconcerted to realise I had no sword at my hip. 'We need to get things moving – and I need a new sword.'

'Take my spare.' Tavie handed me a serviceable sword, a little heavy for my taste and marred with a couple of deep notches. 'It's nowhere near the quality of that Empire blade, though,' he added dubiously.

'Trust me, that's not a problem,' I assured him. The weapon was probably worth about a handful of copper and I accepted it with pleasure. Now that Shiv had the current working with him, our progress down the river was rapid enough to make the newly revived colonists gasp. I noticed that Guinalle spent the trip deep in conversation with Usara, doubtless swapping theories on magic, with Parrail hovering attentively at her elbow while Temar looked on with no small measure of annoyance. I moved to join him at the far rail, finding myself drawn by a sympathy I didn't fully understand.

'If she doesn't want you, lad, it makes no difference, no matter how badly you want her,' I told him.

'Thank you, but I fail to see how it is your concern,' he said stiffly.

'You've been making it very much my concern for most

of the past season.' I raised a hand. 'No, I don't blame you; we've covered that, haven't we? I just thought you might like to benefit from the mistakes I made when I was your age.'

After a moment, Temar smiled faintly at me. 'I lost all my elder brothers, you know.'

'I know, and I lost my younger sister, so I've no one else to boss around any more.'

As the ship sped silently down the rapid river, Temar and I stood in the prow and talked, swapping tales of family and friends, discovering just how it was that we came to have so much in common that the Artifice had been unable to prevent a connection. I also gained some understanding into just why my older brothers Hansey and Ridner sometimes found Mistal and me more than a little trying. Parrail joined us after a while and volunteered some theories about aetheric sympathies, but I have to admit they made little sense to me. Noon came and went and we rounded a bend in the river to see three tall-masted ships securing themselves at anchor in the estuary.

'Dast's teeth!' I swore. 'Elietimm!'

'They must have seen them from the camp.' Livak hauled herself up on to the rail of the ship to get a better view. 'Why hasn't someone raised the alarm? What are they playing at?'

The smoke of several camp fires curled lazily upwards from the walls of the steading. I could see sentries patrolling, bows resting casually against shoulders, no sign that they had seen anything amiss at all!

'It's a ward, a very powerful one. Someone on those ships is using Artifice to make anyone looking out from your camp see only what they have seen before.' Guinalle was at my side, face pale and set. 'Look, the enchantment must be concealing those soldiers, over there. They've landed men to make an unexpected attack.' As she pointed, I saw small detachments of black-liveried troops making their way cautiously through the undergrowth to take up positions to encircle the unsuspecting wizards.

'Saedrin seize it!' I looked round to see Shiv peering at the distant wall, a faint nimbus of green round his hands as he quelled the magelight that would betray us to the Elietimm lurking down river. 'It's no good, I can't reach anyone.'

'We're pissing in the wind, trying to get through Kalion's defences,' Usara cursed with equal frustration. 'He's not Hearth-Master for nothing.'

'What can you do?' I demanded of Guinalle. 'Can you break the ward, was that what you called it? Can you make our people see the truth of what's out there?'

She looked down river, scanning the banks and the distant vessels. 'Until I can find who's doing this, I can't combat the ward. Even then, their Artifice might be too strong, if there are several people working together,' she scowled. 'We need to do something they're not prepared for. The only way they'll drop the ward and betray themselves is if we can really distract them, and they'll be expecting Artifice, defending against it. I can tell from the way they're baffling the wards that Parrail's friends are trying to maintain. Whoever is doing this is a master of illusions.'

'Let's try something a little less subtle then,' Usara breathed and sent a shaft of ochre magic into the river. The waters roiled and bubbled, mud and weed swirling upwards from the river bed. 'I'll give them something they're not expecting.'

'Let me help.' Shiv spread his hands and a dark mossy green light began to glow in the depths. The magic suddenly sped away, down towards the Elietimm ships. As it drew closer, a massive shape erupted from the water in an explosion of foam and noise. If I had thought the sea serpent in the Archipelago was huge, it was a bait worm compared to the monster the two wizards conjured from mud and magic. Rearing out of the water to reach higher than the tallest mast, it crashed down on the deck to split the vessel clean in two, ragged planking embedded in its sides as rose up again, blunt head darting this way and that to snap struggling figures out of the water. Ropes snaked down into the waters as the other boats hastily cut their anchors to flee, sails flapping frantically as the mighty shape dived back into the water, only to rear up once more between the ships and the safety of the open sea. Shooting across the surface of the river, the great beast smashed broadside into one, sending it reeling over to start taking water in every hatch while the monster's tail lashed mercilessly at the remaining vessel, sending splintered spars splashing into the water.

'Wizards keeping shipwrights in work again, are they?' Livak shouted from somewhere behind me. I heard mercenaries cheering as they armed themselves for a fight. 'That should have attracted everyone's attention!'

'Get me something shiny, quick,' Usara was calling to her. 'And a candle, anything that will burn.' Snapping his fingers to light a spill of kindling wood, the wizard angled the magical flame to reflect against some mercenary's rough scrubbed pewter plate.

'Otrick, answer me, curse you!'

What is it? 'Sar, is that you?' The old mage's perplexity travelled clearly enough through the faltering spell.

'Don't you see the ships?' Usara shouted. 'Get Kalion to drop his cursed barrier so I can talk to you properly.'

'Those are Elietimm ships! Saedrin's stones, where did they come from—'

'They're landing troops to attack you! Get ready to defend the walls,' yelled Usara as the spell flickered and weakened.

'Target anyone wearing a metal gorget,' I bellowed as the light died away. 'Do you think they heard?'

Usara shook his head, face aghast. 'Something's happened to Otrick!'

Given the chaos erupting around their ships, the Elietimm had abandoned their attempts at stealth and were charging towards the Den Rannion steading, harsh battle cries sounding across the waters.

'Get us ashore, curse you,' Livak was shouting at the master mariner.

'We can mount a counterattack,' Buril looked up from conferring with his fellow mercenaries.

'Let us at them, Esquire,' one of the colonists urged Temar, receiving nods of agreement from the others. 'We have a fair rate of scores to settle!'

A crack of lightning silenced everyone as black clouds boiled out of nowhere and spears of magic lanced downwards to send black-liveried bodies flying, scorched vegetation burning merrily. Where a detachment tried to stamp out the flames, a surge of crimson fire leaped up from the ground to seize one man greedily by the arm, burning him to the bone despite every effort to quench it, rather transferring itself to anyone who came to the hapless soldier's aid, leaving only charred remnants behind. Screams of fear and pain began to rise above the war cries.

'Do you think they need our help?' I heard one of the mercenaries ask his mate doubtfully.

'Over there, he's over there!' Guinalle gestured wildly at the far bank, towards the ruins of some kind of watchtower. 'Their Artificer, he's over there!'

'Master, can you get us beside that wharf?' I shouted to the captain. 'We have to get off quick if we're not to be cut to pieces as we land!'

'Let us,' Shiv nodded to Usara and the great serpent vanished, leaving only a few swimmers struggling among the flotsam of the ebbing tide. Our boat rode over the water, however, gliding impossibly through the exposed mud flats to wedge itself securely against an undercut shore, the mercenaries leaping over the rail to land on dry grass, which was soon running red with the blood of the Elietimm who charged down to meet our unexpected attack.

After that first success our assault faltered as a handful of our warriors fell to their knees. The air felt heavy around me, almost as if a storm threatened. I wondered if some wizard's magic was going awry. Then one woman, Jervice, Halice's friend, struggled to her feet and I saw her eyes were black as pitch.

'Drianon forgive me!' As Livak whispered her prayer, she threw a dart, hard and true and Jervice crumpled to the ground before she could plant her raised sword in the skull of the man next to her. Others were not so lucky and I saw more than one colonist, so long in waiting, sent straight to Saedrin's door by an unexpected blow from behind. Rage threatened to overwhelm me and I clubbed the man responsible with a heavy hand, sending him bleeding to the ground.

'Tror mir'al, es nar'an,' Guinalle set up a frantic chant somewhere close. 'Parrail, repeat this after me and don't stop, if you love your sanity!'

As the peculiar rhythm built, the sense of pressure faded and our attack was pressed home with renewed bitterness. 'Go for the commanders, the ones with gold or silver at their throats!' I heard Temar shouting. More of Livak's darts went shooting past my ear; anyone she could see with a gorget dropped in their steps. I spared her a glance, hearing her chanting something under her breath. 'What are you saying?'

'Whatever – it is – that she is,' Livak said between repetitions. 'It can't hurt, can it?'

'Over there!' Dragging Parrail along with her other hand, Guinalle grabbed my sleeve and then pointed at the creeper-clad base of the watchtower. 'He's in there.'

'Temar!' I pointed to the tower and looked round. 'Tavie, Buril, with me, and you others!'

'Maintain the ward, whatever you do.' Guinalle dropped Parrail's hand and I noticed the bruises of her finger marks in his flesh. 'It's up to you now. I have to block the source of this Artifice.'

She hurried towards the tower, heedless of danger, Livak and I hastening to put ourselves either side of her as we fought our way through the mêlée. As we reached the entrance, 'Sar sent magic from somewhere behind us to reduce the doorway to rubble and splinters. After an instant of recoiling from that shock, Temar and I led the charge inside. Those who came to meet us died quickly, as I found myself knowing every move Temar was going to make a breath before he did it. It seemed to be working both ways as well. As I darted to the side and an Elietimm sought to follow me, Temar's sword was already moving to spill his guts over the dusty floor. As a second man thought he could smash his blade down into Temar's outstretched arm, I was already poised to drive my crude blade into his head, ripping it out again to smash the hilt into the face of the gorget-wearer hoping to meet Temar's retreat. The rest of the guard died bloodily under the swords of those beside us.

'Upstairs.' Guinalle was flattened against the wall, blood on her skirts, eyes fixed on the beams above her head. Livak, similarly splashed, waited ready to defend her, but no assailants were getting past Buril and Tavie, who had set themselves at the threshold. The two heavy-set mercenaries were drenched in gore, some their own, grimly purposeful as they hacked down any Elietimm trying to seek sanctuary within the tower again.

'Come on.' Temar set a foot on the lowest step of the stair winding up the inside of the wall and I hurried to follow him. I nodded and we both ran up the narrow treads, swords raised, ready to kill whatever we found but crashing helplessly into some unseen barrier that sent agony shooting through my skull. Gasping for breath, I stared into the hollow room in total disbelief.

It was him, the priest from Shek Kul's domain – Kramisak, the bastard who had fled and left me to watch over Kaeska's agonised death. He sat, calm, within a circle of eerie radiance, a mocking half-smile on his thin lips as he nodded towards me in a taunting salute. Stripped to the waist, his hands were raised and he was once more covered in black sigils, shocking against the white of his skin and hair. 'I will attend to you later, Tormalin man, I have bigger fish on the hook at present.'

I glared at him and waved Temar over to test the circle on the opposite side. We found we could move round the enchanter easily enough but could not reach him; even touching a sword to the baleful light sent agony shooting up the arm that held it. As I walked slowly round, I looked over the river to see how the battle fared. The walls of the encampment were wreathed in scarlet fire; Naldeth or Kalion must have set all the creepers alight, which did not suggest the fight went well for our side. Where were Otrick's lightning strikes, which had shattered Elietimm ambitions the year before?

'It's a ward, a strong one.' Guinalle stood at the top of the steps, peering around Livak's shoulder. Livak's face was pale and set and I knew just what it must be costing her to come face to face with the Elietimm magic that had tortured her so foully before. Kramisak's attention wavered for a moment and the circle brightened, but Guinalle raised a hand with a stream of liquid syllables and whatever the bastard was attempting against her went past in vain.

'Livak, do you trust me?' Guinalle moved to one side, her eyes never leaving the Elietimm enchanter. 'Believe me, anything he can do, I can match. Hold my hands, echo my words and understand that he cannot touch us.'

Livak's eyes were wide with apprehension, but she took Guinalle's pale and delicate hands in her own tanned ones and repeated the arcane chant that the younger woman raised, Guinalle's ancient accents, unheard for so many generations, mingling with the cadence of Livak's Forest blood, songs learned in childhood from her long absent father giving her the pattern of the lost magic.

'No, you cannot!' Kramisak leaped to his feet with a shout of outrage as his circle flickered and died. He seized a mace that lay on the floor and launched himself at Guinalle. I dashed forward to intercept him, catching the crushing head of his weapon on the battered edge of my sword. He spat at me, slime just missing my face, and cursed me in his own tongue before hissing a familiar chant at me. I braced myself but no confusion threatened me, no dizziness robbed me of my wits.

'Daughter of whores and mother of vermin!' Kramisak tried to go for Guinalle again but I sent him sprawling backwards into the far wall with a kick in the stomach.

'It's time for a fair fight, you pox-rotted bastard,' I heard myself say. 'There's unfinished business between us, gurry-breath!'

'Then it's my turn.' Temar was circling round behind me now, making sure Kramisak had no opportunity to reach Guinalle and Livak if he somehow evaded me.

'I took you once, prince's man. I can do it again,' the enchanter snarled, hefting his mace in both hands.

Not today, I thought, going in hard against his rapid blows, sweeping his iron-bound mace aside to rip a long tear down his near arm. To have his own blood let like that seemed to enrage Kramisak still more and he came at me with a flurry of furious strokes. For all his ferocity, I found myself evading him with ease. He seemed completely unable to read my moves and equally was unable to stop himself mistakenly anticipating my strokes and stepping into a blow rather than defending against it. I cut him again, a deep wound to the upper arm that weakened his blows considerably. He still managed to get a bruising strike in on my leg, but in doing so laid himself open to a sideways slice that left his ribs showing white bone within the torn red flesh. This ragged sword was sawing into him like wood and I leaned all my strength into my blows.

He was fighting Temar. I saw it in an instant of incredulous understanding. Kramisak did not realise that the mind behind my sword in our battle before Shek Kul had been another's. He was fighting Temar and was losing to me. What would Temar do to that lunge, I asked myself rapidly. He would parry, just so. I stepped in the other direction and slid my notched sword round and over Kramisak's mace to rip into his throat, great gouts of his blood making the hilt slip in my hands as the disbelief in his eyes faded and he fell forwards, the foul and all too familiar stench of death rising from his body as his last spasms ended. I leaned down and cut the belt, with its antique buckle, from his corpse.

Great cries rose from the mercenaries outside. I stepped to the ruined window to see what was going on. To my total surprise, those Elietimm still standing were throwing down their weapons, kneeling, arms spread wide, unmistakably suing for mercy, something the mercenaries were rather more inclined to grant than the colonists, who slew most that they could reach before the mercenaries stopped them. Across the river the fires around the steading suddenly died and Shiv vanished in a flash of azure light, leaving the knot of colonists he had been defending with spears of lightning looking at each other, completely astounded. He reappeared next to me a moment later, chest heaving.

'Is it over?' I demanded, Temar at my side, Livak and Guinalle still clutching each other's hands by the stair way.

'For the present!' Shiv let loose a wild yell of triumph, embracing me, a gesture I returned without hesitation before turning to do the same to Livak, kissing her soundly as well.

CHAPTER ELEVEN

Taken from the family archive of the House Den Rannion, Bremilayne.

From Lyal, Sieur Den Rannion, to Ingaret, Messire Den Perinal, by the hand in person of Milral Arman, of common height with red hair and blue eyes, a scar on his sword arm and a brand of horse theft on his off hand.

My dear cousin,
I write with the sad tidings that my esteemed father, Vahil, late Sieur of this House, was received by Saedrin's grace on the 44th day of For-Summer. I would ask that you convey this news to your mother, my beloved aunt, Maitresse Elsire, in such a manner as you feel appropriate for her age and infirmity. I leave it to your discretion as to whether or not you tell her his final words were of their parents, the friends of his youth, and sorrow over some undischarged vow. I regret to say that this last caused him no little distress and consequently, I assured him that, when circumstance allowed, I would seek to rediscover the lost colony of which I know your mother also still speaks.
Between ourselves, I can only pray that Saedrin is able to pacify my father on this matter, else we face the prospect of his inconsolate shade wandering our halls for some generations to come. Our situation is not as desperate as some, but Misaen will halt the moons before I have resources to spend chasing an old man's disappointments with only half-remembered tales and inadequate records to guide me. The fighting has passed us by for the moment and I am

*in negotiation with sundry Houses in support of the Sieur
D'Aleonne. I would appreciate your thoughts on this matter
and, of course, any assurance of military aid that you might
care to make available, should the situation in your locality
become more stable. You might also care to know that the
Sieur D'Istrac has approached me in respect of a betrothal
between my daughter Kindra and his eldest nephew. How
go your negotiations with D'Evoir?*

Kel Ar'Ayen,
22nd of For-Autumn

'Are you all ready to go?' Shiv sauntered down the wharf, his own baggage slung negligently over one shoulder.

'I think so.' I looked up to the gateway to the Den Rannion steading, now cleared and roughly repaired. Halice and Livak were deep in conversation, Halice in workaday breeches and jerkin while Livak stood with her kit-bag leaning against the wall. I rubbed a hand against my pocket to reassure me that the parchment bearing Halice's account of the healing done to her leg was secure there. If I were going to hand back my oath, I would be rendering a full accounting.

'I was rather surprised when she said she was staying,' Shiv remarked. 'How's Livak taking it? I know they've been close a long time.'

'Whatever else, she wants Halice to be content,' I shrugged. 'Yes, she's sad, and she's done every cursed thing she can to change her mind, but when all the runes are thrown, it's still Halice's decision. Livak can't deny her that.'

'Do you know why, exactly?' Shiv looked curious. 'I haven't liked to ask.'

'Halice says she's had enough of fighting in Lescar, of spending every season losing friends only to have all the runes swept back into the bag and drawn afresh the next year. I can't say I blame her, that's one of the reasons my friend Aiten got clear of the civil wars. Now Halice reckons she's found a place where her skills can be useful and she feels she's fighting for a worthwhile cause.' I grimaced, wondering where I would find such a thing now and still feeling a dull pang at Aiten's name.

'I hope she doesn't have to do any more fighting this year,'

Shiv grimaced. 'Until we can get some more people over here, they're still cursed vulnerable.'

I shook my head and pointed at the walls of the steading where busy figures were repairing the crenellations and wall walk. 'Most of the mercenaries are staying and, with all the colonists we could revive, they should be all right through the winter. They've been putting the prisoners to work building houses and defences as well as picking everything they can find to eat or store, so they're well enough prepared.'

'I still think it's odd so many of them surrendered like that,' Shiv shook his head. 'How can we be sure there are no magic-wielders among them?'

'Guinalle is sure of it.' I shrugged. 'She's been picking their minds apart if they so much as look at anyone sideways. Parrail was telling me it's all connected with a hierarchy of authority in the Elietimm culture.' I did my best to mimic the young scholar's earnest tones. 'Once their leader was dead, they had no choice but to submit to the leader of those strong enough to defeat him.'

'Sounds highly implausible to me,' muttered Shiv darkly.

'I don't know, I've been thinking about it. Remember, those islands aren't like Lescar, able to keep ripping each other apart year after year because so many other people get fat off the spoils or have an interest in keeping the fighting going. If the Elietimm fought like Lescaris, all they'd have in a couple of seasons would be bare rock to eat and cold sea to drink.'

'Maybe.' Shiv did not look convinced.

'The prisoners aren't a threat, Shiv. If they all die of a fever tomorrow, the colony can manage without them.' I wouldn't grieve if they did, I thought, silently acknowledging that I shared Shiv's reservations to some extent. 'No, everyone here will be safe enough over the winter; the Elietimm won't be able to cross the ocean again this year. Better yet, losing their expedition should give them pause for thought before they set sail in the spring, even if they know what happened to them, which I would doubt.'

'Has anyone come up with an explanation for those bastards

having copies of the ancient Tormalin charts of this place, the ones made by Den Fellaemion or whatever he was called?'

'Not that I've heard.' I tried to look unconcerned, not wanting to think about Planir's request that I use my possible new status to investigate this on Messire's behalf. 'I hardly think it's important.'

'I hope you're right,' Shiv sighed. 'I suppose that's one advantage we have over them. We can cross the ocean this late in the year, though Trimon knows I'm not looking forward to it without Otrick or Viltred to help.'

'Dastennin grant us safe passage,' I agreed, none too keen myself at the prospect of the imminent voyage in the teeth of the autumn storms.

'So what will you be doing?' Shiv rummaged in a pocket and handed me a little horn beaker. I held it while he filled it with water, which soon began to steam gently. 'Go on, tell me,' he urged as he dropped a twist of muslin fragrant with herbs into the cup. 'I saw you talking to Planir, what did he have to say?'

I handed Shiv his tisane. 'It seems the Archmage gave your old friend Casuel letters to take to Messire before we started our voyage. Anyway, Cas was asked to stay on, so that Planir could advise Messire directly of the success or otherwise of our quest.'

'And?' demanded Shiv.

'And Messire feels I should be raised in rank from sworn man to chosen man,' I said dryly.

'But that's an honour, isn't it?' asked Shiv doubtfully, seeing my expression.

'It could be, if I choose to accept it,' I nodded, still looking at Livak who was hugging Halice. 'I have the voyage home to decide in, haven't I? Have you another one of those cups?' I wasn't about to discuss this with anyone before I had talked everything through with Livak. 'Anyway, what will you be doing with yourself?'

'After I've taken Pered to Col for the Equinox, you mean?' Shiv grinned as he handed me the tisane, but his expression

suddenly became serious as he made another for himself.
'Planir will have every mage with wits or breath busy testing
everything we learn about aetheric magic, sorry, Artifice I
suppose we should be calling it now. That and threatening
every scholar, university and temple with fire and flood unless
they give up everything they know about the slightest magical
tradition. Saedrin knows, the magic we've won has been costly
enough.'

'Viltred's visions did him no real service, did they?' I commented. 'So much for his predictions of a glorious future with
us all dressed up in our festival best.'

'Auguries are most accurate the closer they are in time.'
Shiv shrugged. 'The warning about the Elietimm was clear
enough; he'd have died if he stayed, no question.'

Maybe so. I hesitated but decided to ask Shiv something
that had been bothering me for a while now. 'Those visions,
the palace being sacked and then us all dressed up in velvets,
was that all true? Not just something to hold me to my oath,
something to tempt Livak with, perhaps, if you could have
got her to watch them?'

Shiv looked round sharply. 'Is that what you thought? No,
Ryshad, that was a true seeing, even if it never came to
pass. All right, I'll admit I hoped the prospect of gambling
at a Sieur's table would catch Livak's eye, but I wouldn't
counterfeit something like that. I knew you to be a man of
honour, what kind of mage do you think I am?'

A disturbance at the gates of the steading saved me from
having to find an answer. I watched with Shiv as a slow
procession made its way down to the wharf, five litters borne
by grim-faced mercenaries and one by Planir, Kalion, Usara
and Naldeth.

'Has Otrick stirred at all?' I asked Shiv gently.

The mage shook his head abruptly, gritting his teeth. 'No,
not since that Elietimm scum tried to take his mind from him.'
The water in my cup seethed suddenly.

'How's Kalion's hand?' The fat wizard was in evident pain
from his thickly bandaged knuckles as sailors helped lift the

frail burden on to the ship. All his learning had not warned him of the damage one can do to oneself. knocking even a small man like Otrick unconscious with a single punch.

'Guinalle has mended most of the damage,' Shiv managed to smile. 'It seems our revered Hearth-Master will still be able to bore his pupils with endless recitals on his flute. Still, it's a small price for him to pay for saving Otrick. I only hope we can find a way to revive the old pirate, bring him back to himself somehow.'

The frail figure of the ancient mage Shannet followed the litter, her stick thin arms clasping a plain urn with a muted grey decoration. A thought struck me. 'Who's going to tell Mellitha about Viltred?' I hoped her grief would be respected by the Archmage.

'Kalion has offered to take the urn to her, since Viltred had no other family.'

Shiv's voice was inappropriately tart, but I could well understand why. I wondered why Planir was giving Kalion such an opportunity to visit a leading citizen of such an important city, where he would doubtless wheedle invitations to meet the great and the powerful of Relshaz. 'I'd say Mellitha is more than a match for Kalion, Shiv.'

'Maybe so,' allowed Shiv with a faint smile.

'And the others who were struck down?' I watched as the motionless form of the woman Jervice was carried gently aboard the vessel. 'What does Guinalle think?' I looked at the slim girl, warmly wrapped in a cloak that I recognised as belonging to Usara, giving Parrail a sheaf of instructions.

'She says it should be possible.' Shiv tried to look hopeful. 'It's just a matter of finding the right approach.'

'Dastennin send you find it,' I said fervently.

'Some deity certainly has a nasty sense of humour,' said Shiv unhappily, 'letting something like that happen, after we arrived just in time to foil the assault.'

'Guinalle reckons it was the other way around.' Usara joined us, his own expression tired and sad. 'She thinks the Elietimm had launched their attack as soon as they realised we were coming down river.'

Shiv shrugged. 'Whatever. So, are you staying or coming with us, 'Sar?'

'Planir wants me back in Hadrumal, so I must do his bidding,' replied Usara briskly, though I saw his eyes following Guinalle as she walked back up the wharf towards the gates. 'Just at present, he's not a man to be argued with.'

'I heard Naldeth trying to get out of staying here,' I agreed with a laugh.

'I don't think Naldeth found Planir's reaction very amusing.' Usara looked sternly at me.

'Chamry seems happy enough,' commented Shiv. 'I think she's had just about enough of the honour of being Shannet's latest pupil.'

'I take it Mentor Tonin hasn't managed to persuade Guinalle to come back to Vanam with him? What success have you had with her, 'Sar?' I asked, straight-faced.

Usara was betrayed by his fair colouring. 'Mind your own business, Rysh. No, I support Guinalle's decision. Of course she must remain here, to safeguard those we still have to revive, if nothing else.'

'So you'll be back here, just as soon as you've found a solution for her, will you?' enquired Shiv.

'Me, or Parrail, or anyone else who finds the knowledge we need,' Usara said repressively.

'I don't think you have much competition there.' Shiv patted him reassuringly on the shoulder.

I held my peace. Guinalle was persisting in tactfully not noticing Parrail's transparent adoration of her, for the lad's sake as much as to divert Temar's manful attempts at concealing his jealousy. I could see him now, sitting on an empty barrel, face like a slapped arse, as he watched the love of his life walk away from him. I shook my head at the remembered pains of youth. 'Excuse me, both of you.'

I clapped Temar on the shoulder. 'Have you made your decision yet?'

He looked up at me. 'What would I do if I came with you? Take this oath of yours to the Sieur D'Olbriot? I have no House or Name to return to.'

'The oath arose for men like that, set adrift in the Chaos after the Empire fell,' I said, recalling this with some surprise. Some of Temar's contemporaries had probably been the first to swear it.

A faint spark of interest lightened the gloom in Temar's eyes. 'Did it?'

I nodded. 'The Sieur offers security, the man swears loyalty in return.'

An echo sounded in my mind, of Messire's words as he stood tall and distant on the dais above me, my own responses striking up from the stone floor as I knelt to offer up my honour all those years ago, the two of us alone in the great hall, as was customary.

'As my walls shall shelter you—'
'So my sword will defend you.'
'As my food shall strengthen you—'
'So my strength will serve you.'
'As my hearth shall warm you—'
'So my heart's blood is yours.'

That was the heart of the matter, wasn't it? Those were the words I would have to ponder as I weighed Messire's loyalty to his oath against my own actions.

A shout from the water broke the stillness of my reflections.

'You don't have much longer to make up your mind,' I said gently.

'What? No, I know.' Temar sighed heavily.

'To make up his mind about what?' asked Livak, as she came up to us and slid herself inside the circle of my arm.

'Should I stay or should I go?' Temar looked up at her.

'Roll a rune for it,' Livak shrugged. 'Anyway, no decision's ever final, is it? Come to Zyoutessela with us. Messire D'Olbriot's invited you, hasn't he? If you don't like it, you can be on the next ship heading this way.'

'Which won't be before the spring next year.' I thought I had better add a note of realism to Livak's cheerful unconcern. I looked at Livak, a woollen wrap incongruous over her jerkin and breeches. 'I know it's a lot to ask, my dearest, and I don't expect an answer at once, but do you think you could possibly bear to wear a skirt when you meet my mother for the first time?'

THE GAMBLER'S FORTUNE

The Third tale of Einarrinn

Juliet E. McKenna

With a gambler's instinct and a nose for profit, Livak
knows how to play the odds. If she didn't, chances
are she'd have found herself in Saedrin's lock-up
long ago.

Having spent far too much time fighting other people's
battles, Livak has now decided it's time she turned
her new-found connections with powerful mages
and mighty princes into solid advantage for herself.
With the threat from the evil Elietimm ever-present, she
knows that knowledge of their ancient aetheric magic
will be of considerable value to both Planir the
Archmage and Messire D'Olbriot. By locating those
who hold the secrets of Artifice first, Livak will hold
the key to untold riches . . .

Magical storytelling and unforgettable characters
combine in *The Gambler's Fortune*, the wonderful new
adventure from a British author who is setting the
fantasy field alight.